For All We Have and Are
1914 – 1915

G. Carlee-Forster

Copyright © 2014 G Carlee-Forster
All rights reserved.

ISBN-10: 1495409082

ISBN-13: 978-1495409080

CHAPTERS

Foreword
Glossary
Prologue, The Death of Innocence   i

PART ONE, The Winter of the World   1
1   August 4th 1914   3
2   August 4th, London   5
3   September 26th, Guernsey   8
4   September 28th, Headingly   15
5   October 2nd – 4th, New Forest   21
6   October 4th, Pateley Bridge   35
7   October, Belgium   38
8   October 28th, Headingly   54
9   October 27th – 29th, British Front Line near Gheluvelt   57
10   November 5th, Leeds General Infirmary   65
11   December 19th, Pateley Bridge   69
12   December 29th, Southern England   85
13   London, New Year's Eve   88

PART TWO, For All We Have and Are   99
14   January 10th, Sussex Downs   100
15   January 17th, Boulogne   103
16   February 8th, Advanced Dressing Station near Fleurbaix   107
17   February 18th, Number 13 General Hospital, Boulogne   123
18   February 24th, Brigade Reserve, Fleurbaix   132
19   February 26th, London   140
20   February 27th, Fleurbaix   145
21   March 3rd, Boulogne   149
22   March 7th, Number Two ADS, 23rd Field Ambulance   157
23   March 9th, Number Two ADS, Farm Buildings Outside Neuve Chapelle   161
24   March 10th – 13th, Neuve Chapelle   165
25   March 18th, London   195
26   April 2nd, Brigade Reserve, La Gorgue – Fleurbaix   202
27   April 23rd, Laventie   205
28   April 27th, Number 13 General Hospital, Boulogne   210
29   May 4th, Pateley Bridge   217
30   May 14th, Front Line Trenches Near Festubert   224
31   May 17th, Number 13 General Hospital, Boulogne   228
32   June 1st, Boulogne   235

33	June 15th -18th, London	248
34	June 22nd, Brigade Reserve, Le Harisoirs	254
35	July 1st, 1st London Military Hospital, Camberwell	257
36	July 14th, Pateley Bridge	266
37	July 24th, Pateley Bridge	276
38	July 31st, Front Line Trenches Near Richebourg St. Vaast	281
39	August 7th, Gonneheim	285
40	August 9th -13th, England	291
41	August 14th, Beccles, Suffolk	300
42	September 3rd, Northern France	307
43	Loos 1915	315
44	October 2nd, Number 13 General Hospital, Boulogne	329
45	October 17th, Paris	331
46	October 30th, Number 23 General Hospital, Étaples	334
47	November 8th, Front Line Near Givenchy	338
48	November 28th -30th, Front Line, Givenchy	343
49	Early December, Number 12 General Hospital, Rouen	370
50	December 24th – 26th	378
	Dedication	393

FOREWORD

This novel is purely a work of fiction. On researching my family tree I came across Corporal William Pratt, my Great Uncle, or is that Great Great Uncle? Intrigued, and following my tendency to become obsessive in all my hobbies, my research led me to look into his life as a Regular soldier both before and during WW1. Unfortunately his records had been destroyed in the Blitz fire back in WW2 and so any hope of finding details vanished. However, I decided to look more generally and made a visit to his regimental museum, the Green Howards Museum (well worth a visit for those military minded) in Richmond, North Yorkshire. The museum curator kindly allowed me to study the war diaries of William's Battalion for the Great War. A wonderful archive that gave an insight, not only to the battles, but also the everyday mundane drudgery of life in France and Flanders from 1914 through to the end of 1915. It was through reading these diaries that I decided upon following up my long held interest in the Great War, or World War One if you prefer, and write a book. This is the result. It is based around those diaries and I have tried to keep to the broad facts relating to the Battalion's movements. I could have written about a fictional Regiment and a fictional battalion but I chose to use the real thing out of respect for William and his fellow soldiers. However, though the circumstances of the Battalion are historically correct none of the characters are real. Neither are they based upon real people and any likeness to anyone living then or now is purely coincidental. I have killed off one or two senior officers purely to remain true to the historical context of the diaries, but the characters ascribed to these unfortunate men are in no way an attempt to recreate a real person. Even their names are fictitious. There are two exceptions to this. One is William. He is not the main character in this tale but a bit player. I know nothing of his true character and so have based him upon the kind of down-to-earth, no nonsense Yorkshire men I have met and know. I hope he would approve and maybe even recognise a little of himself.

I would like to thank a few people for their help and support in writing this book. Firstly to the staff of The Green Howards Museum for their generous assistance during my research. I am indebted to them for two reasons. One, they helped me find out a little about William and two; by allowing me to read the diaries, they gave me the impetus to begin this book.

Secondly I would like to thank my husband Lee for putting up with my antisocial habit of writing for hours on end through winter and summer evenings and for not appearing too bored when I waxed lyrical about some aspect of the Great War or the plot.

Thirdly my sincere thanks to Declan Foy for his honest feedback and his encouragement to carry on when other circumstances almost forced me to give up. For that I am eternally grateful. And it is because of this that Declan became the basis of the one other character in this story to have a real counterpart model. I hope Declan, that you like your alter ego and see in him a little of yourself. You know who he is.

Finally, the title of this book is taken from the famous poem by Rudyard Kipling written in 1914. I have chosen the first line of that poem because it sums up the overwhelming sense of patriotic duty at the outbreak of war. Like many of his contemporary authors and poets Kipling wrote and spoke actively in favour of the war in the early days of the conflict. That all changed following the death of his son, Jack, at Loos in 1915. As this book covers only that early, fervent time I hope he would approve of the title.

GLOSSARY

DIALECT

Alus - Always
Any-road - Anyway
Bairn - Child
Befower - Before
Brung - Brought
Canna (Cannae) - Cannot
Canny - Careful, clever, smart
Chinwag - Chat, talk
Collywobbles - Feeling of anxiety, scared (associated with the nervous fluttering one feels in the stomach region when nervous or scared).
Dickie fit - Mad, angry
Dram - Measure of alcohol, usually whisky
Dunno - Don't know
Eee - Expression like oh
'Ersen - Herself
Ey-up - Greeting of hello or a means of drawing attention to something or someone
Fo' - For
Gi' - Give
Gi' it - Give it
Gonna - Going to
Hame - Home
'Imsen - Himself
Ken - Know
Mebbe - Maybe
Nowt - Nothing
O'er - Over
Outta - Out of
Owt - Anything
Rum (when not to drink, e.g. rum lad) - Odd, strange
Sen - Self
Si thi - See you
Summat - Something
t' - The (the letter is not actually pronounced)
Ta - Thank you
Ta-ra - Goodbye
Tha - You, your
Thee - You

Thi - You (abbreviated and more common version of thee)
Thi sen - Yourself
T'owd - The old
Two shakes (of a lambs tail) - fast, quickly
Un – One (as in the number)
Wa' - Was
Wi' - With
Yersen - Yourself
Yonder - There (as in a place)

ARMY/MEDICAL SLANG

ADS - Advanced Dressing Station
Base wallah - A soldier who remains at base never going near the front
BEF - British Expeditionary Force
Berm - Small shelf on the front wall (parapet) of a trench
Blanco - Block used originally to whiten full dress webbing. Khaki blanco was used on service equipment
Boche - French slang for German, commonly used by British officers, rarely by other ranks
Body Snatchers - Stretcher bearers
Bomber - One trained in the use of hand grenades and other small calibre trench mortars
Brass hat - High ranking officer – refers to gold decoration worn on the cap peak.
Buckshee - Free, for nothing
Camouflet - A small charge detonated in a mine aimed at destroying the enemy's tunnelling activities.
Cap comforter - A sack, about 18 inches long, of khaki or dark coloured knitted wool used for storing odds and ends in and, off parade, and in the line, rolled up and worn as a cap in cold weather, on patrols etc
CC - Company Commander
CCS - Casualty Clearing Station
Char - Tea
Chat - Lice, louse
Chatting - Removing lice or talking
Civvy (civvies) - Civilian(s)
Click, clicked - To strike up a relationship with the opposite sex
CO - Commanding Officer (typically a lieutenant colonel or colonel)
CSM - Company Sergeant Major
Cushy - Easy
Dekko - Look, observe

Devil Dodger - Chaplain
Dhobi wallah - Laundryman
Divvy - Share (also slang for Division)
Dixie - Mess tin for carrying or preparing water/tea/food in- from the Hindustani deachi meaning small pot
DLI – Durham Light Infantry
Dog biscuits - Hard biscuits issued to soldiers as emergency rations (also known as iron rations)
Duckboards - Wooden slats placed on the floor of a trench to try and keep the men within it above the water/mud
Dug-out – Shelter in a trench from shell fire or the weather - men and officers worked, rested and slept in dug-outs
Eat apples – Étaples (soldiers' slang)
Enfilade - Raking gun fire which strikes a body of troops along the length of their formation
Fatigue dress - Without puttees, belt or equipment, in order to work
Fatigues - Chores or other jobs other than soldiering
Firing Step - Raised step at the front of a trench from which soldiers fired at the enemy
Frenchie - Field Marshall Sir Robert French, Commander in Chief of the BEF 1914-November 1915
Fritz - German soldiers, collectively or singly - popular amongst British troops before 1916 when Jerry became more common.
Funk - Fear, nervousness or depression
Glory hole - Any small dug-out or billet usually in very poor condition, sometimes a toilet.
God - Sergeant Major, usually refers to the RSM
Gone west - Dead
Green Howards - Commonly used name (within Army) for the Yorkshire Regiment after their first Colonel
Imshi - Go, away with you
Iron Rations - Hard biscuits issued to soldiers as emergency rations also known as dog biscuits.
Jacks - Military police
Jildi - Hurry, get a move on
Lance Jack - Lance corporal
Loophole - Small opening (often only big enough for a rifle muzzle) within the parapet through which soldiers fired at the enemy
MDS - Main Dressing Station (Army medical services ran an efficient evacuation process by early 1915 which would be honed throughout the war - the evacuation route was field dressing station or Battalion dressing station, ADS, MDS, CCS)
Minenwerfer - German for bomb thrower - a kind of trench mortar, also

given to the actual bomb.
Minnie - The bomb, mortar shell fired from a minenwerfer
MO - medical officer
Moaning Minnie - Name given to the mortar shell fired from a minenwerfer due to the laboured moaning wail it made as it travelled through the air
Moribund - Injured but unlikely to survive - early in the war these unfortunate men were left until last to be treated as it was deemed they were unlikely to survive anyway, emphasis was placed on saving those who might live to fight again
NCO - Non Commissioned Officer
Neurasthenia - Medical term for the psychological phenomenon of shellshock
No-Man's-Land - Term for the strip of land between two opposing trenches that was not controlled by either side - could be as far as a few kilometres (rarely) or as narrow as a couple of metres
Non-stop - A shell passing overhead beyond its intended target
OC - Officer Commanding (of a military unit not necessarily the CO who commanded the Battalion, could refer to the commander of a company, raiding party etc.)
Old Sweat - A veteran or experienced soldier
On the wire - Literally a body left on the barbed wire after an attack also missing or killed in action
Parados - Back wall of a trench (facing back to the reserve lines)
Parapet - Front wall of a trench (facing the enemy)
Pukka - Real, genuine, smart, good
Push - Girl friend
QAIMNS - Queen Alexandra's Imperial Military Nursing Service
QMS – Quarter Master Sergeant
Quick fire - Field service post card - consisted of a number of pre-printed sentences which could be deleted appropriately when there was no time to write a letter
RAMC - Royal Army Medical Corps (RAMC)
Rats After Mouldy Cheese - RAMC
RFA - Royal Field Artillery
Rob All My Comrades - RAMC
RQMS - Regimental Quartermaster Sergeant, warrant officer rank on a par with RSM
RSM - Regimental Sergeant Major
Salient - Part of a military front line or fortification that projects out into enemy territory therefore vulnerable to coming under fire from three sides - the area around Ypres ultimately became known as the Salient
Sarge – Sergeant - became common after 1915 with the increase in volunteers and conscripts (non-regulars). Bemoaned by regular NCOs

Sarn't – Regular soldiers address to Sergeant

Scrounging - Appropriating items or food by bartering, borrowing or stealing

Short arm inspection - Medical inspection of a soldier's penis to look for cases of VD

Short-one - A shell fired by allies that hits or almost hits their own troops

Skrimshanker - Idle, good for nothing

Soldier's Friend - A brand of boot polish

Stand-to - Stand to arms ready to repel enemy attack. A vigil carried out in trenches particularly at dawn and dusk

Star shell - Artillery shell consisting of a flare on a parachute used for signalling or lighting up areas for means of countering an attack for catching raiders in No-Man's-Land

Stay-at-home - Someone reluctant to enlist, a coward

Stuff - Shell fire, heavy stuff = big shells

Swinging the lead - Malingering or otherwise evading duty or work

Terriers - Territorial Force soldiers

TF - Territorial Force (forerunner to the modern territorial army)

TFNS - Territorial Force Nursing Service

Tommy - British (Commonwealth) soldier

Town Major - Officer responsible for organising billets for troops out on rest (usually, but not always, a captain in rank)

Traverses - Thick sandbag or earth partitions in trenches to prevent enfilading and to confine the effects of shell fire.

VAD - Voluntary Aid Detachment

Valise - an officer's canvas kit bag or - a khaki canvas knapsack carried on the back that carried spare underclothing, greatcoat, ground sheet, emergency rations etc.

Very light - A flare fired from a Very pistol

Webbing - Khaki canvas-like cloth worn to carry equipment and act as a belt, as opposed to the leather equipment belt.

Whizz-bangs - Light artillery shell. Name is onomatopoeic referring to the screech of the flying shell and the explosion.

Wind-up, windy - Scared

Wipers - Ypres

Prologue THE DEATH of INNOCENCE

June 1900

A perfect sky blazed glorious summer sunshine across the rolling moors of Nidderdale. Wild flowers nodded and danced in the balmy breeze. Skylarks outpoured their incessant rolling song invisibly from the never ending depth of blue and lapwings wheeled and tumbled over the hay laden fields calling noisily throughout their dizzying display.

A farmer and his workers toiled with heavy horses cutting the long spikes of grass, turning the already mown hay and piling it into loose ricks to dry whilst the rain held off. Their voices carried into the lanes and towards the rugged outcrop of sandstone rocks that suddenly jutted up through the earth like some prehistoric temple. Brimham Rocks. A cluster of carboniferous millstone grit thrust to the surface over eons of turmoil and uplift to sit in stark contrast to the gentle undulating dales around them. Weathered and beaten they clung together in a brooding mass, punctured here and there by bright yellow gorse bushes and heather. Their human past had seen them quarried and pilfered for dry stone walls, but now they remained, for the most part, untouched and unused excepting by the children of the locale and for them the Rocks were an adventure playground beyond their wildest dreams. Amidst the sounds of nature and honest toil the excited shouts of six boisterous juveniles echoed around the resonant sarsens and filled the air with innocent, joyous laughter.

"Joe, be careful!" Elizabeth shouted cringing as her brother scaled the rock they had named Jumbo after the famous elephant of London zoo. Not that it even remotely resembled an elephant in any way. It was simply big.

As the eldest at fifteen, Elizabeth no longer regarded herself as a child. Now she felt she must set an example, act responsibly and ensure the others did not get hurt. She spread the picnic blanket at the base of Jumbo and began unpacking the basket, whilst watching around for any of her companions. They had run off to hide. Joe was 'it' and now he must find the others. What a wonderful place for hide and seek! Elizabeth smiled and turned her face up to the sun, listening to the birds and the quiet munching of the two ponies tethered to a low hawthorn tree behind her. A clatter of pebbles made her start and she quickly gazed to where Joe had been. He was no longer in sight. Anxiously she called out for him, "Joe?"

A smiling face appeared at the top of Jumbo and waved before pressing a finger to his lips begging her not to give the game away. He pointed to the south and grinned. He had already spotted someone, and with that he vanished from sight, sliding down the back of his view point and into a crevice down which he slithered, the coarse grit grazing his bare knees. Joe sucked in a curse, looked about guiltily at uttering a word his mother would not even comprehend and then grinned at his own daring. He landed at the bottom of the 'chimney' and rubbed his knees hard before slinking off in the direction where he had seen Frank desperately trying to squeeze between a massive boulder and a stand of gorse.

Frank was a coup. Being the youngest and small for his nine years he was usually quite hard to find for he could prise his skinny little body into the smallest of spaces. But Joe had spotted him before he was hidden. After that Dora would be easy, her white pinafore would give her away. The hardest pair to find would be Sam and Lily. The twins always stuck together, they were inseparable, and they invariably worked as a team. *They* would not stay put, waiting with bated breath and building excitement for their brother to hunt them down. They would move on, circle around, back-track. Their game would be that of the cunning fox outwitting the hound. The rules meant that they could not move until the first member of the group had been caught, but Joe knew that infuriatingly, once he had Frank, the twins would make their play to get back to Elizabeth unseen.

Frank grunted and gasped as he squeezed through the treacherous thorns of the gorse wincing as one tore his right hand, his body pressed as close to Dancing Bear as possible. He felt another barb catch his shirt, the material snag. He pulled away and with a distinct rip, the shirt came free. He bit his lip with sudden anticipation of what Mother would say about his torn shirt. Then he heard the scrabbling of footsteps and his remorse was forgotten as he dropped to his knees and then his belly and, lying as still as a grass snake in the dusty earth, he waited, hardly daring to breathe.

Dora scampered by, the white of her pinafore flashing brightly in the sunlight. She hesitated, glanced behind her and then ran on. Frank smiled. She would not last long. The pinafore, a beacon that could be seen for miles. She had nowhere to hide. Joe was sure to tag her first and then he could start to try and get back to base. He would have to be careful though, and fast. Joe could run very fast. He ran in the athletics team at his school, a school that Frank was not yet old enough to attend. Sam went, but Sam hated it. Said it was full of snooty, stuck up prigs. Not that Frank knew what a prig was, but he felt sure it was not desirable to be one. A robin hopped into the bush above his head and cocked its head curiously. The boy smiled at its brazen bravery and whistled musically to it. The bird fluttered away.

"Gotcha!" Joe's voice startled Frank so severely that he stood upright, crashed his head into the prickly gorse, scratching his face and scalp. He squealed with pain. His heart sank. He had been caught first, even before Dora. How *humiliating*. Joe stood laughing.

"Come out then you beetle," the older brother snickered.

"I can't. I'm stuck," Frank squirmed within his thorny prison and sucked in a deep breath as another tear opened in his shirt and tore the skin beneath. Near to tears of frustration and panic he cried out, "Help me Joe. I'm really stuck."

Joe wavered. On the one hand he wanted to assist his little brother who looked as if he might cry and, to be honest, was in quite a state with cuts and scratches all over his arms and face. On the other hand he had seen Dora and wanted to catch her before she could get back to Jumbo. "Damn it!" he uttered.

"Joe, p...please," Frank pleaded.

Joe gave in. "*Christ* Frank! Mother is going to kill you when she sees you," he reprimanded as he began to break back branches, opening an escape route. "I should leave you in here really. What a stupid place to hide. You silly bloody arse! I'll give you a bloody good hiding when I get you out." Since Joe had discovered swearing he really did make the most of it when out of earshot of adults. It made him feel grown up, more important. Only men swore.

"No you won't or I'll tell Mother what you said. I'll tell her you used bad words Joe. I swear I will," Frank countered, now wishing he had not asked for help.

Prologue

He did not relish a thumping, especially when he was likely to be in big trouble anyway when he got home. His bottom lip trembled. He wished Lily was here. She would stick up for him.

"You dare say a bloody word to Mother and I'll beat the living daylights out of you," Joe snarled, but the threat worried him. Mother had heard him swear only last week when he stubbed his toe on the fire hearth. He had never thought a woman could move so fast or deliver such a ringing clout to the side of his head. His ear had burned for over an hour and his eyes had watered. Even worse was the lecture he received followed by no supper and he had been starving. It was not an experience he wanted to repeat. He fell silent and casting occasional dark looks fought his way to his brother.

Sam and Lily had been watching from their hollow in a nearby rock formation. It was a good spot. Hidden in deep shadow, partly screened by shrubbery and slightly raised above the winding path, it afforded them a decent view of anyone approaching. Lily stifled a giggle as Dora rushed by and Joe had come onto the scene hot on her heels. They saw the struggle with the gorse begin.

"Oh, do you think we should go and help?" Lily whispered pushing a strand of auburn hair from her face and tucking it behind her ear.

"Don't be stupid. He'll say he caught us too and then Dora would win. Just think of the shame Lil," Sam replied his tone incredulous. At times his twin was too compassionate for her own good. There were occasions when one had to think of oneself first and this was it. Their reputation as the most successful escapers was at stake. He rubbed his forehead smearing it with dirt.

"But Frank might be hurt. Those thorns are vicious," Lily argued.

"Serves him right for choosing such a daft place to hide then doesn't it. Come on Lil, we can't be beaten."

Lily turned to face him and saw the grim determination in his dark eyes. Eyes that sat at odds with his red-brown hair and fair skin, a trait that she shared. She saw no compromise in them. Sam wanted to win, needed to. He hated losing to anyone. It often got him into trouble. She understood. She too had the same determination to succeed, although not to win at all costs. Lily was a little more predictable than her brother, slightly less competitive. Her biggest weakness, or maybe strength, was her compassion for others. She hated to see anyone in pain, whether physical or emotional and looking across at Frank now, she felt truly torn between her desire to win the game and to help her younger sibling.

"Lily, don't you dare!" Sam warned sensing the dilemma within. "Come on. Joe will get him out. We can win easily. Dora probably doesn't know that Frank's been found. It'll be ten in a row," He watched her anxiously. "I'll go without you," he threatened, though he did not want to. They were a team. It would not be the same alone. Plus it would make him look bad, when he could have helped.

Lily hovered on the edge, her lips pursed and brows knitted while she strove to decide. She glanced once again at Joe and Frank. Heard Joe swear. Turned back to her twin with a grin. Sam knew he had won and he returned the expression.

"Come on then," she said and they scampered from their hiding place keeping their heads low and their bodies bent. They hit the path and ran hand in hand laughing hard as they heard Joe shout when he caught sight of his quarry and knew all was lost.

Prologue

"I *hate* you, you snivelling little toad," Joe snarled at Frank as the latter finally squeezed from his prison. "I could have got them if it hadn't been for you."

Frank wiped the tears from his besmirched face and shivered. His arms hurt, his shirt torn and blood stained. He felt utterly dejected, but he still retained enough defiance to show his brother he would not be bullied. With a loud sniff he lunged forward and pushed Joe hard. Taken unawares, the older boy stumbled and fell. He cursed loudly then glared with such vicious anger at his sibling that Frank squealed and ran pumping his little arms and legs as hard as he could. The pounding of feet behind him sent a thrill of fear coursing through his veins and his body found unknown strength from the surging adrenalin and panic. He howled in terror but ran on, not daring to look behind. He swerved to the left and dived between two rocks hoping that they would slow his pursuer enough to allow him to escape. A shout and an oath from behind told him he had a chance and with renewed effort, he pushed on winding along the pathways between the rocks, stumbling and tripping, but never slowing. His breath came in ragged rasps, he had a stitch in his side, but he dare not stop. Only the hill to climb and then over the top would be Jumbo and Elizabeth and he would be safe. Suddenly something hit his legs hard. He lurched forwards falling onto outstretched arms. Flaying and grasping at the earth he tried to get to his feet and then the wind was knocked out of him. He screamed. Joe sat on his back and commenced thumping him on his shoulders and arms. Joe was mad with anger, swearing loudly. Frank yelled and covered his head cowering under the blows.

"*Stop it!* Joe, stop it!" Dora's voice and a pause in the beating. More footsteps arriving.

"*Christ Joe, leave him alone,*" Sam cried.

Lily gasped and ran to Frank pushing her older brother from him and pulling the crying, bloody child close to her for protection.

"Joe, what have you done?" Elizabeth demanded though her voice was barely above a whisper. She stared down at the little brother as he trembled in Lily's arms and then back to the older boy who, now the rage had subsided, turned red with shame and sat panting on the ground. "What were you doing? Look at him. You monstrous bully. He's half your size," Elizabeth chastised.

Joe looked around him. Noted the anger on his eldest sibling's face, the shock that Lily could not hide, the grim disapproval of Sam, but worst of all the reproach of Dora. He dropped his head onto his knees and shivered. *What had he been thinking?* His temper had snapped and all over nothing more consequential than a game.

"I'm sorry. I'm sorry," he said shaking his head. He stood and bent down to Frank. The boy cringed hiding his face in his sister's frock. "I'm sorry Frank, I didn't mean to."

"I think we should go home," Elizabeth announced icily.

"But the picnic Lizzie," Sam remonstrated.

"Frank is in no fit state to stay out here. And you," she pointed an accusing finger at Joe, "You are unworthy of our company. We will let Mother deal with you Joseph Hepworth." Elizabeth turned on her heels and marched back up the rise towards Jumbo. In silence the others followed, Lily and Sam helping their wounded brother, Dora behind them and Joe, sullenly and shamefully bringing up the rear.

"I told you we should have helped," Lily hissed and Sam turned to glare at Joe. The promise of a wonderful day had turned sour and though he was angry at

Frank's treatment he felt more aggrieved at the loss of a picnic and the glory of his win.

Eliza Hepworth was shocked and very angry. She glowered at her five children from her seat on the patio. Dora had ridden home and Elizabeth had insisted that Mother must know the truth despite the twins' sudden plea for discretion and secrecy. Mother might forbid further outings. But Elizabeth would have none of it and now the Hepworth children stood shamefaced and silent as Eliza fixed them all with a stare of utmost disapproval. A stare that softened at the pathetic, battered figure of her youngest son, but hardened once more as it fell upon her eldest. With extreme self control she drew in a long breath and exhaled equally slowly pushing herself up from the garden chair. She moved to Frank and touched his tearful cheek. He really had been in the wars. She smiled faintly.

"Lily, take Frank inside and get Rose to help you clean these scratches. I don't want them becoming infected," she instructed.

Lily made to protest but a warning glance from her mother told her it would be unwise. Instead she guided her hapless brother into the house.

"Sam, go and get washed and change your clothes. You're filthy. When you've done that you can clean the silver, it will save Rose a job now that she has other things to attend to," Eliza carried on.

"Aw Mother. That's not fair. I didn't do anything," Sam whined.

"That's enough young man! It is exactly because you did nothing that you will spend the afternoon inside working instead of enjoying this wonderful day. You could have helped your brother, but you selfishly chose not to. I am disappointed that a son of mine could be so unfeeling," Eliza chastised.

"But…"

"Ah! Not one more word Samuel Thomas or I will stop your dinner as well," his mother threatened holding an admonishing finger towards her most rebellious child. "Now go!"

Sulkily Sam stomped inside. He glowered menacingly at Joe and mouthed the words "I hate you" quite openly before vanishing through the patio doors to his punishment.

"Elizabeth, I have some errands to run. There is a shopping list on the bureau along with my housekeeping purse. You will do this for me please," Eliza instructed her eyes now pinned with steely anger upon her eldest boy. As Elizabeth drifted away her mother drew herself up to her full height, which was no taller than her rapidly growing son before her. That she was gravely annoyed with him was obvious, but what worried her most was his sudden violent outburst, so out of character. If it had been Sam she could have understood, if not forgiven it. But Joe was usually so placid. He took after his father and had not inherited those fiery artistic tendencies that she had been prone to in her youth. She pursed her lips and shook her head. Joe hung his not daring to look his mother in the eye. It was a good ten seconds before she spoke.

"You will go to your room Joseph and you will stay there until your father gets home. He will decide your punishment. I don't know what got into you. What if you had hurt the child badly? He is so much smaller than you. Get out of my sight now and use your confinement to reflect upon what you have done." She turned her back on him. Could not face him any longer. Thomas would know how to deal with the boy. She would leave it to her husband.

Prologue

Joe slunk away, he climbed the stairs to the first floor, felt but did not respond to the carefully and provocatively aimed punch on his upper arm from a disgruntled Sam awaiting on the landing, ignored the accompanying insult, entered his bedroom and flung himself on his bed where he laid on his back staring at the ceiling.

The door burst open and Sam shouted over the threshold. "*I hope Dad beats the living daylights out of you. You git! You've ruined the day for everyone. I hope you can't sit down for a week!*" He slammed the door and Joe could hear his furious footsteps fading away down the corridor and hammering down the stairs.

Many hours later Joe sat by his window peering out miserably at the market town of Pateley Bridge bathed in late evening sunlight. A blackbird sang from the apple tree and the boy thought he had never before realised how melancholy that song was. Beautifully flutelike in its timbre it was also hauntingly mournful. He sighed heavily. A steam train, the six thirty-nine from Harrogate, had pulled into the station in the valley below some two minutes previous and the sounds of passengers talking and greeting friends or family, the noises of luggage, mail and goods being unloaded all drifted up and through the open casement. Some children were playing in the pasture by the river, a raucous game of pirates. He could hear their lusty cries and shrieks of mock anger as they fought for buried treasure. A cricket match had just finished on the green and the players were shaking hands, the spectators drifting away. From the High Street horses hooves and cart wheels echoed and smoke belched from the brewery chimney. Below, in the drawing room, Lily was singing sweetly, accompanied by Elizabeth or perhaps Sam on the piano and Frank's scratchy, but in tune, violin. Joe thumped his head back against the wall and contemplated his fate.

His father had arrived home a half hour earlier. He was later than usual from his rounds, which usually meant a new baby somewhere or a death. Joe hoped it was the former; he did not relish his father's frame of mind if it were the latter. The family would be having dinner soon, he could smell the appetising aroma drifting up from the kitchen window and his stomach rumbled uncomfortably. He had had nothing to eat since breakfast and only water to drink. Despite his deprivation it seemed like nothing compared to the punishment he feared. He wished it was over. He wished he had not lost his temper. He wished he had never hit Frank.

A loud knock at the door brought his heart to his mouth. He stood rapidly from his window seat and swallowed nervously, his hands clutched in tight fists of apprehension by his side. The door opened and his father stepped into the room and closed it behind him. Joe quickly glanced at the man's hands and noting they were free of the slipper that so frequently found Sam's backside he exhaled thankfully.

Doctor Thomas Hepworth pushed his hands into his trouser pockets; he was without a jacket, a waistcoat over his shirt, sleeves rolled up. His dark hair was neatly slicked down with oil and parted down the middle, his moustache waxed into symmetrical points either side of his lips. The moustache had a tendency to twitch when he was amused, but at this moment his expression remained very grave. Father and son studied each other for several seconds before either spoke.

"You have some explaining to do Joseph," Thomas began, his deep baritone voice calm and measured. "Do you want to tell me what happened?"

"I thought Mother would have told you," Joe replied meekly.

"She has, but what she hasn't said is why. This is unlike you son. What got into you?"

"I don't *know!*" Joe wailed and flung himself back into the window seat. "I was just so angry. I don't know where it came from. One minute I was alright, the next I saw Sam and Lily running away and I couldn't do anything about it because of Frank. It was like…, like all the anger and frustration in the world filled me up. I was fighting it and then he pushed me over and I just…, snapped. I don't know why. I seem to get angry a lot lately, but never like that. I didn't mean to hurt him. Is he alright?"

The moustache twitched and Thomas found himself placing a hand over his mouth to hide the smile that threatened to spoil his role as disciplinarian. Yet he understood even if he did not condone his son's behaviour. The boy was growing up. His body flooded with the wayward hormones of adolescence and the lad struggled under their joint physical and emotional onslaught. He moved to the bed and sat down looking up at his eldest boy. He was so like himself with a shock of wayward dark hair, hazel, intelligent eyes and generally a serious, but not sullen demeanour.

"What do you suppose I do with you Joe?" he asked although his mind had been made long before he came to this room.

"I don't know," Joe answered with a shrug. He felt utterly miserable. His father always made him feel so ashamed. It was the quiet intonation. Thomas Hepworth never raised his voice, but somehow his whole being exuded disappointment.

"No? Well there has to be some punishment does there not? Your behaviour was more than unacceptable."

"Yes Father. I'm sorry."

"I'm sure you are. Have you apologised to your brother?"

"Not really."

Thomas held his son's gaze. The boy looked away, his dark fringe falling into his eyes. Thomas stood and walked to the door. The lad was sorry. He was suffering all the torments of a guilty conscience. "You will stay here the rest of the weekend. You may go to the bathroom of course, but your meals will be taken alone. You should reflect on what you have done and on how you intend to maintain control of your temper in future. On Sunday evening you will apologise to Frank and you will tell me what you have learnt. For the rest of the term, until the summer holidays, you will remain at school each weekend," he passed sentence. Joe looked up in unhappy surprise.

"It may seem harsh, but I believe this way you will learn your lesson. You could have hurt your brother. What would you have done then? A bad temper is a sign of ill discipline. It is also one of the quickest ways to ruining not only your life, but that of others. Think on this.

"I will give you a letter to take to your house master," Thomas concluded and turned to go.

"But what about Sam?" Joe blurted.

"What about Sam? He, for a change, is not the one in trouble. He will come home as usual. He is old enough to travel alone."

Winter 1902

"We're not coming," Joe stated with the air of someone who thought the proposition a bore. "Rob and I are going to ride up the Dale, try out his new bicycle. Aren't we Rob?"

Robert grinned and polished the shining red bicycle one more time for good luck. "Too right. You lot can come if you want, but you won't be able to keep up," he boasted glancing at the ancient machines the Hepworth children shared. Bicycles were expensive and the five shared two between them. Joe coveted his best friend's brand new Raleigh with a jealous eye, but at least *he* would get to ride it. All the rest of them could hope for was to examine it with envious longing.

"We wouldn't want to cramp your style," Lily smarted though she shared an expression with her twin that told of disappointment. Sam smirked back and tried to appear as if he did not care.

"Let's go down to the lake. It'll still be frozen. We might be able to skate. Who wants to go on a bike ride anyway? It's far too cold," he added taking her side automatically. Joe grinned knowing his siblings were green with envy that he, above all of them, was fortunate enough to call Robert his closest friend. As such, by way of privileged favouritism, this earned him first place in exploiting the riches bestowed upon Master Bradley by his wealthy and somewhat guilt ridden parents.

"Come on Rob. They're only jealous. Let's go," Joe sneered with superiority and picking up the family's old Rover Safety urged his friend to follow. With a great heaving push on the pedals the pair fought their way up the steep gradient of the drive, waving provocatively at the twins left behind.

Frank ran from the house thinking he had, once again, been left behind, but to his delight found both Lily and Sam still there, staring broodingly at the disappearing cyclists.

"*I hope he falls off!*" Sam shouted as if in conversation with his sister but loud enough for his older brother to hear. The distant laughter in response only added to his chagrin. "Come on, let's go."

"Where are we going to? Wait for Lizzie; she's just putting her coat on," Frank urged as the twins began to walk along the drive.

"*God!*" Sam huffed and stuffing his hands in his pockets scuffed at the frozen earth with his boots. Lily giggled. Ever since Sam had started at Richmond College two years ago, he had begun to swear and blaspheme as a matter of course. After all Joe swore. It had, however, lost Sam more hot dinners than he would care to recount and only his stubborn nature prevented him from admitting so. Besides it amused him to see Elizabeth so shocked and Frank so awestruck. As it was, Frank glanced around as if expecting to find his mother wielding all the disapproval her strong Christian upbringing could muster and he grinned with conspiratorial bravado, although *he* would not dare utter the Lord's name in vain. Not so close to home at least.

"Come on Lizzie! We're not going to wait all day for you," Sam called and as the front door opened and disgorged his eldest sibling he grabbed Lily's hand and with a laugh ran from the others, half dragging her behind him.

Half way up the hill they stopped, panting and clutching their sides, their breath streaming in long vaporous wisps in the frigid air.

"Where are we going?" Lily demanded while watching both Frank and Lizzie hurrying towards them.

"To the lake of course."

"Which way? Lizzie will never go along the railway. We'll have to go round by Bewerley."

Sam groaned. "*Christ!*" he muttered and slumped against a tree. In reality he wanted to be with Joe and Robert. Of course, he wanted Lily to be there too, but Lizzie was too proper, too adult in her behaviour now. Despite his pretence at manhood, Sam was still very much a boy at heart and rightfully so at thirteen, but Elizabeth was almost a woman and her sense of girlish fun which, had never been strong, had diminished notably over the past year. Sam found her dull in the way he found all adults dull.

Frank on the other hand was always too afraid of getting into trouble to rebel against his older sister's common sense and so the twins knew, regardless of their adventurous spirit, that this afternoon would be tempered with a little too much level headed sensibility.

The foursome set off, gingerly sliding down the steep Main Street where the cobbled road had been strewn with sand to prevent the horses and their laden carts from slipping upon the treacherous ice. But the pavements were lethal and folk teetered along the edge of the kerb rather than risk a leg breaking fall. At the bridge they peered down into the black, peaty swirl of water, shallow and almost fordable with its head waters frozen high in the hills and snow blanketing the high peaks. It was bound to flood come the thaw, but as yet the river Nidd appeared benignly peaceful presenting no threat to the surrounding dale. Along its eastern bank the single track railway ran away towards the spa town of Harrogate. Higher than the common pasture on the other bank it would not disappear under a torrent of frigid water once the flood began.

The children hurried across the river, turned left past the cattle market and along the track to Bewerley, a deeply rutted dirt road that was now solid and unyielding underfoot. A better state of affairs than when it turned, as it inevitably would, into a squelching quagmire caking the carts, animals and inhabitants of the tiny village in heavy, clay mud. They sped through the hamlet, the air so cold that despite their many layers of clothes the keen north easterly wind still bit hard bringing a rosy hew to their exposed faces and nipping at gloved fingers and booted toes.

After the village the road became little more than a farm track or driveway, although it was well maintained leading as it did to the grand home of the Yorke family and their farm beyond. It climbed steadily until looking over the dry stone wall the foursome could see the river snaking along far below. Beyond the river a man-made lake, built to ensure the mill at Glasshouses had a constant supply of water through the drier summer months. Its frozen surface glinted in weak winter sunshine, the frost turning it and the surrounding trees white with a coating of rime. Along the lake's eastern edge the railway cut a path, past the mill and into the ever broadening valley.

"Look it's frozen solid!" Frank exclaimed with excitement and they paused to watch a handful of children sliding along the lake edge sending a bemused group of ducks into reluctant flight.

"Oh, we should have brought some bread for the ducks," Lily cried berating herself for not thinking of doing so. "They'll be starving."

Prologue

"They'll be alright. They look fat enough to me," Sam mocked. "Come on, let's get down there. Bet you can't slide right across. I'm going to try it."

"Be careful. It might not be very thick in the middle," Elizabeth shouted after him as he ran off along the lane closely followed by Lily calling him to slow down and, after a moment's hesitation, Frank. "Oooo, Sam Hepworth!" Elizabeth muttered to herself and begrudgingly ran after her siblings. It did not do to run. She was a young lady after all and young ladies were expected to show only modest decorum, not go racing around the countryside in pursuit of wayward siblings. And it was about time Lily acted more ladylike! Huffing and puffing to herself the eldest Hepworth girl skittered down the descending track her boots sparking on the occasional exposed stone, over the river once more and up to the low wall that bordered the lake and the lane.

Sam was already over the barred gate and Lily and Frank were half way there, the former cursing at her unwieldy skirts and wishing she could wear breaches like her brothers. A hand clamped on her arm.

"Lily, you're showing too much leg. Don't climb the gate. We can go through it," Elizabeth chastised and her sister scowled, called her 'prissy' and dropped to the other side. With a loud, disapproving sigh Elizabeth opened the gate and stepped through.

Sam slid onto the ice pretending to skate along its edge. "Come on Lil. I'll race you to the other side and back," he called.

"NO! " Elizabeth grabbed hold of Lily's arm as she stepped onto the lake, "It's not safe. Stay near the edge. Sam, come back here. You'll fall through the ice."

"Nonsense! It's perfectly safe. Look," Sam shouted back and jumped up and down to prove it. The sound of his boots upon the solid surface reverberated around the valley, an almost musical, clanging banging. "Wow!" he exclaimed his face alight with excitement and the thrill of the adventure. "Come on you scaredy cats!"

Lily strained under her sister's grasp and Frank dithered by the edge not quite daring to disobey Elizabeth. "Under no circumstances are you two to go out there," Elizabeth warned and tightened her grip knowing only too well that if she let go Lily would not hesitate to join her brother.

Sam skated further out. He was now a good thirty yards or so from the edge. Beneath him the ice began to creak and as he looked with growing concern at its surface he could make out air bubbles where ice and water met beneath his feet. He frowned and a thrill of excitement edged with fear ran through his body. This was like a real adventure. Ploughing across the dangerous frozen wastes, him alone against nature.

A sharp crack brought him from his daydream and into reality. The ice really was too thin for his weight and looking at his feet he saw a spider's web of minute lines radiating across the surface. He shuddered and his heart raced as fear began to overturn excitement, yet as his sister shouted at him to return he still laughed. However, it was a laugh laced with hysteria as his confidence and bravado vanished. He decided it was time to return. So what if he looked an idiot? Better to get back to the edge. But as he lifted one foot the cracks beneath the other expanded with a sharp report akin to that of a gun. Almost in slow motion he noticed the water seep up through the tiny crevices, he heard himself whimper with terror, heard his name screamed by Lily and, as with a terrible groaning smash the ice gave way, he saw her try to lunge in his direction as he plunged downwards into the biting, deathly chill of black water.

    The effect was immediate. He might as well have been naked for what good his clothes did him. The cold was absolute. It took away his breath so that his scream, half formed as he fell, was swallowed up by the icy, numbing depths. Fear and adrenalin forced him to fight his way to the surface as his head submerged painfully. He fought desperately to reach the air above, but the cold was so complete, so determined to rob him of any strength he had.

    "SAM!" Lilly screamed and struggled to escape her sister's now iron grasp.

    "NO! Lily you'll fall through too. Frank run to the mill get help." Elizabeth ordered, her mind a whirl as she fought back the panic that threatened to overwhelm her. Lily was already out of control. The close bond she shared with her twin and the fear of his drowning had sent the younger girl into hysterical frenzy. She wanted to help her brother, to rush over and pull him free and in doing so, Elizabeth knew, she too would fall through the ice. The other children around them had stopped playing and were now staring at the place where Sam had fallen through.

    With Herculean effort Sam dragged himself to the surface and with thrashing arms lunged desperately to get a grip onto something. He yelled for help as his hands slipped and grabbed the ice edge only for it to break away. He exhaled a dreadful squealing cry and lunged again for the edge his heart now pounding so heavily that he could hear nothing else as panic took hold. Coughing and gasping he struggled to hold on to life, but the cold was so very deep, stealing his breath and his strength.

    Lily started crying and still struggled to break free. Her sister held her with both hands wrapped around her writhing body. Despairingly Elizabeth looked around for help and as yet found none.

    "Come *on* Frank, hurry," she muttered.

    "Sammy!" Lily sobbed reaching forlornly to where her brother thrashed helplessly in a deathly dark pool, only now his splashes were laboured. He was losing the fight.

    Elizabeth bit her lip and looked around again. *Why was no one coming?* It was taking an eternity. She oscillated, torn between common sense that told her to wait and the growing certainty that help would come too late. The latter won.

    "Wait here. Don't follow me, the ice won't take both our weight," she instructed her sister firmly and before Lily could protest she carefully slid her feet onto the lake and edged steadily towards her brother. "Hold on Sam I'm coming," she called. His choked gasp clamped her heart with a terrible fear and she quickened her pace. As she drew closer the ice began to creak. She stopped and glanced up, caught sight of Sam's head disappearing under the surface and in horror she threw herself onto her stomach and reached forward. Her hands delved into the freezing water, the pain of it instantly stinging through her warm mittens. His head came up again, but his face was blue with cold and his eyes dark smudges of fear. "Give me your hands, quickly." She called.

    Sam did not seem to understand her words. In fact he could not hear at all. The world seemed strangely vague and distant. Somewhere his numbed brain recognised a face, realised that he was dying. With super human effort he kicked himself forward and brought his hands to hers. Her grip was strong, but he was so very weak. He wanted to close his eyes and go to sleep. He could feel nothing; the extreme pain of moments ago subsided into resigned numbness.

    Elizabeth pulled her brother with a strength she did not know she possessed, but his weight, combined with the suck of sodden clothes was beyond her powers. Behind her she heard shouts of men. She turned her head and saw a dozen mill workers running along the bank, beyond them the group of children and a handful of women stood around watching the tragedy unfold. "*Hurry, I can't hold him!*" she called. Ladders were being laid on the ice and a couple of men tied ropes around their waists.

Elizabeth felt Sam slipping from her grasp. She jumped with a cry of "NO!" and froze as the ice beneath her cracked, sagged and gave way. Nothing had prepared her for the bone chilling cold. It forced the air from her lungs and she did not have the capacity to breathe. She felt Sam against her body and she pushed him, somehow towards the edge of the ice. The frigid grip of the lake pulled at her heavy winter skirt and coat, she felt herself sinking and with sudden and terrifying horror realised that she had not the strength to keep herself afloat. She had used so much effort in holding Sam above the water that now she had nothing left. She felt her head go under and the aching pain of the cold paralyse her limbs. Somewhere her brain wondered how Sam had kept himself afloat for so long. A disturbance around her registered dimly. She began to sink. Invisible hands drew her downwards. Her legs kicked feebly with ineffectual strokes, but the weight of water was too great and the cold too terrible. Panic gripped her heart and with it she struggled against the fear of drowning, but the urge to breathe became overpowering. She needed to breathe, needed to open her mouth and draw in great lung-fulls of air. Yet all around her was inky, freezing blackness. Inevitably the compulsion won out, the body's urgent requirement for oxygen forced a reflex reaction and Elizabeth inhaled. Icy water raced into her lungs forcing out what little air remained. Yet, the frenzied panic against suffocation was brief. Mercifully the cold had reaped its harvest and she faded rapidly into unconsciousness and final oblivion.

The tragedy, for the players, had felt like an eternity. In reality it was over in less than five minutes from when Sam fell into the lake. The frantic mill workers pulled his unconscious body from the jaws of death and hauled him to the shore where they pumped his arms and compressed his lungs until, with great choking gasps; he coughed, spluttered and then vomited water. They wrapped him in blankets and hurried him away with his terrified siblings into a nearby cottage as the rescuers continued to search for the girl. Sam teetered on the verge of drifting into the same oblivion as his sister, while his hypothermic body fought to conserve heat, to keep his organs alive. A man stripped the boy's sodden clothes from his listless body and helped a woman redress him in her husband's oversized garments. Between them they rubbed his limbs, his hands and feet, his torso. They placed him before the fire wrapped in an eider quilt. Occasionally his eyes opened, struggled to focus on the world around him and then closed as he sank into exhausted insensibility once more. Silently looking on Lily and Frank sat ashen faced, their eyes red rimmed from bitter tears, their fears evident as they held hands tightly.

"Don't let him die. Please don't let him die," Lily pleaded as her great brown eyes sought and locked onto first her twin's pallid face and then that of the man rubbing his frozen body.

"'E'll be right lass. Don't fret thi' sen. Jus' got to warm 'im through," the man replied trying to hide his own doubts. He cast an encouraging smile at the two children and carried on working. His mind, like theirs drifted to the other girl, the one they had not found yet.

Twenty-seven hours later they pulled the corpse of a girl from the mill pond. Her father was there to declare her dead and to take her lifeless body home.

Five days later and the Hepworth family stood in a packed church solemnly staring at the plain coffin placed before the minister. The vicar spouted forth his practised sermon, the congregation sniffed and dabbed their noses, heads hung with respect. Dr Thomas Hepworth held tightly onto the cold hand of his deeply grieving wife. She wore a veil to hide her features and though she tried to be brave, he heard the constant sobs from beneath the flimsy gauze and noted the constant disappearance of a handkerchief. He felt her body shudder and he clasped her hand tighter still, fighting to stem his own pain.

Beside Eliza stood Joe with head bent, never raising it to look about him. Thomas knew his eldest boy wept and, unlike young Frank, was ashamed to show his grief openly. Lily held a kerchief to her nose, her eyes full and the tears spilt unchecked as she sobbed unashamedly while clutching fast to her twin's arm. Thomas reluctantly glanced at the boy. Sam had suffered much, had spent two days bed ridden while he recovered from his ordeal. He was afflicted with tormenting nightmares born of the psychological terror from his brush with death.

Thomas tried not to judge, tried hard to be thankful that the boy still lived and that he had not lost two children, but he could not help the underlying resentment, the deep seated and unshakable conviction that his second son, was culpable in Elizabeth's death. Of course it was a tragic accident. Of course no one was to blame, but as he looked across at Sam's pale face a bitter worm turned in his stomach and he wanted to cry out loud, *"Look what you've done! You've robbed me of my gentle, beautiful, gifted girl."* Why had the boy been so foolish? Why had he not listened to the sensible pleas of his now departed sister?

The parson announced the final hymn and as if sensing he was under scrutiny Sam looked over towards his father. His gaze was met with one that held an instant of flinty hatred and though it quickly vanished to be replaced by an encouraging smile, the initial emotion struck through the boy's resolve. No words of blame had ever passed his father's lips, no punishment had been meted, no question of his behaviour on that fateful day had been aired. Yet at that moment, Sam understood that his father held him responsible for Elizabeth's death and the knowledge of that cut deep into his already wounded and guilt ridden soul. At that moment the bond between father and son was severed and a seed of bitter resentment planted. Over the coming years the seed would germinate and grow and the rift now open would widen.

May 1906

The telephone rang on a bright May morning just after breakfast. Dr Hepworth answered it expecting it to be a patient or news of an accident at one of the Nidderdale mills, but it was neither.

"Dr Hepworth. I'm so terribly sorry to disturb you so early. It is James Wilby, headmaster at Richmond College," the tinny voice on the line announced.

Thomas' mind ran immediately to think of the seventeen year old Samuel.

Prologue

What more trouble could he be in and how bad was it this time that caused the headmaster to contact him personally? Something in the pause and the oddly sympathetic tone of voice quickly dissipated this view. Thomas responded to the call with his anxiety mounting. "Good morning Headmaster, is something amiss?" he dragged the words from his mouth. Eliza had just walked into the hall and stopped on hearing his conversation her eyes questioning.

"I'm so sorry Dr Hepworth, but I must ask you to come here immediately. I'm afraid young Francis is ill. Gravely ill Sir. I hate to bring you such bad news but I'm sure you would wish…"

"Yes, yes, of course," Thomas interrupted as his blood ran cold. He caught his wife's stare and she instantly saw the fear he had hoped to hide. A hand flew to her mouth.

"Thomas?" she questioned her voice shaking.

Dr Hepworth hung up with assurances that he would be at the school as soon as possible. Eliza now had a hand upon the staircase banister as if to steady herself before a blow.

"It's Frank, he's very ill. They think it's Rheumatic fever. I must go to him," he said blankly.

"I'm coming as well. I'll quickly pack some things," Eliza announced suddenly finding an inner strength that always amazed him.

"It isn't necessary Eliza, what about Lily?"

"Lily isn't a little girl, she'll be fine. She won't be alone, there's Rose. Besides, Frank will need his mother. Don't try and tell me to stay behind, he's my baby," she returned with such adamant conviction that he did not have the heart to argue. She hurried away to pack some overnight things calling Rose to help.

Thomas and Eliza were welcomed into the Headmaster's study shortly after the school had sat down for dinner that same evening. Both were fatigued from their protracted journey, both were anxious to hear news of and to see their youngest son. Eliza made little attempt to hide her impatience.

"Dr and Mrs Hepworth, please take a seat. I am so sorry to have to bring you all this way, but under the circumstances I could see no alternative. Perhaps you would care for some…."

"Mr Wilby, I don't wish to appear rude, but I would like to see my son," the mother interrupted not particularly caring if she caused offence or not. However, the Headmaster did not show displeasure, he merely smiled sympathetically.

"Of course. Please excuse me one moment while I find someone to show you the way," he said and briefly vanished from the room leaving the couple alone and afraid. They did not speak to each other. They had no need. Both knew well enough, after more than twenty years of marriage, when words were needed and when they were not. Thomas recognised the raw emotion hidden behind his wife's brave countenance. He understood she was fighting the terror of losing another child. It was a fear he shared, yet his strict Victorian upbringing would not allow him to display sentiment publically. He must be strong, uphold the virtues of masculinity so rigidly instilled within him. Only in private could he exhibit weakness and give in to the terrible aching grief he had felt when Elizabeth had died, when little Mary Jane had succumbed to measles when only four years old. He smiled encouragingly at his wife, though it was a smile that did not reach his eyes, which remained haunted and glazed. She did not return the expression reading his thoughts so very accurately and her expression reflected his own barely hidden terror.

The door opened and Wilby entered followed by a tall, but slight, fair haired young woman dressed elegantly in a fashionably short, ankle length skirt of grey silk and white, French lace blouse. Her blue eyes shone intelligently yet held sufficient sombre melancholy to show she understood and sympathised with the situation perfectly. She was perhaps thirty at the most and so it came as some surprise when the Headmaster, a man in his early fifties, introduced her as his wife.

"Louisa will take you to Francis, Mrs Hepworth. Dr Hepworth, may we talk before you go also? I feel you would wish to understand more of your son's illness. I have requested the School's doctor attend at eight. He is a practitioner in town you understand. However, there is much I can tell you before he arrives."

Thomas almost protested, but etiquette deemed he should stay; the Headmaster evidently wished to speak with him alone. He reluctantly bowed his head in agreement to the request.

"I'll be with you shortly," he uttered to Eliza as she passed by him and he watched her follow the graceful Louisa with more than a little frustration.

"I've had your things taken up to Mr Grantly's rooms. He's your son's housemaster as you know and has very kindly moved into lodgings in town so that you may be near to Francis," the Headmaster began once the women were gone. Thomas' attention drifted back from the sick room and what lay waiting there.

"That is very thoughtful of him Mr Wilby. I should like to thank him. I'm so sorry to put him and you to so much trouble," he responded automatically.

"It is no trouble Dr Hepworth. As for thanks, I'm quite sure that Mr Grantly would expect none. He sees it as his duty to ensure the boy gets the best care and what better care is there than the love of one's parents at such a time. Still, you will have opportunity tomorrow if you wish. I think you have other priorities tonight. Sherry?"

"Er, yes. Thank you," Thomas responded with distracted surprise. He could not prevent his mind from running over the possible course of his son's illness. *How bad was he? When was the school doctor arriving? Was he any good?* Vaguely it registered that the headmaster was speaking again, a glass of sherry extended towards him.

"Please forgive me Mr Wilby, I am a little distracted. Thank you. You were saying?" he accepted the drink and forced a smile.

Wilby returned the expression and took a sip from his own glass. He indicated to a rich, red leather sofa and waited respectfully for his guest to be seated before he took his place in a matching chair opposite. They sat before an unlit fire and from his position Thomas watched the rain cast the distant playing fields into premature twilight through misted, mullioned windows. The dismal turn of weather echoed his mood perfectly. The study, by contrast, was brightly lit by modern electric lights, quite out of character with the antiquated, scholarly interior of the study, but welcome nevertheless.

"Quite a filthy evening after such a bright day. The boys will be happy to remain at study for a change," the Headmaster commented as though partially reading his guest's thoughts. Thomas smiled obligingly at the small talk.

"Dr Hepworth, I am sure that you appreciate the seriousness of your son's illness. I would not presume to drag you here if I did not feel it absolutely necessary. Neither would I insult you by trying to pass on any medical details. That, I will leave to Dr Ashford. It was Dr Ashford that suggested I call you. He fears that Francis may not…, recover. I am deeply sorry Dr Hepworth," Wilby explained his mood becoming appropriately grave.

Thomas took a gulp of sherry emptying half the glass which, he then proceeded to nurse between restless fingers. He stared at the man before him while he gathered his thoughts. He desperately wanted to speak with the school practitioner, to see Frank for himself. He glanced at a clock on the mantelpiece. It was only ten minutes after seven.

"His fever has worsened since you telephoned? Are you keeping him cool? We need to draw the fever down from his head. Is he delirious?" The questions rambled from his lips almost without thought, without pause.

"Yes to all of those. When I last saw Francis he was agitated and not fully conscious. His temperature is very high, but you can be assured that we are doing everything we can for him. We would have moved him to the hospital, but Dr Ashford thought he would be better cared for here, by Matron, and was reluctant to move him in his current state," Wilby replied with a patient smile. "Of course we would have moved him earlier if we had only realised the nature of his illness. I'm afraid it caught us all by surprise. He appeared to have a bad cold, a touch of pharyngitis the doctor thought. I am told that rheumatic fever is notoriously difficult to diagnose. When Francis took a turn for the worst we were all shocked and I must say that we have blamed our short-sightedness since." He waited for a response expecting many questions and possibly anger, yet Dr Hepworth remained quiet and controlled with no outward display of emotion of any kind. Only his occasional distractedness belied the man's anxiety.

As it was Thomas had felt an instant surge of anger, but he was a rational being. He knew the difficulty in recognising symptoms of rheumatic fever in its early stages. The school had done everything it could for Frank and the one to one care he received here was probably better than the small hospital in Richmond could offer and he would surely not survive the trip to one of the big general hospitals at Middlesbrough or Scarborough.

"Thank you for being so candid Mr Wilby. Is there anything else you wish to discuss? If possible I would like to examine my son for myself," he said at length with polite firmness. He noted the Headmaster hesitate, make to say more and then check himself. "There is something else?"

Wilby's moustache twitched and a deep frown furrowed his high forehead as he considered whether he should bring up the other matter. He decided it could and should wait. Now was not the time. "No, no. Nothing that will not wait for a more…ah, congruous time. Come, I will take you to Francis." He rose and, picking up his medical bag, Thomas followed.

They walked briskly along oak panelled corridors and up a wide flight of marble stairs, highly polished from the passage of hundreds of feet over many years. Numerous boys, dressed in their uniform of grey slacks and black blazer, hurried in varying directions. All politely bid their headmaster a good evening, all held an expression of guilt as if caught in some miscreant act. Wilby replied to them all using their surnames with affable familiarity and throwing them a glance that said he knew exactly what they were about.

"The boys are on their way to study," he said rather too loudly as they passed a group of youths loitering on the landing and staring wistfully at the rain drenched grounds through long, leaded windows. The explanation given for Thomas' benefit was aimed directly at the boys and they took the non-too subtle hint and scurried away.

The Headmaster turned into a brightly lit, short corridor with stark white walls and green linoleum floor. At its end a heavy oak door and three wooden chairs. The door was firmly shut and upon one chair a youth sat, his thick auburn hair stuck out in all directions, a result of his constant running of fingers through it. His face was pale and pinched, his dark brown eyes appeared even blacker as they sank into hollows that betrayed a lack of sleep and a deep furrowing frown belied his mood of fraught worry. As the men approached the youth stood, his face expectant and anxious.

The Headmaster glanced behind at his companion and noted the immediate fluctuating emotions of happy recognition, fear and sudden guilt cloud the doctor's countenance all in one fleeting moment.

Oh God. Thomas had forgotten all about Sam. Had never even given the boy a thought. His mind had been totally and understandably absorbed with Frank. Now his middle son stood before him, his young face overwrought, questioning, fearful.

"Dad?" Sam's acknowledgement was a plea, a cry for hope. The news that his parents had been called for had instilled him with a deep and clinging terror. He had great faith in his father's medical prowess and felt certain that his mother could nurse anyone back to life, yet he was plagued by the thought that Frank had already died and this was why Matron refused him entry to the sick room. Was this why his parents had been sent for?

"Samuel, here again I see," the Headmaster commented without irritation.

"Yes Sir. I'd like to see my brother Sir, but Matron won't let me in," Sam replied with a little more defiance in his tone than he had intended. His eyes flitted from Wilby to his father. He took a step towards the latter wanting reassurance, needing some words of comfort, some encouraging sign that everything was alright, that his father understood and cared that he suffered. But Thomas' body language and expression warned the youth that any display of emotion would not be proper and Sam gleaned no hope and received no compassionate embrace. Young men were expected to act with dignity and stoicism. A show of emotion was not acceptable, no matter how terrible the torture. Somewhere inside a pain stabbed deeply into Sam's heart and the memory of a sister's death floated unwanted and unbidden into his troubled brain. His eyes filled and he looked to the floor to hide both his hurt and his shame.

"Perhaps you should let your father see Francis first Samuel. If you wait, we will let you in if your father thinks it appropriate," Wilby suggested.

"*Appropriate!*" Sam ejaculated heatedly, all his pain instantly converted to raw anger.

"Sam!" his father snapped. "Respect, boy."

"Sorry." The youth looked down once more his cheeks burning with indignant passion.

"Not to worry. I understand. This way Dr Hepworth," the Headmaster appeased and pushed open the door. The two men vanished into the sick room leaving behind a resentful youth who fought a complex blend of emotions that flitted between anger, fear, and pain at what he irrationally interpreted as his father's indifference towards him.

Prologue

Frank drifted in and out of consciousness. The fever gripped both his body and mind and he shivered and burned beneath the bedclothes oblivious to his surroundings or the people beside him. Over the last twenty hours he had not recognised any of the concerned adults who tended to or visited him. He did not know that Matron, Louisa Wilby or even his own mother took turns in bathing his sweating, hyperthermic body in an attempt to lower his raging temperature. He was unaware too that his mother barely left his side and that his father had carried out a thorough examination and decided that the next twenty four hours would be critical. He did not hear the grave conversation between doctors when Ashford visited, nor did he perceive Eliza's protest when Thomas finally prised her away, exhausted and pale, to get some long overdue sleep. Instead Frank floated in some black, hot hell where his brain shut down everything except the vital functions to survive. He had sunk so deeply into darkness that he was unaware of how close to the edge of the abyss he had come.

A day after Doctor Hepworth and his wife had arrived at the school and a little after one in the morning the crisis came. The boy who had been fidgeting and muttering incoherently only minutes before lay still, his breathing at first laboured and then barely discernible. Not a sound, not a movement did he make. In the dim light of an oil lamp, thought better than blazing electric lights at this small hour, it was impossible to see if Frank still resided with the living. Matron touched his pallid, burning skin and glanced with concern at Thomas who hurriedly pulled his stethoscope from his bag. With his own heart hammering in his chest he tried to find a vital sign, a beat that confirmed the boy lived. Holding his breath he listened hard, the cold worm of fear turning in his stomach. It was there. Oh relief! Faint and thready, the boy's heart fluttered like a trapped butterfly in a jar. Thomas closed his eyes and sighed. It was not a strong sign, but Frank clung to the mortal world yet.

"We will know in the next few hours," the doctor uttered wearily and resumed his seat by his son's side with his head resting in his hands. Matron, a small round woman of middle age and stern countenance, touched his shoulder tenderly and whispered that she would make some cocoa for them both.

Dawn comes early that time of year in the north of England and with the golden rays of the morning sun Eliza filtered back into the sick room, her brown eyes ringed with dark smudges and her fair hair fastened only loosely behind her head as if the effort of prolonged toilet had been too much for her. She squinted at and turned away from the sun as its glorious fingers of mellow yellow seeped through the tall mullioned windows chasing away the eerie shadows of night from the room. The oil lamp still sat by the bed its rays ineffectual with the brightening day.

Eliza slipped into a seat on the opposite side of the bed to her husband who slept with his head upon the counterpane in a position that would surely leave him stiff necked when he awoke. Eliza half smiled and then with red rimmed eyes, for she had cried often and slept little, she scanned the still, white face of her youngest child. So quiet, so perfectly still. The sweat had gone from his brow along with the flush of fever. He lay there inert, pallid and so totally at peace. Tears of grief filled her eyes and her body trembled with fear as she tried to understand, tried to reconcile the loss of her boy. Shaking, she bent forward and kissed his forehead. It was cool, but not cold. A flash of hope sprang to her breast. She stroked the sodden hair away from

Frank's face and carefully laid her ear close to his lips. Warm breath sent a tremble of relief coursing through her entire frame and she exhaled with a loud and sudden convulsive sob.

Thomas' head flew up from its uncomfortable rest and with it his stomach lurched with dread until he saw his wife smile through a cascade of tears flowing unchecked down her face. He stood rapidly and placed a cautious hand against his child's carotid pulse. Still faint, but stronger and most definitely there! He touched the forehead and with growing optimism allowed hope to flood joyfully back into his heart. Frank was not out of the woods yet, but the signs were favourable.

"The fever's broken. The worst is over. He's sleeping now," Thomas whispered and held a hand out to his wife. She grasped it tightly and wept with unrestrained relief.

That evening, while Frank weakly drank a bowl of soup with help from his mother, Thomas paced back and forth in the housemaster's study. He barely held his temper in check and cast angry, disapproving glances at his middle son who stood before him with eyes fixed upon the faded Persian rug and lips set in a stubborn thin line. Thomas shook his head in disbelief. *What is it about the boy*? He was more than just wilful and obstinately disobedient; he had a total disregard for authority and flaunted it with an apparent arrogance his father failed to understand. The doctor ran over the Headmaster's account of Sam's troubling behaviour in school, the lack of interest in his lessons with the exception of sports and music, his tendency to talk back to his teachers. Sam had been punished for insolence five times this term alone and showed no inclination to change his ways. The Headmaster worried that the boy's academic career was in danger and had stressed the seriousness of failure to his father.

Then there was worse.

The Headmaster had called Mr Grantly, Sam's housemaster, into the meeting and Thomas had been told that his son had been in a fight with some local youths in town. Grantly expressed that he did not think the fight had been started by Sam, but he had been out of school after dark and this was strictly forbidden. If it had not been for a group of soldiers from the garrison, the boy might have been seriously hurt. Unfortunately the soldiers, having rescued him from a beating, took him to a local public house and fortified him with beer. They delivered him back to the school several hours later, dirty, bruised and more than a little tipsy. Sam's punishment had been swift and had left him even more uncomfortable than the thumping from the local thugs had, but it had not deterred his craving for trouble.

The final piece of intelligence related to only last night. The very night when Frank hovered on the brink of eternity, his brother had been caught in the same bar with the same group of soldiers by a teacher who also visited that hostelry. Albeit on an infrequent basis, the Headmaster added as if this reflected badly upon his staff.

Thomas had been at first shocked, embarrassed that his son could cause this much concern and trouble to the school and then he became angry. Not only because of what the boy had done, but because while Sam had been out enjoying his delinquent mischief, his brother had lain gravely ill, near to death. It was shameful.

Thomas stopped pacing, stared at his son with cold, burning eyes and demanded, "Tell me Samuel, what is it that compels you to behave so badly? God knows I've tried to work it out over the years, but I have to confess I am at a loss.

You have been treated exactly the same as your brothers. Neither Joe nor Frank have ever given me half the trouble you have." He paused and waited for a response. Sam continued to gaze at the floor. "Well, have you *nothing* to say for yourself?" Thomas snapped his voice tight and betraying the ire within.

"Lily is always in trouble too," Sam muttered with childish peevishness.

"Oh that is beneath you my lad!" Thomas scoffed. For all his bravado, his claims of adulthood, Sam had just proved himself nothing but a sulky teenager. True Lily could be a worry. She was wilful and had a tendency to disobedience just like her twin, but she also knew when enough was enough. She was infinitely more mature. Thomas dragged his mind from his daughter.

"It would be bad enough Samuel, if it was just your school work. I mean, what has got into you. You have a fantastic opportunity. Durham is an excellent university. Yet, you seem determined to throw that chance away. Mr Grantly says all of your work is suffering."

"My music isn't," Sam interjected indignantly.

"Don't interrupt me boy. *Christ!*" His temper was wearing very thin. With great effort Thomas calmed himself. He inhaled deeply, paced a little more and resumed his interrogation. "Please tell me; please explain why you were drinking in a public house in town with a group of..., of common soldiers."

"They're my friends. I was invited. I play the piano for them and they sing along. We have a laugh. It's more fun than this stuffy hole," Sam replied nonchalantly and for the first time looked his father in the eye. There it was. That arrogance, that confrontation. Thomas glared back and clamped his hands determinedly behind his back.

"Wipe that smug expression from your face boy. You're still not too big to get a good hiding. Do you realise you were breaking the law? It's not simply a matter that you broke the school rules by being out at night, but you're not yet eighteen. It's illegal for you to buy alcohol and drink it in a public house. Have you no concept of how it would reflect upon this school if you were caught by a policeman? What the *hell* do you think you were doing? First a fight and coming back drunk. And then this. My son, entertaining the troops in some seedy bar! I don't pay good money on your education so that you can consort with the lower classes," Thomas finished with incredulity.

"I didn't realise you were such a snob," Sam retaliated provocatively. In a perverse way he was enjoying himself.

Thomas fumed. The boy was pushing his luck. He walked away to the window and back again pushing his red face close to his son's. "You think you're clever don't you? Playing your childish little game. Did you ever consider others? Did you ever consider the school or your mother and I? How we would feel? Did you even *think* at all last night, when your brother lay at death's door and you behaved like a damned navvy?" The cool patience for which he was well known had totally vanished now. The lad had pushed him beyond reason.

"Oh I wondered when Frank would come into it. I suppose if he had died it would have been my fault. You could blame me then, just like you did when Elizabeth...."

"HOW DARE YOU TALK TO ME LIKE THAT? HOW DARE YOU IMPLY.... IF I THOUGHT IT WOULD DO ANY GOOD I'D GIVE YOU A BLOODY GOOD THRASHING," Thomas shouted, his safety valve blown. He

Prologue

balled his hands into fists and seemed to swell as if about to explode. Sam sneered, feeling both fearful and victorious; his own temper had long since overtaken commonsense.

"But it wouldn't would it Dad," he scoffed. A stinging blow across his left cheek wiped the smirk away and brought shocked tears to his eyes.

Thomas exhaled loudly regretting his action, but he did not know how to get through to the boy or even understand him. The jibe about Elizabeth and the intimation that he blamed his son for her tragic death was unjust, yet it hit a guilty nerve. With extreme self control the doctor clamped his hands behind his back once more and turned his gaze away from the red hand print on his son's face and the hurtful expression of hatred that fleetingly clouded it. At that moment he knew he had failed and one more link in the chain that bound them had broken, the gulf had widened. Sam no longer stared at his feet. Instead, with unfocussed eyes and a set, obstinate countenance he gazed directly ahead, his chin high with haughty defiance. For half a minute neither father, nor son, spoke.

"I have arranged with the Headmaster that you will be completely confined to school for the rest of this term. You will spend your free time studying for your examinations. There will be no sport and no music. You will not come home for half term. You can explain to your sister why she cannot celebrate your eighteenth birthday. You can reflect upon the disappointment you will have caused her.

"You have a place at Durham waiting for you and I will not stand by and watch you throw your life away." Thomas impressed harshly.

"I don't want to go to Durham. I don't want to go to university. I don't want to study biology, or law, or medicine or anything at all that *you* decide I should." Why could his father not understand? Always he was compared with Joe. Joe who was at medical school. Joe who had excelled academically. Sadly Sam did not. He was not stupid, but his talents lay on the football field and in his music. He found other subjects boring, science and mathematics were a hard slog and he did not have the temperament for long hours of study to master them.

"You will do as you are damn well told my lad!"

"Why can't I study music in Austria with Lily?" Sam demanded. It was worth one last try was it not? Even though deep down he knew he had blown it.

Thomas sighed heavily and ran a weary hand across his face. "We've been through this Sam. Music is a fine hobby, but there's no money in it."

"But Lily..."

"Lily will marry ultimately. She will not need to provide for a family. She will become a wife and a mother. *You* need a career that will support your own family, when you do, one day settle down. And you will. Be sensible son. You know I want only what is best for you," Thomas explained for what felt like the hundredth time, his tone softer, trying to be understanding. How many times would they have this argument? Why could the boy not see sense?

"I'm going to join the Army," Sam blurted. He had not intended to say it, not this way. Yet the impulse to fight back overcame prudence.

"I *beg* your pardon?" Thomas stared at his son with incredulity.

"I'm going to join the Army. I'm not going to Durham," Sam returned calmly though his heart pounded furiously in his chest. His father did not speak, only continued to gaze with open disbelief.

"Over my dead body you are! You, my lad, are going to Durham, even if I have to drag you there kicking and screaming," Thomas replied at last, his tone steady and low. Then he began to laugh. "My God. You must take me for a fool! I almost believed you. *You*, in the Army, now that is funny. You don't even understand the meaning of discipline and the Army operates by the most draconian rules. How would you cope? Have you any idea how much hard work there is involved in being an army officer. There would be no soft measures there. Break the rules and the punishments are severe. You wouldn't last five minutes."

"I don't intend to be an officer," Sam hit back and allowed a half smile to cross his lips as his father did a double take and almost walked into a chair.

Thomas studied the youth hard. *He's joking surely?* The thought of any of his sons pursuing a military career had never crossed his mind. No member of the family had ever been that way inclined. His ancestors were learned men. Men of science and the law. Eliza came from a long lineage of gifted musicians. To the peaceful Dr Hepworth the concept was alien, yet even if one of his boys decided upon such a path he would never have thought, not for one second, that any of them would intend to enlist as a private soldier. It was simply inconceivable, preposterous. A boy of Sam's background, education and class had only one option, to gain a commission through Sandhurst. Anything else was just too ridiculous to contemplate. Immediately Thomas cast the shocking revelation aside as a rash remark from a sullen and petulant, adolescent boy, aimed to provoke a response. If anything he felt slightly disappointed that this was the best his son could come up with. He sighed.

"Mr Grantly will arrange for your supervision. You will not leave this school again until you have finished your examinations and the term is ended. Then you may come home until you start university. Do I make myself clear?"

"As Crystal, *Sir*," Sam answered facetiously.

His father chose to ignore him; he was weary with this pointless, childish battle.

"Your mother and I will be taking Frank home with us tomorrow. I have arranged for an ambulance. You may wish to spend some time with your brother as he will not be returning this term. I'm sure he will appreciate a moment or two of your time. And you may wish to write to your sister and explain why you will not be home for your birthday celebration, if you can manage to think beyond yourself that is."

The interview was at an end. The final snide remarks and intimations cut deep. Thomas marched from the room leaving his son alone and angry. The insinuation was uncalled for. Sam cared deeply for his family, more than his father had ever understood. His jibe about Elizabeth was born of his own guilt, his deep sense of ultimate responsibility for her death. Throwing that comment at his father had been a clumsy attempt at getting the man to see his pain, to recognise the gnawing guilt within. He had been fraught with anguish over the prospect of losing Frank also; his adventure last night only a means to forget, to allow himself a couple hours respite from the worry. Quite why his father misunderstood him so much he did not know. He had tried to please. God knows he had. Tried to be the son Thomas wanted, to be like Joe. But nothing had ever been quite good enough and eventually he had stopped trying and began to please himself. But he never put his own desires before Lily and now he had to explain that he was responsible for ruining their party. It had been arranged for weeks. Lily had done most of the work herself, making the invitations, supervising the menu, choosing the venue. It was going to be a celebration of their taking the first steps to adulthood. Not yet a coming of age, but the beginning of that journey. Would she understand? Would she forgive him? Of everyone, he needed Lily most. To hurt her was like torturing himself. Perhaps his father understood him after all. This was the worst punishment of all. He swore to himself, kicked a footstool viciously and determined more than ever to carry out his threat. Tomorrow he would go speak with Corporal Beale at the pub and solicit his help.

It was a blow to the family, yet Frank bore the news stoically. He remained cheerful and optimistic and perhaps only Lily was truly aware that he shed bitter tears of regret for a life lost when he was alone. Because of his condition it was decided not to send him back to school and it was because of his condition that he threw himself wholeheartedly into his music. His violin had long played a large part in his life, but over the months when he lay bedridden or restricted to a sun-lounger in the garden, he sought solace and comfort in the instrument. So much so that his musicality, inherited from his mother, at one time only a promise of greatness, blossomed into gifted brilliance. With reluctance Thomas agreed that Frank may study music in Vienna with Lily. He had hoped for something else. Not only because he strongly believed there was no future in music, but also because it was allowing his youngest son to follow a path he had denied Samuel. Only through his desire to allow the younger boy to follow a dream that his frail health may suddenly cut short did Thomas relent to the pleas from Eliza. The joy on Frank's pale and blue-lipped face filled his heart with both joy and sorrow and far in the back of his mind, settled with the guilt that loomed darkly around his middle son. Doctor Hepworth knew by giving this concession to Frank that he had only driven Sam further away.

At the end of the summer term Sam did not return to the family home. Instead he enlisted as a private soldier in the Yorkshire Regiment of his Majesty's Army. Frank and his sister travelled to Vienna, but that path would not be Lily's destiny. Her future, like her twin's, would follow an altogether different and less expected route.

PART ONE

1914
The Winter of the World

> *War broke: and now the Winter of the world*
> *With perishing great darkness closes in.*
>
> Wilfred Owen 1914

On Sunday 28th June 1914 an unknown Serbian revolutionary, Gavrillo Princip, assassinated the Heir Apparent to the Austro-Hungarian Empire, Archduke Franz Joseph Ferdinand, along with his wife, in the Bosnian capital of Sarajevo. During the sabre rattling and political manoeuvring that followed Austria made outrageous demands upon Serbia in recompense or, the ultimate threat, be prepared to go to war. Old allegiances were called upon around Europe. Russia would aid Serbia in any arising conflict. Germany made no bones about declaring its support for the Hapsburg Empire. Of course France would stand by Russia. And Britain?

Outwardly Britain did not consider a minor Balkan state worth the trouble and voiced its intentions to not be drawn into the rapidly escalating situation. However, it had sworn to defend Belgian neutrality and had signed the Triple Entente with France and Russia pledging support should the threat of hostilities arise. That support did not, however, necessarily mean joining the fray and launching herself into a costly European war.

Inwardly, Britain was alarmed at the militaristic posturing of the Kaiser's Germany and had been involved, for some time, in an increasingly expensive naval arms race.

The players were set, the dice loaded and cast ready for the bloodiest conflict in history.

CHAPTER 1.
August 4th 1914.

My Dearest Sam,

    I know you will be eager to hear of our dear brother's wedding that has given us all much cause for celebration this weekend. I know also how saddened you were at not being here for the happy occasion. Therefore, let me paint a picture for you. Matron had so very kindly allowed me to take three days leave in order to prepare and help Dora with last minute emergencies of which there were very few, she being so well organised as usual. I caught the nine fifteen train from Leeds to Harrogate and only had a short wait at the Station before my connection to Pateley came in. You can imagine my excitement as I passed the mill at Glasshouses and knew I would be home within half an hour. To my surprise and great pleasure Frank was there to meet me. I must say that I don't think the London air agrees with him; he's even paler than usual and far too thin. However, his great news is that he is performing at the Proms this year. You can imagine how excited he is about that and mother also. She has already begged Daddy to take her to town for a trip! Sadly I doubt I shall be able to go. I am not due any further leave until the Autumn. What a bore!

    Joe and Robert turned up in style in the new motor car. Obviously a surgeon's salary allows Rob this extravagance. I must say it rather suits him though. Adds to his rather dashing persona! Of course, Mother spent the whole weekend trying to match make! She simply cannot understand that I see Rob as another brother and a dear friend. The thought of marrying him could not be further from my mind. He is a darling boy and more than a little good-looking. Half the nurses at the hospital are in love with him, but I have no feelings for him in that way. Am I a heartless old maid? Mother hinted as much.

    Anyway, enough of these musings. Joe was in great spirits as one might expect and we spent Thursday evening playing music and singing. It was way past midnight when I went to my bed and I had to be up early the next day to help Dora pack her trousseau and pick up the flowers.

    Saturday and the bride looked radiant in cream lace silk as she walked on the arm of Mr Bradshaw down the aisle. The church was a picture and our Joe so handsome in his frock coat. Of course Mother cried and I must admit to feeling a little emotional myself. Frank played a delightful little composition of his own and I sang Ave Maria. I know it's a rather Catholic hymn, but it is so beautiful and one of Dora's favourites so I don't think Reverend Smithson minded at all.

    We had the wedding breakfast at the York Arms in their function room. Joe and Robert made wonderful witty speeches that had us laughing until our sides nearly split, but Mr Bradshaw did rather go on….and on….. I thought Daddy had nodded off. In fact I'm sure of it for he started quite violently when Mr Bradshaw bellowed the toast to the happy couple. Oh and they are happy, so blissfully content and ever so in love. Listen to me, quite the romantic!

    Robert drove Joe and Dora to the Station to catch their train, and Frank had tied some old tin cans to the bumper so that it clattered all the way down the road. Then there was nothing left but for us to all drift back home. It had been such a glorious day, even the weather beamed cheery sunshine upon us. When I finally do get married I hope I have an equally clement day, but knowing my luck it will rain and I shall catch a cold and spend my honeymoon sniffing and sneezing. What a happy prospect for my husband!

    And so dear brother, there you have it. A much précised account of our Joe's wedding. It is a shame that you were unable to be here. We all miss you terribly. I miss you most of all. You will take care Sam won't you? I do worry with all this talk of war, but then Robert and Joe think it will come to little. I wish I felt the same. Now then, I've become all maudlin' as Rose would say.

*I look forward to receiving your next letter. Until we speak again take care and God bless,
As always,
Your loving sister,
Lily.*

Corporal Samuel Hepworth of the Second Battalion the Yorkshire Regiment smiled as he reached the end of his sister's rambling letter. She wrote how she spoke, as if the words were spilling from the end of her pen faster than the thoughts entered her overactive brain. He lay back on his cot and stared wistfully at the ceiling lost in thoughts of home. A home he had not seen for over two years now. He unconsciously smoothed the neatly trimmed *regulation* moustache that he hated so much. It grew ginger, just like his beard if that was ever allowed to materialise, and looked, he thought, ridiculously at odds with his much darker, auburn hair. Like something stuck to his face rather than grown. If it had not been frowned upon he would have long since shaved the damn thing off!

"Eppy? Major wants to see us," Corporal 'Snowy' White peered his head around the door.

Sam sighed and folded the letter into his tunic pocket. He slammed his cap on his head and wandered reluctantly to his waiting comrade. He had only just stopped after a long day and thought there would be a few hours of free time.

"Did he say what for Snowy?" he asked looking around the sun-drenched Guernsey fort where most of the Battalion lounged at leisure enjoying a well earned tea break and a chance to read the mail that had just arrived from home.

"No, but it's serious. 'E wants all t' NCOs now. I'm just rousin' everyone," Snowy returned and hurried off on his quest.

Sam drew a long breath and followed his comrade with resigned reluctance. He had a sneaking feeling there would be no beer tonight.

CHAPTER 2.
August 4th, London

Frank shared a joke with fellow violinist and close friend James Simpson as they carefully packed their instruments into stout cases and turned their thoughts to a late drink. The performance of Mendelssohn's Scottish Symphony had gone down well and the audience, more than appreciative in its final applause, left the members of the orchestra with an abiding sense of euphoric exhilaration. No one felt like leaving the Hall for home. Everyone wanted to celebrate their success. The high spirits demanded celebration and though pubs and restaurants would now be closing Helena had suggested a party at her flat. The younger contingent had agreed unanimously and were now noisily chattering, collecting their belongings together, the ladies wrapping themselves in light evening shawls or jackets. They agreed everyone should bring a bottle of something and they would party until dawn. James had winked at Frank and pushed the paper bag containing two bottles of good red wine from under his seat. Always prepared for the inevitable celebration.

The friends wandered towards the stage door calling goodnights to the few people still remaining and struggling with violin cases, music and wine bottles.

"Hang on Frank. Let's organise this properly. Here, you carry the instruments. Sod the music, leave it here. We can pick it up in the morning. I'll carry the booze. Hey Evie! What's all the noise about out there?" James called as the pretty blonde cellist opened the door and a wave of sound rushed into the building.

"The street is full of people running and shouting," Evelyn answered with a perplexed expression. Then the reason suddenly dawned on her and her face lit with a radiant smile. "My God! You *know* what this is about don't you?" She turned to the two young men approaching her.

"What is it?" Frank began but got no further as another young woman rushed back to the door from the street outside. Her features and eyes were aglow with excitement and she grabbed hold of Evelyn's hand pulling her into the street.

"Leave your cello. Leave *it*!" she insisted and catching sight of the men laughed out loud.

"What is it Helena?" Frank grinned back.

"It's war you dolt!" she cried above the din. "It's eleven o'clock. We're at war with Germany! Come on. Everyone is going to the Palace. We simply *have* to be there."

James smirked broadly and ran his free hand through his somewhat long and dishevelled brown hair, "Ripping!" he exclaimed and rushed to the door, "Come on Frank. What are we waiting for?"

"What about the party?" Frank asked lamely his heart not sharing the same joyful excitement at the prospect of war as the others.

"We can start it at the Palace. Come *on*! Everyone is going to be there. Let's be part of it," James shouted back.

Reluctantly Frank joined his friends, still carrying the violins.

"Leave those here Frank, for goodness sake. We'll pick them all up tomorrow," Helena cried with more than a hint of exasperation. Awkwardly he obeyed, placing his beloved violin in the night porter's room along with Evelyn's cello. It felt wrong leaving it behind, like leaving a part of himself. He hoped it would

5

still be there in the morning and that the porter treated the precious instruments with reverent respect. Evelyn grabbed his hand and pulled him into the street. James and Helena were already heading towards Kensington Road and they could see the crowds of people rushing along towards Knightsbridge and Constitution Hill beyond.

"Not so fast Evie," he protested. She glanced at him a frown crossing her pretty features and reluctantly she slowed her pace.

"We'll get left behind," she complained feeling churlish but at the same time desperate to be part of the crowds, of the buoyant atmosphere. It crowned a perfect evening.

"I'm sorry. But I can't keep up that pace. You go ahead if you like," Frank offered sensing her impatience.

"No, it's alright. I'll walk with you. I should think this will go on for half the night anyway," Evelyn slowed to a walk and linked her arm in his. They entered Knightsbridge and turned into the throng. People rushed past them shouting joyfully that the country was at war, alternately chanting 'God Save the King' and 'Down with Germany'. Some people even held small flags and waved them patriotically as they hurried along. As the couple reached Constitution Hill the crowds grew thicker and they were jostled and nudged as others pushed by. The sound of singing carried on the warm, still air from up ahead.

"Is that James and Helena?" Evelyn asked squinting in sparse lamp light at the forms of two people struggling against the tide back towards them.

"The police are moving everyone on from the Palace. People are moving down the Mall to Trafalgar Square. We thought we'd come back for you," Helena gasped clutching a hand to her side and breathing heavily.

"Sorry old man. We forgot you can't rush off," James added and grinned at his friend. "We'll walk with you." He was still clutching the wine bottles and his face shone with sweat from the exertion of his run. Helena too appeared flushed. They linked arms with their companions and sauntered towards the Mall pleased to slow down and regain a little decorum.

Trafalgar Square seethed with a mass of bodies gathered into two distinct bands. On one side, a vociferous number of anti-war campaigners and on the other, and by far the majority, a horde of Londoners shouting pro-war slogans and abuse at their rivals. A thin cordon of police stood between the two but it seemed the crowd was in no mood for violence other than the hurling of foul and defamatory language at one another. And those against war gradually filtered away, defeated and dismayed that diplomacy had failed, leaving the boisterous revellers to enjoy the heady euphoria engendered by the knowledge that Britain was rushing to the aid of poor little Belgium. Of course the Nation's formidable Navy and unbeatable Army would soon send the Hun packing with more than a flea in his ear.

The foursome joined the throng passing a group of well-to-do young men drinking champagne, of all things, and raising their glasses in drunken salute to the songs and cheers of thousands of merrymakers. The noise was tremendous, the atmosphere electric. What an experience, what a place to be and what a time to be alive! It was impossible not to be caught up in the tide of exultant rapture. Faces beamed with delight. Laughter filled the air along with the spontaneous music of joyous voices. A girl in a blue dress grabbed Frank around the shoulders and kissed him firmly on the lips before letting go with a wild gleam in her eye and exclaiming how wonderful it was to be at war before she ran on hand in hand with another equally ecstatic girl. Despite his earlier reservations Frank could not help but smile back and agree whole heartedly, in the heat of the moment, that it was indeed marvellous and yes we *would* kick the bullying Kaiser back across the Rhine.

Finding a spot somewhere in the midst of the happy mayhem the friends breathed in the hedonistic atmosphere feeling its effects take hold like some psychoactive drug, better than opium, far better than alcohol. The happy hysteria filled their hearts and minds and left them breathless with hearts beating fast and minds reeling with intoxicated giddiness.

James fumbled in his jacket pocket finally pulling out a pen knife corkscrew. He triumphantly waved it in the air to applause from his companions and with great drama drew the cork form the first bottle of wine. Holding the bottle aloft he shouted above the din. "A toast! An end to German tyranny and to swift justice! To the war!" he gulped down a liberal mouthful of wine as the others cheered. He passed the bottle to his friends and one by one they drank to the war.

"To the war and to my brother Sam. God grant that he gets his fair share of Hun bashing!" Frank cried.

"Lucky sod! What wouldn't you give to be in the Army now Frank?" James shouted swallowing another good swig of alcohol and spilling half of it down his shirt when jostled by the increasingly rumbustious crowd.

"I would give my arm and my leg to be him right now!" Frank cried.

"You silly ass. You couldn't fight with only one arm and leg," Helena giggled.

"Then I would give my heart and soul. No, better still my violin," he retorted with inebriated melodrama.

The girls gasped in mock horror.

"Not your precious, darling violin? The love of your life? Your reason for living?" James teased wickedly.

"Exactly." Frank replied with a further salute of the bottle followed by another long drink and cheers all round.

CHAPTER 3.
September 26th, Guernsey

Lieutenant-Colonel Lyons had a dilemma on his hands. Since war had been declared a steady stream of reservists had been joining the Battalion, bringing it back up to full strength. The Depot had become a hive of activity. Peace time equipment had been exchanged for war kit; newly arrived men brought up to scratch by incessant drilling and musketry practice. The officers and men chafed at the bit stuck out here on this island outpost, miles from the action in France. There was no news yet of their deployment and, as the BEF had struggled at Mons, feelings of frustration ran high.

On August twenty-third the Battalion's two Companies based on Alderney had returned to Guernsey. Things were happening at last, they were on the move although as yet no one, not even the Commanding Officer knew where to. What he did know, however, was that he was short of commissioned officers. Not uncommon throughout the Army, but he needed replacements fast and yet all reservists fit and young enough for war duty had arrived. He had permission, and even encouragement, to put forward the names of Warrant Officers or NCOs for a commission. His dilemma, who to choose? In front of him he had spread the service records of those he thought most worthy, who commanded the respect of both men and officers alike; more importantly, who had the right background.

Colonel Lyons was an experienced soldier. He had fought in the South African War, he understood the importance of strong commanders, but more importantly he knew that the Warrant Officers and NCOs were the backbone of the British Army. These men, who had been promoted from the ranks, knew and understood the common soldier better than any officer did. They came from the same class, had been brought up in the same schools, villages and towns. They thought the same way as the men and understood their gripes, grievances and pleasures. They were invaluable to the efficacy of the Battalion and his officers relied heavily upon this knowledge as well as their experience. They had the respect of the men because they had earned it not because they were the privileged upper middle-class that he himself belonged to. And this was the problem.

Lyons struggled to see past the fact that these down to earth, honest and respected soldiers were essentially working class. This alone sat uncomfortably with his requirement to promote at least two, or rather to put names forward, for the exulted position of a second lieutenant in the King's Army. It did not fit with his Edwardian sense of hierarchy. True, men had been commissioned from the ranks in the past yet even now, in 1914, it was rare. Accustomed to making prompt and effective decisions the colonel had to admit that at the moment he was struggling. He sighed and picked up one of the records from his desk, thumbed through it, skimming its contents, although he had read the document several times already. He frowned and put it down again. He rubbed his impressive moustache and swore under his breath.

"*Damn it!*" He strode to the office door, flung it open, saw his aide momentarily absent from the anteroom and catching sight of his approaching batman demanded the servant fetch Major Wilson from D Company and the adjutant, Major Andrews, wherever *he* was skulking. The poor man, in the process of bringing tea, dithered between taking the tray into the office and jumping at once to obey a gruffly snapped order. He stalled, hovered with uncertainty and as the colonel turned back, slamming his door with gusto, the batman decided that tea could wait and ran to find the officers as demanded.

Half a minute later Lieutenant Forbes returned to his desk to find a tea tray and stared at it with a mixture of annoyance and confusion. He wondered why the colonel's batman had left the thing there. It was quite out of character and it sat on top of a pile of papers that required reading and signing. He sat at his desk and glowered at the offending tray not willing to remove it yet resenting its impudent position. Forbes glared at the servant when the man hurried back to retrieve the tea things, would have reprimanded the unfortunate man had he not been followed into the anteroom by two senior officers. The perplexed lieutenant stood from his desk and saluted, made to enquire why the majors were here as he was not aware of a meeting this morning in the colonel's calendar, but was waved back into his seat by Andrews and distracted by the batman retrieving his tray and scurrying away with muttered apologies. The majors disappeared into the CO's office and the servant vanished to make fresh tea and bring more cups. It was all very irregular and Forbes, whose sense of etiquette and order was why he made such an exceptional secretary, felt momentarily flummoxed.

Majors Andrews and Wilson saluted their commanding officer, both anxious as to their sudden summons and both hoping that this was not bad news, that the Battalion was not going to be held back or delayed from playing its part in the war. Already they were desperate to get to France and throw their weight into the struggling BEF. It was unbelievable to them that they were still here on these insignificant islands at all when it was obvious to anyone with even the smallest amount of military knowledge, that an experienced and worthy Battalion such as theirs was desperately needed, right now!

The colonel told his subordinates to sit and offered them both a sherry. Andrews declined and Wilson accepted. Lyons indicated that the major help himself from the sideboard and waited until both officers were seated once more.

"Gentlemen, I have a small dilemma," he paused and both majors exchanged a concerned glance. "I would like your opinion on a matter of promotion. We are in the unfortunate position of being a little light in our numbers of commissioned officers. The options are to either put forward a couple of names from the ranks or take on some untried fellows from one of the Regiment's Territorial Battalions. The latter may delay our departure, but my real worry is their lack of experience. These Territorial chaps are alright and one cannot deny their enthusiasm, but how many of them have done any actual soldiering? With that thought, my inclination is to put two names forward from our existing Battalion.

"I have looked over all the records of our Warrant Officers and NCOs, but I am unable to come to a decision. In many ways I have concerns. One concern is that I am aware of the necessity of retaining experienced non-commissioned officers, the other is their suitability. These men, for the most part, simply do not have the desired background. The obvious choices are RSM Wolfe and RQMS Thompson. They are both, extremely experienced, respected and efficient soldiers. They have rank, but neither of them have even a grammar school education and Thompson is forty-five! I cannot help but wonder how they would fit into the mess." The colonel stopped and stared at his subordinates.

Major Andrews dropped his eyes to his knees and desperately fought to suppress the smile that treacherously twitched at the corner of his mouth. He managed to compose himself and lifted his gaze to that of his colonel. Wilson's expression remained impassive. He had no opinion either way and was simply relieved that the summons had not been for anything serious like a delay in their departure. As neither man spoke Lyons cleared his throat and continued.

"There are another two possibilities, but one is rather junior."

A knock on the door interrupted him. "YES!" he roared with uncharacteristic irritability. Again the majors exchanged a glance their eyes betraying their scarcely hidden humour.

The batman entered with his replenished tea tray and at once the colonel softened.

"Ah Smith. Excellent. You gentlemen will take tea?" Lyons asked although the request was not one to be refused. Both men accented and Smith soberly poured three cups and placed a plate of sardine sandwiches, the colonel's particular favourite, upon the desk in front of them.

"Where was I?" Lyons demanded as Smith retreated from the room and he took a sip of the scalding tea. It burnt his lip and he scowled with pain placing the cup down and checking the content of the sandwiches.

"Two other possibilities Sir," Wilson prompted exchanging his sherry glass for a cup.

"Ah yes. Well one of them is Sergeant Richardson. He at *least* went to grammar school. Quite a good one in fact. His father is a low bank official so he should know how to behave in the mess, or at least one would hope so. He also has fifteen years experience, fought in South Africa with us. Quite a solid chap I believe.

"The other is young Hepworth, one of yours Wilson, our star marksman. I know he's only a corporal, but I know we have all been impressed by his aptitude. He also has the right background. He went to public school, a minor one, but still, he is one of *our* class. His father is a doctor albeit no one very auspicious, just some family practitioner, but I believe his mother comes from money. I don't for the life of me know why he enlisted as a private soldier; he could have quite easily attained a commission to start with. The question now is should I put him forward or not? Would it cause resentment? What are your thoughts gentlemen?"

Andrews looked at Wilson raising one dark eyebrow, his moustache curled in amusement. The old man was serious. Of all the likely dire possibilities that the two of them had discussed on route to his office, neither of them had dreamt that the summons would be for something as trivial as this. Although to call it trivial was hardly fair. In his own way the colonel was anxious that his choice would be the best one for his Battalion and his request for assistance genuine. Still, the adjutant found the situation ludicrous. He could not and did not understand the dilemma. He had no strong feelings regarding class distinction. If the colonel was going to put two names forward for a commission then those names should be the two most deserving regardless of background. He had no dislike for Sergeant Richardson or Corporal Hepworth he simply thought that the two warrant officers were more senior, already carried weighty respect from the men and were tried and tested in positions of command. Wilson probably knew Hepworth best, the man was in his Company after all. Andrews suggested that his colleague voice an opinion first.

"I'm not sure how well it would go down promoting a corporal Sir, with either the men or the officers," Wilson stated evasively, he doubted that Hepworth would want the exulted position of subaltern anyway.

"But his background is far superior to any of the others Wilson," Lyons argued. He had hoped his subordinates would favour this, in his view, most desirable option. Major Wilson placed his tea cup in its saucer and spoke with careful, diplomatic consideration.

"Corporal Hepworth," he began with a sigh. "When he joined up he stuck out like a sore thumb. The men ragged him mercilessly because he is well educated and well spoken. At first he got into one or two scrapes. I had him on more charges in the first year than I care to remember. But he worked hard and settled down. He's a good sportsman; our best centre half and pretty nifty with a cricket bat too. As you already know he's a fantastic shot and the trophy room is testimony to that. He's shown that he is a good soldier, he thrives on the life and the men respect him. He's not one of the bullying NCO's. Other than during drill I've never heard him raise his voice, yet it's very obvious he is in charge. In fact, I'd go as far as to say that he has more influence in his platoon than his sergeant does. He's a very capable, intelligent young man. In my opinion he is a natural leader, but I doubt you'll get him to accept a commission, Sir."

The colonel had liked what he heard, it confirmed his own bigoted beliefs yet the final remark took him aback. "Oh, and why ever not?"

"Well, I don't think he's interested, Sir. You said yourself he could have got a commission from the start yet he chose to enlist as a private," Wilson replied.

Lyons looked crestfallen. "And Richardson?" he asked quietly.

"No. He's not got the same authority as Wolfe or Thompson, Sir and, although I don't know Hepworth as well as Major Wilson, I don't believe that Richardson is as natural a commander as the corporal is," Andrews answered.

The colonel gazed at his two advisors. He was disappointed but they had helped make up his mind, almost. However, he was not going to give up quite yet. "Send Hepworth to see me. Let's see if he dare turn a commission down when it is offered by his CO eh?" he said with a laugh. "Thank you gentlemen."

Dismissed, the majors rose, saluted and left the office. Outside they spoke freely.

"Christ, I thought he was going to tell us we were stuck here for the duration of the bloody war! Why doesn't he simply give the damned commissions to Wolfe and Thompson? They both deserve it." Wilson muttered as they skirted around the busy parade ground.

"He's old school. Doesn't believe that anyone is worthy unless they can trace their ancestry back to Henry the bloody Eighth. What are you going to tell Hepworth?" Andrews asked.

"What I've been ordered to. I'll tell him to report to the colonel immediately."

"You're going to let him know why?"

"No. I get a certain amount of pleasure envisaging the Old Man's face when Hepworth turns him down flat. If I let on what the interview is for, Hepworth will have time to give a diplomatic answer."

"You're certain he will turn it down?"

"Absolutely. He has no ambition that way. He sees himself as one of the men and he has an odd sort of code whereby he believes in advancement through merit rather than one's circumstances. Pity though, he's a good chap. He's the sort of man one would choose as a friend if one was on an equal footing," Wilson replied with a grin.

Sam stood nervously outside Lieutenant-Colonel Lyons' office as he waited for Lieutenant Forbes to tell the Old Man he was here. He was immaculately turned out, his uniform spotless, carefully pressed and brushed, his cap badge and buttons polished until they shone. He would not dare stand before the CO any other way, yet he had no idea why he had been sent for. He was not guilty of any wrong doing, but neither could he think of any reason for praise. Alright, he had been instrumental in D Company's winning goal against A Company last Sunday, but the colonel would not personally offer praise for something as inconsequential as an intra-Battalion football match, even the first of the season. In fact commanding officers did not deem to praise junior NCOs full stop.

Major Wilson had grinned widely when he ordered him to report to the CO, but had not been forthcoming as to the reason why. So, Sam waited wondering why someone as lowly as himself had been summoned to this lofty office. He smoothed his jacket nervously for the fifth time and exhaled loudly glancing furtively at the papers on the aide's desk in hope of finding some clue.

The oak door opened and Sam jumped guiltily as the lieutenant returned and told him he may enter. He caught the subaltern's eye hopefully but received no sign of encouragement, merely a disinterested stare while the young officer held the door open. Drawing himself up to his full five foot seven height, Sam marched through the open door, to the colonel's desk where he snapped a smart salute and stood rigidly at attention before the CO. Forbes discreetly closed the door leaving the two men alone and Colonel Lyons stared with mock concentration at some papers upon his desk. If Sam had dared to look down instead of straight ahead he would have been alarmed to see the papers were his own service records.

After twenty seconds or was it an hour? The colonel looked up and smiled at the young man before him. "Please, stand at ease Corporal," he said benignly. Sam did so and recognising a friendly tone of voice allowed himself to relax with more than a little relief.

"You know why I have sent for you Corporal?"

"No Sir," Sam replied.

"No? Did Major Wilson say nothing? I am surprised, but then he perhaps wished the pleasure to be all mine." Lyons paused and waited expecting to see an expression of curiosity on the somewhat anxious young face before him. But the corporal remained professionally impassive. The colonel liked that, it showed discipline.

"May I ask you a personal question Corporal?"

"Er, of course Sir," Sam replied somewhat taken aback. Commanding officers did not ask junior NCOs personal questions either. Such trivialities were beneath them.

"Why did you enlist as a private soldier?"

"Beg your pardon Sir?" Sam asked with bewilderment.

"Well you come from a good family, you had a private education. You're not exactly one of our normal recruits are you?" Lyons went on.

"I became friendly with some soldiers in Richmond, Sir. They made the Army sound like a good laugh, Sir."

"A good laugh?"

"Er, yes Sir."

"And that was it? What did your family think?" Lyons persisted.

"I, er, had a fall out with my father over it, Sir. I joined up as soon as I finished school Sir."

"Rather a rash decision don't you think?"

"Rash, Sir?" *Where the hell is this going?*

"Yes, rash. I mean you could have had a commission. Rather recklessly compulsive of you wouldn't you say?"

"I suppose so Sir. One of my faults, compulsiveness, Sir. My father said the same thing. I don't regret it though."

The colonel raised an eyebrow and smiled. "No? You never wished that you had taken more thought over your options. I mean, you have been with the Regiment for what, seven years?"

"Eight Sir," *Don't correct him you idiot!*

"Eight. Just so. In that time you would certainly have been first lieutenant, even a captain perhaps."

Sam started to feel uncomfortable with the conversation. He was no fool and he did not like the way the discussion was being manoeuvred. He decided to make his position plain at the risk of annoying his commanding officer.

"Permission to speak Sir?" The colonel nodded. "My father tried to persuade me to apply for a commission, Sir. I'd already joined up and he was, er, not too happy about it. He even tried to get me out. But I was eighteen, I wanted to do something all by myself, without the influences of family and friends. He didn't understand Sir."

The colonel sat back. This young man was a conundrum. "I think *I* understand your motives, though I still think them somewhat ill advised. However, I believe that you have proved yourself Hepworth. Anyway, soon we will be fighting the Hun eh? Soon we will be thick among 'em."

"I'm looking forward to it, Sir," Sam allowed himself to smile at the prospect of going into battle against the Germans. It was what they were all waiting for.

"How would you like to do it as a platoon commander Hepworth?" The question came out of the blue and took the corporal completely by surprise. Two minutes earlier and it would not have done so, but the colonel had out flanked him and caught him unawares. He faltered and actually looked the senior officer in the eye, albeit briefly, before composing himself once more.

"I'm not sure what you mean Sir," he said unconvincingly.

"I have to put two names forward for a commission Hepworth. I am offering one of these to you. You have the right back ground, the respect of the men. You're the sort of young man the Army needs as an officer," Lyons smiled triumphantly. The man could hardly refuse such a request. It was almost an order.

"With all respect, Sir and I thank you for the offer, but I must decline, Sir," Sam returned with barely any hesitation.

"Decline! Decline! Don't be a fool man. This would be the making of you. I refuse to accept your answer."

"I'm sorry Sir, but I believe that there are far more deserving men than myself...."

"You believe! *You*, believe! I don't give a damn what you believe Hepworth. It is what I believe that counts. Don't be so bloody obstinate. I demand you accept this offer!" The colonel had turned puce with frustration and slammed his fist onto his desk. Unfortunately it was the worst thing he could have done if he wished to change the corporal's mind. Gentle persuasion, a gradual play on perceived duty and guilt might finally have swayed Sam, albeit reluctantly, from his stance. But bullying would never work. It was the same tactic his father had used eight years previous and it brought out the worst in his obstinate character. An obstinacy that he had fought to conquer and hide, but at this moment failed spectacularly to do so.

"I'm sorry Sir, I thank you for your confidence in me, but my answer is no," he said and stared dead ahead with only a slight flush on his cheeks to betray his own anger.

Lyons seemed to convulse inwardly. He clenched his fists and finally exhaled loudly. With great self control he forced his rising temper down and placing his hands on the desk spoke quite calmly, "Well Hepworth, I am very disappointed. *Very* disappointed. You may go." He picked up the papers on his desk and without looking up at the man before him; started to place them back into their manila envelope.

Sam saluted, turned smartly and marched from the room. He seethed inside. *Now* he knew why the major had grinned at him and though somewhere deep down he knew that perhaps he was a fool for turning such an opportunity down his stubborn nature would not yet allow him to admit it. He knew he should be flattered at the very least, but at this precise moment in time he wanted only to knock Major Wilson's block off. Instead he returned to the parade ground and took his unspent anger out upon his section with uncharacteristic phlegm.

CHAPTER 4.
September 28th, Headingly

Lily rang the bell of the fashionable North Headingly villa, the home of her brother, and sighed heavily. She felt exhausted after a day of non-stop drudgery on the ward inundated with new patients all suffering from measles as the epidemic raged through the city. In addition she was mightily frustrated. The war was nearly two months old. The British Army, unbelievably, had been forced to retreat from Mons. The newspapers applauded the bravery of the British Expeditionary Force and how well the men had done against a far numerous foe and insufficient help from her allies. The wounded had started arriving back in England. The military hospital at Beckett's Park had been established and despite the fact that she had volunteered for the TFNS, her enquiries had, so far, been rebuffed. As yet she was not needed. *There were sufficient military nurses already employed and if it became necessary that more should be needed, she would receive word through an official letter.* Besides, surely she had more than enough duties at the Infirmary? The civilian population still needed its nurses. *So frustrating!*

The door opened and a maid invited Lily into the house and divested the visitor of coat and hat.

"The Doctor and Missus are in t' drawing room miss," the girl said indicating along the hall. Lily nodded her thanks and taking a deep breath, forcing herself to be cheerful, entered the room with only a brief pause to knock. It was a promised visit for dinner. Robert would be joining them also. She had looked forward to it for days, but now, after her rejection at Beckett's Park she wanted only to go to her room in the nurses' home and feel sorry for herself.

"Lily!" Dorothy exclaimed and rushed to greet her guest with a sisterly embrace. "Oh I'm so glad you've come. The boys are talking of nothing but war and it really is driving me to distraction. Come and take a drink and *please* rescue me from this dreary subject."

Lily returned the embrace, smiled dutiful greetings at her brother and Robert who saluted with a wave of his glass and grinned broadly.

"Sherry?" Dorothy asked.

"Yes please, that would be nice," Lily replied automatically and sat heavily onto the sofa with a barely suppressed sigh.

"Glad you've come Sis. Everything alright?" Joe asked sitting next to his sibling and placing a comforting arm around her shoulders.

"Yes of course. I'm just a little tired that's all. We've been so busy today. The ward is full of measles patients and all of them are really quite poorly," she replied in part truth.

Joe studied her for a moment assessing her answer. He thought there was more to it, but he knew Lily well enough to understand this was the only answer he would get. He kissed her on the cheek and whispered, "Poor you." She smiled recognising he had read her like a book.

They made small talk, enjoyed a brief but energetic conversation about women's suffrage and the rights and wrongs of the Government's policy of cat and mouse tactics, but generally on how the outbreak of war had galvanised militant campaigners into action of a different kind. Their feminist passion and energies being focussed into how best to serve the war effort.

They spoke of how the teacher training college at Beckett's Park had been successfully transformed, almost overnight it seemed, into the Northern Territorial Military Hospital and had already begun to receive its first casualties from France and Belgium. When dinner was called the group were still skilfully avoiding the details of war. Skirting the subject and concentrating on events on the home front, small talk and hospital gossip.

"Shall we take coffee in the drawing room?" Dora suggested as dessert plates were cleared from the table. Lily glanced at the watch pinned to her skirt. "Oh don't say you have to go?" Dora begged noticing.

Lily smiled. "No not yet, but in an hour or I'll miss the last tram."

"I'll drive you back," Robert offered graciously.

"Oh, I don't…," Lily began to protest.

"There. That's sorted then. No rush, Robert will take you home," Dora interrupted happily and seemingly oblivious to any discomfort caused. Lily glanced at her with ill disguised annoyance, but the silent remonstration went unheeded.

"Come Lil. Let's you and I retire. Ada will bring our coffee and the boys can enjoy a cigar and a brandy first." Without waiting for a reply Dora rose and taking her friend by the hand tugged her away from the dining table and away from the men-folk in what Lily considered baffling haste.

In the drawing room the hostess threw herself onto a sofa and beamed happily. "Sit down darling. Oh, you do look cross," she remarked.

"What do you expect? I don't want Robert to drive me back. What if someone sees us?" Lily exclaimed with exasperation.

"What if they do? Since when have appearances bothered you?" Dora returned with amusement.

"I *do* have a reputation to uphold and Robert *is* a surgeon. It's against the rules Dora. Everyone will assume…."

"Let them. That's not why you're bothered. What other people think has never bothered you and you've always broken the rules if it suited you. What bothers you is being alone with him," Dora said perceptively her eyes flashing wickedly. Lily snapped her head around with sudden anger, but the emotion faded rapidly. Dora was right and also wrong. For some time now Lily had been confused about her feelings for Robert; had tried to keep him at a distance. Yet the more she did so the more she found she wanted to see him, to be with him. It was a frightening prospect being alone with him because she did not trust herself to be able to remain aloof. With a sigh she plonked herself down on the sofa just as the coffee tray arrived.

As Ada retired from the room, Dora picked up her friend's hand and squeezed it hard. "I've got something to tell you darling," she whispered. It was the whisper and the intimation of a confidence that caught Lily's attention and stopped her brooding over Robert. "I'm going to have a baby," Dora beamed.

Lily's mouth dropped in surprise and then widened into a bright smile. She threw her arms around her companion and hugged her warmly. "Oh how wonderful!" She cried and drawing back studied Dora's face. "How long have you known? Gosh, you didn't hang around did you? Does Joe know?" she rambled rapidly. Dora laughed.

"I'm nearly two months. Coincided with our honeymoon," Dora giggled as if divulging a shocking secret. "Joe doesn't know yet. I was afraid to tell him."

"Afraid? What on earth for? He'll be over the moon," Lily chastised lightly, feeling for her elder brother. He had a right to know. It was not fair to exclude him.

"Lily, he's joined up. They both have," Dora returned as if this explained her reasoning.

"Joined up? What do you mean? The Army? But they're doctors." Lily felt her heart plummet from the dizzy heights of joy to the depths of despair. *They can't have joined up surely. Not Joe and certainly not Robert.*

"The Royal Army Medical Corps. They did it today. Oh Lily what can I do? I can't lose Joe now. How can I tell him about the baby?" Dora bemoaned suddenly emotional. Lily sidled closer and wrapped her arms around her sister-in-law's body, kissing her head. Relief flooded through her tinged with more than a hint of jealousy.

"That's alright then. They'll be non-combatant. They don't let doctors fight. They'll just be looking after the soldiers. I'm sure they won't even see any fighting. They'll probably be in a hospital somewhere. Still in this country even. I doubt they'll go overseas. Come on you silly child. This is simply the best thing. You *must* tell Joe. It'll make certain he's extra careful. Besides he'll be back home in a no time. They only need sign up for a year you know. He'll feel like he's done his bit and then you can settle down together in a nice country practice somewhere. I doubt the war will last long anyway. Sam's worried his Regiment won't get to fight even."

Dora sniffed and offered a weak smile. Lily must be right. After all, she had put some research into these matters hoping to be able to do her own '*bit*' for the war effort. It was a relief to hear from someone knowledgeable about army medical services. It offered the reassurance Dora needed and gave her courage to let Joe go knowing he would be safe. She wiped the tears welling in her eyes and as the door burst open bringing with it the men and a lingering aroma of cigar smoke she rapidly dabbed her nose with a lace handkerchief. Lily distracted her brother's attention by loudly offering coffee and making a big show of pouring it. She chatted gaily and allowed Dora the breathing space to gather her decorum.

The evening drew to an end with a game of whist and no word was mentioned of the war nor the baby. Just before eleven Lily determined that she should leave. Although not on duty until the following night, she felt it prudent to allow her brother and sister-in-law the chance to talk alone. Her intuition told her that Dora wanted just that, although no words between the foursome indicated anything other than the pleasure of each other's company. And because of this perception Lily was suddenly glad that Robert had offered to drive her home, for now *he* could not outstay his welcome.

As the pair bid fond farewells to their hosts Dora pressed her friend's hands warmly and uttered a soft thank you as they embraced. Lily smiled broadly and in turn hugged her brother with even more warmth than normal leaving him a little taken aback. He looked down into her face with a quizzical expression but received no enlightenment. Both Joe and Dora waved to their guests as they stood arm in arm on their doorstep and with Lily snugly installed in the passenger seat of his car Robert cranked the engine into life. Hurriedly he hopped aboard and with a cheery shout of goodbye the vehicle rattled into the cobbled street shaking its occupants uncomfortably.

For two minutes neither spoke and the Wolsey trundled noisily onto Otley Road. Lily stared up at a star filled sky and beamed. She felt overwhelmingly happy that despite the shadow of war new life had been created and her brother would soon be blessed with a child. She glanced at Robert wondering if she should tell him, but decided not. That should be Joe's privilege. Instead she sighed contentedly and took in a deep breath of uncommonly warm air and linked her arm through Robert's. He turned his attention from the road surprised at the unusual, but not unwelcome, show of affection.

"What is it?" he asked smiling, a tingle of pleasure running unbidden through his body.

"Oh, nothing. It's just a lovely night. So warm for late September," Lily expressed joyously.

"Yes it is isn't it? A lovely night for a ride," Robert returned caught up in her joie de vivre.

"Let's not go back yet. Let's drive out into the country and watch the stars. I miss seeing the stars in town," she announced with girlish enthusiasm.

Robert slowed the car to a stop and stared at his companion unable to comprehend her change in attitude, her sudden abandonment of the wall of formality she built between them whenever they were alone. He could not say it was unwelcome, but it was definitely unexpected.

"Oh, I'm sorry. You're working in the morning. How selfish of me," Lily burst out in apology sensing his obvious surprise yet interpreting it as disquiet or even disapproval.

"No, no, I'm not. Well that's to say I am but…," he laughed awkwardly then putting the Wolsey into gear he swung it around and headed not into Leeds but towards the outlying hills and villages. Lily grinned and clung onto his arm, the other hand holding onto her hat as a gust of wind threatened to whip it from her head.

"You won't get into trouble will you? If you're back after midnight?" he asked as the lights of Headingly fell away and plunged them into inky darkness. The car's headlamps gave only a feeble light and he slowed the vehicle to compensate, bumping through potholes and ruts in the road.

"Only if I'm caught," Lily laughed. "I don't care! What about you?"

She really was quite different. So relaxed and so much more the girl he had first met, before she had built the barrier between them. He did not know whether to rejoice at that girl's return or distrust her mood as an inexplicable show of female fickleness.

"No I won't be in trouble. As long as I'm on duty for rounds I'll be fine," he replied.

"Oh! But that's at seven thirty. Oh Robert, I can't keep you out. You'll never get up in time," she objected unable to keep the disappointment from her voice.

"Nonsense! I've stayed up all night before and still made rounds. Don't worry, we'll not go far. You wanted to see the stars remember," he returned rapidly with a quick glance in her direction. He was not going to let this opportunity slip away. He squeezed her hand and to his extreme delight she pulled herself closer, wrapping both hands about his arm. *God, dare I hope that her feelings for me have changed?*

The car climbed higher into the moorland above the sparkling city sprawling, massively along the Aire valley below. The wind picked up and blew in balmy gusts into their faces bringing with it the aroma of damp earth and that distinctly autumnal smell of slowly rotting vegetation. Lily inhaled deeply, enjoying the sweet scents and the blackness of the countryside around them. Ahead pinpricks of light heralded the next village, but before they reached it Robert pulled off into a lane, drove through a group of trees and parked before a five bar gate. He turned off the engine and they sat for half a minute in awkward silence gazing across a meadow that rose darkly against a sky full of myriad stars; the Milky Way stretching infinitely across the expanse of heaven.

"It's beautiful," Lily gasped and rested her head upon his shoulder. Robert closed his eyes silently uttering a small prayer to a deity he did not believe in and dropped his hand to take hold of hers. He thought she might snatch it away, but she did not. Instead she returned his grip and looked up into his face.

God I want to kiss her he thought and a shiver ran through his soul. She felt the spasm and frowned.

"You're surely not cold are you?" she asked in all innocence. He nearly laughed out loud and his mouth curled into an ironic smirk. "What is it?" she demanded smiling back at him.

"Of course I'm not cold. Don't you know?" Robert challenged and shifted his body around so that he faced her directly. He could see by her change of expression that she did and he braced himself for the inevitable request to take her home, but it never came. Instead she changed the subject.

"Dora told me that you and Joe have joined up," she said her eyes never leaving his.

"RAMC," he acknowledged and dared to believe she might kiss him, might finally feel the same way for him as he did for her. He hoped it was not because of his joining the Army.

Lily nodded sadly. "Yes I know. I had to reassure Dora that Joe would be safe. I wish neither of you had done it. You needn't have. We need doctors at home as well as in France." It was almost a chastisement.

"We felt it was our duty. Besides they might not even want us. The whole thing might be over soon." *Did she really care or was it only for her brother that she worried?*

"Do you really believe that? I'm not so sure any more. Not after Mons. Sam worries that he'll miss out, but I hope that he will. I don't want to lose my brothers and I don't want to lose you." There she had said it. *Was it so hard?* She could feel her face flushing and was glad of the dark. Until this evening she had not wanted to admit her feelings for Robert. She had not wanted to think of loving him. She had her career and she enjoyed it. She had told herself countless times as she lay waiting for sleep that he was merely a friend. The wall had failed to keep him away.

"I didn't think you would care about me," he laughed his eyes searching her face and wishing he could see well enough to read her expression. Her tone of voice told him everything but he still dare not hope too much. He had too much to lose.

"Of course I care. You're a dear friend. I would be heartless if I didn't care," she replied a little too flippantly and regretted her choice of words as he fired them back at her, his disappointment obvious.

"A friend. Yes of course."

Lily sighed and turned away. He looked at the sky feeling it was all slipping away. He had been wrong and despite steeling himself for the worst it still cut like a knife.

"I want you to promise me something," she whispered.

"What?"

"I want you to promise that you won't try and stop me from doing *my* duty if they should ever want me. That you won't try and persuade me to stay at home. I couldn't bear to be stuck here when I can help and when you boys are fighting for us."

"What has it got to do with me Lily? You are an independent woman. You may do as you like," Robert replied unable to keep the bitter edge from his tone.

"Not if I promise to marry you I'm not."

"*What?* Are you serious?" *I'm dreaming. Surely any moment she'll start laughing.*

She turned back and reaching up kissed him on the lips. A quick self conscious embrace but one that imparted the tenderness she felt. He grinned and grabbing hold of her shoulders pulled her into a long and passionate kiss that left her gasping for breath and laughing at the same time.

"You must promise me," she managed after a few seconds during which time he stared at her in disbelief.

"You always said you wouldn't," he said not answering her request.

"Robert."

"Yes. Yes. Of course I promise. How could I stop you anyway? Oh my love. You don't know how happy I am. We must let everyone know. We'll hold a party and we shouldn't wait too long. I mean, well, I should ask your father properly, but then I don't see a reason for any delay," Robert rambled deliriously.

"We *must* wait. Robert. If I marry you now they won't let me carry on nursing. You would condemn me to sitting at home knitting socks. You promised me. We can let family know we are engaged, but please, no one else. Not anyone at the hospital," Lily implored. It was hard not to be carried along with his enthusiasm, but she knew she would die of boredom if restricted to the role of a fiancé and wife. He had to understand. Yet Robert was overjoyed and although he had been carried away with thoughts of matrimony and the longing for all it brought he did understand and he knew to press his desire would only push her away. He clung to the knowledge that she loved him, or at least the thought that she did and the comfort of her willingness to acknowledge an engagement if not publically, at least within the confines of their families. That alone meant she was committed. *Didn't it?* He picked up both her hands and kissed them, his eyes shining with emotion.

"Whatever you wish my darling. I'm happy to wait if that's what you want," he said.

Lily smiled "I think we should go back now."

CHAPTER 5.
October 2nd – 4th, New Forest

The Battalion had spent the best part of four weeks at a camp outside Lyndhurst in the New Forest. Here they became one fifth of the Twenty First Brigade of the newly formed Seventh Division under Major-General T. Capper. They filled their time drawing war equipment, including transport carts, horses and mules, some of which came from all corners of the United Kingdom. The waiting was tedious and no number of long, forced marches, physical training to improve fitness, drills and kit inspections to instil discipline, could alleviate the frustration shared by the officers and men at *still* not playing an active part in the war. Gone were the days when they worried that it would all be over by Christmas and before they reached France. The long retreat from Mons had put paid to that fairytale. But that in itself filled them with desire for vengeance. The BEF had taken a beating and how the men of the fledgling Seventh Division wished to give some pay back.

Now the BEF were advancing, had beaten the Germans back from the Marne, assisting the French in driving the Hun from France. The men of the Seventh Division desperately wanted to be part of that, more than anything to prove themselves in battle, to show the world they were worthy soldiers. Many of the battalions making up the Division had a proud and long heritage and none of them wanted it said that they had done nothing or little in this war. But the cogs of the War Office ground ponderously slowly. Some officers began to worry that there would be Territorial Battalions in France before them and surely that would not do.

Many of the Yorkshires chafed in the knowledge that they may have already been in France, doing their bit, if they had not been ear marked for this new Division and consequently had to wait for other Regular units to return from overseas, from places as far flung as South Africa and India. By the beginning of October things seemed to be building to a head. Something was in the offing. Equipment and rations were complete, battalions had been built up to battle strength from reserve units. Surely the orders to embark for France would come soon.

On the evening of Friday second of October Sam Hepworth finished packing his kit in preparation for his move. He shoved his cap on his head and threw the heavy pack onto his old bunk before stooping to pick up his rifle. On the bed opposite sat Snowy White, watching through a smog of pipe smoke. Sam stood up straight and grinned awkwardly. It felt strange moving on when in fact he had been the least senior of all his fellow corporals. Still, none had shown resentment, only an odd sarcastic remark made in jest.

"Knew it wouldn't be long before they made thi sergeant," Snowy smiled back stabbing his pipe at the freshly sewn third stripe on Sam's tunic. The younger man glanced down at the insignia of his newly attained rank and flushed with mild embarrassment.

"I'll 'ave to be on me best behaviour now wi' thi. Trouble is y' know all me scams," Snowy continued with a laugh in his voice.

"We're still mates Snowy," Sam impressed.

"Aye, but I'll 'ave to call thi sergeant now."

"Only in front of the men and officers."

Snowy sucked hard on his pipe and shrugged his shoulders, "Won't be able to 'ave a pint wi' thi though. Won't be t' same. Still, could've been worse, y' could've accepted that bloody commission. Still think tha wa' mad not to."

Sam dropped his gaze to the ground. He did not want to go through this argument again. Snowy had ranted at length over what he considered bloody minded obstinacy in not accepting the colonel's offer of a commission. "I'll be off then," he uttered feeling there was no more to be said.

"Aye, time y' buggered off. Go on wi' thi sen. Go make a bloody nuisance of yersen to Black Bright," Snowy joked making an irreverent reference to the unpopular Sergeant Bright. He bounced to his feet and stuck out his hand. Sam grinned in response and grasping his friend's hand shook it warmly.

"Thanks for everything Snowy. We'll find a way to share a pint, mate." *Stupid*! It was all so petty. Why should a sergeant not be able to drink with a corporal or a private for that matter? *Bloody stupid rules!* For all he loved his chosen career there were some regulations that he viewed as simply ridiculous. It was an opinion that had got him into trouble in the past. He could not imagine propping up the bar of a favourite pub without Snowy at his side. For the past two years they had been almost inseparable drinking partners even though there was a good ten years between them. When Sam had made corporal, Snowy, at the age of thirty five and the most senior corporal in D Company, had taken a shine to the young man most of his peers thought a little too top-drawer for the non-commissioned ranks. It had been Snowy who had shown him the ropes, kept him out of trouble and took his side, for the most part, in every barrack room dispute and tap room argument.

"It should be you not me," Sam said still clasping his comrade's hand.

"Rubbish! I'm 'appy where I am. Thee," Snowy stabbed his pipe in the young sergeant's chest and his ample moustache twitched with humour, "Were meant for more 'n this. Now go on, bugger off." He dropped Sam's hand and turned away. This sentimental stuff was not to his liking.

For a moment Sam lingered wanting to say more, but not knowing what. They both knew their friendship was stronger than the gulf between their respective ranks, but there was nothing more to say at present. He hitched his rifle onto his shoulder and picking up his heavy pack left the tent walking briskly in the crisp Autumn air the mere hundred yards to his new billet. Only a hundred yards but it might have been a hundred miles.

Two bell tents housed the existing five sergeants of D Company. Sam made the sixth bringing the Company strength up to, or almost, that of the others in the Battalion. His rise in rank filled the space left behind following a series of promotions starting with RSM Wolfe to second lieutenant and cascading down throughout the NCOs within the Battalion. The remaining shortfall in officers had been made up by attachments from the Third, Reserve Battalion.

With attainment of his third stripe Sam had inherited Four Platoon. He hoped a lucky number for he was an untried sergeant of limited experience filling a very competent man's shoes. He knew the twenty five men of the platoon would gauge his performance with critical interest; after all, their lives may depend upon his capability. They were a reasonable bunch of men made up of a couple of hard heads of dubious background, three young lads who might debatably be twenty, four experienced corporals two of whom had seen service in the South African war. The rest of the men were steady and reliable with an average age of twenty seven and more than half a dozen decent sportsmen amongst them. The usual batch of poor, working class lads, joined up due to lack of work, to escape an uncertain future of drudgery and hardship. By comparison, though the life was tough, the Army offered them so much more. It fed and clothed them. Many had not owned substantial and robust clothing until they donned the King's uniform of coarse, worsted wool. They had money in their pockets, even if not much and mostly frittered away on drink. The Army even educated them, taught them to read and write at the very least. Most of all they had comradeship, a feeling of belonging, of being a cog in an important wheel, albeit a very small cog.

The platoon commander, Sam did not know. The lieutenant had joined the Battalion only a fortnight ago from the Reserve and Sam had yet to meet him or even learn anything about him.

He entered his assigned tent and nodded an awkward greeting at the three men who only yesterday he would have considered his superiors. It was a hard habit to break and his deferential mean and hesitant manner must have been obvious for two of the sergeants, a hulking, black haired man in his mid thirties and his stocky silver headed companion of indeterminate age, exchanged a mocking sneer over their hand of cards. The third, a fair man with an open, friendly face and elaborately waxed moustache glanced up from the letter he was writing by the glow of a paraffin lamp. He smiled.

"Come in Eppy. That's your cot lad,"

"Thanks Sarn't," Sam replied automatically and coloured at the sniggers from the card players.

"Fred now Eppy. We're *allowed* to be pals now," the blonde sergeant said with a grin that was aimed to put his young comrade at ease. Sam returned the expression and threw his kit onto the bunk. Fred 'Goldilocks' Beale, as he was known throughout D Company, had been his platoon sergeant for two years, his section corporal and mentor for three years before that. It was Beale who had persuaded Sam, albeit unconsciously, to join the Army. The man knew his nickname and hated it. No one called him Goldilocks to his face, no one dare.

Sam started to unpack a few items of his kit. The tent was not as crowded as the one he had left and each of the three sergeants that shared it had the luxury of a rough hewn locker next to their bunk in which to unload their belongings. The light cast by the two paraffin lamps glowed yellowish and smoky but bright enough to read, write and play cards by and as the new arrival disgorged the contents of his pack the silver haired sergeant swore gruffly, throwing down his hand in disgust. His hefty companion laughed and pulled the small pile of coins towards him with unrestrained glee. Gambling was against regulations, but no one was going to turn informant. The former stood and moving from the rickety card table, stretched and clamped his unlit pipe firmly between his teeth.

"'Ad enough Sid?" his victor mocked.

Sid cursed again mumbling something about his life savings under his breath. He shuffled to his locker and pulled a half bottle of Bell's whiskey from within. He glanced at Sam unpacking his stuff. "Fancy a drop Eppy?" Sid offered having poured a generous measure into each of three tin mugs and handing one to the now recumbent Fred Beale. Sam turned his head, closing the cupboard door on his few personal belongings.

"Better not thanks. I have to report to Lieutenant Fielding in half an hour," he replied scrutinising his watch with more interest than usual.

"Uh, Christ! I feel sorry for the poor buggers in Four Platoon. Some queer reservist in command and an arse wipe of a sergeant to look out for 'em. Didn't y' go to some posh school 'Epworth? God 'elp 'em! They'll soon be in t' shit wi' two poncy bastards in charge," the dark sergeant sneered.

"Knock it off Bright," Fred growled from his bunk.

Sam felt the insult keenly; it sparked his once volatile temper, for so long now held in disciplined control. He clenched his fists and felt his face flush once more. He had worked hard to be accepted in the ranks, but his background always worked against him. He knew a lot of the men and NCOs considered him a 'posh git'. He even changed the way he spoke to fit in, dropping his h's and slipping into colloquial dialect at times. He knew he fooled no one and had earned acceptance through perseverance, his affable nature and by his usefulness on the football and cricket pitch. Added to which, for the last few years he had ensured that the intercompany shooting trophy stayed with D Company. Five years earlier he would have thought nothing about thumping someone of equal rank who had insulted him so openly, but he had learned temperance the hard way and practised it regardless of the difficulty in doing so.

Bright simply sneered and shook his head taking a swig of whisky from his mug.

"Take no notice o' Jake. 'E's just tryin' to wind thi up lad an' he doesn't belong to this tent, so 'e can bugger off if 'e wants to make trouble" Sid stated glancing pointedly at his cards partner. Bright grinned in response and took another drink from his mug. "'E's got a point about yon lieutenant though," Sid added.

"What do you mean?" Sam enquired curiosity pushing through his subsiding anger.

Sid sat at the table and glanced across at Beale. "There's a rumour that 'e's TF. Not a Regular reservist at all. No one's 'eard of 'im. Dunno 'ow right it is, but 'e doesn't look like 'e's done much soldiering. Bit soft lookin'," Sid eventually enlightened.

"Special Reserve?" Sam suggested half in query.

Sid shrugged, "Dunno. Seems a bit intellectual if y'ask me."

"You'll fit in well wi' 'im Eppy." Bright laughed and stared meaningfully at the new sergeant.

Sam smiled sardonically, "I'm surprised you understood what Sid meant, Bright. Bit of a big word for a fuckin' shit shoveller like you isn't it?" The words spilt from his lips without thought. A none too complimentary reference to Bright's previous occupation

Bright stood rapidly, his face scarlet with the characteristic rage that gave rise to his bullying reputation and his nickname. "Y'snotty little bastard! Don't think cos tha's got that stripe that y' can fuckin' talk to me like that. I'll knock tha bleedin' block off!" he roared and took a step forward. That he could do it, the men in the tent had no doubt. Bright was the Company boxing champion and mean with it. Immediately both Sid and Fred leapt to their feet, the former standing between the seething Bright and Sam.

"That's enough Jake. You didn't get owt you didn't ask fo'. I'd go see Fielding now if I were you Eppy. Give Jake a chance to calm down," Beale intervened.

Sam hesitated. Part of him wanted Bright to have a go. Nothing would have given him greater pleasure than to stand up to the sadistic bully. He had more than one score he would like to settle. However, common sense prevailed. Jake Bright was a senior sergeant and any brawling would not be looked upon with sympathy by the company commander. NCOs were supposed to set an example to the men not lay into one another like a pair of drunken navvies. Sam could see his new promotion vanish like smoke in a brisk court marshal. Besides, Bright would probably knock him senseless with one punch. He conceded that Fred's suggestion was the sensible option, shoved his cap back onto his head and left the tent. Outside he paused inhaling deeply. He heard Sid Braithwaite telling Bright not to be an arsehole, followed by Jake swearing loudly and promising to "beat seven bells of shit out of the snot nosed git!"

"Leave 'im alone Jake. 'E's a good kid." Beale appeased.

"Jus' keep the stuck up little shit away from me then," Bright finally growled.

Sam smiled cynically to himself, took another deep breath of cool, fresh air and threaded his way through the moonlit tent city towards the address he had been given for his platoon commander; some place on the edge of town. He walked briskly to stave off the chill of the early Autumn evening and enjoyed the invigorating march of a half mile reaching the distinctly English cottage with five minutes to spare.

Not wanting to be early he gazed for a few moments at the endless swirl of stars and the half disc of a silvery moon. *What a glorious night!* His altercation with Bright was forgotten. He felt at peace with himself and, for the first time, confident in his new position, although he could not honestly say why. Maybe it was Beale's final few words of praise. They meant a lot from a man he had always looked up to, even if they were not lavish nor meant for his ears. All his life Sam had yearned for approbation, strove to please his father, his house master and ultimately his army superiors. His father had always found some criticism. Nothing he had done had ever lived up to the man's high standards. Always he had been compared with Joe. Second best, never first in anything. Even Frank was held in higher esteem. Frank, who had been at death's door and fought his way back to life, who had been allowed to study music, who had become a virtuoso upon his precious bloody violin. No it was only Sam who disappointed his father and only Lily understood the pain it caused him.

He straightened his tunic, needlessly adjusted his cap and knocked upon the door. After half a minute he raised his fist to knock once more when the door opened revealing a woman, impeccably dressed in an old fashioned way, at the older end of middle age. Sam's raised arm dropped to his side and he smiled widely.

"Sergeant Hepworth to see Lieutenant Fielding, Ma'am," he said charmingly with a slight bow of his head. The woman returned his expression and invited him into her house.

"The lieutenant is just finishing his supper, Sergeant," she said as she showed him into a cosy parlour with a blazing fire and a little too much chintz for masculine tastes. "Perhaps you would like a cup of tea?"

"I wouldn't like to put you to any trouble Ma'am," he replied removing his cap respectfully.

"Oh, it's no trouble young man. I was about to make one for myself and Lieutenant Fielding. I'll make enough for three shall I?" she suggested, her blue eyes crinkling rather fetchingly. Sam smiled again thinking the lady must have been quite attractive when young as the vestiges of that English rose quality still clung to her.

"That would be very welcome Ma'am," he returned not wishing to offend and anyhow, he quite fancied a brew.

"Good. I'll let Lieutenant Fielding know that you are here. I've already told him you may use this room. Warm yourself by the fire Sergeant. It's a little chilly outside tonight isn't it?" With that rhetorical question she left him alone.

He wandered around the room thinking it far too hot and stuffy and gazed absently at photographs of what he assumed were family and the cheap watercolour prints of indifferent quality upon the flowery walls. After five minutes of slowly roasting to death he was contemplating unbuttoning his jacket when the door opened admitting a slim man in his early thirties with short oiled, brown hair and a thin moustache. The officer had greenish eyes and a distinctly flushed complexion, whether through wine or the heat of the room was not apparent. Automatically Sam stood to attention.

"*Christ!*" Fielding muttered to himself wondering whether he would ever get used to the rigid discipline of these Regular chaps. He studied the young sergeant before him. He thought he could see a likeness. The colouring was different. Sam Hepworth was shorter and fairer than his brother with a smattering of freckles across his nose; his hair a reddish brown, but the dark eyes were a similar shape, as were the other features. Like the older Hepworth boy, the sergeant had a pleasant looking face; one Fielding felt sure would attract the ladies. Unfortunately the gingerish moustache detracted from his otherwise good looks. Neatly trimmed as it was, and bearing no resemblance to those wonderful plumes worn by older NCOs, it still added a touch of the comical to an otherwise personable countenance.

"Please Sergeant Hepworth, stand at ease, or rather, sit down. I would prefer it if you sit, it is much more convivial to conversation don't you think? God it's stuffy in here isn't it? We'll wait for Mrs James to bring in our tea and then I think we'll dare to open a window. Sit, please do. No need to stand on ceremony we are quite alone," he rambled and noting finally that his subordinate was unlikely to take a seat until he did, he threw himself upon a floral print sofa.

Awkwardly Sam lowered himself into a chair already feeling that the lieutenant was not the usual officer breed. In fact he seemed anything but and *that*, was slightly unnerving. Sam was used to strict discipline and Army protocol. There were rules for talking to officers and them to NCOs. The lieutenant did not appear to be following any of them. At last he allowed himself to take a look at his platoon commander. Immediately the two men caught each other's eye and rapidly the sergeant looked away not wanting to offend, but he had noted the somewhat disconcerting friendly grin, the fragile good looks that were far from soldierly and much more in keeping with a bookish academic or a cherished, spoilt younger son of a country gentleman.

A sudden and slight breath of air announced the arrival of Mrs James. She laid a tea tray upon the low table between the men as both were obliged to stand on her entrance and offer unneeded assistance.

"Now, now. Sit down boys. I can manage quite well you know. I am not enfeebled yet. I thought you might like a bit of cake Sergeant. Lieutenant Fielding does enjoy my fancy buns," she fussed quite innocently.

Sam coughed to hide the snigger that leapt spontaneously to his throat and riveted his eyes onto the gaudy flowered carpet not daring to speak lest he should dissolve into inappropriate laughter.

"There you are then. Just shout if you need anything else," Mrs James said smilingly thinking how pleasant these young men were with their brushed and polished cleanliness and bright cheery faces. Such a shame they had to go to war.

"Will you not stay with us Mrs James," Fielding asked dutifully. The lady returned his charming expression with an understanding countenance of her own.

"You two boys don't want an old lady for company. Besides you have business to attend to and *I* should not be privy to Army matters. Thank you dear, for your kind thought, but I will leave you alone. Goodnight gentlemen," she nodded her farewell and as they uttered the expected response she drifted from the room. After a second or two's pause the men resumed their seats.

"Shall I pour?" Fielding queried as he picked up the pot lid and stirred the contents. He filled two cups with tea. "Milk?"

"Er, yes Sir, please," Sam stumbled in reply feeling as though he were taking tea with a maiden aunt.

"Here you are then Sergeant. Your good health," Fielding raised his cup in a toast. "Funny old stick Mrs James. Quite the innocent abroad you know. She's travelled widely. Doesn't look like she should have and she really is quite unworldly, as you obviously gathered. Sorry, do you take sugar?"

"No Sir. Thank you Sir."

"Cake then. The buns really are very good," Fielding lifted the plate with a wry smile which, despite himself Sam could not help but return. With increasing bemusement he took the offered cake and sat nursing his delicate china cup and plate upon his knee obviously ill at ease.

Fielding sat back and stared once again as the sergeant took a bite of cake and tried to appear comfortable with his situation. "You look like your brother. Fairer though and the hair colour of course is very different. My memory of Joseph is that he has quite dark hair is that not so? Still, I can see the likeness in the eyes and the shape of your face. I take an interest in studying such things Sergeant. I pretend to be an artist," he said at last.

With a piece of bun half way to his mouth Sam hesitated and then replaced it on his plate. "I beg your pardon Sir?"

"Your brother, Joseph. You look quite like him."

"You know my brother Sir?" Sam questioned lamely.

"Certainly. He was in my house at school. As were you, but of course I had left by then. We didn't know each other that well. I mean I was a senior when Joseph started, but I do remember him because he was so very bright and a half decent athlete. I believe you are an even better sportsman. Joseph played in the school orchestra with me, or rather next to me," Fielding explicated.

"You went to Richmond College Sir?"

"Yes, until 'ninety-nine, then I went up to Oxford. Studied history and theology. You can't believe how pleased I was when I found out you were to be my platoon sergeant. I mean, when I found out who you were. Bit puzzled why you haven't a commission though. Still, I'm sure we will be good friends Sam. You don't mind if I call you that do you? My name is Harry," Fielding went on.

Somehow Sam gathered his wits. "You may call me what you wish Sir, but you must know that officers and NCOs cannot be friends. Respected associates maybe, but not true friends, Sir. It's against Army regulations for such fraternisation between the ranks...."

"Tosh!" Fielding interrupted. "Army etiquette at its most ridiculous."

Taken aback, Sam half smiled at the officer's remonstration it was like a breath of fresh air, echoed his own feelings, yet was dangerously close to what the Army would consider anarchy. He hastily took a sip of tea. Fielding was a strange one. Most definitely not a Regular. Perhaps the rumour about him was correct after all. Perhaps the lieutenant had some half baked idea that as friends they may better serve their platoon. Perhaps he had no such idea at all and was simply someone with little understanding of Army protocol and thought he had found a man with whom he had something in common. Perhaps his desire for friendship was just that.

"You seem ill at ease Sam," Fielding prompted as the silence yawned on. "It bothers you, my talking like this? You have belonged to the Army a while have you not?"

"Eight years Sir and yes it bothers me. It is…, most irregular, Sir," Sam returned finding the confidence to speak out. Something in Fielding invited it.

"Irregular? Yes I suppose it is. You do not think we could be friends then Sam? We have more in common than I have with most of my fellow officers I think. I would value your friendship, your help on certain matters. I am not experienced in the art of soldiering. I understand though, that what I suggest is flaunting the rules and you Regulars are sticklers for rules aren't you?" Fielding added the last with a trace of mockery that piqued his subordinate.

"Yes Sir, it's what makes the Army and the Regiment strong. Discipline binds us. We all have our place and know and understand what is expected of us. One cannot simply change hundreds of years of tradition and etiquette on a whim," Sam snapped back and then realising he was not exactly practising what he preached commenced on a softer tone. "Look Sir, don't get me wrong, but even though we went to the same school and our backgrounds may be similar you have to understand that I gave up that life when I joined up. Here, I am not your equal. For friendship you need to look to your fellow officers not to your platoon sergeant, Sir. Anything different would not be right, especially in front of the men." He paused as Fielding appeared to deflate before him. Sid Braithwaite was right and the man had almost admitted it himself, the lieutenant had never been Army.

"You're not from the third Battalion are you Sir?" Sam asked without regard to whether he sounded impertinent.

"No. I joined the fourth, the TF Battalion earlier this year. My brother encouraged me. It seemed a good way to…, well my father has always…., I always felt like I didn't live up to his expectations. Edward suggested if I joined the Territorials that Father might, you know, have something to talk about with me. He was Army. Edward is a captain in the RFA. I never had any aspirations that way, but the TF sounded alright. I mean, it seemed like being a soldier without all the….." Fielding's voice trailed away. He was embarrassed. He had said more than he would have liked and to a man, that for all he knew would go and tell the whole tale to his mates and make a laughing stock of him. He thought not. He thought that Sam Hepworth would have the same integrity that his older brother had. But he was not sure. He glanced at the sergeant opposite and hurriedly took a sip of tea grimacing at the lack of sugar.

For a long moment Sam stared. The lieutenant's blurted confession struck a chord. He understood what it was to feel a disappointment to one's father. It was something they both shared, but whereas Sam felt he had rebelled he saw Fielding's plight as one of seeking acceptance. Still the common sufferance changed his mind in a second about the man before him. His generous nature won through the years of brainwashing and hard discipline of army life.

"May I ask, Sir, how you managed to get here, now?" he requested in a tone that implied his guard had dropped and the olive branch of friendship tenuously extended.

Fielding looked up from his tea cup. His face was still flushed, but he sensed a difference and he jumped to grab the branch with both hands. "I have an uncle in the War Office." He laughed. "It's all very nepotistic really. When war was declared, I decided I had the chance to show everyone that I wasn't just some academic twit. I could have waited I suppose, until the TF were brought in, but I thought it might all be over too soon. I begged a huge favour from my uncle. He was all too happy to oblige. Sadly I'm no damn good at it. The TF was different. Discipline only lasted as long as parade or drill or whatever did. After that we all went to the pub together and became what we really are, bankers, farmers, shopkeepers and the like. Rank meant nothing any longer, and going to the pub did seem to bind us all together as a unit. Here it is all so different. I was naïve enough to believe it could be the same." Fielding smiled a little sadly and eyed the sergeant anxiously.

Sam had his doubts that the lieutenant would make much of a leader, but he seemed a decent fellow and he had rather laid himself bare. Without help he would be eaten alive, figuratively speaking. The men would run rings around him and play him for a fool. "How much soldiering have you actually done, Sir?" he asked quietly.

"Only TF stuff. Basic training, summer camp and I know my Field Service Pocket Book inside out. I know what's expected of me Sam, it's just…, er, I'm not sure how to deliver and it's all a little more rigid than I expected," Fielding returned running his fingers through his hair.

Sam smiled. "Alright Sir, I'll help you. But you must understand that this is a new position for me as well. Until this morning I was still a corporal. There are a few ground rules."

"Ground rules?"

"Yes. Look Sir, you'll get the hang of it after a while, but until then you still have to appear in command even if you don't feel in control. If the men get even a whiff of what you've admitted to me they'll take every advantage they can and we'll both look like fools. I worked too damn hard to get where I am to jeopardise that, so we need ground rules." Sam raised a questioning eyebrow.

"Alright, I agree. What are they?"

"First, in front of the men and other NCOs you address me as Sergeant Hepworth. Anything else is too familiar and doesn't suggest seniority. If you wish, to my face and in front of officers, call me Eppy. That's what everyone knows me as.

"Second, never ask my opinion in front of the men. It's fairly common for officers to discuss tactics with senior NCOs but only in private. *You* are in command. You make the decisions. You work out the tactics by which we carry out orders. I may have helped you come to those decisions and secretly the men might know that, but *never* defer to me or look to me for guidance except in private. Hell, I don't know whether I'll give you any decent help there anyway. I've never fought in anything but a few skirmishes in Ireland.

"Finally, never show me favouritism. If I cock up I get the same bollocking anyone else would. If I break the rules and get caught, you report me to the CO for punishment," Sam explicated and looked for acknowledgment.

"Understood Sergeant and thank you."

"Nothing to thank me for. It's in my interest to ensure you know what you're doing," Sam replied gruffly suddenly feeling awkward under Fielding's beaming gaze and heartfelt gratitude.

"There's, er…, something else you ought to know," the lieutenant added uncomfortably. Sam raised an eyebrow. "I…, er, I can't ride."

"*What?*"

Fielding shrugged. "Just never got round to it. It never seemed important to me and I've always been rather afraid of horses. Flighty brutes! My mother was scared of them and I suppose I inherited her fear."

"*Jesus Christ!*"

"Platoon, fall out!" Sam yelled and the men and junior NCOs of Four Platoon slumped into relaxed posture and began to drift away from morning parade to breakfast. They joked together, muttered about the cold morning, but were generally in good spirits even though there was still no news of orders.

The whole Battalion, the whole Division for that matter, had been ready for several days now. Quartermasters had checked and re-checked stores. The men's personal kit had been inspected, cleaned, polished and re-inspected so much that they were in danger of blinding the enemy with reflected sunlight from their spotless rifles and bayonets. To fill time they marched, paraded, drilled and practised musketry. The rest of the time they waited with increasing frustration, boredom and a little anxiety for embarkation orders that surely must come soon. Where those orders would take them no one really cared as long as it was into action. No one wanted a soft posting. This was the subject of conversation at breakfast, lunch and dinner regardless of rank and this morning was no exception. As the men of Four Platoon sauntered to their tents to discard their kit the banter and chatter once more gave way to speculation and wishful thinking.

Sam followed a group of five men who were arguing amiably about whether the Division would be sent to France or Belgium. One of the five grunted and gave his opinion that there would soon be no more Belgium to be sent to and that France was the only option left. The sergeant interrupted their debate.

"Pratt, a word," he said with enough authority for the pale, brown haired man to blanche paler still, wondering what he may have done wrong. He could not think of anything, unless Eppy had found out about the rum last night? *Surely not?* Although he knew Sam Hepworth was smart. Much smarter than their last platoon sergeant. He thought that the sergeant was fairer than most though, willing to turn a blind eye to the odd misdemeanour. He might have been mistaken in that assumption. He frowned and reluctantly stopped turning to face his superior as his mates hurried away eyeing him with a mixture of pity and almost schoolboy like glee at his misfortune.

"Sarn't?" Pratt said in respectful query.

Sam hesitated, looking about briefly to check there were no eavesdroppers. He noted Pratt's half hidden anxiety and quickly put him at ease. "It's alright Bill. I just want to ask a favour." Pratt eyed him curiously but said nothing. They might have attested in the same year, shared a few drinks together in the past, but Eppy was now a sergeant and he was still only a private soldier. He waited.

"You're a pretty good judge of horseflesh aren't you Bill?" Sam asked at length knowing that the man before him came from a family of farm labourers near

Northallerton and had once spoken at length about his life growing up amongst horses, cattle and the like on a particularly drunken night in Richmond.

"Aye, I'm not bad," Bill replied looking puzzled.

"Good. Look, the lieutenant hasn't got a ride yet. He's asked me to sort one out for him, but I'm no expert. I want you to do it for me. I'll give you his note. I want to make sure he gets a decent ride," Sam explained inadequately.

Bill appeared even more puzzled. The new lieutenant had been with them for two weeks now. Ample time to sort himself out with a horse and why was Eppy worried? He was not the sort of man who liked to ingratiate himself to officers. If the lieutenant had not got himself sorted with a mount the livery sergeant would do it for him, no problem.

"You sure 'e 'asn't got one Sarn't? 'E's been wi' us a fortnight," he said.

"I'm positive. He asked me to look one out for him. Look Bill, I need to be sure he gets the right horse. He's…, he's not a great horseman," Sam explained realising that he would have to be more forthcoming but not wishing to give away too much. But Bill Pratt was not stupid. He quickly put two and two together and made six.

"'E can't ride then." He stated with a broad grin. "Rumour's true; about 'im then. 'E isn't no reservist. Thought 'e seemed a bit wet like. What was 'e? TF?"

"I know nothing about the lieutenant's background Private. He could be from a bloody Highland Regiment for all I know. And you won't go round blabbing your mouth off and spreading malicious rumours otherwise the lieutenant will get to know about that rum jar you and Thornton nicked last night. Do I make myself clear, Bill?" Sam stabbed a finger at the private's chest. Had he made a mistake? He had thought Pratt to be discreet and trustworthy despite his recent misdemeanour. Bill's grin dropped from his face. There were no flies on Eppy. *How the hell did he know about the rum?*

"Aye Sarn't. It's clear. I'll pick the lieutenant a nag. A nice steady un. An' I won't be sayin' nowt. When does 'e want it by?"

"The sooner the better," Sam sighed with relief. "After breakfast. Bring it to the edge of town by ten. Here's the note, you'll need it to get out of camp as well as to persuade the livery sergeant. Thanks Bill, I appreciate it." He handed over the scrap of paper signed by Fielding.

"Not a problem Sarn't. Any time." Bill took the note and stomped off to dump his kit and grab some food before the rest of the platoon ate it all.

At five minutes to ten Sam watched with mounting dismay as Private Pratt led what appeared to be a lumbering old cart horse towards the first few houses that belonged to the small market town. Alright, he had given instructions to pick out something steady, but…. He sighed heavily and ran a hand through his thick auburn hair before slamming his cap on and setting his jaw in obvious rigid displeasure. However, as the private and the chosen steed drew closer, the animal did not appear so ponderous, nor so old. The sergeant allowed himself a glimmer of hope.

"Christ Bill, I thought you were bringing me some old dray nag at first," he laughed as Pratt reached him and steadied the heavy bay gelding to a standstill. The horse snorted compliantly and immediately dropped his head to the lush grass on the verge.

"'E's not pretty, but 'e's steady and docile. Strong too. 'E should be a good ride for someone not used to sittin' an 'orse. 'E'll be alright for t' lieutenant. 'Ad 'ard time persuadin' t' sergeant to let me 'ave 'im. Kept tryin' to give me a dashin' flighty mare. Lovely beast, but she wa' a bit wild like. Didn't think t' lieutenant would stay on 'er back more 'n a minute or two," Bill laughed stroking the gelding's thick neck. "This un wa' earmarked fo' carryin' stuff, but I reckon 'e's just right fo' what y' want. 'E's a bit big mind."

"As long as he's docile we can deal with the rest," Sam stated with relief. The horse was going to be fine. Yes he was a big brute, but he was as placid as anything he could have asked for.

Bill eyed him warily. "We, Sarn't?"

"Yes Bill, we. *We* are going to teach the lieutenant how to ride and I reckon we've got today to do it in."

Bill's eyebrows disappeared under his fringe and his moustache drooped in dismay. "I dunno Sarn't. I 'aven't gi'en ridin' lessons beforer, an' to an officer?"

"Don't worry about it man. I'll do the lessons bit, you look after the horse. Does it have a name by the way?"

"Dunno. Didn't ask. Look Sarn't…" Bill began to protest.

"Stop nattering Bill. Look upon this as a holiday. I've given you the best reason to get out of drill and musketry for the day. Besides I've already arranged it. You're on special duties at the request of Lieutenant Fielding."

Bill scowled muttering that he rather liked musketry practise, but he knew when to keep quiet. Sam Hepworth was a reasonable man, but he was still his sergeant and Bill did not want to be spending the next few days on a charge. With a sullen expression he followed the NCO down a quiet lane, leading the big gelding behind him, to a large pasture in front of a picturesque New Forest cottage. Sam took out a pack of cigarettes and offered one to his subordinate. Never one to turn down a free smoke, Bill gladly took it and the pair lit up, drew appreciatively on the tobacco and waited. The horse resumed his steady munching of grass.

Twenty minutes and two cigarettes later Lieutenant Fielding walked into the field dressed in what appeared to be an old suit stolen from some unfortunate scarecrow. Sam glanced almost apologetically at Bill who dropped his eyes rapidly to hide his mirth under the pretext of dropping his cigarette end and stamping it out into the damp grass. As the officer drew near the two men gathered themselves and saluted. Fielding returned the address and smiled broadly before studying the large gelding with open anxiety.

"Sergeant, Private Pratt," Fielding acknowledged and shoved his hands into deep, workman's pockets on his somewhat threadbare trousers. The only part of his attire that could be described as uniform was his cap. "It's a bit of a big brute isn't it Sergeant?" he said with a worried air.

"He's big, but he's gentle, Sir," Sam replied catching the smirk on Pratt's face which, was rapidly dropped following his hard stare. "Bill here is a good judge of horse flesh Sir."

Fielding looked dubious and edged towards the animal which, the private had now drawn closer, lifting its massive head from the pasture. Sam had told the lieutenant that he had taken Pratt into his confidence, but it was just another worry as far as Fielding was concerned. Now one of the ranks also knew of his inability to ride. How soon before the rest of the platoon? How soon before the whole battalion? He edged closer, reached out a tentative arm to pat the beast and drew it back rapidly as the animal tossed its head in indignation at being pulled away from the long sweet grass. The lieutenant threw an accusatory glare at the sergeant.

"Don't worry Sir. He's a big softy. Let's get you on his back," Sam appeased hoping beyond hope that Bill was right about the horse.

"I don't know Sergeant. He looks like he doesn't like me much. You think he's stable? He won't bolt if a gun fires near him or anything like that?" Fielding asked turning to Pratt with his doubts.

"I think 'e'll be alright Sir. 'E wa' an 'ansome cab 'orse in London accordin' to t' livery sergeant. 'E's used to loud noises like. Been ridden too. Should be steady as a bairn's pony Sir," Bill replied dutifully and with such confidence that the lieutenant actually ventured a smile.

"Okay, what do I do?" Fielding said taking in a huge breath and exhaling loudly.

"Come around this side Sir. You always mount on the left. No, don't worry about him moving, Bill'll hold him still. Bill, take his head," Sam instructed and waited until Pratt stood directly at the horse's head holding tightly onto its bridle. Warily Fielding approached the side of the animal and stared up at the saddle before offering a tentative smile at his platoon sergeant.

"One hand here holding the reins and his mane Sir, the other on the saddle. Left foot in the stirrup. Right, hoist yourself up and make yourself comfortable," the instruction carried on. Fielding obeyed and as he landed in the saddle the big horse barely acknowledged his presence. With growing confidence he gathered the reins as he was shown and sat bolt upright trying to appear as though he had been born there. To start with Pratt led the animal and Sam walked by the officer's side, constantly giving reassurance and advice. After half an hour, the men let the lieutenant take control alone, but remained close by in case of emergencies.

"He really is quite gentle isn't he?" Fielding called from twenty yards away.

"Yes Sir. But he's big enough to look imposing. A good choice you made Sir," Sam shouted back with just a touch of irony that caused Pratt to snigger briefly and the lieutenant to frown in mock remonstration. "See if you can persuade him to trot Sir."

"Trot! God Hepworth, I'm not sure about that. How does one make that happen?"

"Give him a little kick Sir. Gentle though."

Fielding bit his lip in concentration, kicked the big horse a little harder than he should and fell forward grasping the animal's mane in alarm as it lunged forward not at a trot, but a steady canter.

"*Bloody hell!* Quick Bill, head him off that way," Sam cried and lurched after the horse, but his concern was not warranted, after only a hundred yards the beast lumbered back to a walk and nose dived his head into the grass. Relieved, Sam reached its side and Bill took the reins.

"You alright Sir?" Sam enquired looking up at the somewhat wide eyed officer.

"Yes Sergeant I think so. I'm not sure about the docility of this horse though," Fielding returned.

"He's fine; you just kicked him too hard. Made him jump. You need to squeeze his flanks rather than stick your heels in hard."

A couple of hours later and the lieutenant had grown in confidence upon his gentle mount and his serious countenance had brightened. He reined the animal to a standstill and somewhat clumsily dismounted grabbing at the bridle in panic as the heavy horse tossed his head upwards in recognition of a load removed from his back. Fielding patted the broad neck and smiled rubbing his own backside with his left hand.

"Well done Sergeant. An excellent animal," he announced happily.

"Thank Bill, Sir. He found him for you," Sam replied.

Fielding beamed at the private and nodded. "Quite so. Thank you Private. You are obviously an expert in these things."

Bill flushed and grinned awkwardly but did not reply. He took the reins of the gelding and stroked its forelock.

"Does it have a name?" Fielding enquired after a moment's silence.

"He's got an Army number Sir. Probably had a name, but no one here knows it," Sam returned.

"Then I'll call him Samson. He's as strong and as gentle as that biblical hero. Is that alright do you think? Does one name Army horses?"

"I believe most officers name their rides, Sir." Sam exchanged an amused smirk with Pratt behind the officer's back.

"What do I do with him now?"

"Bill'll take him back to the horse lines and let the sergeant know he's yours. He'll be looked after until you need him Sir," Sam explained and gesticulated that Pratt should take the horse away.

As the private led the animal back to the camp Fielding rubbed his behind more vigorously muttering under his breath. "Well he's a good horse, but God my backside is sore as hell. How the blazes anyone can stay in the saddle all day God only knows. Glad I didn't join the Cavalry. Let's hope I can get some more practice in before we move out.

"Private Pratt did a good job there. Will he say anything about it?"

"He wouldn't dare Sir," Sam replied with a sneer and an expression that told of some underhand dealing. Fielding raised his eyebrows in question and his subordinate laughed. "I'd rather not tell you Sir, but Bill won't say anything. He's a good bloke anyway."

The lieutenant never managed to get any further riding practice as the following afternoon at three fifteen the Battalion received orders to return to Southampton.

CHAPTER 6.
October 4th, Pateley Bridge

"I never thought you'd do it. What made you change your mind?" Joe asked as he kissed his sister's cheek and dutifully admired the diamond on her ring finger. They were briefly alone in their parent's drawing room while their mother fussed around Dora and their father conversed with Robert over a cigarette in the garden.

Lily grinned broadly and linked her arm through his. She shrugged. "I don't know. I suddenly realised that I didn't want to die an old maid. When Dora told me she was pregnant I was overjoyed for you both, but I also felt that time was running out. I'm twenty six and I didn't want to be left behind. The maiden aunt left on the shelf."

"You love him though?"

"Of course I do. I've loved him since I first met him," Lily retorted defensively and catching her brother's askance glance giggled girlishly. "Well maybe not that long, but I did like him then; thought of him as another brother. I just wasn't prepared to admit my feelings had ever grown beyond that. I'll have to give up so much. You won't say anything at the hospital? It's a secret for the time being," she added anxiously.

Joe laughed and kissed her cheek again. "Of course not. I've already been sworn to secrecy by Rob. But I think you might have a fight on your hands with Mother. She's got her heart set on marrying you off before Christmas."

"We've no intention of marrying before the war is over and that looks less likely to happen this side of Christmas. Anyway, what about you? Are you happy? Dora seems well," she changed the subject rapidly.

Joe recognised the familiar change of mood, the sudden stubborn set of her jaw that stolidly stated that she did not want to pursue the subject further. He smiled and took his cue, quite happy to talk about his wife and the new life within her. "Yes, she's exceptionally well. Couldn't be better in fact. And I'm over the moon of course."

"Are you going to stay here now? You don't need to go. They'll need just as many doctors here." Lily asked watching her brother closely. She doubted he had changed his mind knowing his strong sense of duty. He stuffed his hands into his pockets and stared at his feet with uncharacteristic self-consciousness.

"Do you think I should?" he replied with a question of his own. Lily had tapped into his own doubts. He was uncertain, something he rarely experienced. Joe had always known what he wanted and had single-mindedly worked to get it. From knowing at the age of eight that he wanted to follow his father into the medical profession to deciding he was going to marry Dorothy Bradshaw when only twelve. Now he felt torn between his responsibilities as a father when his child was born and his duty to his nation. He looked across at his sister, his hazel eyes reflecting his reservations.

"Not necessarily. You should do what you feel is right for you. You've discussed it with Dora though?"

"Yes, we've talked about it, of course we have. She hasn't asked me to stay, but I know that's what she wants. I can't blame her. What woman wants the uncertainty of her husband away at war when she is about to become a mother for the first time? Part of me wants to give her the comfort of knowing I'll be here, but I signed up and I should honour that contract. It's not like I'll be in the fighting. I'm a doctor, I should be safe. Oh they'll probably never call for me anyway. They're more likely to want surgeons like...," he stopped and bit his lip. How tactless of him.

"Like Rob?" Lily finished for him.

"God Lil, I'm sorry. I shouldn't have....It just came out. I'm sorry," he stumbled.

"It's alright Joe. I do understand. We can talk about these things you know. Besides it would be hypocritical of me to try and dissuade him wouldn't it? I mean, I live in hope of being called upon myself. And as for you, you'll make the right decision Joe, you always do," Lily reassured. He smiled vaguely still feeling flustered over his faux pas and stared out of the long French windows onto the lawn to where his father and his best friend stood smoking. He took in a deep breath and exhaled slowly his mind a world away.

"Is there something else Joe?" Lily enquired perceptively. He brought his gaze back to meet hers and for a moment did not answer as if gathering his thoughts or determining whether or not he should confide his deepest fears. She looked at him questioningly with her head cocked prettily to one side. In that instant he determined to say nothing. This was her day. A day of celebration. It would be selfish and inconsiderate to burden her with his worries. She knew she had lost him, that he would discuss nothing more with her and felt, as she always did with Joe, frustrated at his apparent need to suffer in silence. She wondered if he confided in Dora more.

"Let's talk about you. Have you told Sam? He'll be shocked you know," Joe steered the subject away from himself. Lily played along. What else could she do now?

"Yes. I wrote to him last week. There was a letter from him yesterday, full of good wishes. He didn't sound shocked, but then he wouldn't say so much in a letter. He was full of praise for Robert. You know what he's like though. A man of few words."

"Did he say anything about the war? I haven't heard from him for a few weeks. Last I knew his Battalion were leaving Guernsey," Joe continued glad that he had steered the conversation onto another, less personal, footing.

"My, you haven't heard for a while have you? Did you know they offered him a commission and he turned it down?" Lily told with the delight of a seasoned gossip.

"*What?* No, he never said. Well, the stubborn little.... Did he say why? Let me guess, something to do with Father?"

"He didn't say in so many words, but I would guess that was one of the reasons, although I think it had more to do with his own pride. Anyway he turned it down. He's made sergeant though," she added proudly making Joe smile. "He's in the New Forest somewhere now waiting for his Division to come up to strength. He doesn't say much about that of course. They're hoping to get embarkation orders soon, but he says they're all bored to death and terrified it'll all be over before they get out to France."

"Does he believe that?"

"I don't know. Probably not, but you know he's not allowed to tell us much. He wished he could have come home to see us all, but he doesn't think that will happen now," Lily's voice trailed away sadly. It would have been nice to see Sam, especially now. It had been about two years, after his Battalion had returned from

Ireland, since he last had sufficient leave to allow him a trip home and then he had taken digs in Leeds rather than stay at the family home. He had made one dutiful visit to see his parents and the rest of his leave he spent with either Joe or Lily, whoever was off duty at the time. It had caused their mother pain, but what their father thought was anybody's guess. Like Joe, Thomas Hepworth said little of what worried him.

Joe squeezed her hand. "I'm sure we'll all be celebrating together soon enough. The war will not last for long and then Sam will get leave just in time to see you married." He kissed her hand with brotherly affection.

Lily smiled but somehow she did not share his optimism and she doubted that he truly felt it either.

CHAPTER 7.
October, Belgium

"*Christ*! I'm sick to death of marchin'. Me bloody feet are killin' me."

"Quiet Ridsdale," Sam growled under his breath at the muttering private, although in all honesty he shared the view. After arriving in Belgium on the sixth and heading, not to Antwerp where their initial orders sent them, but to Bruges, the men of the Seventh Division had marched backwards and forwards throughout the Flanders' countryside. It seemed no one knew where to send them. Orders were given and revoked. Directions were changed from one hour to the next. Marching on the pavé roads was hell on already blistered, swollen feet and ankles and some battalions of the Division, fresh from overseas, were not as fit nor as used to a long slog on foot as they might have been, given longer to prepare.

"Me bloody shoulders 'urt like 'ell an' all. Bleedin' webbin' cuts right through," Ridsdale continue to grumble.

"Told thi to stick tha socks under thi jacket, didn't I?" another voice piped up sneeringly.

Sam cuffed Ridsdale around the ear and told him to be quiet. The private swore under his breath but obeyed, hobbling dejectedly. His sergeant smirked and reflected on events as he trudged alongside his platoon.

The channel crossing had made him sick. He never could stomach a sea crossing and the longer trip to Zeebrugge had been no exception. His fellow NCOs had ribbed him mercilessly as he hung over the SS Victoria's starboard rails and vomited at alarmingly frequent intervals into a relatively calm sea. Feeling wretched, shaky and his pallor decidedly greenish the arrival at Zeebrugge could not come soon enough. And when it did, what a welcome!

The townsfolk came out in force cheering the second contingent of the Seventh Division through the streets. Women threw flowers and kissed soldiers as they passed by. Some tried to steal, and succeeded in doing so, cap and collar badges. Failing those, buttons were snatched from tunics as souvenirs. Men pressed beer and food into thankful hands and children raced ahead and around with paper Union Jacks as well as their own Belgian flag. The atmosphere was electric and every soldier could not help but be swept along by the euphoria. The Belgian people thought the British Army had arrived to save Antwerp. Little did they or the men striding through their streets realise then that the Commander-in-Chief had given up the city as a lost cause. The Division was sent to Bruges where once more the citizens went wild.

For the next few days, the Yorkshires, along with the rest of Twenty-first Brigade camped in fields and spent laborious days being marched from pillar to post with no apparent aim or objective. The men were fed up. They had seen no action. Not even spotted a German and they were annoyingly unable to enjoy the hospitality of Bruges, skirting the city, tramping around in circles through the flattish countryside under the pretence of patrolling for what appeared to be a fictitious enemy. If it had not been for the distant rumble of guns, they would not have believed there was a war on at all.

Villagers cheered them, showered them with gifts, continued to steel buttons and any remaining badge that might be wrested from its owner. The Battalion became increasingly dishevelled in appearance, much to the displeasure of its commanding officer, but what could be done about it? No one had foreseen a rapturous welcome from the local populace resulting in mass souvenir collecting.

Finally they received new orders that sent them to the wool town of Ypres. Antwerp had fallen, the Seventh Division's task was to cover the retreat of the Belgian Army and, at all costs, prevent the Germans from breaking through to the sea. Ypres, a town no one had heard of and few could pronounce, lay on a crucial crossroads on the edge of a great coastal plain. It was pivotal in reaching the sea ports and the Division had the task of defending it until reinforcements could get up from the south.

And so they marched, footsore and irritable. At least the weather held fine, but oh, for a bucket of hot water to soak aching feet in. Better still, a bath. Sam rubbed his hand around the collar of his tunic. Its coarse material chafed at his neck and he felt filthy, hot and stank of stale sweat. Like everyone else he lumbered under the weight of his kit and with envy he occasionally glanced at Fielding upon his horse. Behind and slightly to his left, Lieutenant Fielding sat astride Samson, looking a little anxious and a little too stiff and definitely *not* like he belonged there. He certainly fidgeted too much, was decidedly saddle-sore. Perhaps he was not to be envied too much after-all.

"Where's this bloody place we're going to Sarn't?" a man called Wagstaff asked.

"It's called Wipers, Waggy," his mate replied before Sam could respond.

The sergeant grinned at the mispronunciation. "Ypres," he corrected.

"Spelt like Wipers to me. Starts wi' a Y doesn't it?" the man grumbled. "Last bloody stand an' all. Isn't right. All them poor folks thinkin' we wa' 'ere to save 'em."

"That's enough defeatist talk Bridges. We'll push 'em back don't you worry. They'll not get through us. No one's ever got passed t' Green 'Owards," Corporal Stanton declared with regimental pride and a push in the middle of Bridges' back. The private swore under his breath.

"You got that penny whistle 'andy Sarn't?" Stanton asked. "Play us a tune to pass t' time."

Sam smiled. They liked a song to march to. It helped them stay in time and relieved the monotony. If he played something catchy they'd all be whistling or singing along. He reached in his pocket for the cheap instrument and started to play Daisy Bell. Before long the whole Battalion was singing along adding their own, uncensored words, to the music. The officers turned a blind eye; they too were fed up and besides, it raised the men's spirits.

It was the fourteenth of October and in the eight days since they had arrived they had barely stopped moving. They marched into the picturesque town of Ypres, across its broad moat like ditch, through its quaint and ancient streets to the gothic splendour of the market square. Here amongst the regal buildings, the spectacular Cloth Hall and rich parade of businesses and merchant's houses, they joined the rest of the Division, once more regaled enthusiastically by local residents and refugees from further afield. They slumped to the ground, accepted beer and bread, vaguely appreciated their charming surroundings and enjoyed the luxury of hot soup. Then, as if a portent of what was to come, it began to rain.

Stand-to at dawn resembled little of what normally passed for men at arms prepared to repel an enemy. The rapidly dug defensive trench was too shallow, despite the hard work throughout the night. It was only three feet deep at best and rather than stand the men knelt, their knees cold in soft damp earth and their joints stiff and aching from constantly maintaining a squatting position. The troops manned the line in soggy, reeking clothes, weighed down and shivering in their heavy greatcoats. They were tired, hungry and dishevelled, but they followed orders without question. They occasionally grumbled and muttered their discontent under their collective breath but, they remained at stand-to for the full hour leading up to dawn, hunched miserably, facing the direction of the enemy, behind the battered parapet of hastily stacked sandbags. No one raised a head or tried to stand and stretch. No one wanted a sniper's bullet through his head.

A weary hour later and with the exception of a few disgruntled sentries, the men were stood down for a breakfast of dog biscuits and tea, meagre rations but welcomed to a man. With his back stiff and sore from constant stooping and his head aching from the sporadic explosions of shellfire and lack of sleep, Sam joined Lieutenant Fielding in an inspection of their section of the line. They squeezed along the ditch passing huddles of miserable soldiers and between them identified areas of weakness from the night's actions, setting parties to work repairing the dilapidated defences.

The two men reached the union with Three Platoon and for a minute or two exchanged a few words with their counterparts there. Sam dropped to his haunches accepting a cigarette from Fred Beale.

"Thanks pal. Smoked all mine," he said tucking the woodbine into his top pocket to be enjoyed later. Beale squatted next to him as their platoon commanders discussed orders.

"Rum business Eppy. Didn't get a wink of bloody sleep. Any idea what's goin' on?"

"Not a damn clue. Fielding hasn't said a word. Hold the line here is all I know. Can't believe we're just going to sit here though. Last night was pretty lively. The Boche are close by and we're spoiling for a fight," Sam returned, rubbing his temple with his left hand.

"Aye, 'bout time we got into some action. Can't be doin' wi' sitting in a God awful 'ole waitin' fo' summat to 'appen."

Sam grunted in agreement and rested his pounding head against the back wall of the trench allowing his eyes to drift lazily skywards and fix on a single blush of a red bloom. "Well, I'll be damned. Would you believe it?" he said.

"What?"

"That flower."

Beale looked at his comrade askance and followed his gaze. "It's a poppy that's all," he said dismissively and with a touch of mockery in his tone.

"Yes, but it shouldn't be here. Not now. It's October. It shouldn't be flowering at all."

"Obviously just as confused as t' rest of us then. God Eppy, you're a daft sod at times," Beale laughed.

Sam grinned and hauled himself to his knees, carefully reaching up to pick the poppy. He sank back to his hunched position to study the little plant with appreciative wonder. Beale shook his head, "Soft bugger," he muttered. His companion chuckled to himself and delving into his tunic removed a small pocket sized volume of Psalms. He delicately placed the flower into its pages and returned the book to his jacket.

"Aye, aye. They've finished their chinwag," Fred observed and the two sergeants rejoined their respective officers and began moving back along the line.

"Any news Sir?" Sam asked as they crawled behind a sentry.

"Word is we might be relieved before lunch," Fielding replied casting a cursory glance at his sergeant.

"Relieved! We're not going to be involved in any attack? Surely we're going to make an advance?" Sam blurted incredulously.

"You sound disappointed. After a night like last I would have thought you'd be happy for the chance of a rest. To get some sleep. I'm sure the men will be."

"I could do with a good kip Sir. We all could. But we're here to fight and so far all we've done is march around Belgium and dig bloody holes, Sir," Sam grumbled with more than a little exasperation. Fielding smiled to himself. He still was not quite used to this Regular soldier mentality. They moaned and grumbled as they worked on their trenches and marched painfully along the awful Belgian roads. Yet they put up with the dreadful conditions of their hastily dug ditch under the terrifying bombardment of enemy guns. They put up with the cold, scant sleep, and the disappointment of a very meagre breakfast when they must all be starving hungry. All of them could do with a wash, a shave, a good meal inside of them and a decent sleep and still they were eager to fight regardless of how exhausted or famished they were.

Fielding shook his head. "Well Eppy, we'll be moving into reserve later this morning whether we like it or not."

True to his word they did. At eleven o'clock the whole Battalion crawled from their trench after the relief took over. It was cramped and awkward to manoeuvre around each other, the occasional shell still burst close by, but they somehow managed to drop into a sunken road in an orderly fashion and march to close billets at Becelaere. They enjoyed a hot lunch, meeting up with their transports and field kitchen and they snatched a few hours sleep, before being set to work preparing ammunition for the front, collecting barbed wire and sandbags for improving defences. They had a hot stew for dinner and just after nightfall, when everyone began to look forward to a proper night's sleep, the order went round to move back up to their original position in the line.

The battalions of the Twenty-first Brigade waited in concealment, hiding behind and within small copses of woodland, in roadside ditches, in and around farm buildings and in some cases laid, spread-eagle in damp autumn meadows. They made up a forward line near and around the tiny village of Terhand. To their right the Twentieth Brigade stretched towards the similarly diminutive Kruiseeke. Within the thin line of troops Sam Hepworth's platoon crouched uncomfortably in the wet, lush undergrowth of a reasonably sized wood along with the rest of D Company. They faced the direction of the Menin road and they waited, shivering in the misty October air, keyed up and anxious to move forward.

They had taken up position at dawn, moving stealthily from their previous entrenchments. The troops knew little of what was expected of them other than they were to wait in concealment until the order to advance on Ghelwe came. When that order would come was anybody's guess and the combination of expectant nervous energy and boredom was exhausting.

Not far away artillery fire echoed around the still, frigid air like the rumbling thunder of a late summer storm. Sporadic, faint, but intense rifle fire rippled across the countryside and crackled intermittently amidst the thumping boom of guns. Somewhere ahead, not far away, a fierce scrap was, and had been, raging all morning. No news had reached the Yorkshires. No one knew what was happening.

The trees dripped, heavily laden with dew and condensed droplets of fog, onto the men below; their uniforms glistened with water. Sam stretched his back and cast an eye around his men. They appeared steady enough although their expressions of frowning concentration spoke of nervous apprehension. The waiting was hardest. Once they were thrown into the fight then the rigid discipline and intensive training would come to the fore and anxiety would be suppressed. Sam knew what they felt, he was feeling the same. His stomach twisted and knotted with every thumping boom of artillery, his heart fluttered wildly in his chest and seemed to bound into his throat with every beat. It was not that he was afraid, for he was not, but he felt tense and if anything, excited. Adrenalin coursed through his body and he was ready and anxious to release that consuming energy.

"Bloody 'ell Sarn't, when we gonna get movin'?" a voice at the side of him asked.

Sam glanced at Corporal Stanton and empathised with his impatience, "Don't worry Stan, you'll get your chance soon enough," he answered although it felt an inadequate response. Stanton grunted in reply. "Check on the men will you," Sam instructed and with a quick nod the corporal shouldered his rifle and headed around their small stretch of woodland.

The rapid tramping of feet through undergrowth lifted everyone's head as they turned in expectant curiosity. A dishevelled and sweaty young soldier stumbled onto the scene. Men eyed him hopefully as the runner glanced around looking for someone in charge. He spotted three stripes on an arm and headed towards the wearer.

"A message for the platoon commander, Sergeant," the youngster gasped.

Sam nodded and led the runner to the end of their line where Fielding held a conference with Second Lieutenant Dodsworth of Three Platoon. The two officers looked up at their approach, the younger man's eyes lighting with happy anticipation. Fielding appeared less keen.

"Sergeant Hepworth?" he enquired.

"Messenger Sir," Sam indicated to the soldier by his side. Fielding raised his eyebrows in question.

"Sir," the young man saluted sharply. "Message from HQ Sir. You are to be ready to move at a moment's notice Sir."

"Is *that* all?" Dodsworth demanded with a disappointed air.

"Er, yes Sir," the runner replied.

"Thank you Private. Carry on," Fielding acknowledged and the messenger scurried away to the next platoon.

"Best ensure the men are ready Sergeant," Fielding instructed and half smiled at the wide grin that filled his subordinate's features. This was what they were all waiting for and if they were all like Eppy they would throw their heart and soul into the fight.

Word passed quickly through the troops and a buzz of electric excitement rippled through the woods. Rifles were checked and packs thrown onto aching backs with quiet banter between comrades and soft laughter indicating a change in mood, a happy expectation of action.

But they were disappointed. A meagre half hour later another order was relayed via messenger and that order was not to begin the attack on Ghelwe, but to return to their entrenchments of the previous day, at the ninth kilometre crossroads on the Menin road.

The frustration within the Battalion as a whole was palpable. They trudged back the way they had come earlier that day with a decidedly fed-up air, muttering under their breath, exchanging their own opinions on the Staff's strategy. At four thirty in the afternoon, they arrived at their previous positions, hungry and grumpy, with only the slightest appreciation, following a chance encounter with a reconnaissance armoured car, that their return was a strategic move following the discovery of two new German corps advancing from the direction of Courtrai. The planned advance had been abandoned. The ground made up at Kezelberg by the Twenty-second Brigade given up. The Seventh Division was digging in to save Ypres and the path to the channel ports and they had to hold on alone until one corps made it north to the beleaguered city.

Another misty, murky dawn brought a tenuous, grey light to D Company's stretch of shallow trench where they huddled at stand-to peering out across the softly rolling ground towards an unseen enemy, somewhere eastwards. The peace of daybreak lasted precisely five minutes. During the night the Germans had brought their artillery closer to the British line and as the first strains of a dull autumn day chased away the shadows of night the guns opened up with a ferocious bombardment. Shrapnel shells whizzed high across the sky, initially bursting short, but soon finding range and scattering the earth and men beneath with white hot bullets and shards of shell casing.

D Company squatted behind their barely adequate defences and watched the horizon keenly with rifles propped ready through hastily prepared loopholes in the sandbag parapet. No time now to worry about breakfast, whether lunch would reach them, whether they would actually get a chance to fire a long yearned for shot at the enemy. Now they were bombarded, deafened and spattered with mud and the blood of their comrades. Every man huddled close to the front wall, cringing at the painful screech of shells flying towards them. It did not take long to distinguish those that would fall short and those that were flying by. To recognise the slowly moaning whine of a missile losing speed and height just close enough to cause alarm; to burst and scatter its deadly cargo within a whisker of one's own head. White puffs of smoke filled the leaden sky and molten lead rained down amidst the cold, chilling drizzle.

Sam and Fielding moved rapidly through the troops, instructing the rapid repair of blasted sandbags and sending stretcher bearers along the line to remove the injured and the dead. A high pitched scream, followed by the piercing detonation of a shell sent everyone diving for the mud at the bottom of the trench. An instant of deathly silence followed, rapidly replaced by ringing ears and then the awful, gut wrenching moans of injured men.

Sam hurried back, crouching low, in the direction of the explosion. They were not his men, they were part of Three Platoon, and when he got there, where the two units converged, his first sight of shrapnel wreaked carnage filled his stomach with bile and sent a wave of wretched nausea through his body. In a cold sweat he stared, for what felt like hours, but in reality was only seconds, at the river of blood mingling rapidly with the mud at his feet. Before him two men lay dying, one was already unconscious, the back of his head glistening pinkish grey where his brains protruded from a fist sized hole in his shattered skull. The other with his face ripped open and a jagged gash exposing his carotid artery spouting blood in a gushing red fountain. Fixed terrified eyes, shining with horrified realisation of his demise. His comrade at his side shouting something at him and holding blood soaked hands over the shuddering man's neck in a vain attempt to stem the flow of life. Sam's eyes fastened upon the open mouth, a black hole amidst a shattered mush of bone and flesh. No sound came from that mouth, yet it screamed loudly with the despair of a dying man before the light in the eyes dulled and his head dropped onto his chest.

Fred Beale hurried up and dragged the blood stained private from the corpse, forcing him back to his post with a bellowed demand for stretcher bearers. Sam shuddered and turned back to his own men, the nearest of whom was clearly shaken and covered with a fair amount of gore.

"Keep your eyes forward Jackson," Sam urged firmly as he passed and clapped a reassuring hand upon the private's shoulder. The man shook himself and returned to his watch across the murky field ahead and only occasionally allowed his eyes to drift back to the ghoulish scene to his left.

Just after noon the artillery fire ceased and an uncanny hush enveloped the front with only the steady patter of rain on mud and caps and the occasional groan of a wounded man breaking the lengthening silence. Sam took up a position against the parapet and unslung his Lee Enfield from his shoulder. He adjusted his ammunition bandoliers and pulled out two clips placing them on the berm in front of him, within easy reach. He pulled back the firing bolt and ensured a round lay ready in the chamber. He cast a glance along the line in both directions, returned the smile from Bill Pratt with a reassuring nod and noted Lieutenant Fielding draw his revolver with a nervous look in his direction. Momentarily their eyes met. Sam raised his right hand, palm forwards showing two fingers at the platoon commander. Fielding nodded, understanding. The message said two hundred yards, its meaning plain, yet a carefully disguised signal between the two men. The sergeant returned to his position, rifle at his shoulder, looking along its sights into a field of misty rain and slowly clearing smoke.

For a long time, nothing, then, steadily and certainly the tramp of many booted feet became unmistakeable as an advancing army splashed and trudged through the wet fields of sticky mud and stubble. Slowly and deliberately the Germans advanced upon their enemy. From the trenches nothing could be seen, only the vast expanse of an amorphous drab field drenched with rain. Sam shifted his weight and lifted his head a touch peering through his loophole, straining to see anything. Cold water trickled down his neck and face. He ignored it, became oblivious to everything except the clatter and trudge of moving infantry somewhere ahead. Yet he had no sight of the foe. Like every man in the line, his heart pounded and thudded loudly in his ears. His mouth was dry, but his hands were steady and his finger caressed the trigger almost lovingly.

Such a tiny movement at first. Like the gentle parting of a curtain or the sifting of mist in a breeze, but it was definite and as the troops watched, the grey swirl in front of them seemed to lift and reveal another, more sinister sight, another mass of grey, only this one moving forward with a relentless and purposeful tread. And it was enormous! Slowly and surely the dark forms of countless soldiers appeared through the drifting rain. Somebody along the line whistled long and low. The man next to Sam muttered an expletive under his breath. Officers voices called out distance, Fielding's closest and loudest. "At three hundred." The clatter of rifle bolts drawn. Steady, cautious advancement.

"AT TWO FIFTY."

Someone sighed loudly. Sam readjusted his stance, made himself comfortable, glanced rapidly at the two spare ammunition clips, and back to the front again. Selected his first target and made a mental note of the second. Men whose features were mercifully blurred by the distance.

"AT TWO HUNDRED. RAPID FIRE, TEN ROUNDS!" Fielding shouted. An order that was echoed and lost beneath a volley of rifle fire all along the line.

The distinctive crack and recoil into his shoulder, the soft chink as the spent cartridge ejected with his next pull of the firing bolt. It dropped heavily, but unnoticed onto his sodden trousers. The next round already flying to its target. Ten rapid shots, magazine emptied and the contents of two more clips shoved into place, recharging the weapon, ready to fire. Sam had counted the men falling under his steady and accurate aim. There was no knowing whether his was the only bullet that hit the unfortunate infantryman advancing towards them, but he was certain that each of his hit their mark with deadly precision. The grey horde twisted and faltered under a shattering barrage of fire, falling en masse in wave after wave.

Fielding yelled an order to reload and commence firing at will. Sam, ahead of the game along with the other good marksmen of his platoon, began to empty the Lee Enfield's contents into the advancing targets with an oddly cold detachment he had never thought himself capable of. Man after man fell before his sights, his brain seeing only targets on the rifle range. The fact that they were moving, living and breathing beings, did not register. He was filled only with the desire to stop them, to hit them with a wall of withering lead. He was unaware that some of his own men were falling around him, that men in his own line were dying.

A screaming roar ripped overhead and burst with deadly accuracy in a flash of yellow-orange light and a spurt of muck. Limbs and heads thrown high in the air as the first of the British shells landed amongst the reeling German infantry. Another scream, another explosion and the enemy was caught mercilessly between relentlessly precise and vicious rifle fire in front of them and the barbarous explosion of shells among their rear ranks.

A cheering broke out further down the line; it grew and spread like a speeding train. The Germans were retreating, turning and running back the way they had come, back through the artillery fire which decimated their numbers further. The temptation to run after them, to turn the retreat into a rout was almost overwhelming and in some places men climbed up onto the parapet only to be ordered down by their NCOs and officers or falling back with a sniper's bullet through the head.

During the short lull that followed, when men shouted congratulations to each other, Sam inhaled deeply relishing the acrid scent of cordite in his nostrils. He shouted at his men to reload and told them to quieten down realising the need for sobriety. Out in the field the nerve racking sounds of the dying and wounded drifted along with a pungent, metallic smell of blood and cordite on the soft breeze that carried the rain along with death.

A quick crawl along the line, checking on the men, a call for stretcher bearers and the latter running doubled up, rain dripping from their caps and down their faces, to retrieve the fallen. A hasty report to Fielding that they had lost Smith and Darley and that Corporal Swales and Private Holdsworth were injured.

"They'll be back. They're only regrouping. They won't give up that easily," Fielding opined and as he did so the enemy artillery opened again with renewed ferocity, crashing all around the British positions, blowing the trenches to pieces, killing the men within. Necessitating short tactical retreats to positions further back and out of the current range.

At four o'clock the bombardment stopped and with a rush the troops returned to their now battered and barely recognisable defences. Half filled with mud, water, blood and shattered sandbags the ditches barely gave enough cover and the men of D Company struggled to keep their heads protected from sniper and machine gun bullets that raked the diminished parapet. They hurriedly piled back some of the fallen bags and hunched with rifles ready for the next onslaught.

It came, different from the last. No steady, cautious approach this time. The infantry charge was as ferocious as the artillery fire had been and it was met with an equally rapacious and withering rifle fire. Countless fell, landing on the remains of their comrades whose bodily parts littered the battlefield. They fell back, advanced and fell back again. Over and over again, until the numbers of dead outnumbered the living and an early dusk put paid to any further attempts to break through the British line.

Exhausted, dirty and shaking with hunger the Yorkshires, along with every other battalion in the line, sank to their knees with relief. But if they thought they would be able to rest and have time to recuperate they had to think again. They managed to grab a hasty meal as amazingly, rations came forward followed by ammunition to be distributed before they set to work re-digging their trenches. Not an easy task as tools were few, being lost or abandoned during the repeated advancements and inevitable retirements of the last few days.

As one unit worked on trench repairs, others moved behind the line and started another in the rear, just as the so called relief battalion did behind them. By dawn, few had slept, but they had at least a shallow network of repaired entrenchments to fall back to should the need arise. It was not much and they were hastily dug, but it was better than nothing.

At morning roll call D Company reported no further losses to its number. Three Platoon had lost Lieutenant Dodsworth, along with two corporals and five other men. They had taken a heavy toll in the previous day's shelling. Two Platoon had seen the demise of Sergeant Sid Braithwaite, an experienced man who could not easily be replaced. There were numerous minor injuries and the weary, sleepless men were brought rapidly from their early morning torpor by the commencement of heavy enemy shelling once more. And this time it was more than just shrapnel.

At seven in the morning the bombardment started, the now familiar whizz of small calibre shells followed by the deafening bang as they exploded scattering white-hot shrapnel bullets and casing to the ground and onto the men desperately trying to shelter there. But worse were devastating high explosive shells that burst with a characteristic shock of black smoke. They wreaked a trail of lethal and merciless destruction, blowing trenches and the men within to pieces. They roared forward at the vulnerable troops like an express train, screaming in a soaring arc through the rain filled sky; plummeting with a deafening, terrifying high pitched whine before the ear-splitting detonation sent men reeling and pounded through their bodies and brains in painful concussion. Those that heard and suffered the explosion were half crazed from the constant explosions. Those who did not hear were beyond suffering, their body parts littering the blasted holes they had been vainly sheltering in.

Time and time again D Company abandoned their trench as a relentless rain of shells pummelled into them. They moved from one tenuous line to another. Hoped the bombardment would stop. Were cheered as the British artillery retaliated, albeit all too infrequently, from somewhere further back. Then a lull and they scurried back to their positions, frantically digging away collapsed earth and anxiously awaiting the infantry charge. It did not come, instead a renewed bombardment forcing them back again to the relative safety of a sunken road. Exhausted, they lay waiting, their nerves jangling with each explosion, desperately thirsty and hungry with no hope of water, food or rest.

Just before three in the afternoon the guns fell silent. Major Wilson, wounded in the left arm, but shouting orders regardless while a stretcher bearer fought to tie a tourniquet around his heavily bleeding limb, sent D company back into their abandoned trench. The orders were to stand and fight, to decimate the enemy with independent rifle fire. The surviving troops dived into their defensive ditch and spread along its curving and battered length. They stepped gingerly over dead comrades, not looking too closely, not wanting to see at this moment, who would not be answering roll call that night. They staggered into position, platoon by platoon, and hastily placed fallen bags above their heads or squatted as best they could with rifles ready and hearts racing.

Sam slammed into the soft mud of the trench wall next to the youngest member of his platoon, a lad of only seventeen whose initial excitement of his first blooding had given way to understandable anxiety. He glanced at his sergeant with an expression of thankfulness that someone with authority stood by his side; someone who could inspire and lead by example. Sam caught his eye and smiled grimly before allowing his gaze to critically follow the length of the line. There were half a dozen more faces missing, but the troops had their section covered, just a little more thinly than before. He caught the nod from Fielding and turned his attention to the pockmarked field in front.

Yellowish smoke still swirled over the piles of up-thrown earth and the grim outlines of yesterday's dead. On the left flank, and only nine hundred yards away, columns of grey clad Germans were massing in their thousands. They formed up into long lines, shoulder to shoulder appearing to be almost linking arms as they advanced. As they marched forward the sound of their voices rang out, clear and proud across the battlefield.

"Jesus Sarn't, they're bloody singing," the young soldier uttered incredulously. Sam gaped in fascination. It was a terrifying yet awe-inspiring sight. Row after row of countless men, shoulder to shoulder with rifles lowered, toy-like with the distance, advancing with a steady, determined tread.

A high, screaming howl from behind and the men in the front line could clearly see the first shell descending in its graceful, curving flight towards the German infantry. It burst in front of them. Several men in the forward column fell; their comrades stepped over them, closed the gap, tightened the ranks and moved onwards. Soon more shells were falling amongst them, bowling the soldiers down like pins and still they came on. Such discipline, such nerve was admirable even in an enemy one was supposed to despise. And still the faint hum of voices in song could be heard between the explosions.

"Christ! They're being annihilated," Sam murmured under his breath as he watched entranced.

"Better them than us Sarn't," the lad replied. Sam only nodded in answer.

The order went out to ready aim and as one the platoon took up position as best they could with weapons facing the enemy. As before they waited, waited until the range was short, when they stood the best chance of hitting their mark. At two hundred yards the command to fire independently was shouted and the already staggering mass of grey shuddered and reeled under a heavy and unremitting rain of bullets. The enemy recoiled, fell back, regrouped and came forward again. Over and over the pattern was repeated. The singing stopped as the massed ranks of Germans were destroyed under a constant stream of shrapnel and rifle bullets.

Along the British trenches, no man dare falter, when someone fell the men redeployed themselves, filling the gaps but inevitably thinning the line. Wearied, sodden, bloody and cold they fought on. Late in the afternoon the enemy broke through a gap on the left between A Company and the Second Royal Scots Fusiliers. The fierce hand to hand battle that followed eventually drove the Germans out and by evening the remnants of the vast Bavarian Reserve Division cut their losses and dug in.

Darkness brought short respite. In between a hasty meal of bully beef and dog biscuits ammunition reached the front and had to be distributed. The wounded and dead had to be carried to the dressing station behind the lines and somehow, somewhere sleep had to be snatched. The sky glowed an eerie orange, a hellishly lurid flickering from numerous fires all around. In every direction farms and barns burned and uneasy sentries watched with nervous trigger fingers as black shapes moved among the dead and dying out between the two armies. The Germans were retrieving their casualties and on the whole they did so unmolested, an unofficial and gentleman's agreement staying British marksmen who watched warily instead.

The sounds were the worst. Distant gunfire still boomed in spasmodic bursts, the occasional crack of rifle fire or spitting rattle of a machine gun added to the heightened nervousness of the troops. But far worse, the soft, spine chilling moans of the wounded laying out in the darkened field. Calls for help in German and occasionally in accented English. Calls for a mother or wife. Sometimes a frantic shout that set the heart racing with fear and then long periods of silence where only the crackle of burning fires filled the still air. It was a hellish, dank night. The rain had petered out and the scene languished under a cold, clinging mist that spread across the gently rolling countryside like the chill hand of death himself.

Sam hurried, bent double along his stretch of trench. The men had eaten, after a fashion, but were still hungry. He had posted sentries and work parties repairing, as best they could with no tools and no barbed wire, the battered defences. He would let them sleep, if they could, in a couple of hours. Until then he had to push them as he pushed himself, hard and mercilessly. He hoped Fielding would have news. Hoped for the chance of relief. Get the men back behind the lines and at least grab some decent sleep. Fielding looked shattered and gloomy when he asked.

"There is no relief Eppy. We're it. We're waiting for One Corps to reach us. Until then we're on our own," he muttered lowly, his eyes looking along the trench to the dirty, unshaven faces of his platoon.

"The men need rest, Sir," Sam stated lamely, feeling as the words left this lips that it was a stupid comment to make. He almost apologised but the lieutenant cut in first.

"I know that Sergeant! For Christ sake man, what do you want me to do about it?" he snapped and ran a grimy hand through mud caked hair. "God, look at them. They look more like tramps than soldiers."

"We've done the Regiment proud though Sir. Look how we've held on. There were thousands of them. Outnumbered us six to one at least I'd say," Sam felt the need to cheer the officer up, to make amends for his thoughtless remark.

Fielding sighed heavily, "Yes, but what a cost," he murmured almost to himself before steeling his gaze and with a set jaw added, "How are the repairs coming on?"

"None too good. The soil here's quite light. It doesn't hold together well and it's saturated. We've got no picks and only a couple of shovels plus our entrenching tools. There's no barbed wire. None's come up with the rations. Good news, ammunition did and has been distributed. Bad news is, we lost another three men today and other platoons have fared worse. I just hope One Corps get here sooner rather than later or there'll be nothing to stop Fritz marching through to Calais," Sam said light-heartedly with a laugh, though in his heart he felt anything but.

Fielding smirked but did not reply. He looked terribly tired. "Make sure the men get some rest Eppy. I think we can expect more of the same tomorrow."

"Already sorted Sir. When they've finished repairs I'll change piquets and the rest can grab some shuteye. I'll rotate them through."

"Don't forget yourself Sergeant. You're no use to me dead on your feet," the lieutenant remarked pointedly. Sam grinned in reply and fumbled in his tunic for the cigarette Beale had given him. When was it? Yesterday? The day before? He had lost track. He brought it out and stared with disgust at its disfigured outline in the softly flickering orange half-light. With a grunt he broke away the mangled end and clamped the other between his lips while he sought a match. Both men were squatting on their haunches and Sam drew appreciatively on the nicotine laden smoke with eyes closed briefly. It was a moment to savour, a welcome fragment of normality in an abnormal world. He exhaled slowly and squinted at the officer through acrid smoke. The lieutenant was watching him keenly with an odd expression. Sam offered the squat cigarette across but Fielding declined.

"No, it's your last one. You enjoy it. I've a sneaking suspicion that their bad for one's health anyway," he said waving his hand.

Sam sniggered, "Undoubtedly," he agreed and took another long drag.

"Can I ask you something Eppy?"

"Of course Sir," Sam answered feeling that another of Fielding's oddly probing questions was on its way.

"Do you know how many men you killed today?"

What a strange thing to ask. "Not exactly Sir, but I've a good idea how many I hit and not many of them will go home," Sam returned with a satisfied sneer.

"Does it bother you? Killing I mean. I was watching you for a while when the fighting got really intense. You never faltered. Never broke concentration. You simply kept on firing, reloading and firing again. The other men glanced around between reloading, only briefly, but they looked to see what was going on. You never did. How did you feel?"

Sam stared through his cigarette smoke at the lieutenant. *You really are an oddball.* He shrugged. "I didn't give it much thought. Our orders were to shoot the enemy. That's what I did. I didn't think about what I was doing. I just did it. I didn't think about them being men. They were simply targets on a firing range. Nothing more."

"And you felt nothing?"

"Exhilaration. Excitement. But nothing for them. No. If anything I...," he stopped the realisation of what he had nearly admitted to bringing a thrill of horror.

"What?" Fielding prompted.

Sam gazed at his platoon commander his own mind shocked by his recognition of a darker self. "I actually enjoyed it, Sir," he confessed flatly.

Fielding smiled with sympathy. "That's what I thought," he said quietly.

It was an uncomfortable moment and one the sergeant was not happy to dwell upon. He hurriedly finished his woodbine and threw the tab end into the mud. "I'd better see how they're getting on Sir," he said and picked his rifle from across his knees. The lieutenant nodded and watched as his subordinate crept away, his body hunched and head low.

A dreadful, rasping groaning woke Sam from a fitful, dream filled sleep. The sky was still lit by unnatural reddish light and he glanced at his watch to ascertain the time, or rather how long he had slept. Barely forty minutes. The horrid gurgling moan again and he sat upright wincing at the pain that stabbed through his temple and trying to focus upon the dark figures around him. He heard frantic voices, muttering in harsh whispers slightly to the left and saw two men, heads together gesticulating in argument.

Dragging himself to his knees and then crawling forward he crept towards the sentries. As he drew nearer the hissing, half choking, gargle of a man's breathing intermingled with an agonised soughing grew louder. The sentries were clearly agitated and as Sam's wakefulness returned he noticed one or two others, supposedly trying to sleep, were instead laid with greatcoats clenched around their bodies and eyes fixed, with sickening realisation in the direction of the awful sound.

"What's going on Dobson?" he addressed the youthful soldier who had stood beside him earlier in the day.

"Fritz out there Sarn't. Sounds like 'e's bad. We wa' wonderin' if we should...'elp or summat," Dobson answered jabbing his thumb towards the parapet, his young face filled with a mixture of fear and concern, eyes bright and staring.

"Bloke's dyin' Sarn't, but this ruddy racket is drivin' us mad. Makes tha blood run cold," the other man added.

"What should we do Sarn't?" Dobson asked.

Sam stared at them both. The chilling cries and moans from over the parapet sending a shiver down his spine.

"Should we bring 'im in?" the other sentry queried.

"He's dying man. Hear that rattle? That's his lungs filling with blood. Christ he must be near. Can you see him?" Sam demanded.

Both men looked at one another with obvious embarrassment.

"We 'aven't dared look Sarn't," Dobson ventured while his comrade stared at the sky.

"*Fucking hell!*" Sam spat with exasperation, though in truth it was his own fear that made him angry. The death throes of the unseen enemy were ominously loud and unnerving. He pushed Dobson aside and took up position at the loophole peering into the night. It was impossible to see at first. Countless dark, amorphous forms dotted the strangely illuminated fields and none of them showed any signs of life. The body snatchers had returned to their lines, abandoning the dead. Sam waited and listened trying to discern the exact direction of the moaning when he realised it was much nearer than he had first thought. Warily he stood, craning his neck over the top of the parapet.

"Watch out Sarn't. Might 'ave a gun," Dobson cried unhelpfully.

Sam frowned and cursed at his own jumpiness, but reaching forward towards a bundled heap to the left of the sentry's loophole he grasped hold of what was undoubtedly an arm. The man attached to the arm squealed like a trapped rabbit causing the sergeant to let go and fall backwards in alarm, his heart in his mouth. The men around him had stirred now and many were sitting up watching with fearful or curious eyes.

"*Shit!* Stoker, give me a hand. He's just over the top. Let's heave him over. At least we can get him down to the dressing station and he can die there," Sam instructed the older sentry.

"Mebbe we should just shoot 'im Sarn't," Stoker offered looking none too keen to risk his neck for a German. He had a point. The man was well on his way to eternity anyway.

"You want to do it?" Sam challenged. Stoker looked away. "No. I didn't think so. Come on give me a hand."

Reluctantly Stoker handed his rifle to a grinning Dobson and followed his sergeant over the top of the parapet. Together they huddled around the crumpled body, keeping as low as possible, not wanting to alert snipers. Sam reached out and grabbed hold of the Bavarian's jacket in order to heave him into a sitting position. As he did so, the injured man screamed loudly, a shrill, ear piercing racket that cut through the still air like a knife. Immediately rifles crackled from the enemy lines and bullets began to spatter on the ground around them throwing up little spurts of mud.

"*Fuck this!*" Stoker cried and dived head first back into the trench. Sam had to agree with him and leapt back over the parapet landing with a heavy thud in the mud and almost on top of Dobson. Everyone was awake now and hurrying towards them, Fielding with revolver drawn.

"What the *hell's* going on Sergeant?" he demanded, his face flushed with sudden anxiety. The rifle fire had died down, but the wounded German still gurgled painfully.

"We were trying to bring in an injured German Sir. Unfortunately he cried out and we were fired upon," Sam said glad that the dark hid his red face. He felt a fool. He should have just shot the man like Stoker had suggested.

"*Christ man!* You could have been killed. Leave him there. He'll be dead by morning. I'll not have my platoon sergeant risk life and limb over a bloody Boche," the lieutenant spat. "What the *hell* were you thinking of?"

"Seemed the right thing to do Sir," Sam replied his cheeks burning with anger at his own stupidity and at Fielding's public reprimand.

An awkward silence fell between them punctuated only by the death rattle of the unseen soldier. Fielding shuddered. It was a horrible, skin crawling sound.

"Do we 'ave to listen to 'im dyin' Sir?" an anxious voice asked from the bottom of the trench. "It doesn't sound 'uman. Gives me t' collywobbles."

"Pull yourself together Ridsdale," Fielding snapped though he knew what the private meant. It certainly was an unnerving and potentially demoralising sound. The lieutenant glanced at his sergeant at a loss. He realised he had just humiliated Hepworth publically in front of six or seven of his troops and he should not expect any help there. But Sam was not a man to bear a grudge and though he smarted from his embarrassment he understood that something had to be done.

"May I borrow your revolver, Sir?" he asked. He could have suggested the lieutenant shoot the German, but that would have been unworthy of him and dishonourable. Instead, he gave the officer a way out.

Fielding hesitated, "You're going to shoot him," he stated blandly.

"Yes."

"I should do it."

"I'm a better shot, Sir," Sam grinned. He did not add that he thought Fielding not up to shooting a defenceless man at point blank range.

"He's not exactly a mile away though is he? Besides an officer should not relinquish his side arm Sergeant," the lieutenant argued.

"I can't do it with a rifle Sir. Not without exposing myself to enemy fire. We won't tell anyone if you don't Sir. It's up to you Sir. We could just leave him. Doubt he's going to last much longer anyhow," Nevertheless Sam stretched his hand out for the revolver. Fielding hesitated. The German gurgled and choked.

"Christ Sir, just give 'im the bloody gun," Stoker cried in exasperation his nervousness overruling years of strict discipline.

The lieutenant pulled the weapon from around his neck and placed it into the outstretched hand with a nod. Sam checked the chamber and taking a deep breath waited below the point where the dying man lay. He listened carefully, but could hear nothing except the terrible rattling of fluid filled lungs. Exhaling loudly, he stood up, took aim and fired two shots into the German's head. A volley of bullets hit the parapet wall as he ducked back down sending small avalanches of earth onto the men in the trench, but the awful, stenorous breathing had gone.

"Thank you Sir," Sam uttered after the last sniper shots had died away and passed back the revolver. Fielding took it with a slight tremor in his arm, but the sergeant's hand was steady and his demeanour unfazed. No one would ever guess that he had just killed a man in cold blood.

"Back on watch Stoker, Dobson," Sam ordered with a glare that could cut flesh. The two men hurried to their loopholes and stared with deliberate concentration across the field in front. Satisfied, Sam moved away following the retreating figure of the platoon commander, dropping back into his previous position to try and get a few more precious hours of sleep. When he had gone Dobson looked around warily.

"*Bloody 'ell* Stokey," he whispered with obvious awe. "Bloody 'ell! I couldn't a done that. *Christ!* Did y' see the lieutenant's face. White as a bleedin' sheet. But 'ell fire. T' Sarn't never batted an eyelid. Bloody 'ell!"

"That wa' cold that wa'," Stoker muttered back shaking his head. "Dunno 'ow a man can sleep after that." He turned to look where Sam lay and saw only a figure hunched beneath the folds of his greatcoat, apparently sleeping soundly. "Look at 'im. Dead to t' world. I'll tell thi this Dobbo. I wouldn't like to 'ave Eppy as my enemy. Wouldn't think 'e 'ad it in 'im to look at would thi? That took guts."

"Too bloody right. Bloody 'ell!"

Beneath his coat Sam stared into the back of his eyelids. Sleep would not come, only the laboured breathing of a dying man, followed by the sharp rapport of a revolver and the deathly silence that followed. He lay and prayed to his God for forgiveness and hoped that he could forgive himself.

CHAPTER 8.
October 28th, Headingly

Dora sighed for the umpteenth time and nervously fingered the brown envelope on her lap. It was addressed to her husband, to Doctor J M Hepworth and it bore the official stamp of the War Office. The thought of its contents filled her with dread. She stood up and placed it upon the mantelpiece next to the clock and she returned to her seat, her mind in turmoil. It was one thing after another. The newspapers were filled with heroic stories of the BEF fighting for some hitherto never heard of town in Belgium. Filled too with growing lists of casualties. It had been weeks since they had received any news from Sam and then it had only been a hurriedly written postcard saying he was alive and well, but hungry. Lily had not heard any more. It was a worry. And now this.

Dora stood again and paced in front of the long sash window overlooking a darkened garden. Large splashes of rain beat against the pane and trickled wearily away. Another sigh. A knock on the door gave her a start and as Ada entered she grasped the heavy velvet curtain with one hand to steady herself.

"Everything all right madam?" the maid questioned noting the wobble and thinking the missus looked a little shaky.

"Oh Ada, yes you made me jump that's all. I was miles away. Did you want something?" Dora replied forcing a smile that faltered before it reached her eyes.

"Cook wants to know what time you want dinner ma'am. On'y t' Doctor is late and she said it won't keep so good in t' oven."

"Then tell her to get it out of the oven. I'm sure we can eat the meat cold if necessary," Dora replied impatiently.

Ada bobbed a curtsey, "Yes, ma'am," she said and disappeared.

Dora returned her gaze to the dark window pane catching her own reflection. She turned sideways and ran a hand over the small swelling of her belly. She turned away, her eyes bright and as the door bell clattered signalling the arrival of her man she forced herself to be calm, pinched her cheeks to give them a hint of colour, for she felt sure she must be pale as death, and took up her seat once more on the sofa. She picked up some knitting and pretended to be busy. In the hall she could hear Joe teasing Ada as the latter divested him of his coat and bag.

The clock ticked loudly and the rain hammered against the glass.

The door burst open and with his usual cheeriness on arriving home Dora's husband regaled her with a hearty "good evening" and kissed her cheek affectionately. She took his hand as he laid it upon her shoulder and embraced it. He thought she looked unwell and a frown of concern clouded his smiling features briefly before he squeezed her hand and drifted to the drinks cabinet.

"Would you like a sherry love? You look a little peaky," he asked and he poured himself one.

"No thank you. I'm a tired that's all. A good day?" she returned and swiftly moved the conversation to his work.

"Quite dull actually. Nothing out of the ordinary. All my patients are doing well for a change."

She laughed, "Well that's good isn't it?"

"Of course, but it doesn't make for interesting medicine," he replied.

"Joe, really! These are people you are talking about. You should not wish them worse off than they are just to keep you interested," Dora chastised with mock disapproval.

He grinned widely showing excellent teeth and for a moment she thought he looked like Sam. It brought back her earlier worries.

"Of course not. You know I don't really," he said and plonked down on the sofa next to her. "When's dinner?"

"As soon as cook serves up I should think. She was panicking about the beef a few minutes ago."

"Good. I'm famished. What are you knitting? Baby clothes?" he asked and fondly rubbed her belly. She removed his hand firmly without hiding the smile that crept to her lips.

"No. It's too early to think of baby clothes yet. These are socks. Mrs Trenchard says the Army need socks, so I thought I'd knit some and send them to Sam. Only I don't think I'm too good at it. I keep dropping stitches."

Joe sniggered into his sherry glass and she jabbed him with a knitting needle causing him to wince and splutter. "Ow, that hurt. You really are quite evil Dorothy Hepworth. Stabbing your poor husband when he's been working hard all day. A good wife would be loving and kind and give me all the attention I deserved."

"You got what you deserved," she countered and pretended to be busy with the knitting to hide her mirth. He placed an arm around her shoulders and kissed her head.

"Love you," he whispered.

She stared up into his face her eyes full to brimming, "I love you too."

"What is it? What's wrong?" his voice filled with sudden concern. *Is she ill?*

"Oh Joe. I know it's silly of me and I'm just being selfish, but I don't want you to go. After what is happening in Flanders, I can't bear the thought of both you and Sam over there."

He pulled her close and laid his head on top of hers as she rested against his chest. He wondered why she was so emotional and would have put it down to her pregnancy, but it was out of character. Normally Dora was so sensible despite the raging hormones.

"Silly girl. They will probably never ask for me. I shouldn't worry about it if I were you. In a few months I'll be too old anyway. Past it at thirty one," he chuckled.

She pulled herself away and wiped the tears from her face with a silk handkerchief. "There's a letter on the mantelpiece. It's from the War Office."

His expression was one of total surprise, but he could not help himself, he bounded from his seat with such enthusiastic excitement that his wife knew she had already lost the battle and her heart sank like lead. She could not stay while he read it. Did not want to hear him announce with unhidden zeal that he had been called up. That the Army would be glad of his services. She rose and muttered, "I'll go check on dinner," and before he could reply she had drifted from the room.

Joe looked up from the brown envelope to see her go. He realised he had been tactless, but it was too late now. He would make it up to her later. He stared at the letter, his heart racing with almost boyish relish. Carefully he slid his thumb along the envelope back and removed the folded letter within, reading it carefully and then re-reading it again. When Dora returned he was still standing before the fire staring into its glowing embers. He turned and smiled guiltily.

"Well?" she asked.

He held the paper towards her.

"I don't want to read it Joe. Just tell me."

"I am requested to report to Aldershot on the tenth of November and there's a list of uniform requirements, a note telling me where I can purchase it all and a payment chit for it," he explained watching her face the whole time, trying to read the emotion within.

"So soon," she uttered, her voice barely audible. "What about the hospital? Your job there? Your patients?"

He shrugged. "This is war Dora. They knew I had enlisted and that this could happen any time. They will have to find a replacement. Besides, it's only for a year unless I want to sign on for longer," he justified.

"Oh," she stared blankly in his direction and for a moment neither spoke. "Well, dinner is ready, we had better not let it spoil," she said eventually and retreated from the room leaving him to reconcile the conflicting feelings of guilt, euphoria and though he would not like to admit it, annoyance that his wife did not share his patriotic enthusiasm.

CHAPTER 9.
October 27th – 29th, British Front Line near Gheluvelt, Flanders

The losses had been heavy. Time after time the enemy artillery had found the trenches with deadly accuracy. Time and again the troops had fought and then retired to a new position slightly behind, digging in, consolidating their defences, fighting off renewed attacks from a seemingly endless stream of grey clad infantry. As the days stretched on the men became ever more weary, ever more desperate for sleep and a decent meal. Still they fought on with such admirable tenacity and formidably withering rifle fire that their enemy was convinced he not only faced a much larger force, but also that a great many machine guns were being used. Yet despite their courage, despite their uncomplaining grit, their numbers diminished with every hour.

After seven days in the front line the remaining men of the Yorkshires were finally relieved on the twenty-seventh of October and with bodies hunched and minds too exhausted to feel anything but assuagement, they staggered rather than marched back, reaching a farm and falling asleep as soon as they found a space to drop in the open barn. The meal that had been prepared for them, for the most part went untouched, too fatigued were they to care. They fell to the ground, their meagre belongings scattered around them. Dirty, stinking clothes, damp with rain and filthy with mud stuck to their backs; boots, caked and crusted with muck and blood, too tight around swollen feet to remove. No officer or NCO had the heart to berate them; they too were dead on their feet.

Sam managed to stay awake long enough to ensure his platoon were accounted for and then he too crashed into a pile of sweet smelling hay. He did not awake for many hours, not until someone kicked him in the ribs and brought him dizzyingly from a deep, dreamless sleep with a heart wrenching start and a curse. It was dark in the barn. A few men were being cajoled to their feet by NCOs and officers. Sam squinted at his assaulter and recognised Fred Beale from Three Platoon.

"We're moving back up," Fred said, his voice flat and weary beyond description. "Get your squad together Eppy." He trudged away leaving his comrade staring with disbelief after him. Two days rest they had said. Two days to sleep and eat and, he had hoped, to clean up; wipe the filth from his face at least, soak his blistered and swollen feet in warm, salty water. Not to be. He glanced at his watch, but could not make out the dial in the gloom. With an audible groan he forced himself onto aching feet and hobbled around his men, shaking them awake, kicking them into consciousness. One by one they roused, dragged themselves to stand, heaving their rifles onto sore backs. When Fielding arrived they barely managed to stand to attention, a subtle straightening of backs and a laborious shifting of rifles was about all they could muster. The lieutenant, grey faced and shattered like his men, returned the salute of his platoon sergeant, noted the sunken, red rimmed eyes of the man and sympathetically stood everyone at ease.

The CO came in and eyed his haggard officers and men with a fatherly pride. They did not look like the disciplined soldiers he had brought to Belgium. They were only half their original number. Many of them slightly wounded. Dirty field dressings covered filthy hands and heads. How many he had lost he dare not contemplate. How many more would die before this was over he could not say. It almost broke his heart to order them back to the Front. They had barely rested, but they were needed.

Everyone was needed. If the BEF was to prevent the German Army marching through Ypres and reaching the coast, every man must fight and they must fight to the end. He gave them a rousing speech. He lauded them with praise. They accepted the pep talk without murmur and with utmost respect for their commanding officer.

Lieutenant Colonel Lyons was a good soldier, he had been with them at the Front all along; he would stay with them. Their weary hearts lifted and their backs straightened. They had received urgent orders to return to the line. They would fight like the devil himself for God, King and Country, but most of all for their CO.

They moved to a new position, to take up the line along with other units of Twenty-first Brigade between Zandvoorde and the Menin Road, inhabiting hastily dug trenches as night fell.

No rest. Lurid night skies, alight with terrible fires behind them in the beautiful city of Ypres and from countless villages and farms, merged into cold, drizzle ridden days. Shell fire, heavy and almost constant shattered nerves and defences alike, killing and maiming without distinction.

Back into reserve for a half day and then up to the Front again. As a miserable, wet and earth shattering morning drew towards a sudden silent close the enemy charged in great numbers, swarming down upon the beleaguered battalions in the British line and breaking through. Mayhem and chaos ensued. Battalions were thrown forward and beaten back, their ranks giving way under tremendous pressure and faltering. They retreated on mass, regrouping in a mixture of units under the command of Lyons, some thousand yards further back.

Sam found himself with Corporal Stanton and Bill Pratt amidst a group of Scots Fusiliers as the advance was called. He had no idea where the rest of his platoon or the lieutenant was. They could all be dead for all he knew. In the chaos of bodies falling back, fighting their way back, they had somehow all been separated. Now they were a mishmash of everyone. The man next to him was a tall, broad backed Scot who talked to himself as he trudged forward.

The going was heavy. Shattered trees and smashed bodies of men made for difficult and gruesome obstacles as they pushed their way towards the enemy. A shell burst somewhere to the right scattering shrapnel indiscriminately. Men screamed and shouted. Still they pressed on. More shells bursting around them now. They dropped to the ground covering their heads with their arms, holding rifles up from the mud. A few days ago these fields had been stubble or pasture, now they were bloody, pitted, quagmires, devoid of colour other the dull grey of mud and the red gore of dismembered and maimed men.

Somewhere through the ear-splitting noise, Sam could hear the colonel shouting orders, encouraging them forward. He struggled to his feet, pulling Bill with him and plunged forward. Rifle fire began to spatter the ground. The big Scot grunted and crumpled to his knees, his eyes dimming as life's spark was snuffed. He fell, his face in the cold mud. Sam pushed on. His heart pounded with exertion and fear, yet he was compelled to advance by the courage of the CO. Someone closed the gap where the Scot had been. He did not know him, could barely recognise the regiment, possibly one of the Bedfords.

They found cover wherever they could. A slight depression in the ground, a fallen tree, a body. And they opened fire, choosing their targets with care and precision. Every bullet had to count. Every aim had to find its mark. The leading line moved forwards, the remainder giving cover. Changing roles as they advanced steadily with rapid short runs forward and longer, fierce fire fights from tenuous ground positions. Shell fire shattered their ranks whenever they stopped. They advanced in deliberate spurts with covering fire from those behind, disciplined, orderly. What did it matter they were a mixture of regiments? They were the BEF and their duty was to retake the ground lost. Painstakingly, they were doing it. Gradually the German horde was being pushed back, but at terrible cost. Shrapnel bullets rained mercilessly amongst the colonel's ragamuffin troops, scything them down in great swathes.

Somehow they made it. Some super human effort brought them to where they had started that morning, pushing the enemy before them. To where they had started, two hundred yards beyond and then they stopped. Dead beat, done in and reduced to a meagre three hundred men. They found cover, began to dig in and held on.

Still beside Bill behind a tumbled down wall, Sam checked his ammunition and reloaded his rifle. His head hurt, his mouth was parched and his left arm stung where a bullet had miraculously passed through his sleeve only grazing his skin beneath. They caught their breath and cautiously raised their heads to peer out into the murky battle ground.

"Where's Stanton?" Sam asked.

"Dunno. Was wi' us a bit since. Didn't see 'im fall. Mebbe, 'e's further down t' line," Pratt replied never taking his staring eyes from the scene in front. A dead German lay about two feet to his left, and without turning he somehow managed to reach out with a foot and kick the body so that it laid face into the earth. "Don't want 'im watchin' me," he grumbled.

Another two men slammed into the wall and hurriedly reloaded their weapons. Sam cast them a quick glance and recognised them as C Company men.

"Christ! We're well mixed up," he said under his breath as he noticed three Scots Fusiliers nearby and a handful of Wiltshires. Orders were being shouted to consolidate the position. Men busied themselves with their entrenching tools, deepening their defences whilst warily keeping an eye ready for a counter attack.

"Sergeant Hepworth isn't it?" a plummy voice called from the left. Sam half turned and saw Captain Gregory of C Company heading his way. "Need to get our men together as a unit Sergeant."

Sam fought the urge to argue. The fact that they were scattered to the four winds did not, at this precise moment in time, seem important. The enemy could counterattack at any moment. Instead, discipline ruled and he merely answered, "Yes Sir."

"Go along the line Sergeant. See if you can find any of ours. Get them organised into groups and when it gets dark enough, we'll move them all together," the captain instructed with ridiculous jollity. He always had been a useless arse, more concerned about appearances rather than sound judgement. Without argument though, Sam heaved himself from the wall and throwing his Lee Enfield over his shoulder began to creep away from Bill who shuffled sideways to allow the exasperating officer a better view of the land between themselves and where the Germans were also busily digging in.

A laboured, screeching whine grew with certain intensity, heading for the crumbling wall. Something made Sam stop. Foresight or intuition or maybe simply that understanding, the recognition of a shell on its final trajectory, heading fatefully to where one cowered, waiting. Whatever it was, he knew, at that instant that the missile was too near, had his name on it. He shouted back to the others, his voice drowned out by the deafening scream. He saw, as if in slow motion, Bill throw himself over the wall, the captain look around with bewilderment and then with a stupid gawp upwards; the other men dropped to the ground. He half turned, his mind racing, knowing that he had no time, no cover; that the thing was going to rip him apart. He was right. His foot slipped throwing him backwards, arms above his head. A terrible, ear-splitting explosion and then pain. White hot, burning, searing into his chest and left shoulder. His body hit the soft mud with a heavy thud as the concussion pounded him to the earth.

Darkness, nothing but black and silence, then sound returning, a constant ringing. He tried to move his head. Still alive, but God it hurt. Like hot irons plunged into his flesh, his breath laboured, his lungs drawing in painful spasm, fighting for air and not finding it. A wave of panic washed over him. He was suffocating. Something had happened to his chest, to his lungs. He could not breathe.

Arms grabbed his body and roughly pulled at his tunic. He distantly heard his rank shouted. Someone was talking to him. They brought him to a half sitting position and fire tore through his chest and down his left side. He cried out, somehow finding the air to expel from his lungs. Realisation that he could inhale albeit with difficulty. Still not enough air, but no longer suffocating. His head swam as hands dragged him against the wall and propped him there. He saw a face through the spasms of pain and the blurriness of fainting vision. He did not know it. It was speaking, but he could not make out the words. They were muffled and sounded foreign? Possibly Scottish. He drifted in and out of consciousness his body relenting to the dark comfort and screaming in protest as his mind forced its way back to the light.

Water on his face brought him nearer to sensible. The ringing in his ears faded a little replaced by the thudding of his heart. His lungs cried out for oxygen and he struggled to keep calm. A voice inside told him he must not die. He must fight and hold on.

Another body plunged nearby, more hands feeling him, steadily firm, but carefully gentle this time. He dragged his head around and saw with thankfulness a red cross stitched on an upper left arm. His eyes roved upwards to a young face, very young, that bore an earnest expression.

The stretcher bearer saw the wounded man staring at him and forced a smile. He spoke, but was certain that the sergeant could not hear him. Shells continued to burst around them, further away, out of range, but frighteningly loud nevertheless. With each concussion the young soldier ducked his head a little and ploughed on with his task. He was certain the wounded man had a collapsed lung. That would make getting him back harder. They could not lay him flat. He needed to be certain of which lung, then they could lay him on that side, leaving his sound lung unimpeded. He explained this to the sergeant and the man who had dragged him against the wall.

"'Elp me move 'im. I need to see where he's 'it," the stretcher bearer said. "Sorry Sergeant, this is gonna 'urt."

Sam saw the lips moving, but could hear only a mumbling drone, a constant whining and the thudding of his beleaguered heart. Vaguely he understood that they were going to move him again and fearfully he braced himself. Searing agony seemed to pierce his whole being, but he bit his lip and did not cry out, though tears sprang to his eyes. They unbuttoned his tunic a little and the young man felt inside, bringing his hand out covered in blood. The already serious face, turned more serious and the stretcher bearer inhaled sharply. "Lot o' blood," he muttered and the Scot next to him nodded.

The splodging of feet and another medical corps man appeared alongside, head bowed cautiously below the wall. By his side crouched Bill, his arm in a makeshift sling made from webbing and a dressing held to his face.

"T' others are all dead. We can bring 'em back later Bunny," the medic shouted. Bunny nodded and turned his attention back to Sam.

"Can you 'ear me Sergeant? We're going to 'ave to lay you on your left side. I think your lung 'as collapsed," the stretcher bearer shouted above the hellish din of exploding missiles.

Sam gazed at him vaguely trying to read his lips, but his vision kept falling in and out of focus. He did not see Bill. He felt terribly weary and wanted to go to sleep. Something told him not to, not yet.

"Never bloody mind explaining te 'im. The lad canna 'ear ye. Just get 'im away," the Scot spat with exasperation. He was shaken enough with that shell barely missing him. The sergeant had taken the blast for him and the last thing he wanted was for the Yorkshire-man to die next to him.

Bunny grimaced, pursed his lips and then instructed his companion to help lift the sergeant onto their stretcher. This time Sam did cry out. He was not prepared for the sudden movement, and the pain was unbearable.

"Go canny wi' 'im," Bill remonstrated angrily.

Sam fainted.

Sometime later a gentle ringing and hubbub gradually building in intensity and volume signalled Sam's awakening. His breathing felt easier, he was aware of that, and as his eyes flickered open he also became aware of the deep aching pain in his shoulder and chest. It hurt when he inhaled, but at least he could inhale despite something sticking him like a knife through his ribcage.

"Ey-up Sarn't. Back wi' us then," a familiar, but muffled voice somewhere to his left. He could hear. With a slow deliberate movement Sam gingerly turned his head to the side and squinted through blood shot eyes at the grimy face next to him. It took a moment of concentration and then everything became clear. The man laid upon the next stretcher, under the faint glow of an oil lamp was Corporal White. Despite his discomfort and general feeling of malaise, Sam smiled.

"Snowy, you old bugger," he croaked through parched lips. God, he was thirsty.

"Glad to see thi' awake Eppy. When they brung y' in I thought y' wa' gonna die. Doctor fettled thi though. Y' wa' makin' a God awful racket. Wheezin' an' gaspin'. He stuck a knife in thi side and put that bit o' pipin' in t' 'ole. Thought 'e was doin' fo' thi, but y' made a weird 'issing noise an' then breathed quietly again. 'Ow do y' feel?" Snowy rambled on in unasked for explanation.

"Like shit."

Snowy laughed, it was a welcome sound.

"Where are we?" Sam asked closing his eyes as a wave of pain spasmed through his torso.

"Advanced dressin' station. They got thi back pretty damned quick. I've been 'ere hours longer. We're waitin' fo' transport to take us out. Problem is, Fritz is 'ammerin' Wipers an' they can't get through. That's what Doc said any-road."

Sam nodded and listened. The constant thump and roar of artillery and subsequent explosion of high explosive rent the air. He wondered how he had not noticed it until now. Odd how the brain cut out the familiar, even something as deafening and frightful as gun fire.

"Awake Sergeant?" a bleary eyed medic queried before Snowy could continue his chatter. Sam turned his head to discern a young doctor of about thirty, his white apron covered in fresh and drying blood, dirt and grime.

"Just about Sir," Sam croaked focussing with difficulty.

"Hmm. We gave you quite a bit of morphine. You've been out of it for a good six hours. How's the pain? Can you bear it? We're running short of drugs," the doctor said apologetically.

"It's alright,"

"Good chap. Ambulance is here. I came over to see if you were up to the move. I need to tell them about that drain. We don't want that lung to go again. I'm sorry though, it's going to be a rough ride," the medic smiled regretfully and wandered away.

Sam exhaled deeply and wished he had not as the pipe through his chest rubbed against his ribs and sent yet more knife-like spasms through his body. He swore.

They tried to lift him gently but every movement was torture.

"Steady on there!" Snowy reprimanded the unfortunate orderlies as he heard his friend's long drawn out moan.

Loaded in the back of a horse drawn wagon, the two men were laid side by side, above them two others, one of whom never uttered a sound throughout the long, painful journey down mud tracks to the main Ypres to Menin road and then along the bone shaking cobbles. It was a journey of intense discomfort, punctuated by periods of extreme agony. Sam's body was bathed in a cold sweat and more than once he passed out, unable to bear the constant torture ripping through his torso. When lucid he became aware of Snowy talking to him. He took comfort in that broad Yorkshire dialect, although he rarely spoke back. He did not possess the energy to do so.

Several times the ambulance stopped for longer, interminable periods. The driver popped his head in to explain their way was blocked. Refugees mainly, leaving Ypres. Daylight now and still shells screeched through the air and smashed the beleaguered city.

"Do you think there's any of our lot left?" Sam asked in a moment of clarity as they waited yet again for the road ahead to clear.

"Course. T'owd man'll still be givin' 'em what fo'. That's why t' bloody Fritz's rainin' all this damned lead at Wipers. 'E can't break us, so 'e's tryin' to break t' civvies instead," Snowy replied cheerfully although his voice held a trace of disbelief in his own words. The man above him groaned loudly. The other remained silent. Snowy thought he was dead, but didn't say so. Sam smiled at the corporal's forced optimism and secretly thought he had a point. Then weariness and pain overcame him again and he drifted into unconsciousness.

Hours later he came to. The world was quiet excepting for the distant booming of guns and a soft hissing of steam. Footsteps hurried by. Voices gave instructions. Grunts of men lifting heavy loads and groans of the wounded. Sam opened his eyes, but saw only blackness. He was very aware of his pain and a familiar smell of soot.

"Snowy?"

"Yeah?"

The relief of hearing that voice. For a few seconds he had thought he was alone. "Where are we?"

"They're loading us onto a train I think. Can't see. It's dark out," Snowy returned.

"What time is it?"

"Dunno. Late. It's been dark for 'ours."

"I'd kill for a drink," Sam added hoarsely. The ambulance driver had helped him to a few mouthfuls of water from a hide flask each time they stopped, but not enough to quench his raging thirst. He suspected blood loss made it worse.

"Aye. I wouldn't mind a beer me sen," Snowy laughed back.

"Snowy?"

"Aye?"

In my right pocket there's a book, psalms, you know," Sam laboured to say. It was exhausting talking and it hurt his chest.

"Aye, I know."

"If I..., you know, if I don't make it, send it to my sister for me. It's got a flower in it I picked for her. You'll do that won't you?"

Snowy stared across to his comrade wishing he could see his face. He thought the sergeant must be delirious though he sounded cognisant. "Tha can gi' it to 'er yersen. Y' not dyin' Eppy," he reassured as a chill shiver ran down his spine. What did he know?

"Promise me Snowy," Sam pressed, his voice weak, but tone urgent.

"Aye, alright. If it makes thi feel better, I promise. But I'm tellin' thi. Y' not dyin'."

Sam closed his eyes with thankful relief. A wave of nausea enveloped him and he forced back the bile. God, he wished this was over.

Fifteen minutes later and a torch shone into the back of the ambulance. Strong hands pulled the stretchers from their racks and their occupants were borne onto a waiting train. A cool hand rested upon Sam's brow. His eyes fluttered open and he glimpsed the smile of a middle aged woman, a nurse. It was such a surprise that he grinned back before his eyelids dropped heavily again.

The nurse frowned. He was bad this one. Might not make the journey. His pale and clammy skin spoke of a body racked with pain, weak and shocked from blood loss. It was touch and go. He seemed to be carrying a fever as well. All too often she had seen it before. Young, fit men in their prime, reduced to filthy, blood stained husks of what they once were. Clothes stuck to their bodies that would have to be cut off. They stank of sweat, blood, sometimes excrement and occasionally gangrene. Their boots would need to be prised away from their blistered and raw feet taking with them a layer of skin. And often, after all this, after holding on to life through the hell of the battlefield and the endless torment of travelling back through the lines to the clearing station and ultimately the waiting trains, often then they let go and softly slipped into the final sleep. The Irish nurse had lost count of those men, just like this one, who had died in her carriage when only a few hours from safety and the comfort of a hospital bed. She noticed the corporal who had been brought into the carriage with him staring at her, an unasked question on his besmirched face.

"We'll try and make him comfortable," she said quietly in a softly lilting Irish accent. Snowy nodded and lay back staring at the ceiling of the converted carriage. He prayed that Eppy would not die. He prayed that he had the strength to give that little book to the sergeant's sister, if he did.

CHAPTER 10.
November 5th, Leeds General Infirmary

Lily sang cheerfully as she restocked the dressings' cupboard. It was late afternoon and nearing the end of her shift, but there was still dinner to serve and the drugs round to be made with Sister. At last she had escaped the medical ward as the long running measles epidemic diminished to a trickle of sufferers. Priorities had changed. With the influx of soldiers from France and Belgium returning to England with horrific wounds the military hospitals were overwhelmed and bad cases, in need of surgery or more than basic nursing care, were being diverted to the big general hospitals throughout the country. Lily had been transferred to a surgical ward in response, where they tended to twenty soldiers alongside a dozen civilian, surgical patients. She still had no word from the military hospital, but at least now she felt that she could help the brave boys returning home, that she was, in a small way, doing her bit.

The soldiers on her ward were not such bad cases. They were those who had been deemed fit enough to travel the long journey north and they were the overflow from Beckett's Park and the military hospital in Bradford. They were mainly amputees, and chest wounds, who were on the mend. As such they were a cheerful bunch, a little cheeky, but ever so grateful and over the moon about being back in Blighty. Few of them would fight again, but there were a trio of fairly lightly wounded Geordies, who would be going back.

The last bandage stowed, Lily smoothed her apron and headed for the kitchen to help the nursing auxiliaries dishing out dinner. They stacked a large trolley with plates of minced beef pie and vegetables and then the auxiliary nurses wheeled it up the ward, serving the meal to ever hungry men. Lily had never seen men eat as much as these soldiers did. At first she had watched with utter amazement as they shovelled whatever fare was placed in front of them down their necks without hardly pausing for breath. They demolished every last morsel and were not above asking for the adjacent man's dish, if someone felt too unwell to eat. Invariably it was the civilians who left the food. Lily did not think she had seen one crumb remaining on the plate of one of their military patients.

She supervised the serving of dinner, ensuring rules were followed, that those who could get out of bed sat at the long table in the middle of the ward and those who could not were propped adequately on pillows, with long white napkins to capture debris. She poured tea into large earthenware mugs and exchanged a happy, but brief few words with the men as they began their meal.

They liked Staff Nurse. She was far more easy-going than the stern and much older sister. She was also much prettier and for the soldiers, so long away from home and female company, she was a sight for sore eyes. She sang as well, when Sister was not around, and her voice was as good as any medicine. They would ask for a song if all was quiet and usually she would oblige with the words, "Just the one then" although it invariably turned into more, ending only when the doors at the end of the ward opened signalling the arrival of Sister or worse, Matron. The auxiliaries and male orderlies were in on the conspiracy and would happily act as look out for such impromptu and forbidden concerts. Hospital rules were strict. Discipline of a military standard, but rules could be broken and circumvented if one had help and Staff

Nurse invariably had help for she was everybody's darling. This evening was no exception. Sister was in her office down the hall and the men were in buoyant mood.

"What about a song, Sister?" a man with only one arm cried as he scooped mashed potato onto his fork. They always called her sister. It was a habit shared by all the Tommies. They did not see the difference and it was a habit that irritated the real sister beyond reason.

"I don't think so Bert. *We're* too close by," Lily responded with a wink. Bert grinned, understanding.

"Later then?" he pressed through a mouthful of food.

"Maybe. We'll see. For goodness sake Bert, don't talk with your mouth full. Did your mother never teach you table manners?"

"Sorry," Bert replied spraying mash onto the table cloth and earning a mouthful of abuse from his nearest neighbour and laughter from everyone else.

Lily rolled her eyes and poured his tea, exchanging a wry smile with the nursing auxiliary next to her.

A discernible waft of air and the soft sweeping thud of closing doors stifled the jollity and brought faces around to the ward entrance in anxious expectation. Lily glanced behind her and saw the stiff figure of Sister approaching. Subconsciously she smoothed her apron again, checked it for smudges; thankfully there were none. Sister was a strict disciplinarian. She ruled her ward with a firm hand, expected her staff to be professional at all times, to not fraternise with the patients, to remain aloof and detached. Her word was law. But she was not a complete ogre. She understood the need for compassion. She was dedicated and efficient and though she would not tolerate the obvious breaking of rules, Lily knew that the fierce countenance belied a soft heart. What Sister did not see for herself, Sister did not question or reprimand even if she might have known what went on behind her back. Sister had heard Lily singing in the ward, but unless she actually caught her Staff Nurse doing so she would say nothing.

Dressed in a sombre, but smartly cut navy dress with apron and veil snowy white, Sister sailed like an eighteenth century galleon towards the centre of the ward. Instinctively the men became quiet and busied themselves with eating. The staff curtseyed respectfully.

"Staff Nurse Hepworth, please would you accompany me to my office?" she requested.

One of the men whistled earning himself a glare from the martinet, but Lily was not worried that she might be reprimanded. Something in Sister's demeanour, her soft tone of voice tinged with concern and the expression of sympathy said otherwise. Lily's heart skipped a beat. This was bad news.

"Is it Sam?" she asked in a small voice the tea pot beginning to chatter in her shaking hand.

The patients stopped eating and watched with curiosity. Staff Nurse had happily and proudly told many of them that her twin brother served with the Yorkshire Regiment.

"Please, Hepworth, my office," Sister insisted and turning her attention to the staring faces at the table sternly added, "Eat your dinner gentlemen."

Nervously placing the rattling tea pot onto the trolley, Lily caught a reassuring smile from Bert before she followed her superior from the ward. The click of heels on the polished wooden floor echoed loudly and gratingly, as if no other sound existed. Lily was aware of only that noise and the heavy pulsing of her own heart beat as she walked behind the briskly retreating figure of Sister to a small, neat room at the end of the long corridor outside. The senior woman paused at her office door and waited for the Staff Nurse to catch up. She smiled sympathetically and opening the door ushered the young woman through. Inside stood Matron, tall and thin, glorious in black and white and for once without an expression that could curdle milk. Sitting on a seat by the desk, Joe, he stood when Lily entered.

Lily covered her mouth with both hands, her eyes filling with tears, she gazed at Joe hoping beyond hope that this was not what she feared. He saw her pain and wanted to rush forward and hold her, but that would not do here. Even though they were brother and sister, Matron would expect rules to be adhered to and discipline maintained even under such circumstances. Lily managed to curtsey to Matron, but her eyes roved to Joe, pleading.

"Nurse Hepworth, please have a seat. No, do not look so grave. Though the news is bad, it is not what you fear."

With fumbling hands Lily managed to seat herself, gripping hold of the chair with white clenched knuckles.

"I received a telephone call from your father half an hour ago. I called Sister to bring you here and Dr Hepworth also. I'm afraid your brother has been wounded. He is currently being treated in France," Matron explained.

"Wounded," Lily heard herself say. The word echoed around and around in her head. Relief washed over her. *Not dead. He's not dead.* She felt herself sink into the chair. "Is he bad? Where is he wounded? Do we know where he is?" she rambled quickly, her brain desperate for information.

Joe spoke, "We don't know yet Lil. Father only told Matron that Sam has been wounded. I don't think he knows any details." The strain of his own fears showed through his forced smile.

"Under the circumstances Hepworth, I am allowing you three days leave. I think you should go home to your mother and father and help them through this time. We can manage here. I have already organised cover for you and Sister is in agreement," Matron interjected. Lily gazed at her.

"Thank you, that is very kind," she answered automatically and turned back to Joe.

"Robert will drive us up. He's off duty at seven. Go pack a bag and we'll meet you outside the Nurses Home at eight."

Lily nodded. She did not know what to think. Her mind raced with countless questions. She suspected they were not telling her everything. Suspected there was worse news to come. She stood and moved towards the door.

"Nurse Hepworth, where are you going?" Matron asked, her tone kindly but puzzled.

"To finish serving tea Matron."

"I'm sure the orderlies can manage without you dear. Go back to your room as Dr Hepworth suggested. You should get something to eat as well. Are you alright my dear? You look quite pale."

"Yes Matron, but if you don't mind I would like to go back to the ward. I don't want to think for too long. This will keep me busy."

Matron looked as if she might object, but catching a nod from Sister assented, "Very well, but once dinner is finished, you must leave."

"Yes Matron, thank you. Sister, Dr Hepworth," Lily bobbed a curtsey and drifted dreamlike from the office and back to the ward. She began clearing empty plates, her face pinched and pale, oblivious to the curious glances cast her way. Obvlivious also to the forced jollity of those around her who vainly tried to make her smile. Automatically she went about her tasks and also those of others more lowly while her mind ran over possibilities, questions without answers, fears. Finally the senior auxiliary nurse took her hand and squeezed it.

"That's my job Staff," she said kindly and relieved her superior of a pile of pudding dishes. The patients were drifting to the day room for a smoke or back to their beds. Lily watched them with detachment for a moment and then moved to the bed-bound invalids, tucking in and straightening sheets that did not need straightening. She did not speak, did not smile, simply occupied herself with unnecessary menial tasks.

"You alright bonny lass?" a middle aged Tynesider asked as she smoothed the bedspread for the second time across the frame covering his amputated legs.

"Yes Wilf, yes, of course I am," she replied but her eyes gave away the lie.

Wilf smiled. "Was it bad news lass?" he enquired.

Lily stopped working and stood upright. She stared into his rugged face, a face that looked older than his forty years, a face that said he understood; he had been there. She nodded and drawing in a deep breath while forcing down the rising emotion she said, "My brother, he's been wounded."

"Bad?"

She shrugged. "Bad enough that they think I should go home to my parents," the sudden realisation of what she had said and its possible implications hit her. *Go home*. They thought that Sam might die. What other explanation could there be? They were waiting for the next telegram that began "we regret to inform you...". Tears welled in her eyes.

"There now bonny lass. It won't be that bad. Look at us. Gave most of us up for dead, but we're still 'ere," Wilf reassured and squeezed her hand.

She did look at them. She stared at the row of injured soldiers, at their armless sleeves, the frames obscuring the stumps where legs had once been. For the first time she saw them for what they were, invalided men, no longer capable of fighting, no longer either, in many cases, of earning a living. She saw the self consciousness behind the cheery smiles, the feeling of worthlessness; the end of active lives. At long last the true meaning of war dawned on her. Not the glorified, jingoistic image portrayed by newspapers and moving picture films, but the wholesale destruction and maiming of brave young men. She could not contemplate losing Sam, but the thought of him limbless and dependent upon others; she knew would be torture for him. Overwhelmed with fear for her brother, she gasped back a long shuddering sob and ran from the ward.

CHAPTER 11.
December 19th, Pateley Bridge

Saturday morning and less than a week to Christmas. The High Street buzzed with bustling activity as the inhabitants of the busy Dales' market town hurriedly made their preparations for the festive season. The butchers' shops heaved with wives and mothers placing orders for a Christmas roast or bird, with cooks from the more affluent houses and inns arguing over prices of turkeys, ducks and geese. The sweet shop window glistened with tantalising candies, its panes smeared from countless, small grubby fingers pressed longingly in hope of a stocking filled with sugary treats. It was also business as usual and the dray horses, what few there were left after the Army had requisitioned more than the locals considered its fair share, hauled heavy carts through the brewery gates and along the dale. The horsepower within Nidderdale had dwindled from over two hundred to less than fifty. Farmers and businesses alike clung to what remained with fierce, guarded possessiveness, casting unwelcome and suspicious glances at any group of men in khaki. And there were plenty of them.

The recruiting offices around the country were in full swing. Any public meeting was fair game for the Army's legions of enlisting sergeants and officials. The market place in Pateley Bridge was no exception and had a stall around which gathered a collection of boys and young men listening to tales from a stout and rather elderly sergeant major as he happily regaled them with heroic tales of Mons, the Marne and Ypres. Not that he looked like he had ever been near to any of them. Still the lads huddled in the cold damp air, their expressions awestruck and their cheers genuine. The banter was the same from town to town, village to village. It aimed to spread enthusiasm for the war, to harvest the young men of the United Kingdom and send them to glorious slaughter. These innocent boys and stolid farm workers would become the backbone of Kitchener's New Army.

Standing against the Post Office wall with a half finished cigarette in his mouth Sam Hepworth watched and listened to the sergeant major's spiel and smiled to himself with cynical humour. He rubbed his aching left shoulder absentmindedly and then deciding it best to move on before the eager war mongers saw and made use of him, he stooped to pick up his kit bag. He took a last draw on the cigarette and flicked it into the gutter. Then side-stepping a singularly determined mother dragging her protesting boy from the crowd around the recruitment stand, he pulled his cap further onto his head, hitched the bag over his right shoulder and marched briskly up the steep incline of High Street. He paused briefly at the top before turning into Ripon road to watch the work force from the brewery spill out into the street following the change of shift siren; then he headed for home.

At the top of the drive he slowed his pace suddenly anxious at what or rather who awaited him. He had not told them he was coming. He had posted one letter to Lily from hospital in France and that was all. Besides, the visit was only for a few days. Yet the prospect of spending time with his father daunted him, no matter how short. He inhaled sharply and allowed his eyes to drift over the Nidd valley to the cottages of Bewerley and the steep green hills that rolled away to Wharfedale. Even in this grey winter light the dale looked beautiful and Sam allowed himself to indulge in more than a moment of homesickness, of longing to stay, of wishing he could turn back time and become a boy again. He shook himself from his reverie and trudged down the drive, green with a winter's growth of moss and in need of someone to brush away the rotting leaves of autumn.

The tree lined drive opened into the wide apron of gravel before the pleasing double frontage of the oddly concocted house that he still called home, though it was more than eight years since he had lived here last. He smiled as fond memories flooded back, but did not head to the front door. Instead he took the path to the side and entered through a smaller portal leading to the kitchen and scullery; to Rose's domain. The bell clanged as he entered and the smell of baking assailed his nostrils in a wave of welcome and also agonising nostalgia. From the kitchen he heard the distinctly irritated tones of Rose tell someone to see who had come in.

"Wi' out even knocking," she muttered grumpily. "If it's that lad sellin' Christmas trees again tell 'im we've already got one. I don't know 'ow many 'e expects us to bloomin' well buy."

Sam grinned at the cook's consternation. Still the same, still full of bluster and grizzle and no doubt still as warm hearted and generous. A willowy, pink faced girl he did not recognise entered the hallway looking flustered and hesitated as she caught sight of him. He lowered his bag to the floor and grinned.

"Rose is still as grumpy as ever I see," he said removing his cap and pushing it into the top of his kit bag.

The girl stared for a second not knowing who this soldier was. Not Mr Joe for certain, though there might be a resemblance, around the eyes. She knew of another son in the Army, but she had never seen him and for a moment she was unsure of what to do or say. The man before her smiled in a way that made her suddenly abashed, like his dark eyes pierced right through her. She flushed further and called behind her. "It's not the lad Rose. It's some soldier."

"A soldier? What are y' talkin' about?" Rose queried testily her voice growing louder as she headed towards the door. She entered the hall, peered along its dim length and with a loud shriek of surprise clasped both her hands to her mouth. Her eyes crinkled with joyous recognition and filled with tears at the same time.

"Ah Rosie, just as beautiful as I remember," Sam laughed and flung his arms wide.

The cook stifled a sob and hurried forward to greet the young man with a long hug of matronly affection, throwing herself into his arms and sniffing happily on his shoulder. He winced as her head hit the shrapnel wound and dropping his cheek on top of her floured hair swayed her ample frame to and fro throwing a cheeky wink at the now gobsmacked girl staring at them both. Rose both laughed and cried at the same time and she clung to Sam for nearly a minute while she fought, not too successfully, to regain her self control. The emotion was contagious and he closed his eyes, battling the rising tide, wanting to be held, wanting her not to let go, wanting to be nothing more than a small boy, comforted and loved. With much effort he maintained masculine composure and prising Rose's arms from around his torso he held her at arms' length and apprised her with a look of affection.

"You haven't changed one bit," he said.

She wanted to say the same, but of course she could not. The last time she had seen him was over two years ago. He rarely came home. That stupid fall out with his father! And now she thought he looked tired, older than his twenty six years.

"*You* look thin my lad," she replied gruffly and behind the smile he caught the concern in her eyes.

"Army and hospital food are not up to your standards Rosie. Any chance of a cuppa and a bit of cake?" he laughed exuding the boyish charm that had always endeared him to her. Of all the Hepworth children, Sam was her particular favourite. Lily came a close second of course, but Sam was *her* boy or rather the one she wished for. She beamed broadly and keeping a tight hold of his right hand pulled him towards the kitchen, shooing the girl through the door at the same time. Sam grabbed his kit bag and allowed himself to be manoeuvred before the stove.

"Take off that coat lad. Kettle won't be a jiffy. Tilly stop gawping! This is Mister Sam. Eee lad it's good to see you," Rose alternately addressed her two companions. "Tilly, kettle! Sit y' sen down lad. I'll cut some cake. Oh, I'm all a dither."

She hurried around the kitchen clucking and fussing like a broody hen. Sam stretched his legs before the stove and watched with amusement, enjoying the moment, the comfortable acceptance he always felt with Rose. He reached in his pocket for a cigarette, got it half way to his lips and then thought better of it. Rose would never countenance smoking in her kitchen. Best go outside for that and at this moment he did not wish to leave the cosy warmth and congenial atmosphere to indulge, what had sadly become, a needed habit. He caught the eyes of Tilly on him and he smiled. She flushed again and quickly looked away. *Bonny little thing, thin and wiry like a foal.* The curl of dark hair that escaped from under her cap coiled fetchingly around her chin. He had the urge to train it back behind her ears.

"Sorry, Tilly is it? I should have introduced myself. Sam. I'm Lily's twin. The black sheep of the family," he explained with a wicked grin and put the cigarette in his mouth without thinking.

"Black sheep's right enough. And master's son or no, yer not lightin' that up in my kitchen sonny," Rose chastised.

With a suitable expression of remorse he removed the offending article and placed it back inside his breast pocket.

"What *am* I thinking of? What about y' poor mam? You'll be wantin' to see 'er right away. Eee I am daft. Been worryin' hersen sick since we got the letter sayin' y' wa' wounded. An' then you only writing to Miss Lily. You 'eartless boy. Come on wi' y'. Upstairs now," Rose blustered.

"No, not yet Rosie. Mother doesn't know I'm here, so she won't miss me for a few more minutes will she? Besides I'm waiting for that cup of tea and cake," Sam protested. He was none too eager to go upstairs, not yet.

Rose swelled with the pride and happiness of one who has been singled out for favouritism. She furnished her guest with his beverage and a generous slice of fruit cake. While he ate she removed her baking from the oven and placed the feast upon cooling trays. Tilly assisted cleaning the oven and running outside for more coal. After a busy five minutes both women sat and joined Sam with a hot cup of tea.

"So how long have you worked for my mother Tilly?" he asked politely.

"Nearly two years now Sir," Tilly replied coyly. It was quite disconcerting having the mistress' son taking tea with them. Of course she had heard all about Sam from Rose, who had always painted a rather dashingly romantic figure of him. The prodigal son, who defied his father's wishes and ran away to join the Army. Rose always told the story as though the master was at fault, but Tilly was bright enough to know there were two sides to every tale. She studied him closely as he chatted amicably to the cook and thought him witty and good looking in a homely sort of way, but she also thought he carried an air of sadness. He had a haunted look about his eyes as if plagued by ghosts and she got the distinct impression that he did not really want to be here, or at least part of him did not. Sometimes the laughter that he so freely gave in to never reached his deep brown eyes. He caught her staring and smiled winningly, she turned away embarrassed.

"Tilly'll show y' through. I've got work to do what with t' 'ouse been full." Rose announced after a half hour, rousing herself from her seat as she spoke and smoothing her apron purposefully.

"House full?"

"Well yes. Miss Lily's 'ere and o' course there's young Mrs 'Epworth, Miss Dorothy."

"Lily and Dora are here?" Sam questioned his heart filling with happy relief. He had thought to call in to see them on Monday, before returning to the Regimental Depot. It had been a hard choice whether to come home or spend his few days leave in Headingly. Only through duty to his mother had he chosen the former.

"Didn't y' know? Well maybe as not. Miss Lily is goin' to France. She must've told you. Maybe you 'aven't got 'er letter yet. What y' mam thinks about it I don't know. A young lass leavin' 'ome to nurse soldiers. It doesn't seem right. But that's y' sister fo' you. Just as 'eadstrong as someone else I know," Rose jabbed a pudgy finger in his direction. "Young Mrs 'Epworth's movin' in wi' y' mam and dad. Mr Bradshaw's 'ardly ever at 'ome these days an' she can't be left alone now, not wi' a bairn on t' way. Besides it's good company for y' mam and good for t' young lady now that Mr Joe's gone. Oh this bloomin' war...." She finished with a sigh, treacherous tears threatening to overflow once more.

Sam had not known. He presumed that Lily's letter had missed him. It was probably in France or Belgium. Wherever the Battalion might be. It did not matter. What did matter was that he could spend his four days with his sister and that was the best Christmas present he could ask for.

"I'll take myself through. Tilly needn't escort me. I haven't forgotten the way Rosie," he said cheekily.

"Didn't think y' 'ad. But it looks better if y' introduced an' Tilly's got to make up yer bed any'ow," Rose insisted and turned to her cook book.

Sam stood and stretched. He kissed the cook on her cheek and stole a mince pie from a plate. "Y'll burn yer mouth," Rose warned with false annoyance and smiled at his laugh as he allowed the maid to lead him away.

They passed through the rear hall and into the grander, red carpeted, inner hall leading to the family rooms and staircase to the upper floor. Before they reached the entrance to the sitting room Sam caught Tilly's arm.

"My father's not here is he?" he asked looking around as if the man might suddenly appear form some hidden recess.

"No Sir. I believe 'e's doin' 'is rounds."

Sam flickered a half smile that barely touched his lips. She noted his anxiety. "You don't need to call me sir, Tilly. Sam'll do. I'm not your master and I'm not an officer. I'm just a sergeant see," he pointed to the three stripes upon his arm. There was a touch of bitterness in his voice.

"Yes Sir, I... mean Sam. It just feels a bit odd like," she answered truthfully. He looked at her fully and grinned. She really was quite pretty and probably very young; she did not look any older than sixteen. He sighed thinking it had been too long since he had enjoyed female company and bearing in mind how this poor girl flushed every time he spoke to her she probably thought him some kind of rakish cad, staring rudely all the time. He briefly wondered what stories she had heard of him.

"You don't have to introduce me Tilly. I'll do it myself. Don't bother with my room either. I'm not used to being looked after," he said at last.

"It's no trouble Sir.., Sam. I'll take your bag up for you shall I?"

"No, I wouldn't dream of it. Go back down to Rosie," he insisted. She dithered.

"I think I ought to make y' bed at least. Rose'll be on me back all day if I didn't."

He bowed his head and acquiesced. "If you insist young lady, but *I'll* carry the bag up."

She giggled girlishly, the first time she had dropped her guard and her face brightened lifting it from seriously sombre maid to pretty, apple cheeked young woman. Something about her sudden cheery openness made him crave her approbation. He picked up her left hand and squeezed it.

"I'm not a bad man Tilly, whatever you may have heard," he uttered quietly

She stared at her hand in his and slowly prised it away keeping her eyes averted. There was a desperation in this man, a childlike desire to be accepted that she found disconcerting. Why should it matter to him what *she* thought? It troubled her and at the same time she wanted to return that steady pressure of his hand and reassure him that she was his friend. Instead she replied, "I'd better go and see to y' room Sir," and slipped away.

Sam watched her lithely climb up the stairs and then with a sigh he walked across the hall, passed the grandfather clock as it chimed the quarter hour, passed the heavy Victorian oak sideboard with its photographs of the family, to the living room door. He stopped, propped his kit bag against the wall, smoothed his tunic, smoothed his hair, ran his fingers over his top lip and laughed at himself for forgetting he had shaved the wretched moustache off. He had never liked it and it was unfortunate it must be re-grown. He took a deep breath and knocked waiting for his mother's call of enter, before he did so.

"SAM!" Lily cried and leapt from the sofa racing into his arms before he could close the door behind him. His mother rose rapidly too and clasped her hands to her mouth, her eyes already overflowing. Dora pushed herself to her feet, a protective hand to her swollen belly and her eyes alight with the pleasure of seeing an old and treasured friend.

"Oh Samuel!" Eliza sniffed, "You didn't say you were coming home." She added the latter as a half hearted chastisement and hurried across the room to greet him. Laughing and with an arm around his sister, he embraced his mother warmly and wiped the tears from her face. A sniff brought his attention to Lily and he saw that she too was crying, with Dora barely in control of her emotions.

"Good God! Anyone would think I had returned from the dead," he exclaimed and kissed his twin heartily as she chuckled through her tears.

"We're just so happy to see you Sam," Dora beamed.

"You look radiant," he said truthfully, thinking he had never seen her look so lovely. "My brother's a very lucky man." She smiled back her face pink, but the compliment appreciated.

They led him to the sofa and forced him to sit, bombarding him with questions and admonishing him for not writing to let them know he would be home.

"I hardly had chance," he protested.

"We tried to visit you, but we couldn't find out where you were," Eliza carried on, her eyes still moist although her composure regained. "Do you want some tea? I'll ring for Tilly. You must be hungry." She rambled on nervously and half rose to pull the bell cord.

"She's making up my room. I've already seen her. I don't want tea Mother. Sit down, please.

"They kept moving me about. I was in Boulogne for two weeks and then they rushed us all out. They needed the beds. I got sent back home. Southampton first, then they moved me up to the London Hospital for an operation. I'm not surprised you didn't find out where I was. Lily got my letter?" he explained. Lily had her head rested on his injured shoulder and nodded in response, it pained him a little but he was reluctant to ask her to move. It had been so long since they had been together.

"Yes, yes. She read it to us. Only the one though..." A reprimand. "It was a relief after the telegram. Wounded in action was all it said. You have no idea how terrified I was, we all were," Eliza replied and the tears fell once more. "Oh, my dear boy. You have no idea...," she sobbed.

Sam disengaged himself from his sister and moved over to sit by his mother. He held her tightly while she sobbed into the pristine khaki of his new tunic. When she was done his eyes too were brighter than usual. She touched his face lovingly.

"This calls for a celebration. Let's have a drink?" Lily pronounced and blowing her nose none too delicately jumped to her feet and headed for the drinks cabinet.

"It's a little early Lily," her mother protested half heartedly though secretly she admitted a small sherry would be more than welcome.

"Nonsense Mother. Sam is home, it's nearly Christmas and what better reason is there than that?" Lily declared and searched for glasses. "What's your poison Brother?"

"A small scotch Sis," Sam answered an arm still encircling his mother.

Lily handed him the drink and distributed sherries to Eliza and Dora. She helped herself to a brandy and sat sipping it while watching her twin with relief and happiness. Just seeing his face again, after so long, was a joy. There was so much she wanted to ask, to know. She almost burst with eagerness to talk to him, but now was her mother's time. A precious reuniting of a parent with a long missed child and the conversation should be light and convivial. But after only a few minutes of exchanged pleasantries and the news of home he insisted they regale him with, the war interrupted and cast its ugly gloom.

"How long have you got? You will be here for Christmas?" Dora asked in all innocence thinking that the Army must allow its soldiers leave, where possible, for Christmas.

"I'm afraid not. I've got four days. I have to report back to the Depot on Christmas Eve. I expect to be back with my unit soon after that," Sam replied. An instant of silence spoke loudly of united disappointment and fear.

"Oh no! Surely they can wait," Dora persisted and wished she had not brought the subject up at all. She knew her words sounded foolish and naïve.

74

"Oh Sam! Only four days. Surely your wound is not healed enough to go back yet," Eliza hurriedly added before he could speak.

"It's good enough. It's a bit sore, but it wouldn't stop me doing my job Mother. The Army can't afford to have soldiers away from action for long. I'm lucky they gave me any leave at all," he explained, his heart sinking with her expression.

"Did it hurt terribly?" Dora asked.

"What? Being shot? Of course it bloody hurt. I got a bullet through my shoulder. It felt like being kicked by a bloody big horse," he returned with a laugh though there was an edge to his response and with regret he noted Dora flush and avert her eyes.

His mother looked horrified. "Please don't swear Samuel," she said quietly.

He sought Lily's gaze, caught the laughter in her eyes at his admonishment and took a gulp of whisky to hide his own rising mirth at his mother's piety. He had forgotten. Never thought of what language he used. Was too used to the rough and ready life of a soldier.

"Is it so awful over there? We hear stories of course and the newspapers say what a splendid job our boys are doing, but they always speak of victories. One doesn't know what to believe, especially when one sees the casualty lists. Your commanding officer was killed, the poor man. I thought a colonel would be safe. It is hard to imagine when one is at home," Eliza asked wanting to understand.

Sam studied her face for a second and finished his scotch. He stood and moving to the cabinet poured himself another. They waited quietly. Lily watching him with professional detachment as well as curiosity. His mother and Dora with obvious anxiety. He turned to face them.

"It's pretty grim, but we are at war and wars are, by nature, grim. We have a laugh from time to time. The fighting is tough, the food is haphazard and we don't get enough of it half the time. We just get on with it. It's a job like anything else."

"Yes, but it's a job that could kill you. Very nearly did," his mother enjoined. "Mrs Yorke lost Freddie at Mons and Mary Featherstone's eldest boy is missing. Naturally we worry and now Joe's going out there too." She glanced at Dora who turned pale and looked away.

What could he say? He dare not tell her the truth. How could she even begin to understand? He looked at his sister as if for inspiration and caught the warning in her eye. It said, don't you tell her Sam Hepworth. Don't you shatter any illusions she might cling to. He took another drink.

"Don't worry about Joe, Mother. He's non-combatant. He'll be well away from any fighting." It was a reassurance for both Eliza and Dora and he thought they believed it. They certainly looked relieved. He could not tell them that the doctors attached to each battalion spent long hours in the front line tending to men, that many came under fire, moved forward and were killed alongside those they were employed to save. His lie widened the yawning gulf that lay between their world and his and his appetite for their company waned a little. He suddenly felt immeasurably weary. He needed to get out of here.

"I would like a bath. Is that possible? It was a long train journey. I was up at four. A bath and forty winks would do me the world of good," he requested.

Eliza smiled understandingly. "Of course dear. You must be exhausted. We can talk this evening. Your Father will be so happy to see you."

I doubt that, he thought as she stood to see him out. Lily bounded up also.

"I'll walk with you and make sure you have everything," she said. She did not need to and with anyone else he would have protested vehemently, but he wanted Lily's company. She would not probe, would not ask awkward questions, but she would listen to what he wished to confide and she would be strong for him.

He pushed open the bedroom door on the first floor. Weak winter sunlight filled the room and temporarily blinded him as he stared into a time capsule. It was just as he remembered. The same blue-grey carpet, a little faded maybe where it caught the sun. The same creamy white walls, heavy, dark blue curtains and the single brass steaded bed with its hand sewn patchwork quilt. He smiled at the bed spread remembering his mother making it from scraps of material when he was a boy of ten. Joe and Frank had one the same and Lily's differed only in that Eliza had sought more feminine scenes of flowers and birds as opposed to the sailing yachts and steam engines to punctuate the plainer squares. The bed had been freshly made with crisply starched, white sheets turned neatly down over the counterpane and pillows plumped and inviting. He noted his kit bag propped against the old, Victorian wardrobe and his great coat, brushed and dried, hung upon its dark oak door. Tilly had brought his stuff up despite his remonstrations otherwise. Glancing around, the only thing that had changed over the years were his own drawings had been taken from the walls and in their place two watercolour prints depicting scenes from the surrounding Dales.

"Are you going in?" Lily prompted from behind his shoulder. He grinned and entered the room, the wave of nostalgia subsiding into renewed weariness. He sat heavily upon the bed and looked up at his sister standing at its end.

"I'm so tired Lil. It's been nearly six weeks since I got out, but I'm still exhausted," he said with a sigh. She sat down next to him and ran a hand through his hair.

"You were injured. Your body needs to heal and in doing so it needs to rest. Why not just sleep. I'll wake you in a couple of hours and you can have a bath before dinner," she uttered softly taking up his hand. He squeezed hers in reply and nodded. Yes, he would like that. To sleep once more in this bed, under this roof. Just like a child, comforted by the knowledge he was safe and warm and loved.

"It was dreadful Lily, really terrible. You can't imagine. We never stopped from the day we landed at Zeebrugge. Marching all day. Hardly enough food at times. The roads were so full of refugees that our transports were always way behind us. You should see them, poor souls. Frightened and dirty with everything they possess in prams and dog carts. They cluttered the roads.

"When we reached one destination they moved us on to another. We finally got to Ypres and then all hell let loose. I can't even begin to describe it. Hell, it was. Sheer hell. Rain, cold, mud. Digging in, moving forward, retreating back, more digging. All the time these great shells whizzing over our heads. The noise, it's indescribable. Like an express train, but louder and non-stop. For hours at a time. And the concussion when they detonate. It feels like your heart is going to burst and your head explode. You can't hear for minutes afterwards. From day break to dusk they fired and sometimes through the night. Men and horses being killed all around. I've never seen so much blood. So much. The earth was red with it. They just kept coming. Hordes of them. We fired into them, rapid fire. Oh and we were good. We mowed them down, but they just kept coming. I can't conceive how many men I've killed or maimed. They fell before us and littered the ground tens deep. I killed a wounded German. Cold blood. Not in the heat of battle. He was making too much noise, moaning, disturbing the men. I shot him!" The memories of the horrors flooded relentlessly through Sam's brain as he felt compelled to unburden himself. He dropped his head into his hands.

Lily wrapped her arm around his shoulders. She did not speak. He needed her to be there, he needed her to listen, but he did not want to be questioned and he did not need to be judged. She wondered how long he had been living with all this tearing away inside of him. After a minute or two he looked up into her face. His eyes were dry, he had not shed a tear, only contemplated his actions with forced detachment. He smiled awkwardly.

"Sorry. It's the first time I've talked about it. Sometimes I dream about it," he apologised with more than a little embarrassment, but now the flood gates were open he needed to carry on.

"Every day there were fewer of us. The Wiltshires were annihilated. Nearly a thousand men killed or wounded. I lost most of my platoon. They're all gone. More than half the bloody Battalion's gone. I don't know how many are left. I was hit before the battle was over and out of it. There were hardly any officers left. My platoon commander, Lieutenant Fielding, was still there, poor sod. He's not even a Regular. Hasn't a clue, but he fought like an old hand.

"When I was hit I thought, oh good, it's over. Just that. I was so tired. We'd hardly slept. Constantly exhausted. I used to fall asleep standing up, we all did. All I wanted to do was close my eyes and sleep forever. It was a relief. I didn't have to go on fighting. Christ it hurt though! Hurt like hell. A shrapnel shell went off amongst where we were sheltering. Two blokes from C Company and a couple of Scots and Captain Gregory copped it and I got the rest, in my shoulder and chest."

"You told us you had been shot," Lily interrupted.

"I lied. I didn't want to worry mother more than was necessary. A bullet wound is so much cleaner, so much easier to understand. I don't want her to think that men are being ripped apart by shards of flying shell casings and shrapnel bullets. It's better that she thinks everything is clean and neat. You know, no one suffers.

"Oh but they do Lil, they suffer the torments of hell itself. Men lie with guts torn out, faces pulverised, limbs shattered and blown off, and they're still alive. Sometimes for hours. There's nothing you can do for them. You just have to keep on firing and hope the stretcher bearers find them and get them out, or that they die quickly. That German didn't. That's why I...

"The sounds are the worst. Horses screaming. I've never heard that before. I didn't know they did. It's a horrible sound. Worse than anything you can imagine. Worse than the men moaning and crying out for their mothers or their wives. Then it would go quiet, deathly, before more shells again and after that another attack.

"I don't know how we are going to keep going. We need more men, more ammunition. Our gunners have hardly any and *they* have so much. I don't know how we continued to stop them. There are Territorials out there now. Terriers for God's sake! They're supposed to look after the Empire and home while we fight. There just aren't enough of us left. If the Aussie's and Canadians don't get here soon, in large numbers, we're done for," he paused, his tone despondent.

"Don't go out there Lil. I don't want you to see what I've seen. No one should see it," he pleaded, suddenly changing the subject.

"I'm a trained nurse Sam. They need people like me," she returned softly. She thought he would try this, knew it would concern him, but he had to understand that she needed to do her part too. "I can't fight like you can. I can't take up arms and serve my country, but I can help those that do. Don't ask me not to go. I need to do this."

He sighed, understanding with reluctance that his sister would do just as she pleased. She was too much like himself to do otherwise. Too independent, too bloody obstinate.

"What does Robert think?" he tried.

A spark of anger flared inside her. She dropped his hand and stood rapidly, walking to the window. She did not want this battle with Sam. She wanted his support not another lecture on why she should remain at home.

"Robert has asked me to stay home. We've discussed it and I'm still going. I made it quite clear when we were engaged what my intentions were. He's not married to me yet," she snapped.

Sam smiled sadly, "I'm sorry Lil. It's just…; it's so hellish, so harrowing. I suppose I just want to protect you from it," he admitted not wanting to fall out, wishing he had said nothing.

She softened instantly, returning to him and kissing his cheek. "I know. I'm sorry too. Come on; you're tired. Go to sleep. I'll bring you a cup of tea in a couple of hours."

He nodded and commenced unfastening his tunic followed by his boots as she hung the former in the wardrobe for him.

"Do you want me to bring you some of Joe's clothes then you don't have to wear your uniform for dinner? You must be sick of it," she said.

"If you like, I'm not bothered," he replied lying back onto the bed. He was too tired to care.

She drew the curtains and fumbled through the dark to the door, "Sleep tight Brother," she whispered.

"Lil?"

"Yes?"

"Thanks for listening."

"Go to sleep."

She heard his sigh as she let herself out of the room. Quietly closing the door behind her she leaned back upon it with eyes closed. *Oh Sam, what nightmare have you lived through?*

At five, Lily knocked cautiously on her brother's bedroom door, a cup of steaming tea in her right hand. His voice bade her enter and with a sense of disappointment she realised he had slept little, he was awake. She pushed her head into the room and found him stripped to the waist and hurriedly fastening a dressing gown over his torso. The light was on and he was not fast enough to prevent her seeing the peppering of vivid red scars covering his left breast and the jagged, knitted rip across his shoulder, along the upper edge of his clavicle and down to the deltoid muscle of his left arm. Her eyes betrayed her shock before she could hide behind a cheery smile and he frowned with a curse under his breath.

"Tea," she said with false jolliness. "Tilly's running your bath. Daddy's home. And Rose is cooking roast lamb for dinner. Your favourite." She gazed at him with wide eyes that despite her best efforts could not hide the horror of her sudden realisation. He opened his mouth to speak but she cut him off, tears welling and spilling down her face. "Oh, Sammy. We nearly lost you didn't we?" The tea cup began to shake in her hand. He took it from her and held her close.

"Shhh! I'm still here you silly ass. Come on Lil, don't cry now. I can't bear it."

With a great shuddering sob, she pulled herself away and gazed into his eyes. "Tell me about it?"

"There's not much more to tell," he tried, letting go of her hands and taking a tentative sip of tea.

"Please, Sam. I want to know."

He exhaled loudly and pulled back the gown. "There were four pieces. They entered here, broke two ribs and one embedded in my lung. This one tore a gash in my shoulder," he pointed to the scars as he spoke. "These were shrapnel bullets. My lung collapsed and, well they thought I might…, you know, not make it. They operated in a tent somewhere. I don't remember anything about it. But some brilliant Army surgeon saved my life, drained my lung and made me fit enough for the trip to base. There were so many wounded coming in. As soon as I was out of danger they sent me to Southampton to convalesce and to remove the splinter. It was a bit near a big vein you see? And it was a jagged piece of shell casing rather than a bullet. They kept me in Southampton for a couple of days and then moved me to the London, for the operation. They radiographed me first. Showed me the image as well. Quite astounding. I've never seen one before. Anyway, that's it. I was there nearly four weeks and then they sent me home and here I am. Still alive you see." He grinned.

"Oh Sam," she whispered. "I wish this awful war was over. They said it would be, by Christmas. That we'd thrash the Kaiser and send his army packing," she continued with frustrated vehemence and plonked herself heavily onto his bed.

"Yeah, it's very different," he agreed absently and gulped down his tea. "Has Dad said anything?" he changed the subject.

"Said anything?"

"Yes, you know, about me being home."

"He's glad you're here, if that's what you mean. He does love you Sam," she impressed guessing his anxiety. He simply grunted in reply and his face clouded with dark brooding memory.

"I've brought you something," Lily announced cheerfully sensing the need to lift his suddenly sombre mood.

"Oh yes?" he grinned in reply, happy to play along.

"Well, two things actually." She delved into her skirt pocket and held out an envelope. "Made with my own fair hands. I hope you appreciate the effort."

He took the envelope with a grin, the irony of her last comment not lost upon him. As children he had always mocked her artistic efforts. He sat next to her and delved into the packet drawing out two bookmarks. One made of card; a pressed flower glued to its surface and then varnished to seal and protect the delicate bloom. The other was made of a strip of heavy cream silk and the same flower had been painstakingly, but not so skilfully, embroidered onto it. Sam smiled at the almost childish stitching and thought that his sister would never possess those desirable, old fashioned womanly virtues. She lacked the patience to persevere at her attempts and as such her embroidery, like her painting was, by a Lady's standards, lamentable.

"It's your parapet poppy you sent to me from hospital." she explained awkwardly. He nodded. "I made it into a bookmark, but then I thought it would probably get all broken up and tattered if I sent it to you, so I made the other one. It's not very good I know, but I thought you'd like it. For luck or something…, you know." She rambled on, becoming more embarrassed as he remained silent. She sighed loudly. "Oh I know its rubbish. You don't need to keep it."

"No, it's not rubbish. I…, thank you. I'll treasure it always," he reassured quickly.

She eyed him suspiciously searching his face for that mocking expression she remembered from childhood. It was not there. If anything he appeared touched by the simple gift, his eyes remained rooted upon the faded, pressed flower and his fingers moved tenderly over the embroidered one.

"Thank you," he uttered very lowly and kissed her cheek. "This one can stay here, my link with home." He waved the card bookmark in the air. "And this one shall return to Flanders with me when I go." He jumped up and placed the silk poppy into the top pocket of his tunic hanging in the wardrobe.

"What time is dinner?" he asked turning back to face her.

She glanced at her watch pinned at her waist. "At seven. You've got a while yet. I'll leave you to get ready. Do you want those clothes of Joe's?"

"I suppose so."

"I'll leave them on the bed for you. Go on, your bath will be getting cold." She hopped off the bed, kissed his cheek and left the room.

Sam pulled the dressing gown tightly around him and delved in his duffle bag for his shaving kit. He had not unpacked. He did not know whether he should bother. He placed the pressed poppy on the writing desk, his eyes lingering upon it a moment longer and thoughts of the day when he picked it, amazed to see it flowering in October, flooded with a certain painful melancholy through his head. He exhaled a long shuddering breath and then, with a sudden determination to make the most of this few days of leave, he headed to the bathroom. One never knew; this might be his last time at home.

Dinner was a pleasant affair, with a delicious roast lamb joint and curd tart to finish. They drank a fine claret; a gift from Dora's father for a special occasion. Eliza argued that this was exactly that. Not that anyone disagreed. The table conversation remained light hearted and just a little contrived to avoid talk of the war. Thomas and Sam shook hands in greeting and if any frostiness existed between them, they hid it well for the sake of others. No one wanted an argument. No one wanted to spoil the sheer joy of being together and though Dr Hepworth studied his son with a critical eye from time to time, no one noticed.

In truth Thomas was as relieved and happy to see Sam as the rest were. He just found it difficult to express that joy openly. There was much in their turbulent past that still annoyed him. He had never been able to understand or forgive Sam's deliberate disobedience and now, more than ever, he failed to comprehend why the young man had, not only joined the Army, but stayed there. Signed on for another five years! Thomas had devoted his life to caring for and saving the lives of others. That his son had chosen a profession that did exactly the opposite remained a huge disappointment to him. That, and the fact that Sam could have been so much more, was the breadth of the river that raged between them.

They retired to the drawing room for coffee and Dora demanded a song recalling the duets the twins had often played with fondness.

"Oh I don't know. I haven't played in a while," Sam protested, but the ladies would hear none of it and his sister pushed him to the piano stool. With mock reluctance he complied and as she took up her seat next to him he began thumbing through a dog eared music score.

"No, nothing serious," Lily protested snatching it from his hands. She delved into a pile of papers atop the instrument and brought out a handful of modern songs. She touched the ivory keys with light perfection and began the introduction to 'It's a long way to Tipperary'. He shoved her sideways along the stool and took over the lower keys.

"You play the melody," he insisted and they began to play, singing at the same time. Soon everyone joined in, with an invitation to Rose and Tilly to join them. A happy, carefree evening, reminiscent of a different age. The only regret was expressed fleetingly by Eliza, who after the final strains of 'Pack up your Troubles' died away, could not help but state how she wished the other boys were home too. It was an innocent remark, but it set a momentary edge in the air. Lily saved the day by producing a new sheet of music with a racy ragtime tune. She began to play and soon her brother picked up the beat and began adding his own improvised harmony.

Eliza smiled proudly and exchanged a glance with her husband. It was a look that betrayed both her love for her children and at the same time echoed his own thoughts. An almost telepathic understanding so strong that he even nodded in agreement to her unspoken regret. Yes, they both could have been so much more. So wonderfully talented. So magical together. They played like they were one. After the initial rustiness had disappeared amongst giggles and teasing jibes, one would never guess that it had been years since they had sat on that stool together. They used to spend hours on wet, miserable days during their childhood simply picking out tunes and composing their own harmonies.

Raucous applause brought Thomas back to the present; he smiled at his beaming daughter and was amongst the loudest crying out for an encore. How would he cope knowing his little girl was over there, amidst the horrors of war? Despite the merry atmosphere a cold fear gripped his heart as he watched and sang and applauded. A fear he could not shake.

"Ooh that's enough! I need a drink, I'm parched with all this singing," Lily announced as the hall clock struck ten.

"I'll make some tea," Rose said and digging Tilly in the ribs indicated that they should leave the family alone.

"Thank you Rose, that would be wonderful," Lily returned and flopped with feigned exhaustion onto the sofa beside her mother.

"Think I'll pop outside for a smoke," Sam declared, his face flushed with enjoyment. He took a pack of cigarettes from his trouser pocket and fumbled for a match.

"Put a coat on, it's cold," his mother called after him as he disappeared into the hall. The sound of his laughter echoed back.

Outside, under a starless sky, Sam huddled under the entrance portico and took long drags on his much needed woodbine. It had been a good evening. He had enjoyed himself. He blew out long tendrils of acrid smoke and watched it curl away into the darkness. Behind him the door opened and his father stepped out to join him. Immediately Sam's posture stiffened; became defensive.

"It's good that you came home. Your mother has been worried sick," Thomas said after a moment during which he lit his pipe. The sweet tobacco assailed his son's nostrils, making his own choice of smoke seem vulgar and foul. He dropped the tab end and extinguished it beneath his shoe.

"They gave me four days leave. I have to report to Richmond after that. It made sense to come home," Sam stated matter-of-factly.

"Is that all? It made sense?"

Sam bristled under the tone of accusation. "No, of course not. I wanted to see everybody. It's been a long time."

"A long time. Yes it has," Thomas agreed.

"For Christ's sake Dad! I'm in the Army. I can't just come home when I want," Sam bit back as the spark of provocation lit the fuse.

"Yes, I know that. Anyway, you're here now," Doctor Hepworth sensed the conversation about to dissolve into yet another argument and he was wearied with such battles. The fact that he wanted to shake some sense into the boy was something he just had to live with. Boy? Sam was a man, not a boy and a man who had, according to Lily, nearly died. Eliza did not know how close she had come to losing a son, but Thomas did. He softened.

"I'm glad you're here. I'm glad you're on the mend. It was a close run thing I gather?"

Sam glared at his father momentarily realising that his sister had confided the details of his injury. He felt annoyed at her betrayal of his trust. "Lily been telling tales has she?" he accused.

"I asked. She told me. Your mother does not know and neither will she from my lips," Thomas appeased.

"It was a close run thing," Sam acknowledged, his anger melting into relief.

"Do you want to talk about it?"

"No. You..., you wouldn't understand."

"Try me," Thomas appealed. It was an attempt to restore the faith. An olive branch extended. It failed.

"It's cold out here. I think I'll go back in. G'night Dad," Sam returned and shrugging his shoulders as if to emphasise the chill, he went back into the house leaving his father alone and the rift unclosed.

The next four days sped by with remorseless rapidity. They were bleak, cold days yet the warmth of the Hepworth household filled them with comfort and pleasant company. The twins spent many hours out walking during the day. The evenings were packed with music and laughter.

Sam caused much hilarity downstairs when Tilly caught him ironing his freshly washed army shirts. She had protested loudly, no longer shy of him, that such was not a man's work. He had refused to return the iron, holding it high above his head and stating that no one else could get the creases in the right places. Besides he found it relaxing. Flustered and flummoxed she had left him to his chores. Never had she heard such a thing. She recounted it to Rose who wisely stated, "Well Mister Sam *is* a soldier," as if Tilly should put the two, seemingly disparate things, obviously together.

The next day he was painstakingly brushing, what to Tilly's unmilitary eyes, seemed his perfectly clean tunic. She almost ribbed him over it, but something in his mien, his dark and sombre expression checked her before the words blurted out. There was something almost reverent in how he worked. The tunic did not need brushing, but he needed to do the work, to cleanse something deeply rooted. He caught her watching him and smiled though the light did not reach his eyes.

"Getting back into practice," he laughed. "RSM would have my guts for garters if he saw it in this state."

"Looks spankin' to me," she replied thinking the jacket was new, how could it be dirty? She moved closer as he held it up for inspection. "What's that stand for?" she pointed to the crossed rifles badge fastened onto the left lower sleeve.

"Marksman's badge. You get more money if you have one of these. Means I'm good at shooting Tilly. Best shot in the Regiment me, didn't you know?" he explained with phoney boastfulness.

"Means your better at killing than anyone else then," she fired back sharply and instantly regretted it. She had not meant to hurt. The words just sprang thoughtlessly from her lips. She liked Sam. He was more approachable than the other Hepworth men, more like her own down-to-earth brothers. But her remark, though meant to be a flippant one, slapped him hard across the face. His eyes narrowed and his jaw clenched. His expression a moment ago so open and light, clouded and darkened.

"Yeah I'm bloody good at killing," he muttered lowly.

"I...., I'm sorry Sam. I didn't mean..., I...," she stammered awkwardly.

"No, don't apologise. You're right. It's nothing to be proud of." He slung the tunic over his shoulder and murmuring something about having to pack his stuff left the kitchen to return to his room.

"Sam, I...," she tried, but he had gone leaving her feeling wretched. He had shown her nothing but kindness and goodhearted, brotherly affection and she, with a careless word, had hurt him.

Early on Christmas Eve, Sam said his goodbyes. He asked that no one accompany him to the Station and put on a stern face at the emotional protestations. He did not want a tearful send off. He wanted his last memories of this leave to be fond ones, with no crying and no miserable goodbyes. Eliza struggled to contain her sorrow and despite her best efforts Lily's eyes were much too bright as he bent to kiss her farewell.

"Look after yourself Sis. I'll write soon," he whispered into her ear.

He hugged Dora and his mother, shook hands with his father and waved a cheery goodbye to Rose and Tilly as he marched up the drive, his kit bag across his back and his greatcoat buttoned against the cold.

With his leaving a temporary frost descended upon the household. It would lift only on the arrival of Frank on the late train. A pity the boys had missed each other. A pity Joe was not home.

A little before lunch Thomas strolled thoughtfully along the first floor corridor. He was in melancholy humour and as he passed his middle son's room he hesitated. There had been so much he had wanted to say. So much he had not said. He pushed the door open and gazed inside. The room was pristine. Everything in its place with military precision. He smiled grimly and stepped inside, walking to the window and staring unseeingly out at the grey winter's day. He turned to leave and something caught his eye. Upon the desk lay a small book neatly placed exactly in the centre of the table. Thomas reached down and picked the little volume up. He recognised it immediately as Sam's New Testament and Psalm book. It had been a

Confirmation gift.

Sitting heavily upon the bed he held the tiny volume in both hands. Within its carefully thumbed pages lay a bookmark with a pressed poppy stuck to it. Thomas opened the page marked and noted some lines underscored and a scrawl of writing in the margin. Curiously he fumbled in his jacket pocket for his glasses and then read the lines. An arrow pointed to Psalm twenty-three whose words began with 'The Lord is my Shepherd.' In Sam's untidy hand the annotation read, *in case I do not return.*

Thomas felt his hand shake. His eyes roved to the underlined passage of Psalm twenty-five. *Remember not the sins of my youth, nor my transgressions; according to thy mercy remember thou me for thy goodness sake.* Then written in the margin next to this the words: *Forgive me for what I have done and for what I will do.*

"Daddy?" Lily's voice from the doorway.

He wiped his eyes rapidly and turned to face her with a tenuous smile. "The room is so neat. I think I preferred it when I used to nearly break my neck climbing over his books and toys strewn all over the floor," he said.

She came and sat next to him sensing his grief.

"He left his Psalm book," she stated seeing the volume in her father's hands.

"I think he left it for me. Here," Thomas handed it to her. They sat silently while she read the words. "He thinks he's going to die doesn't he and I never told him I was sorry," he blurted.

"He'll come back Daddy," Lily comforted though her voice was small and a terrible sense of finality crowded into her brain.

CHAPTER 12.
December 29th, Southern England

Lieutenant Joseph Hepworth, sealed the letter he had just written to his mother and father and stared for five minutes out of the bedroom window of the pleasant country cottage he had the fortune to be billeted in. He was off duty and glad of it. The weather outside had turned sleety and bitterly cold. He could hear the distant crack of rifles as the new Service battalion to which he was attached carried on, regardless of winter squalls, with learning to be soldiers. Something that Joe struggled with despite not being subjected to the same rigours as the other men and officers. That, in part, was the problem.

As a doctor, he was non-combatant and therefore unarmed, not even trained in the use of a fire arm. As a volunteer, he also held only an temporary commission. As such he felt that he did not exactly fit in. Despite this being a Service battalion made up largely of volunteers, it was stiffened by a number of reservists, territorial officers and NCOs. Men who knew the art of soldiering and had little patience with those who did not. They bullied the new recruits into shape and tolerated their medical officer as one might an unpopular child with whom the other children were forced to play.

Joe found Army life tougher than he had expected, not because of the strict discipline, but because he felt like an outsider, which in many ways he was.

He sighed, bringing his thoughts back to the here and now. He placed a new sheet of paper upon the blotting sheet and picking up his pen, began to write.

"My Dearest Dora,

I hope you are well my love and that this dismal winter weather isn't getting you down. You will, no doubt, have heard by now that Robert has been posted to France. He should, as I write, be taking up his role in the British hospital at Rouen. Lucky devil! I know you will not understand, and that you are glad that I am still here in England, but I do envy him. Anyway, at least I can learn my job without the added distraction of having real casualties to deal with.

My duties are varied and a little odd, or rather unexpected. For a start I am responsible for all sanitary arrangements, including supervising the siting and digging of latrines! I suppose the Army considers a doctor knowledgeable in all aspects of hygiene, but I must admit it came as quite a surprise when the corporal responsible for sanitary working parties accosted me to ask my opinion upon the suitability of a certain field and would I inspect the finished article? I've never seen an open air privy in my life! Yet here I am considered an expert in such things.

I have a number of medical orderlies and stretcher bearers as well as sanitary men under my command. The orderlies, like myself, are RAMC men. The rest are from the Battalion. It took a while to get used to being referred to as Sir all the time and also to give orders rather than request work to be done. I think the men and in particular, the NCOs, thought me quite hopeless to start with, which I have no doubt I was. I am getting the hang of it now though, but I tell you dear, I now have the greatest respect for Sam. Quite how he stuck to soldiering I do not know given the strict discipline and the sometimes ludicrous rules. Did you know I cannot even eat with my orderly sergeant? A man who was a teacher in civilian life! If I met Sam, he would have to salute me and defer to me.

Another of my duties is to instruct the men on health, diet and other more delicate aspects of their well being. The latter causes much hilarity within the ranks as you may well imagine and some of the younger officers are terribly embarrassed by it, although I will not enlighten you further.

The men come from all walks of life. Some are from quite rough backgrounds; others are professional, well educated men, who by rights should have waited for a commission but want to be in early. It is a little odd hearing a well spoken voice deferring to a bellowed order from a most colloquial drill sergeant.

Most of the ranks still do not have a uniform or even a rifle. They drill with broom handles and the few weapons there are shared around during musketry practice. The Regular chaps and Territorials have uniforms of course, as do all the officers, but the rest simply wear an old suit or a dark blue one that they all detest as it shows them up as one of Kitchener's men. One or two uniforms have been distributed and you should see the fellows who are lucky enough to have them. They strut and pose like khaki peacocks in front of the rest. It causes no end of jibes and arguments.

They have been spending much time digging trenches and enacting life in them. As such I play my part by visiting them there and generally trying to get to know them. Obviously I am responsible for their health and every morning I hold a sick parade and this is where I have come unstuck. Perhaps I am rather gullible, but I genuinely did believe I was acting in the men's best interest. Sadly the regimental sergeant major (a fierce man who scares the living daylights out of me) did not agree and unfortunately neither did the commanding officer. My fall from grace was my faith in human nature and my willingness to believe that all men are honest. I have learnt, to my subsequent humiliation, that it does not pay to be too sympathetic with these men. You will laugh when I tell you the tale, but believe me at the time I was quite blind to what was going on. So wrapped was I in what I saw as my duty that I failed to notice that I was systematically being taken advantage of.

It started with a genuine case of a strained back. The man involved could hardly walk, he was in so much pain so I put him on the sick list and prescribed bed rest followed by gentle exercise after a few days. As a result he escaped a particularly unpleasant task. It seems that on his recovery he told all his pals this and I suddenly became inundated by a growing number of men on sick parade with a growing number of complaints. Foolishly I believed most of them and placed those I thought needed it on the sick list. The RSM, wondering why his Battalion seemed to be suffering from more than its fair share of ailments, investigated. He gave me a lecture, telling me I was too lenient and that the men were taking me for a ride. Stupidly, and because, I hate to say, my professional pride was piqued, I told him I believed they were all genuine cases.

To cut a long story short I was soon summoned to the CO to explain my actions. After I did so he quite kindly, but extremely firmly, lectured me on the deviousness of men trying to shirk their duties, on how I was gradually reducing the efficacy of his Battalion and that nursemaiding soldiers was not to be tolerated. In his opinion if the men could stand up, then they were fit enough to work.

In short he told me I was too soft and to buck my ideas up or he would have me replaced. I have never felt so demeaned in all my life. The worst of it was knowing that the men saw me as a complete soft touch, wet behind the ears. For days I thought they were laughing at me and I have no doubt that they were. However, I have learned from the experience and as the Americans' would say, I've wised up.

I suppose I will get used to this way of life in time. At the moment I feel about as soldierly as my lead cast toys were! Please do not think I am miserable, for on the whole am not, but to say that there was not some time during every day when I feel totally out of my depth would be to tell a lie. In that respect I am thankful for this extended training period. Think if I were in France and what my actions would have done there!

On a lighter note, my salute is very smart now and I at last understand all the Army terminology that at first was so baffling.

There is no sign of my being sent to France and it may be that I will not go until this Battalion is needed. This will comfort you I know.

Please take care of yourself my darling. I miss you and think of you always.

Your ever loving
Joe.

CHAPTER 13.
London, New Year's Eve

Frank jolted awake as the train lurched out of Leeds Station. He had dozed off somewhere after Harrogate and slept soundly for half an hour without dreams, gently rocked by the steady rolling carriages. He yawned, stretched and glanced across guiltily at his sister. Lily was reading; her forehead creased in concentration.

"Sorry, nodded off," he said and stretched his legs under the seat opposite.

"You were snoring," she replied not lifting her head from her book. He grinned.

They were alone in the carriage and he was glad of it. Travelling was never his favourite pastime. He dreaded having to make polite conversation with complete strangers. At least with Lily along, she would happily chatter away. She was much more gregarious and certainly not shy. He took after his father for shyness and feeling awkward around people. It was a contradiction in his character when one considered that his profession was to entertain, to perform publically.

"Good book?" he tried again.

Lily sighed loudly. "It would be if I could read it in peace," she muttered and closed the volume exaggeratedly. She smiled broadly at him and he echoed the expression. He was happy that she chose to return to London with him; she could have waited another day or so. Now they could spend a little time together. Time they had not truly had since Vienna. She was not due to leave for Dover until the fourth. He could show her the sights of London, show her the Albert Hall, introduce her to his circle of friends, his fellow musicians and....

"Do you want something to eat? I think the buffet car has opened," she interrupted his thoughts.

"No thanks. I'm alright."

She gazed at him as if she thought otherwise, but did not contradict. "I think I'll get some tea. Would you like some?"

"No. You go. I'll probably nod off again soon anyway. Always do on trains. They just rock me to sleep."

"No I'll wait. We can go later," Lily decided feeling she ought not to leave him now he had woken up. She still felt the need to take care of her little brother.

They chatted about Christmas for a while. How good it had been to see everyone. What a shame that Joe and Robert were away. He regretted missing Sam too, but at least Dora and Mother and Dad had been there. They talked a little about Lily's preparations. Where she needed to go to buy her uniforms, what other essential items were on the list the War Office had sent to her. They giggled over items such as fold-up canvas wash bowls, that they even thought it prudent to tell young ladies to pack a vest and corset and that it was essential to own a New Testament and Psalms book as well as a hymnal book of military songs. To Lily it was a great adventure. An escape from the restricted world expected for young women. Her chance to follow her brothers into the patriotic maelstrom of a righteous war. The fact that her view of this war had subtly changed following Sam's wounding, she never let on. Unaware of her nagging doubts Frank envied her freedom, her chance to join in. It was something he could not do.

As they neared Peterborough he felt the tide of sleepiness sweeping over him again. It was wonderful visiting the family, but the long journey, with its change of trains at Harrogate, together with the constant business of visits and socialising that went hand in hand with Christmas, always left him exhausted. Lily recognised the signs and allowed him to drift off again.

At Peterborough two young women joined their carriage, sitting opposite and staring openly at the mousy-haired, somewhat thin faced and somnolent man in his corner.

"Don't worry he doesn't bite," Lily mocked watching their eyes flicking from Frank and then to each other and back again. The taller girl giggled affectedly and her sister, for it was obvious from their appearance that they were related, bit her lip to prevent a similar outburst. Lily thought them asinine and picked up her book. The train shunted into life and Frank snorted loudly. The sisters snickered. Lily rolled her eyes behind the pages of her read. The women began to talk. Inconsequential gossip and chit chat about their plans. It was apparent that they were going up to London to visit a relative and were being treated to a night at a swanky restaurant followed by a New Year's dance. It was apparent because they discussed it so loudly, obviously wanting to impress their travel companions. Lily closed her book with a sigh.

"I'm sorry, did we disturb you?" the shorter girl asked.

As if you didn't know! "No, of course not. It's rather a boring chapter," Lily lied with an insincere smile.

"Are you and your...," the short girl paused and tried to catch a glimpse of Lily's ring finger, "Your fiancé going up to London too?" she finished, her face filled with conspiratorial understanding.

"He's my brother," Lily replied a little too acerbically. "He lives there and I'm on my way to France."

"France! Ooo, how thrilling! Are you...?"

"I'm a nurse," Lily cut the taller woman off. Normally she would have enjoyed a conversation, but she had not taken to this pair with their long, critical stares and their obvious relish of gossip, perceived or real.

"How exciting," the short sister whispered, awestruck.

It was too much for Lily. She smiled sweetly, apologised but excused herself explaining that she needed to get a cup of tea and that if he should wake, would they inform her brother where she was as he might like to join her. As she left the sisters' heads fell together in rapid conversation with occasional glances at the sleeping man opposite.

Frank roused as his head lolled forwards onto his chest. He became aware of girlish, muffled laughter and focussed sleepy eyes on two, well dressed and moderately attractive young ladies watching him. With some embarrassment he pulled himself upright and muttered an apology.

"Your sister has gone for a cup of tea," the fairer of the two said, her eyes alight with humour.

"Oh," it was all he could muster at present.

"She told us she was going to France to nurse our soldiers," the young woman persisted with the conversation. Frank groaned inwardly for he knew now that he was obliged to be sociable.

"Yes, that's right," he answered and averted his eyes to the view out the window.

"I suppose you'll be going soon too," the shorter and darker sister joined in.

"I beg your pardon?" They obviously had not taken the hint.

"To France. I suppose you'll be going too. You know, when you join the Army," the girl clarified with a sideways glance at her sibling.

"Er, no. I won't be joining the Army. I'm not well you see. They wouldn't have me," Frank explained though why he should he did not know. He could have simply lied and agreed with them. The expressions on their round, pink faces made him wish he had.

"Oh," the taller girl returned with a look that said she did not believe a word he uttered. She turned to her sister. "I think we should get some luncheon Sally, don't you?"

They stood to leave and as they did so the shorter woman rummaged inside her handbag, pulled out her hand and stretched it towards Frank. "This is for you," she said her tone cold.

In all innocence Frank held out his hand. She placed a white duck feather in it, the kind that frequently escapes from eider downs and pillows. He stared at it with bemusement.

"Good day," the girl said and together the sisters left the compartment with a deliberate air of disapproval. Frank continued to stare into his palm, his cheeks burning with humiliation, his mind dwelling upon the contemptuous tone of voice. They had not believed him. He sighed.

The door slid open as Lily staggered with the sway of the train, back into the compartment. Caught unawares Frank clasped his fist around the feather a little too late.

"Oh good, they've gone. Terribly anti-social of me, but they were such silly things. What's that?" she asked as she saw his hand hurriedly close.

"What?"

"That in your hand." Lily laughed. "Come on Frank. What are you hiding?" She plonked heavily next to him and picked up his hand.

"It's nothing, just a...," he sighed again and reluctantly opened his fist. Lily stared at the white feather lying there, her jaw working with angry emotion.

"Did *they* give you this? Those stupid women?" she demanded.

He nodded. "It doesn't matter Lil. They don't understand that's all. I mean, I don't look exactly disabled do I? It's just a natural misunderstanding," he tried to persuade himself as much as his sister.

"A misunderstanding! Why of all the heartless, thoughtless.... How *dare* they! Even if you were fit enough to join up, how dare they presume to judge," Lily cried as she built up a head of steam. "I've a good mind to... Where are they? I'll give them a piece of my mind." She stood with fists clenched. Frank grabbed her hand.

"No Lily. Please, don't make a fuss," he implored. She gazed down into his hazel eyes, saw the pain within them and her heart cried out, but she was angry.

"Don't make a fuss...!" she echoed shrilly.

"Please, Lily. For me? Please, just sit back down. Let's talk about tonight. Let's change the subject."

Lily swayed on the spot caught in a moment of indecision. She wanted, more than anything, to hunt down the two young women and give them a few choice words. Yet, Frank's plea melted her ire and her shoulders slumped with forced resignation. She exhaled loudly and squeezed his hand. "Alright," she said and regained her seat. "If that is what you wish. But I tell you Frank, if I see either of those two again I will not hold back. I can't believe they go around with a stash of feathers hidden away. They must make a habit of it. Stupid, thoughtless girls!" She folded her arms indignantly causing him to grin broadly.

"What are you grinning at?" she demanded amazed that he too was not incensed.

"You," he laughed and kissed her cheek. "You're fantastically terrifying when you're angry. Terrifying, but absolutely wonderful."

They disembarked at Kings Cross and took the tube. An event in itself for Lily who had never experienced such an adventure before. It was not one she relished. The underground stations were cramped and stuffy with a lack of fresh air. She felt claustrophobic in the busy press of passengers and the strong taste of soot that lingered heavily in the stale atmosphere. The trains themselves roared through the tunnels like fiery dragons raging along a subterranean world. The screeching steam whistles only added to the nerve jangling horror she felt as they hurtled through the pitch black, the sparks from the engine trailing along the outside of the carriages adding to the Hadean experience. Frank could only smile with amusement at her expression of absolute relief when they climbed the long steps into Covent Garden. He suggested they finished their journey on foot. It was only a few streets to his lodgings. Why bother with a cab. Lily jumped at the chance to finally stretch her legs. She was not accustomed to prolonged periods of sitting and she wished to breathe in, what at least passed for fresh air, for as long as possible.

They wound their way through the Garden and along narrow Victorian streets leading from it until, turning into Wild Street, they halted in front of a modest, brick faced, four storey terrace. The ground floor windows were grimy with decades of dust and soot. The building looked a little in need of tender loving care, but it was sound, no windows broken and even if the paintwork was crumbling, it had an appearance of past grandeur. Taking a key from his pocket, Frank opened the door and helping Lily with her suitcase held it open for her to pass through.

"We're on the second floor," he said and nodded towards the staircase at the far end of a drab and poorly lit hall. "I'll hold the door open while you get to the stairs. It's a bit dingy with it closed. There's a gas lamp, but we're not allowed to light it during the day," he added apologetically.

Lily smiled and took her case from him; he had enough to carry with his own and his violin. She reached the steps and waited until he joined her. As the door shut they were indeed cast into almost total darkness. It took a few moments for their eyes to acclimatise to the gloom. Frank took the lead and with his careful, measured tread, climbed the steep stairs up to the second floor. On the landing a window cast dreary grey light from an enclosed yard at the back of the house. Lily glanced out at the view and shuddered at the oppressive closeness of other buildings. No wonder the place was so dark; everything was built so close to each other. There was barely the space for light to penetrate.

"This way. We're at the end," Frank urged his breathing ragged and short after the climb. "There're only two apartments on this floor. Mr Breslov lives in that one. He's a Russian Jew. Been here yonks. Very learned. Keeps himself to himself pretty much and never complains when we have parties," he smiled broadly at the thought as they passed a shabby green door half way along the passage. At the end he paused and took a deep breath.

"Well this is it. It's not much, but it's cheap and we get it cleaned as part of the rent," he said with another apologetic smile. He tried the door without using his key, something Lily thought strange given that this was London. Still, the front door had been locked. This one, however, was not and Frank cast a somewhat nervous look at his sister as it swung open and he stepped inside.

"Frank darling!" a female voice cried with obvious joy. Lily followed her brother over the threshold and was completely taken aback when a young woman, with yellow blonde hair threw herself into his arms kissing his face affectionately.

With extreme embarrassment Frank prised her hands from around his neck and turning to reveal his sister introduced the two women, "Evie, this is my sister Lily. She'll be staying for a few days."

"Oh!" the girl looked surprised but quickly returned to her previous cheery countenance and beaming, thrust a hand forward. "Hello Lily. I'm *so* glad to meet you. We've all heard so much about you of course. Frank waxes lyrical about all his family."

Lily took the hand and shook it warmly studying its owner at the same time. Evie wore her hair flatteringly curled around her heart shaped face. Large grey-blue eyes flashed with carefree joie de vivre, their lashes thickened with kohl. Her lips were rosebud pink and her skin pale and unblemished, like alabaster. Her clothes were simple, but highly fashionable, the dark blue pleated skirt finishing daringly short at mid calf. By contrast Lily felt plain and prim.

"Oh what am I thinking of. Look at you still standing in the door way. Come in and sit down. You must be exhausted. Frank dear, you look done in," Evie exclaimed and pulled Lily's case from her. She linked arms with Frank and steered him towards a shabby sofa in the middle of a large, airy, but sparsely furnished living room. In one corner a music stand was set up with a cello propped against a stool. Frank dropped his own bags and allowed himself to be led to the seat.

"You must have James' room," Evie declared to Lily, "He's joined up and is off learning to be a soldier somewhere. We all miss him terribly. Would you like a cup of tea or something? Frank darling?"

"Er yes, that would be lovely," Frank returned squirming awkwardly under the questioning stare from his sister. Yes he had some explaining to do. He had told no one about Evelyn.

"Lily?" Evie asked.

"Yes, yes please. That's very kind."

"Not at all." Evie smiled prettily again and with a kiss on Frank's now burning cheek tripped away through a door to the left.

Lily turned her gaze to Frank, her eyebrows raised.

"We've been seeing each other for about six months now," he said in a low voice.

"She spends a lot of time here then?" Lily observed watching his response closely.

"Lil, she lives here."

"Oh. I thought you shared with James. Ah, but he's not here at the moment is he? Well, I shouldn't deprive her of her room, or do you have three?"

"She lives with me Lily. We share a bed," Frank confessed feeling like he was telling a priest. He was not sure what Lily's response would be. Her inability to hide her emotions were, at times, a curse. This was one of them. He saw her shock, her unbelieving horror that her youngest brother could live in sin, outside of matrimony. A scandalous state of affairs!

"Are you engaged?" Lily managed to ask when she had recovered from the bombshell. Her eyes still wide with incredulity.

"No."

"No? Frank, what are you thinking of? What about the poor girl's reputation?"

"It's not like that here Lil. We're musicians. It's acceptable," he justified knowing just how unconvincing and lame that excuse sounded. But it was true. No one cared in his circles. It was still risqué, but it did not carry the stigma that such goings on would in provincial England.

"*Acceptable*! I doubt that Mother and Daddy would think that. What about Evie? Is it what she really wants? Have you thought of that? Frank it's a sin to live together outside of marriage. Does that not worry you?"

"Stop moralising Lily. Look, if you don't like it we can find you a hotel, but Evie lives here with me. I love her and she loves me. We don't need a priest and a piece of paper to prove that. I had hoped you would understand," he snapped back standing up and striding to the long Georgian window.

Lily stared at his back. She was shocked, much more than she thought possible, but she was not angry, just disappointed and a little saddened. She realised she was being a trifle unfair as well. If it had been Sam who had broken such news, she would not have been surprised. The fact that it was her little brother, the quiet, shy one of the family that had done so simply shattered a long held and probably childish illusion of him. He was certainly a dark horse, but if the couple truly loved each other who was she to judge?

"And you really care for each other? This isn't just some..., fling?"

"NO! Lily, I love her," Frank turned to face her, his face flushed but also pleading to be understood. She knew instantly he meant what he said.

"For God's sake, never let Mother find out. You are careful aren't you?" she asked with a frown of concern.

"Of course. I'm not stupid," he snapped back.

"Tea then," Evie announced a little too loudly returning to the room with a tray. It was obvious she had heard everything. She placed the tray on a low coffee table, pushing music scores from it as she did.

"Thank you Evie," Lily returned genuinely.

"I'll make up the bed for you in a minute," Evie offered, her initial cheeriness subdued and her eyes constantly searching Frank's in need of support.

"Oh, there's no need. Just show me where the linen is, I'll take care of myself. What are we doing for dinner this New Year's Eve?" Lily held out the branch of friendship. It was grasped with both hands.

"There's a lovely little Italian restaurant just off the Garden. We go there quite often. The food is cheap enough for a musician's salary and very tasty. Have you ever had Italian food?" Evie rambled.

"No, but it sounds delicious. I shall look forward to it. Cheers." Lily lifted her tea cup in toast and winked at her brother who sighed inwardly with relief and thankfulness. He felt sure she and Evie would get on like a house on fire.

It was with despair that Lily studied her companions as she entered the spacious living room to be greeted with an affable smile from her brother. Both Evie and Frank were dressed for a dinner party in a deep red, richly embroidered evening gown and suit respectively. Lily had not brought such extravagant attire. She had foreseen that she would have no need of it in France, had doubted that she would rarely go out to dinner, let alone be treated to parties. She had a list of clothing to purchase, which included a smart walking out uniform, but as for her civilian attire, she had only her travelling suit, the neatly cut, dark green day dress she now wore and a light-blue cotton one for the summer months. Her letter of instructions had made it quite plain that such would be more than adequate and hardly necessary.

"Oh," she said with dismay, "I feel distinctly under-dressed."

"Not at all. You look lovely," Evie returned, her garnet earrings glinting in the lamp light as she stood and kissed Lily upon the cheek. "If anything *we* are overdressed. Gianni's isn't exactly a smart place. We simply felt like dressing up. We get such little chance these days."

"I'm sorry Sis. I should have thought. Look, we'll get changed," Frank added.

"No, no, please don't. Let's go. As long as you don't mind having your plain sister along," Lily laughed.

"Don't be absurd. You're about as plain as the flower you're named for," he replied earnestly. "Come then. Coats on and let's be away. I'm famished."

The restaurant was packed. Fashionable young ladies with their young men, a number of whom were in uniform. Most, like Lily were modestly dressed; it not seeming right to appear too extravagant with a war on. The exception being the small party of musicians they joined at a long table in the back of the brightly painted dining room.

Candles flickered in empty bottles and subtle gas lamps gave a warm and inviting atmosphere, livening up the terracotta hues of the walls and casting the crisp white table cloths in a pale yellow light. As the trio entered they were warmly welcomed by the host and boisterously greeted by their party, who it would appear had already been enjoying the house wine in abundance. There were three young men under the age of thirty and four women. All were decked in party wear, ready to welcome in the New Year just as they optimistically did a year ago. They were friendly, vivacious, a little bohemian in their dress and views, but fun to be with and Lily at first overwhelmed, soon settled and relaxed in such happy company.

She had never seen Frank so animated. He became a different person. His usual shy reserve giving way to his confident, witty side, so rarely seen in public. His face was flushed with enjoyment, added to by an overindulgence in wine, his arm affectionately around Evie's waist. He laughed louder than anyone at the attempts of one of the men to eat a plate of spaghetti when much of the rich tomato sauce ended upon the unfortunate diner's face and, luckily, the napkin tucked into his collar.

As a newcomer to the group, Lily was regaled with stories that painted a bolder, more adventurous Frank; one that would have given Sam a run for his money. With feigned shock she declared him a shameful reprobate, a title he bowed to with acceptance and some pride. It was good to see him in this carefree light. Always at home and when they had been in Vienna together, he was serious, holding himself in check, not daring to let go. Here, among these gay, young people it appeared he had discovered his inner self.

In studying his body language and that of his companion, it was not hard to see how the transformation had come about. Frank was enraptured by Evie. His eyes lit with a passionate fire each time he laid them on that pretty, pale face. More than in love with the girl; he was obsessively infatuated by her. That Evie cared deeply for him was also apparent, but Lily hoped that the flame that burned so brightly would also last the test of time. All too often, such fires, intense as they are, are also short lived, soon dying to smouldering embers.

The evening ended with the singing of popular songs and affectionate embraces wishing a happy New Year to one and all. Young adults having a wonderful time. A far cry from what their Victorian principled parents would find acceptable. But the atmosphere felt electric, it felt free and despite the shadow of war no one was willing, for this night at least, to let its looming presence spoil the fun. For one night, no one was going to feel guilty for enjoying themselves while their brothers and friends died in the cold mud of Flanders.

It was well into the early hours of the morning when Lily took to her bed and long after ten when she awoke guiltily with a thick head and a dry, stale taste in her mouth. Never had she slept in so late. Never had she drunk so much alcohol. The party had moved on to someone's flat and after that her memories became a little clouded, a little vague. She hoped she had not made a fool of herself and as she crept into the kitchenette, Frank and Evie were still asleep, she racked her aching brains for evidence of impropriety.

She placed the kettle onto the gas ring and drank a long glass of water while waiting for it to boil.

"Oh what a night! I drank far too much," a soft voice behind her stated. Lily turned to see Evie wrapped in a pink, silk dressing gown, her face a little drawn and eyes still heavy with sleep.

"I'm making tea," Lily said. "And I thought I'd have some toast. Would you like some?"

"Ooo no! I couldn't possibly eat a thing. The bread is in that bin, but we don't have anything to toast it on. Unless we light the fire in the living room. There's honey in the cupboard. You could have bread and honey. The bread might be a bit stale though," Evie muttered and sat on a stool, her elbows propped onto the table and her head held heavily in them. "Tea would be nice though, thank you."

Lily took a look at the bread and decided it was none too appetising. She made do with tea, without milk, there was none, and sat opposite Evie sipping it gingerly.

"What a dreadful hangover!" Evie declared and smiled a little ashamedly. "You look fine."

Lily laughed. "I don't feel it. I've been trying to remember what I did after we left the restaurant. It's all a bit of a blur," she confided.

"Oh you were very well behaved. You sang beautifully for us all. Don't you recall? Stephen accompanied you on the piano. I think he was quite taken with you, but you made it quite plain to him that you were spoken for."

"I vaguely remember. That is I remember singing, but the rest.... I hope I wasn't too rude."

"Not at all. You were very lady like, but *very* firm," Evie grinned with approval. She studied her companion for a moment as she took a tentative sip of tea and grimaced at its bitterness. "Urgh, I hate tea without milk and we won't be able to get any until tomorrow." She shuddered.

"We shocked you yesterday didn't we?"

Lily considered her reply and settled on the truth. "Yes, I was taken aback."

"Do you disapprove terribly?"

"I think I should, but..."

"But?"

"But, Frank is so happy. He's so carefree, so alive. I can't disapprove of anything or anyone that gives him that," Lily replied and watched the relief flood into Evie's face.

"We love each other an awful lot. He did ask me to marry him you know."

"You said no?"

"I said we should wait until after the war. He loves his family so much, talks about you all. I feel as if I know each of you as if you were my own sister and brothers. I know he would like you all to be at our wedding. He told me how sad it was when Joe got married and Sam couldn't be there. He said he hopes you'll all be together for the next one. So, I didn't feel I could demand a wedding right away. It wouldn't be fair," Evie explained.

Lily was surprised by her generosity and selflessness. She said so. "You're willing to sacrifice your reputation for his wishes. That is very unselfish of you. You must care very deeply for him."

"I do and around here no one really cares for one's reputation. Amongst our musician family it is quite acceptable. Yet I would not like to think that Frank's parents knew about us. I would like them to accept me as a respectable future daughter-in-law. We *will* do the right thing." It was a request not too subtly put.

Lily smiled and covered Evie's hand with her own. "No one will find out from my lips," she said with sincerity.

"Thank you."

Three days later and both Frank and Evie accompanied Lily, now dressed in the smart blue-grey uniform with red fringed shoulder cape and matching cape and hat, of a Territorial Force nurse, to Victoria Station. A porter pushed her heavy trunk through the crowded troops, their clinging wives, families and sweethearts, to the already burgeoning train. A severe looking matron stood before the first class carriage, clip board in hand and glared at the trio as they approached. She did not approve of men and women fraternising openly and Frank and Evie were holding each other's hand tightly. Worse were the soldiers behind, some of whom were shamelessly wrapped in what she considered brazen behaviour as they embraced their loved ones.

"Name?" the dragon demanded as Lily reached her. "Trunk into the luggage car if you please," she ordered the porter who turned with a curse and fought his way back down the platform. "It is labelled I hope?" the Matron continued.

"Yes, it is. Lily Hepworth, Matron," Lily returned avoiding the eye of her brother who she felt was on the verge of an attack of the giggles and instead caught a cheeky wink from a kilted corporal further down the platform. Lily stuck her tongue into her cheek to hide the smirk that crept to her face. But the matron did not notice, she was sliding her finger down her clipboard reading the names upon it.

"Hepworth, Hepworth, ahh yes. Leeds Infirmary?"

"Yes Matron."

"Well, get aboard then. No lingering goodbyes, we're due to leave in five minutes. That is, if they ever get this unruly rabble on board," the Matron sighed and then turning her attention elsewhere shouted in a tone very reminiscent of a strict headmistress, "Avert your eyes young man. These are young ladies, not a peep show." The unfortunate private to whom she addressed this remark, flushed violently amidst jeers and taunts from his comrades.

"Well, I'll see you when I get leave I suppose," Lily turned to Frank.

He stepped forward and despite a frown and clicking of the Matron's tongue, hugged his sister warmly. "You take care Sis."

Lily pulled away from his embrace her eyes bright with emotion. She hugged Evie next.

"I'll write to you," Evie whispered.

"I'd like that."

She parted from them and climbed onto the train.

"Go up to the front," Matron called, her attention back with her charge. Lily wandered along the corridor until she reached the first of four compartments in which sat seven other nurses, attired just as she and looking just as nervous. One seat remained and she opted for it not wishing to search further. One of the ladies was already leaning out of the window waving, others had their faces pressed to the glass, one cried quietly into her handkerchief. None of them looked as if they were prepared for the rigours of nursing wounded men. But looks could be deceiving.

A shrill whistle sounded and outside hundreds of boots clattered across the platform, shouts of good wishes, catcalls and laughter. The train rocked as the masses of troops hurried on board, extricating themselves from a last embrace. A band began playing some regimental march and the well wishers on the platform began waving to their husbands, lovers, sons and friends on the train. Lily rushed to the window and squeezed in beside two other nurses. She saw Frank and Evie and waved. They saw her and Frank's face lit with a bright smile. He shouted something, but his voice was carried away with the hubbub on the platform.

The train let out a long, moaning whistle and ever so slowly began to pull out of the station; drifts of steam streaming down along its side and obscuring the faces watching it go. With a jolt it picked up a little more speed and began to clatter along the track, swaying and singing rhythmically as it crossed the points and moved onto the main London to Dover line. The platform was gone, vanished in a wreath of steam and smoke and the nurses, with one or two sighs, resumed their seats, eyeing their companions with nervous curiosity as their adventure began.

PART TWO
1915

For All We Have and Are

For all we have and are,
For all our children's fate,
Stand up and take the war,
The Hun is at the gate!

Rudyard Kipling

CHAPTER 14.
January 10th, Sussex Downs

Joe threaded his way through the almost perfectly constructed trench. He hardly noticed the salutes and cheerful greetings from Kitchener's volunteers who, despite the best efforts of officers and NCOs borrowed from reserve battalions and brought out of retirement, still lacked the expected discipline. Not that Joe worried over such details. As far as the regimental sergeant major was concerned Lieutenant Hepworth was one of the distinctly unsoldierly enthusiasts whom he spent many hours lamenting over. Unlike the men, however, the RSM did not look too unfavourably upon the lieutenant because, well, he was a doctor. Allowances could be made for the medical officer, but certainly not for the rank and file. Climbing out of the trench as the fearsome RSM loomed over its parapet, Joe cringed at the bawled abuse fired at the luckless soldiers within. As the language turned particularly blue Hepworth hurried away, head down against the bitter east wind, hands shoved deep into his greatcoat pockets and cap rammed tightly over a snug fitting balaclava. One of Dora's better efforts. Struggling across the undulating field where countless mock battles from the last few weeks had left numerous obstacles, he dodged a 'shell hole', tripped over a stray length of barbed wire, cursed and strove on.

What have I done wrong now? Joe racked his brains trying to remember anything, but he was at a loss. He really had made a huge effort to act like an officer in the King's Army, albeit a temporary one. He tried to give orders rather than request the men to carry out tasks and though he would be the first to admit that he sometimes forgot, he *was* improving. It was just so damned difficult. Joe simply struggled with Army discipline and etiquette. He was not disobedient; such a notion was alien to his character. But his sense of decency and his belief in the equanimity of men put him at odds with his fellow officers and the intransigent sergeant major.

He sighed loudly. The colonel had sent for him and that only ever meant that the old soldier felt the need to reprimand his young medical officer once more.

Joe passed through a gate and into a muddy lane where, trying to avoid the worst of the potholes, he hurried towards Battalion headquarters, conveniently set up in the local village hall. Reaching the main road that ran through the Sussex village before it wound its way up to the top of the downs and into the vale beyond, Joe cursed again as it began to sleet. Great globs of icy slush stung his face and numbed his raw skin. He paused by the cottage where he was billeted and briefly contemplated whether he should change before seeing the colonel. He did, after all, have a greater resemblance to a mud caked farm labourer than the smart officer he had joined the Battalion as. But the message, so earnestly delivered by Private Bartlet, had explicitly said immediately. And Joe's understanding, borne of his own unfortunate experiences, was that immediately in the Army meant exactly that. It did not infer after one had cleaned up and made oneself respectable. He decided against partaking of any ablutions and headed directly to headquarters. Working on the premise that as he was already in trouble, turning up covered in mud could hardly make it worse. *Could it?*

He dived into the village hall glad to be out of the sleet and smiled apologetically at the small group of officers gathered around a central table. One of them smirked back; the others simply acknowledged his presence with a curt nod, a raised eyebrow or an amused twitch of a moustache, before returning their attention to the papers before them. Joe headed for a desk at the back of the room. It stood outside an inauspicious door, the entrance to what had previously been a spacious cloak room, but now passed as the commanding officer's abode. A smart and very young subaltern rose from his seat behind the desk and saluted. Joe returned the address and explained that he was expected. Uncomfortably he noticed the second lieutenant's eyes roving over his besmirched uniform with a mixture of mild amusement and horror. *I should have changed.*

"Wait one moment, Sir. I'll see if the colonel is ready for you," the young man said, hardly able to keep the grin from his face. With a knock he disappeared into the office.

"*Shit!*" Joe muttered under his breath. Hurriedly he pulled the balaclava from his head, smoothed his hair down and stuck his cap back on. He undid his greatcoat and shrugged it from his shoulders, unravelling a thick knitted scarf from his neck and ignoring the soft laughter from the middle of the room telling himself, unconvincingly, that it was not aimed at him.

The subaltern returned and with a wry smile said, "The colonel will see you now Sir." The smile turned to surprise when Joe, with a curt thank you, piled his sodden clothes into the young man's arms.

"Look after these won't you old chap," Joe uttered conspiratorially and knocked on the door. A faint, but firm "Enter" called from the other side and before the aide could object to being used as a coat hanger the doctor had disappeared into the office.

Joe stood before the colonel's desk and saluted self-consciously. As usual an image of his brother drifted unbidden into his brain along with the urge to laugh at this ridiculous necessity for deference. He still had great difficulty in envisaging the rebellious Sam in the same position.

"Hepworth, excellent. Good of you to come so promptly," the colonel boomed in his usual over-loud voice. His eyes wandered critically over the young doctor before him. He saw, but chose to ignore, the blathered boots that had left a trail of muck behind them, the muddy trousers and the smudge of dirt upon the medical officer's chin. "Please, sit down Hepworth. Sherry?" he continued affably. It was easy to be amiable when one was saying goodbye to a fellow.

"Er, no. Thank you, Sir," Joe replied taken aback by the friendliness of his commanding officer.

Colonel Jeffries was an old soldier, had served his whole life in the Army and had come out of retirement when, in his own eyes at least, Lord Kitchener called for him. It was more than a little disappointing to him that he had been given command; not of his old, Regular Battalion, but this hotchpotch mixture of volunteers. He could not criticise their enthusiasm, their eagerness to fight for King and Country, but he did bemoan their unsoldierly ways, their lack of military discipline. And he did object to temporary officers like Hepworth, even if they were only attached to his unit. In his eyes officers were certainly not temporary; they were soldiers while their country needed them, not until their year-long contract was up. Still, they were all improving slowly, and even the doctor showed promise, if he stuck it out.

Jeffries felt almost sad that he was losing Hepworth. The lad was likeable enough, came from a good Christian background; was polite and no doubt very knowledgeable in his field. Such a shame, because now the doctor was almost up to scratch he was being taken away and the colonel knew he would have another namby-pamby civilian in his place.

Jeffries sighed and poured himself a sherry before resuming his seat. He folded his hands on the desk covering a thin, brown envelope.

"It seems Hepworth, that I am to lose you," he said with an unhappy twitch of his substantial moustache.

"Sir?" Joe's heart sank. The old man was going to get rid of him. Probably transferring him to one of the many military hospitals that were mushrooming around the country. He was not going to France after all. Well, at least Dora would be happy. Joe did not even see the point in arguing his case. The colonel had never liked him, had threatened to get rid of him before. It was, he supposed with bitter disappointment, inevitable.

"Yes. I have to say I am quite sorry about it. You are, at last, showing promise as an officer. The men certainly look up to you. No, after a shaky start Hepworth, you're doing quite well."

Glowing praise indeed from a man who had lambasted Joe as a useless academic with the backbone of an earth worm only three weeks ago. The MO was not only astounded he was momentarily confused.

"The worst of it is Hepworth I'll get some spineless sap in your place. Now someone else is going to benefit from all my hard work eh?" Jeffries continued obviously put out. Joe did not speak. He dare not speak. He had an almost irrepressible urge to laugh out loud.

The colonel picked up the envelope and waived it at his subordinate. "These, my lad, are your orders. Unfortunately because you are only *attached* to my unit there is nothing I can do to keep you here. The RAMC have demanded you back. You're going to France. It would seem that MOs are dropping like flies over there. Sickness, frostbite, you name it. They need more trained men. Though I would disagree, you are the nearest they've got spare.

"So Hepworth you will be in France before us. Try to remember what you have learned. I'm sure you'll do alright." Jeffries stood and handed the envelope across to the doctor. Joe, rising also, took it and fingered it nervously.

"Does it say when, Sir?" he asked only half believing his luck.

"With immediate effect Hepworth. You are to travel to Dover tonight. The details are in the envelope." The colonel resumed his seat and started thumbing through forms. Joe, still flummoxed, had not realised he was dismissed. With some irritation Jeffries looked up at him.

"Hepworth."

"Sir?"

"You have some packing to do."

"Yes Sir. Of course." Joe flushed, saluted and turned to the door.

"Good luck young man," the colonel added genuinely as the doctor stepped from his office.

Joe half turned and with a happy grin he answered, "Thank you Sir."

CHAPTER 15.
January 17th, Boulogne

My dearest Sam,

    I hope this finds you in good health and hopefully it has not been so terribly delayed. I am writing this from my room in a small guest house that has been acquisitioned for ten of us nurses in Boulogne. It is the end of my first full week and I am thoroughly exhausted, but quite enjoying myself. <u>At last</u> I feel useful. There is so much to tell you I hardly know where to begin. I promise not to bore you too much.

    Mother was inconsolable of course when I left and Daddy gave me a long, stern lecture on being careful. Anyone would think I was going to be in the firing line! I left with Frank and spent New Year with him while I purchased my uniform etc. (They give one a chit in order to claim back expenses. I can tell you the whole lot came to quite a packet and I am quite low on funds now until the reimbursement comes through).

    Frank has a lady friend, the dark horse. She's a sweet thing, blonde and pretty. Not an ounce of practicality and very artistic in the same way Frank is. They are very much in love and I don't believe it will be too long before we hear wedding bells, although they say they are waiting for the end of the war. Frank is so transformed when he is with her. Not serious at all. Quite the life and soul of the party. It warmed my heart to see him so. The lady's name is Evelyn, although she prefers Evie. I think you would like her although she is terribly scatty.

    I left London on the fourth catching the train to Dover. The Station was heaving with troops and us few nurses were chaperoned by the most fearsome Matron one could ever imagine. She scowled at the poor boys for even daring to glance in our direction.

    We, the nurses, were travelling in First class. We had three compartments and the rest of the carriage was taken up by officers from various units. One terribly young subaltern made the unfortunate mistake of popping his head through the door of our compartment to speak to me and my travelling companions. I think he may have been put up to it by one of his brother officers. Anyway it backfired dreadfully, for just as he did so Matron entered the corridor and saw him. She practically hauled him out by his ear and gave him such a telling off. Poor thing. I've never seen anyone blush so. He hurried away with a flea in his ear, all apologetic and then we received a lecture on not fraternising with young men. Can you believe it? I thought the Infirmary rules were strict, but I now know that army nursing rules are draconian by comparison.

    At Dover we had hoped to embark that afternoon for Boulogne, but there was no room for us on any of the ferries. They were all commandeered for troops. Matron was quite put out and spent at least an hour with some army official trying to persuade him to squeeze us onto a ship. He would not however, and we then had to find lodgings in the town. It was no easy task for Dover is quite full of soldiers, sailors and the like. When we did eventually find somewhere, it was the Grand Hotel and quite out of our means to pay for rooms. Luckily the manager was very amenable. They allowed us to share four to a room, supplying extra cot beds, and agreed to accept a note in lieu of payment from Matron. She was quite confident that the War Office would pay the necessary dues.

    We were stuck in Dover for three days and would have liked to have explored the town a little, but we were not allowed. Myself and two girls near to my age, whom I have made quite good friends with, sneaked out on the second morning. We wanted to have our pictures taken and to have a look around. We did succeed and as you can see I have included a photograph of myself in my TFNS uniform. (I sent one to Frank and Joe also and of course to Mother and Daddy). As you can see it is wonderfully smart, although the photograph doesn't show the colour. We wear blue-grey as opposed to the <u>QAIMNS</u> reserve ladies whose dress is simply grey. I think ours is nicer. Can you imagine the pride I felt when I pinned on my TFNS badge and the little silver 'T's to the tippet? (Gosh, I do sound vain).

Lord, what a fuss when we returned! Matron was up in arms. She did go on so. One would think we were still living in the last century (I think perhaps she is). Such a lecture we received on the harm that could have befallen us, how our reputation and the reputation of the TFNS could be sullied by our escapade. Emma was almost in tears by the end of it. I kept my eyes rooted to the floor for I felt sure I was going to laugh. It was such a storm in a tea cup. Sadly after that we were never left alone and we spent the rest of the time confined to the hotel.

Finally, on the eighth we sailed for France. Such excitement! But it was a bitterly cold day and the wind, blowing down the Channel from the east, cut right to the bone. Any hopes of strolling around the deck were cut short though we suffered a reasonably comfortable journey in the First Class Salon amidst a few well-to-do French ladies and gentlemen and a number of army officers. Through the windows we watched hundreds of poor Tommies huddled against the cold. I thought of you and hoped that NCOs are afforded a little more luxury. The sea was quite rough, but I must say I am an excellent sailor. I know you are not, my dear, so I shall not boast too much about it.

Boulogne was teeming with people. I have never seen such crowds. Most of them were in uniform of one kind or another. I kept wondering if anyone I knew was there. Whether you could be. I do not know when exactly you are to return to your unit. Your last letter told of a training course.

We were ushered into a massive waiting room and after about an hour, Matron hurried over with another nurse, a Sister Beddows, whose job it is to greet new nurses and arrange accommodation for them. She seemed quite flustered, but was very efficient and thankfully we saw no more of our dragon-like chaperone. I believe she returned to England.

We were taken, by hired charabanc to the Hotel De Louvre. They had no information about any of us and we were questioned on our experience, where we had nursed, for how long and the like. Our uniform and kit were checked for deficiencies also and where any were found, arrangements made to bring everyone up to scratch. They allotted placements to us. I am staying in Boulogne at Number Thirteen General hospital. It is in the Casino, of all places, and is quite grand.

We had one night at the hotel and then we were all sent our separate ways. Unfortunately Emma was posted to Rouen although Gladys Forbes is with me and we were lucky enough to be sent to the same hospital and billeted in the same guest house. We share a room in fact. Gladys is thirty and comes from Birmingham. She has a wonderful sense of humour and we get on tremendously.

The next day we were formally presented to the colonel. Quite a pleasant chap, but very much the army sort. He smiled a lot, but seemed a little embarrassed at talking to a group of five nurses and I got the impression that he wished we were all soldiers instead. Then Matron gave us a lecture on how we were expected to behave and the dire consequences of not doing so. It went something along the lines of:

"Ladies, we expect great things of you. You will work long hours, see terrible sights, suffer many hardships, but I know, as professional nurses that you will rise to every challenge. And you will be challenged. It is hard for our young men away from their loved ones and as such they are want to form ready attachments, especially to young ladies from their own country, namely you. You must, therefore, remember that you are all on active service and as such you must not fraternise with members of the opposite sex. All relationships must be strictly professional. As nurses and sisters it is your responsibility to maintain discipline on the wards. Rules must be obeyed and strictly enforced for all patients.

"You will find that a small number of VADs have now joined us. These ladies are not trained nurses and should not be given the same responsibilities. It is down to you to ensure that they act in accordance with the rules. As many of these ladies tend to be somewhat younger than yourselves, you may find they have a rather overly romantic view of the patients and are apt to readily declare themselves in love with some wounded soldier. As such you must discourage any unprofessional behaviour. Members of your wards will remain detached but compassionate. We are here to nurse these young men back to health, so that they might continue to fight for our cause, or recover enough to be repatriated home. Idle chit chat is to be discouraged.

"It is worth stating that it is forbidden for any member of the nursing staff to accept a dinner or tea invitation, to go walking, driving, dancing or boating with any member of the opposite sex and that includes RAMC officers. On your day off you will wear your walking out uniform. Civilian clothing may only be worn when on leave. When off-duty you must return to your lodgings by eight pm or dusk whichever comes soonest.

"Uniform skirts must be no shorter than three inches off the ground" (At this she stared hard at both mine and Gladys' skirts, which I swear were regulation length)

"If you break any of these rules you will be dismissed and sent home to England. Please do not make the mistake of thinking that any of you are indispensable."

What a tartar! I was already frowned upon and I must say if she thinks I'm going to ignore all those poor boys in order to appear professional, she can whistle!

We started working on the tenth and haven't stopped for six days. I'm on a surgical ward, Amputees mainly, poor things. They're all so cheerful outwardly. Happy in the knowledge that they will be going home, but what future is in store for them God only knows. Some of them are so young, boys really. I make sure I keep a smile on my face and a kind word for them all. We are not allowed to call them by their Christian names. We either use their rank or their surnames.

I share the ward duties with Sister Slaytor. She's QAIMNS and quite strict, but no worse than my sister at the Infirmary. She is wonderful with the men and I think they look upon her as a motherly figure (she is in her fifties and nursed in the South African War). I have learned so much from her already and so far I don't think I have given her cause to be disappointed in me.

We have a number of male orderlies, who can be quite cheeky and have to be kept in check, but Sister knows how to handle them and I am learning. They're not bad really. They just tease a little.

I will not bore you any longer my dear. This letter is already turning into a novel and I have to be up at five tomorrow (it is nine o'clock now). I will only add that I received letters from Joe and Robert yesterday. They had been posted before New Year and only just caught up with me. Joe is hoping to be in France soon. He is struggling a little with army discipline and has had a run in with the colonel in charge of the unit he is attached to. Nothing serious, but he has been told he is too soft with the men. I had to laugh. You know what Joe is like.

Robert should be in France now. He was being posted to Rouen. I think he was rather disappointed not to be posted to a regiment or a field ambulance, but I am rather glad he is well away from danger. I only hope Joe is as lucky. And you dear, I wish you were safe too. Please try to be. I know that is probably a foolish thing to say to a soldier, but I do worry so for you especially after what you have already been through.

Well, dear brother, I will close now. I send you my warmest love and may God keep you safe until we see each other once more,

Your devoted Sister

Lily.

"Have you finished it at last?" a weary female voice uttered from the bed opposite.

"Yes. I'm sorry," Lily replied.

"Who is it to, your fiancé?" Gladys enquired, curious despite her desire to sleep.

"No, my twin brother, Sam. He's a sergeant in the Green Howards. You know, the one I told you was wounded."

"Ah yes. Well, may we have the light out now?"

Lily laughed as she sealed the already addressed envelope. It read, Sgt. Samuel Hepworth, 2nd Battalion, The Yorkshire Regiment, British Expeditionary Force. She hoped it would reach him. Leaning across to the oil lamp, she turned off the flame and without removing the woollen socks from her feet, huddled deep into her bed, shivering with cold.

CHAPTER 16.
February 8th, Advanced Dressing Station near Fleurbaix

A screaming whine, piercingly shrill and ominously close caused the men to stop their chatter and stare fixedly at the vaulted ceiling. A deafening detonation, the ground trembled and another cascade of dust and loose masonry fell onto the half dozen or so sick soldiers below. The ruined farmhouse cellar was becoming increasingly untenable as a dressing station in Joe's opinion. A direct hit would pulverise the stretcher section above and bury them all. He cringed instinctively with each concussion and wondered if he would ever get used to it. Whether he would ever stop being afraid. He watched the soldiers in his care and the men under his command with guarded interest. They were nervous as the shells drew closer, but they were not afraid. Not obviously anyway. They seemed to take a fatalistic view. If their number was up there was not much they could do about it. It was a kind of defence mechanism, a shared bravado that they joked about to hide their anxieties. It was something Joe did not yet possess and wished he did.

The reality of his experiences in France, like the Army, were far from what he had envisaged. His own reactions to being under artillery fire a disappointment to him. He had thought himself braver than this and he was not even in the front line, but a good mile back! It had sounded a long way back when the major had asked him to take a spell at Number Two Advanced Dressing Station. Well behind the lines. He had even had the audacity to laugh derisively when Newbould had gloomily wished him luck and held out a shaking hand. Newbould's expression had been one that said thank God it's not me. At the time Joe had thought his colleague cowardly and had barely hidden his contempt. Now he understood. Number Two sat next to the supply road. Excellent for evacuating casualties and sick men, but well targeted by the German artillery and shelled with monotonous regularity. Another shuddering detonation brought Joe's concentration away from his patient's chest he tried in vain to listen to.

Sickness. Most of the men arriving from the Front were sick not wounded, although every bombardment brought the odd casualty, even an occasional body. But at present the biggest enemy to the man in the trenches was disease and the weather. It never stopped raining and when it did not rain it snowed. The trenches were mires, the front line and the land between it and the dressing station, a swamp. In places men stood thigh deep in freezing mud. Joe had seen more cases of frostbite in just four days than he had in his entire career previously. Frostbite and now this odd phenomenon they were calling trench foot.

The men's feet just rotted and despite edicts from above, threats against commanding officers and down to lowly privates, nothing seemed to help. To the doctors it was obvious that until the water had gone and the weather warmer nothing much could be done. It was heresy to suggest the troops be removed from the trenches, though subjecting them to long spells at the Front was sure to increase their chances of sickness. All that could be done for trench foot was to prescribe and enforce the liberal application of whale oil, a ready change of socks and hope for the best.

The man under Joe's stethoscope coughed hackingly and winced from the pain of it. An obvious case of bronchitis that if not treated might turn into something worse, something like pneumonia.

"Bit close that one, Sir," the Irish orderly corporal assisting said understatedly.

Joe forced a smile. "You might say that Fallon. Bloody stupid place for a dressing station. Don't know why HQ hasn't moved it by now. We get shelled every day," he muttered and returned to listening to the sick man's laboured breathing.

"Nowhere else to put it Sir. Weren't so bad a week or two since. It'll quieten down again. Fritz likes to t'ink he's softening us up that's all," Fallon added feeling that he ought to offer some glimmer of hope. He liked Lieutenant Hepworth, had actually learned from him. The new doctor was generous with his knowledge, appreciated an inquisitive and interested mind. Not to mention he did not relish the idea of breaking in another inexperienced medic if this one crumbled like Newbould had done. Fallon thought Hepworth could take it. He was afraid, but he was in control and his sense of professional duty drove him to grin and bear it.

"Alright Corporal, this man needs bed rest and warmth. Let's transfer him up to the Main Dressing Station. Get a couple of stretcher bearers lined up. He can walk, but I'd rather he ride," Joe instructed with a sigh.

"Might have to keep him here a while Sir. Fellas won't want to go up the road with this goin' on," Fallon murmured quietly.

"Hmm. Let's get them warned in any case and a hot drink down him. You'd like that Private? Tea or cocoa?" Joe turned his attention to the sick man.

"Cup of char would be grand Sir," the soldier wheezed with an appreciative smile.

This is what Fallon liked about the new medical officer. He was not Army. Did not really care for the expected hierarchy and subservience deemed necessary by Regular officers. Hepworth welcomed suggestions as long as they were discreetly made and the corporal was very tactful.

"Who's next?" Joe asked straightening his back and looking around in the candlelit gloom. *God, what a dreadful hole this is.* Perhaps it made some sense to place a dressing station in a cellar, to surround it with sandbags for added protection, but it made for a lousy working environment and after the pristine sanitary conditions of a modern general hospital, it felt like a step back into the dark ages.

"Fella over there wit' bad feet, Sir. He's the last from this mornin's sick parades," Fallon replied.

Joe groaned inwardly at the prospect of another pair of swollen and sloughing feet and climbed carefully around the other men. The corporal instructed another orderly to inform the stretcher section there was man to take down the line and saw to it that hot drinks were prepared and distributed. Often that was all that they needed. A hot beverage and a good few hours sleep then they were back on their feet again and with their Battalion. For the most part they were tough men. This was a Regular Division, they were used to hardship.

Joe finished examining the last man, ensured that his feet were dressed suitably and fresh, clean socks donned. He stood from his work, stretched and surveyed the scene. His domain consisted of a large subterranean room. Along one wall racks held space for stretchers to be stacked along with their inhabitants three deep. He could collect and hold up to twenty men here. In the middle of the room four trestles allowed stretcher cases to be placed for immediate treatment and along the other wall a long bench could hold up to thirty sitting or walking wounded. Six men this morning, the ones that did not pass muster at their respective sick parades.

Quiet. Three of them he could send back in an hour or two. He would give them the luxury of rest for a while though. The others were in need of more than warmth and rest.

"Cup of tea, Sir?" an orderly asked holding out a tin mug.

Joe smiled and took the beverage gratefully. "Thanks Thomas," he said genuinely and moved to the end of the cellar where he had his bunk and a desk, or rather an old kitchen table rescued from the derelict building above. It was optimistically referred to as the MO's office. Here he slept, often like the dead.

He slumped into a rickety chair, sipped the tea and grimaced at its strong taste of chlorine and petrol. He pulled a pile of forms towards him. The Army loved forms. They had one for everything. Turning up the paraffin lamp he sighed and began to fill in the details of each man being sent down the line.

A shuddering explosion rocked the makeshift hospital. The low conversation between its inmates and carers abated temporarily. Everyone paused, waiting for what might come next and then continued as they were before. Joe brushed the pall of dust from his papers, his heart rate slowing to something approaching normal. Soft laughter amongst the men and their attendant orderlies signalled all was well. Joe continued to write moving from the forms to his notes, trying to ignore the intermittent pounding of guns and muffled detonation of shells. After an hour they stopped.

He sat back listening and gazing upwards as if by staring hard enough he could see through the vaulted roof, through the mountain of sandbags, the stretcher bearers' dug-out and the transport section and across the desolate landscape beyond towards the Front. He looked down the dressing station and caught Fallon's eye.

"Do you think they'll attack?" he asked lowly as the corporal approached his 'office'.

Fallon shook his head. "No. That was only so we don't forget they're there. It'd be much worse if they were up to somet'in'," he replied in his gentle Irish lilt.

Joe nodded wondering if he could stand something worse. He supposed he would have to.

"How long have you been out Donal?" he enquired feeling the need to fill the quiet with conversation. He found Fallon easy to talk to. Was comfortable with the man's easy going nature, his natural tact and obvious compassion for the injured and sick men that came their way. Joe preferred the corporal's company in many ways to most of his fellow officers. Preferred it to Captain Foster in charge of the stretcher and transport section above. Foster was too much a dyed in the wool Regular Army surgeon, well versed in the mantra of his creed and a little condescending to a mere temporary officer like Joe. Not to mention that Lieutenant Hepworth was a physician and not a surgeon. That, in the eyes of Foster, made him good for dealing with the sick, administering basic first aid and dressings and that was about all. In the captain's opinion a good orderly could do all that for a fraction of the pay.

"Since last October, Sir. I came out wit' the Seventh Division and I've been wit' them ever since," Fallon answered and pulled up a stool opposite. He recognised the lieutenant wanted to chat and though it would be frowned upon by their respective superiors he did not really care. Hepworth did not treat him with the same patronising contempt the majority of British officers and his fellow NCOs did. He saw beyond background and nationality and held none of the prejudices of his class. In Fallon's eyes, Hepworth was a true humanitarian, altruistic and compassionate.

Within the dictates of Army regulations the lieutenant treated everyone the same.

"You're not a Regular though are you?" Joe carried on glad that Fallon had joined him.

"No sir. I volunteered and because of the number of losses t'rough August and September I was posted to the Ambulance and sailed wit' the rest of the Division at the beginning of October."

"What made you volunteer? I mean you're an Irishman. You're heart can't really have been with the English."

Fallon paused, his grey-blue eyes searching the inquisitive face before him. He detected no provocation in the question, merely curiosity. "It seemed the right t'ing to do at the time, Sir. Some of me friends joined infantry regiments, but I'm not one for fighting. I joined the RAMC. T'ought I could help. What about you Sir? You must have had a good position at home."

Joe laughed and stared into the empty mug on the table. He leant forward and twisted it around absently. "Like you. It seemed a good idea at the time. I thought the Army would need doctors. I was right, but it's not what I expected," he admitted.

"What did you expect, Sir?"

"Uh, I don't know. I think I rather naïvely thought it would be more heroic if that makes sense. I thought I'd be treating wounded men, saving lives. I never thought my days and nights would be spent treating the same illnesses I saw in the hospital back home."

"There'll be plenty of wounded soon enough, Sir. Next push we or old Fritz over there makes and we'll be wishing we only had sick fellas to deal wit'," Fallon observed.

"Perhaps. Are you married Donal?" A sudden change of subject.

"Was Sir. Me wife died last year. Tuberculosis."

"Oh Christ! I'm sorry. What a clumsy arse. I feel dreadful now," Joe apologised sincerely.

"Tis alright Sir. I'm over it now. Still miss her though. She were a shining star my Mary. Dark, dark hair and blazing blue eyes. Like forget-me-nots they were. I was the envy of Balbriggan when we married. For seven years I was the luckiest man in Ireland. Our only regret was we had no kiddies. Just as well in the end I suppose," Fallon spoke with animated feeling that dwindled to quiet reflection. It was the most Joe had gleaned from the corporal who was generally a laconic individual preferring to listen to another than talk himself.

"What about you Sir? Are you married?"

Joe shifted uncomfortably. After what he had just heard it did not seem fair to wax lyrical about his own recent matrimony. "Yes, her name is Dorothy, Dora," he answered simply and hoped that Fallon would enquire no further.

"Children?" the corporal pressed, his honest, smiling face filling his companion with uneasy guilt.

"One on the way. Our first," Joe returned desperately trying to think of a way to turn the conversation. *God, this must be painful to hear.*

"You must be t'rilled Sir. Nothing like family. Is she pretty, your wife? I'm t'inking she must be."

It just got worse. Joe groaned inwardly. "As a picture. Look Donal. Christ! I'm really sorry man. I didn't mean to pry and... Well, you don't want to hear about my life when you've..." He faltered at a loss.

"Don't worry about it Sir. Life goes on as they say. I'd be a miserable bugger if I didn't accept that. Me Da were a miserable sod. I don't want to end up like him. My Mary's wit' God now. That's the best place for angels," Fallon grinned broadly.

"Do you truly believe that?" It was a subject Joe struggled with, God. His upbringing had been Christian, his mother a devout woman, but a lot that the Bible preached, that he had been taught, did not fit with the science he practiced. Yet unlike Robert, he was not a self proclaimed atheist. He still sought answers.

"I have to, Sir. Besides," Fallon chuckled, "If it isn't true we're wasting our time out here."

Joe smiled in response, posed another question but was distracted by movement near the stairs. He grimaced. "Look out, CSM Cross, due south." He stood and pushed the forms towards the corporal. Fallon took the hint and jumping to his feet also, picked up the papers.

"I'll take these to the stretcher section then Sir," he said with a wink and scurried away before the sergeant major could detain him.

"Sergeant Major, what can I do for you?" Joe asked with all the military bearing he could muster. He felt it had failed as Cross gazed down his lengthy nose and cast a slow critical eye around the cellar.

"A number of casualties coming in Sir. You'll need to get rid of this lot." Cross jerked his head towards the sick men. "I'll send some men down to move 'em out right away."

"Do you think that's wise Sergeant Major? I mean, what if Fritz starts shelling us again? Maybe we should just move them into the transport shelter," Joe challenged without much conviction.

Cross fixed his superior with a supremely condescending stare before answering. In an instant Joe understood what Sam had meant when he had referred to all sergeant majors as God or His right-hand-man.

"We need the room Sir. We'll take a chance," Cross said eventually with obvious sarcasm. "There's about ten wounded coming down the line. Shell burst right over the top of 'em, poor buggers. Let's see if we can't save 'em eh, Sir? You're going to be busy," Cross smirked and marched away leaving the medical officer feeling foolish as usual.

Within the next five minutes the room was emptied of the sick. The experienced orderlies bustled around without need of instruction, preparing trestles and racks for stretchers, piling dressings onto a bench, fetching water by the gallon can. Fallon returned and mucked in as his superior donned a surgical smock and pulled a bag of instruments from a shelf. Hepworth sighed a little nervously. This would be his first big test. Before this he had only treated an occasional wounded man and nothing serious. His job was to assess the casualties, ensure those most in danger were hurried to the main dressing station with minimal delay, check dressings and make whatever temporary adjustments he could, to administer painkilling morphine where necessary and get them all away as quickly as possible. If no more came down the line, there would be time to ensure the casualties were warmed to reduce the threat of shock.

As the first stretcher was precariously man-handled down the steep stairs a nasal voice called loudly from behind and for the first time Joe felt pleased to hear Captain Foster.

"Thought you might like a hand old chap," the captain announced with as much jollity as he could manage through his streaming head cold.

"Thank you Sir. That would be most welcome," Hepworth responded genuinely while indicating where the injured should be laid down. Foster rummaged through the shelves along the back wall and returned to the nearest stretcher fastening a handkerchief around his face.

"Don't want to drip all over the poor blighters," he explained happily, pulling on a smock over his uniform.

The two medics, any differences forgotten, rapidly worked around the injured soldiers assessing as far as they could at first glance, who required the most urgent treatment; who could wait. The orderlies brought in blankets, cut away filthy, mud-caked clothing and washed down bloody, grime covered bodies to reveal the true extent of the damage. One of the wounded moaned and cried alternatively, his fuss disturbing the others whose pained expressions and vacant eyes gave way to either an anxious look or an angry gaze in the unfortunate man's direction. Joe grabbed the arm of a passing orderly and instructed him to give the fretful man morphine. The private nodded his understanding and hurried away to the drugs shelf. There were others worse off who needed attention before the soldier making all the din. Hepworth squeezed through the space between two stretchers up to a man with a gory dressing around his head, a pallor as grey as death and fixed staring eyes.

"Leave that one old chap. I've seen him. He's beyond our help I'm afraid," Foster called from where he was busily re-dressing an abdominal wound. "*Damn it!* Someone get some more light down here. I can't see a bloody thing!"

Joe hesitated by the dying man. He looked so young, not much more than a boy really. It was true he was too far gone. His pupils were fixed and dilated, sightless and glassy. His breathing shallow and ragged. It would not be long now. Even so it was hard doing nothing. It felt wrong. Against everything a doctor stood for. Resignedly Joe moved along the rows of stretchers to work upon those who could be saved.

Three men were rapidly checked, their dressings adjusted and sent immediately onwards. They needed more care than could be delivered in this dingy cellar. Their bodies ripped and torn by shrapnel, a lower leg hanging by the merest sinew, a corporal with half his lower face missing and only a garish hole to show where a mouth had once been, the abdominal wound with its guts held in place by Foster's dressing. These men needed surgery urgently. Their removal provided a little more space both in which to work and to breathe.

The remaining casualties were less serious. Bad enough to get them a trip home or a long spell at a base hospital, but there was time to clean them up first. A mixture of deep muscle and flesh wounds, a couple of head wounds, quite deep, one missing an ear, a shattered shoulder. All the cases were serious enough that without proper treatment they might die from complications. The biggest killer was gas gangrene. All too quickly the open wounds began to fester and suppurate. Within a day in some cases. The soil in northern France was well manured and rife with bacteria that bred and multiplied within the slashed and broken bodies of men left for too long in squalor.

Care was needed to ensure the wounds were cleaned thoroughly, dressed so that air could reach the lacerated tissues yet prevent further dirt entering. It was a challenge that faced the medical corps on a daily basis. Working in cramped, far from sterile environments, often with little light and no running water, it was difficult to ensure that injuries were as well tended as required to prevent infection. A challenge also for the wounded who suffered, for the most part, with brave fortitude, grimacing or swearing quietly. Filthy dressings were cut away and cold water or salt solution washed through and around their damaged bodies.

"D' ye think they'll send me hame, Sir?" a private asked in a soft Scottish brogue as Joe tied off the bandage around his head.

"I'm sure of it Private," the medical officer replied with a smile. That's all they wanted when they were so badly hurt. To go home. This lad would be back though. "For a while at least. Private Stubbs here will get you a drink. Tea or cocoa, just let him know."

"I'd prefer a dram Sir," the young soldier grinned.

"I'm sure you would, but tea or cocoa is all you'll get here I'm afraid," Joe laughed and moved aside to let Stubbs take over. He stretched and looked around. They were done. He caught Foster's eye and they shared a satisfied grin. A grin that fell from both their faces as the moribund patient finally issued his last shuddering breath. The silence that followed it, though brief, was unnerving. That sound had filled the cellar for the last three hours. It had pervaded everywhere. Could be heard above the occasional groan of pain during a dressing, over the low hum of conversation. Now it was gone and momentarily it left a void, until the quiet chatter of the injured and their attendant orderlies commenced again. The death accepted with relief. Joe clamped his jaw, a hard knot of guilt filling his stomach. He went over to the body and gently closed the wide staring eyes.

"Don't beat yourself up over him Hepworth. The poor blighter is better off dead. Doubt if he knew anything about it. You couldn't have helped him, you know that?" Foster murmured with uncharacteristic sympathy.

"I just feel we should have tried, Sir," Joe returned not lifting his gaze from the dead man.

"Waste of time. We have to attend to those we can do something for. If we'd worked on this one, he still would have died and maybe some of those other buggers we shipped off earlier also. We can't work miracles, especially out here. We were lucky today. There were only a few. During a battle we would be overwhelmed and we might lose hundreds. Today was one hard decision, during a push one has to make them every minute. Welcome to the war Hepworth!" Foster laughed sardonically and clapped a comradely hand on his subordinate's shoulder. Joe looked shaken.

"Come on Hepworth. You did well today. Damned well for a civvy street physician."

Praise indeed! Despite his sudden despondency Joe sniggered. "Thank you Sir. I think."

"Get this lot something warm down them. I'll sort out transport. I'll leave the paper work to you," Foster instructed with a wry smile and bustled away. There were only six men left and already a pair of stretcher bearers were heading down the steps to collect the first and take him to the main dressing station well behind the line.

Joe caught Fallon watching him from where he was helping the odd one out, a victim of a gunshot wound brought in with the rest, pull on his coat.

"Hot drinks for them all Corporal," the medical officer called.

Fallon acknowledged the order and scurried off to chivvy along the tea makers. Joe half turned away, the pile of paperwork beckoning, when something about the soldier Fallon had been assisting caught his eye. He paused and looked again. It was the cap badge. Though hard to see in the dim light of paraffin lamps and candles, and though blackened and tarnished so as not to glint in the sun, it looked familiar. Not being a military man, apart from the Medical Corps badge, he recognised very few others. It was different from the Scotsmen he had treated. Foster must have done this one. Joe stared at the cap badge.

"Is owt wrong Sir?" the owner of the badge asked, his filthy face a picture of anxious concern. Had the doctor noticed something wrong? Was he worse than he thought?

Joe shook his head and stepped closer. "No, I'm sorry. It's just your badge," he pointed to the man's cap. "Which Regiment are you with?" It was a stupid question. He already knew the answer. The soldier grinned proudly and sat up straight.

"Second Battalion, Yorkshire Regiment, Sir. T' Green 'Owards," he announced loudly.

Joe nodded distractedly. *Yes, of course.* Quite why it had not dawned on him before he did not know. *How stupid am I?* "The Seventh Division," he muttered to himself with realisation. Sam's Division, Sam's Regiment. Why had he not thought about it when he first arrived?

"That's right Sir," the private confirmed thinking the officer a little weird. Surely he knew the units in his own Division.

"Do you know a man called Hepworth? A sergeant." Joe enquired.

"Do I? Course I do. Plays centre 'alf for us. Scored twice t'other day when we thrashed t' RFA seven to nowt. Bloody good goal second one wa' an' all. Good footie player is Eppy. Sorry Sir, I mean, Sergeant 'Epworth. 'Ad to come off in t' second 'alf though. Don't think 'e's right fit yet. 'E wa' wounded summat bad at Wipers. To tell t' truth, a lot on us thought 'e wouldn't come back. Were a surprise when 'e did," the soldier rambled happily. Joe smiled that his brother was popular and at the image painted.

"D' y' know 'im Sir?" the man asked.

"Yes."

"Good bloke is Eppy. Won't stand fo' no shenanigans though. But 'e's alright. Used to be in my platoon. When 'e were a corporal like. Befower t' war tha wa'. Wi' Three Platoon now. Since 'e got back. Still D Company though," the private went on. He was obviously of a garrulous nature.

"He's at the Front then?"

"Aye, we went up yesterday, Sir."

"Where abouts?"

"Battalion HQ's at Dead Dog Farm, Sir."

"Dead Dog Farm?" Joe queried his right eyebrow raised and a half smile on his lips.

"Aye. Named after a dead dog like," the man stated obviously with a grin. "Don't know what its proper name wa'. Be summat y' can't pronounce."

Joe smiled.

Fallon returned and handed the soldier a cup of strong, hot tea.

"Ta Corp," the private said gratefully.

"How do I get to this place?" Joe pressed. Fallon watched him quizzically.

"Y' don't want to go up there, Sir. Bloody God forsaken 'ole. Battalion'll be out again in a few days. We on'y spend about four days in t' line. I'd wait 'til then if I wa' you, Sir."

"But you're not me are you Private? Please, tell me how to get there," Joe insisted.

The man stared at him as if he was quite mad and then with a shrug explained how to reach Dead Dog Farm. *Bloody bonkers! Another idiot wanting to visit the trenches. Just like those bloody staff officers. Didn't know when they were onto a cushy number.* "Y' want to stay in t'com trench for as long as y'can. It's full of stinking water though further up. But in day light all that field is covered by snipers," he added feeling he ought to warn the doctor of the dangers. He seemed a little too green to work it out for himself.

"Thank you," Joe said and moved away to his desk. Fallon followed.

"You're not seriously considering going up the line Sir?" the corporal asked in a hushed voice.

"Any o' these men to go first Sir?" a stretcher bearer called from the other end of the cellar.

"No Smith. Take whoever's finished their tea," Joe replied and then dropping his voice, "Yes I'm going."

"It's not a good idea Sir. You'll get into trouble for leavin' your post," Fallon impressed. The lieutenant stared at him with a half amused, half angry expression.

"Then I'll go when I'm off duty."

"You're never off duty while at the ADS Sir. You know that."

Joe sat down heavily and ran a hand through his hair. Hair that had not been washed for five days and consequently stuck out at all angles. "Then I'll go at night when it's quiet. The private said it wasn't safe during the day. What's it to you anyway Donal? It'd be me in bother not you."

"Just wouldn't want to see you get into trouble Sir. Besides, it's bloody awful in the trenches and they won't t'ank you for dropping in to say hello."

Hepworth leaned back on his rickety chair, it creaked under his weight. He thought the corporal oddly interested in his well being and though he did not need to explain his reasons his sense of decency demanded he should.

"Donal, I thank you for your concern, but this is something I really need to do. You see, my brother is up there. For the life of me I don't know why I didn't twig earlier that we were in the same Division. Stupid of me I know. So, I want to go and see him. We haven't seen each other for over two years."

Fallon considered this explanation but did not give up so easily. "Well then, why not wait until he's back in reserve. What difference does a few more days make if you haven't seen him in so long. Sir," he continued to argue realising he was perilously close to insubordination. With any other officer he would not have gone so far. Then again, with any other officer he would not have been bothered.

"Christ! Frankly Corporal, this is none of your damned business. Now, I've had enough, just get on with your work and leave me to do mine," Joe snapped with a flash of uncharacteristic temper. He was not a man to rant and rave. His annoyance showed as little more than irritated grumpiness. Unlike his brother he possessed none of the fire that could get him into the deep water. But he was annoyed now. He could not understand the corporal's interference. He picked up a pen and began filling in forms with obvious bad humour.

"I'll be coming wit' you then Sir," Fallon said quietly.

Hepworth stopped writing and stared. "Like hell you will! This is personal. It's got nothing to do with you. I don't need a chaperone."

"No Sir, but you'll be needing a guide. Easy to get lost at night. No lights, lots of men passing up and down. There's a fair maze of communication trenches and they all lead somewhere different. Get lost and you'd look a right arse, Sir," Donal countered with more than a little disrespect. He gambled well. With any other officer he would be on a charge for speaking out of turn like that. The lieutenant gazed with disbelief and then laughed shaking his head.

"Very well Donal. If we lose our guests and receive no more by seven we'll have ourselves a little expedition to this Dead Dog Farm. In the mean time *you* have work to do!" Joe returned to filling in forms and with a canny grin Fallon drifted to his own duties.

With great disappointment Joe stepped from the ruined remnants of the farm house that acted as Battalion Headquarters of the Yorkshire Regiment and into a cold and misty February night. He saw Corporal Fallon leaning against a crumbling brick wall sharing a smoke with a sentry and with a toss of his head he indicated they should leave. Shoving his hands deep into his greatcoat pockets he contemplated his brief conversation with the Battalion commanding officer. A man who had made it quite plain that he would not tolerate sightseers and whom, in front of several of his officers, had also been at pains to point out that he did not think much of junior, temporary medical officers wasting his time.

Embarrassed at the recollection and extremely frustrated Lieutenant Hepworth exhaled deeply into the frigid air and watched his breath stream away like smoke on the barely perceptible breeze.

"No luck Sir?" Fallon asked guessing correctly the outcome of the venture.

Joe sighed. "No, you were right. It was a waste of time. Or rather, *I* am a waste of the CO's time. He made it quite clear that a battalion in the line could not afford the luxury of allowing visitors to speak to its members. That senior NCOs in particular were far too busy to be given up to the whims of anyone less than a general. He also stressed that officers do not socialise with NCOs regardless of whether they are brothers or not."

"Got a bit of a roasting then Sir?"

"Huh, you could say that. I haven't felt so stupid since... Well actually I find myself feeling stupid quite a lot lately. Come on let's get back, it's freezing out here." Joe began to trudge away, the corporal hurrying to catch up with him.

"Doctor Hepworth!" a voice from behind called. The two men stopped and turned peering into the gloom. Though no lights burned it was possible to see, just. Frequent Very lights punctuated the night sky, often too distant to cast the scene into stark relief, but close enough to lift the blackness into tenebrous shades of charcoal grey. A figure hurried towards them, tall and slender. Slightly out of breath from stumbling through the boggy field, a tired looking officer with a thin moustache and a none too flattering sheepskin jerkin tied over his coat halted in front of his counterpart and offered his hand.

"Joe isn't it? Joe Hepworth. I'm sorry, you probably don't remember me. Fielding. Harry Fielding. We played in the school orchestra together. I was a senior when you started," the officer explained.

Joe shook the outstretched hand and studied the man before him. He could not place the face although the name was familiar. "You're Sam's platoon commander," he said remembering that much at least.

"Yes. No. Well, I was. I wish I still was. When Sam returned his position had already been filled. He went to Three Platoon to replace Sergeant Beale who is now the CSM," Fielding gabbled in his usual eccentric way.

"Oh," Joe answered simply, wondering why every man he met from this Battalion felt the urge to explain everything. "I'm sorry Lieutenant, but can I help you? We were just about to return you see." He ignored Fallon's barely hidden snort of amusement.

"No, no. Forgive me I should explain," Fielding breathed and looked around furtively. Both Joe and Donal followed his stare, both feeling surreally comical. "No, look. I was in HQ and overheard your, er, discussion with Colonel Andrews. I can help. It's a little unorthodox, but I think I owe Sam more than the odd favour. His platoon is next to mine in the firing trench. He'll be busy, but I think I can persuade his commander to spare him for a few minutes. I know a good place you can meet; it's an old dug-out in one of the support trenches. If you still want to that is. Otherwise it's a safe bet that we'll be in billets at Fleurbaix in a couple of day's time."

Joe glanced at Fallon who shrugged signalling he did not mind either way. They were here now were they not?

"I would very much like to see my brother. Thank you Lieutenant Fielding. I don't want to get you into trouble though," the doctor admitted.

"Harry, please call me Harry. It's no trouble at all. Let's just hope we're not caught eh? These Regular Army types are sticklers for rules. You've probably realised. It's much less rigid now than it was in the beginning, but it's still real pain in the backside. All these regulations over who can socialise with whom and the like. Sam gave me quite an insight into it when we first met.

"This way. Stay close there's quite a few holes big enough to lose a cow in. In fact there are several lost cows in them!" Fielding explained with morbid glee.

Fallon sniggered and Joe dug him in the ribs with a barely hidden grin. They fell in behind their guide, skirting obstacles and unseen shell holes filled with fetid, chest deep water. They dropped into the communication trench and waded through thick, cloying mud, standing aside to allow blathered working parties carrying ammunition, sandbags or wire to pass. The soldiers acknowledged the two officers apologetically and grumbled onwards. The three men fought their way forwards, their feet pulling heavily in the soft muck and aching as the icy water seeped into their boots.

"Bloody hell! Is it always this bad?" Joe muttered as his left leg submerged up to his knee in perishing sludge.

"It gets better when it freezes. But every thaw brings more rain and more mud. Grim isn't it?" Fielding replied and dodged a couple of engineers struggling to carry a pump up the line.

"It's no wonder they get frostbite and their feet rot," Joe mumbled to himself. He found it appalling that men were working in these conditions let alone living in them. Harry cast him an askance glance but did not comment.

After fifteen minutes staggering through the glutinous mire they stopped. Fielding pointed to a low opening in the trench wall. "Wait in there. Like I said it used to be an officers dug-out but we abandoned it after the last thaw. There's only about a foot of water in it now. No good for sleeping in but it'll serve well enough. I'll fetch Sam. I need to feed his platoon commander some cock and bull story. Don't worry it won't be hard, the lad's as green as grass. Sam runs rings around him and he can't see it," Fielding smiled though his expression was lost in the dark. "Give me about ten minutes. Here's a candle. Don't light it until you're in there." He handed over the stub of wax and trudged away into the night.

Joe and Fallon hesitated briefly before stooping beneath a wooden lintel and into a black stinking void. Hepworth choked on the stale, reeking air and the corporal lit the candle.

"Nice place Sir," the Irishman said with grim humour.

Gazing around the MO agreed. The dug-out was no more than six foot square. A ledge ran along two walls and held evidence, in the form of a couple of mouldy blankets, of fairly recent occupation. A stray tin mug floated haplessly in the murky water at their feet. The air smelt noxious, a mixture of stagnant swamp tainted with urine. "Buckingham Palace has nothing on this place," he replied with a laugh.

"I'll wait outside for you Sir," Fallon offered thinking privacy was a good excuse to get out of this hole.

"There's no need Donal. My brother won't mind you being here," Joe replied.

"All the same, I'm sure you'd both like a chat in private. Like you said, it's been a while and, well, you won't want some stranger lurking in the background, listening while you catch up. Besides, I'd rather be out there than in this sump anyway," Fallon admitted with a wide grin.

Joe nodded in reply. He could not argue. The dug-out was disgusting. "Hang on until they get here though hey?"

Several minutes later the squelching and slithering of boots heralded the arrival of men. The entrance grew darker as two silhouetted forms stood in front of it. Joe heard a man swear in disgust. Sam's voice.

"Bloody hell Sir, you could have cleaned up a bit first. It's a right glory hole this," Sam joked and with a grimace dropped into the stinking water. "Hiya Joe," he smiled but it fell warily from his face when he noticed the corporal.

"Would your man like a cup of tea? Some of the men have just brewed up. I'm sure they won't mind," Fielding called inside.

"Would I?" Fallon replied "Excuse me Sir, Sergeant," he pushed by and waded back to the entrance. The brothers watched him leave.

"I'd not be more than fifteen minutes if I were you Eppy," Fielding added.

"Understood Sir," Sam acknowledged.

Left alone the brothers shook hands warmly, their faces all smiles.

"It's good to see you Sam," Joe said happily as he apprised his sibling in the dim glow of the candle. He thought his brother looked tired and thin.

Sam grinned broadly, his mud splattered face resembling a ploughman more than a soldier. Beneath his cap his hair stuck to his scalp and the horrible goatskin jerkin he wore was filthy and stank of wet musky animal, discernible even above the other mephitic odours within the dug-out.

"Never thought to see *you* here though. How long have you been out?" Eppy asked still clenching the hand offered in greeting. He let it go aware that they had been holding onto each other for a little too long.

"A few weeks. I'd have tried to see you earlier, but stupidly it never dawned on me that we were in the same Division. How are you?"

"I'm filthy, I stink, I'm covered in lice. I ache all over after our fucking football match against the RFA and my shoulder gives me jip in this cold, but I can't grumble. Life's a ball!" Sam replied sarcastically and they both laughed. "Tell me what you're doing. You're not with a battalion are you?"

"No. ADS. But you don't want to hear any of that. It's fairly mundane stuff. Just patching up a few bullet wounds and mainly looking after men with common ailments one sees at home. I'd rather hear about you. Tell me about your life. What's it like in the trenches?"

"You can see for yourself Joe. It's like this," Sam replied evasively.

"No you clot! I mean really. What's it like," Joe persisted.

"You don't want to know."

"Yes I do. I mean, we get a few shells drop near at the ADS. Scares the living daylights out of me, but it can't be half as bad as it is down here. You had it rough at Ypres from what I heard. Tell me all about it. I feel very ignorant. I should know. Should understand."

"Believe me ignorance is bliss."

Joe recognised the tone of voice, the stubborn trait that said he would gain nothing by pushing the conversation. He also realised his brother did not want to awaken what might be painful memories. He dropped the subject and for a moment they stood in silence.

"Sit on the ledge. It'll save our feet from freezing and your coat won't get sodden," Sam indicated to the shelves that had once acted as bunks.

They waded to the wall, stuck the candle in the middle of the ledge and jumped up either side of it. For a few seconds they sat with legs dangling like small boys, gazing with wide eyes at their surroundings. The tramp and squelch of feet outside reminded them that this was no cave and no childhood adventure, but for a spell it had almost felt like that. Joe chuckled.

"I was thinking of the mine shaft. Do you remember? You scared the hell out of Frank. He ran out screaming for his life and I never laughed so hard," he reminisced.

"Yeah I remember," Sam laughed. "Poor Frank. He told Mother though and I got a bloody good hiding from Dad."

"You deserved it."

"Uh! Probably. I usually did. I hear he's got a lady friend."

"Frank? Has he now? The dark horse! Since when?" Joe leant back against the wall, intrigued.

"Dunno. Lily met her when she stopped off in London. Another musician. Very pretty from what Lil says."

"Serious?"

"Lily seemed to think so," Sam revealed.

"Well I never. Better hurry Sam. You'll be the only one left on the shelf." Joe teased. His brother sniggered.

"How's Dora? She looked grand when I saw her before Christmas. Baby must be due soon?"

"April. She's fine. Not too happy about me being out here though. I told her it's only for a year," Joe answered as though he was trying to convince himself of this.

"Isn't it?"

"I don't know. Maybe. I can't say it's been an enjoyable experience so far. Bloody rules and paperwork drive me mad. But it seems wrong somehow. Only staying in for a year when everyone else is in it for the duration."

Sam studied his brother's face. It was hard to assess his emotions in the flickering half light of a single flame. Then it would have been hard anyway. Joe always kept his feelings close. The sergeant smiled at the image of his fair minded and somewhat socialist sibling struggling with the rigid discipline of the Army with its myriad of petty rules, half of which seemed, to the lay person, to serve no purpose. He took out a pack of cigarettes from his pocket, selected one and lit it from the candle.

"The duration might only be a year," he said squinting through acrid smoke as he exhaled. He offered the pack to Joe.

"Do you think so? No thanks. I still don't," the doctor waved the cigarettes away.

Sam shrugged drawing on his smoke. He leant his head back, appreciated the nicotine and considered his reply. "I don't know to be honest," he said at length. "Must be nice though," his mind drifted away from war.

"What must?"

"Being married, becoming a father."

"Bloody hell Sam! How did you get back round to that one? Yes. Yes it is," Joe smiled proudly. It was nice. More than. It was the best thing that had happened to him and he had left it behind to come here. "You should try it," he suggested not wishing to dwell upon home.

Sam chuckled to himself, "Wouldn't suit the life."

"Other soldiers marry."

"Aye well, it's different for officers and a sergeant major. Their wives travel with them. But it wouldn't be fair really would it? I mean, I'm out of the country half the time. Some of the blokes are married and they hardly ever see their wives. And I'm not one for cheating either."

"Cheating?"

"Yeah you know. It gets awfully lonely for a man away from home for so long. It's not only sailors who have a girl in every port," Sam hinted obviously.

"Oh, I see." Joe felt suddenly naïve and found himself oddly embarrassed by the conversation. Ridiculous when one was a medical man and had given lectures on the dangers of casual sexual encounters to groups of soldiers back in Sussex. Despite this he realised that, compared to that of his brother, his life had been very sheltered. He had still been a virgin when he married Dora, at twenty nine. It would seem that Sam's sexual experience began at a much earlier age. "And do you?" he asked trying to sound worldly and knowing he failed abysmally.

"There's been a few," Sam admitted, the smirk evident in his voice. He took another drag on his woodbine and exhaled slowly allowing his eyes to follow the smoke, his mind elsewhere.

"You are careful aren't you?" Joe could not help the question. It fell from his lips unbidden and crash landed between them. They were worlds apart. Tied by the bonds of blood and distant memories of childhood but little else.

Sam squinted through the smoke at his elder brother and started to laugh, throwing his head back against the wall and staring at the dank ceiling. He laughed so hard that tears rolled down his grimy cheeks. Joe flushed. *What a stupid thing to say*!

"Oh Joe!" Sam hiccoughed at last. "Man, you really are priceless. You sounded just like the padre then. He's full of that holier than thou shit! What do you think? I'm not bloody stupid. I don't want the fucking clap!" He sniggered some more and flicked his tab end into the evil swirling water.

"Sorry. Professional habit," Joe offered in explanation, his own amusement at his ridiculous question pushing through his discomfort. Sam spluttered and they both giggled childishly together. It took some minutes and aching sides before sobriety was regained.

"Lily said Rob was out here as well," Sam changed the subject.

"Yes. He's at Rouen and from all accounts, getting lots of surgical practice. He wants to be nearer the action but they need all the surgeons they can get at base hospitals. It's different up here. My work is mainly glorified first aid. For Rob it's real challenging stuff. He enjoys his work. Gives me all the gory details in his letters, yet he longs to be at the Front," Joe gave a swift account of his best friend's experience. He waited for his brother to respond, to ask another question or make a comment. After all Robert was Sam's friend too and soon to be brother-in-law, but the sergeant said nothing. Instead he stared at his sibling, his expression undecipherable. Uncomfortable with the silence Joe rambled on.

"He says there are some really interesting cases. You know, the sort of thing one would never see in a civilian hospital. He really enjoys it when something like that comes his way." Slowly it dawned on him that he had made a mistake, that his brother did not share this professional detachment where men became cases rather than human beings.

"*Enjoys*? Ah, well I suppose it would be very interesting for a *surgeon*. Working with shattered bodies that is. Very *interesting*," Sam agreed with bitter irony. "Still, if I were you Brother, I would try to get a job like that. You don't want to be up here long. Especially not when there's a push on. Gets a bit *nasty* then."

Joe studied his sibling. He was aware of the sudden tension and not sure whether he was being mocked or not. It was impossible to tell with Sam. Was he being sarcastic or merely showing concern? The doctor preferred to believe the latter.

"I'll be alright," he said. "Do you think there's something likely then? A new offensive?"

Sam shrugged. "If I was running this show I'd plan a spring offensive. Hit them before they could get to us. And you don't have to be a genius to notice that there's a hell of a lot of new troops in this sector. Unusual for a quiet stretch of the line. More guns too. I wouldn't mind betting old Frenchie's got something up his sleeve. But what do I know; I'm only a lowly sergeant."

A long ten seconds of silence filled only with the murmur of disgruntled men passing outside and the distant rumble of artillery somewhere else down the line.

"You'll be back in reserve soon?" Joe asked feeling that the connection between them was faltering.

"In a day or two."

"We should get together for a drink."

"Officers and NCOs are not permitted to socialise together Joe."

"I know that, but we're brothers. I'm sure they'll make allowances for us."

"*Jesus*! This is the Army Joe. They don't make allowances for anyone. It's against the rules," Sam retorted with an exasperated air.

"Since when have you paid any attention to rules?" Joe challenged feeling his brother drifting away from him.

"Since I joined the Army," Sam snapped back.

Joe felt deflated. He had looked forward to seeing his brother, but somehow after the initial joy of meeting the visit only served to highlight their differences. As if he sensed it too Sam said, "It's been good to see you Joe. I need to go. I've got a working party to check on. If I don't keep on their tails they'll be slacking in some dug-out or other." He held out a hand. Joe shook it warmly.

"I wish we could have more time to talk," he said regretfully.

"Maybe another time. Take care, Sir," Sam returned. The acknowledgment of rank seemed to widen the gulf that threatened to separate them.

"Sam," Joe called as his brother reached the entrance, "Promise me that you'll take care of yourself."

The sergeant smiled broadly. "No need to worry about that. I'm not daft," he stated and with a wave of his hand vanished out into the trench.

Alone, Joe felt bereft. Nothing was as he had expected. Everything was cold, dark and miserable and in his eyes, the rigid discipline of the Army thwarted what should have been a worthwhile and enjoyable venture.

"You alright Sir?" Fallon's voice broke through his reverie.

"Let's get back Donal. This place stinks."

CHAPTER 17.
February 18th, Number 13 General Hospital, Boulogne

"I'm sorry Hepworth but we're in a bit of a jam. I know you've never been on the head ward before, but you're my only qualified nurse. I daren't put any of the VADs on it. They're not up to this. I need someone with real nursing experience," the night sister of C floor apologised with a deeply flustered expression.

Lily had found, in her few weeks at the busy military hospital, that many of the Regular Army nurses, those who belonged to QAIMNS, struggled with running such a large venture, with so many sick and injured men. They were highly skilled and unquestionably professional, but they were used to peace time numbers. In Boulogne the patients numbered thousands. British, Canadian, a lot of French and Belgians, even some Portuguese, a few Indians and the inevitable German prisoners. And Number Thirteen General was not the only hospital, there were several more in Boulogne alone and numerous springing up along the coast down to Étaples and beyond. The scale would have been unimaginable only a few months previous. Huge tented and roughly hutted cities had been erected all along the northern coast of France. They housed the new recruits and returning soldiers now flooding into the theatre of war. They comprised of training camps, rest camps, punishment camps. Camps for prisoners and those for the rehabilitation of the sick and injured. And all these men needed feeding, clothing and looking after when they became ill. The number of hospital beds were struggling to keep pace, not only with the wounded brought back from the Front, but with the growing number of medical complaints suffered by hundreds of men thrown together.

Outbreaks of influenza and childhood illnesses were rife. Soldiers arriving from the remote highlands or overseas colonies succumbed to epidemics of measles and chicken pox in droves. Inevitably the camps and accompanying hospitals spilled into the hinterland and sprawled for miles joining one French seaside town to the next like a bizarre kind of encroaching suburbia.

This was war fought on an industrial scale. Quite unlike anything anyone had seen before. The highly trained Army nurses had more than proved their worth amongst the countless wounded since last August, but they failed to cope with the administrative nightmare of running what were effectively large, general hospitals. Lily had found that she had as much, if not more experience, in nursing large numbers of patients and that the older, QAIMNS Reserve and TFNS sisters and matrons, were far more able to accommodate the administrative duties than their Regular counterparts.

Lily loved her work. She loved the excitement, the bustle, the noisy, uncouth lads fresh from Blighty and full of exuberance and eager patriotism. Boulogne was a hub of ceaseless activity. It was an adventure on a scale she had hitherto only imagined. Not that it was easy. She worked hard. Her shifts, twelve hours for five days each week. She received one and a half days off, but sometimes, even this was revoked. Like today, when someone went sick.

She had seen horrors too. Young men dismembered or mutilated beyond description. Those dying helplessly from gangrene despite the medical organisations' best efforts. Boys dying from tetanus because they had not received the serum in time. Others simply died. Too weak through blood loss or sickness to pull through. It was heart wrenching, but at the same time it could be rewarding. For every horror story there were at least two or three miracles of recovery.

At no other time in her life had Lily felt so needed and so fulfilled. She knew she played only a very small, yet important role and even if no one but the boys she nursed said thank you, that was payment enough. To know she had helped, had given comfort, care and hope was a greater reward than any higher accolade.

But the toll on nurses was high. The winter had been hard and cold and many had succumbed through exhaustion to the same epidemics the soldiers suffered. The sick sisters' hospital had a fresh face every day. Some returned to duty after a week or so, others were sent home, never to return. One or two had even died.

"I hope Sister Madley is not too ill?" Lily queried as she walked beside the night sister through the corridors of the third floor. Electric lights blazed from ornate brackets on the walls, a reminder of the Casino's illustrious past.

"Oh I do hope not. We badly need all our experienced nurses fit and well. Matron told me there are some new ladies arriving in the next week. But I have no doubt we will have to share them with Abbeville and Calais. I never thought I'd hear myself say it Hepworth, but thank goodness for the VADs. Some of them are coming along quite nicely now."

Lily said nothing. She did not fully comprehend this aversion many of her counterparts had to the Voluntary Aid Detachment girls. Much of it was professional pride. The highly trained and skilled nurses resented the arrival and use of untrained, though eager, well-to-do volunteers. There was a fear that these VADs would usurp the qualified nurses, be allowed to carry out duties only someone with the necessary proficiency should do and therefore undermine the importance of true nursing care.

Lily thought it a disproportionate reaction. She was not immune to such pride, but anyone with an ounce of sense could see that the volunteers had a role to play. Without them, there would be far too much work for everyone else. They filled the same role as nursing auxiliaries and probationers in civilian hospitals. They had their place. It did not help however, that those few who had landed in France were mainly from the upper classes and possessed an air of superiority born of privilege. It was a trait soon knocked out of them by the no nonsense discipline of military nursing. But the jealously remained even if it had tempered a little.

"Here we are. I hope you'll be alright. I'll pop in every hour or so, but I can't promise more than that. I've got the whole floor to supervise. Sister Poole will brief you."

"I'll be fine Sister. Don't worry. I can manage," Lily replied confidently feeling the need to reassure the flustered night sister. The older woman smiled with an expression that showed both relief and uncertainty. She liked Hepworth. Found the girl sensible and competent. A good nurse. Never fazed by whatever task she was given. If she was ever upset, or anxious, the young woman hid it well. She possessed a self assurance and self belief that the night sister thought admirable in one so young. Her only flaw, a tendency to flaunt the rules. The shortening of her dress had induced a severe reprimand from Matron and she had more than once been chastised for being over familiar with the doctors.

"Very good. I'll see you about nine then. If you have any trouble, don't hesitate to call for me," the night sister impressed.

Lily walked the length of the ward with Sister Poole, taking careful note of instructions and any information regarding each patient. The room had once been a private salon, splendid with crystal chandelier and gaming tables. Now the chandelier had been removed and the tables replaced by a dozen beds, each of which were occupied.

"They're not all injured. Number three and number eleven are suffering from shell shock. Outwardly they show no trauma, but obviously something has disturbed their brains. Major Hargreaves believes that shells bursting close to them causes some kind of internal injury that manifests itself psychologically. Either way, they are fairly quiet. Number three says nothing, but does as he's told. Number eleven has nightmares and he can scream out and carry on. It varies though. From day-to-day.

"The others to watch are number seven, he has a tendency to get out of bed and run a-mock. And number five is prone to fits. If he has one you must call the medical officer immediately. Numbers two, four and nine are permanently sedated. They'll take their drinks and medication but they'll give you no trouble. Number eight has lost a leg, so even though he can be noisy, he can't cause much disruption. Twelve and one are always quiet and the others, poor souls, well they will probably never wake up," Sister Poole finished sadly.

Lily took it all in, mentally made notes to keep an eye on number seven and five and wished the sister had used the men's names instead of numbers. It was a tendency of the Army to dehumanise people by giving them numbers, but Lily found it unnecessarily heartless when men were wounded and in desperate need of comfort and help. She vowed to read each man's notes to learn their names as soon as Poole had left.

"Well I think that's everything Hepworth. Is there anything you wish to ask?" Sister finished.

"No, I don't think so. Should I expect a visit from any doctors?"

"What over night? I shouldn't think so, not unless you have any problems. Your night orderly should be here within a half hour or so. His name is Fergusson. A bit of a dour Scot, but he's a decent enough man and knows his job. He looks after this ward and the medical ward next door. I know he makes a lovely cup of cocoa." Poole smiled and glanced around the quiet ward at her charges. "Well, they're all yours Hepworth. I'll see you in the morning. Good night."

"Good night Sister," Lily echoed and once alone traversed the ward once more, reading and memorising the names of the men in each bed. Those who were conscious watched her with haunted eyes or stared unseeingly at the ceiling. Number eleven, a corporal called Sanders, grinned at her once and returned to counting the letters on the magazine he was supposedly reading.

The doors at the end of the ward banged open and an RAMC orderly burst in with a trolley full of hot drinks. Lily jumped out of her skin and those men that were able, sat up gleefully, almost childlike in anticipation of their evening drink of cocoa. The orderly began doling out his drinks.

"One for ye Sister?" he asked Lily without even acknowledging that she was not the usual night nurse.

"Yes please. It's Fergusson isn't it?" Lily responded.

"Aye."

"I didn't expect you to bring the men a drink."

"Well, poor buggers like a cocoa before lights out. I'll gi' 'em a wash then and a bottle. Wi' luck they'll not wet the bed," Fergusson grinned his eyes watching the new nurse's response.

Lily smiled. She knew his game. "Well if they do Fergusson, I know I can count on you to help me change them," she countered. He nodded sourly and wheeled his trolley from the room.

"I'll be back in half an hour te wash 'em."

"Very good. I'll help you," Lily answered much to his surprise and he actually returned her smile.

Well that was a step in the right direction.

By ten o'clock all the patients were washed and ready for lights out. Fergusson piled his fresh trolley high with empty cups, a wash basin and used towels.

"Will ye be alright Sister? I have to go next door now."

"Yes Fergusson. I'm sure I will be fine. They all seem to be settling down. Once the lights are out they'll go to sleep."

Fergusson smirked. "Aye, well don't get too comfy. Their demons come out at night. Some of the poor beggars are passed it, should've been put to sleep if we were more humane, but then there's them with somthin' not right up here, if ye know what I mean." He pointed to his head. "The dark for them holds terrible memories. If ye need me just shout. I'll be back and forth anyhow, but not for a while. I 'ave te look to the poor buggers next door for a time." He nodded a sombre farewell and wheeled his trolley for the second time, from the ward.

Lily strolled from bed to bed. Checking on her charges. Speaking a word to those she thought could respond. She received in reply only a toothy grin from Sanders and blank stares from the others. She checked on the sedated men and those who were deeply comatose, tucked in their blankets and ensured the cot sides were securely in place. She did not want them falling out of bed, and then she lit her lantern and turned off the bright electric lights.

An eerie silence pervaded the salon; the lantern producing long shadows that cast the night nurse a ghostly figure. Sanders closed his eyes tight shut and whispered the Lord's Prayer to himself over and over, his repeated soft incantation setting a steady rhythmic undertone, which number seven countered with the odd random shout out loud. Lily let them be for five minutes before deciding they might disturb the other men and cause unnecessary agitation within the ward. She decided to tackle Sanders first and picking up her lantern stepped over to his bed casting an eye at number seven, whose name, annoyingly she found she had forgotten, as she passed. He was waving his arms in the air as if fighting off some imagined attack and she hesitated wondering whether she should deal with him first. Suddenly his arms dropped to his sides and he lay still. She watched him for a moment and then carried on to the now frantically whispering Sanders. As she approached he pulled the bed clothes over his head and began weeping like a child.

Oh my! "Corporal, Corporal Sanders, come now, there's nothing to be afraid of here. You're quite safe you know. You're in hospital, remember," Lily tried not knowing whether he did know where he was. She had no experience of this odd phenomenon called shell shock. She had attended a lecture on it, and had seen wounded men jump at the slightest loud noise, their nerves raw and frayed, but this was different. The corporal did not seem to know where he was and somewhere in his tortured mind he fought those demons that Fergusson had talked about. He whimpered.

Lily set down the lantern on his bedside cabinet and gently pulled back the sheets from his head. Wide, staring eyes met hers, his face contorted with fear. She took his hands and his vice like grasp caused her at first to recoil anxiously, before she realised he was terrified and that grip a desperate need for comfort. She sat on the edge of his bed and carefully releasing one hand stroked his forehead, like a mother reassuring a little boy. She decided to forgo formality and talked quietly to him using his first name.

"Is it the dark, David? Don't you like the dark?"

His huge eyes stared at the lamp and he nodded. The dark, claustrophobic, cold and filled with the dead. They came for him in the dark, at night when no one else could see. It started with the steady boom of his heart pounding in his ears. A pounding that rose in pitch and became indistinguishable from the guns. Guns thundering through his head, never stopping, constantly wearing away at his nerve and with the guns the faces drifted by. Cheery boys and men he had known. Not cheery now. Now they haunted him, condemned him to a life of torment because he was alive and they were not. He still breathed that fresh, sweet air; still felt the touch of another human being and by rights he too should be dead. He should be with his comrades, marching endlessly across that execrable barren hell, through mud and cold to confront the eternal enemy.

Who is this woman? What is she doing here in this purgatory? She was speaking to him. *What did she say?* Such a soft voice. So warm and real. Like home. Slowly Sanders fought his way out of his private hell and came half way to recognising the real world.

"Shall I sit with you until you fall to sleep? David?"

Is it mother? Am I really home? He wanted to believe it. Oh how he did. To believe that he was back in his bed with his brother Sid at the other end and dear Mam telling him it was only a bad dream and that she would sit with him until he went back to sleep. *Is it true?* His grip on the slight hand remained fierce, his eyes fixed on the pretty nurse beside him, but seeing an altogether different woman. A woman who had been with him through childhood, who had nursed him when he was ill, chastised him when he was bad and held him close when he was hurt or afraid. He had thought that woman had died a long time ago, but no, she was here for him now.

"They frighten me Mam," he uttered so very quietly, in a small childish voice that Lily had to strain to hear him.

Number Seven suddenly shouted out making Lily jump, but Sanders didn't seem to notice.

"Who do, David?" *The poor soul.* He was not in his right mind. Thought she was his mother.

"The men from my section. They frighten me. They come for me when it gets dark. They want me to go with them," Sanders answered and made a low whining noise in his throat as he looked around frantically to see if the malignant ghosts were watching.

"There's no one here David. It's just you and me and a few other men in hospital remember. You're safe. No one will come for you." Lily crooned.

"But they're angry that I'm here. I should be with them."

"No. God wanted you to be here, not with them," Lily said quite firmly, realising he spoke of dead comrades. "Now you must go to sleep David. You need to rest and get well again." She moved her hand to try and get some feeling back into it. His grip tightened with panic.

"NO!" he shouted terrified she was going to leave him. Lily started and looked around the ward. Number seven cried out again and began his battle with the air above his bed, and number three sat upright. *Oh Lord!*

"Don't leave me alone Mam," Sanders begged.

"David, you must be quiet. You'll disturb the other boys." She gazed around trying to assess the ward. Number three was watching her, his name was George Cuthbert she remembered and she wondered if she ought to tell him to lie down. Sanders grabbed at her arm. She dare not leave him; he was too distressed and likely to shout out again. *God, what do I do now?* Number Seven was becoming more frantic in his fighting and George was... *Oh no, where is he?*

"Come on David, out of bed. You can help me with the others," She tugged his hand and bemusedly he obeyed, still holding tightly onto her. She did not know what else to do.

"Where are we going Mam?" Sanders asked his eyes even wider than before.

Lily picked up the lantern and led the way down the ward. "To find George. I think he's hiding."

"Hiding? Like hide and seek?"

"Yes David, just like hide and seek. I think he's frightened too."

"Maybe they've come for him and taken him away!" Sander's voice climbed an octave as his imagination threatened to overwhelm him.

"No, I don't think so. I told you, no one will take you away from here. George is only hiding." The idea to make this a game for the corporal struck Lily as the only way to keep him calm. He had regressed to his childhood by way of escaping the trauma in his life, so she would treat him like a child. Let him think that this was a game of seek and find. Hopefully he would not become more of a handful when they found George.

Number Seven called out, crying at some imagined horror. His words unrecognisable gibberish.

"What was that?" Sanders demanded apprehensively. He stopped dead and squeezed Lily's hand tight causing her to wince with pain.

"David, you're hurting my hand. Please don't squeeze so hard," she chastised.

"Sorry Mam. That noise?" he whispered and huddled closer to her grasping at the sleeve of her uniform. If it had not been so tragic it would have been a comical sight. He, a nearly six foot tall guardsman, towered over her, but his actions and stance were those of a small boy.

"It's just one of the other boys trying to frighten you. You're not afraid are you? He's just being naughty. Take no notice." She moved on again with Sanders clinging to her. He looked around occasionally to see if he could see this naughty boy, but he shuffled along beside her compliantly enough. They reached Number Three's bed.

"George? Are you under there?" Lily peered under the bunk. The young private sat there, cross legged.

"Is he there Mam?" David giggled.

"Oh God! Don't tell me you've brought that nutcase down 'ere," George moaned.

Well, at least this one is compos mentis.

"I couldn't really leave him. He's afraid. Why are you hiding under your bed?"

"I'm not. This is my dug-out. Well, it's Captain Mayhew's actually, but 'e don't need it no more. 'E's dead y'know. Blown to bits. BOOM! Like 'e'd never been there."

Alright, maybe he isn't compos mentis after all. "Don't you think it would be more comfortable in bed George?"

"Not safe out there. Shell's dropping all night. Don't want hot shrapnel down me neck."

Lily stood upright and glanced at David. What should she do now? Number Seven screamed. David jumped physically in the air and trod on her toe trying to get as close as he possibly could.

"I don't like that boy Mam. He makes scary noises."

"Yes he does. Don't worry I'll sort him out when we get George back into bed."

Lily stared along the ward. What was she doing? She wished Fergusson would come back. She was out of her depth and she hated it.

Suddenly she had an idea. "David, we're going to make a new den for George. Come on; help me pull this blanket off." Sanders obeyed smiling. This was a new game.

"There's a curtain over there, on wheels, do you see it?" Lily asked pointing into the corner of the ward. Sanders nodded. "Will you fetch it for me?"

He took a step forward, hesitated, and turned to look at her, his face anxious. "What is it?" she asked.

"He's a bloody coward that's what," George opined from under the bed.

"Be quiet Private," she snapped back.

"It's dark over there," Sanders quavered.

"But you're a brave boy David. I'm only here. I can see you all the time. Run along and get it and then we can build this den."

Carefully he edged towards the curtain rail. George sniggered from the safety of his dug-out.

"I don't know what you're laughing at young man. You're not staying there."

"Well I'm not coming out. It's not safe I told you. And I don't want to share some bloody 'ole with nutters like 'im."

"You don't have to. I've found you a new dug-out. Look George, that one is no good anyway. It's too low. It'll get flooded," Lily argued remembering that Sam often complained of having to sleep on the firing step of a trench because everywhere else was full of mud and water.

David returned with the curtain, his face flushed with fearful excitement. Just like a child.

"Thank you David. Let's put it here." Lily wheeled the rail to the end of the bed and half opened it so that it enclosed the lower part of the bunk but left the rest in view. "Now, can you put the blanket over the bed stead at this end and the rail down there? I'm not tall enough," she asked the corporal. He grinned and did what she asked, fastening the blanket as instructed with a couple of safety pins she delved from her pocket.

"Right Private Cuthbert, out of that dug-out that's an order," she instructed.

"Who're you. You're not an officer," George challenged sullenly.

"Oh yes I am my boy. Now unless you want to find yourself on a charge and before the CSM, you'll get your backside out of that dug-out now!"

George faltered, thought about it, worried about being on a charge. They might give him a field punishment again and he didn't want that. At last he climbed out.

"Gotcha!" David cried and tagged George on the arm.

"Fuck off you looney!"

"Private Cuthbert! Language," Lily upbraided.

"Sorry Sir."

"I should think so. This Private, is your new dug-out. Get inside. As you can see you will be quite safe from whizz-bangs and whatever else the Hun wishes to hurl at you."

George looked at the tent like den sceptically, but not wanting to disobey an order, climbed in. Once on his bed and sheltered beneath the blanket, he settled back. "Is it all mine? I don't 'ave to share with 'im?" he asked pointing a David.

"No, it's all yours. Now, Private, get some sleep. Stand-to at dawn."

"Yes Sir. Thank you Sir," George replied and closed his eyes.

Lily sighed and looked at Sanders. Now for Number Seven. Strange, she had not heard him for a while. Only an odd wheezing sound came from his direction. Frowning, she picked up the corporal's hand and hurried towards the other end of the ward.

"Oh my God!"

Number Seven was half out of his bed, had climbed over his cot sides and somehow got his sheets fastened around his neck. He was half strangled and fighting frantically for breath, choking and gasping.

"David, quickly, lift him up."

Sanders looked bemused.

"Here, like this," Lily took hold of Number Seven under the arms and tried to heave him up, but she was not strong enough. David cottoned on and took over from her. Hurriedly she unwound the sheet and loosened it from the hanging man's neck. He started to fight, scratching at her and at Sanders, making the task almost impossible.

"Hey!" the corporal protested and dropping Number Seven in indignation he thumped him squarely across the jaw. A powerful blow that knocked the struggling man senseless.

"David!"

"Well, he hit me first."

"Never mind. Pick him up for me, I can't get this loose."

Sanders obeyed and between them they managed to get the sheet away from Number Seven's neck and lift him back into bed. Lily quickly examined him. He was a little blue in the face, but his breathing was steady. No doubt he would have some nasty bruising around his throat in the morning. His bandaged head lolled onto his chest. She had him propped up on his pillows, didn't want to risk laying him flat just yet. Better call for the MO just to be sure. She groaned a sigh of relief and dropped her head onto the cot sides. A warm hand rubbed her shoulders.

"It's alright Sister. He's OK."

Lily looked up and found David watching her. But it was not David the boy. It was Corporal Sanders, the guardsman.

"Gave us quite a fright didn't he?" Sanders said.

"Yes he did. Are you feeling alright yourself David?"

"David! You know, no one's called me that for a long time. My dear old Mam always called me David. To everyone else it's always been Sanders or Dave."

Lily smiled. Somehow the act of saving Number Seven's life had brought the corporal to his senses. It was a relief and it might only be temporary, but for now it was very welcome.

"You need a good cuppa, Sister," Sanders declared.

Lily laughed. "And you need to get back to bed."

He grinned. "It's not fair is it?" he said as they walked back towards his bunk.

"What isn't?"

"These poor lads and that one down there not right in his head," he jerked a thumb towards George's 'dug-out'.

"No David, it's not fair. Will you be alright now?"

"Course I will. It's not like I'm afraid of the dark you know. I'm a big boy now," he joked. He seemed to have no memory of earlier.

"Of course you are. Good night then David. Thank you for your help."

"Oh you're welcome. Little lass like you would never have managed him alone. Good job I was here. 'Night Sister." He climbed back into his bed and dropped to sleep almost as soon as his head hit the pillow. Lily stared at him for a good half minute, her own head reeling from the last hour's exertions. She returned to the desk in the middle of the ward and sagged into the chair behind it, weary with stress. The ward doors opened and Fergusson strolled in. He reached her desk and looking around declared, "Well, it's really quiet in here tonight."

Lily laughed and shook her head. He raised an eyebrow in question, but she did not enlighten him.

"What's that on Cuthbert's bed?" he asked at length. He did not use numbers. They were men in here, even if they were not all with it.

"It's his new dug-out," she replied.

Fergusson smiled. "Aye, so it is."

CHAPTER 18.
February 24th, Brigade Reserve, Fleurbaix

A rare hour or two of leisure time. Recently promoted Sergeant Snowy White peered into the newly opened reading rooms in Fleurbaix. They were not half bad considering the Battalion had been requested to help with their creation only yesterday. Already filled to the brim with men grateful for somewhere warm to relax other than billets. A place they could find some normality, read an out of date newspaper or magazine, leaf through a dog eared book, get a hot drink and a bun for nothing, even write home. Following a much needed and relished bath, a shave and a good meal, the reading room would soon be next in popularity. It already was. It gave a natural alternative to the ubiquitous estimanet with its inflated prices, watered down beer and rough vin rouge. Made a welcome change for those seeking peace and quiet or those whose pay had already been spent. Only the distant rumble of artillery remained a reminder of where they were and most men, by now, were immune to its thunder unless its missiles crept closer.

Fleurbaix had been well and truly shelled, most of its buildings damaged to some extent, some pulverised completely. But today it remained quiet. Fritz was bashing someone else. Today the Battalion relaxed as much as they were allowed to, caught up with much needed sleep, read letters from home and penned carefully sanitised replies.

Snowy looked around the crowded, smoke filled room. It was impossible to make out the man he looked for through the tightly packed bodies. With a sigh he pushed inside, returned a few greetings and squeezed his way to the rear. There, in a threadbare corner armchair sat Sam Hepworth, a letter in his hand and a frown on his face. Snowy smirked and pressed his way towards the chair.

"Ey-up Eppy. Fancy a drink?" he asked with a grin.

Sam looked up from his letter. "Beer?" he affirmed knowing very well that his comrade was not inferring they have a cup of tea.

"Aye, unless tha wa' gonna do summat else, but I fancy a beer an' a look at that pretty mamselle," White smirked. His friend returned the expression. Yes, a beer and the chance to watch Mademoiselle Collet bring forth beverages and soup as she worked around the tables of leering Tommies was a better prospect than replying to his sister's long epistle just now.

The letter disturbed him. He had not liked what he had read. It had only added to his long held discomfort at his sister's decision to come to France. Stubborn, headstrong creature that she was. No regard for her own safety or what it would mean to their mother if anything should befall her. Why could she have not stayed at home? She had worthwhile work there. Now she was in Boulogne, exposed to sights, that in Sam's opinion, no woman should ever see. And, from what she said, he gathered the nurses were dropping like flies with the usual winter ailments made worse because of the hard work and long hours. It was almost with glee that she had informed him she had asked to transfer to a hospital train. She had not even been out here two months and she might be travelling perilously close to the danger zone. She had to have her adventure. *Silly little cow*! No, Sam decided now was not a good time to reply. He might write something he would later regret. A beer was a much better option. He picked up his cap and pulled it onto his head.

"What we waiting for?" he said bounding to his feet. Beaming, Snowy led the way into the street. They skirted a passing transport column and headed towards the little café at the end of the main road. It would be just as crowded, if not more so, than the reading room, but at least they could get alcohol and Sam always managed to get beer well before his turn. Snowy teased that Mademoiselle Collet had a soft spot for Sergeant Hepworth and that her father turned a blind eye to their flirtations because he actually bothered to speak French, albeit badly, rather than shouting in pidgin English hoping to be understood. And the music helped.

The early evening sky glowed menacingly orange in the east, the sound of guns louder in the street even above the crunch of wheels and horses hooves. Neither man cared. It was just a night like any other. They could scarcely remember what it was like to see pitch black, star studded skies and hear nothing but the wind or everyday traffic. War had clouded their memories of normality. This was about as peaceful as it got.

They ran across the road between two horse drawn wagons, saluted an officer striding purposefully in the other direction and dashed into the dark doorway of what appeared to be a boarded up house. Inside bright yellow light momentarily dazzled the two men and the noise and fug created by a mass of men hit them with a blast of warm, fetid air. If half of the Battalion had been in the reading rooms it seemed that the other half was here, although in reality the number was only around fifty, mostly from D Company, who were not on duty this night. In the cramped room it seemed there were many more.

"Lucky to get in," Snowy commented as the middle-aged proprietor pushed past them with a scowl and grumbling turned the sign on the door to fermé and locked it.

"Bonsoir Monsieur Collet. Comment allez vous?" Sam asked in schoolboy French and gazing around, searched for a feminine form.

"Très bien. A quoi vous-pensez?" the proprietor replied with a reluctant smile. The Frenchman never liked to appear happy when serving British soldiers, yet the fact was they were making him reasonably rich and as long as he could keep their hands off his daughter, he was actually very happy. This one, however, he did not mind. This one was decent, polite, spoke a little French, albeit with an abominable accent, and played his old piano very well. Monsieur Collet liked having this one in his establishment; he added free entertainment and in way of payment asked for nothing other than beer. It was a mutually convivial arrangement.

"Vous jouerez ce soir, Sergent?"

"Oui. Mais d'abord, je voudrais une bière," Sam replied and smiled as he caught the eye of a dark haired, attractive young woman serving vin rouge to a group of Medical Corps corporals. She returned his expression coyly with a slight flush and quickly returned her attention to her task.

"Mais naturellement. S'il vous plait, venez avec moi tous les deux. Je vous trouverai une table," the Frenchman pushed his way through his vociferous clientele, the two sergeants following behind.

"Ahh, Eppy. This is what I like about comin' out wi' thi. Alus get a seat and a buckshee drink," Snowy sighed appreciatively as the proprietor roughly pushed a couple of privates from their seat near the piano, much to their consternation, and shouted to his daughter to bring over two beers and not the watery stuff either. The special brew!

Within five minutes two tall glasses of amber liquid were placed before the men.

"Merci Mariele," Sam thanked her softly, his dark eyes holding hers just a little too long. She smiled back brightly.

"De rien….Jouerez vous quelque chose ce soir?" she asked nodding towards the piano at which a group of men were gathered, one of whom was picking out a half decent melody.

"Naturellement. Que voudriez-vous entendre?" he asked ignoring the kick under the table and the knowing grin from Snowy.

"Quelque chose de beau," she returned knowing he always played something sentimental for her and that it would shut the men up for a while before they clamoured for something they could sing along to.

"Vous êtes belle Mademoiselle."

Mariele beamed and flushed prettily.

"Oy love! Can we get a drink over 'ere?" an impatient voice called from across the room. Mariele smiled apologetically and hurried away. Sam turned to his drink and Snowy. The latter batted his eyelids and pursed his lips mockingly.

"Ooo Monsewer," he said in falsetto and sniggered into his beer.

"Fuck off," Sam growled back smirking at the friendly banter.

"Tha's clicked there alright. I never get a piece like that."

"You're too bloody ugly that's why."

"What d'y' say to 'er?"

"None of your bloody business."

Snowy snickered. "Oh aye? I'm glad she fancies thi though Eppy. Wouldn't get this pukka stuff if she didn't."

"I see Black Bright's in. Thought 'is platoon were on Picket?" he nodded in the direction of the detested sergeant.

"Probably are. He'll have posted sentries and left 'em to it," Sam commented with dislike.

"Bastard! I 'ope 'e gets caught one day."

"Wouldn't half the Company? Come on Snowy, forget Bright. I need cheering up. Got any fags?"

"Smoked all yours again?" Snowy laughed reaching in his pocket for a pack of cigarettes.

"No, but you owe me about half a dozen. Come on you stingy bugger," Sam returned dryly and held out an expectant hand. With a curse, his comrade handed over a smoke and they lit up and fell into easy conversation.

A half hour later and, following a series of imploring looks from Monsieur Collet, Sam waved his empty beer glass meaningfully and indicated towards the piano. The proprietor nodded gratefully casting a none too pleased glare at the lance corporal bashing away at the keys of his prized instrument with all the musical flare of a charging rhinoceros.

"Time to earn some more beer pal," Sam muttered to his companion. "Comin' over?"

"Stupid bloody question. I won't get none if I stay 'ere. On'y that watery slop an' then I'd 'ave to pay forrit," Snowy grumbled and the two men drifted over to the misused piano.

"Clear off Corbett," Sam pulled rank with a jerk of his head. The lance jack pulled a face but said nothing and with his mates, he shuffled away to prop up a wall. He was not really put out. His disgruntlement merely a show of bravado. Like everyone else, he was happy to let Eppy have free reign over the instrument. They'd get some decent entertainment and enjoy a good sing-song.

As Hepworth sat on the stool Mariele brought two more beers and placed them atop the upright. Snowy thanked her appreciatively and took a long, satisfied swig. Sam merely smiled and, with uncharacteristic coyness, fished in his tunic pocket bringing forth a neatly folded wad of writing paper. Unfolding it he revealed a hand written music score.

"What's that?" Snowy asked curiously, wiping beer froth from his moustache.

"Pour vous Mademoiselle," Sam spoke to Mariele, ignoring his comrade. He began to play.

The piano was not the most wonderful of instruments although it was, at least, in tune. Its chords and tone were more favoured for music hall sing-alongs than for refined pieces of classical composition. Yet Sergeant Hepworth was an accomplished and gifted musician despite the long years of scant practice. Whenever and wherever possible he had taken the opportunity to play, usually in some bar, and though he knew his playing fell well below what it could be, his less discerning comrades thought it as good as any professional. As he played the café grew unusually quiet, the boisterous conversation subdued to hushed whispers. It was not a piece that one would normally assume the rough and ready Tommies would appreciate, yet its melodiously soft, melancholy air caught many a man reminiscing with happy nostalgic reflection. Lightly and expressively Sam caressed the keys into creating something hauntingly beautiful, as delightful and compelling as any birdsong. As he reached the last bar, his fingers kissed the keys in a lover's goodbye and ended with a chord so soft it could barely be heard. A spontaneous applause broke out. Sam blushed self-consciously and took a drink of beer. He smiled at Mariele who gazed back mesmerised with tears in her eyes.

"C'est enchantant," she whispered. He bowed his head in thanks.

"Bloody 'ell Eppy," Snowy muttered, his eyes wide and feeling not a little emotional. "That wa' reet good. Did y' write that thi sen?"

Sam laughed shaking his head.

"Give us summat we can sing to Sarn't" a voice called from across the room, a number of others joined in the request. Sam folded up his score and tucked it back inside his jacket. He winked at Snowy as Mariele moved away to serve more drinks and accepted a lighted cigarette.

"No, our Frank did, but she doesn't know that," he answered at last.

"You're in there chum," Snowy muttered knowingly. Sam grinned, drew contentedly on his woodbine and played a rapid flourish before launching into a melody of popular songs. Soon the whole café reverberated with happy and slightly merry voices, somewhat lacking in tune and with many a verse that would be unrecognisable to its composer. No one left the building. No one would now, not until they were kicked out or until the music stopped. This was what Monsieur Collet had banked upon and why he had been happy to lock his door.

The music stopped, however, sooner than anyone would have anticipated. A shocked, girlish squeal followed by a torrent of angry French and a resounding slap across a face brought laughter from the nearby men. Nothing more should have happened. Everyone would have carried on singing if the drunken molester on the receiving end of the strike had been any other man but Jake Bright. The heavily built sergeant leapt to his feet knocking the drinks from the table and spilling the men from it. If only the bar had not been so crowded Mariele would have easily escaped his grasp. As it was she stepped backwards into an already unbalanced soldier, who unknowingly blocked her exit and Bright reached out with a massive hand and clamped it around her left wrist. With a vicious tug he pulled her towards him, growled some obscenity and with his free hand struck her hard across the left cheek. The girl shrieked with pain, fell backwards into the same unsuspecting private as before and reeling dizzily crumpled to the floor.

The scream, clatter of furniture and crash of breaking glass arrested all laughter and singing. Men scattered from their tables, someone stooped to help the young woman to her feet. The piano playing stopped abruptly and Sam jumped up onto the stool to see above the heads of the swarm of men, all of whom were craning their necks to find the cause of the hubbub. He could hear Monsieur Collet shouting angrily in French, caught sight of him pushing through the crowd towards Bright. From his position Sam could not see Mariele; the sea of khaki hid her from view. It was only when Bright shoved away the Samaritan helping her to stand, as Monsieur Collet clasped his hands across his mouth in horror, that he realised the brute had hold of the girl by her hair and was dragging her back to her knees. Sam saw a fist drawn back and before anyone else had reacted, had even realised what was happening, he launched himself through the throng, pushing and elbowing his way. He heard another scream, angry shouts, the sound of a struggle and the smash of a bottle.

Wondering why no one had rescued the girl, why Monsieur Collet stood motionless, his face horrified and pale, Sam barged his way forward and there, before him, saw the answer. Bright had his back to the wall. One hand held Mariele's hair, pressing down on top of her head. She knelt on the floor her fingers clasping her scalp, her face displaying a purpling welt and her nose bleeding. In the other hand the sergeant clasped a broken bottle by its neck and waved it menacingly at the girl's face whenever anyone took a step towards him. On the floor, with a comrade hurriedly dabbing at his head, a private crouched, blood oozing from a nasty gash in his forehead. At the other side of the room someone unlocked the door and scurried out into the night.

The inhabitants of the café collectively held their breath. Every man's eyes flicking with morbid fascination from the scene before them to each other. Everyone desperate to help but not daring to step forward for fear the glass would sweep into the girl's terrified face. Tears rolled down her battered cheeks and her eyes locked momentarily with Sam's. He took half a pace toward Mariele and her tormentor. Bright saw him and with an insane sneer flashed the bottle. A hand clasped Sam's arm to stay him. It was Snowy.

"Sergent, s'il vous plait. Ma fille," Monsieur Collet pleaded, but the brutish drunk roared at him to shut up.

"Jake, put the bottle down man. Let 'er go. For God's sake man they'll crucify yer," another man tried to reason. Two men either side edged closer.

"Don't even fuckin' think about it," Bright warned menacingly and yanked the girl's head back. She screamed and closed her eyes in pain and fear.

Something inside of Sam snapped. Some long restrained emotion held in check by years of discipline. His stomach knotted and his chest tightened with deep, choking hate. It was a base, primal instinct he had not experienced since adolescence. Since he had learned, through systematic punishment, to quell it. His long buried and fiery temper rose inside his breast like some demonic beast, his heart pumping, his skin crawling as the hairs upon it stood on end. But this was no red mist. That would come later. This was cold, calculated loathing so deep that he could feel his body shaking, yet his head stayed clear. He knew what he was going to do. He knew that it could cost him dear. He did not care. Snowy's hand touched his shoulder, he shrugged it off.

"Eppy don't," Snowy whispered. His words went unheeded. Sam watched Bright like a hawk, waiting for his moment, the antipathy within swelling with every passing second.

"Sergent, I beg you," Monsieur Collet cried desperately in strongly accented English. It briefly caught Bright's attention, but it was enough. Without hesitation Sam launched himself at the big sergeant and grabbed the arm wielding the bottle. Bright bawled angrily and as his massive, puce face turned towards his assailant, a head butted him hard on the nose, followed by a swift and crunching knee to the groin. The victim groaned with pain, blood gushed from his broken nose and letting go of Mariele's hair he sank to his knees.

That should have been enough. Someone gathered the girl to safety. Passing her, trembling and sobbing, into the arms of her father. It should have been over. Bright overwhelmed and held fast until the military police or an officer arrived. But the beast had been unleashed and years of repressed anger and frustration let loose. Before anyone could react, Sam launched into Bright with the frenzy of a mad man. Now the calculation had given way to the mist. Now discipline cracked and sadistic, thuggish pleasure took over. The attack was remorseless, vicious even, and no one stopped him. The men watched with ghoulish fascination. Many had longed to see a day such as this. Many had suffered the malicious bullying of Jake Bright, both physical and psychological. No one in D Company particularly felt compelled to show mercy toward someone who had tormented them throughout their careers. This was a moment of justice and they were enjoying it. Especially so as judge, jury and executioner was Sergeant Hepworth, probably the most mild mannered and self controlled man in the Company.

He was not self controlled now. Red in the face, breathing hard, Sam threw blow after savage blow with shocking ferocity upon the now helpless and bleeding man at his feet. The more blood he saw, the more he enjoyed it. He did not want to stop although by now his lungs burned with anaerobic exertion. He wanted to pummel Bright into oblivion. He wanted him dead.

"For fuck's sake someone stop him! He'll kill the fella," the Irish voice of Donal Fallon shouted above the cheering soldiers all encouraging Sam to cause more damage.

"Good," someone sneered back.

Snowy snapped from his trance-like fascination and turned to the medical corps corporal who had begged that sanity be restored. Suddenly the seriousness of the situation dawned on him. Eppy was not going to stop. He would carry on until he killed Bright or he collapsed himself, from exhaustion.

"Christ! They'll 'ang him," he muttered and exchanged a glance with Fallon as he finally realised his best friend was about to commit murder. An unspoken understanding passed between the two men and together they rushed forward and dragged Sam to the wall slamming him hard against the cool plaster. A series of disappointed jeers and catcalls assailed their ears. Their prisoner struggled with the strength of a wild animal. They had difficulty holding him, until swearing profusely, Snowy took hold of his raving comrade's hair and shoved his head roughly against the wall. Instantly Sam saw stars, pain shot through his skull and made him feel sick. He slumped, the insane ire dissipating with the force of the blow.

"Ouch! I bet that hurt," Fallon laughed.

Snowy grinned sheepishly. "Thanks pal. I've got 'im now if tha wants to see to 'im," he said with a nod towards the groaning, huddled form at their feet. Hepworth had stopped struggling and both men relaxed their grip. Fallon indicated to one of his colleagues and between them they examined Bright. Sam coughed, breathing hard and looked at his bloody hands. His knuckles were split and now that the adrenalin had subsided they, along with his head, hurt like hell.

"You fuckin' idiot," Snowy spat angrily. "What the 'ell got into thi?"

His comrade merely shrugged. Too exhausted to answer.

"Come on. Let's get thi outta 'ere befower t'bloody Jacks arrive," Snowy muttered.

Too late. The front door banged open, two red capped police entered, followed by two armed infantrymen, the CSM and God.

"No one move. What the *hell* is going on 'ere?" a distinctive and resonant voice demanded.

"Shit it's the RSM," Snowy hissed and slumped visibly. There was no escape for Eppy now.

The room instantly fell into respectful silence, the sea of khaki parting with men standing rigidly as the senior warrant officer moved through them, back ramrod straight, cane under one arm. Behind him followed the military police men and Company Sergeant Major Beale. Snowy glanced pityingly at his friend. God and his right hand man. "Fuckin' idiot, tha's forrit now," he muttered and let go of Sam who slid to the floor with a mixture of weariness and wretched resignation. With his head on his knees he breathed deeply and wondered what had got into him. He fought the urge to laugh hysterically.

Regimental Sergeant Major John Tebbit cast an apprising eye around the now orderly room. He noted, with practiced insight, the many guilt ridden faces, it showed in the way they averted their gaze from both him and the two bloody sergeants by the back wall. He noted also, the proprietor attending to his daughter by the bar. A pretty, dark haired girl, he thought pleasing to the eye. Now that bonny face was bruised and battered, her right eye swollen and nose bleeding. With growing anger he noted also the now sitting form of Jake Bright, a dressing clutched to his mouth and nose and wincing in pain as a medical orderly felt at his torso. And finally, Tebbit's glowering eye fell upon Sergeant Samuel Hepworth, a man he had thought of steady temperament, intelligent, promising, and his heart sank with disappointment. He was not alone. Fred Beale caught Snowy's eye and shook his head forlornly, his lips pressed into a thin line.

"Get these two men locked up," Tebbit growled at the police behind him.

"Sir, this man needs attention before he's moved," Fallon interjected while still examining the extent of Bright's injuries.

"Can he stand?" Tebbit demanded.

"With assistance Sir, but...," Fallon faltered under the unflinching and unsympathetic gaze of God.

"Then he's fit enough to be moved. You can finish seein' to 'im when 'e's locked up. Get 'im out of 'ere," Tebbit growled. "And you lad," he pointed his cane at Hepworth. "On your feet. NOW!"

Sam struggled to his feet and staggered dizzily as his head protested at the movement. Snowy instinctively put out a hand to steady him.

"Don't you dare Sergeant White. 'E's not 'urt. 'E can walk out of 'ere and if 'e can't, 'e can crawl," the RSM snarled.

Sam shuffled towards the two waiting police guards. He cast a sideways glance towards Mariele and caught the nod of thanks from her father answering it with a half smile.

"You can wipe that smirk off your face son. It's a Court Martial for you. You're a fuckin' disgrace to the Regiment," Tebbit warned in a low voice, then louder, "Get 'im out of my sight!" to the guards. They escorted him, one either side and as he passed he could not look at Fred Beale though the CSM's words cut deeper than any blow.

"You're a bloody fool Eppy. They'll throw the bleedin' book at you fo' this. I thought I taught y' better than that."

CHAPTER 19.
February 26th, London

Frank sat nervously twisting his cap as he waited his turn amongst the dock workers of London's East End. It was another gamble. His fourth attempt to join up. The first two had failed out of hand when at the beginning of February he had tried to enlist initially in the London Rifle Brigade and then the East Surreys. Both recruiting sergeants had been willing, their job not to notice the shortcomings of eager volunteers. But each were accompanied by a doctor and before any man signed anything they looked at teeth, feet and importantly, listened to chests. Frank's chances were scuppered from that moment on. The doctors were simply too keen to ensure the Army received only able bodied men. He had been sent on his way.

Vowing not to give up and much against Evie's wishes, he tried again a week later. This time he got a little further. He looked physically fit. A little pale maybe and thin, but no different from many of the poorer Londoners queuing hopefully at the numerous recruiting offices, makeshift and official. Frank had learned his lesson. Do not try and enlist at the regimental barracks or official office. There was always a doctor on hand there. Try one of the temporary centres, in a church hall or a community centre. Somewhere with only a sergeant and an officer to swear one in. Get in and one only had to pass the medical later and surely once enlisted there was a higher likelihood of a blind eye being turned. Again he had failed. His stumbling block, once more, the physical examination the following day. In a black mood he had walked home and consoled himself with music. Playing his violin with frenzied fervour. Not resting to eat or drink until he practically collapsed with exhaustion only to be discovered, fevered and shaking by Evie.

Oh how she had chastised him. Stupid, idiotic boy! How could he even contemplate joining the Army when he had neither the strength or the stamina. Vain folly!

If he had been able, Frank would have stormed from the flat, banging the door in a fit of rage worthy of his brother. If he could, he would have done what Sam so often did after an argument with their father. He would have gone for a long, strenuous walk, ten miles at least and finished it with a visit to a pub, where he would have had several beers. But Frank could barely stand without feeling faint. His damaged heart laboured heroically in his chest and he cursed his bad fortune.

Over the next few days he had mulled over his options. Maybe he should try for a non-combatant role. The RAMC like Joe? They needed orderlies as well as doctors. As long as he got into khaki. He had little knowledge of what the Army required, other than men to fight. A conversation with a fellow musician one evening led him to believe that his chances of enlistment would be greater in the poorer parts of town. The East End, for example. Word was that the medical examination over there was carried out by a lax doctor who seemed only too eager to send the sick to their fates in France and Flanders.

So here he sat. He had reached the dreaded medical and it did not look promising. So much for the lax doctor. In this dimly lit warehouse there were three doctors doing their bit to ensure the Army received only fit, young men, each ensconced behind a meagre curtain on wheels. They were furnished with victims by an RAMC corporal from his desk piled high with official looking forms.

Frank sighed. His optimism failing. Around him, a dozen or so well built and powerful dockers, with hands like shovels and arms bigger than his skinny legs. He stared at the attestation paper in his hand. Middlesex Regiment. If he could only get past the doctor. He wondered whether they could be bribed. He sat back and watched the motes of dust floating in a shaft of sunlight filtering through a high window and he waited.

"Hepworth, Francis Michael," the corporal shouted making Frank jump.

With growing trepidation he got to his feet and walked over to the desk.

The corporal looked him up and down, his face emotionless and stern. He thrust a hand forward, "Papers," he demanded.

Frank handed over his forms and watched the official read through them with frowning concentration. He made a note of Middlesex Regiment in his ledger and thrust the papers back. "Number three," he instructed and pointed to the partition furthest down the massive room.

The hopeful recruit hurriedly approached and then peered around a wheeled curtain; a paltry concession to preserving modesty. Behind it a table, neatly stacked with official documents, a stamp and an assortment of medical implements such as one would see in a doctor's surgery. A set of scales sat on the concrete floor beside the table and next to this a rule for measuring height. The only other object, a long, angled lamp, at this present moment switched off. A white coated doctor, middle aged with greying dark hair and clean shaven, stooped over the table busily writing notes. Around his neck the dreaded stethoscope. He did not appear to be wearing any kind of uniform beneath his doctor's garb and indeed his oxford brogues belied him as a civilian. Thankfully not an Army medic. Hopefully then he would be less rigorous in his examination.

Frank hovered by the curtain unnoticed and after a moment or two coughed to announce his presence. The doctor did not look up but merely stuck a hand backwards and demanded, "Papers." His next patient obliged.

"Remove your clothes," the medic instructed as he read the documents in his hand.

"All of them?" Frank asked.

The doctor sighed. Another shy wallflower. He turned around to eye a slightly built young man with wayward brown hair and striking hazel eyes. A sensitive face, almost girlish. He sighed again. "You may keep your drawers on," he said and returned his attention to the papers.

Nervously, Frank began undressing, taking his time, not wanting to rush himself and agitate his heart. *What am I doing here? This is never going to work.*

"Hepworth, Francis Michael," the doctor stated.

"Sorry?"

"Is that your name?"

"Yes. I prefer Frank."

The medic ignored the comment. "Age twenty four and seven months?"

"Yes."

Musician? Interesting. In work?" A change of tone. A softening and mildly interested.

"Yes."

"What type of music?"

"Er.., classical mainly. I play with the London Symphony," Frank explained as he removed his shirt and folded it neatly on top of his trousers.

"Really? I was at a concert on Sunday evening. You must have been there. Well, well. What do you play?" The cold punctiliousness of before had been replaced by friendly intrigue. Obviously the doctor was a music buff. A good sign perhaps?

"Violin. I play piano as well, but it's not my specialism."

The doctor smiled and Frank shivered as he stood barefooted on the cold, warehouse floor, dressed only in his underwear.

"I'll need the vest off. Sorry; it's damned cold in here I know," the medic pointed out sympathetically. "I need to confirm a few details, ask a few questions, alright?"

Frank nodded and wondered why could he have not kept his clothes on a little longer, he was frozen stiff.

"They've got you down for Middlesex Regiment, that right?"

"Yes."

The doctor nodded. "And you've stated that you're willing to be vaccinated."

"Yes."

"Excellent. Any illnesses? Chronic respiratory disorders, anything like that?"

A pause. Only momentary, but noticeable. "No."

The doctor hesitated, eyed the young man before him with mild suspicion and then carried on. "Childhood illnesses then. Please confirm which, to your knowledge, you have had. Measles?"

"Yes."

"Chicken Pox?"

"Yes."

"Mumps?"

"Hmm. I don't know, maybe."

"Whooping cough?"

"I think so, yes."

"Any others? Scarlet fever, Diphtheria?"

"No."

"Good. Please stand under the rule. I need to get your exact height."

Frank moved to the measuring yard and the doctor, a much taller man than he, stooped to read the result.

"Five feet nine and one quarter inches," he muttered scribbling the height onto a form. "Scales. Let's see. Nine stone and...two pounds. A little on the light side young man," he chastised affably. "Feet. Let's have a look. No fallen arches, not flat footed? No, excellent."

Another positive. Frank felt his optimism growing.

"Any trouble with your teeth?" the doctor asked.

"No."

"Well, the dentist will have a proper look and confirm. I don't do teeth. Eyesight. Wear spectacles?"

"No."

"See the chart over there on the wall? Please read the second from bottom line to me."

"C,E,Z,M,O,U."

"Excellent. Right let's have a listen to your chest."

The stethoscope was wielded and Frank's optimism plummeted. He might be alright. He felt relatively calm, had done nothing strenuous, but as the doctor moved behind him his heart fluttered nervously. The instrument was placed upon his back.

"Big breath in – and out again." The stethoscope moved to the other side. "Once more. Breathe in – and out. Good, lungs are clear." The medic moved around to face his patient. "Just listen to your heart."

A wave of apprehension and Frank fought to remain relaxed, tried to think of anything that would keep his heart from beating a frenetic pace and giving the game away. *Could they tell anyway? Did it sound different even when at resting pace?* For a long time the doctor listened. Too long. The wordless vacuum yawned into deafening silence as Frank's anxiety mounted. He could hear his own pulse, thready and unsteady in his ears. Other sounds, mute before, grew inordinately loud. The curt instructions barked at other recruits, the click of segged shoes on the hard floor, a door banging shut. After an eternity of exactly one minute, the medic straightened, sighed and shook his head.

"You know I can't pass you fit don't you?" he said and watched the expected disappointment cloud the young man's face.

"Can't you ignore it? I pass everything else. I have to join up. You *must* understand," Frank pleaded with no heed to pride. He was desperate.

The doctor shook his head. "I'm sorry. I can't do it. It wouldn't be fair to you and it would be a waste of the Army's time to try and train you. Go back to your music. Forget the war," he turned to write on the forms. Frank grabbed his arm urgently.

"No! *Please*. Pass me fit for home duties. I don't know. Desk work. The Army must need clerks. What about drivers? I can drive," Frank lied despairingly knowing full well he had never sat behind the wheel of an automobile. Had only ever been a passenger.

"Look son, I can't do it and I won't. Your patriotism is admirable but you'd never make it through basic training and even with a desk job or as a driver, you still need to learn how to march and the rest. How far can you walk without becoming breathless? Honestly?"

"But I *must* do something. You don't understand. My brothers and my sister are all out there. My sister is a nurse in Boulogne. I can't do nothing. Look, look at these..." Frank stooped to his pile of clothes and fished a tobacco tin from his jacket pocket. Opening it he shoved it under the medic's nose. The doctor looked down and saw the little white feathers stuffed within. There must have been half a dozen of them. He felt the anger grow within and inwardly cursed the cruel intention of these otherwise innocuous items. He understood the young musician's desperation, shared it himself to some degree. At forty six he had been turned down by the Army as too old. But at least he could serve in other ways and it might change if things became bad enough. For this young man, there was no hope.

"Please Mr Hepworth, put your clothes back on," he uttered softly.

Frank's eyes smarted with disappointment. His arm dropped to his side and he visibly slumped and morosely began to dress. He was doomed to a war of inactivity, to be branded a coward by every girl or soldier he met and he despised himself for it.

The doctor stamped the papers as unfit for service and scribbled his reasons why. He cast a quick glance at the despondent musician. The lad was barely in control of his emotions, looked as if he would break down and cry. He hurriedly wrote an address on a slip of paper and when Frank was ready, the doctor handed back the Army forms.

"Give these to the corporal outside. Take my advice son, don't try any more. No one will pass you fit and even if you did find someone unscrupulous enough to do so, you'd not last five minutes in training. It's hard. Too hard for someone with a weak heart. It could even be the death of you. Do you understand?"

Frank nodded miserably. He stared at the UNFIT stamp on his papers and dare not look at the doctor.

"There are other ways you can serve your country. If you really want to do something think about using the talents you have."

Franks snorted derisively. What use were his talents? The medic was like all the rest. He did not understand. Had no idea what it was like to have to listen to the cruel jibes, to suffer the accusing stares and pointing fingers. Even when performing he saw, or was it only imagined, the recriminating glare of the audience? He pulled his cap onto his head and forced himself to face the practitioner.

The doctor smiled. "Here," he said holding out the slip of paper. "If you're interested there are things you can do. The lady at that address is a good friend of mine. Her name is Mrs Davidson. She works for the Red Cross. She has started a project to put together a group of musicians, singers and comedians to entertain our wounded soldiers. It's only a small affair at the moment, but she organises evenings, sometimes in hospitals, sometimes in church halls. I've been told the soldiers love it. Keeps their spirits up. Gives them something to look forward to. You get to wear a Red Cross uniform. I'm sure she'll welcome you. Give it a go eh? Tell her Brian Baxter sent you and highly recommends your services."

Frank took the slip of paper and stared at it. He did not know what to say. His anger at his rejection a few minutes ago melted and once more emotion threatened to overwhelm him. He looked up, his eyes bright and his face flushed. "Thank you," he mumbled.

"My pleasure. Good luck," Baxter offered his hand.

Frank shook it with a bashful grin and carefully folding the slip into his breast pocket, walked from the warehouse dropping his failed papers on the corporal's desk on his way out. But instead of a demoralised gait, the doctor saw a young man with hope and just a little pride in his step and he smiled to himself thinking that was his good deed for the day done.

CHAPTER 20.
February 27th, Fleurbaix

Summary justice had become the norm by late winter in 1915. Had become so as a matter of necessity. It was not practical to remove able bodied men from the theatre of war in order to carry out a lengthy Court Martial, whether they were the accused or more importantly, one of the witnesses called forward. The need to try and convict men swiftly so that the majority could return to their units and serve their punishment in the field often made far more sense than locking a man, capable of fighting, away for a lengthy custodial sentence. There were many exceptions of course, but it made more sense that felons remain to face the enemy, rather than be removed to the safety of prison. For this at least, Sam Hepworth was grateful. For the fact that his Court Martial was presided over by two officers from his own Battalion, one of whom was his company commander, Major Wilson, filled him with hope that he would receive a fair hearing. Captain Smith-Bridges of A Company was, he thought, a reasonable chap although he had had little dealings with him. The staff officer, a distinguished looking major by the name of Richards, he did not know. Some brass-hat from Brigade.

The greatest source of hope, however, came from the numerous witnesses called, all of whom gave the same story. Almost as if it had been rehearsed between them they spoke of extreme provocation, of Bright's vicious violence against the young French woman and how Sergeant Hepworth had acted out of compassion to prevent further injury to, or possibly even murder of, a helpless and innocent civilian. The fact that this was purely conjecture, that the witnesses could not know with any certainty that Sergeant Bright would have actually used his broken bottle on the girl, was irrelevant. There were no lawyers to pick up on such a detail.

A number of his fellow NCOs and three officers, including Fielding, gave testimony to Sam's good character, his undoubted worth to the Battalion as a more than competent non-commissioned officer. The court even had a statement from the girl's father pleading for leniency.

Yet despite all this, Sam knew he was in serious trouble. They had read out the charges and detailed the injuries he had inflicted upon a fellow NCO. It was a damning list. A broken nose, two broken ribs, multiple contusions, a fractured cheek bone, two lost teeth and a black eye. By rights he should be gaoled. In the pre-war world a substantial custodial sentence would have been a certainty along with demotion to the ranks.

The Court Martial had already found Jake Bright guilty of maliciously maiming a soldier in the King's Army, of bringing the Army into disrepute, of drunkenness and most damning of all, of assaulting a female civilian. Sam did not know it, but Bright's sentence had been severe.

"Thank you Lieutenant Fielding, for your testimony. You may step down," Major Richards said as he scribbled more notes onto a pad of official paper before him.

Fielding saluted and turned from the three officers at the table. He marched from the room casting a quick glance at the solemn faced sergeant standing between two armed military police. He smiled encouragingly but Sam's gaze did not falter from the wall behind the presiding court members. He remained, as he had stood for the past two hours, at ease, but unerringly rigid.

The three judges conferred briefly before the Staff officer spoke. "Sergeant Hepworth."

"Sir," the accused snapped to attention glad to move his legs at last, though they apparently did not reciprocate the feeling.

"Have you anything you would like to say in your defence?"

"Only that I regret the severity of my actions, Sir. My intention had been only to prevent Sergeant Bright from doing more harm to the young lady or anyone else, Sir. Unfortunately I lost control."

"Lost control? Yes, you certainly did Sergeant. Can you shed any light upon this loss of control? It would appear, from what we have heard today, that it is somewhat out of character," Richards demanded with sarcasm.

"No Sir, I cannot. I am truly sorry, Sir," Sam replied.

"You should save your apologies for those you have let down Sergeant. Thank you. You will leave the room now."

Sam saluted and turned smartly his guard following suit and they marched him from the makeshift court and into a pantry that served as his cell. He sat on the floor with his head pressed back against the cool, whitewashed wall and cursed his resurgent volatile temper and Jake Bright for rousing it.

Inside the once comfortable French salon the presiding officers held conference.

"Popular fellow. Even his previous platoon commander felt the need to speak for him. He's one of your men Wilson, what are your thoughts?" Richards questioned.

"I don't want to lose him. He's one of the best NCOs I've got. Bright's a bully and a thug. Always has been, but he's a clever blighter. No one's ever managed to catch him in the act. I'm surprised something like this has never happened before; the men taking matters into their own hands. I'm even more surprised, however, that it was Hepworth who finally cracked. It's a disappointment and quite out of character," Wilson replied with regret.

"Yet you have said yourself that you have needed to punish him in the past for fighting and insubordination," the Staff officer challenged.

"Yes, but a long time ago. Hepworth was a hot headed youth. He needed a firm hand, but he's no fool and now, I would say he is an outstanding soldier," Wilson countered.

"Captain, your views?" Richards turned to the man on his right.

Smith-Bridges shifted in his seat and stared at the pencil in his hands. For a few moments he contemplated his response. "I don't know the man as well as Major Wilson, Sir and I cannot speak from personal experience of his character. That said, he did have a hell of a lot of support today and RSM Tebbit told me there were many more willing to speak on his behalf.

"I believe there may be some justification for leniency in this case. Firstly, because we could really use a man like this for the next offensive. We don't want to lose another experienced NCO. I agree that Bright was a liability and had to be removed for the good of his Company if nothing else. However, this man is different. My second reason for advocating a less severe punishment is because of his popularity. The men see him as a bit of a champion. In their eyes he meted out justice upon someone they despised. I think if we are too harsh, we will make a martyr of him."

"Interesting argument Captain," Richards stated with raised eyebrows and a half smile. "I quite agree that with plans for a fresh offensive well underway we cannot afford to lose experienced men. Unfortunately, thanks to Sergeant Hepworth we *have* lost Bright."

"With respect Sir. I would argue that Bright is responsible for his own actions. Had Hepworth not assaulted him, his Court Martial for attacking both the girl and Private Danes was still inevitable," Wilson threw in realising that he was beginning to sound as partisan as his men had done.

The staff officer grunted with reluctant agreement. "Yet we cannot let him go unpunished. We cannot have NCOs brawling in front of the men and beating the living daylights out of each other. They are responsible for maintaining discipline not inciting a riot," he asserted and looked to both his fellow officers for agreement. They nodded with little enthusiasm.

"Well, his record hitherto is quite exemplary. He was wounded at Ypres I see," he carried on noting the lacklustre support.

"Yes, quite badly. But he seems to have recovered well enough. Look, he's the best damned shot in the Battalion, he's popular and respected by the men and he's bloody good at his job. I don't want to lose him Richards," Wilson threw in his hand. He knew he had already blown any pretence of impartiality; he might as well come clean.

Major Richards considered his colleague for some time. As Staff Officer he had seniority and his was the final decision, yet in all his experience of Courts Martial he had never come across a case quite like this one. Martial law would recommend the same punishment for Hepworth as Bright, but Richards was a fair minded man. He had been impressed by the support, even amongst the officers, of the accused. His instincts told him that both Wilson and Smith-Bridges were correct in their own summations. He scribbled his decision upon the form before him and showed it to the two men either side. They read it and agreed. It was a fair punishment.

"Very well. Let's bring him back. Captain, if you please?" Richards requested and Smith-Bridges went to the door and shouted for the accused to be brought back.

The swiftness of the judgement caught Sam by surprise though he did not really know what he should expect. With mounting dread he marched, between his guards, back into the room with his mouth dry and heart pounding anxiously in his chest. He saluted and stood rigidly at attention, eyes forward.

"Sergeant Hepworth, all I can say is this is a sorry state of affairs. You have not only let yourself down, but your Company and most of all the good name of your Regiment. For a man with your background and character it is a severe disappointment. Military law indicates that I should give you a custodial sentence and reduce you to the rank of private," Richards paused for effect. Sam swallowed fearing the worst.

"However, there has been an overwhelming amount of testimony given, both regarding the events that culminated in this whole unfortunate business and to your character. Not least amongst this is a letter from Monsieur Collet in which he has begged for leniency on your behalf due to, in his opinion, your saving his daughter's life. Quite melodramatic as the French have a tendency to be.

"We will, of course, never know if Sergeant Bright would have grievously injured, or indeed murdered the girl, but conjecture and opinion run to that he would.

For this reason alone I have concluded that in some respects your actions were done with the best intentions. However, it did not give you licence to beat the man senseless.

"In coming to our decision the Court has taken these testimonies into account and we all three agree that your sentence is a just one all circumstances considered. You will remain with your unit. You will not go to prison. Nevertheless we must mete out a punishment that sets an example. A senior NCO or anyone else in this Army cannot take the law into his own hands. Discipline is what makes us strong Sergeant and you have shown a great lapse in that discipline," Richards paused again and watched the young man before him. He noted no emotion, no betrayal of relief or fear. The man was completely master of his anxieties, for the major had no doubt that Hepworth must be anxious. He could have lost everything.

"Your rank will be demoted to private effective immediately and you will forfeit two months wages. Do you understand this sentence?" Richards concluded.

"Yes Sir," Sam replied stiffly. His body flooded with relief, yet his face remained impassive. Shortly the loss of rank would hit him hard, but for now he was glad to get off so lightly.

"I hope this is an episode that will never be repeated Hepworth," Richards warned. "Major Wilson?" He offered the final words to his colleague.

"Return to your billet Hepworth and pack your things. Report to RSM Tebbit at six o'clock this evening. I need an hour or two to decide what to do with you, but you should count yourself very lucky Private. You may go." Wilson dismissed.

The title slapped Sam hard in the face. Private. There it was; the realisation of what he had thrown away. Not an unfair decision by any means. In fact a very lenient one, but it pained him greatly. He had been proud to make sergeant, especially at only twenty-six. Now his own stupidity had cost him dear. He fleetingly thought of his father's reaction. All he had ever wanted, in his own way, was to make Thomas Hepworth proud of him, to show he could achieve something on his own, by his own hand. There was no pride in a Court Martial and only shame in being demoted. He thanked the officers formally, saluted and marched from the room a free man but one very much demeaned.

CHAPTER 21.
March 3rd, Boulogne

"Hurry up Glad! We've only got four hours," Lily called from her shared room to the bathroom down the hall. Impatient to get out, she was already dressed suitably for the cold with a warm coat over her walking out uniform. She held her hat in her hands, turning it around and around with increasing restlessness. Gladys always spent too long putting up her hair. It was a habit that had caused her to be late on duty more than once, but still she laboriously went through the process of pinning and gripping even the most wayward strands. Lily, on the other hand, found a plait the easiest way of taming her auburn mane and then coiling it into a semi tidy bun, which could be pinned quickly. Under a ward scarf it worked very well, the white, veil-like headdress hiding a multitude of escaped tresses. It was not so tidy when not hidden, but the hat always did the trick and one was not expected to take it off. Quite why Gladys had to be so punctilious Lily could never quite fathom. It was an irritation, albeit a minor one.

The door to the bathroom opened and the fair headed Gladys hurried up the hall, pushing in a final pin.

"At last!" Lily gasped.

"I haven't been so long Lil," the other nurse returned begrudgingly. Her friend's impatience always annoyed her.

"Come on Forbes. If we're lucky we'll get a table by the window." Lily hastily fastened her grey hat with its bright red ribbon to her hair, disturbing a side wisp as she did so. With a tut of irritation she curled it around her ear and hurried down the stairs. Sighing, Forbes followed, heaving on her coat over her ample frame and carrying her hat in her teeth. Not that Forbes was fat, but simply a well built girl who struggled to obtain that desired sylph-like figure. Hepworth was always at a run. Probably why she remained so thin. She stepped out onto the street and groaned.

"Oh it's raining again!" she complained.

"It's always raining. Don't be such a baby. Here take my arm. You don't need to look in the window, the hat looks fine. *Come on*," Lily urged.

With another sigh Gladys linked arms with her energetic friend and together they whisked into the downpour, hurrying across the road and into the side street beyond. Keeping their heads down they dodged and jumped over puddles, huddled together, ignoring the odd shout from a friendly Tommy. It would be more than their life was worth to converse with a man in public. It was strictly forbidden. Lily wondered at this draconian regulation, that seemed ridiculous to a young woman who had grown up with three brothers and who found male company as pleasant, on the whole, as female. For your protection, Matron had explained.

They turned into a wide and busy street, waited for a lorry to pass; in the back smiling lads waved eagerly. The girls found it impossible to suppress a smile and giggled conspiratorially together, Gladys checking behind just in case someone was watching. They ran across the road, lifting skirts higher than Matron would deem seemly, but one did not want to get them drenched, and lighted on the pavement in front of a busy café.

"Oh, all the window seats are taken," Lily moaned and then shrugged and headed for the door. Her friend had not moved. "Come on Forbes, we're getting wet if you hadn't noticed."

Gladys joined her companion and grabbed her arm. "We can't go in," she breathed nervously her face flustered.

"What do you mean? Of course we can. Look there's room further back."

"No, no," Forbes made an odd little flap with her hands and hopped from one foot to the next as if on hot coals. She turned to face the street and whispered, "Captain Thewlis is in there."

Lily grinned wickedly. "He isn't, is he?" she pressed her nose against the glass pretending to look. Poor Forbes had one hell of a crush on the Canadian doctor.

"Don't! He'll see you then we'll have to go in," Gladys whined.

"Well, I'm going in anyway. I'm cold and wet and I'm hungry. I would like to have something decent to eat on my afternoon off." Lily depressed the handle and pushed the door, a waft of warm air rushed past them carrying with it cheerful conversation and appetising aromas of freshly baked bread and onion soup. Gladys groaned and followed her inside.

They stepped into a dimly lit room, a little shabbily decorated with red and white chequered tablecloths cheerily hiding the ancient tables beneath; the walls filled with a mismatch of paintings and photographs, some of seascapes, some of the town and others of distinguished looking French gentlemen. The place was small and cramped and apart from two tables it was full, mainly with local clientele excepting for three British officers and a group of what appeared to be journalists huddled in a corner. There were no other nurses that either woman could see and in many ways that was a relief. It was nice to be away from work. The officers were a different matter. Lily smiled to herself.

The proprietor hurried over to greet them.

"Mademoiselles, a table for two?" she asked.

"Yes," Lily replied and glanced across at the table where Captain Thewlis and two fellow officers sat drinking cognac and coffee. He noticed her watching and raised his glass. She smiled and waved.

"*Lily!*" Gladys hissed.

"Just being friendly."

"Ici is good, yes?" Madame offered a corner table.

"Oh, could we sit over there," Lily pointed to a table for two just behind the officers.

"Certainement," Madame acquiesced with a knowing smile and picking up two menus led the way.

"No, Hepworth! We can't!" Gladys protested vainly hiding behind her rather more confident friend.

"Why not? We're not doing anything wrong. Just having dinner at a table behind the best looking doctor in Boulogne. You *do* like him don't you?"

Forbes mumbled something that Lily did not catch and sulkily insisted on having the seat with its back to the men. Not quite what Hepworth had planned, but it might still work. They removed their coats and Gladys buried her head in her menu, which for ten seconds she held upside down, before self-consciously righting it and scowling as her companion giggled mockingly.

Madame wandered over and lifted an enquiring eyebrow. "Ready?"

"Yes. I'll have the seafood soup and the beef to follow with vegetables. You have vegetables?" Lily ordered.

"Mais oui. And you Mademoiselle?"

"Oh, I don't know, the same. Thank you."

"And to drink?"

"I think we will have a glass of white wine Madame," Lily requested and ignored the daggers look from her friend.

"Very good."

Madame drifted away again and Gladys leant over the table and whispered harshly. "We're not supposed to drink!"

"Oh don't be such a bore! It's one glass of wine. It won't hurt you."

"What if someone should see?"

"No one is going to see. Look, I can see the door from here; if anyone comes in we'll hide the wine under the table. Enjoy yourself; you are three feet away from your perfect dream."

Forbes glowered and sat back huffily with folded arms. She leant forward after a few seconds and hissed, "You're a wicked girl Hepworth. It's alright for you. You're engaged. You're safe."

Lily laughed out loud and the officers on the table behind them paused in their conversation momentarily. Thewlis smiled across at the ladies and then resumed his chatter with one eye observing the nurses while sipping his brandy. He adjusted his seat so that he could watch without being seen to be doing so.

"You're such a ninny Glad. This is a public place and those strange being's on that table are officers and gentlemen. I thought you'd want to sit near him. Breathe deep dear, you can smell his cologne." Lily teased.

"You're incorrigible Hepworth. I ought to walk out now!"

"What and miss a delightful dinner? I don't think so. Come on Glad. I'll behave now. I'm only teasing. Let's enjoy ourselves."

Soup arrived and the nurses settled down to eat and talk quietly between themselves, savouring the delicate flavour of the food and sipping the white wine with only a trace of guilt. By the time their meal was over, they had forgotten the men next to them who were still, for some reason, in the café. Perhaps hoping the rain would stop?

Lily finished her wine and sat back smiling, as she did so she was surprised to see Captain Thewlis on his feet in front of her and the other two officers half turned on their seats. "Oh, hello," she said for want of something else. Gladys looked startled and flushed violently red.

"Ladies," Thewlis drawled in a soft Canadian accent, his face holding its usual half amused expression. One never quite knew whether he was making fun or whether he was simply a jolly sort of chap. It was preferable to believe the latter. He bowed his head politely. "My friends and I were wondering if you would care to join us for coffee."

The nurses caught each other's eye. Forbes took on an expression of alarm and half shook her head.

"It's very kind of you to ask Captain, but you know it's against the rules and we would be in terrible bother if word got back to Matron," Lily answered and tried not to smirk as her companion sagged with relief.

Thewlis smiled. "Indeed. But we won't tell if you don't and as you can see, there is no one else here who could know us. I think we are safe. If you like we will simply pull our chairs around and push the tables just a little closer. That way we are still all seated separately should anyone happen upon us. We give you our word of honour that we will behave impeccably," he placed his hand across his heart.

Lily giggled. "I'm sure you will Sir. What do you think Glad?"

The expression of alarm returned. "I, er, I."

"Oh do say yes Miss Forbes," the lieutenant sat directly behind her urged in a voice that held only a trace of a tease, a slight lifting of tone to something nearing the feminine.

"Yeah, come on Glad old girl! Be a sport," Thewlis added picking up on the nickname.

Gladys folded and with a glowering glare at Lily nodded and shifted her seat around a little way so that she half faced the men. They rearranged their seats accordingly and the captain ordered coffees all round and cognac.

"Oh no, we mustn't." Forbes protested.

"But I insist. It'll help stave off the cold when you make the dash into this torrential downpour once more. It'll do you good, Glad," Thewlis pressed and resumed his seat now directly opposite Lily. He took a sip of his brandy. "We all know each other?"

"No I don't believe I've met the ladies before," the other officer chimed cheerily. He was a fresh faced young man, probably not long qualified. He looked barely older than twenty but must be at least twenty six or seven.

"Sorry, of course not. Freddy Dickenson, Staff Nurse Forbes and Staff Nurse Hepworth. Feddy's a lab rat. Not likely to step foot upon your turf ladies. Note the white skin and the blood shot eyes indicative of hours of staring down a microscope," Thewlis mocked.

Dickenson laughed and even Gladys smiled coyly.

"Aitken, you know of course."

The other lieutenant raised his glass and the nurses nodded in polite acknowledgement.

"Ah, excellent our coffee and cognac. Merci Madame. Et permettez-moi de régler le repas de dames," he finished in perfect French.

"Oh no, we can't let you do that," Lily protested understanding.

"Yes you can and you will. It's my birthday, thirty five today, and I feel generous. Indulge me," he smiled winningly and for the first time Lily felt uncomfortable. She dropped her gaze from those soft grey eyes that searched and held hers so boldly.

"A toast then," Aitken declared holding his brandy aloft. "To our generous host who by great misfortune today passes into middle-age."

"Oh no, not middle-age. Thirty five is quite young still," Gladys interrupted and blushed once more, her outburst shocking herself. Everyone laughed.

"Thank you Glad," Thewlis said with a failed attempt to appear hurt by the lieutenant's words.

Aitken sniggered. "To Alex," he toasted and in an undertone, "You old boy!"

"To Alex," Freddy echoed and the nurses a little less boisterously. They took a sip of cognac and Forbes pursed her lips at its biting heat.

"Gosh!" she exclaimed. "That's a little keen isn't it?" The men laughed, the ice was broken and Gladys smiled with growing confidence. "I've never had brandy before," she admitted and took another sip.

Lily glanced at Thewlis, caught him smiling at her and promptly looked away.

"You mean you've never taken a nip from the medicine cabinet Glad? We had a sister at Leeds, who used to do so frequently. One night she got quite drunk. Unfortunately Matron found out and Sister had to resign. It was quite a scandal," she dived into conversation. An escape from that odd feeling of discomfort.

"The old devil!" Freddy feigned horror. He commenced upon a story of his own and soon the group were laughing together like old friends at reminisces of indiscretions past. They avoided talk of war, of their work and even of their own lives. It was a time to enjoy only the present, a brief hour of respite from a dark and austere world. A glimmer of something better, although unreal. Old world barriers were forgotten, the rule against friendships between sexes ignored and Victorian principles scorned. It was a daring little gathering that would shock the high principles of Matron and no doubt the mothers of all involved, but it was a step into a future. A future, that war permitting, they would own and shape, not their parents or the old generation of puritanical warmongers who had put them here.

After an hour they were by far the liveliest table and Gladys had quite come out of her shell, surprising even Lily. Perhaps it was the alcohol. With some dismay, Lily realised that Staff Nurse Forbes was a little tipsy having finished her third cognac. She glanced outside, the rain still poured down and the sky threatened an early dusk.

"Would you like another?" Aitken asked noting the empty glass.

"Oh, I don't know. I feel quite giddy," Gladys giggled.

Time to go, thought Lily. "I really think we ought to be leaving now. It's growing dark already and we will be in hot water if we don't get back before the lights are lit," she offered by way of an excuse.

"But it's only just gone five. It won't be dark for another couple of hours yet," Freddy protested and Gladys nodded gazing at her companion with hopeful anticipation of staying a little longer.

"Perhaps on a bright day, but not with this rain. I'm sorry gentlemen, but you must understand that by dark, our superiors mean once the lights need to be turned on and that, is imminent," Lily insisted and stood, pulling on her coat. The men rose also and Forbes sulkily struggled to her feet, grasping the chair to steady herself. Freddy helped her with her coat.

"Must we go Lily?"

"Yes, I'm afraid we must. Thank you gentlemen for your company, it has been a most enjoyable afternoon," Lily held out a ten franc note to Captain Thewlis.

"You can put that away young lady. I said I wished to treat you both and treat you I shall," he clamped his hands behind his back and set his mouth stubbornly. She stared at him with annoyance for some seconds and then with a sigh relented and thanking him placed the money back into her purse.

"Come on Glad," she linked arms with Forbes and after another thank you and polite goodbyes, carefully steered the tipsy nurse out of the restaurant. On the street the rain lashed into their faces and the rush of oxygen sent Gladys into a dizzying spin.

"Oooo Lily. I do feel queer," she gasped clinging on tightly and swaying.

"You're drunk. Why didn't you say you don't drink? I should have listened to you to start with. It's all my fault."

"But we had such a lovely time. I really enjoyed myself, thank you," Gladys replied, smiling. She spoke with a little slur.

"Yes we did. But we had better hurry now, come on," Lily tugged at her arm and made to run across the street, but Forbes stumbled and almost fell.

"Oops," she giggled.

The door behind opened. "Need a hand?" Thewlis asked with genuine concern.

Lily almost refused thinking this was the worst thing that could happen, but realising that she could not manage Gladys on her own relented. "I'm sorry, but could you? I'm afraid she's a little tipsy."

"I am not!"

"Sure. Here Glad, take my arm and hold tight. Oops, there you are, I've got you," Thewlis chuckled as Forbes stumbled into him, he propped her upright, his arm supporting her.

"Sorry," she slurred.

"Hell! She didn't drink that much!" he stated with a questioning amused glance at Hepworth.

"It's not funny. She doesn't drink normally. It's gone straight to her head and this fresh air has only made it worse," Lily explained. "Please, we must get her back and I must get her to bed before anyone notices. There'll be hell to pay if we're caught."

"I'm sorry Lily, I wouldn't have bought her another if I'd known," Thewlis apologised sincerely. He pulled Forbes' arm around his shoulder and pushed his cap back straight where she had knocked it askew.

"It's alright. It's my fault really. I should have realised."

"Lead the way, ma'am. I've got her," he indicated with a grin.

Hurriedly they crossed the street and headed back to the guest house. Like a naughty child, Lily peered around the corner of a house to check that street was clear before they made their final dash through the rain. There was still a chance that someone might be watching from a window and it would be bad enough for Gladys to be caught intoxicated never mind in the arms of a British Army officer. She bit her lip.

"What's the matter?" Thewlis asked as he stopped behind her.

"I don't know how to get her into the house. Look at her, she's even worse now. I can't carry her and...." she indicated forlornly.

"Don't worry. I'll make something up." He suddenly picked Forbes bodily from the ground carrying her in his arms. She giggled and her head lolled onto his chest. "Lead the way."

Lily frowned, hesitated and then thought what the hell. She even admitted to be quite enjoying the adventure. It was the risk of being caught breaking the rules. It reminded her of childhood, of being with Sam. She ran across the street with the captain in close pursuit and hurriedly entered the small hotel holding the door for him to follow. No one was in sight.

"Where's her room?" he demanded.

"You can't go up there!" Lily reacted wide eyed.

"Hey, I'm a doctor, I have a sick lady in my arms," he grinned.

She returned the expression and led the way to the first floor.

"Hepworth! What on earth are you doing? Who is...excuse me Captain, but..." a flustered and indignant woman protested but she was cut off.

"Sister Peters. I fully understand your concern and ordinarily I would not dream of entering this establishment, but I'm afraid Miss Forbes has taken a turn. Luckily I was nearby and able to assist Nurse Hepworth to bring her home," Thewlis lied convincingly.

"A turn. Oh dear. She isn't ill is she?"

"I think it is just a chill Sister. She came over all faint and I could not possibly carry her back alone. Thankfully Captain Thewlis came to our rescue," Lily conspired.

Sister Peters considered them both for a moment, while the captain took the opportunity of indecision to place Gladys upon her bed. Quite conveniently the drunken nurse moaned.

"Oh dear, she sounds quite poorly, poor thing. I do hope it isn't influenza," Peters continued.

"No, no, I don't think so. Probably just exhausted poor girl. You ladies do work so hard. Let her sleep for a few hours and then wake her with a nice cup of strong coffee or tea. I'm sure she'll be right as rain in the morning," Thewlis instructed confidently. Lily had to rivet her eyes to the floor to stop herself from laughing. He closed the door and faced Sister Peters, whose gaze drifted away from the door and to him. She returned his smile and nodded.

"I'd better go. I don't want to get you ladies into trouble," he said causing the older woman to jump guiltily as she realised in these circumstances she appeared to be as culpable as anyone if someone should see them.

"Yes, quite. Hepworth, you had better see the doctor out," she bustled.

Lily nodded and led Thewlis back to the entrance. She opened the door and he passed her, hesitating on the threshold with a frowning glance at the sky.

"Thank you Captain," she said offering her hand.

He shook it affably. "Alex. Call me Alex. I'm happy to help."

She nodded. He reminded her of Sam. He had the same reckless quality that brought out the rebel in her. Not necessarily a good thing, she thought absently to herself, but one that felt completely comfortable. He did not move. "You're getting wet," she prompted.

"Yeah. Say, could we do this again?"

"What carry poor drunken Gladys back home and lie to Sister Peters?" she mocked.

He grinned. "No, you know. Have dinner or something."

"I'm engaged Alex," she replied firmly wondering why she felt disappointed.

"Oh! I see," he slumped, dropping his eyes to the floor. "We could still be friends. You can always bring Glad. I promise I won't get her drunk again." He faced her, his expression hopeful, his eyes shining warmly and the boyish smile charmingly crooked.

She felt her heart flutter. "I don't know. It wouldn't look... I'm not sure that Gladys would...," she stammered. He looked crestfallen but what could she do? She was engaged to Robert. It was against the rules to go to dinner with any member of the male sex without permission of Matron. It did happen of course, but at the perpetual risk of being seen and reported. How would she explain that to Robert? Yet she liked this man. She liked his easy going ways, his humour. She liked his warm, grey eyes and the way he continually seemed to laugh at the world, his lopsided grin and expressive mouth.

"I think we would both regret it," she uttered at last and glanced behind her at the sound of a door opening. "You'd better go."

She started to close the door and he touched her hand briefly. "Think about it," he urged and then hurried into the darkening evening. She shut out the rain and leant back against the door her head in turmoil. *Don't be a fool Hepworth. You're simply flattered by a handsome man's attention. Go upstairs and look after poor Gladys and forget charming Alex Thewlis.*

CHAPTER 22.
March 7th, Number Two ADS, 23rd Field Ambulance

The Advanced Dressing Station was quiet. The heavy enemy shelling of a few days ago, an onslaught that had brought many more wounded through the dingy cellar than Joe had thought possible, had ended as abruptly as it had started. During those days and nights the ADS had worked around the clock augmented by men and officers from neighbouring Ambulances whose fronts were not so heavily bombarded. It had been a period so intensely busy that Lieutenant Joseph Hepworth and his men had barely noticed the thundering explosions that crept so terrifyingly close. Compared to a few of weeks ago, Joe had become hardened and oddly oblivious to the dangerous situation he worked in. The time flew by like an express train, the flow of casualties steady, but unrelenting.

Afterwards, in the bitter chill of a weirdly peaceful dawn, the members of Number Two ADS had collapsed into exhausted sleep, too tired to reach their bunks, curling where they had stood, utterly drained. No one had eaten in over fifteen hours, all were hungry, but all were too spent to be bothered and they slept like the dead. Joe had sprawled onto a recently vacated trestle table, where only minutes before he and Private Stubbs had finished dressing a man with a shattered jaw. For six hours no one had disturbed their rest, though visitors had come and gone, finding nearly everyone stretched out in varying somnolent poses. Captain Foster had grinned at the scene and let them be. If the bombardment started again it would wake them. Anything else could wait. They had earned their rest and God knows they would need it for during the next push the sustained pressure of the last few days would seem like a picnic by comparison.

Now it was business as usual. The odd injured man, the inevitable sick. Each were treated with the monotony of routine and dispatched back to their units or down to the Main Dressing Station for convalescence or further treatment. Now only the occasional boom of artillery disturbed the peace up and down the line. It was sporadic and scarcely a British gun answered it.

Something was brewing. The batteries behind and in front of the ADS were uncannily quiet and the number of troops in the area swelling to almost plague proportions. Canadians had moved into Fleurbaix and Joe no longer knew the whereabouts of his brother's Battalion. Somewhere close by, but whether in the line or at billets, he had no idea. This bothered him. Fallon had told him there had been some trouble in Fleurbaix. That Sam had been arrested. Arrested! Joe could not believe it and any thoughts he might have had about discovering the truth had been cut short by the shelling. Now, he did not know where Sam was and consequently had little chance of finding any information pertaining to the alleged incident.

The RAMC lieutenant stretched and sat back on his rickety chair. It groaned under his weight and lurched alarmingly so that he hurriedly leant forwards again grabbing the table to stop himself falling. He cursed and vowed to replace the damned seat. He cast an eye around the cellar. It had suffered from lack of care over the hectic period. The pump had broken down twice and only when Stubbs noticed a growing number of puddles had they spared someone to fix the temperamental engine. At least it was working now and the place, though unhygienically damp, no longer filled with water.

Only four patients remained; the remnants of this morning's sick parade. All of them from the Wiltshire Regiment and suffering the ubiquitous low fever that Joe now associated with this God forsaken place. Fever, pains in their legs, at times it was quite debilitating. The cause of it? No one had any idea. It had appeared with the trench system and was obviously linked to the conditions in which the men were forced to live, but more than that was a mystery. Joe gave the unfortunate soldiers twenty four hours bed rest. Most of them were then recovered enough to return to their unit, some might require further rest. They always recovered only to relapse after five days or so. Ultimately many of them would have to be evacuated behind the lines for a spell in hospital, but they all got better, eventually. These four were not so bad and he hoped by the morning they could rejoin their Battalion.

He glanced at his watch. A quarter to eight. It would be dark outside and he contemplated going up to get some fresh air when he received an unexpected visitor. Footsteps alerted him to the arrival of two men. One was Private Stubbs, the night duty orderly, and the other an officer. Joe stood and peering through the dimly lit cellar recognised Fielding as Stubbs stood aside and pointed towards the medical officer.

"Lieutenant Fielding," Joe said warmly extending a hand. "An unexpected pleasure."

Fielding shook hands and smiled. "Harry. Please call me Harry. May I?" he indicated to a stool opposite the desk.

"Please. Is this a social call or business?" Hepworth asked wondering whether he should be worried. A knot of tension tightened in his stomach.

"A social call, yes, I suppose so. I was passing near-by. We're moving up to help dig reserve trenches. I thought I'd pop in to say hello. You don't mind? I'm not disturbing you?"

Joe relaxed and inwardly sighed with relief. "Not at all," he said cheerily. "Welcome to Number Two ADS. My universe at present. We are very quiet at the moment, as you can see." He swept a hand around the room.

Fielding glanced about and smiled grimly. "Don't get too used to it. There's a push in the offing. Don't know details yet, or exactly where, but we're not digging reserve trenches for the hell of it and there's enough men and guns being moved up to fill the Isle of Wight. Soon we won't be able to turn around without falling over one another. Have you noticed how quiet our artillery are? Saving ammunition for something big."

Joe had not really thought about it like that. In truth he had been too busy. Even so, once more he felt militarily disadvantaged. He knew and understood so little of this world. Sam had once written of Fielding being as green as grass, without an ounce of soldierly knowhow. But to Joe, the infantry lieutenant seemed every inch a veteran.

"I'm sorry Harry, would you care for a drink? I have some brandy or I could get Stubbs to make some tea if you prefer," he offered thinking he ought to play the host. The surroundings may not be civilised, but that did not prevent him from being so.

"A brandy would be splendid. Better be a small one though. Can't stay long anyway. Have to supervise my men," Fielding replied with a grin.

Joe grabbed a bottle from the shelf behind him and poured a generous measure into two tin mugs upon the desk sliding one across to his visitor who took an appreciative sip and sighed.

"Don't your NCOs supervise your men?" Hepworth queried nursing his mug. He knew the answer, but he wanted an opening to ask about Sam. He need not have bothered. This was the reason Harry Fielding was here.

"Of course they do and more efficiently than I can, but I would be a poor commander if I did not show my face from time to time," Harry took another sip of brandy and then placed the mug with careful deliberation onto the desk, twisting it around and staring at the reflected lamplight in its burnished contents.

"Did you know that Sam was back with me?" he asked a little awkwardly.

"No. I haven't heard from him since we met the other week. Corporal Fallon, my orderly NCO, told me he was in some trouble but I haven't been able to find out more. He was in a fight? Is this true?" Joe returned, glad he could talk openly. He watched Fielding's response closely.

"Yes it is true. I'm afraid he rather let himself down," Harry confirmed understatedly. "There were quite serious charges. Assault, effectively. If it hadn't been for certain mitigating circumstances he would be serving a prison sentence."

"*Prison?*" Joe repeated, shocked. He had not considered that the Army dealt with offences amongst its men in this way. Fielding sighed and explained. When he had finished the medical officer took a long swig of brandy, nearly emptying his mug.

"Of all the stupid...," he began angrily. "*Christ!* He was like this when we were kids. Fighting I mean, getting into scrapes of one kind or another. My mother used to despair and he and Father were forever at loggerheads. It was why we were all dumbfounded when he joined up. Discipline and Sam just did not fit together. We were amazed when he stuck it out. I thought he had finally learned to control his temper. It seems I was wrong." Joe sat back in his chair wearily. For some reason, probably instilled in him from childhood, with being the older brother, he felt responsible for Sam and his behaviour. It was a ridiculous notion. They were grown men who had gone their separate ways years before. But he could not help it. Always he had heaped the burdens of his siblings' woes upon his own shoulders. Often unasked for and always unnecessarily.

"No you weren't wrong. I know Sam fairly well by now. I've seen him working with the men. I've seen him fight in battle. A more self possessed and disciplined individual I have rarely met," Harry disclosed.

"Uh! Sounds like it," Joe spat back. Fielding glanced up at him, surprised by his anger.

"It *was* out of character. That's partly why he got off so lightly. Very lightly in fact. In truth, he really *should* be serving a custodial sentence. That's what the rule book says anyway. Still, I'm rather glad he isn't.

"I thought you ought to hear the full story from someone who could give you a balanced view. Sam is being hard on himself. Volunteering for any shitty work that comes our way. It's his way of making amends I suppose, but he *is* heaping the punishment upon himself."

"Well, so he bloody well should! Brawling in a bar and over a woman. God, I thought he had more sense than that," Joe's tone was unforgiving and he was too incensed to understand.

Fielding smiled. "I don't think it was as simple as that. Jake Bright is a nasty piece of work. I've often wondered why he hadn't been dealt with before. The Army has funny ways and traditions. I'm still learning many of them. If you saw the man you'd wonder how Sam could have come off the better. Bright's twice his size.

"Anyway, like I said, Sam's back with me. The CC thought it better to move him out of Three Platoon. I'm glad to have him. Despite this set back he's a good soldier and there's another thing. It could only happen in the Army. Our CO, Anderson, has reinstated him to corporal. Used the excuse that Sam has proved himself over the last few days. The reality is we need experienced NCOs as simple as that.

"Well, better go. They'll be missing me. Thanks for the brandy," Harry concluded and stood. Hepworth followed suit and they shook hands.

"Why did you feel you had to explain for him?" Joe asked.

"Well, he wouldn't would he? He's too proud. And I wouldn't want his family ashamed of him should anything happen. You know, the last thing you heard was he had been court martialled. What he did was wrong and he has been punished. But, it was also quite a noble thing in its own way. It's increased his popularity with the men you know. They respected him before, now they practically love him."

"Love him! Why?" Joe laughed incredulously, thinking the notion absurd.

"Because in their eyes it was Bright who was the villain and Sam stood up to and bested him. Then he was punished for what they see as meting out justice. He's a bit of a martyr. I'm not a violence loving man Joe and neither do I generally condone it, but I have to admit in this case I tend to agree with the men." Harry explained and tipped his cap with his cane. "Goodnight Doctor."

"Goodnight," Joe murmured back astounded. His anger had melted away and in its place, despite his reluctance to admit it, he could not deny the spark of pride the lieutenant's words had ignited in his breast.

CHAPTER 23.
March 9th, Number Two ADS, Farm Buildings outside Neuve Chapelle

"Fallon isn't it?" a quiet, northern accented voice asked from the dark causing the Irishman to stop unpacking the last crate and squint into the gloom. A shape stepped forward followed by another. They were carrying rolls of barbed wire, but did not seem too hurried to get forward. The voice sounded vaguely familiar and as the two men moved closer Donal recognised the nearest as Sam Hepworth.

"Aye, that's me Sarn't," he replied.

"Corporal now pal, was private up until two days ago," Sam corrected with a laugh and the barest hint of bitterness. "This is Dobson."

Fallon nodded a greeting but did not speak. He was wandering why the two men were here, near to the ADS, heading for the communication trench without the rest of their unit.

"Christ man, you lot were hard to find. We've been trudging around for hours. I've come up to see my brother. Is he around?" Sam carried on.

"Yeah, he's down in the barn. I t'ought you were on the way up," Donal returned indicating to the wire.

Sam grinned, "Bit of a ruse so I could get up here. We're going into the line later. I might not get a chance again. Could you tell him I'm here?"

"Of course, but why not go in. It's bloody cold tonight. I've just made the lieutenant some char, and there's enough left for two more," Fallon offered.

"I don't know. I don't want to get young Dobbo in bother," Sam hesitated uncharacteristically and looked to his companion.

"Aw come on Corp. I'd kill for a nice cuppa," Dobson protested.

"Alright. Lead the way," Sam turned back to Fallon. "Leave the wire out here Dobbo."

Donal instructed his men to finish unloading the supplies and then to get some rest before he escorted the visitors towards the remains of a farm that now consisted of a few crumbling walls behind which a series of tents had been erected and reinforced with a large sandbag edifice. Next to these stood a medium sized barn that looked more or less intact. A hand-full of vehicles, covered by muddy tarpaulins waited nearest the road, two of which were horse drawn, the animals tethered in the lee of a wall and munching lazily on a pile of hay. The three men threaded through the canvas village and pushed through into the building. The sound of men busily setting up the makeshift hospital faltered briefly and then continued, a low hum of conversation and instruction. The smell of paraffin lamps and candles hung heavy on the damp air. Directing the construction of trestle tables Joe stood with his back to the entrance.

"Someone to see you Sir," Fallon called and then turning to Dobson, "Come wit' me lad, I'll fix you up wit' a cuppa. Do you take sugar in yours?" he asked Sam.

"Good God, do you have any?" Hepworth questioned back gobsmacked.

"No, but I could stir some jam into it if you like it sweet."

Sam grimaced. "No thanks. Just as it comes," he said noticing Joe leaning back against his desk with a quizzical expression and arms folded. He muttered to Dobson that this would not take long and headed towards his brother. "Joe," he acknowledged awkwardly as he stopped before the medical officer half wondering whether he should salute or not.

"*Corporal*," Joe returned pointedly. Sam's heart sank. He opened his mouth to speak but his brother cut him off. "You really are a stupid arse, you know that don't you?"

Sam turned his head away fighting the rising anger and the disappointment that his sibling had reacted exactly as he had thought he would. "I don't really want to talk about it Joe if you don't mind," he said at length with quiet self control.

Joe was surprised, he had expected a reaction. He did not get one. He softened his attitude and indicated to a stool just as Fallon appeared with a mug of tea.

"There you are Sar..., er, Corp. No jam, no milk, just strong tea," the Irishman said.

"Thanks pal. Eppy, call me Eppy," the infantry corporal proffered with a grin. Donal nodded and catching his superior's eye discretely left the brothers alone.

"What are you doing here Sam?" Joe asked as his sibling took a testing sip, seemed to approve of the beverage and followed it up with a longer gulp.

"Not bad char that," Sam observed. "I wanted to see you. Might not get another chance. You took some finding I can tell you. I only had a sketchy idea where you'd moved to. Me and young Dobson were just about to give up when I saw Fallon there. Good bloke that."

"Look Joe, I've not come to explain myself or say I'm sorry. I've had my punishment and I don't need any holier than thou crap from my family. I've no doubt Father will have something to say if he can even bring himself to write, but that's not why I'm here. I don't really care what any of you think anyway." He launched into what was obviously a prepared speech and a lie at that, because he did care. He cared deeply what Joe and ultimately his father thought of his misdemeanour. "Anyway, this might be the last chance I get. We're going into the line in a few hours. We're at Laventie and I haven't been able to get to Fleurbaix since the fight. I wanted to ask you a favour," he finished hurriedly.

"A favour? Sam, what the hell are you doing? You're in enough trouble without sneaking off from your unit to see me. What do you think will happen if your platoon commander finds out you've gone?" Joe could not hide the exasperation in his voice. He could not believe that his brother was so stupid to risk getting himself into further dire straits.

"Nothing. Nothing will happen. This was Fielding's suggestion. We're bringing wire up to the Front. Volunteered for the job. Deliver it and then return before ten, they're my orders." Sam replied cockily with the cheeky sparkle in his eye that Joe remembered from childhood. He could not help but return the grin.

"Alright, what's this favour?"

Sam pulled a grubby envelope from his breast pocket and handed it across the table. Joe took it and examined the unmistakable scrawl of his brother's handwriting on its front. It was addressed to Mademoiselle Collet, Maison Rouge, Fleurbaix. The medical officer frowned. "What is it?" he asked.

"It's a letter. It's for Mariele and I haven't been able to deliver it to her. You're an officer. You can get out and about more easily. I thought you wouldn't mind if..., you know, if I don't come back," Sam explained a little sheepishly.

Joe looked up at him, studying the earnest face. There was no jollity, no sign of bravado or arrogance. Sam was deadly serious, too much so for comfort. It did not feel right.

"Do you really think you might not?" the medic asked. He had not given such an eventuality a thought before and now the question sounded ridiculously naïve. His brother had been seriously wounded at Ypres. Of course he was right to think that something might befall him again. Surely that was only being realistic. Joe's blood ran cold at the thought and the sudden realisation that within twenty four hours he might find himself fighting to save Sam's life in this draughty barn. He shuddered.

"It's a possibility isn't it? All I'm asking is that if the worst did happen, will you take this to her? It's a kind of last request," Sam laughed, though the laugh rang hollow.

"Yes I'll take it, but better still, I'll keep it safe so that you can take it yourself. Just make sure you keep your head down this time," Joe agreed and tried to lighten the conversation.

"I'm not going looking for trouble. Thanks Joe," the corporal stood and held out his hand.

"You're going already?"

"Yeah. Better had. Got to get the wire up the line and then get back and it's a good hike in the dark. Easy to lose your way."

Joe stood and shook his brother's outstretched hand. "Good luck Corporal," he said with feeling.

"You too Sir," Sam answered with a smirk. The judgment had gone, they understood each other. He turned and called out for Private Dobson. The young man hurried to join him.

"Best of luck Eppy and you too lad," Fallon wished as they passed through the doors.

"Cheers pal. Look after him for me. He's not too good at taking care of himself when the pressure's on and I don't think he knows what's about to hit him," Sam nodded back towards Joe and waved a hand in farewell.

"Aye, I'll watch out for 'im," Fallon promised.

"Thanks. When this is over I'll buy you a drink or two. I think I owe you."

Fallon watched the infantry men disappear back into the night and with a sigh wondered if the lieutenant would see his brother again or whether he would ever get the chance to hold Sam Hepworth to the promise of those drinks. He hoped that he would.

Joe stared at the envelope in his hands, his mind racing in a turmoil of emotion. He had been angry, but that ire had soon melted. He had been sorry. Sorry that he had thought badly of his brother. Sorry that they could not spend more time together. Sorry that they might never meet again. Now he was afraid. Afraid that Sam would die. Afraid that he might have to watch him die. Ludicrous as that thought may be for there would be thousands of men involved in tomorrow's battle. Joe could not help the dread that tightened his stomach and left a sour taste in his mouth. He wished he had said more. Wished he had thought of something meaningful to say, but like so many times in his past the vocabulary had escaped him. It was always so hard to express his feelings. He felt uncomfortable and embarrassed at admitting his affection for his male siblings. He thought they knew he loved them, but he could not say so. How did a man openly admit such a thing? To one's sister, wife and mother, fine. Women were different. They expected to be told such things, would be hurt if they were not. But for a man to tell his brother, be careful, I love you too much to lose you. Well, it just was not done was it? He sighed heavily.

"You alright Sir?" Fallon asked.

"Yes, thank you Donal. He gave me a letter to deliver if anything should happen to him," Joe replied with another sigh. "I'm not sure what I'll do if..., if he ends up here tomorrow. Christ what was I thinking! And what the hell do I do with this?" he waved the letter in the air.

Donal did not know what to say. The question, he thought, was rhetorical. At last he simply smiled and suggested, "Why don't you get some sleep Sir? It'll be a busy day tomorrow."

Joe smirked cynically and pushed his dirty hair from his forehead so that it stuck upright, in spiky tufts. "It's addressed to that girl. The one he got in the fight over," he continued ignoring the advice.

"He doesn't know?"

"Know what?"

"Well, Fleurbaix was shelled heavily a few days ago. Lot of the buildings were hit. The café amongst 'em," Fallon explained.

"Good God, was she killed?"

The corporal shrugged. "I don't know, Sir. Might have been or she and her father might have moved away. All I know is the place is gone. Shame, because it was one of the few out here that didn't water the beer down too much and he had some good stuff for special customers. Your brother was a special customer from what I heard. He and the monsieur had an arrangement. Free beer for musical entertainment. I didn't know you came from a musical family Sir."

"Yes, Sam has a real talent. All my siblings do. I'm the least musical of the lot. What do I tell him about his girl?" Joe asked.

"The truth Sir, but not until he comes back. You wouldn't want to have his mind on anything except his job just now Sir. You'd never find him anyhow," the Irishman advised wisely.

Joe nodded and muttered that he would try to get some rest. He drifted to his bunk at the far end of the barn. He did not wash, did not undress, but laid upon the hard, makeshift bed and stared at the ceiling. He heard Fallon clearing away the debris of his hurried supper and the tea mugs, he heard Stubbs snoring from the men's bunks behind the curtain partition and in the distance he heard the soft crump of a shell exploding. He waited a long time for sleep to come and all the time his mind was a whirl of regrets, of words unsaid. He tried to think of Dora, to bring back memories of home, of their first night together, of the unborn child she was carrying. But instead of bringing peaceful happiness to his dreams these thoughts of another world only brought sadness, loneliness and a deep and burning desire to be there, to run away from this hellish place and never come back. He vowed that come the end of his contracted year, he would do just that.

CHAPTER 24.
March 10th – 13th, Neuve Chapelle

10th March.

"Jesus Christ, Corp. They're gonna kill us all if they drop any nearer!" Dobson cried above the thunderous din. Sam had all on to hear what the lad said, but still put his finger to his lips to signal silence. Now was not the time for youthful chatter.

Never had they heard anything like it. The noise was more than deafening, the scream of heavy shells and subsequent explosions vibrated the earth, ear drums and their insides like nothing anyone had ever imagined. Huddled in the reserve trenches the men of the Yorkshires waited behind the Scots and trembled with a heady mixture of excitement and fear as the sky was rent by a continuous and deadly wall of wailing metal. Relentless and viciously painful to the men waiting beneath its fiery rain the bombardment was both terrifying and marvellous. Poor old Fritz was taking a real battering this time and it was hard not to feel sorry for him.

Another ear-splitting salvo flew over. The men instinctively crouched lower even though the hellish missiles were nowhere near, were flying to seal another man's fate across the lines. Faces were taut; jaws clamped tight, a few nervous smiles exchanged. Dobson started to laugh manically. Sam grabbed his tunic front and shook the lad soundly.

"Calm down Dobbo," he said through gritted teeth. *God, this must be what it's like in hell.*

Dobson's wide eyes searched his and the young soldier shook visibly. He was scared, but at the same time euphoric. Sam hoped he would hold together. He thought he would. It was not the first time the lad had gone into action. The waiting was the worst. Keyed up, tense, waiting for the order to advance. It would be a while yet in coming. The Twenty-first Brigade were in support to the Twenty-third. They would be going nowhere soon.

Sam leant his head back against the trench wall and watched his breath stream out into the frigid air. *God it's cold.* It had even tried to snow and a few flakes still drifted lazily around, reminiscent of goose feathers and a remembered, but distant pillow fight as a boy. A smile touched his lips and faded as the ground trembled with force sending his heart racing into his mouth and then back to the pit of his stomach again.

It was different this time. Different from Ypres, because he knew what to expect. They had seen it before and the illusions of the past had faded to be replaced by stark reality. Still, this time they were on the offensive not the Germans. This time, *they* would be the ones pushing through.

For a long half hour the shells shrieked and tore across the heavens, exploded with terrible force, ripping open the frozen mud and sending its troglodyte inhabitants to oblivion. For a long half hour the Tommies waited, shivering from cold and anxious exhilaration, exchanging a grin with a comrade, swearing at the crash of the never ending bombardment. Until at last it fell silent. For ten precious seconds, no sound, not even the shuffle of feet or clatter of equipment. Temporarily deafened for a few brief moments and then the world returned.

The thrilling shrill of whistles blown and a mad cheering as the Twenty-third Brigade went over the top. Desultory rifle fire and for a long time nothing else. Far distant a machine gun sputtered into life. From their position in the reserve trench it sounded as if there was little opposition. A few opinions shared about the fate of poor old Fritz. A low murmuring hum spread amongst the men as they conjectured over what was happening only yards ahead.

The platoon sergeant pushed down the line, hushing the men with a glare or an uncompromising remark. As he drew level with the rear section he turned and caught Sam's eye and maybe for a moment a slight flush of embarrassment coloured his cheeks.

"Any news Sarn't? We moving up?" Sam asked, voicing what the men wanted to know.

The sergeant shrugged. "Dunno Eppy. No one's tellin' me nowt!" he said and trudged back the way he had come.

"God, Corp, what're we waitin' fower?" someone muttered behind him.

Sam shook his head, "Not for us to question why Ted."

"Christ, I'd kill for a fag," someone else grumbled.

"Me too pal."

As the bombardment stopped so the wait for casualties began, but it was not long before the first were being stretchered into the barn, their faces haggard with pain and blackened or yellowed from muck and cordite fumes. The ADS swung into action augmented by two more medical officers sent up from the Main Dressing Station.

Captain Foster and Joe hurriedly assessed the needs of the wounded, leaning heavily upon their orderlies for assistance, knowing they had to make fast decisions. Keep the man here or send him down the line? Was it worth working on this one? Forget him he's gone. Move him into the moribund tent, he'll die soon. Give him some morphine and put him to sleep, he'll pass quietly then. No this one's fine, only a flesh wound, he can wait or walk up to the MDS. We need to re-dress that one. Christ his guts are out and spilling onto the floor! Watch it pal, don't stand on 'em!

A blur of anguished faces, some obviously relieved to be out and alive, others too far gone to care. Joe laboured on with either Fallon or sometimes Stubbs by his side. They cleaned and dressed the injured men. Gave them a hot drink where time allowed. Tried to keep them warm until they could be moved out. Soon the stretchers were all over the floor and they were stepping over them.

A man shouted through the barn doors that another twenty were on their way in.

"Hell man we don't have the room for 'em," Foster bellowed as he pulled shrapnel out of a bleeding neck and hurriedly dabbed it with weak peroxide solution. "Dress this Private," he instructed and marched to the doors to filter out the worst cases.

Covered in blood and sweating despite the cold, Joe moved to his next case, a gunshot wound to left thigh the label fastened around a button on the man's tunic said. It need not have been there, the wound was bleeding profusely. Fallon had already cut the lad's trousers back revealing a yawning gash that had evidently clipped an artery and was hurriedly re-tying a tourniquet to stem the scarlet flow. The soldier stared at his leg with morbid fascination.

"Didn't know I 'ad that much in me?" he mumbled awestruck as Joe stooped closer to examine the damage.

"You've a lot more yet, but we need to plug this up. Donal, sutures," the MO instructed and took the cleansing solution from the corporal. "This'll sting," he apologised and liberally swabbed the limb. The soldier cursed loudly.

"Sorry Sir," he muttered afterwards, his hands gripping the side of the stretcher with white knuckles.

"Don't worry about it. I'm going to stitch you up and then the corporal here will bandage you and we'll get you out of here."

"Thanks Corporal." Joe took the suture needle from Fallon. "You might want to swear a bit more," he suggested to his patient and set to work.

Stretcher bearers hurried into the makeshift hospital and removed those who had been seen to and those who needed more specialist care. Foster was diverting the worst cases outside, moribunds in that tent, abdomens, amputations and heads straight on down the line. Nothing could be done for them here. And still the numbers poured in.

The other two doctors worked alongside Joe, experienced and efficient, they crunched through the load with quiet perseverance.

"Where do you want this one Sir?" a bearer called as he and his mate staggered, exhaustedly with their load through the open doors.

Being nearest, Joe looked around forlornly for a space. He could see none. "Can't he wait outside? There's no room in here."

"Captain told us to bring 'im in, Sir," the man replied his face grimly set.

"Oh hell! Put him down there then if you can squeeze him in. Can't you take any to the other dressing stations? We're full to bursting here," Hepworth said exasperatedly.

"The others are all full too Sir," the stretcher bearer answered causing Joe to colour at the realisation of his ridiculous request.

"Of course they are," he mumbled under his breath and tied off the dressing to a chest peppered with deep lacerations. "This man's ready Stubbs. Label him up and get him away," he added and carried on.

Ten minutes to nine and they still shivered in the reserve trench. Things sounded a lot livelier ahead of them now. The enemy had recovered from his initial shock of the heavy bombardment and was fighting back. Shrapnel zinged through the still, frosty air and machine guns stuttered frantically with regular monotony. Young Dobson, who had been quiet for some time, moaned and dropped his head onto the barrel of his rifle propped against his legs. Sam glanced at the lad, a frown of concern upon his face. For too long they had waited in nervous anticipation. Only so long could a man stay positive as the surge of adrenalin forced conflicting emotions through his tense body. Only so long that a man could remain excited in anticipation of a fight before the hormone wore away at his cheerful resolve and fear wormed its invading path to the fore.

Sam rubbed the lad's arm encouragingly, "Not long now Dobbo," he reassured. "Soon be up and in the thick of it." Though in truth he did not know. They had been here, crouching in the bitter cold since two thirty that morning and now they were stiff and blue and agitated.

A familiar, well spoken voice coming down the trench brought hope of news. Fielding passed through his men with Sergeant Kelsey at his back. It was a moment before he reached the last section and by then the soft and eager murmuring amongst the troops had given away the news he brought.

"Moving up at last then Sir?" Sam asked as the lieutenant drew level.

"Yes Eppy. We're moving up to the support trenches in Rue Tilleloy at nine. I don't want any stragglers. It's likely to be a hot run. Fritz has the ground covered and is dropping shrapnel, but they want us up now," Fielding explained as though he disapproved the idea and probably did. He had reverted to calling all his men by their names or nicknames now. They were his family and rank meant little to a man who had always struggled with the rigidity of the Regular Army. He also struggled with the insistence of waiting for orders. If they had moved up an hour ago after the Twenty-third Brigade had advanced, they would not be running the gauntlet of enemy fire. He smiled sadly wondering how many of these lads he would lose.

"Cheery bugger," Sam muttered as the lieutenant hurried back the way he had come and the men of his section sniggered in cynical agreement.

At nine the whistle blew and the whole of the reserve trench erupted its contents into a pock marked field, racing hell for leather across the open. As they emerged machine gun fire enfiladed their ranks and shrapnel shells exploded indiscriminately amongst the surging troops, ripping flesh apart and tearing clothing from their battered bodies. In front of Sam, Dobson froze in horror as something whooshed close to his head and a warm wet mush hit his face. The man ahead of him slumped, his cranium split in two revealing a jagged, gaping slash of red-grey pap. The body dropped and lay twitching face down in the churned up earth. Sam shoved a firm hand against the lad's back and pushed him forward, swearing and encouraging alternately, his own heart pumping wildly.

An odd crack of wood followed by a stinging vibration ran into his right hand where it gripped his rifle and something hit hard against his pack. He did not stop; he carried on pushing at Dobson's reluctant form until the private overcame his terror and lunged towards the eternally distant goal of the support trench dug across the main road to Armentières. Dobson dived into the refuge head first landing heavily on Ted Little who cursed wildly and pushed him to the ground. Sam jumped in after narrowly missing both and sat panting for breath.

"Christ that was a laugh a minute," he gasped cynically. "You stupid little bugger! If you fuckin' stop dead like that again I'll shoot you myself," he stabbed an accusatory finger at Dobson.

"S...sorry Corp, but it wa'... " the young soldier apologised shakily. He put a hand up to wipe his face and puzzled, stared at the pinkish, jellied ooze coating his fingers. His face turned white and he squealed like a girl flinging the gore away. "Oh fuck, *Jesus Christ*! I've got 'is fuckin' brains all o'er me face. Fuck, fuck," he cried and dropping his rifle began rubbing his visage vigorously with a dirty handkerchief while jigging up and down on the spot. If it had not been so tragic it would have seemed comical and indeed Sam could not help but smile though a cold disgust also churned in his stomach.

Ted laughed and then pointing said, "You won't be shootin' anyone with that rifle Corp," His grin spoke more of his relief at getting into the safety of the trench rather than at the unfortunate weapon his section leader still gripped in a blood spattered hand.

Baffled, Sam looked down. Saw his hand lacerated and bleeding from splinters and the trigger of his Lee Enfield buckled and useless. "Fuckin' 'ell! How the fuck...?" he cursed. He emptied the magazine and threw the useless weapon against the trench wall. He pulled a handkerchief from his pocket, tied it around his hand that, now he had seen the deep gouges in it, had decided to sting like mad. Then he cautiously peered over the parados of the trench back in the direction they had come. He cast about the field noting the few stragglers diving to safety along their line, a handful of wounded dragging themselves pitifully forwards or back, whichever way seemed the nearest to cover and amongst them the still forms of the dead. He saw what he was looking for, not twenty yards away, glanced up as if expecting to see something overhead and attempted to hoist himself back out into the field. Hands on his hips pulled him back down with a curse.

"Bloody 'ell Corp, what d' yer think yer doin'?" Ted gasped horrified.

"Getting a fucking rifle. I can't shoot anyone with this one. What do you expect me to do, use harsh language at Fritz over there? Get off me. I'll be back in two shakes," Sam shrugged the private's hands from him and clambered up out of the trench. He lay face down on the frozen earth and waited a couple of seconds before crawling, snake-like towards the nearest body. Twenty yards seemed a mile away. He dare not move fast, did not want to catch the attention of the machine gunners or a sniper. Slowly and deliberately he inched closer to the outstretched arm flung in death above a surprised and blankly staring face. Reaching out he grasped the barrel of the dead man's rifle and with painstaking deliberation pulled it towards him.

An explosion to his left sent his head instinctively beneath protecting hands. A hard rain of muck fell onto his back and arms. He waited breathing hard. Had he been seen? Was a bullet heading his way? For almost a minute he did not move, not daring to lift his head or flinch a muscle. Eventually his nerve returned and he renewed his grasp on the Lee Enfield and slowly, with utmost care, began to shuffle back towards the support trench.

"Where's Corporal Hepworth? Did he not make it?" Lieutenant Fielding asked with obvious concern as he reached the last of his men. He had lost, until now, only four, but his heart filled with dread as he realised the man he cared about most within his extended family, his favourite son, was not here.

"'E's gone to get a rifle Sir," Ted replied matter-of-factly as if the corporal had simply walked down to the armoury.

"He's *what?*" Fielding demanded aghast.

"'Is got shot up Sir," Dobson explained equally unsatisfactorily pointing at the forlorn weapon behind him.

The lieutenant stared at them both with exasperation. With a steady and deliberate tone, as if talking to a small child, he questioned, "And where has he gone to get a rifle?"

"Back t'way we came, Sir," Ted jerked a thumb westwards.

"*Jesus Christ!*" Fielding muttered looking upwards and jumped as a foot appeared above his head, followed by another and then a man fell, tumbling down into the ditch.

Sam landed with a thump and laughed out loud with unchecked relief, his heart still racing from the adventure. He had not noticed the officer and waved the rifle triumphantly above his head. "Got the fucker!" he cried.

"Glad to hear it Hepworth," Fielding snapped back.

Shit! Sam jumped to his feet his expression becoming suitably serious.

"Don't let me catch you doing anything so downright foolhardy again Corporal. You could have got bloody well shot, you stupid arse!" the lieutenant chastised.

"No Sir," Sam returned apologetically not daring to make eye contact and striving to check the laughter that hovered near to the surface. Laughter that if it had broke free would have betrayed his relief at getting back, that would have been a touch hysterical.

Fielding made a grunting noise and muttering something unintelligible trudged away. In his wake a wide grin crept over Eppy's face and he winked with feigned nonchalance at the smiling, youthful Dobson. Then he began to wipe the congealing blood from the rifle.

"*Christ!* What are we waitin' for now?" Someone grumbled as they squatted uncomfortably in the support trench. Occasional shells exploded nearby but their range was off and apart from the incessant rifle and machine gun fire around the village of Neuve Chapelle a little to the south, this section of the line was relatively quiet.

"Why aren't we bloody movin'? There's bugger all resistance 'ere. We could get well forrad," Corporal Pritchard muttered to Sam as they hunched together through lack of space, bored, cold, frustrated and more than a little edgy.

"Dunno," Hepworth replied though the question had been rhetorical. He felt the same. They had not met too much opposition while running across the open. Casualties had been relatively slight compared with further south. Surely that meant that Fritz had scarpered or was at least keeping his head down. The British shells that screamed overhead met only perfunctory retaliation. But for some inexplicable reason the whole of the Twenty-first Brigade languished in support trenches, cramped and waiting for orders to advance. God knows there would be hell of a mess if one of those German five-nines finally hit the mark!

Lieutenant Fielding crept along the line counting and checking on his men.

"What's happening Sir? Why aren't we moving up?" Sam took the opportunity to ask.

"Haven't the foggiest Eppy," Fielding answered with a shrug. "All I know is Twenty-third Brigade have moved up and we're waiting."

"What the 'ell for, Sir?" Pritchard gasped with incredulity at this news.

"I'm as in the dark as you are Corporal," the lieutenant snapped back. God this was frustrating. He knew no more than the men. *What a way to run a bloody war!* He hurried away again and his troops unhappily resigned themselves to wait.

Sam took the opportunity to clean his purloined rifle and shared a furtive smoke with Pritchard.

"You alright Dobbo?" he asked the private crouched and shivering at his other side. He was worried about the lad after crossing the field. Dobson showed signs of losing control, of his fear getting the better of him and this damned waiting game did nothing to help frayed nerves.

"Not bad Corp," the private mumbled, yet his eyes roved restlessly and he jumped with every crump of shells.

Sam studied him for a few seconds and passed him a cigarette. "Here, it'll take your mind off it. Try and relax Dobbo we're not going anywhere fast and Fritz is way off the mark. He hasn't a clue where we are."

Dobson took the cigarette gratefully but still looked around for anyone who might take him to task over lighting up.

"No one will say owt Dobbo. Two much smoke around anyway to give the game away. Here," Sam reached across with a match.

"Thanks Corp," the youngster acknowledged and drew heavily on the woodbine.

"Just think what you can write home about after this. It'll be some letter. Keep 'em occupied for a month!" Eppy laughed. Dobson's letters home were notorious. He was a prolific epistle writer and they had been known to run to ten pages. Needless to say they were not too popular with Fielding or the CSM who had the joy of censoring them. "The lieutenant will have a dickie fit."

"Aye," Dobson sniggered. He smiled at the thought for a while and then his eyes drifted far away, back into some torment. "Ridsdale got it, Corp. I saw 'im lyin' there, just starin' like. Think 'e wa' dead though," he said quietly at length.

"Aye well, Ridsdale was a slack bugger anyhow. Forget him. Nothing you can do for the poor sod now. Come on; tell me about this girl of yours. You gonna marry her or what?" Sam persisted. Get the lad thinking of something else. His girl, sex, anything to stop him dwelling on the dead.

"Dunno Corp. Do y' think I should?"

"Christ Dobbo, she's your push," Sam laughed through exhaled smoke and flicked his tab end into the mud.

The flow of casualties arriving at the barn had settled into a steady stream rather than the initial frenetic rush. Joe was glad of it. It gave him time to examine the men properly, to re-dress their wounds before sending them on to the next stage. Even Foster had rejoined his team and was no longer directing stretchers into carts to be rushed away or diverting the walking wounded to the Main Dressing Station another mile behind the lines. It was busy, but the chaos of a couple of hours previous had evolved into a well organised system of examination, treatment, dressing and evacuation. The ADS worked like a well oiled machine. For the present.

"Hepworth, go take a look at the moribunds will you old chap? If there are any you think might have half a chance, send them in here. Otherwise, just do what you can for 'em eh!" Foster delegated as it became apparent they had broken the back of the work and had time to address the hopeless cases. The ones that were unlikely to live. Not all might be that bad. Given the time, the right treatments and a sterile hospital environment, many of the seriously injured would have a fighting chance. But out here? Most would die before that chance came.

Joe wiped the blood from his hands onto an already reddish-brown stained cloth and without reply to the captain made his way to the tents in the lee of the barn. Three of these housed men waiting transportation to the clearing station, a fourth held the moribunds. Once inside Joe was struck by the comparative silence. An occasional soft moan punctuated the otherwise eerie quiet of the shelter with its rows of pathetic bundles on stretchers. It was no place to keep dying men. A cold, draughty tent in the middle of a muddy field with artillery pounding resonantly all around and the constant ripple of distant rifle fire. It was an undistinguished and undignified end for a soldier.

Glancing around Hepworth held little hope for the battered forms, covered only by a coarse blanket, only the meagre canvas of the stretcher between them and the frozen earth. Most of them would die of shock or hypothermia.

The two orderlies acknowledged his entrance and continued to move from one casualty to the next, checking for signs of life, writing slips of paper and tying them to tunic buttons, covering faces when all was lost and retrieving an occasional identity disc and personal belongings.

Joe leant out of the tent and called for two stretcher bearers. He ordered them to accompany him in case there were any men worth working on and he sent an orderly for morphine. At least if he could not save them, he could help them sleep.

In solemn procession he and his attendants moved amongst the stretchers. A quiet conversation with one of the orderlies had pointed him to the most promising cases, those who were at least awake and cognisant. An elderly sergeant with his legs blown off and breathing stenorously. They had thought he might die quickly, but he was hanging on and had not deteriorated much. Joe checked him over and sent him into the barn. They might as well give the old boy a fighting chance.

Next a lad who looked too young to be in the Army. Probably lied about his age. His face was clear and girlish, devoid of anything that could resemble whiskers, not even the soft down of a pubescent beard. His abdomen had been ripped open and his guts spilled from the jagged hole. Someone had thrown on a rough field dressing, but it hardly contained the loops of bowel, their form could be seen bulging under a blood and faeces soaked wad of gauze. The boy's eyes were bright, lucid and frightened, his face deathly pale. Those eyes never moved from the medical officer as the latter carefully unwound the sodden bandages.

With all the self control and professional detachment he could muster Joe fought the urge to recoil from the foul stench and the torn, glistening ropes of intestines that tumbled from the boy's body. He could see it was hopeless. That even if they succeeded in sewing the lad back together infection was inevitable, its first signs were already evident, and death a certainty. Yet the private was too young to die surely? God, it was so desperately unfair.

"I'll be alright Doc won't I?" the boy asked. It almost broke Joe's heart.

"Yes son, you'll be fine. Are you in much pain?"

"A bit. But I can stand it, Sir," the brave reply.

"I'm sure you can Private, but you don't have to. I'll give you something to help. It might make you a little sleepy, but I'm sure you won't mind a good long kip," Joe took a syringe and the morphine bottle from the orderly.

"No Sir. I could sleep 'til Christmas, Sir. Only it keeps wakin' me up," the private gesticulated to his abdomen. That he was in some agony there was no doubt. The sweat on his face gave too much away.

Joe smiled. "Help me get a vein up Davies," he asked the orderly and between them they rubbed the lad's cold arms and hands, tying a tourniquet first around one arm and then the other. It was useless. The veins had shrunk and shrivelled as the first signs of shock took hold. With no other option the medical officer decided on an exposed vessel within the boy's abdomen. He plunged the needle into the purple vein and slowly depressed the syringe as poor Davies held aside loops of bowel.

"There you go son, you go to sleep now. Everything will be alright," Joe uttered gently into the private's ear; already he was drifting away. The morphine would not kill him, but it was doubtful he would ever wake again. They re-dressed the wound and moved on.

They by-passed a faceless lieutenant with a fist sized hole in his head through which the pinkish grey mush of pulverised brain pulsed. Somehow the officer's chest rose and fell and bubbles of air formed around what once had been a mouth popping with each gurgling breath. God only knew, if he even existed, how the poor man still lived. The only consolation was the certainty of unconsciousness, or so Joe hoped as he shuddered and bent to examine another soldier with a gaping chest wound.

At two after noon the Twenty-first Brigade finally moved forward and linked up with the Twenty-third in the re-captured old British trenches of 1914. Although the enemy guns were busy any other resistance remained light. Optimism ran high. They could see the church spire in the village of Aubers. It would be so easy to take. Move on to the next trenches, overrun the fleeing Germans, suffer very few casualties, for opposition would be minimal and Aubers would be theirs. But once more they were ordered to wait. Some garbled message reached Lieutenant Colonel Andrews at his forward headquarters suggesting there was a strongly fortified redoubt in the orchard just to their south east. The advance could not progress until reinforcements had dealt with this stronghold.

Disbelieving his men were held up once more for some cock and bull fantasy of Divisional HQ he furiously snatched the field glasses from around his adjutant's neck and marched along the trench, ignoring salutes and apologies from men he pushed out of his way as they struggled to reverse the parapet to give more cover. He stomped, in high temper, all the way to the southern extent of his Battalion, to the position where A Company abutted with the Royal Scots Fusiliers. He threw his elbows against the sandbagged wall and with little heed for his safety, gazed through the glasses towards the ruined orchard only a hundred yards away. He had a fine view. Not a movement from within its tumbled down walls, its smashed and shattered fruit trees whose skeleton forms had been pulverised to stumps and ragged splinters of wood. There was no redoubt. *What were Division thinking of?*

Andrews swore to himself and strode back to his headquarters. If he could move forward now the Battalion could take the village before dusk. Well before. The enemy was more than simply wavering; they had crumbled and fled. If only he had the authority to act independently. He felt sure the OCs of the Scots to his right and the Wiltshires on his left would agree. Cursing once more he glanced at his adjutant and then scribbled a curtly worded message and gave it to his runner. The message ran along the lines of "No enemy between our line and village of Aubers. No redoubt in orchard. Permission requested to advance. Can take objective before nightfall."

The runner vanished, slipping and slithering through the soft mud. The frost had lifted but the air remained raw. Staring up at the lowering clouds, Andrews reflected that at this rate it would be dark before he received a reply and by then it would be too late.

An eternity passed before the order came and when it did the brooding sky had brought a premature dusk and light sleety rain. But at long last they were moving again. Straddling the old German line three Companies headed out into the open keeping in touch with the Scots. D Company hurried along the trench where it curved north-eastwards. All advancing towards a derelict mill directly in line with Aubers in the distance. It was too optimistic to make the village by dark now, but they could gain the mill, advance the line a good way forward.

They made good progress, pushed on out of cover and into a sudden and heavy hail of machine gun bullets. The enemy had made use of the delay. D Company found themselves enfiladed, fire seeming to come from all directions. They teetered, staggered forward trying to link up with the rest of the Battalion who were furiously digging in on the right, and finally they were forced back some hundred and fifty yards or so to a shallow drainage channel. The men started to entrench hard and fast.

Sergeant Kelsey wriggled on his belly along the shallow ditch as bullets zinged and spat at the earth just above his head. The ground gave little cover, but at least there was some; at least if they kept their heads down they were out of sight of the enemy. He grabbed the leg of a corporal working furiously with his entrenching tool to pile more earth in front of them. The men alongside laboured with the same purposeful concentration.

"Eppy, Eppy!" Kelsey shouted above the rifle and machine gun fire. *Christ! We must be surrounded.*

Sam turned to look over his shoulder, his face muddy and streaked with sweat despite the chilling cold, his tunic caked in muck.

"You seen the lieutenant?" Kelsey demanded. He'd already asked three other section leaders all with the same response.

"No Sarn't. He hasn't come this way. You sure he's not up yon end?" Hepworth answered with a nod northwards. He stared and a worm of dread shifted in his stomach. Something in the sergeant's manner was disconcerting.

"I think we've lost 'im," Kelsey confirmed the fear.

Sam shuffled his body downwards and turned his head either way to look up and down the ditch as if by some remote chance he might see Fielding strolling along towards him.

"You sure?" he asked lamely. "He's not just up with the new bloke in Three Platoon?"

Kelsey shook his head. "Been that way. They 'aven't seen 'im." He hesitated and then leant forwards speaking directly into the corporal's ear. "What do I do Eppy? I don't know what to do."

Sam stared at him with surprise while his brain still rejected the idea that Fielding was gone.

"Eppy?" the sergeant pressed urgently.

"Better report it to the CC Sarn't. Might find yourself in charge of a platoon. You sure though?"

"Look man, I can't find 'im. It's not like he can 'ide 'imsen in 'ere is it? 'E must be dead or dyin' out there somewhere," Kelsey gesticulated angrily into the field.

"We'll have to look for him. Make sure," Sam said not willing to give up on the lieutenant.

"Like 'ell we will. Not wi' bullets ricocheting all around us."

"We can't just leave him Sarn't."

"We don't even know where 'e is Eppy for God's sake!" the sergeant snapped. "I'll go report 'im missin' then." He sighed, struggled to turn around in the narrow space full of men sprawled on their stomachs digging or keeping careful aim with ready rifles, and hurried on hands and knees back the way he had come. For half a minute Sam stared after him, his mind racing.

Fielding had been with D section when they were advancing, he was sure of it. He dropped his entrenching tool and to his men's surprise scurried off to their right, squeezing by semi-prone bodies, crawling over legs and abandoned packs. Twenty yards and he found his man.

"Bill, where's Fielding?" he shouted above the din.

Lance Corporal Bill Pratt slid away from his makeshift parapet to hear what his comrade said. "What?" he asked frowning.

"The lieutenant. He was with you. Where is he?"

Pratt looked puzzled and shrugged his shoulders. "'Ell Corp, I dunno. You sure 'e wa' wi' us?"

Sam groaned with exasperation. He took a deep breath and holding it half knelt, tentatively raising his head above the mud piling up in front of the ditch.

"Jesus man! Watch out," Bill exclaimed and cringed expecting the corporal to have his head blown off.

But Sam was not completely reckless. The German line was a good seventy to a hundred yards away, the light poor, he wore a black cap-comforter, a woolly hat, on his head. His face was smeared with muck; he would be hard to see. Besides the bullets that sprayed the top of the slowly deepening trench, were on a routine traverse, hopeful of catching some unwary fool, but content to keep the British heads down. He had waited until the firing had passed this section before he dared to look and he would not stay with head and shoulders unprotected for longer than a few seconds. It was risky, but not stupidly so.

He stared across the expanse of No-Man's-Land, trying to ascertain if any of the handful of bodies strewn across it were officers. If anyone was still alive. It was hard to see clearly through the drizzle and vapours of smoke that drifted across his line of vision. He had to concentrate his gaze for several seconds at each human shaped mound as they merged seamlessly into the mud. All the time he tempted fate and he counted to himself in his head as the raking machine gun fire grew louder and closer. Suddenly Sam dropped back.

"*Fuck!* You been 'it?" Bill cried his heart racing and his eyes instinctively checking for holes in his comrade's head and shoulders.

"No. I've seen him," Sam exclaimed excitedly. He started unloading his kit, except for a water bottle. He propped his rifle against the ditch wall. "Don't fall back onto that," he grinned.

"What you doin' Corp?" the lance corporal asked dumbfounded. He had a good idea.

"I'm going to fetch him back."

"Is 'e alive?"

"Think so."

"Bloody 'ell Eppy, leave 'im fo' t' body snatchers. They'll fetch 'im in when it gets dark. Just tell 'em where 'e is," Bill argued. "You'll get thi-sen killed goin' out there now."

Sam shook his head emphatically. "It's a good couple of hours 'til it gets dark proper and if this rain lifts it could be longer than that. He could die in that time."

"If 'e's that bad, 'e's as good as dead any'ow," Bill grumbled.

"Look, I'm going for him and that's that. You are going to give me covering fire, but only if that machine gunner passes this way. You understand? Bill, he's only twenty yards or so away. There's a shell hole to his left. I'll pull him in there and check him over. Let Kelsey know and get some SBs once I've got him."

"I dunno Corp. Still think it's best to wait like. Sarn't 'll give me a right bollocking if..."

"I'm not asking Bill. I'm going anyhow. It's up to you if you want to cover me or not," Sam interrupted and held the lance corporal's gaze.

Bill nodded reluctantly. "Tha's fuckin' mad." He shouted at his men to stop digging and take up position along the ridge of earth ready to give covering fire on his say so.

"Thanks pal," Hepworth grinned and waited while the men readied themselves, curiously looking from him to Bill and until Fritz decided to move his concentration of fire.

As luck would have it the German machine gunner must have become bored with firing at nothing because at that moment the firing stopped. Sam hesitated, waited a moment longer and then taking a deep breath climbed out of the ditch, scampered and slithered across the morass, keeping his body as low as possible, towards Fielding. He threw himself into the earth by the lieutenant's supine body and reached out a hand to grasp the officer's arm just as Fritz caught movement out of the corner of his eye and commenced a random spraying of bullets at the British lines. A shout from the ditch brought a return volley of rapid rifle fire zipping over the two men where they lay in the mud and momentarily silenced the Maxim.

Fielding flinched at the touch of a hand on his. "Keep still Sir. It's Eppy. *Jesus!*" Sam cried and planted his face soundly into the mud as a hail of bullets fizzed barely a foot above his head. They were not meant for him, but he was not going to risk moving just yet. He waited for the firing to stop then he pulled with all his strength dragging the lieutenant into the shell hole.

"As 'e got 'im?" Lance Corporal Pratt asked the man next to him as they both ducked back into the trench. Retaliatory missiles spattered the mound above and Bill checked along his section to make sure everyone was safe. They were.

"Think 'e did Corp, but if they aren't both dead then I'm a Dutchman," the private replied breathing hard.

"WHO THE FUCKING 'ELL IS FIRING!" Sergeant Kelsey bawled as he crawled towards D section. Behind him, a little distance away, followed Major Wilson.

"*Shit!*" Pratt muttered.

"What the *hell* is going on?" the company commander demanded as he caught up with the sergeant. He glared from Kelsey to Bill and back again. "Well?"

"Givin' coverin' fire Sir," Pratt replied economically.

"Covering fire. for what? Under who's orders?"

"For Corporal 'Epworth Sir. They wa' 'is orders. 'E's gone to fetch Lieutenant Fielding, Sir."

"*What?*" Wilson stared incredulously. He was furious, but at the same time staggered. "Is the lieutenant alive then?" he questioned and briefly caught Kelsey's eye.

"'E wa' a minute ago, Sir," Bill answered.

"God Almighty! Why didn't Hepworth wait until it was dark?" It was a rhetorical question. Wilson merely voiced his thoughts aloud, but the lance corporal answered him anyway. "Dunno, Sir."

"Do you think he made it? Hepworth I mean," the major quizzed after a second or two. By now the enemy fire had died away again.

"'E wa' next to t' lieutenant when Fritz started shootin' again. I 'aven't dared look since, Sir."

Wilson nodded. He bit his bottom lip and waited for half a minute, then he took his cap off, handed it to Kelsey and pulled a dark woolly cap-comforter, similar to Sam's, onto his head. Slowly and with the utmost caution he pulled himself up to the top of the heap of muck and peered out across the grey landscape.

"*Good God*," he cried and slid back down. "Better get some stretcher bearers down here Sergeant, but they can wait until it gets dark before going out there. No more firing Pratt, not without proper orders." Wilson put his cap back on, but did not remove the comforter.

"Are they safe, Sir?" Bill dared to ask.

"Well I don't know about safe, but Hepworth seems to have managed to get the lieutenant into the cover of a shell hole at least. Let's not take any more risks gentlemen. We wait until nightfall to bring them back." Wilson half smiled and crept away before he betrayed his approbation. The stunt was foolishly reckless and he proposed to make that very clear to Hepworth when the man returned, but secretly he was rather impressed.

Sam and Fielding slid unceremoniously into the watery mud of a decent sized crater just as Major Wilson peered from the trench. The lieutenant groaned lowly as pain stabbed through his left thigh and his head thumped in protest at the forced movement. He had not wanted to move, had wanted to rest where he fell regardless of the bullets spraying around him. But he had been bullied and dragged into action. Sam pulled his superior to a semi-seated position and squatted before him.

"Right Sir, let's have a look at you. Where've you been hit? Do you know?" he asked light-heartedly. His mood was exuberant. He had done it!

Fielding swallowed. His throat felt parched and his brain ached. He wanted to go to sleep. "Left leg..., thigh. Head hurts too," he croaked and closed his eyes.

"Aye, you've got a nasty cut across the top of your nut. It'll smart a bit I'd say. Brains are still in place though," Sam reassured cheerfully after taking a quick look. Why did he feel so exhilarated? His heart pumped like the devil and he had a ridiculous urge to laugh out loud.

He examined the leg wound.

"*Shit!*" he muttered under his breath. The lieutenant was bleeding heavily, the bright red flow indicative of an arterial haemorrhage. If he did not get help soon, Fielding would bleed to death.

Hepworth unravelled part of his right puttee cutting a length off with his pocket knife. Hurriedly he tied it tight above the six inch tear in the lieutenant's tattered and stained trousers. Fielding moaned and grasped his rescuer's shoulder.

"Sorry Sir. Had to put a tourniquet on. Does it hurt badly?"

Fielding shook his head. He was too exhausted to speak. Felt too sick and weak. He dropped his head back into the mud with a sigh. The corporal continued to work retrieving a field dressing from his tunic and ripping away the trouser leg to reveal a ragged, gaping gash in the lieutenant's thigh. It peeled right through the muscle, exposing the pinkish white glint of bone beneath. It was impossible to see the offending torn artery and Sam could only assume, with some relief, that it must be a minor vessel or surely the officer would be dead already. He pursed his lips and threw iodine powder into the wound, ignored Fielding's shouted curse and deftly applied the dressing. This done he took another look at the scalp wound. A lot of blood, some of it drying and matting the lieutenant's hair, but it was only superficial. A nasty cut that could do with a stitch or two, but nothing more.

"Thirsty Eppy," the injured man muttered.

"Here, take a sip. Steady, don't gulp it you'll choke." Sam held his water bottle to Fielding's lips, brushing pale clammy skin at the same time and he knew he had to get back to their lines soon. It was no good waiting until dark.

The lieutenant shivered, "God, I'm cold."

Shock. He was going into shock. Sam bit his bottom lip thinking. Somehow he had to keep the lieutenant warm. What else? *Don't let him go to sleep. Keep him talking.* He glanced up at the sky and back in the direction of the British line. Dare he go now? It was still light enough to be seen if anyone was watching and they were sure to be. But dare he wait until dark? Fielding coughed and shivered violently. The corporal swore wishing he had a greatcoat to wrap the man in at least. He knelt up and rubbed the officer's arms vigorously.

"What are you doing here Eppy?"

"I came for you Sir. Didn't want to leave you out in the cold. You'd catch your death Sir."

Fielding laughed. It turned into a hacking cough followed by a groan. "I don't think I'm going to make it. You wasted your time and risked your life for nothing Eppy."

"Rubbish! It's nothing a few stitches and a good long rest won't put right. Just think of all those nice pretty nurses looking after you, Sir," Sam responded with a knowing grin.

"I'm married Eppy."

"I won't tell if you don't Sir."

The lieutenant laughed again and winced with pain. "Tired. I'm tired Eppy. Just let me go to sleep. Leave me here. Thanks for trying," he uttered morosely.

"*Bugger that!* I'm going nowhere Sir. Not without you. And if you think I'm letting you go to bloody sleep.... Like you said, I've risked my bloody life for you. You can at least have the decency of staying alive until I get you back. Come on, we're going," Sam retorted angrily although the anger was born of fear. Fear of losing a friend. The revelation struck him. Of course that was why he was out here. He was not risking life and limb for his officer; he was risking it for a friend. He grunted.

"Come on Harry, arm around my shoulders." He grabbed the lieutenant's arm and pulled him upright.

"Leave me Eppy. I'm dying anyway," Fielding protested weakly.

"Like hell you are! Hold tight Harry I'm taking you home. Just think of those nurses." Sam hoisted the man up, slipped back in the mud, swore and tried again. This time he managed to get the lieutenant upright.

"I can't Eppy. I can't. I haven't got the strength," Harry cried.

The corporal waivered. Fielding was like a dead weight and somehow they had to get out of the shell hole and the twenty yards back to their lines, probably under fire.

"*Sodding hell.* Okay. Sit there just a sec." He lowered the lieutenant back into the mud and then crouched in front of him. "Right Harry, on my back. Come on, *move* man."

With great effort Fielding obeyed as he was bullied and berated, sworn at and cajoled by the determinedly forceful corporal. Somehow he managed to claw his way onto Hepworth's back. Somehow he managed to hold on. And somehow Sam managed to crawl out of the pit, half choked by the lieutenant's desperate grasp around his neck. With superhuman effort, the blood pumping in his temples with the strain, he staggered and stumbled through the pock marked quagmire. Waiting for and praying that the bullets did not seek and find them. Slowly, painfully the corporal carried his platoon commander back to the lines. Twenty yards, it seemed like twenty miles. Twice he almost fell, almost dropped his burden. Miraculously he stayed on his feet. Miraculously no one fired at them. True the light was poor now, but they surely could be seen?

Across in the German trenches Leutnant Gunter Dressler watched the heroic struggle of a man carrying his officer back to the British lines. He had a hand upon the shoulder of the machine gunner, holding his fire. Dressler knew he should not prevent the Ersazt from mowing the men down, but something in that desperate struggle through the mud moved him. He had seen the man drag the wounded officer into the crater. Had thought him both foolhardy and brave. He had been astounded when, not fifteen minutes later, the pair had struggled from the pit. Why not wait until dark? He could only surmise that the officer was in need of urgent treatment.

Dressler was a humanitarian by nature. This brazen act of pointless heroism appealed to his German sense of honour, his faith in human altruism. He wondered if any of his men would do the same for him.

He stayed the machine gunner until he saw the two men tumble into the British trench and then he ordered a raking fire along the pile of mud serving as a parapet.

The casualties had mounted again, chiefly, as Captain Foster explained, because now it was dark and the stretcher bearers could comb the battle field for wounded without fear of being seen. Other than a couple of hours during the quieter part of the day Joe had not stopped. He ate between cases, a bit here and there, a gulp of cold tea. He had managed to catch forty winks when Foster suggested they work a rota while it was less busy. Now they were run off their feet again and he felt exhausted; his head ached, but he slogged on. Whatever he was going through the men at the Front were suffering far worse.

The battle had been raging for over fifteen hours now and though it no longer heaved and shook the ground and the rapacious rifle fire had become sporadic, it was by no means over. Both sides were digging in, retrieving their wounded, clearing out the dead. All in preparation to start over again in the morning.

And the wounded continued to pile up. As fast as they could move a man out from the dressing station another two or three more were brought in. *It must stop soon. Surely there cannot be many more.* Joe found it hard to visualise the carnage up front, the sheer numbers of troops lying dead or injured. He lacked sufficient military knowledge and field experience to estimate the cost in human sacrifice. He was vaguely aware that some men brought in were from units he did not recognise. Apparently they were having it much worse south of Neuve Chapelle and the dressing stations down there were overwhelmed. God only knows what it must be like!

Someone had said the day had gone well. Joe could not remember who. Looking around at the battered and torn men within the barn he found it hard to believe or agree. Still, Foster had said this was nothing compared to Ypres. Doctor Hepworth had shuddered at the thought and more than once, as he cut away the filthy, bloody uniform of some patiently quiet and terribly maimed soldier, he hoped that his brother was safe.

"This one's done Fallon," he indicated to the blood soaked man on the trestle before him. "Get him shifted and bring me the next."

At least they had managed to get a system going. Foster had stationed the RSM outside to direct the walking wounded and light cases onwards, the moribunds went straight into the tent behind the barn where Lieutenant Shenton assessed them further. Urgent surgical cases, except bleeds, were also rushed through. The ADS kept the rest and inside the draughty barn the remaining three medical officers worked through the constant stream of injured men in turn, assisted by competent orderlies who ensured that each case was removed and replaced with quiet efficiency.

Joe stretched his back and rubbed his face vigorously to try and stave off sleepiness while he waited for his next patient to be lifted onto the trestles.

"Light head wound, arterial bleed to left t'igh," Fallon read the label aloud. "Field dressing only and tourniquet on."

Joe sighed and bent over the officer. "Alright, I need sutures and swabs. Let's deal with the bleed first, if we can and get him cleaned up a bit. How's he look? Any sign of shock?" It was a question aimed at himself. In his current state of fatigue he found speaking his thoughts and tasks aloud helped his concentration. Fallon shouted for supplies and began cutting away the casualty's trousers and unravelling the grimy dressing. The doctor quickly assessed the man's general condition.

"Good God!" Joe cried recognising the besmirched face before him. Fallon paused, glanced up, saw the expression of surprise on the MO's face. Someone he knew. But the lack of emotion, the quick return of professional detachment indicated it was no one close. The corporal peered at the patient, acknowledged a face he had seen before and continued with his task.

"Sutures, swabs, iodine, Sir," the orderly tasked with fetching supplies said as he deposited them in a wheeled tray by the trestle.

"Hello Joe," Fielding mumbled faintly having recognised the doctor. He felt dreadful, weak and sick. His head pounded and his thigh throbbed agonisingly. The pain sapped what little strength he had.

"Harry," Joe acknowledged.

"Ready Sir," Fallon prompted having completed his work.

"Right. Swab down the leg please Corporal. Iodine solution.

"It's alright Harry. We'll get you sorted and out of here in a jiffy." He selected a suture needle and examined the wound. Fallon had made a good job of cleaning out the blood and dirt. The damaged artery was ragged, beyond stitching up, but it was only a minor vessel. Just as well. Even so, Joe was concerned about the amount of blood loss. Fielding's pallor was whiter than white and his skin waxy. The medical officer decided to tie off the artery. No use doing anything else and he lacked the surgical skill or time to repair it. The job rapidly done he instructed Fallon to slowly release the tourniquet. He wanted to make sure his work did not give way under the pressure of pumping blood. It did not. He sighed.

"Okay Corporal, let's pack this hole and then I'll have a look at his head."

They laboured quickly and smoothly, an efficient team. Joe almost took for granted the way the Irishman seemed to second guess his instructions. They had only worked together for a few weeks, but already they shared an understanding that usually took months or years of teamwork. This natural empathy was something they both guarded jealously, striving to be placed together. It was not purely selfish indulgence; they were more efficient this way. It was a matter of practical common sense. Something generally woefully lacking in the British Army.

Throughout the whole painful procedure Fielding remained quiet. He wanted to sleep, but his discomfort was too great. He hoped they would give him some morphine, but so far they had not.

"Sorry Harry. I'm going to have a look at your head now, but the bandage has dried on and is stuck to your hair and scalp. We'll wet it but it's going to pull a bit. How are you feeling?" Joe asked sympathetically as he left Fallon to finish fastening a clean dressing around the leg.

Fielding spluttered a cynical laugh. "Oh, just fine and dandy," he replied faintly and winced as the doctor sponged cold water onto his head and began unravelling the blood blackened bandage.

Only a scalp wound as the label stated. It was soon cleaned up with a liberal amount of iodine solution and a neat row of five stitches inserted. As the corporal took over to redress the injury Joe moved around to the front of his patient and asked, "Are you in much pain Harry?"

Fielding nodded with mild irritation, the answer to the question seemed glaringly obvious surely?

"Two grains of morphine please Corporal," the doctor instructed and began scribbling notes upon a label. The particulars of Fielding's injuries, treatment and medication. He fastened it onto the lieutenant's tunic. "He's done; let's get him out of here."

"Harry, you've lost a lot of blood, but you'll live," Joe reassured while waiting for the stretcher bearers. *If you don't get gangrene.* "They'll give you anti-tetanus serum at the MDS and before you know it you'll be in a warm comfortable bed. Probably in Blighty." He smiled.

Fielding returned the expression weakly.

The stretcher bearers hurried to the table.

"Harry, did you see Sam? Was he alright?" Joe entreated laying his hand upon the lieutenant's chest and staying the bearers momentarily. He had to know. It had been running through his head ever since he recognised Fielding.

"Saved my life," Harry replied through a morphine haze, his world growing dim and comfortably warm. Sleep crowded in.

Joe wanted to ask more, but the lieutenant had become insensible.

"Sir?" one of the stretcher bearers questioned politely. The doctor removed his hand and nodded allowing them to go.

Fielding's answer was a frustration. What did it mean? Had Sam saved the lieutenant's life and died himself or was he unhurt? Joe had an overwhelming urge to rush to the moribund tent and search for a familiar face. His eyes rapidly scanned the rows of casualties. A ridiculous notion. He did not have time to search and neither was it certain his brother would be brought here. He could have moved straight through or gone to another ADS. He could be perfectly alright, still in the Front Line. He could be dead. Joe caught Fallon's eye, smiled self-consciously and called for the next case.

11th March.

Effectively on the left flank of a salient, raked by machine gun and rifle fire, shelled by enemy guns; it was impossible to move forward or make any progress at all. They had waited too long.

One light shone in the darkness of stalemate. Following a daring raid by the Battalion bombers sixty two prisoners had been taken. But the euphoria of that success was blighted by the inability of D Company to get forward, to link up with the rest of the Battalion and the Wiltshires. The reason? Two strongly defended redoubts barred the advance and mercilessly enfiladed the British positions. Overnight and under cover of darkness the enemy had crept stealthily back into their second line trenches and were reeking a terrible revenge. The British line was too thinly held, too exposed, their artillery, so far, ineffectual on the redoubts, not even finding the range.

Lieutenant Colonel Andrews fretted and cursed. Until the redoubts had been dealt with he could not move, could not bring his rear Company forward. He had no Forward Observation Officer to guide the artillery and the runners he desperately sent back to the Brigade battery, with messages aimed at helping to direct fire, were obviously either ignored or unable to get through.

By mid-afternoon the Twenty-first Brigade had moved exactly nowhere and to make things worse their own Batteries were now enthusiastically dropping shells well short of the enemy, hitting their own trenches. With mounting frustration Andrews tried again to redirect the guns, sending message after message. If the artillery could not get the damned range they may as well stop shooting altogether for what good they were doing. The CO could not afford more casualties through friendly fire.

D Company's front was lively to say the least. They had dug in as best they could overnight, but they were stuck. No one dare raise his head an inch above the trench wall. The three sentries who did were already stiffening with rigour mortis, their comrades edging around their bodies if they needed to move.

Sitting miserably in the muddy clay the men and officers were hungry, cold and fed up, yet could do nothing but wait. Wait for the artillery to flatten that bloody redoubt directly in front of their tenuous position, to wipe out the machine gun on the left. But the shells that fell were short more often than not and casualties were growing.

The men worked carrying the dead out of the way, crawling on hands and knees, shifting the corpses into a hastily prepared, short trench at right angles to the existing line. No more than a ditch, barely three foot deep, it was somewhere to pile the bodies so that they maintained some space up front. The increasing numbers of wounded sat in the same ditch, dull eyed, exhausted, not wanting to share their position with ghosts. But it was impossible to get back. The one or two who had tried were lying spread-eagled in the open, blankly staring at the overcast sky. With no cover it was suicide. Best wait until darkness and hope not to bleed to death in the meantime.

With no rations coming forward, the dead were rapidly relieved of their meagre supplies, the tins of bully and the rock hard biscuits being shared amongst their living comrades. The scant food barely filled a small hole in a man's stomach after a day of fighting and a night of working. Hunger gnawed at empty bellies, thirst tore at parched mouths and throats, but there was nothing for it other than to wait and hope for a breakthrough soon.

A low whistling moan droned heavily through the leaden sky. The men instinctively ducked low, huddling as close to the ground as the seeping mud would allow.

"IT'S SHORT, IT'S SHORT!" someone cried out. Another voice yelled back telling him to shut it. Young Dobson whimpered, his nerves shattered, his head aching and light from lack of sustenance and the constant pounding of artillery, the concussion of shells. Sam slipped a comforting arm around the private's shoulders and like a frightened child the young soldier buried his head into the corporal's chest. The men covered their heads vainly and prayed.

The weary missile detonated ten yards away, its explosive force throwing muck high in the air to rain heavily upon the troops sheltering in their make-shift trench. The blast bowled sandbags backwards onto the helpless soldiers beneath. They dived spontaneously into the mud, deafened and reeling.

"*Make it stop! God please, make it stop!*" Dobson shrieked clinging desperately to Sam as the latter lifted his head and rubbed the dirt from it.

"Come on Dobbo, pull yourself together lad. We're still alive," Hepworth snapped, his own nerves frayed and his temper irascible because of it. He shook the private roughly. This funk was beginning to affect them all. Dark looks were cast in Dobson's direction with every cringing squeal he uttered. They did not loathe him as a coward, but they resented his lack of self control, it unsettled them all.

Sam glanced around, trying to ignore the trembling youngster at his side, and check the rest of his section for casualties. There were none, but somewhere to the right a man was screaming. Stretcher bearers were called for and squeezed by, clambering over the cramped legs of their comrades, crawling through the slime. Dobson began to cry.

"Christ Corp, can't we get 'im out of 'ere? 'E's no bloody use to anyone like that and 'e's givin' me t' bloody collywobbles," a private two men to the left grumbled loudly.

"Where's 'e supposed to go to Stan? Kid isn't injured is 'e," another retorted irritably.

"Well someone fuckin' well shoot 'im in t' foot or summat," Stan spat back bitterly.

"Don't be a bloody idiot!"

General murmuring broke out. Angry words and arguments exchanged.

"SHUT UP! Arguing amongst ourselves won't make it any better. Like a bunch of bloody kids! Save your energy for fighting Fritz," Sam bellowed above the din of guns and men. The muttering died away. The corporal understood their edginess, sympathised with it and though Stan's suggestion of shooting Dobson was not even to be contemplated it did give him an idea.

"Jacko, hold onto the kid for a while. I won't be long," he pushed Dobson away towards Private Jackson, prising claw like fingers from his greatcoat. Such strength in fear, the lad's grip was like a vice.

"Dobbo, Bert, listen to me," Sam shook the private until his eyes focussed in concentration. "I'll be gone five minutes that's all. Jacko will... *Shit*."

A searing whoosh and a bang and more earth splattered into the trench as another British shell narrowly missed landing in it. Dobson screamed, Jacko swore.

"BERT, FUCKING LET GO OF ME, THAT'S A FUCKING ORDER,"

183

Sam yelled.

"Where the 'ell you going' Corp?" Jacko demanded none too keen to be lumbered with a snivelling youth.

"To rob the dead," Sam replied with a grim smile and wrenching himself free from Dobson's grasp scrambled on all fours, rifle slung across his back, towards the casualty ditch.

He reached the pile of dead and the white faced wounded with only one half hearted challenge from a fresh faced subaltern to which he had confidently replied that he was on an errand. He quickly assessed the bodies. They were propped three deep. The huddle of injured men five yards further back instinctively averted their eyes from the corpses. Amongst them a couple of RAMC stretcher bearers worked, too busy to notice anything amiss.

Sam took a deep breath and lunged into the heap of cadavers, pulling bodies away until he reached an officer. On finding one he glanced around furtively checking that no one was watching. The officer was Second Lieutenant Garfield. Two Platoon's commander. A good man. A good officer. *What a waste*! He began to rummage through the lieutenant's pack and pockets. His revolver and ammunition had already been recovered as per Army protocol. The corporal hoped that the other stuff might have been overlooked. He was in luck. In Garfield's breast pocket Sam's hands grasped a small, sodden box. Hurriedly he pulled it out, grimacing at the thick, sticky congealing blood that covered it and his hand. The unfortunate subaltern had been hit in the chest by shell casing and the massive hole it left behind was now a black and sickening mess of gore, lung and bone fragments; the dead man's tunic and trousers soaked in a great deal of it.

Sam swallowed back the rising bile and hoped the contents of the disintegrating box were still there, intact. He let the body drop back. It did so with a disconcerting and squelching thud.

"What are you doing here Hepworth?"

The corporal spun around in guilty shock quickly folding his fist protectively around his ill-gotten gains. The box scrunched soggily into pulp.

"I was asked to collect any rations that might have been missed Sir. From those that won't be needing them anymore. The men are hungry Sir," he answered the lie spilling forth easily.

Major Wilson eyed him askance and then nodded, his face grave and sad. "It's a poor show Corporal. Fine men gone to waste. Didn't even get a chance to fight. Christ, bloody useless gunners!" Wilson swore with frustration and anger. His eyes drifted from Sam to the dead and back again, his face softened into resigned fatigue. "You didn't find any?"

"No Sir, not yet. The job's a bit grim, Sir."

Wilson nodded in melancholy agreement. It was indeed grim. "Well, like you said Corporal, they won't be needing any food now will they? Carry on Hepworth."

"Yes Sir. Thank you, Sir."

Wilson squeezed by and pressed on to the wounded. Sam sighed with relief and returned his attention to the corpses. He had to look for rations now. The major was no fool and would smell a rat if he simply disappeared.

Pulling back the prone corpse of a dark haired private he jumped back with a yell as the head lolled heavily onto the cadaver's shoulder, held in place only by thin sinews of tattered muscle and flesh. It nodded obscenely, the man's eyes staring upwards, his mouth open. The bile rose uncontrollably and Sam vomited.

"*Fuck*!" he cursed and spat into the mud, wiping his mouth with a shaking hand. His eyes held those of the partially decapitated private. Ernie Fellowes, nice, quiet man from Hawes. Even quieter now, poor beggar!

"Sod this!" he glanced to where the major crouched amongst the injured and, deciding he would not be noticed, crept away.

Wilson saw the movement from the corner of his eye and briefly turned to watch. He saw the corporal vanishing around the traverse and he frowned thinking the man was up to something. He had not believed the story about searching for rations. The dead had already been relieved of anything so valuable. Still, the major had neither the time nor inclination to follow up his suspicions at this juncture and when he had, he would have forgotten the whole episode.

Returning to his section Sam squatted against the wall and carefully peeled apart the mushy cardboard in his bloody fist.

"What's that?" Jacko asked curiously. A few other men leaned forward to see, intrigued. Sam did not answer. Grimacing, he pulled apart the mess no longer particularly squeamish about having someone else's blood all over his hands. At last he retrieved the foil packet within. It was intact and inside should be five precious grains. He glanced at Dobson and tried to calculate a reasonable dose. He wanted to send the lad to sleep, not kill him and Bert Dobson was a skinny kid. Cannot have weighed much more than eight and a half stone soaking wet! Sam had often wondered how the private had managed to persuade the recruiting sergeant that he was old enough to enlist. Yet somehow he had done so and the scrawny youth had been with the Battalion now since June of last year. Everyone knew he was only seventeen. That was mainly why they had put up with his childish whimpering for so long. But even the most tolerant amongst them had his limit and patience and sympathy were wearing thin.

Sam decided that two grains would suffice. He ripped the foil open and emptied its contents into his hand.

"*Bleedin' 'ell Corp!*" Jacko exclaimed realising what the tiny grains were. The corporal glowered at him but said nothing.

"Here Bert. Here, take this," Sam pressed two grains between the boy's teeth and handed him a water canteen. "They'll make you feel better."

Dobson obeyed. Why should he not? Eppy always looked after him. Might have given him the odd clout now and then, but would never intentionally harm him. He swallowed.

Jacko's eyes bulged with alarm and he looked about anxiously. "*Christ!*" he muttered under his breath.

"I'll take him," Sam said and pulled the young soldier into a protective, fraternal embrace. It should not take long.

"What's 'e gi'en 'im Jacko?" Ted Little asked in the closest the bombardment would allow to a whisper.

"Morphine I think," Jacko answered equally low. The revelation filtered through the section.

"'As 'e done for 'im?" Stan questioned his eyes wide.

"Don't be so bloody stupid Stan," another man laughed nervously.

"'E'll be shot if 'e's killed 'im," Stan persisted undeterred.

"Shut it Stan! Dobbo'll just go to sleep. Eppy wouldn't do 'im in y' daft bugger," Ted added.

"I dunno. Y'never saw 'im shoot that bloody Kraut at Wipers. And then there wa' that business wi' Black Bright. Beat seven bells o' shit outta the bastard wi'out flinchin' once. Not that the bugger didn't ask for it like," Stan concluded.

A screeching whine, everyone ducked low and another shell sent hot shards of metal zinging into the sandbag parapet and shook the earth. Dobson moaned but did not rouse.

"Is 'e asleep Corp?" Jacko enquired raising his face to look.

"Yeah. Look, you didn't see anything, any of you. Pass it back. I don't want anyone else getting into hot water. This is my responsibility alright?" Hepworth urged.

Too bloody right it is! Jacko nodded. "Whatever y' say Corp. What y' gonna do wi' 'im now?"

"Get him out of here. Shell concussion," Sam grinned and shouted for stretcher bearers.

Jacko sniggered, "You clever bugger!" He passed the word back that Dobbo had been knocked out by a shell blast.

"Thank Christ!" Stan laughed and echoed his corporal's shout.

The body snatchers came hurriedly, closely followed by Sergeant Kelsey who had recognised the calls from part of his platoon and feared the worst.

"What 'appened?" he demanded with obvious relief that there was only one casualty.

"Think he was concussed by that last shell Sarn't," Sam lied

Kelsey looked around for verification. The men nearby nodded solemnly. A few mumbled "Aye".

"And no one else's 'urt or owt?" the sergeant questioned, gobsmacked that only one man could be injured.

"Rum business isn't it Sarn't?" Jacko added with such seriousness that it took all his self restraint for Sam to keep a straight face.

"Certainly bloody is," Kelsey agreed scratching his head. "Alright, get 'im outta 'ere. 'E better go back wi' t'other wounded when it's dark. Bloody weird though." He instructed the stretcher bearers and laid Dobson's rifle with the unconscious soldier.

"Ammo," Sam prompted and took Bert's ammunition bandolier from the sergeant to distribute amongst his men.

Kelsey crawled away following the unconscious Dobson upon the stretcher, shaking his head and muttering in disbelief.

Jacko laughed and his humour spread infectiously through the section.

"I 'ope they never find out though Corp. They'll 'ave them stripes off thi again as quick as a flash," Ted observed seriously after the amusement had died down. It had lifted their mood. Removing Dobson had relieved their nerves.

Sam shrugged with a grin. Dobson had been a liability and had to be removed. It had seemed the only way. He reflected how strange that the boy had gone to pieces like that when at Ypres he had remained steadfast.

"'E'll be alright though won't 'e Corp?" Stan asked having moved closer. Unlike his superior, Stanley Smith felt remorseful. On consideration he had probably been responsible for the corporal's actions.

"Thought you wanted him out of the way Stan," Sam responded and wished it was foggy enough for a smoke. But it was not.

"I did, but I didn't really want to 'urt 'im. 'E's just a kid. Drives me bloody nuts, but 'e's just a kid," Stan admitted.

"Don't worry. He'll sleep like a baby for a few hours. When he wakes up he'll be at the first aid post and Doc'll want to keep an eye on him for a while. He's out of this one. Hopefully he won't remember owt though, otherwise I'm buggered."

Stan stared and nodded. "Stupid little bugger shouldn't be out 'ere any'ow," he grumbled in reply and they all dived into the mud as another short one droned by.

12th March.

Furious rifle and machine gun fire from the three right-hand forward Companies broke the dreary misery of morning stand-to. Shouted orders sent hearts racing as the men of D Company stared into the mist with weapons ready and saw nothing. Yet somewhere out there a frenetic fire fight was underway.

A German counter attack; someone passed the message along the line. But it was impossible to see from this rear position. A strong and acrid smell of cordite hung heavily in the cold damp air and drifted slowly over the trenches. The persistent discharge on the right did not let up. Sounds both familiar and strange floated over the ditch where D Company waited on tenterhooks. Screams and shouts. Cheering, followed by the unmistakeable detonation of bombs. That the lads were busy there was no doubt. Flashes of yellow light rent the mist only to be engulfed into its grey shroud seconds later. Calls for stretcher bearers during an eerie lull. Another ear-splitting volley of rifle fire, unremitting and ferocious.

For some minutes an unseen battle raged before very gradually the firing petered out, became sporadic and then ceased only to be replaced by the blood chilling moans and cries of dying and wounded men.

"*Jesus*! What's 'appened? D' you think our lads stopped 'em?" Ted asked his eyes wide and staring uselessly into the grey dawn.

"Sounds like it," Jacko muttered back optimistically.

They remained at the ready for another couple of hours during which time a short and sudden burst of bombing rent the silence. Again out of sight. They could only guess at the cause and trigger fingers twitched nervously, but discipline staid their fire.

By mid-morning the fog lifted and word passed that a German raid had been repelled. Half the Company stood down to grab some food. A meagre supply of rations had somehow made it to them during the night. Apparently there had been more, but it had met a sticky end when hit by a German five-nine.

Sam rubbed his eyes smudging fresh dirt across his already filthy face and forehead. He readjusted his position and kept his head down, peering only through his loophole. His mouth was dry and his stomach ached from want of food. He hoped nothing would happen before he got a chance to eat.

Something did happen, but it was way off to his right and he could not see through his miniscule field of vision. A whistle blew followed by manic cheering. Immediately machine gun fire replied angrily from the right hand German redoubt. Some foolhardy attack! Sam cursed to himself in frustration and anger. Did the damn commanders at Division not know that the bloody artillery had not taken out any of the enemy strongholds? The attack was sure to fail and end in futile carnage.

Inevitably the shouting diminished and the machine gun stuttered to a halt. Once more the cries of injured men filled the vacuum. A few shouted orders, clanking of equipment and distant voices carried blindly on the still air. Pungent cordite fumes made his eyes smart and with relief Sam swapped places with Stan Smith as the order to rotate the watch was called. He squatted in the mud at the bottom of their makeshift trench and tucked greedily into a tin of bully beef washed down with a mug of cold tea and fought the urge to rub his eyes again.

The CSM squeezed along the ditch, pausing to speak to any NCO huddled there, before pushing on. Wherever he came across an officer he spent a little longer.

"Ey-up, Goldilocks is on 'is way. What's this about then? Summat must be up. Must've found out about young Dobbo, Corp," Jacko teased and rapidly shovelled his beef into his mouth. God knows when they would get anymore and he did not want to lose out now. Sam swore at him in reply and watched Beale approaching curiously.

"Eppy," the sergeant major acknowledged as he drew level. His cap sat slightly askew upon a bloody bandage inexpertly fastened around his head.

"Sir," Sam respectfully returned.

"Artillery is going to take out these redoubts. When t'barrage lifts, two platoons will push forward and join up with C Company. Three and Four Platoons 'ave drawn t' short straw. Better get your section ready Eppy. I'll be leading you lot with Sergeant Kelsey."

"No officer with us, Sir?"

"None to spare. We've lost over 'alf of 'em," Beale replied tetchily as if he thought this should be obvious.

Sam reflected that it was and nodded. "We'll be ready Sir. Let's hope they get the range right this time though."

Beale smirked. "Well they can see further today and word is they've got the proper co-ordinates this time. They don't 'ave an excuse not to." He noted the cynical sneer on the corporal's face and ignored it. He too was not overly confident after yesterday's fiasco. He leaned forward and muttered lowly, out of earshot of anyone else. "I'm relying on you Eppy to keep the platoon steady. Kelsey's alright, but 'e's isn't as steady or reliable as you." He smiled and hurried off before Sam could reply.

The artillery fire was vicious and, for once, on target. At long last the Battery observers had been able to reconnoitre German positions, adjust calculations and finally throw enough steel at them to dislodge or obliterate their occupants. Vast numbers of the enemy surrendered, walking out into No-Man's-Land with hands aloft. The barrage lifted and the order was given for the two Platoons to advance and straighten the line. They pushed by grey-clad, exhausted prisoners moving back to the British lines and hurried to take up a new position. They got a little more than half way when the bullets cut into them. Only one redoubt had been destroyed. The other was barely touched and its occupants had raced back to their positions and began to rake both advancing Tommies and surrendering Germans, with indiscriminate enfilading fire.

Running hell for leather, aware of the zip of missiles whizzing by his head, aware of the occasional grunt of a man nearby and a glimpse of someone falling through the corner of his eye, Sam raced towards their goal. A second before leaping into the trench a dull thud against his pack impressed a narrow escape. Vaguely he thought "that's two in there now," and vowed never to part with this lifesaving knapsack. He landed heavily next to Jacko who must have run like the wind. Others tumbled in behind him. A few seconds only to catch his breath and set men to work reversing the parapet and a number covering their front. A quick head count. Men were still dropping into the trench, but it was already apparent that Four Platoon had suffered a good few casualties.

"Anyone seen the CSM? Sam shouted above the racket. A few grunts pertaining to the negative replied. The sudden spark of concern had to be pushed away, buried along with other anxieties, for later. There was no sign of Sergeant Kelsey either.

Still, men crawled into the shelter; many of them now were wounded to some extent. They crumpled in a heap of relief and utter fatigue, the strain and pain evident upon their blackened, stubbled faces.

"Right get this fucking trench reversed. JILDI! No bloody lounging. Fritz isn't going to wait until we've had a bloody rest. COME ON. SNAP TO IT!" Sam bellowed kicking and pulling men to their feet. There seemed to be no one more senior to take charge. Moaning and grumbling they obeyed him and wearily began to rearrange the German trench, reversing the parapet with hurried care. It would be a rudimentary job. No point in risking too much. When darkness came they could make a better go of it. At least the trench was deep. Fritz knew how to dig a safe hole.

The machine gun fire had dwindled to an occasional stutter, but a heavy fight raged once more further south and bursting shells ensured that all instruction had to be shouted above the din.

Sam strode along the ranks setting a number to cover the workers, organising the work, bullying where he needed to, cajoling where he knew it would have better effect. He searched for surviving NCOs and first came upon Bill Pratt.

"Bill, take a couple of men and look for dug-outs. Don't want some dirty Boches sneaking out of the ground and doing for us."

The lance corporal grinned and scurried away with two men. With everyone working, Sam instructed two runners to head along the trench, in opposite directions, and make contact with any officer they came across. Three and Four Platoons were in position, but all officers had been lost. Keeping his head low, Sam turned to check on the wounded. None seemed too bad. A couple of superficial head injuries, the others flesh wounds, painful, but not life threatening. The worst cases would be still out there, unable to get forward or back by their own hand. In the absence of stretcher bearers, he gathered the casualties together and instructed them to take care of each other's injuries. Once dressed they could join the watch.

Things seemed to be coming together. The first runner returned with news that Lieutenant Charlesford from C Company would inform the company commander and then would be down as soon as possible to assess the situation. In the meantime, Three and Four Platoons were to carry on as they were.

"Corp, Corp! Over 'ere," a voice shouted above the rattle and thunder of weapons. Crouching where the trench wall was still too low to stand, Sam hurried towards the cry. A group of soldiers, 'A' section men, including their own corporal, were huddled around a form sitting in the mud.

"What is it? What's up? Dixon?" he addressed his counterpart. The NCO looked around at him, his expression changing from anxious to relieved.

"Eppy, it's the CSM," he yelled above the noise. "I've sent a runner for body snatchers, but...," Dixon faltered and stared at the ground.

Sam pushed passed him and squatted before the wounded man. *Christ Almighty*!

Beale's tunic was soaked with blood in one gory mess from his chest down to his waist. His trousers too were sodden. He smelt strongly of urine and faeces and his breathing came shallow and laboured.

Sam's heart missed a beat; he swallowed hard biting back the horror and outrage, the terror that threatened to overwhelm his self control. He snapped at the men to return to work. Dixon crouched behind him.

"Don't know 'ow the poor sod's still alive Eppy. Dragged 'imsen over a couple o' minutes ago. Christ! Look at 'im."

"Thanks Dix. Look, see if you can chase up these stretcher bearers. He needs help fast."

"Jesus man, 'e's dyin'! Nowt'll save 'im." Dixon returned.

"Just fucking do it Dix! He's not dead yet."

Dixon stood as high as he dare, thought about retaliating, about making some retort to the effect of who put Eppy in charge, but refrained. He understood the aggression was born of the pain at seeing old Goldilocks shot to bits. He knew that Eppy held the CSM in almost fatherly esteem. He nodded and placed a sympathetic hand on his comrade's shoulder.

"Aye, alright," he uttered and sauntered off.

A swell of emotion rose in Sam's stomach. A mixture of fear, anger, frustration, love and hate. Love for the man slowly dying in front of him. The man he had learned so much from, whom he had looked upon not only as a fine and respected soldier, but as a mentor, a father figure and a friend. Hate for the German bastards who had done this to him.

"Sir, can you hear me? It's Eppy, Sir. *Oh Christ*!" He spoke loudly into the sergeant major's ear, his last phrase a cry of despair.

Beale choked a half laugh and his eyes fluttered open. "Eppy," he breathed and coughed. Little bubbles of pink froth formed at the corners of his mouth. Sam stared at them in morbid fascination. He felt his eyes prick and his throat constrict. Somehow he managed to stem the rising tide and steel himself. He began to unbutton the warrant officer's tunic. A bloody hand grasped his weakly and dull, heavy eyes held his horrified stare. Beale shook his head.

"No use Eppy. I'm riddled through. Can't y' smell 'ow rotten I am?" he tried to laugh again but started to cough hackingly. "Shot me through the guts, the bastards!" he gasped.

Sam *could* smell him. The sergeant major's abdomen was ripped apart by bullet holes through which bodily fluids other than blood seeped unchecked, soiling his clothes.

"Are you in pain?" he asked feeling desperately helpless. *What a stupid question.* Beale's eyes had closed again, his hand still on the corporal's. He did not respond. Sam squeezed the hand and the eyes fluttered painfully open.

"Give us a drink Eppy, there's a good lad," the CSM begged at last.

Sam let go of the clammy hand. Far too cold and damp to be good. He reached for his water bottle. It was nearly empty, but he placed it to the sergeant major's lips and helped raise his head to allow him to drink. Beale groaned as a wave of agony tore through his wrecked body. He swallowed deeply half choking and desperately thirsty. He was glad it was Eppy with him at the end. Eppy was a good lad. A little headstrong at times, but a good lad. Bright as a button and full of spark. Best kid brother a man could hope for. And they were brothers.

Sam gazed with despair as the wounded man slaked his thirst and the water he swallowed so voraciously seeped back out of his holed torso, spreading rivulets of pink fluid onto the gory tunic, before soaking in with the rest. He made a soft mewling sound in his throat and stared heavenwards, "*Sweet Jesus!*" his eyes smarted with salty tears.

"I've got some morphine Sir," he offered loudly turning his attention away from God and back to his comrade.

Beale shook his head. "Don't waste it on me lad. Save it fo' when it can do some good eh?" He closed his eyes again and his face clouded as a spasm of pain shook his frame. He groped with his hands, searching for comfort. Sam grasped them and choked back his emotion.

Corporal Dixon returned with two stretcher bearers and Lieutenant Charlesford from C Company.

"Alright Corporal, the bearers will take him now," Charlesford shouted above the constant barrage of exploding shells.

Reluctantly Sam made to pull away, but Beale tightened his grasp and his lids flew open. Blearily he focussed upon the officer and the body snatchers. He shook his head violently and spoke, but his words were lost to the cacophony of the battle. Charlesford crouched nearer the sergeant major's face to try and hear him. He glanced once at Sam, his expression sympathetic and he nodded his understanding.

"Leave him," he ordered the stretcher bearers. "You're needed further down the line anyway. Stay with him Corporal. Until it's over."

"Sir, the men. We have no officer and no NCOs above corporal," Hepworth explicated as the lieutenant turned to go.

"Understood Corporal. I'll send one of our subalterns down and Sergeant Beresford. Looks like the men are in hand anyway. Stay with CSM Beale," Charlesford answered with a faint smile. How could he turn down a dying man's last request? There was little time left to rob him of.

Sam nodded and sat back into the mud next to Beale, still holding his hands tightly.

Men splashed back and forth around them. Some stopped briefly to say a word, but on the whole they were too busy to stay. The sergeant major drifted in and out of consciousness, each time coming round with a sudden lurch causing his companion to start.

"Eppy?" Beale cried half in panic. It was getting dark. He could not see and he was afraid of being alone in this final dark.

"I'm here Sir," Sam squeezed the clutching hand and squinted upwards at the milky sky where a weak sun filtered onto the earth below.

Beale relaxed. "Don't call me Sir, Eppy. Call me by my name. Don't want to die wi' a friend callin' me Sir.

"Eppy?"

"Yes?"

"Write to Sally fo' me. Tell 'er I wa' thinkin' of 'er and the boys. Major's letter won't say so much. You tell 'er proper Eppy."

"Of course," Sam promised and blinked rapidly turning to watch two men piling dirt into sandbags to his left. They cast furtive glances in his direction but doubled their efforts when he met their gaze.

"Eppy?"

"Aye?"

"Don't leave me alone. I don't want to die alone."

"I'm going nowhere Fred. Here," Sam wrapped an arm around the sergeant major's shoulders and gently pulled him closer at the same time grasping his right hand tightly.

Beale gasped and breathed heavily with sickly fluidity for a moment. His body convulsed and Sam tensed screwing his eyes closed and pursing his lips.

"Do y' believe in God Eppy?" Fred asked, panting for air and sweating from the rigours of the latest spasm.

Did he? He had done once. He was no longer sure. *How could God let anything like this happen? He was supposed to be kind and merciful wasn't he?*

"I don't know," he answered truthfully. Maybe he should have lied.

The sergeant major laughed, "No, neither do I. But I believe in 'ell and this is it." He spluttered again and retched.

"You'll tell Sally won't y' lad?" he repeated. Had he asked that already? He could not remember.

"Yes, I'll tell her."

"It's gettin' dark Eppy, must be late."

Sam looked up into the bright sky and swallowed hard. *Not yet, please not yet.* He wasn't ready. There were things he wanted to say.

Another terrible spasm shook the CSM's body, his hand clasped agonisingly around his comrade's. He choked, making an odd gurgling sound in his throat. Sam clutched him tightly resting his wet cheek upon the matted head. The convulsion lasted a long time, about ten seconds in all and then with a long wheezing sigh the racked body fell limp.

The corporal closed his eyes and let the tears fall from beneath his lashes. He could not hold back the sorrow. Did not want to. For five minutes he let the grief pour forth and then, with the greatest effort he forced it back. He allowed pain to be replaced by rage, anguish by hate and he vowed vengeance. His soul screamed denial of God and he wanted to shout it out loud. To rant and rave. He did shout. Shouted his disbelief in the mercy of the Almighty. Only the Devil walked here.

"Corp?"

Sam looked up, his grimy face red and streaked with the tracks of tears. He rubbed it rapidly, smudging away the signs.

"What is it Bill?"

"No Germans 'iding and Lieutenant Charlesford wants to see thi," Bill Pratt said with as near to quiet respect as conditions would allow. "'As 'e gone then?"

"Aye, he's gone." Sam gently laid Beale's body back against the wall. "Go through his pockets will you Bill. I don't want someone nicking his stuff. Don't think anyone would, but... It should go back to his wife. Then you'd better get him moved out of the way."

"Alright Corp," Pratt replied flatly. He too was affected by the sergeant major's death. They all would be. He had been a popular and respected man.

"Where's the lieutenant?" Sam demanded.

"Back yonder. Round t' first traverse."

Hepworth moved away stealing only one last look at Fred's body before dragging himself together and returning to duty.

13th March.

In the early hours of the morning the Battalion was relieved by the Gordon Highlanders. Exhausted and depleted further by enemy shellfire throughout the afternoon, the Yorkshires staggered back behind the lines to the reserve trenches. Dead on their feet and faint with hunger and thirst they tripped and lumbered over potholed fields, stumbling over bodies, blindly trudging by the many RAMC men combing the area for survivors or simply collecting the dead. The worn out troops practically fell into the reserve trenches, sleeping, in most cases, where they landed. A few managed to stay awake to eat the breakfast of boiled bacon and tea that had been prepared for them. For the rest, it would be there when they awoke, albeit cold and unappetising.

Forcing down the bacon and gulping the tea, he never could stand being hungry, made him feel ill, Sam shuffled along the trench, finally finding an unoccupied shelf above the mud. He fell onto it, wrapping a greatcoat tight around his cold, fatigued body and drifted into welcome unconsciousness. Too tired to notice the discomfort of his bed, too tired to be disturbed by the constant thunder of artillery as dawn brought another bombardment and far too tired to notice the steady stream of wounded trudging or being stretchered back from the Front.

In the barn the night had brought a non-stop flood of wounded. Overwhelmed and overwrought the medical officers and orderlies had striven to do their best, but in truth they barely scratched the surface. Restricted by the sheer volume of numbers of casualties they administered basic first aid only, redressed a few and sent the poor blighters on.

As dawn filtered grey, smoky light into the Advanced Dressing Station and the guns thundered into life, Joe groaned audibly and wiped the sweat from his forehead on the back of his sleeve. It was freezing in the barn yet his body burned with fevered enervation.

"You need to rest Sir," Fallon observed quietly, his own head thumping in exhausted protest.

Joe laughed a little hysterically and finished tying the dressing to a severed hand. "He's done, move him out. Next one up!" he called.

"Sir?"

"How the *hell* can I rest Donal? Look at them all. Poor buggers," the lieutenant snapped back. Fallon raised his eyebrows but said nothing. The man was past it.

"Sorry Donal. We're all shattered. Another hour and it's our turn to rest, until then we keep going," Joe apologised with a sigh. They had started a sleep rota again at Foster's suggestion once the casualties began to mount up. A couple of hours only, just enough to make one crave more. Hepworth and Fallon were scheduled their rest at eight thirty. It could not come soon enough.

"Any news from the Front?" Joe asked. Talking helped keep him awake although his head was light and his vision occasionally blurred. *How the hell am I supposed to do this job properly under these conditions and this strain? Christ! I'm probably killing more men than I'm saving.*

"T'ink some progress was made from what the lads are saying. Looks like the cost was high though," Fallon muttered morosely, lamenting the futility of war.

"We're holding Fritz's trenches Sir. They won't push us out. Not the Immortal Seventh," the young soldier lifted onto the trestle said with a smile. He wore the badges of the Wiltshire Regiment and had a huge wad of dressings fastened bloodily to his neck.

Joe returned the expression wearily. "Glad to hear it Private. Now hold still while I have a look at you."

"Bloody great piece o' shell hit me in the neck Sir. Wham! Cor, you should've seen the blood. Spurting out everywhere," the youngster rambled with excited pride.

The doctor paused, his hands perfectly still upon the knot he had been endeavouring to unfasten. He glanced at Fallon who pursed his lips.

"Spurted out did you say, son?" Joe asked.

"Yeah. Like having a piss, er, if you'll excuse me Sir. Right from here." The private pointed to the thick pad of gauze plugging a hole in his neck.

"What's his label say?" Hepworth demanded his heart fluttering somewhere near his mouth.

"He doesn't seem to have one Sir," Donal replied.

"*Christ!*"

"Arterial?"

"Sounds like it. *Hell!*" Joe ran a blood stained hand through his hair.

"It's alright Sir ain't it?" the private asked in a frightened voice, his euphoric bravado suddenly dampened by the doctor's sudden hesitation and obvious anxiety. He did not know what the medics were talking about but it sounded like they were worried.

"Yes, yes it's fine. Only thing is we haven't got the right facilities here for you. I'm going to have to send you straight to the Clearing Station. I don't want you to touch your neck and I want you to keep your head as still as you can until you get there and a doctor sees you. Do you understand?" Joe explained carefully and took the label Fallon handed to him. On it he scribbled arterial bleed, left neck. Query carotid laceration. "Private, do you understand?" he pressed again.

"Yes Sir. Am I going to die Sir?" the soldier asked his eyes wide with fear.

The doctor smiled, he hoped reassuringly. "As long as this padding stays here you'll be fine. You need an operation that's all and we can't do it here. Can you do as I asked?"

"Yes Sir," the private uttered with the barest relief.

"Good lad. STRETCHER BEARERS!" Hepworth called as he tied the label to the young man's uniform. "Ambulance to CCS, urgent."

The men bundled the private away and Joe sagged visibly resting his hands on the trestle top, his head hanging. "God Donal, that was close. Too bloody close. How could I have missed it? It was bloody obvious, all that packing. *Jesus!*"

"It's exhaustion Sir. He didn't have a label. You noticed before any harm was done. That's all that matters. I didn't pay any heed either. We're both done in Sir."

Joe smiled grimly, wiped a shaky hand over his face "I scared the kid half to death. Poor sod!" he said and stood upright. "NEXT!" They carried on.

CHAPTER 25.
March 18th, London

The dark blue serge uniform felt horribly itchy. Thank goodness for the shirt underneath. Frank adjusted his tie nervously and stared at the facade of what had once been an orphanage, but had recently been transformed into Number Three London Military Hospital. He looked at his chit of paper and back to the grand Victorian edifice before him. What he could not see from here was the small town of huts that sprawled through the extensive grounds, replacing playing fields with convenient bungalow wards. It was still under construction, growing, it seemed to those who worked here, on a daily basis, like some miniature suburban sprawl. Evie squeezed his hand.

"Everything alright Frank?" she enquired smiling up into his face.

"Yes. It's really odd, but I feel quite nervous. Don't you?"

She shrugged. "No not really. It's not like performing at the Albert Hall is it? I mean there'll be a hundred or so faces at most, instead of thousands."

"That's what's making me nervous. It seems more intimate. You know, like a private concert," he tried to explain his sudden and illogical stage fright and laughed at how ridiculous it sounded.

"Well it's not like you're performing alone and we've been practising every night for two weeks. I doubt there will be many discerning ears amongst the audience anyway. A few of the officers maybe, but the rest..."

"Evie you snob! Are you telling me that the average Tommy Atkins will not appreciate our classical repertoire?"

Evie scowled. "I didn't mean it to sound so... It's just, you know, I think most of them will prefer the more popular stuff. I doubt many of them frequent a classical concert, but I'm willing to bet that they all go to the music hall."

"Just as well we're not playing anything highbrow then isn't it?" he mocked her once more and she squeezed his arm hard in reproof.

"Come on let's go in, it's cold out here."

Inside they were directed to the recreation hall, a large, high ceilinged room with a stage at one end. It had evidently been some kind of assembly room with a highly polished wooden floor and rows of long windows allowing an abundance of natural light, but affording no views to anyone gathered within. Upon the stage a number of musicians busily set up their positions.

Not a full orchestra and neither was it anywhere near as proficient as the London Symphonic, the majority of its members being able and enthusiastic amateurs rather than professionals. Even so, they could belt out a decent tune, as dear old Rose would have irreverently stated, and with Frank as lead violinist, they could not go far wrong. They would perform a few of the more popular classics, William Tell Overture, Rule Britannia, the overture from Carmen. Rousing stuff that always caught the mood of the audience. The rest of the concert they would accompany the singer, Grace Pemberton as she would undoubtedly engage the Tommies in a sing-along to the usual programme experienced in music halls all around the country. A comedian would rouse some laughs and then the performance would close with the National Anthem.

"Darlings you're here!" a distinctly theatrical voice boomed from in front of the stage. Frank and Evie exchanged a grin and headed towards the expansive and jolly figure of Mrs Davidson as she likewise dodged awkwardly around hospital orderlies setting chairs in readiness for the audience. Wielding her massive bulk with remarkable grace the august lady reached her youngest musicians without overturning or nudging a single seat. A feat that apparently dumbfounded one orderly as he stared with disbelief, scratching and shaking his head at the same time.

"Francis, darling," Mrs Davidson offered her wobbling cheek and Frank obligingly kissed it. "Evie, my sweet little child." The same cheek was proffered once more. "What do you think of our theatre? Quite grand isn't it? I am *most* impressed. Far better than at Number Two. But there you are. We must work in whatever is offered us. It is the performance that is important not the locale. Our meagre offerings bring joy to so many poor suffering boys. One should not grumble at our surroundings. But, this.., this is wonderful," the lady effused without drawing breath. "Come, come. We must get you to your positions. Grace isn't here yet, of course. Never, my dears, never burden yourselves with singers of even the obscurest celebrity. They are the most difficult of creatures and one frets so over their reliability."

Taking Frank by the arm, Mrs Davidson led him to the stage, leaving Evie to struggle alone with her cello case. Muttering under her breath the young woman barged through the chairs knocking one or two flying and apologised profusely to the disgruntled orderly who now stood stern faced with his hands on his hips.

"Can I carry that for you Miss?" he asked, determined that this small, pretty woman should not disrupt his militarily arranged seats.

"Oh, would you? Thank you so much. I'm so sorry, I've rearranged some your chairs." Evie thankfully handed the instrument to the middle-aged soldier.

"Not to worry Miss. I'll see no *more* damage is done," he replied pointedly causing Evie to flush with guilty embarrassment.

"Are you not placing any seats at the back, or have you not got that far yet?" she enquired trying to engage the surly man in conversation to hide her discomfort.

"That space is for the wheeled chairs Miss. Some of our lads won't be able to walk down 'ere. They ain't got no legs see, or they're still too poorly," he enlightened, his tone impatient like he thought she should know this. This *was* a war hospital after all.

"Oh yes, of course. How silly of me," Evie muttered in return feeling even more stupid than before. She climbed onto the stage behind Frank and offered thanks to the orderly as he handed up the cello.

"'S alright Miss," he grunted and hobbled off to finish his task. For the first time she noticed he walked very stiff legged, a lack of fitness that condemned him to war service at home rather than at the Front, though he looked far too old to fight anyway.

"Are you alright my dear?" Mrs Davidson bellowed causing Evie to jump as she watched the retreating orderly.

"Yes. Sorry Mrs Davidson. I was distracted for a moment."

Mrs Davidson beamed and then made a high pitched squeak of surprise. "Oh thank goodness. She's here. Excuse me my darlings," and she waddled off towards the back of the hall, where the star turn, Miss Grace Pemberton had just entered adorned in elaborate furs and a decidedly extravagant feathered hat.

"Are you alright? You look a little pale," Frank whispered and waved in acknowledgement to the second violinist.

"No I'm fine, it's just..."

"Just what?"

"Well, it's just struck me that the whole audience will be injured men."

Frank laughed. "Of course. What did you expect?"

"I don't know. I just hadn't given it much thought that's all. The orderly said some of them will be in wheeled chairs because they have lost their legs. I never really..., I'm not sure I should be here," Evie uttered forlornly.

"Don't be ridiculous. They'll be no different from any other audience except maybe a bit more appreciative," he encouraged, but watched her face with critical interest. He had never thought Evie to be squeamish or pathetic in any way. She always gave the impression of being strong. He frowned and reached out to squeeze her hand. Her distant and anxious expression melted and with determined cheeriness she returned his encouraging smile.

"I'm alright. I'm just being silly that's all," she said and picking up her cello drifted to her seat upon the stage.

The babble of men died down to an expectant hush as the commanding officer of the Number Three London took the stage. He coughed to clear his throat, looked down upon the sea of faces, the few nurses and medical officers dotted amongst their patients, the bandaged heads, the slung arms, limbless sleeves and the crowd of wheeled chair occupants at the back. All stared back with almost childish expectation, their faces bright, happy, looking forward to the concert. The colonel coughed again.

"Ladies and Gentlemen," he began wondering if he should have been more military in his approach. "I will not bore you with a long speech. I know that it is not I you are here to listen to. So without further ado I am more than happy to introduce this evening's entertainment, kindly brought together by the splendid Mrs Davidson of the Red Cross. Please, put your hands together in welcome and I bid you enjoy your evening."

The colonel swept his arm across the stage and as his final words were lost in rapturous applause the conductor lifted his baton and the orchestra burst into life with a spirited rendition of William Tell. Classical merged seamlessly with contemporary music. Grace lustily regaled the crowd with their usual favourites, A Long Way to Tipperary, Who's Your Lady Friend and the like. Mr Crichton, the comedian, had them rolling in the aisles with his risqué jokes and amusing ditties.

Frank thought it wonderful. He had played to some appreciative audiences in his career, but none more so than this flotsam and jetsam of the battlefield. The Tommies roared with laughter and shouted uproariously for encores from every performer. It was impossible not to be buoyed on a wave of euphoria with them. And because of the avid appreciation, the surge of adrenalin, he played better than ever. When the orchestra finished its final piece the crowd clamoured for more by chanting and banging their tin mugs on chairs and floor alike. The din was unbelievable. It was fantastic! The conductor flourished his baton and the orchestra reprised the last verse of Rule Britannia, the invalids joined in, singing with unrestrained pride at the top of their voices. At the end the performers stood and bathed in the applause, grinning nearly as broadly as the men below them.

Grace Pemberton stepped over to Frank and leant to whisper in his ear. "Do you know it?" she asked.

He nodded. "Yes of course. You wish me to accompany you?"

"If you can manage it. I think you can," she smiled. He returned the expression and moved with her to take centre stage. The cheering throng beat frantically with their mugs and as the singer raised her hands they grew reverently silent, waiting for her to speak with almost breathless anticipation.

"Thank you. On behalf of all of us here I thank you for your most wonderful appreciation of our meagre endeavours." She paused whilst the shouting and whistling died away again.

"Before we finish with the National Anthem, I would like to sing to you a particular favourite of mine. It is a song from an Opera by Puccini and is called O Mio Babbino Caro. The words are in Italian, but the music speaks for itself. And I have the pleasure of being accompanied by Mr Frank Hepworth who normally plays with the famous London Symphonic." She waved an arm towards Frank who bowed in acknowledgement to both her generous introduction and the enthusiastic applause of the audience. He had no nerves now. Gone were the jitters of before the show. Now Frank had taken on the mantle of his alter ego. The performer. The artist. No longer the shy young man who scorned the company of strangers.

He placed his violin under his chin and lifted the bow and following the barest nod from the songstress, an indication that she was ready, he closed his eyes and felt the opening bars of the aria. They drifted pure and clear across the hall, a hauntingly beautiful melody played by a master of his art. Grace joined with a strong contralto. A good voice, powerful and clear, but it lacked that purity and pathos that the aria truly deserved.

The men went wild, obviously moved by the melancholy sweetness of the impromptu duet. Grace bathed in the limelight while Frank smiled abashed, suddenly shy again at the ecstatic attention.

"We perform well together I think Mr Hepworth," Grace leaned over between curtseys and uttered lowly. "We should do it more often." She took another deep curtsey and Frank bowed self-consciously once more before looking around and, taking his cue from the conductor, gladly hurried back to his seat.

A drum roll signalled the National Anthem and as if by magic the cheering stopped dead, a scraping of chairs filled its place where, those men that could, struggled to their feet. The hall burst forth with a lusty rendition of God Save the King and when the last bars died away the hospital orderlies began to move the less able patients and those that could walk drifted happily and noisily back to their wards. It had been a grand evening. An evening to write home about. The entertainment first class. The performers began to pack up their instruments and other belongings.

"So what do you say Mr Hepworth?" Grace interrupted Frank's conversation with the other violinists. He glanced at her thinking her intrusion rude though he was far too polite to say so. She was, as Mrs Davidson alluded to, a minor celebrity who had a high opinion of herself and although he could not deny she had a fine voice, a good ear and the attractively curvaceous figure that would always ensure she remained a favourite with the not too discerning Tommies, he found her rather vulgar.

"I'm sorry?" he said, though he knew only too well to what she alluded.

"My suggestion that we should perform together," she reminded with the mildest touch of exasperation.

"I rather think that is down to Mrs Davidson, don't you?"

"Tosh! I do not work for Mrs Davidson. I merely agree to offer my talents to her," Grace dismissed airily.

"Perhaps. But I *do* work for Mrs Davidson, or rather the Red Cross and as such my loyalties firstly have to lie with her. If she is in agreement, then I would be honoured to accompany you." His reply firm, but diplomatic.

"Oh, of course. Then I shall have words with her. You cannot deny Mr Hepworth, that the audience loved us."

Frank could think of no suitable remark worthy of him and so merely bowed his head in acknowledgement and watched the prima donna flounce away to accost a rather red faced Mrs Davidson who was enjoying the attentions of the hospital's commanding officer. Catching Evie's eye he intimated that they should go. He felt tired now that the adrenalin had subsided and he wished to go home. Evie seemed reluctant and only slowly finished packing her cello and music, her eyes constantly drifting to the few remaining patients in the hall who seemed to be waiting, probably for Miss Pemberton to make her exit.

"What's the matter?" Frank gave up and went directly to help Evie with her things.

"Nothing. I just don't want to go while *they're* still here," she nodded towards the little band of men. Frank looked across at them. Dressed in the hospital blue uniform there were about a dozen, all able to stand, a couple with an arm missing, three whose bandaged eyes assuredly meant they were blind, the others sported crutches and some showed no obvious injury at all.

"Why not? They won't bite. It's no different to well wishers after any other concert. They're probably all waiting for Grace anyway. Come on. I'm tired. I just want to get home." He picked up her hand. She snatched it away irritably. He stared dumbfounded.

"What's got into you?" he demanded.

"I just don't want to go past them. I can't face them. Look at them Frank," Evie moaned, tears welling in her eyes.

Why is she so emotional? "They're wounded men Evie that's all," he tried, not understanding her aversion.

"I can't stand it Frank. All the time we were playing I kept looking at them. It makes me feel so... I don't know, but I can't face them. What would I say to them if they spoke? I couldn't look them in the eye. My God Frank, some of them can't even see."

He could not understand her fear. It seemed totally irrational and completely out of order. He had never thought Evie capable of such selfishness. Angrily he grasped her hand.

"Come on, you're being a complete ass. We're going and if they talk to you, then you politely speak back. They're human beings Evie, not monsters!" He marched her off the stage and towards the exit where the group of wounded soldiers stood. As they drew near the men nudged one another and smiled expectantly. They were all officers; no doubt the only one's allowed the freedom to linger.

"I say, that was a cracking show," one armless lieutenant said as the pair drew level.

"Thank you. We're glad you enjoyed it," Frank replied conscious that Evie had slumped by his side and was gazing fixedly at the floor.

"Best show I've seen in a long time," another fresh faced subaltern joined in though his eyes were covered, his beaming young face spoke of his enjoyment. "Will there be another?"

Frank suddenly felt awkward. For a moment he understood how Evie felt. Here he was, seemingly able bodied, at least able to earn his living and live a normal life, whereas the men before him had sacrificed their fitness. Whether any of them would make a complete recovery he did not know, but it was certain that the blind men and those limbless individuals would not. What had the future in store for them? They had given so much. Would their country be grateful to them? Frank felt humbled by their jollity, their lack of self pity and also their lack of judgement towards him. He realised he must appear a fit man, but they had not spurned him or acted with scorn, only open friendliness.

"I'm sure there will be. That is our role after all," he replied.

"That Puccini aria you played with Miss Pemberton was delightful. You and she should tour the wards. There are a lot of chaps who can't get out of bed, who would give their right arm to hear something like that," the armless lieutenant suggested affably and chuckled as he realised his pun and waved his stump. His companions laughed. Evie shuddered.

"I hadn't thought of that. I'll suggest it, thank you," Frank returned with a grin.

"Excuse me," Evie muttered prising her hand from his and with the barest of nods at the men she hurried with her cumbersome cello away outside. Frank found his anger piqued and flushed with embarrassment on her behalf.

"Something wrong with your girl?" an officer on crutches with no foot asked as he appreciatively watched the rapidly retreating cellist.

"Just a little tired I think. A long day, you know." The reply felt inadequate and was. Frank imagined they knew why she had disappeared so quickly, he could see it on their faces. "I suppose, you're all waiting to speak to Miss Pemberton?" he offered casually.

"Oh yes. Quite an adorable creature isn't she?" armless number two eagerly replied. His friends sniggered.

"Old Dashforth here is quite smitten with Miss Pemberton. We've been telling him she's far too old for a boy like him and far too discerning," another blind man teased and his victim swore genially.

Frank grinned. Dashforth did not appear that young, well no younger than he anyhow, but then Miss Pemberton was a lady in her thirties and would no doubt find the attentions of this young man, though flattering, somewhat inappropriate. Or perhaps she would be happy of the attention. She was a performer after all, with an artist's ego.

"Er, you wouldn't do us a favour would you old chap?" armless number one asked.

"You want me to introduce you?" Frank guessed.

"If you wouldn't mind."

"Certainly. Let me go and fetch her." It seemed the least he could do and quite harmless. Evie, would no doubt be loitering outside. Well, she could wait.

He had no trouble extracting Grace from Mrs Davidson. The intimation that a dozen young men were waiting to make her acquaintance was more than motive enough for her to take her leave. She glided behind him and waited with false modesty while he made the introduction.

"Gentlemen, may I introduce Miss Grace Pemberton," Frank obliged and as the injured officers shook hands with the lady and bashfully acquainted themselves to the star he quietly took his leave.

He found Evie standing outside the main door on the steps. She looked miserable and tearful.

"I'm sorry Frank. I had to leave," she offered in pathetic explanation.

Frank stared at her with contempt. That he was angry was obvious. That he did not understand, more so, but she could offer him no substantial reason for her behaviour other than an abhorrence to invalidity and how could one admit to that? She dropped her eyes to the ground.

"Let's go home," he said coldly and stepped out into the night. He did not offer his arm as he usually did and neither did he speak. His disappointment and disapproval too great as yet to offer friendship and deep down his own fears had been aroused. Fears of Evie's ability to cope should he become ill. Would she? At this moment in time he very much doubted it.

CHAPTER 26.
April 2nd, Brigade Reserve, La Gorgue – Fleurbaix

It almost felt like Spring at last. The sun shone benignly, no rain for a change, though the roads were still knee deep in places and the countryside a bog. A few birds tentatively gave voice to a few bars of song like an orchestra warming up before the performance. Not quite ready yet to shout joyously from the tree tops, but preparing themselves for when the long, grey winter finally did loosen its tenacious grip. It seemed a long time since the hot summer of 1914. A long, dreary slog through a Hadean winter of brutal cold, hardship and death.

With his face turned to the warm sun, Sam Hepworth strode briskly through the French countryside, hopping through a hedge and over a ditch, leaving the road for the fields. It was a good five or six miles across country from La Gorgue, where the Battalion were enjoying a rest, to Fleurbaix. Further by road. And despite the fine weather, it would still be dark by eight. The going was not easy either. Shell craters littered the fields; filled with water they posed significant obstacles along with the debris of war; a shattered gun carriage, abandoned, or rather, forgotten tangles of barbed wire. Working parties were doing their best to clear the detritus away, but it was a mammoth task.

The mud piled up on the soles of his boots sucking at his feet, making the going heavy. He started to regret his route, thought it might have been better to go the long way round after all, by the road. Stumbling across a heavy battery desperately fighting with a team of horses and about thirty men to move a gun carriage from the quagmire, he decided to skirt behind it, not wanting to be seen or challenged. He had permission to be out and about, but if stopped by an officer it would waste precious time explaining and they would probably put him to task helping. Unseen, he ducked behind a ruined barn and pushed on, the sounds of men and horses dropping behind him, swallowed up by the intermittent thunder from the Front.

As he drew nearer Fleurbaix the country changed. Gone were the stands of trees and the greening fields he had passed through on leaving La Gorgue. Here the countryside was war torn. Shattered copses, demolished buildings, abandoned homes left to decay. Not even nature dare venture here yet. The shell holes were more abundant, dead horses and mules, though not numerous, were evident enough to add an unwelcome stench to the air. Depressing! A miserable reminder of Hell, as if one needed it. Sam cut through the remnants of a wood and dropped into a sunken road, busy with transports and troops moving back and forth between the village and the Front Line. No one paid him much heed. They were too busy with their own tasks. Most were working parties, moving up with picks and shovels to repair trenches or dig new ones. He did not know and cared less, but allowed himself to be carried with the stream heading back to their billets.

What a change! The village had been pummelled to a crumbling ruin. Hardly a house remained in-tact. Hard to believe the Battalion had been reasonably comfortable here only a few weeks ago. Most of the inhabitants had gone. Had made some half hearted attempt to protect their property before leaving. Boarded windows, padlocked doors. But artillery had little respect for such punitive efforts and properties lay in various states of devastation with walls ripped apart and the wreckage that had once been someone's pride and joy strewn to the four winds or left ripe for looting.

With an increasing feeling of dread Sam quickened his pace, side stepped the numerous pot holes and craters, avoided the rumbling wagons which invariably became stuck in the pitted road and had to be levered out with much swearing and cursing from drivers. He clung to the tumbledown walls of shops and houses and made for the café, ignoring the mayhem around him and hoping beyond hope there was something other than this destruction, something and someone left.

He turned a corner onto what had been the main road to Armentières and stood aghast, his heart thudding in his ears, his eyes wide with shock. The café was nothing but a shattered husk, its walls a pile of rubble and its red tiled roof a heap of debris within. Sam ran forward, stopped, stared and threw his hands on top of his head in a gesture of despair. *They can't be dead. Please, not her. Not Mariele*!

Someone passed near-by. Sam lunged towards the Canadian soldier and grabbed his arm. "The family that lived here, do you know what happened to them?" he demanded.

The Canadian looked first at the crazy British corporal and then towards the ruin. He shrugged. "Ain't a clue Corp. Either dead or gone," he replied unhelpfully. Sam gazed at him with angry frustration, his hand still grasping the man's arm.

"Do you mind?" the soldier indicated that he wanted to move on; it was a polite though unsubtle way of saying let me go. Sam dropped his arm, muttered an apology. Of course this man would not know, why should he? The Canadian trudged on.

"Hey, are there any civvies left here at all?" Hepworth called after him.

"Try the church," the soldier shouted back.

The church. Of course. These catholic priests were averse to leaving their flocks while any remained to be tended. Although Sam cynically considered that their devotion had a closer link to the riches within their churches than to doing God's work.

He ran across the street, dodging between trucks and dipped into the lane that led to the church. Like everything else the building had suffered the attentions of shell fire. Even God's house was not immune to the ravages of artillery. The tower had been reduced to a remnant; dangerously precarious pinnacles of mortar were all that remained. The transept fared little better with hardly any roof and its windows blasted in. It appeared deserted.

With growing pessimism he approached, stepped over a heap of stones that had once been a wall, noted a number of freshly dug graves marked by meagre wooden crosses and felt the hairs prickle on the back of his neck. *What am I doing?* There was no one here. He would never know her fate. Forlornly he sat on a fallen tomb stone and dropped his head in his hands. *So tired.* He felt so desperately weary. The glimmer of hope that had been the promise of a tender female caress, a dream held as light against the dark, had faltered and died. Extinguished along with the rest of his faith. *How many more?* Who else would he lose? The memory of Fred Beale drifted into his bereft mind, painful and cruel. The others at Ypres. There were countless names. *Harry Fielding? What had happened to him?*

"Can I 'elp you?" a quiet, accented voice asked making the corporal start violently and whirl around unbalanced. He slipped from his seat onto the damp earth and the kindly smiling old priest stepped forward to help him to his feet.

"I'm alright padre, you just startled me that's all," Sam responded, jumping up before the clergyman could reach him. Somehow the thought of those holy hands touching him was abhorrent. Like he was too sullied and tainted by evil and beyond the help of God.

The Priest sensed the recoil and dropped his arms. He studied the young Englishman before him; saw the exhaustion of spirit, the haunted eyes that held too much pain. "I'm sorry to startle you. You were looking for someone or only resting?"

A pause. A chance to know and now Sam was not sure he wanted to. It might be better to imagine she got away than know that she had not. The Priest smiled and cocked his head questioningly.

"I was looking for you I suppose," the answer at last.

"And now you 'ave found me. 'Ow can I 'elp you?"

Sam looked away towards the direction of the café and bit his bottom lip. He had to know. He sighed loudly and asked, "The Collet family, who ran the café, do you know if they..., where they are?" There it was done and now he held his breath waiting for the reply.

The Priest nodded and smiled kindly. "You wish to know what 'as become of Mariele?" he asked astutely. Sam flushed and nodded.

"She and 'er father are safe as far as I know. They left two weeks ago and went south. Monsieur Collet 'as family in the South. I believe they were 'eading for Paris and then on to Toulouse."

"Toulouse." Relief. Disappointment. So far away, but safe.

As if reading his mind the Priest echoed those sentiments. "It is a long way from 'ere, but you must be glad she is safe now. You 'arboured an affection for the girl?"

"An affection?" Yes he had. More than he had wanted to admit, or was that the war? Was it simply the need for comfort, for something as basic as sexual gratification and the delightful diversion of feminine company he had craved? A gentle fantasy in a brutal existence. "No more than any other man who knew her," he answered coldly. It was untrue, but he tried to convince himself. "Thank you Padre."

"You are welcome my son," the Priest responded quietly and watched the English corporal walk away. He hoped he had lifted a little of the load, but his feelings were that this one was close to becoming one of the lost flock. He shook his head sadly and returned to replanting the daffodil bulbs that the shells had torn up. They would not flower this year, but in time they might bloom once more.

CHAPTER 27.
April 23rd, Laventie

Cursing at the sudden downpour Joe pulled his cap firmly onto his head and hurried down the pock marked street. A group of Labour Corps men were busy filling in holes and they stopped to salute him as he passed by, still regimental and disciplined despite the atrocious conditions in which they worked.

Unusually the 'Town Major' had been most helpful in identifying the whereabouts of Sam's billet. The officer had been a little surprised perhaps when the RAMC lieutenant had explained the reasons for wanting to find Corporal Hepworth. But once he understood, he had been very accommodating. Even offered his congratulations and wrung Joe's hand joyously. The happy tidings were a glimmer of normality in an otherwise austere world and even an army billeting officer was not immune to the hope and joy such news brought.

As quickly as it started the rain ceased and warm sunshine broke through the scudding clouds. Somewhere close by a blackbird began his fluting song while up the line artillery boomed and thundered. A bizarre mix of peaceful serenity and the obscene.

Joe grinned. He could not help himself. Nothing could blight his mood. Not the showery weather, the constant noise of guns or the mud that seeped into his boots as he sank ankle deep into an unrepaired hole filled with cold, murky water. He had to share his joy with his brother. Had already told everyone in his own billets; dragged Fallon out of the NCOs mess and regaled him with unchecked exuberance. The smiling Irishman had shaken his hand most affectionately and wished him hearty congratulations before Joe had felt the need to find Sam and left the orderly corporal shaking his head in amused wonderment.

Begging a lift with the rations transport out of Estaires, the buoyant doctor made his way, somewhat impatiently, to Laventie, treating the driver to enthusiastic chatter. The poor man probably wished he had refused the lieutenant, but how could he? Yet it was most irregular to find oneself engaged in heartfelt conversation with an officer and the driver had been relieved when he dropped his passenger off at Battalion Headquarters.

At last Joe strode purposefully down the main thoroughfare through town towards a billet at a farm on the outskirts. Apparently D Company was housed up there, with the officers in the half ruined farmhouse, the men in the barn and the NCOs in a stable. It did not sound too auspicious. The Town Major had laughed when he had commented as such and said that with so many troops in Laventie it was the best that could be done. Besides, the billet lay on the quieter side of town and was rarely troubled by shelling. Corporal Hepworth would be there, probably, unless they were out training or working. More likely they would be preparing for parade at this time. Joe had not really listened and was still not fully familiar with the everyday tasks of soldiers out of the line. This so called rest puzzled him, for it seemed the troops worked harder and suffered more pointless discipline than ever they did at the Front.

He found the farm. Asked a young private leaving a large and noisy barn where he might find Corporal Hepworth and was directed through an archway into a cobbled courtyard beyond. The property had obviously once been quite respectable and of greater affluence than the majority of farms in this part of France. However, it now had a slightly knocked about appearance; too many loose tiles on building roofs, the odd wall tumbled down and windows of the house boarded where once glass had allowed light to enter. Across the yard a low brick stable enclosed the northern edge, the doors of which had seen better days and had been hastily repaired with little skill or care. Where the roof was damaged a tarpaulin had been slung to stave off the rain. It flapped precariously in the stiff breeze causing the dozen or so men within to gaze up anxiously just as the doctor entered. Someone called that an officer was present and everyone jumped to his feet, standing at attention.

God! He would never get used to this. Joe blushed, once again feeling like a fish out of water. He looked around, noted that despite its ramshackle appearance outside, the billet was a picture of military order and cleanliness within. Bed rolls lay on clean straw at precisely measured and equal intervals. Neatly stacked next to them were each man's valise and his kit. Rifles were propped in wigwam fashion in the middle of the room. A few oil lamps burned to give extra light and many of the NCOs present were jacketless and in the process of brushing tunics, polishing buttons, insignia or boots. One man was half way through a shave.

"Sorry to barge in. Er, please, carry on as you were," Joe stammered self-consciously and looked about for his brother.

The men returned to their chores casting an occasional, curious glance in the doctor's direction. He had not said why he was here. Simply walked in. Perhaps it was an impromptu hygiene inspection although he was not their Battalion MO. Well, he would not find anything untoward here.

"Can I 'elp you Sir," a pale faced corporal, nearest to the door asked. He held a button stick in one hand and a tin of Soldier's Friend polish in the other. A blast of fresh air and a sudden brightening of the stable indicated someone had opened the door. Instinctively Joe stood to one side to allow the entrant to pass.

"Er, yes. I'm looking for my... er, for Corporal Hepworth. Is he here? I can't see him."

"Behind you Sir," a familiar voice answered causing the lieutenant to jump around. The pale faced corporal smirked at his comrade from behind the officer's back and sat back to his polishing. Sam saluted and failed to hide his own amusement. "You wished to see me Sir," he said.

"Yes. Er, would you walk outside with me Corporal? Joe replied trying to sound authoritative. It came out like a request.

"Certainly Sir," Sam indicated that his brother should lead the way. He winked at Bill Pratt who sniggered and shook his head. *Bloody temporary officers!* They were pains in the arse most of them. The RAMC blokes were usually alright, but they were about as soldierly as a troop of boy scouts.

The brothers walked in silence across the courtyard and out into the lane leading back into Laventie. Joe turned right and headed into open country, Sam following with growing apprehension. *Had something happened at home?*

"Is everything alright Joe?" He asked after about fifty yards without a word passing between them.

"I'm a father Sam!" the doctor blurted, his joy spreading across his face. He started to laugh.

His brother grinned broadly at both the news and his usually reserved sibling's boisterous expression of happiness. "That's grand Joe. What is it?"

"A boy. I have a son! Robert Joseph Hepworth. Seven pounds seven."

"And Dora? She's well?"

"Blooming by all accounts. My God Sam! I want to tell everyone. I *have* been telling everyone. I think half the Brigade must know by now. I never felt so proud."

Sam laughed. This ecstatic man before him was so unlike the restrained and serious brother he knew. He held out his hand. "Congratulations! I'm overjoyed for you," he offered with feeling.

Joe clasped the hand tightly in both of his and wrung it exuberantly. "I had to tell you. I couldn't wait or send it in a note, so I cadged a lift with Transport. Poor bloke driving must have thought he had a lunatic next to him. I never shut up. I must have made quite an impression on your Captain Swain as well, because he couldn't have been more helpful. Let's celebrate. Let's have a drink."

"Joe, I've got Parade in half an hour and you're an officer remember," Sam reminded with only a hint of exasperation.

Disappointment momentarily clouded the doctor's face. He had not reckoned on Sam being unable to get away, although he should have done. The rumble of wheels and laboured groaning of an engine caused him to look around and they both stepped cautiously out of the road and onto the long grassy verge as the ponderous lorry wheezed by. They watched it pass incuriously, lost in their own thoughts momentarily.

"I didn't think you might be busy. I still don't understand this Army concept of rest," Joe admitted. "Still, you've got a few minutes. We can have that drink," he pulled a small hip flask from his tunic pocket.

Sam grinned and shook his head. He glanced at his watch. "Ten minutes then. I'll have to clean my bloody boots again." He jumped up onto the remnants of a wall and the MO climbed up next to him offering the flask. He took it and offering a toast took a swig of rather good brandy. "That's good. Where did you get it?"

"Charles sent it. I've got a couple of bottles. You can keep the flask if you like. It'll do you good on a cold night in the trenches," Joe replied still smiling as he handed the brandy back to his brother.

"Thanks."

"Quite alright. I wish..., that we were at home. I wish we could... you know, just go down to the pub. You, me, Frank and Dad. It'd be grand to wet the baby's head in the Wagon and Horses."

"Lily would be miffed if she couldn't come too," Sam stated as he took another sip of brandy and thought he better not have more.

"Women are strictly not allowed at such a gathering. Wetting the baby's head is a male preserve," Joe answered in all seriousness but smiled at his sibling's chuckled response. He too could envisage the remonstrations of their sister at being excluded. A brief silence ensued; he was not sure how to ask the next question. Not sure how it would be greeted. The future was so uncertain. In the end he decided that the straight forward approach was best.

"I know it could be a long while before we all get home, but would you be God Father?"

Sam nearly choked on his final sip of Brandy. He coughed and his eyes watered. "Jesus Joe, why not kill me with shock?" he spluttered. "What about Robert?"

"I've asked Robert already. We need two remember. Two God Fathers for a boy. Lily will be God Mother of course."

"What about Frank?"

"I don't think Frank will mind do you? What do you say?"

Sam studied his brother for a second. To say he was surprised was an understatement. He was not sure whether he set the best example. A God Father should be upstanding and respectable should he not? Still, Joe seemed serious and so he felt duly humbled. "It would be an honour Brother. Thank you."

"No, thank you."

"Better keep Frank in reserve though just in case I buy it," Sam added with a cynical chuckle. "*Christ*! Look at the bloody time. I have to go Joe. Sorry. It's been great. Thanks for the brandy. Thanks for thinking of me," he leapt from the wall in a sudden flurry and thrust his hand out. Joe shook it warmly.

"Look after yourself."

"Of course. You too. Ta-ra then." Sam turned and had taken three strides when his brother called out to him.

"Sam wait! Sorry. I forgot to return this. You'll be wanting it back." Joe held a familiar, dirty envelope in his hand.

The corporal stared at it for a second his expression unfathomable. "Chuck it. I don't need it anymore," he said at last.

"What? But why? I thought..."

"She's gone." The tone was flat, unfeeling.

"Gone? She's not...? She hasn't been killed has she? I heard Fleurbaix was badly shelled."

"No. Left with her Dad. Gone to Toulouse or somewhere that way. The village priest told me," Sam enlightened with apparent nonchalance.

"Oh! That's a relief then," Joe returned still holding out the tattered envelope. "I'm sorry though. You really liked her didn't you?"

"What makes you think that?" An edge now, in the voice.

"Well you wrote this to her. She must have been special enough for you to..."

"She was just a welcome diversion that's all and *that* was a means to an end," the interruption was curt, its intimation disagreeable.

"A *diversion*? Really? Come on!" Joe could not hide the sarcasm. He did not believe a word of it. Sam might like to play the hard nut, but anyone who knew him knew he was really soft as shit!

"Yeah, really," the corporal bit back.

"So you don't want this?" Joe waved the envelope in the air.

"No. Like I said, chuck it."

The doctor nodded.

"Any chance of leave?" Sam relented changing the subject. He was being an arse and he did not want to quarrel and spoil his brother's mood.

"Maybe. Not yet though. Maybe at the end of May."

"That'll be good. Give my love to Dora."

"I will. Why not write yourself?"

"Yeah. When I get chance. I owe her a long letter to thank her for the socks," the corporal laughed again. "See you Brother."

"Bye Eppy," Joe used the nickname for the first time and they exchanged a grin. He watched his sibling hurry away, jumping over the worst of the mud filled puddles in a vain attempt to prevent his already blathered boots becoming even filthier. They would take some getting clean and he had precious little time to do it in.

Joe felt a pang of guilt that he may have got his brother into trouble, but then he doubted it. The impression he had of Sam the soldier was one of competent ingenuity.

He stared at the envelope and sighed folding it back into his pocket. Joe looked up at the sky, saw another shower was on the way and decided to find a lift, if possible, back to Estaires.

CHAPTER 28.
April 27th, No. 13 General Hospital, Boulogne

Lunch. At last a chance to read Joe's letter. Lily had a good idea of the news it would hold as she had already received long correspondence from both her parents and Dora telling of the birth of a baby boy. And she needed some good news. The hospital was burgeoning with casualties from Ypres, where another battle raged. They had had to clear the wards and evacuate boys to England, who really should not have been moved, more times than she could count. Or so it seemed. Each time to make room for a fresh, relentless stream of torn and battered men. It continued yet. On a still day they could hear the guns from here and each day more train loads arrived. At present they experienced a minor lull. The numbers arriving not so great. It gave respite for the nursing and medical staff and rest for the wounded soldiers within the hospital. They all, of course, longed for the blue ticket to Blighty, but many needed careful nursing and treatment before they left.

Lily felt exhausted and fed up. The news that her application to transfer to the hospital trains had failed had cast her in a sombre mood for a day or two. A mood quite out of character and worsened through lack of sleep and long days. Polite, but to the point, the notice had informed her that as she was only a Staff Nurse she could not as yet be considered to work on the trains. The authorities demanded only the most capable of nursing sisters for this role and currently her level of experience was inadequate.

What did they know! The disappointment had been compounded by a severely disapproving letter from Sam. *As if it was anything to do with him! He was a fine one to talk about consideration given to what their parents might think!* Lily had fumed angrily. Felt hurt at both the rejection and her twin's moralising. But in the end, as was her nature, she made the most of it. She still enjoyed her work at the hospital and at least now she would not have to broach the subject with Robert. He would most certainly have objected. Been angry even. *It was alright for men! They had everything so easy!* An unfair presumption perhaps, given the state in which many entered her ward.

So the letters brightened an otherwise unhappy week and now as she read it, Joe's hand spilled joy unbounded onto every page. Lily smiled broadly. She could not remember when her eldest brother had last, if ever, expressed his feelings so deeply. Possibly at his wedding, briefly, after a little too much champagne. His words filled Lily's heart with happiness and her eyes shone with emotion.

"You look happy. May I join you?" Gladys asked wearily and slumped into a chair opposite before her friend could answer. She stared at the food on the tray and dropped her head into her hands. "Oh God!"

"What is it Glad?" Lily put down her letter and touched her roommate's arm.

Gladys shook her head and stared tearfully at her lamb chop. She picked up her fork and began pushing the hard peas around the plate, making no attempt to eat.

"It's simply awful Lily. Awful! We lost another two over night and one this morning just as we were doling out breakfast. I don't know how much more I can stand. There's nothing we can do for them. We can't even alleviate their suffering. I've never felt so useless. And they're so frightened the poor things... Oh Lil!" She dropped her fork and began to sob into her hands.

A couple of sisters on an adjacent table glanced across curiously and a group of gossiping VADs fell momentarily silent. Lily hurried round the table and sat by her friend wrapping comforting arms around her shoulders. She made quiet soothing noises, trying to calm the distraught nurse.

Gladys worked on a medical ward and it had borne the brunt of victims exposed to the latest, horrific weapon to be deployed by the Germans. Gas.

The worst cases had been the French colonial troops. Poor Zouaves who spoke no English and heavily accented French making communication difficult if not impossible. They suffered doubly as a result. They did not understand the doctors and nurses who tried to treat and comfort them. But school room French was a far cry from a fluent native patois.

Blinded, the colonials battled to breathe through necrotic lungs in a terrible, fearful darkness. Ultimately so many died and were still dying. Drowning in their own bodily fluids as the noxious chemicals destroyed sensitive, vital tissues. It was a heartbreaking death. Painful and prolonged. The victims suffered hideously until the very end when they slowly suffocated, terror stricken and fully aware of their passing. For their helpless carers it was harrowing to watch and even the strongest will and the coldest soul could be reduced to pitying tears.

The cases amongst the Canadians and the British troops had, so far, been less severe. Even so, some were permanently blinded or would forever spend their lives struggling and wheezing for breath. The fear of an asphyxiating death gripped even those with only minor affliction for they had seen the stuff. Had seen what it did. Seen the greenish, silent, insidious vapour roll across the battlefield, sinking into trenches and hollows. They had seen what it did to the inhabitants of those spots. Had smelt and tasted its pungently nauseating aroma. Had vomited and wretched with eyes streaming.

The medical authorities were horrified. Scandalised even. It was a breach of the Hague convention. An indefensible and shameful assault on humanity and surely the perpetrators of this heinous crime would find a passage only to Hell come their day of judgment. There was nothing honourable in this weapon. It brought neither a glorious or swift death. It was becoming evident to everyone, even those whose patriotic zeal had led them to France to fight for the noblest of causes, that there was nothing virtuous in this increasingly cruel and vicious war. Humanity had found new and more sinister ways in which to kill and maim. Ways that had until now only been imagined by the most depraved minds as the most barbarous torments of Hell.

"Come now Forbes. This won't do. You have to pull yourself together. Everyone is staring at you," Lily whispered not unkindly, aware of the curious glances from around the canteen.

"*I don't care! You don't know what it's like. You don't have to nurse them!*" Gladys wailed and began sobbing uncontrollably. Lily rubbed her back vainly; not knowing what to say. What could she? Forbes was right. She did not know.

"What's going on here Hepworth?" a strong authoritative voice demanded. Lily jumped to her feet respectfully, recognising Matron's commanding tone immediately. Gladys slumped into her dinner tray.

"Matron. I'm afraid Forbes is a little overcome," Lily replied inadequately with a curtsey.

Matron's eyebrows flew into her hair. "Hmm, so I can see. Something to do with her work?" She continued to talk as if Gladys was not there.

"Yes Matron. Gas patients, Matron," Lily enlightened. She need not say more.

The senior nursing officer's stern countenance softened. She took a hurried step forward and gently helped the distraught staff nurse to her feet.

"Come now Forbes. Come with me," the sombre lady soothed. "I'll take over now Hepworth. Thank you." It was a dismissal. A reminder that there was work to be done elsewhere.

"Yes Matron," Lily replied and grabbing her letter headed back to her ward of cheerful amputees and surgical cases. Oh how lucky they were. If it could be described as lucky to have lost a leg or the use of an arm.

Back on ward five tea was being served by Davies, the ward orderly and Mabel Parkinson, the more than capable VAD. Mabel was a clergyman's daughter. Very robust. Used to accompanying her father on trips to help nurse his poorer parishioners. She was strong stomached and definitely not faint hearted. At thirty eight she was one of the older VADs. Very plain with a hard red face and straw like blond hair. Consequently she was a spinster still. She looked after the men well enough, was firm but compassionate, but oh was she pious! Too pious and too Quaker-like for the down-to-earth Tommies with their irreverent humour and blasphemous language. Far too pious for Davies, a lad of twenty four from the valleys of South Wales. His flat feet had prevented him from serving with a front line battalion, but they had not stopped his entering the Army.

Davies liked a joke, a pint or two; loved rugby and consequently his language had a tendency to be colourful. A railway worker by trade he was a cheerful rough diamond with a stout frame, mop of black hair and, like most of his creed, possessed a fine singing voice. Unfortunately his choice of music, popular with the patients, rarely met with the approval of the prudish Miss Parkinson. As a result the two did not get on and Lily was far from surprised to find the strapping lad and the demure Quakeress not speaking to each other on her return.

The Staff Nurse sighed knowing at some point both would divulge their petty grievances. In the meantime it did not make for a happy ward and that would not do. A harmonious and cheerful staff imbibed a similar quality in the patients and if the boys were happy, their sufferings were less. Lily firmly believed this. It was a phenomenon she had witnessed time and again. Even the poorliest casualty could improve no end and that was always worthwhile even if short-lived.

Hepworth decided to leave the disgruntled duo to their task. They might come around and after witnessing Gladys' emotional breakdown she felt in no mood to listen to the gripes of others. Instead she began preparing for the medical officer's rounds scheduled to commence after tea. The prospect, so normally taken in her stride, was today a little unnerving. The current duty MO always left her feeling, well, flustered really. Made worse, she was sure, by the fact that he knew he did.

She began her tour of the beds, checking the notes were up-to-date, that each incumbent was as he should be and no one had deteriorated in her brief absence. She assumed not as neither Parkinson nor Davies had rushed over with dire news.

"Cor Sister, these two are a right pair of bleedin' miseries today. 'Scuse me French. I'm glad you're back," the cockney private in the first bed divulged.

Lily frowned in an attempt to show disapproval at his swearing. "Your language does not improve as well as your leg does Mr Vaughan," she scowled yet could not help a half smile at his cheeky grin.

"Sorry Sister. Keep forgettin' like. It's better than it were in the trenches though," he apologised none too sincerely.

"Thank goodness for small mercies."

"What's up wiv 'em any'ow?" Vaughan returned to his observations.

Lily sighed and glanced at her assistants. "At a guess I would venture religion and blasphemy Mr Vaughan." She winked at him and moved on.

It was no good. The whole ward had picked up on the frosty atmosphere of ill feeling. Six men commented on it and the new boy, with his jaw wired together, looked decidedly downhearted. She needed to lift his spirits and having two surly faced and snappish staff members was not conducive to cheerfulness. Lily slammed down the notes of a young Somerset boy whose left knee cap had literally been sawn off by slicing shrapnel. He started at her sudden irritability and grinned widely as she marched purposefully towards the VAD and the orderly now engaged in clearing tea cups with frigid exactitude and a far too obvious clatter of crockery.

"Office. Now!" Lily ordered and strode onwards to the small partitioned cupboard aspiringly known as sister's office.

Parkinson and Davies glowered at each other but their hearts sank. Staff Nurse Hepworth was an easy going young woman, much more approachable and patient than sister. Very likeable in fact. Popular with the patients and, as Davies often recounted to comrades, pleasing to the eye. But boy, did she fire on all cylinders when she lost her temper. The signs did not bode well.

Parkinson tried to bolster confidence. Staff Nurse was over eleven years her junior. Very young for a qualified nurse in fact. Nevertheless, the Yorkshire woman was, in sister's absence, in charge regardless of age.

Davies drew a deep breath as they approached and entered sister's office. He hated being told off by women. It was so intimidating. Much more so than when the sergeant major shouted at him. It always reminded him of the thinned lipped anger of his mother just before she clouted him with whatever came to hand, whether it be rolling pin, sweeping brush or, on one occasion, a good sized fillet of fish! He braced himself for the onslaught.

Like two naughty children the duo stood before the diminutive form of Staff Nurse who waited with arms folded and face set into an expression of severe disapproval. Small red patches of colour on her cheeks betrayed her anger and somehow, with her back ramrod straight and head held high she seemed to stretch her five foot two inch frame into something more gargantuan.

Outside on the ward all conversation stopped. Everyone wanted to hear this and the meagre hardboard wall was no respecter of privacy.

"Bleedin' 'ell! They're for it now," Vaughan muttered with glee to the man in the next bed.

"Christ mate! On'y seen Sister mad once, but bloody 'ell, for a little un she sure scared the shit outta me," his Lancastrian neighbour admitted with a grin and both waited and listened for the tirade to begin. It started quite calmly.

"I am both disappointed and displeased with the pair of you. I expect everyone on this ward to get along or at least make the effort to," Lily began her voice quiet but stern.

"We do get along Staff," Davies interjected eagerly.

"Don't interrupt me Private!" Lily snapped back. The young man winced and took on an expression of suitable gravity. "I left you for half an hour that's all and when I return the atmosphere is so frigid it could freeze Hell over.... No, I don't want to hear you're grievances Parkinson," she held up a hand to silence the VAD who had drawn breath, probably to object to the blasphemous reference to Hell.

"Your behaviour, both of you, is childish, unprofessional and unacceptable. I should report you both. You to Matron, Parkinson and you, Davies, to RSM Wilson." Lily paused for effect. Davies looked suitably alarmed.

"I'm sorry Staff, but Private Davies got a little out of hand and took offence to me reminding him of his role," Mabel interjected hurriedly.

Davies whirled on her. "I did not! You started one of your holier than thou lectures. I wasn't..."

"THAT'S ENOUGH!" the patience had snapped. "Children! That's what you are. Silly, puerile, children. Well, it stops now. Both of you are culpable so don't... No Parkinson, don't you dare to interrupt me or you will find yourself outside of Matron's office faster than you can say Jack Flash!

"I don't care for either of your arguments or whether one of you offends the other. All I care about is the well being, physical *and* mental, of those boys out there. You two and your selfish and egotistical conceit are irrelevant. Your role is to support me in ensuring these brave lads are cared for in the manner they deserve. They *do not* deserve to put up with your infantile behaviour and ridiculous feuds.

"Now this is what is going to happen. You will both forget your differences and make every effort to work together. There will be no more arguments and no more bickering.

"Davies, you will show Nurse Parkinson due respect as warranted by her status. She does, whether you like it or not, rank above you. You will follow her instruction without question. If you have an issue or believe you are being unfairly treated, you first come to me. If you cannot abide by these rules I can arrange for RSM Wilson to find you duties elsewhere; like the mortuary for instance. Do you understand?" Lily threatened her face now red and neck blotchy.

"Yes Staff," Davies answered glumly. He dare say no more. If he argued she would carry out that threat, he felt sure.

"Parkinson," Lily turned her attention to the VAD. "You will kindly remember this is a hospital not a church. You will keep your more pious opinions, therefore, to yourself. You will treat both Private Davies and the patients with respect and you will not impose your sanctimonious views upon them. Is that clear?"

Parkinson drew herself upright offended and humiliated that she should be lectured in such a way and in front of a ward orderly! "Staff Nurse Hepworth, I must object to being spoken to in such a way. It is both demeaning and...," she began.

Lily cut her off. "I frankly don't care Nurse. As I said, the only thing I care about are those lads on the ward. Your feelings don't come close. If you have a grievance you can take it up with Sister when she returns from leave, or Matron, but I would think carefully before you do. If you are terribly unhappy here I can ask Matron to place you somewhere else. The moribund ward might be more suited to your solemnity."

Parkinson flushed crimson from the neck of her dress to the roots of her yellow hair. Yet she bit back her retort. Answering back to a trained Staff Nurse was akin to a private soldier insulting an officer. It was insubordination.

"Good. Now we all understand one another. Davies, keep your language clean and behave like an orderly please. This is not the rugby field now! And Parkinson *try* and smile more. Stop being so straight laced. There are enough rules here that cannot be broken without making everyone feel so miserable all the time. Are we finished?" The question was a statement requiring only acknowledgement.

"Yes Staff," the assistants echoed in unison.

"Good, then get back to your work. The MO is due any minute I don't want him finding the ward in disarray." Lily dismissed them.

Once the pair stepped back into the ward the conversation, as if by magic, resumed; every man seemingly involved in serious discourse with his neighbour. That they had been listening was obvious. It made the humiliation of the chastisement all the worse.

"Jesus! I have to say Parky, she's magnificent when she's angry. Scared the sh..., er living daylights out of me. Just like me mam," Davies sing-songed in undertone.

Parkinson seethed inside, but the orderly's words brought a rare smile to her face. Hepworth was scarcely two years his senior and yet he compared her with his mother. It was an image she found amusing despite herself. The fact she thought the woman a jumped up little upstart was momentarily forgotten.

Lily sat heavily into a chair and exhaled deeply. Her hands still shook with adrenalin fuelled passion and she reflected that she had, perhaps, gone too far. Her fiery temper had got the better of her.

"That was inspiring Lily, truly inspiring. I almost quaked in my own boots waiting outside," a laughing North American accent broke through her thoughts and she jumped to her feet as the doctor entered the office.

"Captain Thewlis! Oh, don't laugh. I went too far. They both have every right to make a formal complaint now. Especially Parkinson. I should have dealt with them separately," Lily moaned feeling wretched.

"Nonsense! And spoil the effect? The whole ward has been entertained for the past five minutes," Alex teased.

Lily flushed scarlet. "Oh don't say that. Really? Oh no! How unprofessional of me. It's unforgivable." She dropped her voice low. Had never considered that the patients could hear everything. And Thewlis. How long had he been here? He said five minutes. She groaned and dropped her head into her right hand.

"Aw, come now. It was first rate and from what the men said, more than deserved. I'm sure as hell certain they'll toe the line now," Thewlis grinned boyishly and sat on the edge of the desk a smirk lighting his face.

"Captain, please. I feel so ashamed."

"Rubbish! You shouldn't. Anyway come on. We've got rounds to do. Joining me or are you gonna sit there brooding?"

"I am *not* brooding, Sir," Lily bit back and he smiled broadly.

"After you Staff," he indicated with a short bow and the sweep of his hand. Glowering with all the sternness she could muster, which was very little, she led the way into the ward.

They slowly worked through the patients. Alex taking his time examining each man, each dressing. Listening with studied interest while Lily ran through the notes. He passed a few words with all. Thewlis was a popular MO. More relaxed, less stuffy than his British counterparts. Always ready to have a little joke or a chat with the ordinary Tommy. Before long the smile had crept back on Lily's face, her embarrassment forgotten. He had a way of doing that, of making her smile. It was his generosity of spirit, his refusal to allow the war to depress him; his willingness to laugh at the world and at himself. Yet at the same time he made her uncomfortable with his informal chat, his disregard for all the rules and his way of watching her with that slightly amused expression when his eyes lingered a moment too long on hers. She felt awkwardly abashed in his presence. She had never followed up his dinner proposal, even though it extended to Gladys. She thought it would be inappropriate to do so and the necessity of breaking the rules gave her suitable excuse not to.

As they moved towards the last bed he whispered next to her ear, "I hear Glad had a bit of a breakdown at lunch."

Lily stopped still for a second and stared. "Who told you that?" she enquired too shocked to deny it.

"Oh, one of the VADs on ward eight. Said the dear girl was weepin' bitterly," he replied seriously.

Lily studied his face and saw no teasing now, only concern.

"She ought not to spread gossip like that. It could be hurtful," she stated with prim disapproval at the indiscrete VAD. She had an idea which one it was. A silly girl with a crush on just about every doctor who wore a uniform.

Alex caught the irritation in her voice and smiled. "She's on the ward with the gassed boys ain't she? Sad business Lil. Was she really bad?" Genuine concern.

"Bad enough. I don't think she can stand it there much longer. She needs a break. Leave or a change of duties. The thing with Glad is she can't switch off to it. Not enough anyway," Lily divulged quietly, they were now in front of bed twenty.

Thewlis raised an eyebrow as he pretended to read the chart. "And can you?"

She looked hard at him, trying to discern any trace of mockery. She detected none; for once he was very serious. "Mostly," she confided. He smiled.

"Maybe she won't have to put up with it much longer. Maybe Matron will move her somewhere less trying for a while.

"Hey, you should both take me up on my dinner offer. That'll cheer her up," he laughed and Lily scowled.

"Sergeant Jones. Gunshot wound to left shoulder, fractured clavicle and scapula. No recurrence of infection. Responding well to eusol washes and iodine tincture," she iterated the details of the last patient with tight-lipped solemnity.

Alex grinned and stooped to examine Jones. "Doing well Sergeant. Soon have you on your feet hey?"

"Was 'oping for a trip to Blighty Sir," Jones hinted with hopeful anticipation.

"Oh yeah? Well, there's no doubt about it man, but let's get you well and truly on the mend first hey? Don't want to be turning up to see the missus until you're fit enough do you?" Thewlis winked and the sergeant smirked with a cautiously coy glance towards the nurse.

Lily acted as if she had not understood a word they said or the intimation made.

CHAPTER 29.
May 4th, Pateley Bridge

Dora put baby Robert into his cot and momentarily closed her eyes. No one had told her that mothering would be so tiring. She quite marvelled at how the working class women, with their hordes of children and relentless labours to clean, feed and nurse, managed. By no means a delicate woman herself, Dora had learned new respect for her less fortunate countrywomen. She at least had the wherewithal to employ a nurse. Even so, the nurse did not sleep in the same room as Robert, nor did she wake in the night to feed him. Dora felt perpetually exhausted and consequently overly emotional. Eliza, and the nurse, both wisely stated that it would get easier, but secretly the new mother wondered how and more importantly, when?

She slumped back into the chair allowing her mind to think of Joe. How she wished he was here. How she wished this dreadful war was over and that he was back home safe, along with Lily and Sam. It would be so nice to be together as a family again. Lily and Robert could get married. Everyone could come to the Christening. A Christening that Dora reluctantly acknowledged would have to be postponed indefinitely or decide on different God parents.

The baby whimpered and Dora's eyes flicked open in alarm, but he settled almost at once, her anxiety uncalled for. Why was she so nervous? She had never been like this before. Always self assured and resilient. Yet nowadays she felt constantly in turmoil, fraught with seemingly irrational worries. Again Eliza had said this too would get better. That many women suffered from some form of depression or emotional instability after giving birth. It was quite normal. Dora hoped she was right for at this moment in time she felt anything but confident or happy even and it was a state of mind she struggled to cope with.

She sighed again and glanced out of the window and across the valley. The sun fleeted in and out of fast scudding clouds. A promise of rain to come. April showers had forgotten to cease when May breezed in.

In need of solace Dora pulled out a dog eared and much read letter from her skirt pocket. She fingered the envelope lovingly, caressing the spiky letters of Joe's handwriting, hoping by doing so that she could make some connection. She took the pages out and read them again, relishing the intimate language and obvious love they held. The green envelope had ensured this letter, for a change, had not been censored. No one had read its contents and as such Joe had expressed his feelings freely. The letter also gave an account of his life, how he spent his days and nights, the friends he had made. It was obviously sanitised for her consumption. Yet Dora was no fool and though ignorant of what it meant to serve at the Front she understood enough to realise that her husband's work must be, at times, both arduous and dreadful. The sights of wounded soldiers in Leeds and Ripon told her that.

Dora skimmed through the letter to the last page, which enclosed more treasured wishes and an intimation that Joe might get leave at the end of the month. Not a certainty by any means, but operations permitting, it might be possible.

As usual she found herself crying over his words and feeling both desperately lonely and afraid. She missed him so much. He should be home now! He should be with her and their child. For all her father's love and that of her parents-in-law, Dora longed to be back in the Headingly villa with only her man and her baby.

Below in the hall the doorbell chimed. It would be the postman. A cheerful fellow whose arrival was equally eagerly anticipated and dreaded. Dora listened carefully, almost holding her breath, to Tilly's conversation with old George, trying to hear any shocked gasp or intimated condolences that might herald bad news. It had become a daily torment, the Sabbath being the only respite. Another nerve racking ordeal she struggled to overcome. Today the conversation between housemaid and postman remained light, no low mumblings only a tinkle of girlish laughter and a cheery goodbye followed by footsteps to the drawing room, a knock on the door and a loud proclamation to Eliza that there were three letters.

Dora sighed with relief, only then realising she had been holding her breath. She glanced at Robert sleeping peacefully and decided she could steal away for a while. He would not awaken soon though she did not like to leave the child alone. It was the nurse's day off and Dora briefly contemplated asking Tilly to sit with the baby. *God, this indecision and frustrating over protectiveness.* The boy would be fine. If she left the door open she would hear him cry and she so desperately wanted to hear the news. The housemaid's loud declaration of post was, by now, a family ritual. It signalled letters from France and it summoned the family together. Only the green enveloped correspondence was not shared.

Dora left the nursery, leaving the door ajar, and hurried downstairs rapidly dabbing her eyes to remove all trace of emotion. She arrived in the drawing room just as Thomas drifted in from the garden. It being a Saturday he had no surgery today and his locum partner had agreed to make house calls.

The family gathered in anticipation and on cue, Rose brought in tea. They waited until she had left, no one speaking except Eliza to thank the cook. Thomas stood by the empty fireplace one hand upon the mantel piece the other holding his unlit pipe to his lips. His face betrayed no outward emotion. It remained calm and impassive. Only his quick abandonment of planting his summer bedding belied his eagerness to hear the news.

Eliza pursed her lips. "Three at once. I swear the Post Office holds them back Thomas," she said with a frown and accepted the cup of tea handed by her daughter-in-law.

"Coincidence, I'm sure," Thomas replied sucking thoughtfully on his pipe.

"Hmm. I do hope so. I would hate to think they have them for days before delivering them. Well now," Eliza paused to put on her reading glasses. "We have one from Sam; that's the thinnest I'm afraid. One from Lily and the last is from dear Robert, God bless him." She glanced at the others; the unspoken question of which one to read first indicated by a rise of her eyebrows.

"Robert's first. We haven't heard from him for weeks," Dora expressed gaily.

"Very well," Eliza opened the note and cleared her throat.

"My Dear Folks,

Such joyous news and such a happy honour to have the new arrival named for me. I cannot express my delight and gratitude enough. I only wish I could be there in person to extend my felicitations and share what must be a wondrous time. My love to you dear Dora. I trust and hope you are well and that the pleasures of motherhood are all that you expected. My sincerest best wishes to the proud grandparents. You must both be overjoyed."

Eliza paused and smiled first at Thomas and then at Dora.

"*You will all laugh when I tell you that on receiving the good news I shouted it out loud to everyone within ear shot. I'm sure the fellows thought me quite mad. I gave them such a start when usually they look upon me as a quite serious body.*

"*I received a long letter from Joe. He sounds so rapturously happy. I know he is desperate for leave. I hope he gets some soon. He expressed the possibility of perhaps later this month.*

"*I too am hoping for leave. I have been here for six months now and I am ready for a rest. I have been endeavouring to arrange it to coincide with Lily's, but as yet neither of us has had notification. My commanding officer, being another temporary type, is sympathetic, so I am hopeful.*

"*We have been dreadfully busy throughout April and though the initial influx of casualties has died away we are still full to overflowing. My work cannot be said to be dull. Exhausting yes and at times I am left wondering at man's ability to inflict such grievous harm on his fellow man. It is such a terrible waste. Still, I have not written to depress you all with my dark thoughts of the war. Suffice it to say that I wish, like so many others, that this conflict will reach a swift conclusion. There is hope that our troops may break through this year and push the Germans back home with one large flea in their collective ears. We shall see. Let us hope this is not false optimism.*

"*We have been learning all about the new method of blood transfusion. Thomas, you would find it most edifying. The method has been developed with great success in the United States of America. A number of venerable practitioners from Harvard have brought that invaluable know-how here to France. The method is truly simple and brilliant, but I will not bore you with it here. This is a discussion for you and I to share at our leisure Thomas. Over a cigar and a brandy, in civilised surroundings. However, I am sure that very soon we will be able to carry out transfusions as close to the Front as the Clearing Stations and how many lives this would save!*

"*The Hospitals here at R_____ are expanding massively. I've moved to one on the Race Course! It is quite a grand spot and, now that spring has arrived, is very pleasant and sunny in its aspect. I am not so optimistic about winter though. It is very open and I suspect will be apt to catch the wind. Most of the wards are in massive tents and temporary huts!*

"*My billet is a bell tent that I share with Lieutenant Charles Winters. A very amiable chap from Nottingham, but he is want to snore quite sonorously. I have appropriated myself a supply of ear plugs to mitigate the effect.*

"*Sleep is very precious to us all and the Army has a tendency to not respect its refreshing and healing properties. We are disturbed by bugle calls most of the day long. Reveille awakens the day shift at five a.m. The night shift are disturbed by the bugle for breakfast, lunch, tea and dinner and then another to rouse them! I hate night shift. One is lucky if one catches four or five hours sleep. Tents do not afford adequate soundproofing and if the sun is shining their interior is unacceptably bright and often hot. I have consequently learned the Tommy's art of scrounging and have managed to 'acquire' several army blankets. These, Winters and I have shared to fashion ourselves an inner tent, like a hairy wool mosquito net. When on night shift, we crawl beneath the suspended blankets which, at least give the allusion of twilight. Sadly, they also keep in the heat and we may have to open the tent sides when the summer arrives.*

"*Well my dear friends it is ten o'clock now and I am up at five, so I must say adieu for the present. Hopefully it will not be too long before we are all together again, even if it may only be for a brief interval. If we manage it, Lily and I will travel home together and be with you for a few days. We will send a telegram in advance.*

"*Until then, my best wishes and love to you all.*
"*Yours affectionately, Robert.*"

Eliza looked up smiling. The seed of hope for a visit well and truly planted. "Oh I do hope they get leave together. It would be so nice," she voiced glancing at

Thomas. He nodded in agreement reading more in that look than she had expressed. Poor Eliza. Having all of her children away from home was hard upon her. He knew she especially worried over Lily as a single woman in a foreign land. Nothing he could say would assuage that persistent anxiety. He decided to take a seat at last and mulled over the contents of Robert's letter. He had been intrigued by the mention of blood transfusions and already a plethora of questions were crowding out his sympathies with his wife's wishes. He wanted to see Robert to discuss this exciting advancement and he had no doubt that Lily and Joe would have some interesting anecdotes as well.

"I'm so glad he approved of us naming little Robert after him. Joe was worried he would be too embarrassed by it," Dora chimed in, her mood lifted by the letter and her words interrupting the private thoughts of her in-laws.

"Of course he approved. How could he not? It is an honour surely. What was Joe thinking of?" Eliza asked, her tone disbelieving and surprised.

Dora shrugged. "You know how he worries about offending. He can't help it. That's just Joe."

"Yes, I know dear," Eliza smiled and patted her daughter-in-law's hand. "Which next?" she held up the two remaining envelopes.

"Might as well get Sam's out of the way. It won't say much anyhow," Thomas muttered while helping himself to another cup of tea. He had not meant to sound accusatory, but somehow he did. Eliza picked up on it and frowned deeply. Still this disapproval and disappointment. It had not been helped by the postcard they had received some six weeks ago. It had come for Sam and had asked them to send mail to Corporal Hepworth, not Sergeant. No explanation why. They could only guess at its meaning. Discreet enquiries to both Joe and Lily revealed only some hint at misconduct. Nothing more. Neither Thomas nor Eliza knew the extent of Sam's misdemeanour. Had no idea of the Court Martial and subsequent demotion to the ranks. As far as they were aware, and through their ignorance of military matters, they believed their son had somehow only lost one stripe and could only guess the reason why. It was, in Thomas's eyes however, another proof of Sam's delinquency. Another disappointment and it served to keep the rift open.

Eliza drew the single sheet of paper from its mud smeared envelope. Eyed the spidery handwriting written hurriedly in pencil and wished her middle son would write more. She sighed and then with frowning concentration as she struggled to decipher the scrawl, she began to read.

"Dear Mother, Father and Dora,

"Thank you for the parcel and letters. I received them yesterday. We are in reserve so at last I get some chance to write. Your letters confirmed the happy news, though Joe had already beaten you all. He came eight miles from his billets to find and tell me, bringing a hip flask of brandy to wet the baby's head. He managed to scrounge a lift over, but I think he had a long march back. Not that he was bothered. He was so over the moon I don't think his feet would have touched the ground any of the way.

"On 12th April we had a visit from Sir John French. He came to Brigade and made a short speech followed by an inspection of each battalion. He cut quite a dashing figure on a fine bay horse, but he did not stay long.

"We've been mainly on fatigues this month and done an awful lot of marching! My feet are sore from it, with blisters as big as my thumbnail despite my boots being well worn in. We've been so used to being in the trenches that our feet are no longer used to long marches.

"Thanks for the pipe and tobacco. It will save on cigarettes and might make me look a little more distinguished! The socks are most welcome and any more you can send will be gratefully received.

"Shared the cake and whiskey with some of the lads. They went down well as you can imagine. Saving the tinned fruit for my birthday. Speaking of which, I could really do with a new watch. A wrist watch if you can run to it. I've broken my old one, or rather a piece of Fritz's shrapnel did!

"Love and best wishes, Sam X"

"What does he do with all those socks? We send him two pairs with every parcel," Dora asked with a laugh.

"With Sam, one never knows," Eliza replied trying to hide the concern. She did not like the image conjured by the admission of a broken watch. It spoke of danger and it was only with reluctance that she admitted any of her children might be in danger. It was how she coped. Denial of the truth.

"Do you think we can get him a watch Thomas?" It was not really a question.

"Save trying to think of what else to send him," Thomas replied.

"I wish he would write more. We never know what he is doing or where he is," Eliza continued folding the besmirched sheet back into its envelope.

"They're not allowed to say," Dora said.

"He probably doesn't get too much chance to write anyway. At least he sends a note reasonably frequently so that you know he is safe." Rare words of support from Thomas for his estranged son. It took both women by pleasant surprise and they stared at him enquiringly.

"Well, for all his faults he has always written home," he felt obliged to add feeling his cheeks flush. He picked up his pipe and clamped it between his teeth. "Next letter Eliza. Let's hear what our Lily has to say." He changed the subject rapidly.

Eliza obliged with an unsuccessfully hidden smile.

"Dear All,

"Please forgive me for not writing to you all individually. We are so busy at the moment with all the fighting going on at_____."

"Oh, it's been blanked out," Eliza commented at the big black smear across the offending name.

"Censored. Lily hasn't quite understood what can and cannot be divulged, obviously," Thomas chuckled. His wife nodded and carried on.

"I'm still on my surgical ward. They wouldn't transfer me to the trains. Apparently one has to be a sister. As if that should make any difference! Anyway, we are dreadfully busy. We cleared all the wards before the fighting started and we do the same every two or three days. Only the really bad cases stay. The poor boys are simply streaming in and we no longer have the luxury or space to nurse them back to health. They are treated and then even the slightest wounded are shipped to England so that we may take in more. Of course this is very popular with the Tommies. They get impromptu leave and rest, but for us it is back breaking work.

"Today is my first half day off in ten days. I am supposed to get a day and a half each week. I'm exhausted and shall take to my bed early.

"*The Germans have been using a dreadful new weapon. No doubt you've read about it in the papers. We first experienced it effects when lots of _____*"

"Oh more censoring. They've blanked out the whole paragraph," Eliza commented with annoyance. She sighed and resumed.

"*Gladys had a bit of a breakdown and has been moved onto a light surgical ward to give her some respite. I think the poor dear will not last the course though. Her nerves are quite frayed and were made worse the other day when she learned that her brother had been wounded. He's been taken to _____ and they have let Glad visit. I think he is alright, but she's in such a dreadful state. She might transfer home soon. I shall be sad of course for we get along so well together.*

"*I received your letters and parcels. Thank you. I cannot wait to come home and meet little Robert for the first time. I hope you are not worn out Dora dear. I am sure he is a little treasure though and quite as good as gold.*

"*Joe wrote too and was obviously so full of pride and joy. I think he wished Sam to go for a drink with him to celebrate, but that is not allowed. The Army is full of ridiculous rules. One would think they would make an exception for brothers. It really is quite draconian. For example, if either Joe or Sam came to see me I would have to obtain permission from Matron to meet them. They are boys and nurses are not allowed to socialise with boys even if they are one's brothers. If I was lucky she might agree for me to have tea in her rooms or, with Joe, in a café. As long as we also had a chaperone. With Sam, it is doubtful she would allow it at all. He is an NCO and technically I am ranked the same as an officer. Therefore, nurses are not supposed to fraternise with other ranks! Ridiculous isn't it?*

"*Oh I do long to see you all again. With luck I should get leave soon, but not until the fighting has died down. We need all hands on deck at present. We seem to be taking the brunt of the casualties up here. Robert says it's a little quieter in R_____.*

"*They're building a massive hospital complex at _____. It is to serve the training centre there as well as to relieve some of the pressure up here and at C_____. About time too! There is talk of a reorganisation at the same time. The Canadians are opening their own hospital and we may lose some of our medical officers to it. I believe they will have a choice, but I'm not sure. It is unlike the Army to give anyone a choice! It could mean that we lose Captain Thewlis. He is the quite charming Canadian surgeon I told you of in my last letter. It would be sad to lose him as he is very popular with the men and quite a few of the nurses too!*

I have finally managed to keep Nurse Parkinson and Private Davies on speaking terms, although I had to resort to threats of dire consequences to do so. Nevertheless it paid off and the ward was quite harmonious for Sister's return. Davies, being a Welshman, has a marvellous singing voice and when Sister permits, we often treat our boys to an impromptu concert. It goes down well with everyone except Matron, who does not approve, so usually Parkinson or Sister act as look out for us. But, Lord! We've had some narrow escapes!

"*I was in trouble last week for shortening my dress. Matron made me take it out again. I had only done it for practical reasons. It is so cumbersome with a skirt only three inches off the floor. I only took it up another three inches. It could hardly be described as immodest. I will wait a week or so and take it up again. She may get fed up of chastising me.*

"*A new draft of nurses arrived yesterday though I haven't had chance to talk to any yet. Most are QAIMNS Reserve, but there are a couple of TFNS ladies so I shall not feel totally alone if Glad leaves.*

"*I received a letter from Sam. Short and to the point as usual, but he sounds in better spirits than before. He was quite upset about the injury to Lieutenant Fielding and then the death of*

Sergeant Major Beale at _____. Did he tell you about it? You will remember that Mr Beale always looked after our Sam. We met him once at the Station in Richmond before they went to Guernsey. A quiet, unassuming chap. Cheerful with lots of blond hair. His men called him Goldilocks. Sam was with him when he died. He leaves a wife and three children. It is so terribly sad.

"*Sam suspects they are being sent back up the line soon so don't expect much in the way of letters. You may get the odd Quick Fire postcard. I hope he manages to celebrate our birthday and he isn't at the Front then!*

"*Oh my goodness! I've just seen the time. It's nearly half past nine and I was hoping to catch an early night. I will close then until next time when hopefully I should be able to give you news of my leave.*

"*God bless you all and keep you safe. My warmest love, Lily.*"

"I had no idea about Mr Beale. I thought he was a sergeant the same as...," Eliza stopped and pursed her lips glancing at her husband. "Do you remember him Thomas?" she finished.

"Vaguely."

"I wonder why Sam didn't tell us."

"Why should he? I'm sure he would not have thought it was something we would wish to know. It's not as if we knew the man," Thomas opined.

"No but we knew of him. We knew he took a particular liking to Sam and that they were friends. Oh, his poor wife and those children! I do hope they will be looked after."

"I believe the Army provide a pension for men's families," Thomas offered without much interest. He did not wish Eliza to dwell upon the death of some soldier; it would ultimately start her worrying about her own sons.

"Trust Lily to get into trouble for shortening her dress," Dora said in an attempt to prevent the mood from plummeting into morbid reflection of death. Thomas eyed her thankfully.

"I do hope she is careful. She is far too wilful at times. She and Sam are so alike. I don't want her to offend Matron again. I shall write and urge discretion," Eliza stated diverted from her previous train of thought.

Thomas smiled to himself but offered no comment. He stood, stretched and declared his intention to return to the garden.

"Well don't be long dear. Lunch will be ready at twelve," his wife informed and carefully folded Lily's long epistle into its reluctant envelope.

Dora picked up her knitting. Another baby jacket for Robert. She was becoming quite adept now. However, she placed it aside and selecting fresh needles began to work on another pair of socks for Sam.

CHAPTER 30.
May 14th, Front Line Trenches near Festubert

Heavy retaliatory shelling from the Germans met only by the occasional return of fire from the British batteries behind the pummelled lines. The enemy used a new kind of high velocity shell to scatter deadly shrapnel upon their huddled foe as they tried vainly to shelter behind breastworks and in trenches. Already christened whizz-bangs on account of their speedy zipping flight and subsequent explosion, the missiles were consequently viewed with dread by groups of soldiers trying to move forward into shelter or worse, work in the open fixing multiple broken signal wires. As if the enemy bombardment was not enough, few and far between as they were, too many British shells once more fell short. Uncomfortably so. And commanders in the front line, beleaguered and fraught with the frustration of not being able to get forward, desperately sent ever more anxious messages to the Brigade Batteries to hopefully rectify the wayward range.

C and D Companies of the Yorkshires waited at stand-to in the firing trench. They had hoped to be going over the top, but they were stuck, without clear orders, half expecting a German attack. C Company were having a particularly rough time of it and seemingly taking the brunt of whatever Fritz could throw their way. Exploding shells ripped at the parapet, scattering debris over the men beneath. Casualties were steadily mounting and they had gone precisely nowhere.

Constantly at the ready, constantly repairing walls, digging out fallen earth, the men were fatigued before the assault could even take place. With nerves frayed from the unending pounding of guns the Yorkshires stood miserably, cursing and grumbling or silently contemplative. This was not the warfare they had trained for. Bore no resemblance to the practised pitched battles fought on open ground, rushing forward, scrabbling for hasty cover, felling the enemy with accurate deadly and rapid rifle fire. This was squalid, nerve shattering attrition. They fought an enemy they rarely saw and still they died in great numbers, either in some ill thought out rush to take a German trench or, more often, from the destructive force of a mortar bomb or indiscriminate shell. This was siege warfare on a grand scale and for the remaining soldiers of Britain's Regular Army it was as alien and bewildering as for the numerous new volunteers. Still, the Army commanders placed their faith in this dwindling, bedraggled remnant of a once great fighting force. Placing the few they could least afford to lose in positions of gravest danger. Asking the impossible of a loyal, disciplined force, who would never say no despite the hopeless futility of their task.

Corporal Hepworth leaned heavily against the trench wall, his Lee Enfield propped through the loophole, his head never venturing above the parapet. The sentry next to him watched across No-Man's-Land through a makeshift periscope some bright spark engineer had put together. The attack, the postponed attack, was due to take place tomorrow. In the meantime there was no rest, no respite. Fritz might come lumbering across, taking the initiative. He was certainly throwing enough metal over to advertise the possibility. The corporal shrugged his shoulders trying to make himself more comfortable. At least it was dry, but God was he tired. He rubbed his eyes and watched the sentry with little interest other than he felt he should appear alert. Hardly anyone in the section spoke. Hardly anyone had the energy or inclination to. They were strung out, filthy, lice ridden and utterly exhausted.

Another whizz-bang detonated near-by. Young Dobson cringed, dropping his head onto the butt of his rifle with eyes tight closed. Then, the moment over, he glanced at his section leader and grinned self-consciously. Sam smirked back but his gaze held the private for much longer.

He was better, Dobson. A spell of leave had done wonders following his presumed shell shock at Neuve Chapelle. Hepworth had been glad to see the lad return as cheerful and cheeky as he had been before. Yet there was a difference. It showed in his eyes. A far away, slightly haunted look that all the bravado in the world could not hide. A look manifest in a number of men. It told of disillusionment, of fear and above all, of the need for rest. Not Army rest, but a long spell at home, away from the war and the horrors of their everyday existence. Yet despite the increasing numbers of men reaching the Front, there seemed very little opportunity for leave even for those who had already served with the BEF for so many months. Morale had slumped and soldiers now talked of catching a Blighty one; wishing for a wound bad enough to send them home. Not bad enough to maim them for life.

Dobson had achieved the coveted return to Blighty and only his section and its leader knew the truth. Even so, even after a proper rest, Sam considered the lad near the edge and watched him with brotherly concern.

Another explosion. This time rocking the earth with seismic force. No shrapnel shell that. Far heavier, far more destructive. Dirt, kicked high in the air from No-Man's-Land, rained copiously upon the inhabitants of the trench. Covering his head with his arms Sam cursed loudly at the hail of muck and small stones. Nearby Jacko wiped blood from his face as a sharp fragment of jagged rock or metal grazed his cheek.

"Eppy!"

Sam turned around to see Second Lieutenant Fisher hurrying, stooped almost to a crouching position, towards him.

"Mister Fisher?"

"CO's on his way up with Major Sherringham. CC wants you to go meet and escort him forward," Fisher shouted above the din of the bombardment.

Sam raised his eyebrows in surprise. "Me Sir?" he yelled back.

"Well, he asked me to send someone reliable. Doesn't want the colonel delayed in the CT with all this shrapnel flying about. Thought it might be safer for him if someone guides him up," the subaltern continued, ducking instinctively at another resounding explosion.

Sam did not agree. In fact, he thought the idea ridiculous. Quite why the CO had decided to wander forward during the worst bombardment for weeks God only knew. Sending anyone back to meet him would not make the slightest difference to the man's safety and would only put more lives at risk. His life for instance.

"Eppy?"

"Yes Mister Fisher. On my way Sir," Sam responded and withdrew his rifle from the loophole slinging it around his shoulder.

"Take Dobson with you. Looks better a two man escort I think," Fisher added and hurried away.

Just as well, for if he had stayed the flabbergasted corporal might have said something he would later regret. Instead he stared after the retreating officer and swore under his breath. "Come on Dobbo," he said. "You heard the man."

They squeezed by a couple of men hastily filling a sandbag, ducked another spray of muck that liberally peppered the trench and after giving way to two stretcher bearers dived into the narrow communication trench and trudged along its tortuously zigzag path.

"What's t'owd man comin' up 'ere fo'?" Dobson called.

"How the hell should I know? Christ Dobbo, you ask some bloody stupid questions at times," Sam shouted back pushing on in a semi-hunched position. It was a question, however, that he would like to know the answer to. *God! It's a damned stupid time to visit troops in the firing line with all this metal flying around. Has the colonel taken leave of his senses? Why not wait until dark at least?*

A long wailing and tired moan droned heavily towards them. Instinctively and with the benefit of experience the two men dropped to their knees and covered their heads. The missile plummeted into the ground a few yards to the left of the communication trench detonating with fearsome and deafening force. Piles of dried mud cascaded into the winding ditch half burying them as the earth bucked violently.

"*Fuckin' 'ell!*" Sam cried spitting dirt from his mouth, shaking it from his hair and clawing himself out of the debris. "That was fuckin' close. Dobbo? You alright kid?"

Dobson stared with wide, frightened rabbit eyes through a filthy, fearful face. He nodded but did not speak and Sam felt a tremble in his body as the private accepted a hand to pull him to his feet.

"Come on. That was one of ours. Bloody artillery!" he grumbled and after a quick inspection of his rifle turned it muzzle downwards before slinging it back around his shoulder. They carried on, Dobson quiet and pale. Every few seconds the corporal turned to check the young soldier was still there, but he always was, right on his tail.

They stumbled around a corner and hunched lower as the trench wall barely reached four feet high at this juncture. Up ahead, only yards away, two senior officers crawled likewise towards them.

"Hepworth, what the blazes are you doing back here?" Lieutenant Colonel Anderson demanded.

"Major Wilson sent me to escort you up to the Front Sir," Sam replied.

"I don't *need* a damned escort! Does he think I might get lost? Nowhere to bloody go but forward!" Anderson shouted irritatedly.

"I think he was concerned for your safety Sir," Sam offered knowing it sounded ludicrous and agreeing inwardly with his commanding officer.

"My safety? And what were you two supposed to do to ensure that eh? *Bloody safety*. I'll give him bloody safety. Go on, about turn and double it back. You can tell Major Wilson I don't want or need any babysitters!"

"No Sir. I mean yes Sir," Sam flustered back. He turned around urging, without a word, Dobson to follow suit.

The screeching groan grew steadily louder drowning out the background racket of explosions and booms. Too slow. Too laboured. The droning missile was surely going to drop near. Dobson felt it too. Both men stopped dead, hesitated, listened and knew. Together they turned to face the CO and his second-in-command, shouting wordlessly above the wailing din. Dobbo made a sudden, brave dash towards the startled officers. Sam groped desperately at thin air to try and stop him.

Anderson too had realised the imminent danger. He was no stranger to gun fire, but for some inexplicable reason he did not move. His reactions were too slow.

As Major Sherringham dived to the ground the colonel remained hunched and frozen in position his mouth open in a surprised O.

With a last minute and desperate lunge Sam grabbed at and caught Dobson's rifle and with super human effort pulled on it. Hard. As the shell burst the pair fell backwards, one screaming on top of the other. Red hot shards of steel sliced through the air splitting sandbags, shredding material, carving flesh.

Colonel Anderson slumped to his knees, eyes dulled by death and fell face down into the trench.

Aware only of a massive concussion, like a huge blow to his head and body, Sam was unconscious before he hit the ground unaware of his young comrade landing heavily on top of him.

When the debris stopped falling and the ringing in his ears faded, Major Sherringham lifted his head and gazed horror-struck first at his dead commanding officer and then at the shrieking and writhing, shattered and bloody body of the private. Reeling with shock the major groped forwards checking the colonel for signs of life. He found none and stepping carefully over the body, his whole being still trembling and his head thumping, he crawled to the two men, tried to calm the lad offering his hand for comfort and peered at the corporal beneath. Bizarrely Hepworth appeared unscathed except for a few scratches. He was unconscious but breathing steadily. Sherringham shouted at the top of his voice for stretcher bearers.

CHAPTER 31.
May 17th, No. 13 General Hospital, Boulogne

Blood red brightness and excruciating pain pulsating through his head. Sam struggled towards the oddly muffled sounds that for some time now had drifted wave like into his fevered brain. His eyes fluttered open, closed in protest at the dazzling light and tentatively, almost involuntarily, twitched open again. Instinctively he raised a heavy arm to offer shade and frowned deeply at the thumping pounding in his head.

A figure hurried over and blocked out some of the brilliant glare. Vaguely he became aware of a female voice speaking to him. The words were unclear, strangely distant. He tried hard to concentrate and groaned audibly with frustration and at the constant, unremitting throb through his skull.

A face close to his. It reminded him of Rose only a much slimmer version. He smiled at the memory and the face returned the expression. It wore a white starched scarf covering its hair. It smelt of lavender and carbolic. An odd mixture of scents, both powerful and evocative; not unpleasant but a reminder of another time. Hospital. He was in hospital. The face belonged to a nurse. Almost like a slap across the face the realisation brought him to full consciousness. Had he been wounded again? He could not remember. He lifted his arms and squinted through pain at them. Still whole. He wriggled his toes. Still there. Relief! But what about the headache? Slowly and with great deliberation he felt his cranium. No bandages.

The nurse was speaking yet her voice seemed odd. He could not explain why. It was indistinct but if he turned that way, just a little, the words became clear and loud. It hurt his brain to think and he screwed his eyes against the constant ache.

"Does it hurt badly? Corporal, can you hear me?" the nursing sister asked raising her voice just a little.

Yes he could hear. Sort of. He moved his head slowly to one side, his neck stiff and sore. She spoke again but he could not decipher her words. Carefully, excruciatingly he turned back to look at her and caught the last few words.

".....understand me?"

It dawned on him. He was deaf in his right ear. That was why everything sounded strange.

"I can't hear," he replied a little too loudly pointing to the defunct organ and then he cursed as another spasm shot through his tormented brain.

The sister sucked in her breath at the uttered oath, but she had heard worse. The poor man was obviously in agony. She called out to an orderly to fetch the medical officer and returned her attention to her charge.

"Corporal, Corporal, can you hear me at all?" she gently prized his hands from his scalp and stuck her face close enough that he might see her lips move. He seemed cognitive. No delirium, no confusion. Just pain. The doctor had been worried about potential brain damage. There might yet be some. But other than extreme discomfort and difficulty in hearing the patient appeared alright; a little disorientated perhaps. That was only to be expected. He had just woken from a three day coma. He lay in a hospital bed, clean instead of lice ridden and filthy. Obviously he would be perplexed.

"Yes I can hear you, but not at this side," Sam answered breaking the nurse's thoughts. "My head's killing me."

A surprisingly cultivated voice. Northern, most definitely, but without the laziness of dropped aitches or colloquial dialect. She smiled kindly. "I know. I've sent for the MO. Now that you are awake he may prescribe some pain killers."

"I bloody well hope so." Sam grumbled. He might be conscious but he was confused enough to forget to whom he spoke. To forget good manners. She was speaking to him again, this thin Rose. He wanted to tell her to shut up, but he could never speak like that to Rose. Had he just sworn at her? It was the pain. The constant, thumping drumming. It was almost unbearable. He grasped his head again with a groan.

Sister frowned. Poor man. She hoped the doctor would acquiesce to morphine. Yet one had to be careful with such patients. The corporal had arrived unconscious two days ago from a Casualty Clearing Station near the last push. Apart from a few bruises, a scratch on his chin, there was not a mark on him. He had simply lain, not moving, in a coma while the orderlies undressed and bathed him, while the medical officer examined him. He would swallow when they dribbled water from a wet sponge through his lips and he had winced when they had inserted a saline drip, but he had not awoken. They had suspected brain damage though he responded well to tests. He had reacted to speech with an odd twitching of his mouth and rapid eye movements. His pupils had never been dilated. Now he was awake they could ascertain more. Hopefully he only suffered from severe concussion.

"Thirsty," he interrupted her thoughts once more. She helped him to a drink of water, firmly preventing him from swallowing too much too quickly. Not an easy task for now his mind had realised the extent of his need and he desperately tried to drink furiously, as if his life depended on it.

"That's enough for now. You'll choke if you're not careful," she chastised softly. As if on cue he began to cough and splutter sending more spasms of pain through his skull. Sister leaned him forward and vigorously rubbed his back.

"Better" she queried. He nodded looking pale and shaken.

Sister smiled at him then straightened on hearing her name. She walked over to meet the medical officer, briefing him as they returned to the bed side.

"He's in considerable pain and he says he can't hear anything in his right ear."

The Army doctor bent over Sam whose eyes were screwed tight shut again. "Yes, his ear drum is perforated. I don't know if there's any other damage. Ear's aren't my thing," he muttered in reply to Sister and then in a loud voice to his patient, "Good morning Corporal Hepworth. Glad to see you've decided to return to us. Bit of a headache though?"

Sam started at the booming voice and his brain protested violently. "Fuckin' 'ell! No need to bloody shout. I'm not fuckin' deaf," he cried his voice slipping into dialect.

The doctor grimaced and smiled apologetically at the nurse. "Better prepare some morphine I think Sister. I'll just give him a quick check over, but I think we're safe." He made no reprimand to his patient, neither at the discourteous or insubordinate response. Head cases were funny. They could be lucid one moment and completely confused the next. It seemed likely that the corporal acted instinctively, not fully aware to whom he spoke or what his surroundings were. It was not unknown for men to think they were still in the trenches. Besides, the MO was a civilian doctor, temporarily commissioned into the Army and as such he was far more understanding than the Regular Army physician.

"Sorry I shouted Corporal. I just need to have a quick look at you then we'll give you something for the pain. Do you know where you are? Can you remember what happened to you?" he asked as Sister hurried away and he sat on the bed to look into Sam's eyes with an ophthalmoscope.

"I'm in hospital. I don't know how I got here. I was with Dobbo and the CO. Something.... No. I just remember a sound, a screaming whooshing noise, then nothing. A short-one got me I guess," Sam answered with frowning concentration. *Why do they keep asking me questions? Why not just give me the morphine?*

The doctor, a swarthy skinned lieutenant looked at him. Nothing confused about him now. "You swore quite badly just now you know. It isn't acceptable in front of the nurses," he said thinking a rebuke would not go amiss.

"Did I? Sorry Sir. I keep forgetting. You made me jump and I thought I was...," Sam paused.

"Thought you were what?"

"Thought I was back there. At the Front. I keep thinking I can hear guns. You know. Pounding...in here," a finger pointing to his head.

"Yes. I think that's your concussion. Certainly one can hear the guns on some days, but they are very distant. It should pass in time. Have you any other symptoms. Double or blurred vision? Numbness or tingling sensations?" the MO asked still staring into his patient's eyes.

"No Sir. Just one hell of a headache and this ear."

"Hmm, well that's good to hear. Any dizziness when I turn your head so?" The doctor grasped Sam's head and twisted it quickly from one side to the next.

"*Jesus Christ!* No, maybe, a little. Bloody agony though. I'd rather you not do that again Sir." Sam's hand flew to his cranium and his eyes watered. The MO smiled apologetically.

"Sorry Hepworth. You can have some morphine. Ah, here's Sister with it now." He took the syringe from the nurse and administered the drug through a prominent vein. "There you go. That should make it easier for you. You might get sleepy. Best succumb to it if you do. Sleep is nature's great healer." He turned to go.

"May I ask you a question Sir?" Sam called before the medic retreated.

"Certainly."

"Do you know what happened to me?"

"Shell shock we think. Not the neurological kind, but literally. It seems the concussion from an explosion rendered you unconscious. You're really very lucky. I've seen other cases where the casualty has suffered quite severe brain damage as a result," the doctor explained with a quick smile.

"And the others? Do you know about the others? My CO, Private Dobson?" Sam struggled with the creeping somnolence that had already begun to dull the pain and wrap his body in a warm embrace. His eyes became heavy and threatened to close even as the MO answered his question.

"I don't know. I'm sorry. I'm a brain specialist so I only see head cases. They might be on another ward, but they could also have gone to a different hospital. You came in with so many. Why not give their names to the orderly and let him see what he can find?"

"Yes Sir. I'll do that Sir. Thank you." The eyes dropped closed and the corporal fell into a drugged sleep.

Sister and the doctor moved away.

"I think, that you may let Staff Nurse Hepworth know that her brother should make a full recovery. She may visit him when he awakes, but let's give him another day first."

"Very good Doctor," Sister acknowledged glad at last to give some good news to a fraught colleague.

"It may also be prudent to warn her that he may still be a little confused at times and that his language on such occasions is apt to be particularly foul," he concluded.

Sister simply smiled.

Lily listened impatiently to Sister Madley, trying to appear professionally interested and outwardly calm. Unfortunately for too long she had lived on tenterhooks waiting with fervent anxiety to see him. Terrified that he might not wake up. Afraid that when he did he might not recognise her; might not be quite normal. The relief she felt yesterday when Private Fergusson had entered her surgical ward beaming from ear to ear had almost been indescribable. She had nearly broken down with thankfulness. Hastily, last night, she had scribbled a letter to her parents and another to Joe. *Sam is awake and all seems well.* She wrote with a promise of more details later.

She had not been permitted to see him then. He was sleeping, they told her. The wait had been intolerable. All through another shift, another long day. For the first time in her life she found herself clock watching and oh how those hands dragged so painfully slowly across the white enamel face. All the time she fretted that he might get worse or be asleep again and she would have to wait yet another day. Even the heavy workload could not detract her mind from dwelling upon him. The new arrivals, four shattered young men fresh from the Front, bodies torn and infection rife, could not keep her thoughts from a beloved brother longer than a few minutes at a time.

Finally, at six o'clock Sister Slaytor had told her to go early. Go and spend a few precious minutes with that even more precious soul. Lily did not need telling twice. She had hurried from the ward, run up the long, sweeping flight of stairs and almost knocked into two VADs in her haste to get to his bedside. Then, the final hurdle, she had to ask permission of Sister Madley.

"He's in some pain still. Lieutenant Emery thinks it will subside in a day or two, but he may always be prone to headaches now. We simply know so little of these things," Sister Madley explained sympathetically. She noted the restless disquiet in her junior colleague and smiled. Would she be any different? "Go along. Spend a little time with him. Not too long. He tires quickly. And remember, he cannot hear you in his right ear," she gave in and released the Staff Nurse.

Lily thanked her profusely and vanished in a whirl, almost running into the ward.

She was at his side before he became aware of her. They had told him she might be allowed to visit and he had watched hopefully all day long. But how his head ached and now he sat with eyes closed and face strained.

"Sammy?" Lily uttered tentatively taking care to approach his left side and fearing he was asleep. He looked so tired, so gaunt. Old even. Her eyes filled and she battled the rising tide of sentiment. It would not do to cry now.

Sam thought he heard his sister's voice. It sounded far, far away. His eyes snapped open hopefully and she was there, crying in front of him. She kissed his cheek clutching and wrapping both his hands in hers.

"Oh Sammy?" she cried.

"Hey, I'm not dead! Stop this. This isn't my tough little Lily," he soothed feeling his own emotion threaten to overwhelm him. "Christ Lil! I want cheering up not making bloody miserable," he muttered with false gruffness.

She laughed. It worked. He understood the tears were only relief, but it was the thoughts behind them that disturbed him. The obvious thankfulness. Far too stark a reminder of what might have been. A cold, spine tingling shiver ran through his body and he pushed the spectre of a narrowly escaped death back into its dark recess.

"I came last night, but you were asleep and they wouldn't let me see you. How are you dear?" Lily enquired dabbing her eyes with the corner of her apron before grasping his hands once more. She was reluctant to let him go. Holding on meant she could keep him safe.

"I'm alright I suppose. I don't remember much. Don't remember yesterday really either. Apparently I swore a lot. Sister made a point of telling me," he grinned. "My head hurts like hell and I'm deaf in this ear." He pointed to the right side of his head.

"Your ear drum is perforated. Did they tell you?"

"Yeah. Might be more damage too. I've got to see a specialist," Sam said.

Someone further down the ward cried out and set another patient muttering.

"God Lil! This place is full of nut cases. Can't you get me out of here?" he whispered casting a wary glance at his somnolent neighbour. "This bloke's been like that for two weeks. Fergusson told me. Look at him. Poor sod! Had half his brains shot up. If he was a horse they'd shoot him, but instead they keep him lying there and let him die slowly." He shuddered not wresting his eyes from the comatose man.

"I know. I worked on here for a few nights. It was quite challenging. But they're not all that bad. Some have shell shock. They get better."

"Like me?"

"No. Your injuries are physical. A different kind of shock. More psychological. We don't really understand it. The doctors are calling it neurasthenia," Lily explained.

"They're waiting for another brain specialist to see you before they move you. They want to make sure there's nothing wrong." Sister had told her this a few minutes earlier.

"Bloody hell! What else could be wrong? Don't tell me I'll get worse," he laughed nervously.

"No, they don't think so. They're just looking after you Sam. They're worried about the headaches," Lily appeased wishing she had said nothing. He looked anxious now and she did not want to upset him. Had not meant to.

"They're worried? That's reassuring," he laughed sarcastically.

"Sorry. I didn't mean... I... They're just being careful." Her voice drifted away. He had closed his eyes. He looked strained. She felt awkward and tactless. What had she been thinking of? Whatever horror he had gone through the last thing he needed was her cold and clinical explanations. He needed comfort and reassurance. He needed love. Tears sprang unbidden to her eyes again and she squeezed his hand tentatively.

"It's okay," he said responding to her touch and reciprocating in kind. "I'm

For All We Have and Are

just tired and grumpy that's all." He rubbed his head, frowning and she realised his surliness was born of discomfort.

"Poor you. You really will have to consider a more sedate profession when this is all over," she joked.

He smirked. "This one was alright until this bloody war. I quite liked the odd skirmish. Found it exhilarating. But now. Now, I'm just tired and everyone... everyone is going." A distinct trace of regret.

"Going?"

"Dying. Getting killed. There aren't many of the original crowd left. Probably even less now. I don't know," he elucidated faintly with growing melancholia.

"Don't you remember anything at all?" Lily decided on a slightly different tack. He was beginning to get morose.

"No. I've asked Fergusson to find out what happened to the others. I mean, if I'm alive the others should be too, right? I want to know Lil. I want to know what happened to Dobbo. Hell, the poor little bugger is probably dead." He turned away the corner of his mouth twitching and his eyes stinging.

"Do you want me to ask around as well? One or two of the MOs might know something. He could have been taken to another hospital. Sam?"

He swallowed hard and took a moment before facing her. She recognised the fight with emotion. Saw the over brightness of his eyes.

"I'd like to know," he answered at length.

"What's his full name?"

"Bert Dobson. Albert I suppose. He's only a kid. Not even eighteen yet. I can't remember his number."

"I'll see what I can do," Lily promised.

"Thanks."

A discreet cough interrupted their conversation. Sister Madley stood at the end of the bed.

"It's time for dinner and I think that is enough for today," she said kindly as the pair turned to face her.

Sam opened his mouth to object but Lily placed a finger on his lips. She stood and kissed his cheek. "I'll come back tomorrow. Get some rest. Bye Sammy," she whispered in his good ear.

He nodded, his disappointment apparent but resignation there too. "Bye Lil. Be good."

She returned his cheeky grin and accompanied Sister to the end of the ward turning once to wave and finding him watching her avidly as though she were leaving for good. It left her feeling coldly disconcerted.

"He's a little depressed," she observed to her companion.

"Yes. They often are for a while. The pain doesn't help," Sister agreed.

"Will it get better? You said the doctor thinks so."

"Oh yes I'm sure it will, but it may take some weeks."

"I hope they don't send him back too soon. I wish he could go home," Lily confided.

Sister Madley stopped and looked back to her patient. He still watched them, a pained expression on his face. "It's difficult isn't it? We want them to get well, but we know when they do they'll be sent back to the Front. If they don't, well, they have the rest of their lives to learn to live again with whatever deformity or torment they are scarred with. War is a dreadful thing Hepworth," she imparted sadly, then smiled. "I'm sure your brother will be just fine. Come back tomorrow. I'm certain you'll see an improvement."

CHAPTER 32.
June 1st, Boulogne

Lily left Matron's office her head reeling with a long list of do's and don'ts. It had taken some negotiating, using all the powers of persuasion she possessed, to finally get approval and permission from the strict martinet. Agreement for her to take her own brother out for tea. The issue, as far as Matron had been concerned, that the brother was not only a patient in her hospital but also an NCO in the King's Army. On paper it was against all the rules and being a military nurse for the last twenty years, Matron believed in rules. However, she did have a softer side and was capable of great generosity. It just rarely showed itself. For several days she had refused point blank. But Staff Nurse Hepworth was tenacious if nothing else and had repeated her request, once her brother had been removed to a convalescence ward, at every opportunity. Finally the austere matriarch relented. However, she had stipulations.

They must wear uniform. Lily in her walking out dress and hat and her brother in khaki. They must be back before dinner at six. They were to visit one of the approved cafés and they must go straight there and straight back. No detours. No walks.

Lily had ensured her face remained impassively respectful. Answered "Yes Matron" and "No Matron" where appropriate and secretly kept her fingers crossed behind her back hoping Sam would behave himself. He was making a rapid recovery, though he still suffered headaches and tended to be overcome with light-headedness rather too readily to be classified as fit. Yet the doctors reckoned another couple of weeks and he would be ready to return to his unit. Lily thought it too soon, but had no power or influence to fight the Army.

She hurried to his ward and found him sitting by the door, cap in hand, shaved except for the ridiculous ginger moustache, and wearing his cleaned, rough serge uniform with two stripes on the upper arms. It was more than a little shabby, but buttons and insignia gleamed indicating a fresh polishing. He smiled when he saw her and stood, wincing briefly at the protestation of his brain to sudden movement and eyeing with suspicion Sister who had noticed Lily's arrival.

"Matron has spoken to you about the rules and you have her note?" the senior nurse asked her subordinate as Lily reached her brother's side and hooked her arm in his.

"Yes Sister. We will be back by six and we must go straight to the café, without dalliance," she replied refusing to make eye contact with Sam, who coughed to hide the little laugh that escaped him.

Sister glanced at her patient with a stern eye. "These rules must be obeyed Corporal Hepworth. Matron is making a great concession on your behalf. Do not deviate from the instructions you have been given. Do I make myself clear?" she stressed firmly.

"Yes Sister. Very clear," Sam returned matching his gaze to hers, maintaining the well practised expression that, throughout his life, had persuaded the naïve that he could be trusted. He felt Lily squeeze his arm thankfully. He must not spoil this now. She had worked too hard to get the authorities to relent.

"Very good. I will see you at six. Enjoy your tea," Sister offered satisfied that her warning had been heeded. She returned to the ward and with her withdrawal Sam raised a cheery arm to wave at a group of his fellow inmates who eyed him with envy and gestured back rudely.

Outside the hospital they paused and took in the fresh sea breeze, a little cool for the first day of June, but the sky was a perfect, dazzling blue and the sun felt warm on their upturned faces. Sam took in a deep breath and exhaled slowly. For the moment he could forget, pretend the war did not exist, that it had never existed. For a few hours he could once more be with his beloved sister. Corporal Samuel Thomas Hepworth could vanish and the boy that once lived in his body could reappear. Just for a few hours. He looked down and saw her smiling up at him.

"Penny for them?" she asked.

"Nothing really. I was just thinking I can't hear the guns," he replied.

She cocked her head to listen. Sounds of the town and the crying of gulls assailed her ears and very faint, a long way away the soft thud of artillery. Perhaps he could not hear it. The ear specialist had said he may remain permanently deaf in his right ear. "They're very distant. Are you sure you're up to this Sam?" She knew he would say yes even if he was not.

"Of course I am," he answered as expected.

"You've taken your pills?"

Sam squinted up at the sky and tried to ignore the dull thump in his head as a result. The headaches were much better, but they had not gone away. They said he might have to learn to live with them. "Don't be such a nag Lil. I'm fine. They're sending me to convalescent camp next week, so I must be alright," he said with a hint of sarcasm. "Let's go to the beach. I haven't walked on a beach for ages."

"We're not supposed to deviate from our instructions remember," Lily reminded with a convincing impersonation of the ward sister.

Sam laughed. "Sod that! Come on. I want to feel the sand between my toes. It's too nice a day to sit for hours in a stuffy café with a load of garlic reeking Frenchmen. He took her hand and pulled, setting off at a brisk pace, then stopped realising he did not know the way.

"Over here." Lily laughed and took over, leading him to the promenade where they strolled in affable silence arm in arm until they reached a flight of steps to the sand and scurried down like children. Sam immediately removed his boots and socks, stuffing the latter in a pocket and tying the former together by their laces and flinging them around his neck. He rolled his trousers up and dashed to the water's edge. Lily laughed and followed casting a cautious eye behind in case anyone, who may disapprove, was watching. Whereas her twin never did, she always worried that they may be caught.

Only a few children played on the beach and elderly French couples, and the occasional group of soldiers walked along the promenade. None of them paid the pair any attention. While Sam played a childhood game of trying to avoid each breaking wave, she strolled along the firmer sand wishing she dare do the same. Sadly she lacked the courage to take her shoes and stockings off while wearing the responsible uniform of a Territorial Force nurse.

"I have some news about your friend. I was going to tell you over tea, but..." she began.

Sam stood still ignoring the wave that splashed chillingly around his feet. "About Dobbo?" he interrupted. He had almost given up hope of hearing. He had read in the out of date English papers of Colonel Anderson's death, but had found out nothing of Bert. He may still be alive but, as a mere private he did not warrant an obituary. It was impossible to tell. Now that Lily had news, he was not sure he wanted to hear it. Not if Dobson was dead.

"Yes. Do you want to talk about it now?" she sensed his hesitation, his anxiety.

"No. Not here. I don't want to spoil this memory."

"But it's not all..."

"*I said no,*" he snapped. His head responded with a violent stab of pain and he screwed his eyes holding a hand to his temple.

"Sam?" Lily's fingers touched his arm gently her face full of concern. He was not well enough to return to the Front whatever the doctors said.

He cursed softly under his breath, barely audible and ran his hand over his eyes. "I'm sorry. I didn't mean to shout. Tell me when we get to the café. I don't want to talk about him here," he apologised as the spasm subsided.

"Alright," she said, understanding. She had always understood his moods and emotions. She alone had seen the vulnerable boy years ago and still saw the vulnerable man now. He began walking slowly, splashing through the water, the previous game forgotten. She kept up with him wondering what he was thinking, worrying that he might be suffering and saying nothing. Suddenly he looked at her and grinned. That wicked, mischievous grin that she both loved and dreaded. Instantly she became wary reading trouble in that face. She backed away a little and then as he lunged towards her she shrieked girlishly and ran away.

"No way Sam Hepworth!" she cried reading his intentions with telepathic accuracy.

"Come on spoil sport. Get your feet wet," he laughed and tried to head her off. She squealed and side stepped just in time. He tripped and fell, caught his hands in the sand and pushed himself upright again. Lily stood facing him, out of reach, hands on hips. Her face shone brightly and for a moment they were both children again playing an age old game. A middle-aged French couple sauntered by smiling at their exuberance. No doubt they thought the pair lovers.

"That's *enough!*" Lily warned but he was undeterred and after pretending to be out of breath with hands on knees he darted towards her again. She yelped with alarm recognising the danger, knowing he was faster and lifting her skirts she ran, her heart beating hard while her stomach fluttered half with fear, half excitement. Hands grabbed her waist and she screamed in giddy protest as she was swung around and bodily lifted from the ground. She slapped his back with half hearted annoyance as he flung her over his shoulder.

"Put... me... down!" she demanded, giggling. He seemed to stagger, loosened his grip and then caught it again. With a laugh he headed mercilessly to the sea.

"Sam! NO! Don't you dare! Don't...NO!" she shouted and giggled alternately.

He swung her down and out. She screamed, but he did not let go. At the last moment he pulled her back and dropped her so that only her feet hit the next wave. Cold sea water seeped into her shoes. She turned on him and punched him hard as he stood guffawing at her consternation.

"It's... not... funny! You...." She punched him again her face red with passion.

"Ow! Lil. Bloody 'ell! Stop it!" he hiccoughed between chuckling at her temper and defending himself. His head thudded dully, but he tried to pretend it did not. Had to hide it from her.

She gave up punishing him and stomped onto drier sand, ringing the edge of her dress as she did so, her back turned against him. She heard his sigh and the splash of his feet approaching and she waited.

"Sorry Lil. Couldn't help it. You looked so prim and proper. Had to do it. You understand, eh? Come on, don't sulk," he apologised insincerely, the amusement evident in his voice. He rubbed his head. *Damn this pain. Go away!*

She still had not turned. Waited until he stood right behind her, until she could sense his warmth, hear his breathing. Then, like a tigress, she spun around and with all her might shoved her hands against his chest and pushed. His face reflected the shock at her deceit as he fell sprawling backwards.

"Ha ha!" she shouted gleefully. "Who's laughing now?" And then she ran, as fast as she could, to the steps and the safety of the promenade. He would not dare carry on the game amongst the citizens of Boulogne, but she had to be quick. He was still fast, injured or not and her stupid skirts got in the way.

She heard him swear and with a wild squeal she ran harder through the soft sand. He was gaining, rapidly, yet she was almost there. She heard cheering, shouts of encouragement and she looked up to see half a dozen Tommies on the promenade urging her on. They waved her to safety. Any thoughts of decency and decorum were lost in the hysteria of the moment. Lily paid no heed to the nagging conscience that tried and failed to remind her of her position. She was eleven again and running for her life from the brother she had just pushed into the river at home.

She reached the steps and strong arms hoisted her unceremoniously over the balustrade. With ungainly relief she rolled over the railings landing amongst the joyful soldiers who had aided and abetted her escape. And just in time. She had felt Sam's hand brush against her disappearing ankle, but then she had whirled through the air and was safe.

"There you are lass. 'Ow about a kiss for your rescuers?" one of the soldiers asked cheekily. Out of breath and flushed Lily eyed him askance and he grinned toothily.

"Ey, you alright Corp?" another voice asked with some concern. Lily's attention snapped back to her brother. She leant over the railings where two of the Tommies were watching Sam. He stood below, stooped with hands clutching his head. With a staggering step sideways he fell. Immediately the two men vaulted the railings and Lily ran down the steps.

"Sam, Sam!" she cried as the Samaritans helped her brother to sit.

"You alright?" the soldier asked again.

Sam blinked away tears from his eyes and rubbed his temples with his fists. In a moment Lily was knelt by his side clutching his face. She was speaking. His head screamed in protest at his activity and he did not hear what she said. He felt faint and for a few seconds his giddiness threatened to overwhelm him.

"Do you want a 'and Miss? To get 'im back?" the other soldier asked. Their comrades watched with quiet respect from above.

Lily glanced at them. Did she? "Sam, Sam are you alright? Oh Lord. Yes, yes please help me take him back," she cried her eyes filling uncontrollably.

"NO! No, I'm alright. Honest. It's okay. I don't want to go back," Sam responded at last.

"But Sammy..."

"No, please. Let's go have tea. I'll be alright," he grasped her hand tightly. His face showed the strain of the spasm but his eyes begged her to relent. She dithered, looked to the two soldiers as if they might make the decision for her. One of them shrugged.

"Are you sure dear?" she asked softly.

"Yes. Please."

She nodded and stood.

"Give me a hand?" he asked and the two Tommies obliged.

"You sure you're alright Corp? Look white as a sheet to me?" the toothy soldier called from above.

"No I'm fine. Thank you," he turned to his helpers and thanked them also.

"Don't mention it pal," one replied. They loitered while Sam slowly climbed the steps, Lily following with pursed lips and then they bounded up afterwards.

"Thank you," she said as they rejoined their friends and headed at a sauntering pace in the opposite direction. They waved cheerily but she caught the hushed question between them. "What's 'appened to 'im d' yer think? Looks proper poorly."

Sam evidently did not hear and for the first time Lily felt thankful for his partial deafness. He offered his arm, his colour returning to his cheeks, but she thought he still looked ill. *Oh how could they think of sending him back?* Slowly they made their way to the Café Renoir, the same establishment Lily and Gladys liked to frequent on days off. As usual Madame greeted her warmly and steered brother and sister to a secluded corner at the rear of the room. The table was screened further by local clientele and opposite, a very young subaltern sat nervously with an equally anxious VAD. Lily did not recognise her, but it was obvious theirs was a clandestine meeting. Matters for the secretive couple were made worse by Sam's smart salute which the second lieutenant acknowledged with alarm, a furtive glance around the room and a hurried removal of his cap. Lily smiled reassuringly hoping to put them at ease.

"Eet is neer ze back door Monsieur. If you need to leave," Madame hinted conspiratorially as Sam took his seat and she handed him the menu. He gazed at her with bewilderment and merely answered "Thank you."

"What was all that about?" he asked as the dame hurried away to serve another customer.

"Madame has an arrangement whereby young men may vanish through the back yard if someone in authority comes in. Nurses are not permitted to socialise with men remember. That is why she has put us here, at the back in this gloomy corner and opposite those two love birds. You scared him half to death with your salute. It drew attention to him," she nodded towards the subaltern and his blushing companion.

Sam half turned to look, thought better of it and picked up his menu instead. "God!" he muttered under his breath.

"Anyway. Madame obviously assumes you are my beau."

"You sound like you have experience of this arrangement," he teased.

"Very funny. I just come here often that's all. Everyone who comes here knows the drill. Luckily Matron and most of the senior sisters don't. It's too shabby for them."

"I don't know. It has a kind of rustic charm," Sam laughed and she scowled.

"Coffee then. Do you want buttered toast as well?"

"I thought it was tea."

"The French can't make tea. Safer with coffee. Toast?" Lily said.

"Yes. That would be nice. Am I allowed a beer?"

"No. It's more than my life's worth. You've already scared me half to death with that turn on the beach. I can't let you have alcohol now."

"Just one won't hurt," he pleaded knowing she would relent. He pulled a cigarette from his jacket pocket and searched another for matches.

"Oh do you have to smoke in here? Those things are particularly foul," Lily protested.

"Christ! No beer and no fags. This is going to be fun," he grumbled putting the woodbine back in its wrapper.

Madame returned and Lily ordered buttered toast, coffee and a small beer. Sam grinned his thanks. "Happy Birthday," she said and pushed a small parcel towards him. "Sorry it's late. I'm afraid it isn't much either."

Sam looked taken aback. He flushed with embarrassment. "Thanks. I'm sorry. I didn't get you anything. I meant to when we next came out on rest, but…"

"It doesn't matter. You hardly had chance did you? Anyway you haven't seen what that is yet. You might not like it," she joked.

"It's not another embroidered poppy is it?" he teased and she scowled reprovingly at him.

"Open it!"

Their order arrived while he unwrapped the little parcel. He smiled broadly at the packet of pipe tobacco and small silver match box within. "Thanks Lil."

"Daddy said he'd sent you a pipe and all the Tommies complain about their matches always being wet and useless. It's engraved, on the back, look." She pointed.

He turned the box over and read the plain text. *To my dearest brother Sam, with love Lily.* He picked up her hand and kissed it. "You're a treasure."

"Toast?" she offered the plate smiling happily as he carefully stashed his gifts into his pocket and took a sip of beer. Good beer. Not the watered down stuff he was used to. It reminded him of La Maison Rouge, of Monsieur Collet, of Mariele. He frowned and pushed the thought aside.

"Tell me about Dobbo," he requested through a mouthful of toast. *Get it over with Sam and then move on.* He tried to sound nonchalant; tried and failed.

Lily smiled and reached inside her pocket for a folded piece of paper. With a glance at her brother, he was watching without expression, his face impassive, she checked her notes. She took a deep breath. "Private Albert James Dobson. Second Battalion the Yorkshire Regiment. Number 10992. Is that him?"

Sam nodded his eyes fixed on the paper in her hand.

"He was taken to Number Eight British Red Cross hospital in Calais. That's why no one here knew anything about him. They shipped him home to England two days ago, but I don't know where to. Could be anywhere," Lily continued.

"He's alive," Sam uttered to himself, relief flooding through his body only to be plunged back into an abyss of fear again. "He's badly hurt?" he asked, guessing the truth. Knowing it to be true.

Lily sighed. "Yes. Do you want to know?"

"Yes."

"He lost his left eye through a shell splinter. Quite a lot of damage to his face, although they said it would not be so bad in time. He had another injury to the left leg and unfortunately it became infected," she paused watching her brother's face for signs of emotion. His dark eyes bored into hers, asking her to tell him something else, not to reveal the last gruesome detail, yet he had to know.

"They amputated," he said matter-of-factly before she could tell him.

"Yes. His leg became gangrenous. There was nothing else they could do. We just can't fight that kind of infection Sam."

He looked away blinking furiously and swallowing the treacherous lump that emotion brought to his throat. Mutilated! Dobbo had been horribly mutilated. It made him feel sick. Sick of the war. Sick of seeing friends killed and maimed. He wiped his eyes hurriedly.

"He's only a kid," he muttered so quietly that Lily could barely hear him.

"I know. He's safe now. He's home," she tried to comfort placing her hand over his.

"Safe. Yes, I suppose he is. Not sure what future he'll have though. What is there for a young, uneducated man to do if he's not physically whole?" It was a rhetorical question filled with bitterness and anger.

"I don't know," Lily answered anyway. She wished she had not told him. Not today. It spoiled the mood and she had wanted today to be memorably happy for him, before they sent him back to Hell.

"*What a fucking waste!*" he exclaimed vehemently.

"Sam!"

"Sorry. I'm sorry." His head dropped into his hands and his body seemed to quiver. Lily sat startled. She had only ever seen him like this once before. When Elizabeth had died. She wanted to wrap her arms around him and let him cry onto her shoulder like she had then. But it was different now. He was no grieving child and although it took all of his self control he fought against the emotion and sat back to drink his beer, his face a mask of determined indifference, his eyes cold.

"You were close?" she blurted thinking it would do him good to talk. Not liking the unfamiliar, sudden hardness. He said nothing, just continued to drink, his gaze distant. His mouth set in a thin line. "Sam, it's alright to talk about it. Don't bottle it up. Don't do a Joe," she pleaded.

He flicked his eyes back to hers; saw the anxiety and his resolve melted. He ran both hands through his hair and sighed loudly. "He used to drive me mad," he said at last. Yes he could talk to Lily. No one else. But she would never judge. Never think him weak. She understood him. "Always bothering me. Used to cling to me like a bloody puppy." He smiled at the memory.

"He looked up to you."

"Yes, probably. Although I'm not sure I was the best role model he could have had. He was a good kid though."

"Is. He's not dead," Lily reminded.

As good as. He nearly said it out loud. "I'll miss him Lil. He was like a kid brother. Getting in the way. Making a nuisance of himself. You know like Frank used to. I wonder who else has gone." His voice trailed away as he lost himself in dark thoughts, memories and fears of loss. Lily squeezed his hand reassuringly, but did not have the words of comfort. How could she? There were none to give.

A discreet cough startled them both and their hands flew apart as if caught doing something they should not.

"Hello there. Not disturbing something am I?" a slow Canadian drawl queried.

Catching sight of the officer's uniform Sam jumped to his feet before clutching at his head as a spasm of pain ripped through his skull. He staggered and both Lily and the officer reached out to him.

"Steady on man. Here, I got ya," the Canadian reassured. "Here, sit down. Sorry, I didn't mean to startle you," Thewlis apologised his face a picture of penitence as he caught Lily's eye. "You alright?" he asked Sam as the latter regained his seat.

Sam rubbed his temples and nodded. The thumping began to subside. "Yes Sir. Thank you Sir. Sorry I..."

"Hell don't apologise man. It was my fault. Shouldn't have sneaked up on you like that. Just wanted to see what.... Christ, I should've guessed. You must be Sam. Alex Thewlis," the Canadian doctor stuck out his hand and without invitation pulled up another chair to the table. Lily stared at him with reproof but her brother had accepted the handshake, albeit warily.

"God, I'm no good at this. Sorry I'm causing you some embarrassment. I came over because I recognised Lily. Thought to save her from unwanted attentions," Alex laughed. "But I got it wrong, thankfully. I'm sure pleased to meet you Sam. Your sister is always talking about you. Am I bothering you being here?" he asked and looked from brother to sister.

Lily smiled awkwardly, both at Thewlis' enthusiastic chatter and at Sam's expression of surprise. Yes he was bothering her. *Why has he come in here today?* She opened her mouth to protest at his invasion of their privacy, but her brother spoke first.

"No Sir. You're not bothering us. You're a friend of Lil's?" Sam questioned respectfully and with a hint of mischievous mockery as he caught his sister's eye. That wicked glint had returned. He suspected something and he would play a game to get to the bottom of it. She should be glad. Thewlis' rude interruption had snapped him from his mood of despondency. But she was not. She sighed.

"Captain Thewlis is one of our MOs at the hospital. *He's a colleague,*" Lily stressed and squirmed uncomfortably at her sibling's broad, knowing smile. He was in his element now and she would suffer his relentless, playful taunting later. She knew he had jumped to all of the *wrong* conclusions.

"Alex. Please call me Alex. Lily insists on using my title. She's very proper, but we're quite good friends really aren't we Lil?" Thewlis enlightened with an openly cheerful smile. Lily flushed at her brother's grin.

"Shouldn't really address you by your Christian name Sir. Against the rules for NCOs and officers to be so familiar," Sam dragged his attention back to the affable doctor and thought he ought to at least make the effort to follow military etiquette even if Thewlis was determined not to. Something of his Regular Army pride was irked by this lack of discipline.

"Oh yeah rules! Get in the way a bit don't they. You Brits are very hot on rules. But then I think you only play by 'em if you have to, eh Sam? And there's no one here to snitch. That weasely subaltern made a dash for the back door as soon as I walked in, poor kid. So, like I said, Sam, call me Alex," the Canadian insisted with a grin. "Would you like a cognac?"

"Eppy. The lads all call me Eppy, even my company commander. Yes, I'd like a cognac," Sam replied warming to this brash officer.

"No, you shouldn't," Lily interjected with a daggers drawn stare at the doctor."We should get back."

"No we're alright Lil. We're not due back 'til six *remember*," her brother argued pointedly. "I'd love a cognac. Thanks." He turned back to the MO.

"Great. Do you want one Lil?" Thewlis asked his eyes alight.

"Certainly not!" she replied somewhat rudely. He was incorrigible.

"Alright just the two then." Alex leaned back on his seat and signalled to Madame, his order understood seemingly by telepathy.

"What are you doing here Al..., Captain Thewlis? I thought you were on duty today," Lily demanded ungraciously. She noted her twin sit back with his hands in his pockets and an amused smirk on his face. She tried to ignore him.

"Hey you know my shifts better than I!" Thewlis mocked. "I changed my day last minute. Not me actually. It was Robinson. I owed him a favour so... And, I knew this was your afternoon free. Thought I might find you here for a chat.

"I keep asking your sister to dinner, but she resolutely refuses. Against the rules you see," he winked conspiratorially at the increasingly astounded corporal whose eyes grew brighter with impish pleasure at each revelation. The maudlin mood that possessed him earlier had quite vanished with this new sport. Only his headache threatened to spoil the fun.

"Ah! Merci Madame," Alex thanked the proprietoress as she placed two brandies before him. "There you are Eppy. Your good health. I trust and hope you are regaining your strength." He raised his glass in salute.

Sam returned the gesture and savoured the brandy. It was a good one. Not the usual rough stuff served to the troops. Another perk of being an officer. "Yes thanks. I'm much better. Soon be back with my unit."

"Too soon. You're nowhere near fit enough," Lily jumped in with uncharacteristic gruffness. Both men regarded her for a moment.

"I'm *much* better," her brother insisted with a warning glare. She sighed loudly with exasperation. "So how long have you worked together," he changed the subject and enjoyed Lily's growing agitation. She was a close one, he thought. Had never mentioned this *friend* and now she sat glowering at him, arms crossed and decidedly put out and flustered.

Lily slumped in her chair and begrudgingly watched the two men warm to each other. Her feelings were confused. Angry with Alex for barging in upon their intimate little get together. Time with Sam was a precious rarity and she desperately missed his company. She was also disconcerted by the obvious conclusions her brother had jumped to. Quite incorrectly, she thought. His sneering glances and his arched eyebrows which, perpetually challenged her conscience, both exasperated and annoyed her. Still despite all this part of her rejoiced in the fact that they liked one another. And they did. It was evident in the way they both relaxed regardless of rank, the way their laughter came spontaneously and easily.

She joined in the conversation when forced to, frowned when they lit up cigars and puffed acrid smoke into the already stifling atmosphere, but smiled inwardly at their instant camaraderie. Most of the time she listened and watched enthralled. A kindred spirit was being born before her very eyes. It seemed as though she observed two old friends reunited after months of being apart. They chatted about everything, exchanging anecdotes, giggling boyishly at ridiculously childish jokes, exchanging serious views on the progress of the war, its futility versus its necessity. They did not argue. Their minds and souls agreed. As the minutes passed by, Lily thought Sam closer to Alex than he had ever been to anyone other than herself. Strangely and irrationally she felt jealous of this and became confused by her feelings.

"Say, I'm having dinner here. Do you two want to join me?" Thewlis announced snapping Lily from her musings. She looked up, saw Sam's hopeful happiness, Alex's affable, charming smile and her heart bounded along with unexpected emotion to her mouth.

"No. Thank you. We have to get back to the hospital for dinner. It was one of Matron's stipulations," she replied rather snappishly.

"Aw come on Lil. I can talk the old gal around," Thewlis tried.

"No Alex! You *can't* talk her around," she spat with sudden ire. "Come on Sam. We're going." She waived a hand to attract Madame and fumbled agitatedly for her purse.

The men exchanged an eyebrows raised glance.

"Well if you're sure...," Thewlis began.

"Yes I'm sure," she cut him off. Sam looked to his empty brandy glass in embarrassment.

Madame hovered not sure who to hand the bill to. Mademoiselle had called for it, but there were two gentlemen with her.

"I'll take care of that," the captain offered reaching out for the invoice.

"No you *won't*!" Lily snatched it from Madame's hand causing the woman to jump in surprise. Thewlis looked astounded.

"Lily, there's no need...," Sam began also taken aback by his sister's seemingly irrational outburst. It was unlike her. But Lily had already thrust the French notes into Madame's hand and muttered that she keep the change. She ignored her brother completely and turning to Thewlis managed to speak to him with forced civility.

"Captain Thewlis, nice to see you." And she set off, before he could even lift himself from his chair. Both men gazed after her retreating figure. Sam swore.

"Look, I'm sorry Alex. I don't know what's up with her. Women eh?" he muttered feeling he needed to apologise. "I'd better go after her. Glad we met." He offered his hand.

Thewlis stood and shook it warmly. "I'll pop in and see you before they move you. Don't worry about Lil. I usually exasperate her. Not sure why." He grinned as if he knew well enough. Sam echoed the expression, shoved his cap onto his head and hurried after his sister.

She waited outside on the pavement watching a convoy of old London buses roll by with distracted interest. As soon as he joined her she began walking rapidly towards the hospital.

"What the *hell* was all that about?" he demanded hurrying to catch up. His head began to pound as soon as his activity increased. *Damn it!* "Lil, slow down for God's sake!"

She relented and slowed her pace. "He always thinks he can push his way in. Anywhere he likes! Never bothers to think whether he is welcome or not. And then he thinks he can dictate what everyone should do!" she began waving her arms agitatedly.

"Lil, the man asked us to have dinner with him that's all," Sam reasoned. *Why is she acting so irrationally?*

"That wasn't all!" she retorted almost hysterically. "He thinks he can sweet talk everyone. Even Matron. He wouldn't have managed that one I can tell you. And it would not have been him having to explain. He just can't see it. The trouble he could cause. I could have lost my job Sam!" she declared furiously and increased her step to a fast march again.

Sam hurried after her, grabbed her arm and pulled her to a stop. "Slow down will you. My head's thumping as it is without pumping tons of blood into it on a forced route march!"

"*God*! Fine soldier you are!" That was unkind. He had been hurt. His pain was real. The remark had been unworthy of her. She apologised and slowed to a miserable saunter. *Why did she feel so angry*?

"It's Captain Thewlis you should apologise to Lil. You were bloody rude to him," he remarked and got in step beside her.

"Yes I know."

"Well why were you? I rather liked him. Decent chap. Down to earth. Can tell he's not Army though. He rather reminded me of...."

"*Give me strength*! Can we stop talking about Alex Thewlis?" she cried throwing her arms in the air with exasperation.

Sam gawped thunderstruck. After a moment he shrugged and strolled in silence for a while until he felt uncomfortable with it.

"How's Robert?" he asked in a voice as near to innocence as he could muster. The opportunity was too good to miss but he was unprepared for the response. He had thought, erroneously it would lighten her mood, make her realise what an idiot she had been, give her the chance to laugh at herself, but he had miscalculated the depth of her emotion. She wheeled on him, face flushed in temper.

"Are you deliberately trying to provoke me Samuel Hepworth?" Her eyes flashed vehemently. This was dangerous ground. Those little fists were quite capable of causing unladylike damage. Still he ploughed on. She needed to talk about this. She just did not know it yet.

"Of course not. I just wondered that's all."

"Wondered what?" she demanded warily. Did she want to pursue this? Her temper subsided a little to be replaced by anxiety. She could never hide a thing from Sam although almost up until this moment she had successfully hidden it from herself.

"Whether Robert knew about Alex," he answered and pretended to gaze at the sea as they turned automatically onto the promenade rather than back to the hospital.

"What are you suggesting?" A hint of warning in her tone. He did not care. She knew he did not. He would just carry on until she admitted it. *Why not just admit it then? Confide your worries and hopes. Because you hardly dare admit it to yourself. You coward*!

"You know."

"No Sam, I don't. You'll have to tell me." *Please tell me then I don't have to say it myself.*

Something had changed in her voice. It begged for help, for understanding, he thought he saw a flicker of pain behind her eyes. He lost his playfulness and sat upon a bench and looked across the Channel to the distant white cliffs on the horizon and the multitude of boats and ships plying their way back and forth. He patted the seat and she sat next to him resting her head on his shoulder as his arm slipped around hers.

"You know, I never thought Robert the right man for you," he said softly.

She stared at him, her eyes bright and face flushed, but she did not speak.

Sam sighed. "You should end it, before it's too late. Come on Lil. Think of yourself for a change. You don't love Rob, not enough to marry him."

"And what do you mean by that?" she demanded feeling wretched. *What a mess*!

"Would you rather live a lie? Marry a man you didn't love? It wouldn't be fair Lily, not to you or him," Sam reasoned at the same time wondering where all this wisdom came from. He was a fine one to talk. His relationships had never lasted more than a few weeks, in some cases only for a night of lust followed by a cold goodbye at the break of dawn. He smiled. "Thewlis is charismatic and rather dashing. He sets your heart racing doesn't he?" He shut up and watched her.

She gazed at the far away shores of England feeling the fresh sea air cool on her face, fighting the conflicting emotions within. Sam had made her face what she had not wanted to and she was not certain whether to thank him or slap him for it.

"I don't know what to do," she sighed at last. "We were trying to get leave together. Go home and see Dora and the baby."

"Do it then. Pull whatever strings you can, ask whatever favour. Spend some time together and see how you truly feel. If you find yourself imagining he's Thewlis or wanting to get back here, then you'll know."

"And then what? I call off the engagement. I don't know if I can do that to him. What would everyone think?" Lily bemoaned.

"Sod everyone else! This is about your life not theirs. They might be shocked, but they'll still love you. And Rob would get over it in time. I mean, does he really love you? Or are you just the only girl he feels comfortable with. He's not the most outgoing type is he? Only child and all that," Sam challenged becoming frustrated by her dithering. This was not the daring Lily from childhood. This was someone else in her skin. Someone who felt bound by duty and followed etiquette, a usurper that the expectancy of polite society had put in her place.

"God Lil! Let me spell it out for you. Rob is a wonderful man. He's a great friend. He's handsome, rich and successful. Everything, in fact, a woman could wish for in a husband. He's kind and sensible. He'll make a loyal husband and a doting father for your children, but he's also a boring fart! He'll never make you laugh until your sides split or do something spontaneous just for the hell of it. He'd never even try to get you into bed before you were married and you'll never want him to!"

"I should think not! He's a decent, well brought up gentleman. Sam, I'm appalled you could even..." Lily protested haughtily but he interrupted her.

"He's a red bloodied man, Lil. Any bloke who isn't queer wants to get his girl into bed. He wouldn't be normal if he didn't. Hell most blokes would...," he stopped short. Her face looked a picture of alarm. He was forgetting himself. It was not the same for Lily. Middle-classed young ladies did not receive the same education in life as their male counterparts and neither were they expected to. By her expression he realised he had probably just destroyed some feminine illusion. An illusion gently nurtured by well-to-do families to protect their daughters from the coarse world of men. Judging by her reaction he was correct.

"You should not judge others by your own standards Sam Hepworth!" she retorted hotly, her face flushed and lips pursed in a thin, disapproving line, yet beneath her shock she felt ridiculously ingenuous.

"All I'm trying to say," he continued softly, "Is that I don't think Robert is right for you. You have more passion, more zest for life than he has. He will stifle you in time. You may be content as the wife of an eminent surgeon with five or six kids, but you were meant for more than that Lil. You have always wanted more than that. And I don't want to see you disappear." He smiled a little abashed at his sentimental argument.

Lily stared at him for a while her eyes searching for answers she knew he could not give. "And you think Alex would be right for me?" she asked at length in a small voice.

Sam shrugged. "I don't know Lil. He's certainly more fun and more like you. But I don't know the man do I? You do. Just think twice before you commit to an ordinary fate that's all. I'd rather see you galloping across the plains of Canada after Thewlis than an old before her time mother of five."

After a long pause Lily sighed and turned to watch the little fishing boats and much larger troop ships vying for position to enter the harbour. There was no more to discuss. She had a decision to make and Sam could take no more part in it. "How's your head?" she asked changing the subject.

"Pounding."

"Let's get you back then."

CHAPTER 33.
June 15th -18th, London

Oh it's good! Really good. Frank played the haunting melody once more; his eyes closed between glances at the scribbled score, feeling the emotion, the soft longing in each beautiful, sorrowful note. His bow glided delicately over the strings of his violin. Music made for this instrument. Sam was right. *How could I have thought it a piece for the piano?* It was too exquisitely mournful to truly be given justice by anything else.

He finished playing the piece for the fifth time, opened his dewy eyes and exhaled tremulously. Nothing he had written before compared to this. The emotion it provoked was intense. What passion, what deep despair. He stared at the spiky notes and allowed his mind to imagine it performed by the whole string section drawing in the deep melancholy of the violas. It would be magnificent orchestrated. He could do it. He had to.

He was still listening to the evocative strains running through his head when the door of the flat opened and Evie breezed in, shopping in one hand and an umbrella, dripping water onto the floor, in the other.

"Oh it's awful out there. So much for flaming June!" she exclaimed and kicked the door shut with her left foot. "What is it? What's wrong?" She pressed suddenly alarmed and completely misreading the tears still standing in his eyes.

"Nothing. Sorry, nothing at all." He laughed and wiped his eyes. "It's just.... Evie, sit down and listen to this," he added hurriedly and swung the instrument under his chin once more.

"But the shopping. Let me put it away first," she protested frowning.

"No. No it can wait. Sit down and listen." He was so persistent, so animated that she obeyed without further question, propping the sodden umbrella against the wall and perching herself on the sofa, the basket of groceries at her feet.

Frank closed his eyes and played, not needing to read the score, but feeling and living the harmony. With the last achingly soft note he opened his eyes and lowered his bow. He glanced across at Evie and found she too was on the verge of tears. She had her hands pressed to her mouth, her gaze unflinchingly astounded and so utterly moved.

"Oh Frank, that really is too beautiful for words. Oh you clever darling. When did you write it?" she said at last.

"I've been tinkering with it for a while. I wrote it for piano and sent it to Sam. You know, just to get an opinion. He suggested it should be played on strings." Frank laughed. "What do you think? Should I orchestrate it? I think it would be marvellous played by the orchestra."

She stood and walked over to the music stand. Picking up the dog-eared paper she read the sheet for some seconds before replying.

"You've got to. It *has* to be played. But maestro would hardly deem to listen to..." she began.

"No not the Symphonic. The Davidson Orchestra. We could play it at our next concert. Maybe not. They'd need more practice than that. But soon. I could orchestrate it in no time. I can hear it already. I don't know why I didn't see it myself. Too close I suppose." Frank enthused.

Evie frowned. It seemed too good a piece for such an amateur airing, yet every work of art had humble beginnings. "Play it again," she insisted and stood directly before him. Frank obliged and she listened critically, yet still it brought tears to her eyes.

"It really is cleverly woven. It pulls you into a whirl of emotion. I can almost feel the passion you must have felt while writing it. But there's something cold as well. As if you..., I don't know; as if you...," she faltered. "Oh do *something* with it Frank. You must," Evie pleaded knowing he needed no encouragement. He nodded returning her smile and not quite having the courage to let her know he had written it for her.

"Were there any letters?" she asked returning to the sofa and picking up the basket of shopping. She disappeared into the kitchenette while he fumbled for paper and a pencil. He meant to start work straight away. "Frank?" she called after a few seconds with no reply.

"Uh? Oh yes. One from Sam. Came with this in it. He's returning to his unit, er, tomorrow I think he said. He's asked if I could find a friend of his who has been wounded. Didn't know which hospital he'd been sent to, but he's given a name," he returned absently, scowling at the second pencil with no point and starting to rummage through a pile of unfinished manuscripts for a sharpener. "There you are you little bugger," he muttered finding it.

"But his friend could have been sent anywhere. Do you want some tea?"

"Sorry?"

"Tea?"

"Oh, yes please."

"And his friend. He could be anywhere," Evie prompted peering around the doorway with a grin. He was so lovable when he became distractedly eccentric like this.

"Hmm? Yes I suppose he could. Well I can only ask around the London hospitals can't I? If he's not here, then Sam will just have to write to the man's family."

He had not really expected to find Albert Dobson and if truth be told, had only half heartedly searched, but surprisingly the private was listed on the recent casualty list entering the First London Military Hospital, an annexe to Bart's and comprising of an old college building and numerous, purpose built huts. Now that he had found Sam's friend Frank dithered about what to do. He could of course, simply write back to his brother and pass on the news. Then it would be up to Sam whether he wrote or not. But that did not seem the right thing to do. Surely he should visit the man, find out how he fared and then write with the information gleaned in a sympathetic letter.

Evie was very much against a visit, but Frank felt duty bound and did not suffer the same squeamish revulsion to injury and illness as she did. In the end, after a morning's deliberation he approached the hospital and enquired whether Private Albert Dobson may receive visitors. He could, from three until five in the afternoon.

Frank left a brooding Evie that very afternoon and made the trek across London to Camberwell with a small bottle of scotch, it seemed only right to take a gift, and an umbrella just in case. It was a warm and sultry day, just the sort of weather to spawn thunder storms although, as his bus clattered to a halt outside of the red brick edifice of the First London, the sky could not have been more benign. A deep azure blue studded with soft white, innocuous clouds.

"You are the first visitor he has had," the ward sister explained as she pointed out the correct bed. "Poor boy. None of his family have been. The Army offered to pay their way, but they have so far, declined to come. He's quite perky though. Nice boy. Try not to tire him too much." She smiled kindly and pointing the way once more, watched the visitor cautiously enter the ward before hurrying away to chase the orderly making tea.

At first Frank had to catch his breath as he entered the long hut, with its two endless rows of pristine beds. Despite the almost overpowering smell of carbolic there was a pervading, sickening aroma of malign infection. Gangrene in all probability. All of the men, nearly forty of them, were surgical cases. Some would not make it. Some lay stupefied and either unaware of their surroundings or too ill to care, their eyes gazing forlornly at the tin roof, their pallor grey, deathly.

Those who were not so sick sat up in their beds. Some read, some were writing letters, some chatted to their neighbour and a few had visitors. All of them were bandaged to a greater or lesser degree. Many had lost limbs. Some had their faces shrouded in lightly stained dressings, hiding some gruesome horror beneath. Bed thirty-three seemed a long walk amongst this wreckage of humanity and Frank found his courage waning as he approached.

At the foot of the bed, he paused, glanced quickly at its occupant and consoled himself that there was nothing too shocking to see. Dobson sat propped against his pillows. He had a substantial dressing covering his left eye and part of that cheek. His amputation was hidden from view beneath a wire frame and his bed clothes. He stared back at the young, pale musician with open curiosity, not knowing who he was and wondering why the serious, thin man had stopped by his bed.

"Albert Dobson?" Frank asked and offered what he hoped was a friendly smile.

"Aye," Dobbo replied feeling even more curious. This bloke did not look like some Army official though he wore a uniform of some sorts, a dark blue one with a war worker's silver badge and a red cross on its arm. Was he another orderly come to take him for some treatment? They had said they would probably measure him up for a leg, although Sister had intimated that would not be for some time yet. The Red Cross man did not look like the usual orderlies though.

Frank stepped forward and held out his hand. It seemed the right thing to do. "Hello, I'm Sam's brother," he said by way of explanation.

Dobbo frowned as he shook the soft, long fingered hand. City hands. Definitely not an orderly. "Sam? Oh, Eppy, I mean Corporal 'Epworth," he said grinning as at last it dawned on him.

"Yes that's right. He asked me to call on you, see how you were. Do you mind," Frank gestured at a chair next to the bed.

Dobson nodded his head to imply that he was happy for this man to stay. He looked nothing like Eppy. Maybe the eyes, but that was all. Quite a bit taller for a start, darker and thinner. The private pulled himself more upright and half turned to face his visitor. "Y' don't look much like 'im," he said after a moment of awkward silence.

Frank laughed. "No, I'm more like Joe, our older brother."

"I met 'im. 'E's a doctor with t' field ambulance. We dropped in to see 'im at Neuve Chapelle. Just before t' push like. Didn't think 'e looked much like Eppy either. What's y'name?"

"Sorry, it's Frank. I should have said."

"Frank that's right. Couldn't remember. You're the musician."

"That's me." Another pause while the young invalid stared, apparently assessing his visitor. "I, er brought you this." Frank reached in his jacket pocket and pulled out the whisky.

Dobson rapidly looked towards the other end of the ward where Sister was talking to another patient. He lifted the bed clothes a fraction, "'Ere, shove it under 'ere. We're not allowed booze. 'Cept a beer if the Doc says it's alright," he winked conspiratorially.

"Oh!" Frank responded, alarmed that he was now aiding and abetting the breaking of hospital rules. He hesitated, but fear of being seen overcame conscience and he hurriedly stuffed the bottle under the sheets.

"Ta. That's real nice o' thi. I'll 'ave a nip wi' me tea when it comes," Dobson grinned. "Eppy alus used to share a nip wi' me. Shouldn't 'ave really; 'im being a corporal like. But 'e never cared. Alus looked after me did Eppy. Is 'e alright? I worried 'e might be dead."

It was an odd revelation. Stated with a mater-of-factness that seemed almost obscene. Frank was quite taken aback by its bluntness and surprised at his own indignant shock. At first he thought the private callous, but then thought he detected concern behind the one sparkling grey eye.

"Yes he's fine. He was concussed and spent a little time in hospital in France, but he should be back with his Battalion now," he explained. Yes he had been right. Dobson was clearly moved by this news, his apparent callousness of a few moments ago merely bravado.

"I'm glad. Right glad," Dobbo muttered almost to himself, his eye glittering even more brightly. He sagged back into his pillows and seemed to lose himself in some quiet reverie. Frank waited, not sure whether to speak or not. In the end he decided he should.

"He was worried about you. Wanted me to make sure you were alright. Are you?" *What a stupid question! Of course he's not alright. Look at him.* Frank blushed.

"Ah that's just like Eppy. Alus thinkin' about t' rest on us. Never 'imsen. You should a seen 'im go fo' Lieutenant Fielding. 'Eart in me mouth I 'ad. Bloody 'ell! CC wa' boilin' mad, but I reckon 'e wa secretly pleased. Never said owt to Eppy afterwards any road." Dobson revealed and his eye roved to the roof and back to his visitor. It was obvious the private practically hero worshipped his corporal, revered him almost. Without expecting to Frank felt a welling of pride for his brother.

"And you. You are being looked after?" the musician pressed.

"I'm alright. Yeah, they look after us 'ere. And I won't be goin' back there either. 'Ome fo' me now," Dobson chuckled, but the light dimmed in that eye, just a little. "They're supposed to measure me up forra leg, but Sister says I aren't ready yet. Stump not 'ealed enough. They might move me to Bradford or Leeds first. Be nearer me mam then. She won't come down 'ere. Too far for 'er and she's scared o' comin'. It'll be 'ard enough to get 'er into Leeds. I think she's been there once. No one to look after t' bairns any'ow," he rambled cheerily.

Frank thought it a shame that no family had come to see the lad. It obviously bothered him, but he was putting on a brave face. He smiled. Dobson rambled on.

"I got a girl at 'ome too. Right bonny she is. On'y sixteen though. 'Er mam and dad won't let 'er come down on 'er own and they won't bring 'er neither. Miserable buggers. Eppy reckoned I should ask 'er to marry me." He beamed brightly.

"Did he now? Sounds like the sort of advice he'd give," Frank commented with amused sarcasm. It passed the private by.

"Yeah, full o' good advice Eppy. Good laugh too. Never shouted at us like t'other NCOs. Well, not unless we were been bloody stupid. Then, boy did 'e blow. Got a right temper your brother 'as. Not often 'e lost it though. 'Cept when 'e beat t'shit outta Black Bright. Lost 'is stripes fo' that. Bloody good to see though," Dobbo smiled sheepishly as if he had divulged something he should not. He shrugged. "Any road, like I said, alus put us before 'imsen."

Frank was intrigued by the tale. No one in the family, at home at least, had known the details behind why they had been asked to address letters to *Corporal* instead of Sergeant Hepworth once more. None of them had the faintest inkling of military discipline and no one in France enlightened them. Not even Joe.

"He had a fight then? We did not know what had happened. Was he demoted to a corporal for it? Is that what happened?" he asked.

Dobson screwed his good eye up as if pained and gazed at his visitor a long few seconds before replying. "'E didn't tell thi? Shit! I shouldn't o' said owt then. Bugger it!"

"It's alright. I won't say anything," Frank reassured thinking he would find out no more. Perhaps it was just as well.

"Sod it! Look; y' don't just lose a stripe in a Court Martial. 'E wa' busted back to t' ranks. S'on'y cos CO knows a good NCO when 'e sees one that Eppy got any stripes back at all," Dobson relented.

"Court Martialled? But I thought that... Was it that bad?"

"Bad? It wa' bloody glorious!" the private laughed bringing a smile to Frank's face despite the shock.

"And will you marry your girl?" Frank asked warming to this simple, affable boy with his devotion to Sam and his readiness to laugh despite what had happened to him. He thought it best to not dwell on Courts Martial and fights.

"Dunno," Dobson said his face darkening. "Don't really think she'll want an 'alf blind cripple," he mumbled, for the first time looking morose.

Frank did not know what to say. He could hardly argue the point, he did not know the girl and neither did he wish to prolong the pain of doubt. "Sam asked, if you were well enough, would you write to him. He said your letters are legendary and he could do with cheering up," he changed the subject once more.

"Did 'e?" a laugh, unforced and boyish. "I'd like that. 'E's back wi' t' Battalion y'said?"

"Yes, I think so. He was due to rejoin them on the sixteenth."

"I'll write there then. 'E's still a corporal?" Dobson asked seriously.

"Er, yes. Shouldn't he be?" Frank thought the question odd.

"Thought they might o' gi'en 'is stripe back by now. Especially after Fieldin' and then this. Didn't want to send it to Corporal 'Epworth when it should be Sergeant. E'd go spare."

"I don't think he would. Anyway, why don't you just call him Sam or Eppy? He wouldn't mind. I mean, you're not likely to be in the Army for long now." *Tactless Frank. Look at the pain that caused. Stupid, thoughtless comment!*

"Still gotta address it to 'im proper though 'aven't I?" Dobson replied determined to hide the disappointment and aching regret he felt. "I liked been a soldier. Weren't much good at it, but I still enjoyed it. Eppy's a good soldier. I tried to be like 'im, but I weren't as brave or as clever. 'E's smart your brother. Good piano player too. 'E showed me a few bits to play, but I wa' all fingers and thumbs. 'E plays like a proper musician. 'E said you wa' brilliant. Is that right?"

Frank smiled at the way the private's thoughts spilled one after the other into words, as though his brain could not keep them to itself a moment longer. Probably a symptom of nerves, but it was also part of who Dobson was. Sam had said in his letter that he might ramble so, if he was well enough.

"I'm quite good, yes. I play for a Red Cross Orchestra. We come to hospitals and play for the patients. We also play in some of the smaller theatres. I think we've got a concert here in a couple of weeks. You should ask to come along. I'll play a request for you. What would you like?"

"I mighta been moved by then," Dobson replied with an expression of disappointment. Then he grinned. "But if I 'aven't, would y'play summat posh. The lads' alus wanted Eppy to play us songs to sing along to, but sometimes 'e used to play some posh stuff first. Real nice it wa'. I'd never 'eard owt like it befower I met Eppy. Sometimes used to make me all maudlin, but I alus enjoyed it. Yeah, summat posh. I'd like that."

"Alright. If you're still here, I'll make sure we play something posh," Frank laughed.

They chatted a little longer, until the orderly rang a clanging great bell to signal that visitors should leave. Not knowing whether he was relieved he could go or disappointed Frank stood and offered his hand. "Well Mr Dobson, looks like I have to go."

"Dobbo. Eppy alus called me Dobbo. Will y' come again?"

"Would you like me to?"

"Yeah, I would. It's borin' as 'ell 'ere and no one from 'ome is gonna come. Bring yer violin and gi' us a private concert."

"Alright. I'll come back on Monday. I've got concerts over the weekend. Nice to meet you Dobbo. Don't forget that letter to Sam. I'll tell him to expect one," Frank said and picked up his umbrella. "And don't get caught with that whisky or Sister won't let me in again."

"Don't worry pal. I know ow to 'ide stuff I shouldn't 'ave. Eppy taught me," the private grinned back and watched his unexpected visitor leave with the first real feeling of optimism he had felt since arriving back in England.

CHAPTER 34.
June 22nd, Brigade Reserve, Le Harisoirs

"Corporal Hepworth Sir," Private Hodges, batman to D Company commander, Major Wilson, announced through the doorway of what had been a particularly well appointed parlour before the war. The wealthy merchant's house no longer had that look of well kept affluence; its gable end crumbled where a German shell had hit, the shutters hung from their rusting hinges and the glass windows had been replaced by hard-board. That said, its roof was nearly intact, the rain only leaking through here and there. The upstairs rooms were still reasonably comfortable sleeping quarters; especially luxurious for a handful of war hardened officers who did not mind the mice in the mattresses or the wind that rattled the hastily covered windows. Downstairs still had a functioning kitchen, capable of delivering a tasty meal. The cellar even held some wine, which had been requisitioned and the appropriate army chit left in lieu of payment should the owner ever return. The drawing room made a wonderful place in which to relax; the dining room a comfortable officers' mess and this, what had been the family parlour, was the CC's office.

Wilson looked up from his chair behind a marvellous eighteenth century writing desk rescued from the ruined library and told Hodges to let Hepworth in. He returned his attention to the papers before him and as the corporal entered, saluted and stood at attention, he covered the pile of letters with a bible. Another sad heap of condolences to an ever growing number of bereaved families. It was a task Wilson hated; a task every officer dreaded, and sadly, one that consumed ever more of his free time. He glanced up at Hepworth and smiled briefly.

"At ease Eppy," he said and waited while his subordinate assumed the more comfortable stance. "I suppose you're wondering why I sent for you?"

Stupid question, Sam thought. Of course he was bloody well wondering. *It was unlikely to be for tea and biscuits was it?* "Yes Sir," he replied economically.

"Well, it's good news actually. In fact it's more than good news. I am delighted to tell you that you are to be awarded a medal," Wilson paused for effect.

"A medal, Sir?" Sam echoed with surprise. "What for, Sir? If I may ask."

"For saving Lieutenant Fielding's life man, that's what for. You did know I had put your name forward on his request?"

"No Sir."

Wilson laughed. "Well I did. Sadly, we have not got the result we would wish for, but the powers that be have granted you a suitable award nevertheless. It is my great honour to tell you that you have been awarded the Distinguished Conduct Medal for an act of unselfish bravery that saved the life of your platoon commander. Well done Eppy," he offered his hand.

Sam hesitated, not knowing what to think. It was a surprise and one he should feel proud to receive, but having seen so many acts of bravery, so many men selflessly give their lives, it was an honour he was a little embarrassed to receive. Yet he was learning the art of diplomacy and he shook the major's hand with an answering, "Thank you Sir."

"Is that all you have to say Hepworth; thank you?" Wilson laughed again.

"It's a surprise that's all Sir. I don't rightly know what to say yet. It...it is a great honour, but I think there are others more deserving than I," Sam tried to explain, at the same time making every effort not to sound ungrateful.

Wilson understood. In fact he had to agree that in many ways there were others just as worthy, if not more so, who would never see recognition. The letters on his desk stood testament to that. All letters about men who had died bravely, doing their duty, yet none of them would receive a shiny medal to pin proudly to their heroic chests. He nodded and resumed his seat. "Sit down Eppy. Pull up that chair over there," he indicated to a dining chair.

With another expression of surprise Sam did as he was told and sat, uncomfortably, opposite his company commander, no longer easy, feeling awkward. He would have preferred to remain standing if the major had more to say. Now he was out of his depth, in uncharted territory. He did not know what to do with his hands. He could not link them together behind his back. The situation reminded him of his first meeting with Fielding. An odd situation of being treated as an equal, or almost so. In the end he folded his hands upon his lap like some demure maid and with the same discomfort.

"How are the headaches? The MO said he had to give you some more aspirin yesterday?" Wilson asked with unexpected concern.

"Er..., they're not too bad Sir. Getting better all the time," Sam replied once more taken aback.

"You sure? You're not lying out of some stupid sense of duty. I don't want sick men cluttering up the ranks. You're no good to me unless you're A one fit."

"Yes Sir. No, I'm not lying Sir. They're worse if I get tired Sir, but they aren't nowhere near so bad anymore. I'm alright," Sam thought to mention that he still could not hear properly, but decided against it.

Wilson studied his subordinate carefully for a moment and eventually decided he was telling the truth, although he had the distinct impression that Hepworth was an adept liar. He sighed. "Eppy, I'm giving you your stripe back. I think you've proved you've earned it and we've lost too many NCOs over the last two shows. Reinforcements have helped, but we've taken a hammering recently and we need men with experience, men who know both the troops and the ropes," Wilson explained leaning across the desk.

Sam stared with astonishment. He could hardly believe his ears. Was this a joke? He expected that any minute the major would start laughing and say that it was. He opened his mouth to speak, closed it again, stared at his hands and then shook his head in disbelief. Finally he returned the major's smile. "Thank you Sir."

"Don't thank me man. I think you've learned your lesson, but if you do anything like that again we'll throw the bloody book at you. Anyway, you won't be staying with D Company. A and B Companies are desperately short of NCOs. I have been asked to transfer you to A Company and Corporal Pratt to B," Wilson stated brusquely although he too shared the disappointment he noted flitter across Hepworth's face.

Sam's smile faltered, the joy he felt moments ago plunging into bitter disappointment. Not that he should be surprised. He knew he had been lucky to return to the same Company twice after a spell in hospital. Hell, some men were beginning to be transferred to completely different units. At least he was staying with his own Battalion. Even so he had been with D Company a long time now. His friends were amongst its men, what was left of them.

"I see Sir," he said at length realising the officer expected a response. "I shall be sad to go. It has been an honour, Sir."

The major smiled. The expressed sentiment was one he shared even though Hepworth was, militaristically at least, his inferior. "Take this chit to the quartermaster and then report to CSM Morris, he's expecting you. Announcements will be posted regarding your award, and Mister Wise, A Company, One Platoon, knows he has a new sergeant." Wilson handed over an official note paper.

"Thank you, Sir," Sam repeated again. The medal was an embarrassment, but the rank was not. It was a greater source of pride than any lump of tin could be. The chit for issue of a stripe to be sewn onto his tunic far more precious than a card telling him of recognition for an act of bravery. With mixed feelings he stood and paused. Wilson looked quizzically at him.

"May I ask how Lieutenant Fielding is Sir? Do you know?" Sam asked.

"He is making a good recovery I believe," Wilson returned with a smile.

"Would it be appropriate for me to write and thank him?"

Wilson sat back and considered his reply. Hepworth was a strange one. Appearing cool and distant when required but affable and generous by nature generally. "I think it would Sergeant. Do you have his address?"

"No Sir."

"Write to the Princess of Wales' Nursing Home, Portsmouth. He'll be there still I think."

Sam nodded. "Thank you Sir."

"And Hepworth?"

"Sir?"

"Behave yourself in A Company. I've stuck my neck out to get you that stripe back. Don't let me down," Wilson requested with a smirk.

"Wouldn't dream of it Sir."

CHAPTER 35.
July 1ˢᵗ, 1ˢᵗ London Hospital, Camberwell

Frank angrily unpacked his violin, stacking music scores upon the stand with uncharacteristic bad humour. Mrs Davidson frowned in his direction and pursed her lips wondering whether to attempt to cheer the young man or leave him to his brooding bitterness. One did not like to interfere. She hovered, vacillated and decided it was probably no more than a lovers tiff. These artistic types were so temperamental. The hospital matron caught her eye and instead of assailing her first violinist, Mrs Davidson drifted to the prim nursing superintendent and put him, temporarily, from her mind.

Around the hall chairs were being dragged into their final resting place with irritating, jarring racket. It was the last straw and Frank glowered at the laborious manoeuvrings with venom.

"WILL YOU *PLEASE* BE QUIET!" he shouted, bringing the hall to a standstill, surprised looks from his fellow musicians and a nervous giggle from one of the girl oboists. Mrs Davidson and Matron gazed with astonishment, open mouthed and incredulous at such a rude outburst. The orderlies, merely shrugged their shoulders, smirked at one another and carried on as clamourously as before.

With the majesty of a galleon, Mrs Davidson sailed to the violinist's side. "Francis, please control yourself dear. Whatever is the matter?" she both remonstrated and requested in hushed tones.

Frank flushed violently red, painfully embarrassed and muttered an apology.

"Do you feel unwell?" the dame demanded in a flurry of concern that belied her worries for the success of the concert rather than the well being of its principal musician.

"No, no. Yes, well a little maybe. It's awfully stuffy in here isn't it?" he lied.

"Why don't you get some fresh air dear? These dreadful men will not have the hall ready for another ten minutes or so. One wonders why the Army employs them. Such slovenly creatures. I'll ask Matron to see that the windows are opened. We must have some air in here. You are quite right. It is far too hot and stuffy. I can't have my musicians becoming ill," she concluded and glided with her usual surprising grace to address the matter.

Frank took her advice. Not that the air outside was very fresh. With July had come a stifling, humid heat that only London could make even more unpleasant by adding the further ingredients of coal smoke and the foul stench of rank drains to the foetid concoction. Even so he needed a few minutes solitude if only to quieten his temper. Jumping from the makeshift stage, he pushed his way around struggling men and disappeared into the relative cool of the wide entrance hall and then into the oppressive heat of the midsummer evening. Leaning against the wall beside the door he lit a cigarette and drew on it appreciatively allowing the nicotine to soothe his frayed nerves. He closed his eyes and with increasing calm ran over the argument between himself and Evie of an hour earlier. He had wanted her to come to the performance. It would be the first time the orchestra played his composition to a live audience and although she had heard it at rehearsals her refusal to participate any longer, because of her ridiculous fear of sick people, meant that she would not witness its reception.

Frank felt certain the audiences would love the piece. It had a captivating melody that could not fail to move even the most emotionless individual. Its magic lay not only in its hauntingly beautiful lyricism but in its ability to mean something to everyone. Anyone who had loved, anyone who had seen beauty, anyone who had witnessed death. All the emotions that any of these experiences roused were evident in his moving masterpiece. And Frank felt certain it was a masterpiece. Now that he had orchestrated the work, relying heavily upon the mournful passion of the strings, he understood it truly was a great work. It captured the mood of the times and he intended to dedicate its first semi-professional airing to Albert Dobson. He felt certain the young private would approve. Yet the one other person he wanted to be there had refused to come.

Frank inhaled cigarette smoke and determined to push his bitter disappointment away. Instead he thought of Dobbo, how the young man would react. He had asked if the private may be brought to the front of the hall. Matron had promised to see what she could do, but that space was usually reserved for officers.

In the two weeks since they had first met, Frank and Dobson had formed a firm, if odd, friendship. It was odd because in reality they had absolutely nothing in common. Dobbo was a working class lad from a poor family in Middlesbrough whose father had died in a pit accident and left a wife with six children. This had been Dobbo's reason for joining the Army, underage and before the war. Nearly all his pay went to his mother to supplement the meagre pension she received from the Union and the money she made doing other women's laundry. He knew little of anything other than the Army and Middlesbrough. Despite his reputation for long letters, his literary experiences ran only to newspapers and a couple of children's novels which, he confessed, he had read over and again until the covers dropped off. His upbringing could not have been further removed from Frank's privileged childhood, with its expensive education, music, plentiful food, good clothes and an opportunity to be whatever he wished to be. Yet despite their differences and the age gap, Frank could understand why Sam liked the young private so, why he had gone out of his way to look after him. It was impossible to dislike Dobson even though it was impossible to say exactly why.

The tooting of a car horn broke through his thoughts and looking out at the street, with a sinking feeling, Frank returned the exaggerated wave of Grace Pemberton. He flicked the tab end of his smoke into the gutter and graciously waited for the singer to totter up the steps in her ridiculously high shoes and tight skirt. Always dressed, what he considered, inappropriately she tiptoed towards him a vision, or was it a nightmare, in gaudy pink chiffon with a hat that would have rivalled any at Ascot on Ladies Day. She offered her hand; dutifully he bent to kiss it and turned to escort her inside.

"Had you sneaked out for a smoke you naughty boy?" she teased with her usual condescension that sent prickles of irritation down his spine. He fought not to show his annoyance and instantly knew he had failed as she laughed affectedly and pinched his nose. "I won't tell," she whispered and pulling his arm into hers and his body far closer than he felt comfortable with she proceeded to chatter about her tedious journey to this God forsaken part of London. As they passed into the hall, she sneered with distaste at an elderly orderly who nearly bumped into her and, even though the poor man had not so much as brushed her skirts, she recoiled as if burnt.

Another stupid woman. Frank thought. *They're all so puerile. Why couldn't they be like*

Lily or was she alone amongst her sex?

"I should not speak to you at all Francis if truth be known," Grace stated.

"Sorry? What do you mean?" *I don't care. Truly I don't. In fact I'd rather you didn't.*

"Well, you still refuse to join me in a little duet. We would be sensational you know."

"I'm flattered. But I also work. When I am not rehearsing with the Davidson orchestra I have other rehearsals with the Symphonic. I did try to explain Miss Pemberton. There is no slight on your dear self intended," Frank returned with as much tact as he could muster.

She sighed. "Well I do think you should consider quitting this second class outfit. You are far too good for it you know," she squeezed his arm. "Ahh, Mrs Davidson," she called and letting go of her captive teetered towards the benevolent lady.

"I'm too bloody good for you," he muttered under his breath as she disappeared out of view. He returned to the stage, unpacked his violin and with the rest of his colleagues tuned to the middle C of the less than perfectly pitched piano brought with great effort onto the stage.

As the orchestra scraped and scratched into tune the hall began to buzz with the excited chatter and laughter of nearly two hundred injured Tommies. Before long any further attempts to achieve a musical concord had to be abandoned as the scraping of chairs, the clatter of wheels and crutches, the incessant and collective babble of the multitude of blue clad soldiery drowned out all but the brass section. Frank took up his seat allowing the excited atmosphere to seep into his body and take him over.

He looked for Dobson, craning his neck to see a familiar face amongst the sea of strangers. They had not brought him to the front. All the seats here were taken by officers. Frank felt disappointed. He could not see his new friend and became worried that he might not be there at all. Then an arm waved vigorously near the back of the hall. The musician strained to see, caught the half bandaged head with its covered, eyeless socket, caught the characteristic grin. He waved back and getting up, jumped down from the stage and hurried down the central aisle. Pushing past a wheeled chair with a muttered pardon, he reached Dobson just before an orderly wheeled another invalid into the space next to him.

"This young man's to go to the front," Frank shouted above the din with an air of superiority.

The orderly gazed at him and shook his head. "Officers at the front. 'E stays 'ere," he argued.

"But I have agreed it with Matron."

"I don't bloody care if you agreed it wiv the King. More'n me life's worth to take 'im up there," the orderly shouted back. Dobson eyed both with amusement.

Frank made to say some more but decided it simply was not worth the effort. The orderly was not going to oblige. He drew in a deep breath climbed in behind Dobbo to take the handle of his chair. He stared at the orderly who, with his own charge, stood in the way. The orderly stared back.

"Well move then. I'll take him myself," Frank insisted. By now the group of men around them had fallen quiet and along with the two chaired invalids were watching the confrontation with comic interest.

"'E can't go I tell yer. Leave 'im there," the orderly shot back becoming agitated.

"I tell you man, I have permission to take him to the front. Ask Matron if you don't believe me."

"I ain't asking 'er," the reply.

"I insist you move. I shall not ask again," Frank raised his voice higher. The men all around were enthralled by the additional entertainment now.

"Who d'you think you are orderin' me anyway. Bloody toffee nosed musician. Come in 'ere an'..."

"It's alright Frank. I'm 'appy to stay 'ere," Dobson interrupted hoping to restore conviviality.

"Shut up Dobbo, I'm dealing with this. You're coming to the front," Frank snapped.

"Yeah you bloody stay out of this," the orderly joined in and then stabbing his fingers against his antagonist's chest roared, "Bugger off back onto that stage and do what yer paid to do. Y' bloody stay-at-'ome."

Indignation at the intimation swelled like an enraged beast in Frank's chest, his temper snapped and he bellowed back, "I AM NOT PAID YOU BLOODY IMBECILE. NOW GET OUT OF MY WAY YOU IGNORANT MORON!"

The orderly swayed and then grabbed Frank by his jacket collar and bodily heaved him back into the aisle and pushed him to the ground. The hall had now fallen into awed and deathly silence not that either man noticed. Frank bounded to his feat, his heart beating laboriously in his chest and his head swimming dizzyingly, but his temper knew no bounds and quite to the orderly's surprise this skinny, white face lad planted a dazing punch squarely upon his nose. Blood spurted everywhere, the men cheered, the assailed man swore. Feet rushed to the scene and a steely, female voice echoed chillingly through the uproar instilling the hall into sudden and expectant silence.

"JONES, *MISTER* HEPWORTH! May I remind you both *this* is a hospital and not the dock yard. Jones, report to Sergeant Stockwell immediately. Mister Hepworth, you, I believe are required on stage. Move, both of you, NOW!"

Grasping his streaming nose Jones muttered a distinctly nasal "Yes Matron," glowered at his attacker and scurried away. Frank dithered, his temper subsiding into mortified humiliation. He tried to speak but the senior nursing officer cut him off. "Do not try my patience young man. You are only still in my hospital because you owe these men a concert. Private Dobson will remain here." It was a firm and just rebuff.

Frank glanced apologetically at Dobbo who, behind Matron's back, sat grinning happily. He gave a thumbs up and with a half smile, the embarrassed musician hurriedly returned to the stage trying to ignore the stares and laughter of the men. What had come over him? His behaviour was reprehensible to say the least. He had not felt blind rage like that since a boy when Sam laughingly held him at arm's length and his fists flayed widely at thin air, never quite reaching his mocking brother.

As he retreated two orderlies were signalled to clean up the blood, Matron caught Mrs Davidson's surprised and horrified eye and intimated through a method of thought transference only possible to those of formidable authority, that they should have words later. As Frank climbed back onto the stage painfully conscious of the shocked expressions, and one or two distinctly amused ones, of his colleagues, the sardonic smile of Grace, a spontaneous applause broke out amongst the audience.

He took his seat to cheers and despite the fact he felt like a complete idiot and he shook from the trials of the exertion he could not help but be buoyed by the comradely support. He had no doubt that Matron and Mrs Davidson were furious, but as he picked up his violin he could not conceal the smile that stole unbidden to his lips.

Mrs Davidson rushed to centre stage, glowered meaningfully once at her young violinist and held her arms aloft to request quiet. The cheers dwindled to happy anticipation as the lady called the audience to pay attention. Joyful faces locked on hers and two hundred men hushed to listen respectfully.

"Gentlemen and of course, Ladies," Mrs Davidson bowed her head in acknowledgement of the few nurses scattered amongst their patients. "It is a great honour to perform for you this evening. I will not make a long and boring speech, do not fret. All I wish to say is, I hope that you enjoy our humble concert, that it fills your brave hearts with joy. This is our small way of saying thank you, of bestowing a meagre, but well deserved gift in lieu of something more worthy. We cannot imagine what you have been through. We cannot hope to ever fully understand. But we can say thank you. All the musicians and the comedian performing tonight give their time freely. Many would gladly swap places with you if they could. Please, enjoy..." She backed away clapping her hands and the crowd erupted into exuberant applause and cheering.

The conductor took up his baton and with a count of three beats brought the orchestra into resounding, exhilarating life with the uproariously, uplifting Pomp and Circumstance March Number One. The Tommies sang along proudly and at its end the hall reverberated with a cacophony of boisterous clapping, shouting and banging of tin mugs in appreciation. The members of the orchestra grinned at one another their hearts aglow. How could one not be inspired and excited by such acclaim? These audiences of battered and maimed soldiers were the most appreciative and demonstrative of any. What more could a performer ask for? As the clamour died down, the musicians moved into their usual repertoire, punctuating boisterous classical with popular melodies, accompanying the vivacious and much admired Miss Pemberton and providing theatrical music hall backing sounds to the comedian's simple, but topically hilarious jokes.

After an hour the pace slowed, Grace sang a brace of sentimental songs and bowed long and repeatedly to the bright eyed applause. She held up her hands and winked across at Frank who glanced back with a sudden flash of nervous apprehension. He was going to have to speak. This was the point when they would play his newly orchestrated composition. He had given it a name, something he felt fitting, but now he was unsure whether to play it or not. What if they did not like it? What if it was too moving, brought back unwanted memories? Too late now, he heard Grace begin her rehearsed introduction.

"Ladies and Gentlemen, please, may I ask for quiet. Gentlemen? Thank you," she shouted above the din. The crowd fell quiet.

"Sing us another one love," someone called from the back of the hall. A spattering of laughter followed.

Grace smiled. "Later. First I would like to introduce you all to our fabulous orchestra's lead violinist. Ladies and Gentlemen, Mister Frank Hepworth," she started to clap, Frank blanched, hesitated and as expectant eyes followed the singer's outstretched hand he realised with dread he had no choice. Slowly he stood, the audience recognised him as the pugilist from earlier and cheered encouragingly, he smiled coyly and moved to the front of the stage. Flushing furiously he held his hands for quiet. It took some seconds for the shouting to die down.

"I am overwhelmed," Frank began his voice wavering with pent nervousness. "However, I feel my sudden popularity may have more to do with my rather ungentlemanly behaviour of earlier than my musical ability tonight." They cheered and laughed, he smiled warming to his role. He waited until they became quiet again and carefully avoided Mrs Davidson's glowering eye from her seat in the front row.

"Gentlemen and Ladies," Frank bowed low to Matron who watched him with a steely, disapproving stare. "The orchestra will now perform a new piece of work and I would like to dedicate this music to a friend who is in the audience tonight. He wished us to play something *posh* for him. So to Private Albert Dobson of the Second Battalion the Yorkshire Regiment I dedicate this to you and hope it meets with your expectations." A few cheers probably from fellow soldiers of the Regiment. Frank looked to where the young invalid sat although he could barely see him, only make out the top of his head. "This is for you Dobbo and for all soldiers who fight so far away from home. It is called Reminiscing."

He glanced once at the orchestra behind him and then lifting his bow began to play the slow, haunting melody immediately losing his nerves and becoming one with the music, eyes closed and expression serene. Gradually the string section joined his lone instrument, violins first, then violas, finally cellos and double bass. Over an exquisite five minutes they caressed and wove the tune with spellbinding beauty, building the piece into a magical, stirring crescendo before falling to the initial gentle strains of a single instrument once more and fading into a long, final plaintive note. As the last vibration disappeared from his fingers Frank opened his eyes and gazed, with slightly blurred vision, upon the previously boisterous crowd. Their faces reflected an odd, stunned awe. For a second or two there was silence and for one awful, heart stopping moment he thought they did not like it. Then they began to clap, falteringly at first, then with wild enthusiasm. Those who could stand did so, some called for encores, others cheered, many were incapable of either but applauded until their hands were sore.

Frank stood and shook; he could not prevent the tears filling his eyes or stop them from falling from his long dark lashes. He ushered the string section to stand and accept acclaim. They did so bowing once and then joining with the cheering Tommies, acknowledging him.

After that the remainder of the concert vanished in a whirl of noise and boisterous singing. As usual Grace insisted upon the lead violinist accompanying her in a duet, but for once it was not the show stopping event despite her charm and popularity. That moment had already been sealed. They finished with the National Anthem, lustily sung by the audience. As the last applause died away and the inevitable scraping of chairs began, Frank exhaustedly loosened the strings of his violin and carefully returned it to its case. Members of the orchestra came over to congratulate him and say goodnight, a few exchanging views.

"Thought they weren't going to clap at all to start with old chap," a trumpet player stated.

Frank laughed. "Me too," he confessed.

"Bloody brilliant! I've never felt so damned proud to be in an orchestra as tonight. You're a bloody genius man," an exuberant Welsh cellist cried in a voice much louder than it needed to be as he pumped his colleague's hand with a passion.

"Thank you," Frank returned flushing coyly.

"Francis my dear boy," Mrs Davidson's bulk parted a respectful way to where he stood politely returning thanks for the congratulations while trying to see whether Dobbo was still in the hall. Above everyone, it was the private's opinion he wanted to hear. He frowned at the dame his heart sinking a little as he remembered her stern countenance of earlier and the intimation that a remonstration was due.

"Francis you are forgiven," she gushed and grabbing his shoulders kissed either cheek in a demonstrative Gallic embrace. Frank blushed even redder, feeling the rush of blood to his skin. "That was sublime my dear. Sublime. Worthy of the greats. I will be speaking with Sir Frederick first thing tomorrow. That work cannot be ignored. It has to be aired upon a more discerning audience. You, my dear, dear boy, are truly wonderful." Mrs Davidson continued, her eyes sparkling with dewy pride and her fat cheeks wobbling with emotion.

"Thank you." It was all he could say. Part of him still revelled in the afterglow of success, the remainder wished only to be left alone now, to find Dobbo and then go home. He felt elated, yet so very tired. He busied himself with his music, shook a few more hands, was glad that Grace had vanished without seeking him out. Mrs Davidson sailed away to speak with one or two distinguished looking officers waiting discreetly at the bottom of the stage and finally Frank could look up, free from well wishers, out into the hall.

Far at the back, near to the doors, a little knot of men stood awkwardly. With them sat Dobson in his wheeled chair, a VAD nurse standing behind him. Dobbo caught his gaze and waved. Grinning, Frank jumped down from the stage, ignored the dizzying giddiness that momentarily assailed him, it happened so often he scarcely gave it a thought these days, and hurried to join his friend. The little group smiled with abashed awe as he arrived.

"Well?" he asked.

"Aw Frank, that wa' blood..., er fantastic." Dobbo replied nearly forgetting the nurse behind him. "Fair made me cry it did. An' I wouldn't want to admit to that normally. But it were so... I can't find t'words. I'm not clever enough. It got me right 'ere," he clamped a hand to his heart. "Made me think of all me pals, an' of France an' everything we've been through. T'wa right sad, but at t'same time made y' feel right proud. Does that make sense?" He laughed.

"Yes. It makes sense."

"You writ it?" one of the other men asked.

"Yes."

"Frank's Eppy's brother Loll," Dobbo half introduced.

"That right? Bloody 'ell. Didn't know 'e 'ad a famous brother," Loll laughed. "Y' don't look much like 'im."

"You know Sam?" Frank asked smiling broadly.

"Aye. 'E's D Company like young Dobson 'ere. Good centre 'alf, bloody good marksman. Uh, sorry Sister. Plays piano like a good un an' all. 'E still alive then?" The question, blunt and out of the blue.

"Mr Randall, really, what a question," the VAD reprimanded.

"It's alright Nurse," Frank laughed as the straight forward Yorkshire man muttered an apology. "Yes, he's still alive."

"Good. I'm glad to 'ear it," Randall grinned back toothlessly, it appeared he had lost them recently for much of his face showed the remnants of yellowed bruising along with various superficial contusions. What else was wrong with him was not apparent.

"We're all Green 'Owards," a slight, fair haired man with a missing left arm admitted. "We wanted to say we enjoyed the concert especially that tune. Dobbo 'ere wa' tellin' us 'bout you too. 'Onoured to meet y' Sir." The man stuck his right hand out. Without hesitation Frank shook it and soon found himself doing the same with the other three men. The nurse and Dobson beamed happily.

"Please don't call me Sir. I'm not anyone special. I'm just glad you enjoyed yourselves tonight. That's what we come for."

"Aye, we enjoyed it. Thanks. Makes it feel worthwhile. Like we're appreciated or summat," Loll Randall said.

"Well gentlemen I think we should allow Mister Hepworth to get home. Thank you Mister Hepworth," the VAD decided to bring the gathering to an end. It was more than her job was worth to keep these men out of bed any longer. Matron would be lurking somewhere nearby. The men scowled with disappointment, but they did not argue. They thanked the musician once more and hobbled or slumped away, following the nurse.

"I'll call in tomorrow Dobbo," Frank called after them. A cheery wave acknowledged him and then they were gone.

"Coming for a drink old chap?" a fellow violinist asked as he made his way to the doors.

"No thanks John. I'd best get home. Evie will wonder where I am," Frank smiled. He did not wish to celebrate. The thanks of those men were enough. Meant more than any other plaudits could. With a warmth born from satisfied altruism he headed out into the humid July night, returned the farewells of colleagues and caught a bus, the first of three, and headed home.

It was past midnight when he crept into the apartment, fully expecting Evie to be in bed. He stole into the kitchenette and filled a glass with water, gulping it down in long drafts then refilling it once more. He doubted, despite his tiredness, that he could sleep just yet; his mind still reeled with the events of the evening, with the success of *Reminiscing*. He wanted to share his happiness with Evie, but knew he should not wake her, it would be unfair. He picked up his glass and returned to the living room only to find her seated upon the sofa, wrapped in her red silk dressing gown. He thought how lovely she looked with hair tousled and loose around the creamy skin of her face and neck. Lovely and vulnerable.

"Hello. I didn't mean to disturb you. I was trying to be quiet," he offered softly and took a seat next to her. He wanted to pick up her hand, but memories of the earlier argument prevented him. What if she still hated him?

"You didn't wake me. I couldn't sleep. I've been thinking about earlier. I'm sorry Frank," she uttered meekly and held his gaze with sad blue-grey eyes.

He pulled her close and kissed her, happy that they were friends once more.

"How did it go?" she asked.

He told her, explaining the performance in minute detail, but omitting his altercation with the orderly. She did not need to hear that and she would only chastise him. Instead she listened with her head resting upon his chest while he played with her hair and stroked the back of her neck.

"Good. I'm glad it went well. Do you think Mrs Davidson really will see Sir Frederick? It would be so grand if the Symphonic would play it. You'll have to publish it."

"Yes. I want to publish it anyway, but I don't know whether she will. You know what she's like. I'm not really bothered."

"But you should be. It's important," she lifted her head to catch his eye and then pulling away from him sighed.

"What? What is it?" he asked perturbed by the sudden change in mood. Was she angry over his lack of ambition?

"There's something else important you need to know."

His heart sank. Had something happened? To Sam or Joe? "What is it? No one's hurt are they?" he looked around for a telegram.

"No, no. No one's hurt. Frank, stop fretting, listen," she laughed, her mood lightening again and she picked up his hands. "It is serious though. I'm pregnant."

"*What?*"

"You heard me. I'm having a baby," she repeated and her expression changed from smiley to anxious.

He stared at her open mouthed, his head trying to take in the news. Slowly his face lighted into a wide and joyous grin. "Oh my beautiful, beautiful darling! That's wonderful. Marvellous. I'm speechless!" He pulled her into an amorous embrace and kissed her over and over until she was helpless with laughter.

They snuggled together, warm in their shared pleasure and love.

"I thought you might be angry. I was afraid you would not want me anymore," she whispered.

"How can you say that?" he demanded lifting her chin and kissing her. "You know I adore you."

She giggled and laid her head on his chest once more. "I love you Frank."

"I love you too. But you know what this means don't you?"

"What?"

"We have to get married now."

"But..."

"No buts. No arguments. I'm going to make an honest woman of you. I'll cable my parents tomorrow."

"Oh, don't tell them why. Frank, they'll despise me," Evie pulled herself upright once more, her face fraught.

"Did I say I would? No one needs know why. Besides the answer is obvious. It's because I love you. Come on, let's go to bed," he grinned with boyish charm and pulling her by the hands lead her to the bedroom.

CHAPTER 36.
July 14th, Pateley Bridge

Joe stared at the bundle that was his sleeping son. It still had not really sunk in that this little pink and white, helpless infant was his; a product of his and Dora's love. He wanted to reach out and touch the child but feared to wake him, so instead he watched with awe and a warmth inside he had never felt possible. His heart swelled with pride and overflowed with love. What a wondrous miracle of creation. Despite being a doctor the thaumaturgy of creation never ceased to amaze him and roused the eternal doubt that battled within. Was this child merely a result of Darwinian evolution or did some Divine being wield a more powerful magic? It was an answer he forever failed to resolve and even now, after his experiences in France, where the horrors of war drove God from the most devout, he remained unsure. It seemed impossible that something so exquisitely perfect could be the product of mere chance.

The nursery door opened and a soft breeze from the open window wafted warm, hay scented air into the room. Swifts screeched around the house their calls invoking cherished memories of this place, of home. He half turned, caught sight of his wife and smiled wistfully. She reached his side and covered his hand where it lay on the cot side, with hers.

"I thought I might find you here," she said gently.

He had been home just two days, had slept as long and as contentedly as the babe he watched over and spent much of his waking time coming to terms with fatherhood.

"I'm sorry, I'm neglecting you," he returned tearing his eyes from the infant to look at his wife. *God she is lovely.* He had missed her so much.

"Nonsense," she dismissed and with a stab of emotion read both the love and the fear in his brown eyes. It shook her and with a trembling hand she touched his face. "What is it?"

"Nothing. I..., I just missed you that's all." An inadequate reply but as usual he struggled to express his feelings.

She smiled and her eyes filled, "I missed you too. But now your home..., for a while." *Shouldn't have said that. Look at the pain it caused.* Dora stood on tiptoes and kissed his lips. "I love you," she whispered.

"Oh God!" He pulled her to him and held her with fierce longing in a tight embrace. His whole body shook and she thought he was weeping, but she would not pull away, would not place him in a position of embarrassment. She held on while he buried his face in her hair.

"Oh, begging your pardon Madam," a shocked voice announced as the thin, middle-aged nurse bumbled into the room half hidden behind a pile of flannelette nappies.

Joe broke away from his wife and with his back to the room gazed out of the window onto the drive below. He blinked rapidly and fought to gain control, his face flushed and hot. Dora's eyes followed him, feeling his discomfort. She wanted to shout at the nurse to get out, but it would be unfair, the woman had not known that husband and wife would chose their son's nursery in which to cling to each other like long lost lovers.

"Shall I leave?" the nurse hovered uncertainly. She had not meant to intrude but goodness knows what she would do with this washing. Take it back to the scullery she supposed.

"No, no. We were just leaving. Please, carry on," Joe replied brusquely and strode purposefully to the door. Dora glanced down at her boy and then followed him with a shy smile at the maid.

"Shall I fetch him down when he wakes Madam?"

"No Edna. He'll need feeding. Come and inform me and I will come up," Dora answered.

"Very good Madam," Edna bobbed a curtsey and teetered to a chest of drawers where she started to fold the squares. As the door clicked shut behind her, she turned and smiled to herself, before placing the clean washing neatly away.

Dora hurried down the stairs trying to catch up with her husband, but he was already out in the garden, pacing up and down the drive, his face furrowed and lean. She leant against the threshold and studied him her heart wanting to rush to his side and her head warning her to give him space. He looked different. He had lost weight, not that he was ever fat. His face had lost any trace of the roundness of youth. Before he had left she thought he still held vestiges of boyhood despite being thirty. Now those remnants had gone. It was not simply because he had grown thinner; it showed in his eyes as well. Somehow they seemed smaller, lacking in the vitality they once had. Maybe it was simply because he was so tired. He had said as much. Yet he had a remoteness about him, a haunted restlessness that she could not reach. He was glad to be home and still he seemed sad. Whether because he knew he must go back or because of what he had experienced over there she did not know. He would not say. She had tried to ask, but he had only said it was not something he wanted her to hear about.

"Oh talk to me Joe. I'm here to listen. Don't shut me out," she muttered under her breath as she watched his preoccupied pacing.

The raucous clatter of an internal combustion engine and the crunching of gravel aroused both husband and wife from their private reverie and a cheerful, shouted greeting from the portly figure of Charles Bradshaw brought a smile to his daughter's face and his son-in-law's endless journey to a halt. Waving what appeared to be a periodical in the air, somehow the mill owner brought the Daimler to a controlled stop and laughed with characteristic jollity as Dora almost skipped to the car, happy for the unexpected diversion. He offered his cheek and she dutifully kissed it, taking his arm and half pulling him from the vehicle. Joe sauntered over and offered his hand.

"My dear boy. So good to see you," Charles boomed in his usual overly loud, resonant voice.

"And what about me Daddy? You've been in London for the last month and you haven't even missed me. We weren't expecting you. You should have called or sent a telegram," Dora teased, smiling at her sanguine father.

"It is always good to see you my treasure," he laughed and kissed her heartily on her face. "I wanted to surprise you all. I've invited myself over. Got to celebrate. Is Thomas in? And Eliza?"

"Father's at his surgery. Mother's in though. Celebrate? I wasn't expecting a celebration," Joe laughed feeling a little awkward. He liked Charles Bradshaw immensely, esteemed him as a sound businessman and respected him as a father-in-law, but he had not really wanted his leave to be treated as an excuse to celebrate.

Charles guffawed loudly causing Joe and Dora to share a quizzical glance. "No, no my dear boy. As much as I am glad to see you and my beautiful daughter and my precious grandchild, none of you dears are the reason for our celebration. Don't you know? It's in here. I thought *you* might have heard Joe at least." He shook the magazine clutched in his left hand.

"Know what Daddy? You're not making sense. Oh! Is the war over? Have they called a…a truce," Dora gasped hopefully and flushed foolishly as she caught the half exasperated, half sardonic sneer that Joe failed to hide in time.

"No my dear, sadly not. Here, look…," Charles flourished the periodical. It was a copy of the Sportsman magazine, which he opened at a well thumbed page. Inside were two torn pages from the London Gazette. He glanced up guiltily with a coy smile. "Here, it's here. Let me read it. Damn, where did I put my spectacles?" He fumbled in his jacket for his glasses. "Here, you read it Joe. He's your brother anyway." He thrust the pages at a bewildered young man and stood back with satisfaction as Joe first read the citation to himself, opened his mouth in amazement and then widened it into a broad, bright grin.

"What is it, Joe?" Dora queried becoming frustrated with the prolonged anticipation.

"It's Sam. Not here. Inside. Find Mother. I'll read it to you both. Fetch Rose and Tilly as well. Dad should be here." With a laugh he shot inside and began shouting for the servants to come to the drawing room. Dora stared after him with astonishment and then up at her father who raised his eyebrows and beamed.

"I've brought champagne. The very best," he confided and led her into the house.

In the drawing room Joe practically pushed his mother into her favourite chair as his wife and father-in-law entered. He lunged to the door behind them and bellowed, "Rose, Tilly, in the drawing room now!"

"Charles! What a pleasant surprise. Have I you to thank for turning my son into a raving lunatic?" Eliza greeted her old friend affably with only a hint of perturbation and offered her hand.

Charles chuckled and kissed it. "I'm afraid so Eliza. But it gets worse. I have invited myself to dinner and I have brought champagne."

"Have you now. Well whatever…?"

"Shhh Mother. Ah, Rosie sit there and Tilly, here," Joe interrupted and placed the flustered cook and maid onto the sofa where they sat looking at a loss and distinctly out of place.

"Joe, really! What on earth..?" Eliza tried once more wondering why her son had brought the servants in and sat them down in the family drawing room.

"Listen. Listen to this. Dad should be here too, but it can't wait." Joe waited for silence and cleared his throat glancing conspiratorially at Charles as he began to read. "Two bits. First the index, heading; Distinguished Conduct; name; Hepworth Samuel Thomas; rank; *Sergeant*." Joe paused for effect as his mother gasped. "Second bit, the citation," he fumbled the pages to read the second with theatrical affectation. "Distinguished Conduct Medal Awarded to *Sergeant* Samuel Thomas Hepworth of the Second Battalion the Yorkshire Regiment, for an act of devoted bravery when, with total disregard for his own safety he ran into No-Man's-Land to rescue his badly injured platoon commander, Lieutenant Harold John Fielding. In the face of enemy fire and with no means of cover, this *fine* non-commissioned officer showed great courage in seeking and recovering his fallen commander, administering life saving first aid and carrying him back, single handedly, to safety."

Eliza covered her mouth with her hands in shocked surprise. Dora squealed with delight and bounded to her feet to grab the papers from her husband and read the citation again. Rose clapped and sobbed alternately. It was her Sam, her lovely boy. Tilly smiled happily, glad for the family, glad for the soldier she had met and liked last December.

"Oh Sam! Oh Joe, you must fetch your father. Charles, I think we must have more than one bottle of champagne," Eliza managed at last.

"I've brought half a dozen my dear," Bradshaw laughed.

"Rose, are you able to rustle up something special? I know it's short notice."

"Don't worry Mrs 'Epworth, I 'ave just the thing. Come on Tilly, there's much to do." Rose bounced to her feet and hoisted the housemaid to hers, bustling her through the door and back to the kitchen. They should not stay, this was a family matter, but oh how her heart fair burst with pride. Her favourite boy, a hero.

"Your father dear. You must fetch him," Eliza reiterated having seen no inclination in her son to move from his position in front of the unlit fire.

"Mother, he's in the middle of surgery. It can wait. He wouldn't come anyway," Joe patiently reminded and smiled at his parent's restless frown. It was easy to see from where Sam and Lily inherited their impetuous traits.

Eliza sighed with sudden irritability and reluctantly agreed that her son was correct. She asked for the Gazette pages and re-read the notice, her eyes filling once more and threatening to overflow. "Oh Sam," she uttered lowly and pressed slender fingers to her lips.

"We should put these in the cellar to chill," Charles waved his bottle of Champagne and taking the cue Joe offered to help fetch the others from the car.

The house descended into busy preparation for the unplanned celebration, with fresh flowers cut and arranged, toiletries carried out earlier than was usual, Charles Bradshaw delivered to a guest room and, at Eliza's insistence, everyone dressed for an occasion and carefully orchestrated back into the drawing room ready for when Doctor Hepworth Senior returned home.

It was all so unnecessary, so ridiculously excessive that Joe could not help but wonder at his mother's grip on reality. Still he did not protest, understanding that she needed this one piece of excellent news to lift her from the constant fear she felt for her children. The celebration was merely an escape into a by-gone world, a means of coping with her stressful existence. He was not sure how Sam would have viewed it. He would probably be horrified and no doubt, to the bitter disappointment of their mother, disappear to the pub instead. Joe felt certain that his brother would not welcome such a party on his behalf. Just as well he was not here to see it then.

At four-thirty Tilly stood peering through the side window at the driveway. She occasionally smoothed the crisp white apron over her best, black serving dress and glanced fretfully up the stairs. The Missus had said everyone had to be in place for when the doctor returned, but young Mrs Hepworth was upstairs with baby Robert. Tilly's first job was to warn Dora of imminent arrival and her second, if necessary to waylay the Master of the house. Quite how she should do the latter she had no idea. She peered through the window again and with a jolt recognised the swinging gait of Doctor Hepworth as he strode, blissfully unaware of what awaited him, his jacket thrown over his shoulder and shirt sleeves rolled up. In his right hand he swung his medical bag and in his mouth he contentedly clamped his pipe.

"'E's 'ere. Mrs 'Epworth, 'e's 'ere!" Tilly cried at the top of her voice.

Scurrying footsteps upstairs as Dora handed a, thankfully, sated baby to a bewildered nurse and rushing to her own room flung off the nursing blouse she wore replacing it with one of fine, pale blue silk. She glanced in the mirror, scowled at the loose hair but thought there no time to redress it and hurried downstairs. Outside the open door she could hear Tilly engaged in some conversation with the doctor and she ran breathlessly into the drawing room, slowing only to a more ladylike pace as she reached the entrance.

Tilly, in desperation had rushed out doors and with some trepidation, for she hated to lie, begged her employer to please take a look in her eye. She felt sure there was something in it, it was hurting so. She had even managed to rub the innocent orb hard enough before hand to make it appear red and watery. Ever the obliging physician, Thomas placed his bag on the floor and lifted the girl's face to the sun. He placed his spectacles on the end of his nose and examined the eye.

"Can't see anything Tilly. It must have come out on its own. Probably just a speck of dust. What have you been up to?" He did not comment upon the singularly oddness of being accosted by a servant before he entered his home. It did not occur to him that it was odd, but something else did.

"I've been cleaning out the attic Sir," Tilly lied again feeling she would surely rot in Hell if she carried on regardless of the intention behind the lie. To make matters worse, Doctor Hepworth looked at her askance as if he detected the lie.

"Well, it seems alright now. I'll find some drops for you to help the irritation. Tilly, why are you dressed in your best frock?"

The shock of the question caught the maid unhappily by surprise and she stammered with her reply, "Oh, er, well, you see, Madam wished me to wear it." *What a stupid answer. Now he surely smelt a rat.*

In response Thomas raised his eyebrows and half smiled at the girl's discomfort. Something was going on. With a leap of his heart he thought perhaps that Lily had come home on leave, or that Frank had ventured north with his new fiancé. "Did she now? And why's that?"

Tilly groaned inwardly and visibly slumped. "I don't know Sir," she replied dejectedly.

"Ah, I see. Sworn to secrecy eh? Had to waylay me did you?"

Miserably the maid acknowledged his guess. "Yes Sir. Sorry Sir. I couldn't think of..."

"Never mind. You've done your job well enough I think. Now let us go inside so that I might be surprised," he chuckled with a conspiratorial wink. He followed her to the door, noting Bradshaw's Daimler discreetly parked behind the old stable building and his grin broadened further. Obviously something warranted a celebration. He had not even known that Charles was back in the county.

Depositing his bag and jacket onto the large oak chair that lived permanently behind the door for such purposes he asked of Tilly where the family were waiting for him.

"T' drawing room Sir," she answered and as he unrolled his sleeves and headed that way she tidied away his divestments with relief that her part in the subterfuge was over.

"What's all this then?" he demanded as he entered the drawing room, gazed with feigned surprise at Charles and the family dressed for a much grander occasion than a weekday dinner and felt a momentary pang of disappointment that there was no Lily or Frank to greet him.

"Thomas," Eliza lighted from her seat and with face aglow took him by the arms. "Such wonderful news." She added and pressed a glass of Champagne into his hands.

"What..?" He looked at them all, their smiling faces. His lovely daughter-in-law whose immaculate appearance was belied as sham serenity by the obviously hurried re-pinning of her hair. His dear wife, who stood next to him so apparently overjoyed and yet so near to tears. Charles with his usual affable, wide grin waving a glass in his direction and finally to Joe, the only one who really appeared embarrassed by the whole ludicrous pageant. Whatever it was, his eldest son viewed the resulting exhibition as disproportionate to the event.

"Here darling, read this," Eliza interrupted him and pressed the London Gazette pages into his hands.

He gazed at the papers, placed his glass on the coffee table and replacing his spectacles on the end of his nose scanned down to a circled citation. He read it silently his lips moving, his head nodded an approval, his eyebrows raised and his eyes crinkled happily. Not quite believing what he had just seen, he read the name again.

"Well, well. I never would have... Well, it seems our boy's done something good at last," he said not meaning the words to sound condescending, but they did.

"What do you mean at last?" Eliza demanded somewhat indignantly. She had been watching with glowing pride and his words, to her, seemed cruelly unjust.

"Nothing my dear. I meant nothing by it. Don't misunderstand me. I see now why you are all dressed for an occasion. This *is* a celebration and a worthy one," Thomas appeased and kissed his wife's hand. He lifted his glass. "To Samuel," he toasted. The others did the same and only he saw Joe's half smile at his desperate diplomatic recovery.

"I never would have believed it though. Not because I don't think our son to be brave, but I never gave such possibilities a thought," Thomas admitted. Charles laughed and poured out more Champagne for everyone. No one's glass was going to remain empty.

"When was this? It says Neuve Chapelle. That was when?"

"March," Joe answered and swung onto the sofa picking up his wife's hand and taking another gulp of wine. He had already drained one glass and on an empty stomach it was surprising how quickly the stuff went to one's head.

"March! I wonder why he has not written to tell us." Thomas thought aloud, beginning to share Eliza's pride.

"Probably he did not know himself. He still might not. Do you think Joe?" Eliza asked in all innocence.

Joe finished his second glass of Champagne and waved it at Charles for a refill. An action of uncharacteristic rudeness that brought a frown to Dora's and his mother's brow. He watched the bubbles in his replenished wine for a moment and swallowed another mouthful.

"Joe?" Eliza pressed with obvious disapproval behind her question.

"Oh I think he'll know by now. Takes a while for these things to be announced, but they would have told him as soon as the decision was made. Rather indecent not to," Joe replied a little thickly and played with a wayward strand of his wife's hair. She pulled away from him shocked by his matter-of-fact, almost callous tone and his disrespectful manner. This was not the considerate, polite man she had married. Something in him had changed. She hoped it was simply the drink heightening his sombre mood of earlier.

"Then why has he not written to tell us?" Eliza plodded on regardless.

"Perhaps he hasn't had chance," Dora ventured nervously. Joe scoffed into his wine glass. "Joe!"

"Well, listen to you all for God's sake!" He stood and threw the rest of his beverage down his throat.

"Joseph, not in front of the ladies," his father admonished.

Joe bowed his head in a mocking apology.

"I never thought that you would be jealous of your brother. It is unworthy of you son," Thomas added further, angry and disappointed with his eldest child's behaviour.

"Jealous! Uh, is that what you think? I'm not jealous of Sam. How could I be? I'm as proud of him as you are, probably more so knowing the dangers he faces on a daily basis. Sam probably hasn't written because *he*, in all likelihood, is embarrassed by the award," Joe enlightened ruthlessly and filled his glass at the same time. The party eyed each other tensely.

"Embarrassed? I don't understand. What do you mean dear?" Eliza asked, her voice deliberately calm.

Joe laughed derisively. "You have no idea do you? You all live in this cosseted little world, keeping the war nicely at a distance. Sam's lost a lot of friends. He probably feels they are more deserving of a medal than he is. I was at Neuve Chapelle. I actually treated Lieutenant Fielding. He told me Sam had saved his life. But there are many others that save men's lives and go unrecognised. Either because they were not witnessed by an officer who thought it worthy of praise or they were killed doing it."

"But that doesn't make his heroism any less. He should be proud of his achievement, proud that he's been recognised," Dora opined trying to comprehend this philosophy.

"*Heroism*! That's just it Dora. Don't you see? Can none of you see? He probably doesn't see himself as a hero and he isn't. Not any more so than any of his comrades who fight and die with him," Joe tried to impress on them the logic behind his conclusion, but their faces told him they did not understand and could not. His stomach filled with knotted exasperation and he fought to control his emotions, but too much wine and no food were against his efforts.

"I wish you wouldn't talk about dying when there is something glorious to celebrate," Eliza commented indignantly in the silence that followed. She was determined to still celebrate the news.

"*Glorious*! *Christ*! You really are all so naïve. You sit here in your cosy warmth and knit your socks and hats and gloves. You don't know where they go or care as long as you feel you're doing your bit. But you have no understanding of the filth and squalor our soldiers live in, of the constant fear of death or worse. The knowledge that tomorrow, or the day after, the man standing next to you might be dead, rotting on the wire out in No-Man's-Land. Where's the glory in that?"

"Joseph, that's enough," Thomas warned quietly.

"Tell me? What will you say if a telegram comes tomorrow telling you that Sam is dead. Dear Dr and Mrs Hepworth, I regret to inform you... Will that bit of tin they pinned to his chest be a comfort to you? He died a hero so that's alright. Is it? Is it Mother?" Joe ranted, red in the face with a passion he had not released for years.

"JOE!" Thomas stood in reprimand, his features dark with anger; his hand clasping Eliza's whose white, shocked face stared with disbelieving bewilderment at her son.

Joe looked drunkenly at their faces. The horror they displayed at what he had said. Why had he? Why had he spoiled his mother's illusion? Why not let her believe what she needed to. He ran a shaking hand through his hair and with a muttered apology hurried from the room leaving an uncomfortable, perplexed atmosphere.

"I'm sorry. I'm so sorry. He's not himself," Dora excused on her husband's behalf. "Daddy, what must you think of us?"

"Nonsense. The boy's bound to be nervy. Don't bother yourself about it. We're all family. Here have some more wine," Charles reassured.

Suddenly the party atmosphere no longer felt appropriate to Dora. "I think I should go to him," she uttered.

"Oh leave the lad alone for a while. He'll come around. Thomas?" Charles waved the champagne at his friend.

"No, I'd better go. I won't be long," Dora stood and drifted from the room. She found Joe sitting on the low wall out in the garden, staring down unseeingly at the dale and the town drenched in glorious summer sunshine. She wandered over to him and sat by his side, not speaking but covering his hand with hers. He sighed and entwined his fingers with hers.

"I really was a pompous arse in there wasn't I?" he said

"Yes."

He smirked. "I deserved that."

"You hurt your mother and embarrassed them all," she returned softly. A gentle chastisement.

"I know. I shouldn't have said it all. I don't really know why I did."

"Frustration. You're right, we don't understand. But don't expect your mother to. She lives each day in dread of that telegram. She needs these little glimmers of joy to keep her sane. Don't despise her for that."

"I don't despise her. And I really am proud that my brother has been recognised for what he did, but that doesn't make what I said untrue. I just shouldn't have said it that's all. I should have kept it to myself," he explained.

"No, you shouldn't have kept it to yourself. But you could have unburdened those feelings on me. I'm here to understand Joe if you'll let me. But please don't torture your family like that. Eliza needs hope not darkness."

"I didn't want to tell any of you anything. It just came out. It's the wine," he confessed.

"Undoubtedly. But why not? Why not tell me?"

"Because the truth is too awful to burden anyone with."

"I love you," Dora whispered and kissed his cheek

"What, after my despicable behaviour?" Joe smiled and clamped her hand tightly.

"Yes, even after that. You should come back in. Let Eliza have her party and be graciously apologetic."

"In a few minutes. I need to clear my head and think of what to say. You go. I won't be long I promise," he placed her hand to his lips and stroked her hair.

"Alright." Dora stood and squeezed his shoulder.

"Father was right though," he admitted. "I am jealous of Sam. Not because he has a medal, but because he is brave. I'm not. I quake with fear at every shell that falls near us. I live in mortal dread of being killed or wounded and I don't even go to the front line. Sam's nearly been killed twice and still he shows no fear."

"That doesn't mean that he isn't afraid," Dora attempted to appease, kissing the top of his head, her heart full from his honest revelation. It must have been hard to admit to himself let alone to say out loud.

He shrugged. "Maybe not, but he's always been adventurous. Some might say foolhardy. When we were kids he was always in scrapes. Not me. I was too afraid. Afraid of being caught, afraid of getting hurt. Pathetic really."

"That's why he became a soldier and you a doctor. What you do is brave too. Saving all those lives. It is very honourable and worthwhile Joe," she stated with conviction. She really believed it to be so.

"Is that what you think? That I save lives?" he asked with a scornful laugh.

Dora sat once more and looked into his face. "Don't you?"

He shrugged again and turned away staring with unseeing eyes at the valley below. "I suppose I do, some. When there's no push on the work is mundane, you know, sickness, a few accidents, the odd wounded man. We have more time; can do more before sending them back or onto hospital. During a push it's hell. There's no time to think. We administer first aid that's all and send them down the line. We hope they don't die. I might save one or two. I probably kill many more through exhausted incompetence and what's the point? If we save them, they fall into one of two camps. They either end up going home to a life of disablement and charity or they get sent back to the Front to be killed all over again." Joe spat the last words vehemently, his sense of futility more pronounced now that he was away from the war.

Dora did not know what to say. She could only vaguely imagine what he was talking about, had no real inkling of the horrors he alluded to. She followed his gaze and tried to picture a scene different from this golden tranquillity of rural beauty, but she failed abysmally. How could she envisage what she had no experience of? She had always thought of him working in some romantically ruined chateau where brave Tommies were brought in fleets of ambulances, like she had seen in Ripon, perfectly dressed with pristine bandages; neat wounds to heads and chests and legs. He talked about squalor and exhaustion. Her only experience of squalor, the view of the slums from the train as one pulled into Leeds. Was it worse than that? Somehow she thought it must be, but she could not push through the ignorance of her privileged upbringing to truly understand.

"Well, at least you don't have much longer to go," she offered at last after failing to identify with his world in the Army.

"What do you mean?" his head snapped around rapidly, his eyes piercing and tone aggressive. It frightened her a little and she replied falteringly.

"Well, you will have done your year soon. Your contract was only for a year remember. Soon you can leave the Army. Come home. We can be a family again. You, me and little Robert. You can forget the war." Her voice trailed away and her heart sank at the look in his eyes. It was almost contempt. Contempt for her. She shivered.

"Come home?" he repeated incredulously. She really did not understand did she? Had no idea.

"Y...yes. You have done your bit Joe. You've served in France. Many others haven't and they are returning to their practices. I was speaking with Sarah Mortimer, David is..."

"Do you honestly think I can come home when Sam is still out there, when they're crying out for doctors?" Joe interrupted unable to keep the disbelief from his voice.

Dora hesitated. "Well... yes. I thought... I mean. It was only for a year wasn't it? That's what you said when you joined up."

"I couldn't live with myself," he said heatedly.

Dora felt her lip tremble and her throat constrict with emotion. She fought hard to fight back the tears. He had promised it would only be for a year. Had reassured her that they would be a family again come next December. That thought had sustained her through the dark days of waiting anxiously for the next letter, dreading the fearful telegram. "B...but you promised," she stammered weakly.

He turned away unable to face the distress in her swimming eyes. "I'm sorry, but I've already committed to signing on for the duration of the war. Don't ask me to do otherwise Dora. It is my duty to do this. Sam's out there. I should be too."

"Damn Sam!" she cried hotly with a passion he had never expected. "He's a soldier. You're not. You're a doctor Joe. We need doctors at home as well you know. And where is your duty to your wife and son? What will I tell Robert when he's old enough to ask why his daddy didn't return from the war? Shall I tell him it's because you thought more of your duty and how you would be compared with your brother than you did of your own son?"

Joe gawped, shocked by his wife's sudden outburst. Her words hit him hard. He had not expected this response. Had thought she would stoically accept his decision. He had not expected a fight and such a damning accusation. "That's not fair Dora. Please, try and understand," he soothed feeling the sting of her words like a slap across the face.

"NO! No I won't try and understand, because I don't. You hate it out there. It's made you moody and rude and then you tell me it's your *duty* to go back. Well to *hell* with duty Joseph Hepworth!" she ranted and shaking with anger and emotion she ran back to the house and vanished from sight.

He stared after her, shaken by her vehemence, astonished at her open hostility towards him or rather, towards his decision. The turmoil within him deepened and tore at his conscience, but it did not change his mind. It could not. He had not been flippant when he had said he could not live with himself if he returned to civilian life. For all he despised about the Army and his role in it, he saw no alternative but to remain a servant of the King.

CHAPTER 37.
July 24th, Pateley Bridge

Evie combed her long blonde hair and began the careful task of curling tresses onto her head and pinning them into place. It was a chore she took pleasure in, appealing to her artistic flair and her vanity. She knew just how to dress what was arguably her best feature, to bring out the most in her deceivingly fragile looks. She had already dressed for dinner in a modest, cream lace dress trimmed with rose coloured ribbon. It was a flattering garment and completely hid the tiny bulge of her belly that she self-consciously dreaded would be noticed by the family. Frank had laughed at her concerns, saying there was nothing to see, but she knew the bump was there and that it *could* be seen and their secret discovered if she did not take the utmost care with her clothes.

Pushing another pin into place she reflected upon her welcome into the Hepworth household. They had been met at the Station by Frank's brother and his wife. Together they pushed the delightful baby Robert up the steep hill of Main Street and along the relative flat of Ripon road to the oddly jumbled house where she now sat. She had instantly liked Dora and found Joe friendly if a little aloof. She had thought him very dashing in his uniform and found herself trying to imagine Frank in the same garb and slightly resentful of the fact that he never would be.

Mrs and Doctor Hepworth were gracious and nowhere near as formal or austere as she had expected the north country middle-classes to be. They had treated her with kindness and respect and, whether they approved or not of their youngest son's sudden decision to marry or of his future wife, they went out of their way to make her comfortable and at home. They had given her Lily's room for her visit saying it afforded a better view than any guest room. And so it did. The panorama of the town below and the rolling purple hills enclosing the pretty dale was captivating. Far more enchanting than she could ever have imagined. Even the smoking chimneys from the brewery and the scarred quarry works on the hillsides above the town, could not detract from the chocolate box beauty of the leafy valley with its serenely dark, glistening river snaking through fields and woods towards the mills downstream.

Evie placed a rosebud comb into place and sighed happily. She was happy. This was a lovely place; the Hepworths a lovely family. She felt at home with these people even after so short a time. Now she had met the family, her nerves had subsided and she longed to be a part of them, to be Mrs Frank Hepworth. She ran her hand over the hidden bulge of her belly and smiled.

A knock on the door and Frank's voice. "Are you decent? May I come in?"

"Yes," she called and stood from the dressing table to face him as he entered. He stopped in the doorway and grinned.

"You look lovely," he said, his happiness shining radiantly upon his pale features.

"Thank you."

"Are you ready? It's time for dinner."

"Yes, of course," she glided over to him and took his arm, he kissed her lips gently.

"Don't you want to close the window? It might be cool later," he nodded to the open casement as they turned to go.

"No, I'm enjoying the freshness of this air. I want to drink in every last drop of it."

He laughed and led her down stairs.

At dinner the talk was all about the forthcoming wedding, of regrets that not all the family could be there. It was doubtful that Sam would make it and sadly Joe had to return to his Ambulance unit in France in two days time. Evie revelled in the conversation. Never before had she been the centre of attention for so long. It was giddying and threatened to go to her head.

"We are all so pleased my dear. Though we scarcely knew of course. Frank is such a dark horse at times and now we have a wedding. And I was expecting it to be Lily and Robert. Well there you are. They have chosen a long engagement because of this frightful war and you dears have decided upon the opposite. I must say, that although it was a surprise, I prefer the latter," Eliza confided as they commenced with their first course.

"We didn't think it worth waiting Mother. The war is likely to go on for years and who knows what might happen. There have been bombing raids on London you know. The danger is not confined solely to France and Gallipoli," Frank explicated quickly, rescuing Evie from a potentially awkward moment.

"Oh don't say that Frank dear. I like to think that at least one of my children is safe. London bombed! It doesn't bear thinking about."

"Tell me dear, who will give you away?"

"My Grandfather Mrs Hepworth. My parents are in Singapore," Evie responded and noted the look of surprise upon her hostess' face.

"Eliza dear. Call me Eliza. You are soon to be my daughter-in-law."

"Your Grandfather you say. And are we likely to meet this gentleman before the event?" The tactful query was aimed as much at her son. Best not to ask too many awkward questions about families.

"We'll arrange a dinner before the wedding in Suffolk. Evie's Grandfather is quite frail Mother. He cannot easily travel far."

"Of course. So Frank dear, tell me of your work for the Red Cross. It sounds quite intriguing." Eliza changed the subject and engaged her son in small talk. Evie took the opportunity to observe her hosts. Thomas ate with solemn quiet. Apparently he never spoke at the dinner table, at least not during courses. Yet, though he obviously thought this habit rude, he did not check the others. Instead he quietly munched on his food and listened to the chatter, sometimes with an amused air, sometimes with an expression of exasperation at the banality of the talk. Dora likewise was quiet and Evie thought a little fatigued. Perhaps motherhood had its downside in disturbed nights or perhaps the affable young woman felt a touch under the weather. Joe, having finished his first course sat back and sipped white wine delicately. He occasionally joined in with questioning Frank upon his exploits but for the most part listened and laughed at the various anecdotes. He was no longer dressed in his uniform, but in a dinner suit. Dark and good looking, as tall as Frank but broader, Evie thought him very desirable as a brother-in-law. She had not met the other brother, Sam, but if he were as handsome she was more than happy to be marrying into this attractive family. For Evie, outward appearances were as important and as obligatory as an agreeable character.

"You are not wearing your uniform Joe," she commented during a lull in the conversation.

Joe glanced at Dora and then smiled. "No. I try not to wear it at home. One must put it on when one goes outside, but in the home it is not the most comfortable of garments," he explained.

"Oh, what a shame. It looks so dashing too. Quite heroic," she returned flashing an almost flirtatious smile. Joe grinned awkwardly. It was quite a forward pronouncement and other than his sister, he was not accustomed to responding to forward young women.

"Do you think so?" Dora said instead, folding her napkin neatly by her side plate and lifting her wine glass to take a sip.

"Yes I do. I think all of our young men look very gallant in their uniforms. Don't you?" Evie answered happily unaware that she may be offending. She did not notice the slight rigidity in Frank's bearing or the vague flush to Joe's cheeks.

"No I hate it. I think them nothing but an obvious and unnecessary reminder of this ghastly war. The sooner we can throw them all on the bonfire the better," Dora expressed forcefully.

For a moment silence descended over the dinner table. Embarrassed Evie began to apologise. "I'm sorry. I didn't mean to say anything..."

"Don't be silly dear. You haven't said anything you shouldn't," Eliza patted her hand.

"No Evie. I'm sorry. I'm tired that's all and soon Joe has to return. It just wears on ones nerves a little that's all," Dora added graciously.

With her usual discretion Eliza rescued the mood and returned to questions about life as a female musician in London, regaling at the same time, some of her own experiences from youth before she married and became a mother. The atmosphere, which had briefly threatened to dissolve into strained politeness at once lifted, no one really wanting to travel down that road once more.

Two days later, on a bright but breezy morning, Evie and Frank accompanied Dora and Joe, pushing baby Robert in his perambulator, down to the Station. Joe's leave was over. They stood on the platform waiting for the train to disgorge its passengers and the engine to be re-coupled to what had been the rear. A number of khaki clad soldiers tumbled onto the Station, saluted the RAMC officer standing seriously with his wife and infant child. Joe returned the salutes handing baby Robert back to Dora and moved to shake his brother's hand.

"Goodbye old chap. Wish I could have timed my leave better. I would have liked to see you get hitched. Send me a photograph," he said.

"I will. Take care Joe," Frank replied.

Joe turned to Evie and kissed her cheek with brotherly affection. "A pleasure to meet you Evie. I look forward to calling you sister." She smiled in return and linked her arm through Frank's with possessive pride.

"Here. I'll help with your bag," Frank offered.

"No, I've got it. Well, farewell," Joe smiled with effort, the wrench of leaving becoming painful. Part of him wanted them all to walk away now, to leave him alone so that he could forget the comfort of home and the pleasure of being with loved ones. But the rest of him wanted to cling on until the very last moment.

He returned to Dora and took up her hand. Leaving the others to hold onto the pram the couple sauntered along to the first class carriages where Joe allowed the porter to stow his bag aboard. As the clanking of rolling stock signalled the installation of the locomotive at their head and a hiss of steam swept along the platform enveloping its occupants in a transient mist he bent to kiss his wife holding her in a tight embrace.

"Please come back. Please don't get killed," Dora whispered through tears she could not prevent from falling. He buried his face in her hair and drank in the scent of her perfume, soft and delicate, a smell he could imprint on his memory to recall when he thought of her.

"I'm sorry darling. I'm sorry I can't do what you ask. You do understand don't you?" he uttered fighting his own emotion.

"Yes," she lied. "Just promise me you'll take care. That you'll look after yourself, for Robert's sake."

"I'll try."

The guard blew his whistle and called for remaining passengers to board. As if in fear of losing him forever, Dora suddenly clung with fierce strength to her husband. He felt her body tremble with her barely constrained sobs and his own throat constricted and ached with emotion.

"I love you," he said and prised her hands from around his waist. The pain in her eyes was unbearable and he had to turn away, to go now. The shrill whistle from the engine caused her to jump nervously and with a jolt they parted. He leapt onto the carriage and the guard closed the door firmly, parting the couple with ominous finality. Dora held out her hand and he grasped it as the train lurched forward. She walked with ever quickening pace, holding onto him until the very last moment, until the platform plunged away and she had to release him. Their fingers drifted apart, their final touch like the softest brush of a feather and then he was gone, his face disappearing in a wreath of steam and smoke as the eight fifteen to Harrogate rocked and clattered out of sight.

Dora stood alone at the end of the platform. She sobbed silently into her handkerchief for some minutes before forcing herself to regain control and return to the others who discreetly waited some distance back. Dabbing her eyes and delicately wiping her nose, she straightened her posture and returned to her companions.

"I'll take him," Frank said turning the perambulator around with a smile and pushed it from the platform.

Evie wrapped her arm in Dora's and gently steered her future sister-in-law back into the bustle of Main Street. They strolled without speaking for some minutes with Frank ahead, quite lithe in his step.

"He'll make a good father," Dora said at length. "He enjoys it, look."

Evie stopped still with a thrill of anxiety. Did she know? Dora smiled at her. "My dear, it's obvious. But don't worry, Eliza will never guess and I will never tell. She's too innocent to think such things happen, but the war has changed all that hasn't it? When are you due?"

Evie commenced walking. It was almost a relief to talk about it. "January. An awful month to be born in I think," she confessed. How liberating to discuss it with someone else and not to be judged.

"I envy you."

"Envy me! Why?"

"Well, you will be blissfully happy. You will not have to wave goodbye to your husband with the crippling uncertainty that he might never return.

"You said on your first day here that you thought Joe looked heroic in his uniform. It affronted Frank, did you know?" A glance at Evie told Dora that she did not. "I know you meant nothing by it, that it was simply a careless comment, but don't wish it for him. Be happy in the knowledge that he will always be with you and cherish that. I would gladly swap places with you for that precious security." She laughed self-consciously. "Listen to me. I sound like a moaning old woman."

Evie kissed her companion's cheek and tugged her forwards once more. "No you don't. You sound like a woman who loves her man. Come on, let's catch him up. Did I tell you how we first met?"

CHAPTER 38.
July 31st, Front Line Trenches Near Richebourg St Vaast

The nights were definitely drawing in. Dusk pervaded the sultry summer evenings by nine now. It gave both sides greater opportunity to carry out repairs, as long as they were careful; send out patrols, as long as the moon was not too bright and move up equipment and rations. As such, work parties were numerous and in attempts to stave off boredom and keep men active, maintain fitness and discipline, their commanders ensured the front line remained a hive of industry, at least by night.

Once more the Western Front had ground shatteringly into stalemate with both sides licking their wounds and consolidating. While generals considered the next offensive, the decimated battalions of earlier disastrous battles rebuilt their numbers, rebuilt the trenches and enjoyed, for want of a better word, the relative quiet of high summer.

The New Kitchener's Army was trickling into France, new divisions and new battalions. They were sent to so-called quiet sectors to learn the art of trench warfare from those already blooded and more grizzled than they. The remnants of Regular units still bore the brunt of the more active areas; wearied and jaded, but too disciplined to be resentful; they accepted the drafts of pristine reserves, tried to forget the friends who had gone, rejoiced in the return of an old comrade and simply got on with it. They did not ask why or when or who, they would not have been told anyway. Curiosity was not encouraged in the King's service; it was not conducive to good discipline. The men were expected to fight and to work so that is what they did. They did not begrudge the eager volunteers of Kitchener's troops their quiet sectors. They understood that they were the professionals, that they were the back bone of the BEF. How could anyone expect these raw and enthusiastic recruits, with their shiny inexperienced officers to hold their nerve under heavy bombardment? No, the old sweats did not resent the new bloods, they maybe smiled at their naïvety, made coarse jokes at their expense, looked down on them with a superiority born of pride and experience, but there was no animosity. The poor buggers would learn soon enough the price to be paid for being a patriot.

Sam moved into the support trench with his picked band of ten men, passing as they did so a group of wide eyed young officers from some new Service battalion being given a familiarisation tour. He respectfully acknowledged them and the weary looking, dishevelled captain who was their guide and instructor rolled into one. The latter tried to hide a smirk and returned the address with a roll of his eyes heavenwards. The look spoke volumes. It said, look at me Sergeant, babysitting boy scouts now.

The working party turned a corner, the men commencing their banter now out of ear shot of the officers, laughing at a particularly ribald joke. They carried picks and shovels slung over one shoulder with their rifles over the other, weighed down by these and the compulsory ammunition and rations to get them through the night. Still they did not mind. They were used to carrying their lives with them and at least they would be busy, not bored and miserable on sentry duty.

They stumbled through the half-light frequently cursing as they tripped over unseen obstacles and kicked debris away. The trenches were in a mess after an earlier, haphazard bombardment courtesy of Fritz. Of course he had to remind them there was a war on and that he had not gone away, skulking back to Germany with his tail between his legs. Far from it. A mild shelling was a daily occurrence in this part of the line. You could almost set your watch by it and have a bet with your mate on whether it would be shrapnel or heavies coming over this time.

Still, they were not here to clean up the trench. Someone else would do that. And really it was not all that bad. At least it was dry, baked into hard, unyielding rock by the summer sun. A far cry from the quagmire of six months previous. The trenches were much safer too. The necessity of living in these squalid, cramped ditches had forced improvements that the enemy constantly tried to destroy. The parapets were built up to a good covering height; duckboards lined the floor in case a sudden downpour returned the solid pavement to mushy swamp. The bodies of past encounters had been removed leaving no grim reminders to stumble across. The odd dead mule on the way up maybe, but no semi-decomposed cadavers of forgotten comrades. If only Fritz left them alone, it would not be so bad.

Sam turned another corner, shouted at the men to close up and hitching his rifle further onto his shoulder squinted at the silhouetted figure ahead. The MO had got there before them. Sam liked that. He thought it showed leadership, set the right example. He tripped over a discarded ammunition box, swore out loud at the lazy so and so who had left it there and, stooping to pick it up, threw it over the parados. Its clatter hushed the men temporarily and brought the doctor from whatever private musings he indulged in.

"Is that you Lutterworth?" his well spoken baritone demanded as he peered into the gloom. The damned corporal was taking his time.

"No Sir, it's Sergeant Hepworth with your working party Sir," Sam called back and climbed over a heap of dislodged sandbags. He turned and instructed three men to replace them onto the parapet.

"Hepworth. Splendid! I've lost Lutterworth I think. Probably taken a wrong turn." It was easily done. The trench system was a veritable maze, a confusion of semi-subterranean tunnels open only to the sky. Very easy to take a wrong turn and get lost, especially in the dark.

"Do you want me to send someone to look for him Sir?" Sam asked as he and his men drew to a stop before the medic.

"No, no. We'll end up losing everyone. He'll turn up eventually. How many have we got?"

"Ten Sir and myself."

"Excellent. Well, gather around. I'll just light up this lamp and show you what I want."

They did as bid, crowding as best they could in the limited space, struggling to see the vague pencil sketches held up by the MO in the dim glow of a trench lamp.

"Do you think you can do it in one night?" the doctor asked uncertainly. Pouring over his drawing of the new latrine pit made him think that perhaps he had been a little over ambitious. But something had to be done. The old ones had been badly shelled. Not only were they unhygienic now, but they were dangerously unsafe. Somehow Fritz had got the measure of their whereabouts and the men's grim humour about dying on the pot was turning into a foul reality. He looked at the grimy, rough faces around him.

Hepworth grinned. "Not a problem Sir. We'll have 'em dug out in no time," he replied and efficiently set his men to their task taking on dual role of foreman and labourer. Before long the party were stripped to the waist, sweating profusely and piling freshly filled sandbags around the deepening pits.

After about two hours the long lost Lutterworth returned, flustered and apologetic, but bringing with him three stretcher bearers carrying bags of lime and a dixie of tea for the workers. Sam stood his men down for a break and gladly accepted his mug of nearly cold, strong tea. He plonked himself on an upturned bucket, drank his beverage and chewed on iron rations, which he dunked in a vain attempt to make them softer and more palatable. He listened to the banter, throwing in his own two pennyworth from time to time, enjoyed a cigarette and was totally unaware of the MO's approach on his, still deaf, right side. Consequently he started noticeably and with a curse as the medic spoke and the men sniggered as they jumped to attention. The doctor laughed and bade them sit once more.

"Sorry Sir" Sam apologised glad that the dark hid his flushed face.

"Don't apologise Eppy. Still can't hear properly eh?"

"No Sir. Not quite. It's better than it was though Sir."

"Hmm. Is it? Is it really?" the MO asked his disbelief evident.

No flies on Lieutenant Lord. Sam smiled and stared at his feet. He liked the lieutenant. A youngish doctor somewhere in his thirties, he had a high regard for the men in his care. Not much passed him by. He could smell a lie before it was even thought of. No one could pull the wool over his eyes; he was much too savvy for that. He knew almost instinctively when a man was shirking or putting on a brave face. He had no time for the former treating them with short shrift, and sympathy and respect for the latter. But neither would get away with their subterfuge.

"No, not really Sir," Sam admitted.

"Thought not. We must get it looked at Eppy. What about the headaches?"

"Better Sir. Most definitely."

"But not gone?"

"No Sir."

"Hmm," Lord sat down and indicated his subordinate should do likewise.

"Ought to get the men back to work Sir," Sam protested half-heartedly.

"Give them a few more minutes Sergeant. They're ahead of schedule. Cigarette?" The MO offered selecting himself one from a silver case.

"Thank you Sir," Sam accepted the smoke and bent forward to the offered lighter. He drew appreciatively. It was a better brand of cigarette than his own, smoother, less acrid, definitely an officer's smoke.

"When did you last have any leave Eppy?" Lord asked leaning back against the trench wall.

"Not had any really Sir. I got four days when I came out of hospital last December, but that's all. I've had chance to rest though. Not all the men have."

"Rest! In hospital? Good God man, hardly. The body works hard at healing itself. You know, I said when you returned to us that you should have had a spell of leave. If you were an officer you would have. I think it would see off those headaches once and for all."

"Not much chance yet Sir. I'm about 120 on the list," Sam laughed.

The doctor eyed him for a moment or two. "Your father's a doctor isn't he?" he said at length.

"Yes Sir and my older brother. My brother's out here Sir, with the RAMC."

"Is he? Do I know him do you think?"

"Don't know Sir. His name is Joe. He's with Twenty-Third Field Ambulance or he was. I haven't heard from him for a week or two. He went home on leave."

"I don't recognise the name. So two doctors in the family and you joined the Army as a private? Very strange Eppy," Lord commented with amusement.

This old chestnut. It always caused someone some amount of curiosity. "Black sheep of the family Sir," Sam returned wishing he was not so much of a conundrum, with his middle class upbringing, his public school education and his posh voice that he so vainly tried to hide. He flicked his tab end onto the floor watching its dull red sparks extinguish as it vanished beneath the duckboards.

"Well I'm sure your father, being a medical man, would never forgive the Army if we didn't take care of that ear. There's no reason why we shouldn't. I'll arrange for you to see another specialist. Would London be acceptable to you? I could send you to Rouen, but..."

Sam looked up and grinned. "That would be very acceptable Sir."

"Well. I'll see what I can do. If I sell it to the CO that you could combine the examination with leave, I'm sure he'll look upon it more favourably. I mean he wouldn't lose you twice then would he?" Lord conspired.

"No Sir. He wouldn't," Sam laughed. He considered the doctor and wondered just how much clout the RAMC officer had. After all, he was only a lieutenant. How much did the CO pay heed to his advice? *It's worth a try though isn't it? No harm in asking.* "My brother's getting married on August fourteenth. It would be nice to get leave then Sir," he said, not bothering with subtleties.

Lord laughed. "I'm sure it would Eppy. This your doctor brother?"

"No my younger one. He's a musician."

"Well, leave it with me; I'll see what I can do. Better get your men back to work Sergeant," Lord finished with a wink.

"Yes Sir," Sam stood with a grin and picking up his shovel shouted at the semi-prone working party to get back at it. He had no idea why the MO felt he should act on his behalf and quite frankly he did not care, as long as the result was what he hoped for. Perhaps Lord was simply a truly altruistic man, more medical practitioner than Army officer and all the more human for it.

CHAPTER 39.
August 7th, Gonneheim

Out at rest. Although rest actually meant a substantial amount of work. At least they were away from the trenches, away from billets in ramshackle, disintegrating villages, away from stray shells, the constant, deafening roar of artillery, the indefatigable clatter of machine gun fire. Away from uncertain rations, filth and for a brief spell at least, from the mind numbing tedium of trench life.

Out at rest the guns became a heavy rumble of omnipresent thunder, an oddly comforting rhythmic pounding. Not the terrifying crump and high pitched screeching whine with its subsequent earth shattering blast. Out at rest the small arms fire became a distant crackle of fireworks on Guy Fawkes night. Nothing to worry about. Unrelenting, but far enough away to forget about. Remote. Reassuringly so. For a while.

The Battalion had taken a bath removing several weeks of ingrained grime, luxuriating for as long as they dared in hot water, actually hot, not tepid. And joy of joys their mud spattered uniforms, stinking with accumulated sweat and dirt, crawling with vermin, had been laundered and fumigated. Every man had been issued with clean underwear and two fresh shirts. Trousers and tunics had been collected, if not in pristine condition, at least clean, smelling of carbolic and naphthalene, temporarily devoid of lice.

Buttons, cap badges and other insignia had been polished until they gleamed; boots had been brushed and dubbed until they looked respectable once more. The holes in soles had been repaired until new footwear could be scrounged. Webbing had been blancoed and rifles stripped, cleaned, greased and reverently reassembled.

The Battalion looked like professional soldiers once more rather than the rag tag vagabonds who had marched out of the line six days ago. And today extra effort had been made. Today Sir Douglas Haig, Commander of the First Army, would be visiting them. The troops had been informed at morning parade. All companies would spend time on the rifle range where the auspicious visitor would observe musketry practise. Later, following lunch, the whole Battalion would be paraded for inspection and some awards made to a couple of men, a pair of DCMs needed presenting.

Sam ruminated over his instructions as he watched, without much interest, the final thirty men of B Company take their last shots. A shouted order and the field echoed with sharp cracks as a rapid volley of ten rounds followed by another ten ripped across the hundred yard range to a row of corresponding paper targets pinned to bails of straw. He only vaguely registered that the accuracy of all of those shots was not quite as good as delivered by a platoon of mainly different men a year before. Of the thirty soldiers laid in the fresh cut hay, deliberately pumping round after round at their distant targets with frowning concentration, only five had sailed to France last October. One of them was Corporal Bill Pratt, transferred from D Company to stiffen the ranks of new men, and Bill had never been the greatest marksman anyway.

Sam smiled critically at the peppered targets as scores were shouted back and the prone men climbed to their feet. He smiled at the shaking of heads, the smug expressions of a few, too few, but still his mind would not switch off from those infernal instructions.

For All We Have and Are

He and Lance Corporal Dawes would be in the front ranks. Is that the best uniform you have? *Well of course it is we don't carry spares!* Maybe another should be borrowed from one of the newer men, just for the presentation. You understand Hepworth. Wouldn't do to look like a scarecrow in front of Sir Douglas Haig would it now? *Scarecrow? What do you mean Sir? It's only a little frayed; I've darned all the holes, bloody neatly too.*

Haig would be inspecting the troops first, then, he would stand before them all, give a rousing speech, praise the Battalion on their staunch performance etcetera. Finally they would be marched to stand before General Haig on the commands of RSM Tebbit and the CO would read out the citations of each man in turn. The general would pin the medal to their chests. The men would cheer. They would be dismissed, salute, step back and march back to their original position. If the general spoke to either of them they must answer only briefly and with the utmost respect. Do not make eye contact. Do not smile. This is a serious business. Did they understand these instructions? *Yes Sir.* Were there any questions? *No Sir.*

God! Why is all this happening to me? Next time let the bloody officer die!

A shouted command snapped Sam from his brooding and he exchanged a grin with Pratt as he passed. "Pretty crap shooting that Bill," he muttered as the corporal reached his side.

Bill swore. "You think tha's still got it then Sarn't?" he challenged grumpily, although he was not really grumpy. It was an act on behalf of the raw recruits with him. None of them knew Eppy. None of them had been here until a few days ago when they arrived in their smart, clean uniforms, eager faced and full of bravado.

Sam winked. "I know I have," he boasted and moved forward to take position.

"Bloody 'ell Corp. 'E's a big 'eaded git isn't 'e?" one new lad said.

"Bet 'e misses," another muttered.

"Fancy a bet then d' thi?" Bill suggested. They were falling prey. Couldn't help themselves.

"Two francs says 'e misses one," the first private took the bait.

"Two francs. Come on lad, make it worthwhile," Pratt mumbled back. Better not be overheard.

"I 'aven't got any more. Lost what I 'ad playin' crown an' anchor last neet. Two franc's all I can afford," the private said glumly.

"Wouldn't want take it from thi then," the corporal laughed.

"Y' think y' would Corp?" the second private asked.

"Know it pal. An' summat else, e'll get 'ighest score an' all."

"Nah! 'E's not that good. Not better than Budgie wa. 'E on'y missed wi' a couple an' them on rapid fire, didn't y' Budgie?" the second private ascertained cockily. Budgie nodded proudly.

"Well, put y' money where thi mouth is then," Bill challenged.

"Fags! I got twenty fags. Bet them on it," Budgie said.

"Fags'll do. Yer on. You in Gundill?"

"Aye alright. Twenty fags. 'Ope y' ave enough to pay us wi' though Corp," Gundill accepted and the three men surreptitiously shook on their bet. Pratt folded his arms, grinning widely, knowing he had already won. So gullible these new lads. Like lambs to the slaughter. Alright, it might be a little unfair. They did not know Eppy was good and the rotten bugger had taken his marksman's badge off, pinned it inside his tunic. Between them, they would be forty fags the richer tonight.

The men of one platoon A Company were ready. Thirty aimed shots to be taken following the command. A break for change of targets and then twenty rapid fire. It should be more, but ammunition was rationed. Smugly Bill watched as Sam's carefully aimed shots ripped into their target one after the other, clustered neatly near the centre. Ten, reload, ten reload, final ten. Hand in air to signify finished. *Not bad Eppy. Faster than the rest and very neat, very close.*

As scores were being shouted out Bill glanced sideways at the two gamblers. Not so cocky now. A little pale. *You 'aven't seen nothin' yet lads.* He took out his pocket watch. Gundill nudged his mate.

"What's that fo' Corp?" he asked.

"Timin' 'im. Twenty rounds rapid. Should take 'im 'bout one five I reckon. Mebbe one ten if 'e's 'aving an off day." He smiled at their worried faces and glanced from the watch to the men about to take their shots. A racket of deafening rifle fire, spurts of muck from the field, tufts of straw forcefully ejected, paper targets shredding under relentless attack. Bill counted, "Sixty, one, two three, four come on Eppy, nine. Ah ha."

Sam's arm was in the air. Pratt focussed on the pulverised target and smiled. The men next to him stood agog. The firing faded away and scores shouted back.

"Fuckin' 'ell!" Budgie gasped. His pal groaned. All those fags lost.

"Told thi'. That's forty fags y' owe me between thi.

"Good shootin' Sarn't," he praised as Hepworth strolled to his side.

"Time?" Sam asked and unbuttoning his tunic took out the crossed rifles badge and pinned it back to his sleeve. Gundill swore under his breath.

"One nine."

"Uh! Need more practice then. Not gonna get it are we? I was a bit wide on a couple too. You were right Bill, not as sharp as I was. Worthwhile?"

"Oh aye. I'll find thi' later," Bill winked and with a nod the sergeant moved away. "Right lads cough up."

"Fuckin' 'ell Corp, y' didn't say 'e warra marksman. Weren't a fair bet that. 'E weren't wearin' 'is badge," Gundill grumbled fishing in his pocket for the precious cigarettes.

"Well, I didn't lie to thi. Y' never asked. I told thi 'e wa' good. Anyway thought y' knew. Best shot in t' Regiment three years runnin' befower t' war wa' Eppy. Come on 'and 'em over."

Grumbling the men did so, with conspicuous ill grace. "Anyway, teach both o' thi a lesson," Bill continued grinning from ear to ear.

"What's that Corp?" Budgie said staring in his top pocket to see if he had any smokes left.

"Not to gamble. It's against t' rules tha knows. Get caught an' tha's on a charge." He laughed and wandered away.

In a car at the back of the field General, Sir Douglas Haig lowered his binoculars and nodded with approval at the commentary from Lieutenant Colonel Yarwood on the display they had just witnessed. There had been some damned fine shooting there.

Four hours later, Sam stood rigidly and self-consciously at attention in a tunic hastily borrowed from Sergeant Blandford for the price of half a dozen of his ill-gotten cigarettes. Beside him stood an equally uncomfortable Lance Corporal Dawes. They could sense each other's embarrassment, but dare not glance sideways in an attempt to show solidarity. The ordeal was only bearable because of the knowledge of each other's presence. They had been marched out in front of the whole Battalion by RSM Tebbit, and both inwardly cringed as their citations were read aloud.

Sam had not wanted this, and judging by Dawes' demeanour, what he could feel of it, neither did he. If one had to receive a damn medal why could it not be presented in some private courtyard? Buckingham Palace would be better than this. At least there they would have been one of many, anonymous, known only to the loved ones who may have accompanied them. But here? Christ! It was cringingly public.

The pair stood, ramrod straight, eyes fixed on some point in space directly ahead, immaculately smart and inwardly squirming with the knowledge that there were nearly eight hundred pairs of eyes staring at their backs. In front of them stood the neat, scarlet and gold braided, unassuming figure of the VIP visitor. White haired and not as tall as Sam had expected, Sir Douglas Haig's eyes twinkled with fatherly pride as he listened with the odd approving nod of his grey head to Colonel Yarwood's words. On their completion he picked a dark blue and burgundy ribboned medal from a box carried by a smiling aide and stepped to pin it to Sam's chest.

"It is with honour Sergeant and great pleasure that I award this Distinguished Conduct Medal to you. Be assured that you can wear it with pride," Haig spoke quietly in a soft Scottish accent. "Well done man."

"Thank you Sir," Sam replied wondering with a pang of doubt whether he should have spoken at all. But the general seemed not to mind and indeed carried on speaking with haughty affability. "Colonel Yarwood tells me you are a fine marksman Sergeant. Indeed, I had the pleasure of watching you this morning. Very good shooting. Very admirable."

"Thank you Sir." *God shut up will you and move onto Dawes.*

"You've been out from the start I believe?" Haig went on.

"Since last October, yes Sir." *Shit! Don't correct him you idiot.*

"Quite." A hint of a reprimand in the quiet voice. "At Ypres?"

"Yes Sir."

"Put your rifle to good use there then."

"Yes Sir."

"Well Sergeant, let's hope you get the chance to do so again. Our next push will drive the damned Hun out of his trenches and I've no doubt a fine and gallant soldier such as yourself will look forward to routing him all the way back to Germany eh?" Haig said with a hint of passion and a crinkled smile. He believed it. It was no condescending rhetoric.

"Yes Sir. Very much so Sir," Sam returned, his gaze still forward, somewhere over the general's shoulder. It seemed the right thing to say even though he did not truly believe the next push would succeed. How could it? None of the others had worked and Fritz was even more securely dug in than he had ever been. Unless the Brass had radically changed their tactics they would all still be fighting over the same bit of ground for another winter.

Haig, however, seemed pleased and he moved on to Dawes commencing another brief, but admiring commentary. Sam exhaled with some relief and waited.

Haig stepped back, they saluted him smartly, he returned the gesture, the CO called for three cheers, which the troops obliged with gusto. It was good for morale if nothing else, seeing mates honoured. Discomforted and humbled, the duo were marched back to their place where they exchanged a relieved and awkward grin and waited, along with everyone else, until the Brass Hats had climbed back into their shiny automobiles and driven away.

At long last the Battalion was dismissed and the curious gathered around the reluctant heroes to catch a glimpse, perhaps hold the insignificant circle of silver pinned to two chests. Questions about what the Great Man had said, cheerful banter and mickey taking, but also quiet reverence. If it had been an award for his marksmanship or the lifting of a footballing trophy Sam would have relished the comradely approbation vainly. As it was he found the whole experience an embarrassment and the praise something he was unworthy of.

"'Aven't you miserable lot got something better to do? Clear off the lot of you. Sergeant 'Epworth, drag your arse over 'ere lad!" a distinctly authoritative and instantly recognisable voice demanded. Never before had Sam felt quite so happy to be summoned thus by God. As the crowd of men drifted away, buoying Dawes along with them, Sam straightened his cap and under Tebbit's inscrutable gaze hurried over to the RSM.

"Mister Tebbit." he respectfully acknowledged.

"You made leave Eppy. You can pick your papers up this evenin' and the MO wants to see you," Tebbit imparted indifferently. He watched without emotion as a wide smile crept over the young sergeant's face. "Pleased Eppy?" he asked gruffly.

"Yes Sir. Very," Sam replied.

"Well I'm bloody well not! You'll miss sports day and I'd a bet with CSM Lockwood that you'd win t' 'undred yard dash."

"Sorry Sir."

"Like 'ell y' are. Go on, get out of 'ere," Tebbit growled and as his subordinate scurried away he smiled to himself glad that the lad had turned himself around once more.

Blandford insisted he get his tunic back. Understandable really. It was in a much better state than Sam's. With his travel papers signed, his leave permit dated and his duffle bag and few belongings retrieved from transport stores, Sam really needed something a bit smarter. He'd tried Snowy, the only other sergeant of similar height and build. But Snowy's uniform was in a worse state than his! There was nothing for it but to try and scrounge a new one and Christ! That would cost him.

He sauntered up the road to the shed, previously an automobile repair workshop, where the Quartermaster's stores had been set up. He took off his wrist watch and stuffed it in his trousers' pocket. No way was the thieving bastard having that! Pushing through the door and nonchalantly loitering against the wooden planked wall, he waited until the quartermaster sergeant finished totting up numbers in his impressive, black leather bound ledger. After a deliberately long three minutes the six foot four QMS closed the book and stood with hands resting on his makeshift counter staring at his visitor.

"After summat Eppy?" he queried brusquely, knowing the answer was yes. They were all after something. Mostly buttons or extra underwear. They liked to have spare underwear. They were supposed to bring a chit signed by an officer or warrant officer, but most of them were on the scrounge. He always told them the same. The answer was no. He had to make the books balance. The stock out had to reflect exactly the number of chits and the stock in. Thing was, bright sparks like Eppy knew the game. Knew the QMS fiddled the ledger sheets; that he always had more than the book said and for a price, fiercely negotiated, they might get what they came for.

Sam sauntered up to the trestle table acting as a counter. "I've got leave," he said and lit a cigarette.

"Lucky you. So what d' yer want?"

"My brother's getting married," Sam exhaled smoke upwards and watched it coiling lazily into the stale air of the shed. It was best to act this way, like he could not care less.

"O aye?"

"I need a new tunic."

The QMS sucked in a deep breath and stood upright with a grin. This was his lucky day. Eppy needed a tunic. That would not be cheap and Eppy always had money. Came from money. Smelt of it even.

"I 'aven't got any," the big sergeant lied.

"Come off it Titch. How much d' you want? I'm not expecting to get it buckshee," Sam recognised the game but did not have the patience to play it well. He wanted the tunic then he could jump a lorry out tonight and get an early boat from Boulogne in the morning.

Titch frowned. Eppy wasn't playing. Shame because this was his favourite bit. Still he recognised stubborn obstinacy when he saw it. "What's it worth to yer?"

"Christ! Just tell me what you want," Sam retorted with exasperation.

Titch smirked and folded his massive arms. "A quid," he said.

"You're kidding! Bloody 'ell Titch."

"That's t' price Eppy. Don't tell me y' can't afford it. Y' want to look good fo' y' brother's weddin' don't y'?"

"Ten bob and I'll bring you back a bottle of Scotch. Can't get it over here Titch." Sam knew the QMS had a predilection for whisky and whisky was hard to come by in France.

Titch hesitated, "Two bottles," he bartered.

"Fuckin' hell! Alright two bottles."

The QMS grinned and disappeared into the murky recesses of his domain. "Thirty six or thirty eight?" he called after a moment.

"Thirty eight."

A few seconds later Titch returned and dropped a neatly folded tunic onto the table top. Before Sam could gather it up a pair of huge hands pressed firmly on top of it. "Money first," the QMS grunted.

Sam grumbled under his breath and pulling out his wallet searched its well worn folds for the equivalent in francs of the ten shilling price. He handed the notes over and made to take the tunic, but the big hands would not relinquish it.

"I want summat good. Bells or Famous Grouse. Nowt rough and cheap," Titch demanded.

"You'll get something good you miserly old bugger. Now give me the bloody tunic," Sam bit back. *You wouldn't know a good whisky if I threw it in your face you ugly git.*

The QMS laughed and let go. Eppy was as good as his word even if he was a stuck up little sod! With quiet satisfaction and ten bob richer he watched the younger man leave the store and then he returned to his ledger.

CHAPTER 40.
August 9th – 13th, England

The train chugged laboriously into Harrogate station its carriages swaying and clanking noisily, shaking its occupants from their musings or conversation. The guard on the platform shouted the town name unnecessarily as the passengers were already shaken into action and busy gathering belongings.

Sam opened his eyes and tipped his cap backwards, blinking at the sudden and unexpected brightness as sunlight suddenly streamed into his compartment. His fellow travellers, a thin, elegant woman with three impeccably dressed children sniffed with disapproval though whether it was because he stretched and yawned with great appreciation or because she had shared her first class compartment all the way from Leeds with a sergeant in the Army was not clear. As the children giggled at his exaggerated awakening the woman hushed them severely and Sam suspected that he was perhaps viewed upon as not of the right breeding to be installed into the comfort of a Pullman coach. He smiled at the two girls and a boy, not caring what the mother thought, and stood before the train came to a stop pulling his kit bag and rifle from the overhead racking. He glanced out of the window at the platform and the expectant faces of onward passengers waiting there before checking his watch. Three thirty. Another hour before the connection to Pateley Bridge. Time for a smoke and a cuppa in the station café. The train shuddered to a stop and he steadied himself against the window.

A sniff from behind indicated the well dressed woman wanted something. He half turned and noticed her eyes drift once, with subtle intimation, towards her shopping the guard had stowed above her seat. Half thinking he should ignore the unasked request for assistance, she had spent the whole journey casting dark, disapproving looks in his direction after all, he hesitated before deciding it would be unforgivably ungentlemanly. He smiled winningly and reached up to lift the heavy basket down.

"There you are madam. Would you like me to carry it from the train for you?" he said in his most educated voice. The soft and well spoken accent obviously surprised her. Apparently she expected a rough and heavily dialected speech for she arched her eyebrows with amazement and smiled despite herself.

"No thank you," she replied after a short pause and accepted the basket with a little more good grace than her previous demeanour.

"I'll hold the doors for you then," Sam continued relishing the discomfort he caused. *Snotty cow*! He stepped to the compartment door and slid it open standing well back to allow her and the three children to pass. She did so with the barest nod of her head in lieu of thanks and hurried away along the corridor the little boy gazing backwards at the soldier with wide eyes. Sam winked at him and the child giggled and waved before his mother ushered him in front of her with a reproving stare backwards.

Sam grunted and after waiting for an elderly couple to pass by he too followed and stepped out onto the platform into bright summer sunshine. A lovely afternoon. The tiredness of the long journey, of the past months of hardship seemed to drop away from him and he beamed with pleasure at the prospect of being back in God's county. He looked around him, exchanged a hello with a couple of young women who eyed him with coy appreciation and allowed his gaze to follow them as they hurried away arms linked and heads together conspiratorially. Nice looking girls. Undoubtedly silly, but he would not have minded either on his arm or even both. He grinned at himself, heaved his bag onto his right shoulder, the Lee-Enfield onto his left and was about to head to the little station cafeteria when another girl caught his eye. Tall and willowy, although he thought she had filled out a little since he had last seen her, quite curvy in fact, she suddenly caught his eye and a slow, shy smile lit up her face.

There was something about Tilly he really liked. She was not particularly beautiful, in fact most of the time she appeared quite plain, although the unflattering maid's uniform she usually wore probably did not help. But when she smiled he thought her the prettiest thing, with bright, intelligent blue eyes and pink cheeked innocence. As their eyes met he felt his stomach flutter and his heart quicken. It surprised him, but it was not an unwelcome feeling, just very unexpected. He strode over to where she stood and fought the urge to kiss her cheek. Instead he lifted his cap in respectful greeting.

"Hello Tilly. This is a pleasant surprise," he said brightly. *God Eppy get a grip, she's only a kid.*

"'Ello Mister Sam," Tilly responded with that half embarrassed flush he always thought so attractive.

How old was she anyway? "Just Sam remember," he corrected not liking the formality or its implication that she felt inferior to him in anyway. She nodded and looked at her hands. Staring. He always stared. It made her feel uncomfortable though he meant no harm by it.

"I didn't expect to see you 'ere," she said feeling awkward under his gaze. He seemed to realise her discomfort and tore his eyes away.

"Home on leave for our Frank's wedding. Didn't you know I was coming? Thought Mother would be all of a fuss and bother over it," he chatted nonchalantly.

"She is, but didn't expect to bump into you like. Y' know," she admitted and blushed again.

"No well, I suppose not. Waiting for the Pateley train or are you going somewhere else?"

"No, Pateley."

"Good. Fancy a cuppa then? I'll buy you a cake as well if you say yes."

She looked at him. That cheeky, boyish grin. Those intense deep brown eyes that pierced disconcertingly into hers. Oh he made her feel all of a fluster, but she liked his company despite her ridiculous embarrassment. She had been looking forward to him coming home on leave, though she thought she should have no reason to. She barely knew him and he was so much older and so much her better. She could not help but return the wide smile he gave her and then any attempt at finding an excuse to decline his invitation was futile. She did not speak but he offered her his arm and tentatively, with a self-conscious look around, she accepted it and he steered her, not to the station café, but off the platform and up into town.

"Where are we going? We'll miss our train?" she remonstrated half heartedly. This was a strange feeling holding onto the arm of a good looking soldier. Their passage up into the fashionable spa town drew curious and smiling glances from passersby. It was an experience she had never encountered before and quite exhilarating.

"We'll catch the later one. There's a nice little place up here that my sister likes. A while since I've been there, but I think you'll like it. Is that alright? We can go back if you prefer to get home. I just suddenly don't feel a rush to get there and it's nice to have a pretty girl on my arm," he said with a mischievous smile.

Oh that look again. She could feel her face glowing hot and half turned her head away, but she did not protest. He squeezed her hand softly where it lay on his arm and quickened his pace towards the tea shop. This was an added and unexpected pleasure and he determined to make the most of it. He turned a corner; up ahead a small but exclusive café spilled its well-to-do clientele onto the broad pavement outside where they sipped tea or coffee amidst decorative flower pots under a bright, Parisian style awning. Inside those not relishing the sunlight took refreshment in cool, stylish, yet homely surroundings. Tilly stopped, her face betraying something close to fear.

"What is it?" Sam asked.

"I can't go in there. It's too posh for someone like me," she uttered very quietly.

"Rubbish." He tugged her arm, but she did not move. "Come on Tilly. You'll like it. I promise. It's not too posh for you."

"It is Sam. I'll look out of place. I'm not dressed for somewhere like that. Never would be. I'm not like them," she protested nodding at the well dressed ladies sitting under feathered and flowered, expensive hats.

"No that's true enough. You're better than they are. Look Tilly. I'm not exactly dressed like a prince am I? It's a café for goodness sake, not some high class restaurant. Trust me, it'll be fine. I promise." Gently he pulled her towards the tea shop and reluctantly she let him. They took a seat outside on the last remaining table and if anyone stared or thought they should not be there, he did not let her dwell upon such matters. From the moment they sat down he engaged her in conversation breaking off only to order their beverage and cakes.

An hour soon passed affably with frequent, easy laughter. Tilly relaxed finally and enjoyed his company. He always made her laugh. Such a ready wit. A little teasing maybe, but not unkind and happy to listen to her thoughts. She had never met a man who did that. Her brothers were often too full of their own wishes and desires to have any interest in hers. And the boys she knew were only after one thing to her mind and she was not that kind of girl. The other men in her life she thought far too superior to even consider her worth speaking to, although her employer was always kind, but she could never bring herself to speak to him without a question being asked first. Sam was different, although why she did not know. Somehow he managed to give her some notion that her opinions were important enough to be listened to and whilst she understood that she was hopelessly ignorant by his standards, he never made her feel that way. She smiled at him with open appreciation and he stopped talking.

"What is it?" he asked noticing the change in her gaze from nervously childish to warmly relaxed and...? A joyful thrill rippled through his body leaving him momentarily bemused and for once, uncharacteristically coy.

"Nothing. I was just thinking this is nice. Being 'ere an' listenin' to your stories. You alus make me laugh," she replied strangely confident.

It was his turn to feel awkward. He watched her for a moment as conflicting emotions flickered through his mind. The sudden realisation of his desire and the guilt that crowded in after it. *God she is lovely, but God she's far too young. Those thoughts are indecent Sam Hepworth.*

She laughed. "What are y' lookin' so serious about?" she asked innocently.

He sat back and smiled slowly before shaking his head. "Don't know. I'm glad you've enjoyed yourself. It's been nice hasn't it? I haven't had tea with a pretty girl since... God, I can't say when. May I ask you something Tilly?"

She looked at him warily. He had that searching expression again, the one that gave her goosebumps. "Depends what it is Sir," she answered with a hint of cheek and trying to sound nonchalant.

"Sir?" he raised his eyebrows and she giggled girlishly. The grin dropped from his features and leaning forwards, arms resting on the table, he became very solemn staring first at his hands and then her face. His shift in mood increased her nervousness and she blushed prettily.

"How old are you Tilly?" he asked, the suddenness of the question taking her completely by surprise. It was not what she thought he was going to ask and her relief manifested itself in a self-conscious snort of laughter.

"I wa' eighteen last month," she said proudly as if this was some great achievement.

"Eighteen," he echoed quietly. Nine years between them. *That's not so young after all is it?* A flicker of hope, or was it something else warmed inside of him? His smile returned. She looked younger.

"Why d' you want to know?"

He shook his head. "Just wondered." He sat back again with a sense of disquiet. *There's no harm in a bit of flirtation with a pretty girl is there?* "Suppose I'd better get the bill," he said and looked around for the waitress. There was no one to be seen. With a frown of frustration and a glance at his wrist watch, better not miss the next train, he sighed and excused himself to go into the establishment in order to pay.

Inside he found the proprietoress and waited for the change from a five shilling note not really taking heed to his surroundings.

"Samuel isn't it?" a woman's sophisticated contralto lifted his attention from fumbling with the coins to leave an appropriate tip. He turned his head to find a fashionably and elegantly dressed lady of around fifty smiling at him from her seat by the window. "I thought I recognised you my dear. Home on leave?" she continued.

"Mrs Yorke, what a pleasant surprise," he acknowledged thinking it anything but. An acquaintance of his mother, an intolerable gossip and a woman who had no compunction in voicing her opinions loudly without a care for the offence they may cause. He had suffered her acid tongue in the past. Involuntarily his eyes drifted through the window to where Tilly waited. Mrs Yorke followed his gaze and too late he knew he had given her ammunition for her favourite pastime. Anger flared within his stomach yet he could say nothing without making the situation worse. Maybe she would not recognise Tilly. Maybe she would not hurry to spread the rumour that was already implanting its embryonic seed into her head. Sam desperately tried to distract her from the girl outside.

"Yes I'm home for Frank's wedding. I trust you are well now Mrs Yorke? I was very sorry to hear about Freddie," he kept his tone soft, hoping the offer of condolences for her loss last year would prevent her bored and malicious brain from working overtime.

She turned back to him and took on an air of long suffering grief. "Thank you my dear. I am tolerably well under the circumstances. Freddie did his duty and died a hero that is some consolation to a grieving mother. It is a shame that we must lose so many of our brave young officers, still, men need to be led and an example set to them." Her nose seemed to wrinkle with disgust as she pointedly stared at his uniform, her eyes lingering upon the stripes on his arm. Her insinuation and blatant snobbery stung just as they had intended. His retort spilled acerbically from his lips before thought checked his tongue.

"Bravery is not the sole preserve of officers madam. If you will excuse me." He bowed his head and angrily marched from the café. Heading straight to Tilly he ensured that Mrs Yorke was watching as he offered the girl his arm and without a word he steered her away hurrying back to the station; she nearly running to keep pace. The afternoon was spoiled. Spoiled by the knowledge that some busybody would make his innocent tea with a pretty housemaid into something far worse.

They travelled back separately despite his offer to pay for a first class ticket. No, she already had hers and she knew her place even if he did not. Yet on arrival in the Dales town he walked her home determined to rescue some of the joy that a chance meeting had soured. Why should it? Why should he not be friends with Tilly? Why should he not walk out with her even? He thought to ask the question. Glanced at her smiling face and thought to leave it for another day

Somehow the opportunity to speak to Tilly never seemed to materialise. Sam found himself caught up in family visits during the first two days of his leave and, when he happened to find time to sneak down to the kitchen, the housemaid had a day off. Then, on the eleventh, Lily came home and any time he had to himself was greedily taken up by his sister who demanded his company to save her from some of the more dreary dutiful visits. Not that he minded. He relished and enjoyed his twin's companionship; it was a rare and cherished pleasure and so he packed Tilly into the recesses of mind along with the rest of his regrets. Until the day before his brother's wedding.

The house was topsy-turvy as last minute preparations were made and bags labelled ready for the train. Eliza hurried about both flustered and excited at the same time as she supervised the collecting of the family's luggage. She scowled at the kit bag and rifle thrown with careless abandon by her middle son and wished once more that he had chosen a different career. The last thing she needed was a visit from Mrs Yorke at that moment. Especially when Lily had so inconveniently disappeared on a walk with Sam and Thomas was seeing to last minute cover arrangements at his surgery with his partner. It was a visit enjoyed even less when the spiteful caller divulged her hurtful gossip before feigning to notice that the family must be going away and considerately curtailed her stay.

When Thomas returned he noted with relief that most of the bags had disappeared and mentally acknowledged his wife's ability for organisation. Entering the drawing room, expectant of a happy greeting he was surprised to see Eliza more than a little distraught and when he heard the tale she had to tell his surprise turned readily to anger. Anger directed at not only the vindictive busybody who had so maliciously hurt his wife, but also at his son who once again was the cause of her distress. With his temper barely in control he marched to the kitchen door and demanded that Tilly come to see him in his study, at once.

At midday the front door burst open and a laughing Lily, clinging lovingly to her brother's arm pulled him inside the hall. It had been a grand walk on a lovely hot summer's morning, but they had to be home before one and ready to go to the station by two. It did not give them much time for final preparations and Mother would be disapproving in the least that her daughter had left her to sort the luggage on her own. With a sigh Lily noted that the bags, excepting Sam's and the rifle, had gone and a twinge of guilt pricked her conscience, her broad smile evaporated into a frown.

"Uh oh! I reckon you're in trouble Lil," Sam whispered gleefully into her ear earning himself a wicked dig in the ribs. He opened his mouth to remonstrate at the jab when the study door burst open and a tearful, red-faced Tilly ran out. She caught sight of the astounded twins, sobbed heavily and vanished into the kitchen corridor.

"Whatever is the...," Lily began as her brother turned to follow the maid, his thoughts full of concern.

"Samuel! In here now," the sternly disapproving voice of his father interrupted them both. His tone reminiscent of severe reproof from their childhood. The twins stood still and stared, Sam taking a mechanical step towards the scene of so many punishments before remembering he was no longer a child who feared his father. He stopped and his posture stiffened into obstinate defiance.

"Daddy? What is the...," Lily began.

"Go and help your mother. You should have been here an hour ago. Leaving everything to her as usual you selfish, spoilt girl," Thomas snapped at his bewildered daughter with a glowering look.

His words struck Lily like a slap in the face and doubled her guilt. Flushing scarlet she glanced briefly at her brother before hurrying away, upset and cowed.

Sam set his jaw angrily but still did not move. From his father's demeanour and Tilly's obvious distress he already had a good idea what this was about and he had no intention of taking any reprimand with good grace.

"That was uncalled for Dad. It's my fault Lily's late," he said keeping his voice deliberately low.

"Why does that not surprise me?" Thomas snapped back, his irritation rising further as he recognised his son's antagonistic disposition. Why did the boy irk him so? He stood to one side and stared unseeingly at the door frame, waiting. With a derisive snort Sam took the hint and, not wishing to cause a scene in the hall where everyone would hear it, he marched into the room throwing himself into a seat. When his father turned from closing the door Sam faced him wearing a determinedly smug expression.

"You can wipe that look off you face young man," Thomas snapped.

"Or else? I'm a bit big to whip now Dad," Sam bit back childishly.

Thomas chose to ignore the provocation and took a deep breath to quell his temper. He strode to the window and clasping his hands behind his back, a little too tightly, he paused long enough to gain control of his ire before turning to face his son.

"Your mother has had a rather unpleasant visit from Mrs Yorke," he began.

"Oh yes? And what has that got to do with me?"

"Don't play games Sam. You know damn well what it's got to do with you. What I want to know is how long has this..., this relationship, for want of a better word, being going on?"

"Relationship?" Sam spluttered through a sneering laugh, his eyebrows raised with incredulity. He had not quite bargained on this conclusion. Why not?

Thomas reddened, his anger churning within his chest. He wanted to step forward and wipe that ridiculous smug smile from the boy's face. Boy? Hardly. Though the wayward son was acting very much like one. He balled his hands into fists as they dropped by his sides.

Recognising that his father's safety relief valve was about to blow Sam uncharacteristically relented with a long exhaled sigh. He had no stomach for a fight.

"There is no relationship Dad. I bumped into Tilly at the station in Harrogate the other day. We had a wait for our connection so I took her for a cup of tea. That's all there is to it. Mrs Yorke must have been there...."

"Don't lie to me! You know damn well she was there. You spoke to her just before you made a spectacle of yourself and that poor girl by..., by..., embracing her publically," Thomas interrupted almost beside himself with rage.

Sam stared, his expression betraying the surprise of this unforeseen gossip. This was ludicrous.

"I did not... embrace her as you put it. I offered my arm that was all," he managed to keep his voice level, then he laughed.

Thomas exploded, his resolve to remain calm vanished. "Don't lie to me!"

Sam stood rapidly his own anger piqued, but still he managed to maintain control. "I'm not the one lying. That stuck up cow is the one telling tales and adding her own vindictive embellishments for good measure. Oh, but you'd prefer to believe her rather than me wouldn't you?"

Thomas hesitated.

"Whether you did kiss her or not is not the point," he said at length feeling he had been drawn into a childish game.

"Seems very much the point to me. I took the girl for a cup of tea. We had a nice time. I like her company. I might have wanted to kiss her, but I most definitely did not. Look Dad why the fuss?" The game wearied Sam. He could not understand the depth of his father's anger. A much ado about nothing.

"Because you did not think about your mother. About the affect this would have on her?"

"What's Mother got to do with it?" a wary query.

"Oh don't be so bloody naïve. This sort of malicious gossip affects her. How can she hold her head up amongst her friends with this scandal hanging over the family? Hmm?"

"Scandal! *Jesus*! It was tea, nothing more. Hardly a scandal. If you want scandal you're looking to the wrong son," Sam flapped his arms with exasperation. So what if he had shocked the genteel society of Pateley Bridge's middle classes. It was nothing compared to... He froze. The expression of complete bewilderment upon his father's face spoke volumes. They did not know. None of them? He had thought it obvious. Surely his father...?

"You don't know," he stated, his voice suddenly silkily calm, a smug expression upon his face.

Thomas felt a worm of apprehension turn in his stomach. A reluctant thought, cast far into the back of his mind, crept into the light. He did not want to hear this. Did not want to admit what he already suspected to be true. Did it matter? Of course it did. Sam was right about the scandal. If he acknowledged what his errant son was about to tell him then tea with a housemaid would fade into insignificance.

Doctor Hepworth paled and gripped the back of his study chair tightly.

"Oh ho! Oh this is sweet. This is really sweet. All these years I've been the wayward son, the black sheep, the one you would rather did not exist, but it's not me you should be lambasting this time. My dear, precious little brother has outdone even me and you didn't know," Sam gloated and laughed maliciously. He was enjoying this moment. Years of pent up anger and frustration prevented him from seeing the pain behind is father's eyes, from caring whether he hurt the man or not.

"What are you insinuating? I don't care for your tone," Thomas managed to ask through gritted teeth. He did not want to hear it, but better hear it now than allow his smugly self-satisfied son to make a game of it.

Sam cocked his head on one side his expression triumphant. "Mother's darling Frank has got his girl into trouble Dad. In the family way you know. And I would have thought, as a doctor of your experience, that you would have realised that. I mean, the suddenness of this marriage. You didn't even know the girl existed until when? A month ago? It's not hard to fathom what's happened. After all they've been living together for some time now."

"Living together?" Thomas had been about to challenge his son's assumptions, he could still deny the truth, but this new revelation was a further blow. It showed on his face. For the first time Sam suffered a pang of guilt. The smile vanished. He looked to his feet and knew he had gone too far. At last the realisation of his selfishness hit home and he understood the pain he caused.

"For how long?" Thomas demanded, his tone stern.

Awkwardly Sam shrugged his shoulders. He felt wretched now. The fun had gone out of his game and unfortunately the damage had been done. He had betrayed Frank. More than anything he had destroyed an illusion his father held dear. And what of his mother? It would be more than she could bear to know the truth. "I don't know," he muttered at length.

"DON'T LIE TO ME!" Thomas roared. His son flinched.

"About a year I think. I don't know for certain, but they were living together last New Year when...," Sam stopped before incriminating his sister.

"When Lily visited," his father finished for him. A long silence ensued while both men contemplated the possible repercussions of this revelation.

"Look Dad, I'm sorry. I shouldn't have said anything. Please, don't hold..."

"No you should not have, but as usual you have done what a better man would not have even considered. I am not sure what part of this..., this shocking disclosure I am most disappointed with. Not you. I would have expected nothing else of you. You continue to live up to your poor character and fail to rise above puerile disaffection. I am not surprised by your misplaced pleasure in this. But Frank..., and Lily. I...," Thomas found that words failed him. Overcome by a deep sense of betrayal his anger melted into profound sadness. "I think you should go now. An apology to your mother and to the unfortunate Tilly would be in order," he uttered quietly turning his back and staring unseeingly out of the window.

"Of course. What will you do? You won't tell Mother any..." Sam hesitated before leaving, his remorse heavy in his heart.

"No, no. She would not..., understand. Any of it. She does not need to know. Leave her with her illusions," Thomas returned still facing the window.

"And Frank?"

"I think you should go." A final dismissal.

Sam stared at his father's back for several seconds racking his brain for words that might appease, that might heal. He could find none and quietly slipped from the room.

CHAPTER 41.
August 14th, Beccles, Suffolk

The wedding was disappointing only in that the sun did not shine all day long. For a brief hour a thunderstorm drenched the quaint market town of Beccles on the border between Suffolk and Norfolk. A drowsy little town whose inhabitants carried out their simple affairs with the slow, steadiness of country folk that had remained unchanged for eons. A very different scene from the bustling vigour of Pateley Bridge with its brewery, cattle market and numerous mills and quarries. Beccles sat, not amongst high rolling, purple hills, battered and shaped by violent northern winds, but nestled by the lazy river Waveney in a broad valley whose soft slopes barely lifted the land a hundred feet or so above sea level. A place of oak woodland, big skies and gentle undulating farmland, drenched by long sunny days through the summer months and frosted by a cruel north easterly through much of the winter. Other than the relative bustle of market day one would think Beccles, with its old Georgian mansions, its Dutch flavoured buildings and pastel painted facades merely an echo from another time. A time untouched by war, without the daily clamour for young men to lay down their lives for their country. The contrasts of the two towns could not have been greater, their inhabitants less similar, but this was where Francis Michael Hepworth married Evelyn May Parker at the impressive parish church of Saint Michael.

The smiling onlookers could not help but notice the wedding party as it left the church and gathered together at the entrance on New Market. It was obviously a well to do affair. There were two expensive motor cars waiting and being enviously coveted by a number of small boys and young men alike. The ladies of the party were richly and fashionably dressed, the bride in French lace. The gentlemen appeared distinguished with two in uniform, although oddly the best man wore a sergeant's garb and not that of an officer like the other, darkly handsome man standing beside a pretty, auburn haired bridesmaid and a pleasingly attractive young mother with a baby. The sergeant wore a ribbon of some decoration on his tunic. Perhaps he was one of the eager volunteers of 1914, a few curious members of the small crowd decided and cheered happily as the newlyweds posed for a photograph. The couple dodged a barrage of rice before climbing into one of the waiting cars. The older members of the group, a white haired gentleman, whom some of the crowd recognised as one of their own, the parents of the groom and the young mother, huddled into the other vehicle. The uniformed young men and the bridesmaid waved them off and followed behind on foot. It was nice, the crowd acknowledged, to see such a happy union amidst the dark shadow of war. It was a reminder that life went on despite the bloodshed and would continue to go on regardless. As the wedding party dispersed the townsfolk did also and carried on with their own affairs.

Lily linked arms with her brother and her fiancé as they strolled leisurely towards the river and the Riverside Hotel for the wedding breakfast. The sun beat hotly upon her hatless head and she wondered whether the flowers fastened into her hair were wilting under its heat. It was marvellous to see Frank married regardless of the hidden reason for it. The wedding also added a welcome diversion to her leave, a light respite from the oppressive claustrophobia of home with her mother's fussing and Dora's exacting need for reassurance that Joe was safe in France. It allowed her some time with Sam and ensured that she and Robert could not spend too much time alone; something she dreaded yet also desired. She had not broached the subject of their engagement although she thought she must. Yet he seemed so blissfully unaware that anything about her had changed. She had hoped by now that he might have noticed her coolness and her deliberate detachment.

They had travelled home separately, their leave not exactly coinciding. She had journeyed with Gladys who was returning to England for good. He had arrived in the country only two days previous. This was their first meeting.

Lily had arrived in Pateley Bridge on the eleventh and had hoped to spend precious time with her twin and yet all too soon the burden of duty had overshadowed those hopes. All too soon she had to share her brother with the rest of her family, spend hours in an atmosphere of feminine domesticity with her mother and Dora, cooing over the baby or visiting other ladies of the town. It was a duty she found stifling and tedious and it highlighted the widening gap between her life and that of most women left at home. With every hour spent in their company she realised how different her world was. A terrible, harrowing world, full of death and suffering and at the same time wonderfully adventurous, inspiring and fulfilling. Contrasting that non-stop, relentlessly exhausting adventure with the mundane existence of home life with its seemingly insignificant worries over food shortages and the dwindling supply of domestic servants, the distance between herself and her contemporaries had never seemed greater. For the first time Lily understood what Sam had meant when he had said she would never be happy as a wife and mother, not if it meant living in the choking, Edwardian atmosphere of the English middle class.

Until coming home she had been undecided, thinking that once reunited with Robert her love for him would vanquish all doubts. Now she knew it was not to be and should not be. It was wholly unfair to him. He deserved a good wife. Someone who would support and cherish him, who would be contented to live a peaceful and ordinary life in an affluent and fashionable town, amongst other wives of equally successful and deserving men. It was not a life for her. She knew that now. Despite the horrors of war and the endless drudgery of her work, Lily knew she was made for more than domestic bliss and she wanted more. She was not, as her brother had thought, torn between Robert and the enigmatic Alex Thewlis, but between her perceived duty and her own ambition and desire for independence. The engagement had to be called off, but how to do it and when she remained uncertain.

The trio ambled down the surprisingly steep hill from the town to the hotel and the river. They laughed and teased one another for a short and blissful few minutes before a suddenly darkening sky began to splash rain upon them with an accompanying crack of thunder that rivalled any artillery gun. They quickened their pace to a run and hurried, as the heavens opened, into the welcoming dry of the fashionable hotel, joining the rest of the wedding party with a burst of youthful gaiety.

Eliza smiled as her wayward twins rushed inside; Robert a little flushed and much more dignified behind them. It was hard to reprove the pair regardless of their lack of decorum. Thomas, she noticed, merely frowned as his daughter declared loudly that she was soaked to the skin and winked in a most unladylike way at her grinning brother.

"Lily come and sit down dear. Please act like a young lady for once. Whatever will Mr Parker think of you," Eliza chastised half heartedly and more because she thought she ought to than because she believed in what she said. Lily sobered her expression and took up a seat beside Dora; she motioned to Sam to sit on her left with a pleading glance. They were seated around a large rectangular table, the elderly Mr Parker conspicuous by his absence and the Bride and Groom also missing.

"Where are the happy couple?" Robert asked placing himself with some disappointment opposite his fiancé. He had hoped to sit next to her. Despite his understanding of the twin's close bond he could not suppress the stab of jealousy that soured his expression momentarily.

"They are having a photograph taken in the garden. Although, if it is still raining I have no doubt they will be back very shortly," Dora enlightened and accepted a glass of sherry from a grave and smartly dressed, but very young waiter.

"It's only a shower. And Mr Parker?" Lily enquired accepting her aperitif with a winning smile that caused the attendant to blush to the roots of his very blond hair. Only a boy, the waiter moved onto the soldiers, still scarlet and awed by men who had so obviously served in France. He stared fixedly at the sergeant's medal ribbon, looked as if he wanted to say something, but only managed a shy smile instead and hurried away.

"Mr Parker will be back with us directly," Thomas replied with emphasis.

"Oh. I see," Lily said with a look of amused understanding and sipped her sherry.

The return of Mr Parker, Evie's aged grandfather, and the newlyweds prompted the serving of the wedding breakfast. A very private and modest affair yet enjoyable enough. With a war on it had seemed obscene to throw money away on a lavish reception and a good and exclusive dinner was deemed far more appropriate. Fine wine and champagne to be enjoyed and a delicious roast beef joint. The war forgotten for a few hours, the party laughed and rejoiced in the occasion, discourse was pleasant, buoyant and far away from dark thoughts and worries. A toast was made to absent friends and family, the only hint of a more sinister reason for Joe not being present, or Evie's parents not wishing to return from Singapore.

Sam made a speech as best man, a short yet witty chronicle of Frank's life. It brought laughter and applause from the group, colour to the groom's cheeks and ended with a gracious tribute to the lovely bride. He resumed his seat pleased with his efforts and beamed with satisfaction as Lily squeezed his arm for a job well done. And perhaps only he noticed his father's frosty gaze and aloof manner. No one else seemed to.

Sam banged the table demanding a response from his brother. Frank stood and surveyed his family, the snowy haired and affable Mr Parker and his new wife.

"Er, I suppose I should thank Sam for that enlightening speech. Needless to say I am only glad that we are few in number and the tales he told were already known, to some extent, to Mother and Father. I only hope this has not tainted Mr Parker's view of me," he began with an embarrassed air. The party chuckled and Mr Parker shook his head smiling. Thomas sighed and stared into his champagne glass.

"I would like to thank Mother and Father for footing the bill today and Mr Parker for giving away his granddaughter. I know Evie would have dearly loved her parents to be here, but we know that though many miles away, their thoughts are with us. I would also like to thank Lily for acting as bridesmaid and Robert for taking time out of his precious leave to be with us. Let us hope that it is not long now before it is you two who are tying the matrimonial knot and beginning a long and happy life together." He paused and grinned at his sister.

Lily flushed and dropped her eyes aware of everyone's gaze upon her. She stared at her hands fighting the conflicting emotions within. She knew Robert stared longingly at her, she knew he wished more than anything to marry and saw little reason for delay. The whole family anticipated her wedding with the exception, perhaps, of Sam. He leaned across to her now and whispered in her ear, "Be brave," before sitting back with an encouraging wink. The gesture could only be construed as some slightly risqué remark pertaining to marriage. They all saw Lily blush deeper and smile awkwardly at her twin.

"Thank you, my sweet sister-in-law, for making the long journey when your little man is so young still. I am only sorry that our Joe couldn't be here with you," he spoke directly to Dora who smiled back with bright eyed emotion. She had nearly declined making the trip. Nearly used the baby as an excuse, but that would have been unforgivably rude. This was, after all, Joe's family. Her family now.

"Of course I would like to thank Evie, my wife," Frank continued, "For allowing me to marry her and making me the happiest man alive." He lifted his champagne glass and silently offered a toast to his bride who beamed with rosy joy into his face. Everyone clapped and joined in the toast.

Thomas silently contemplated the couple. Could he forgive his son's indiscretion? The boy was certainly doing the right thing now, but what had gone before? What debauched lifestyle did the pair lead in their London love nest? The bitterness grew within his breast. He threw a dark look at Sam. The blame for his disillusionment lie there, with that wastrel. Thomas wanted to leave the room, to get some air, the atmosphere of happiness stifled him, but Frank had not finished. He held up his hands and delved into his frock coat inner pocket bringing forth what appeared to be a carefully folded pamphlet tied with a dark blue ribbon.

"Finally I would like to share with you all some wonderful news. I have not spoken to any of you regarding this subject excepting my wife of course who has known from the start and without whose encouragement the venture may not have reached a conclusion.

"A few months ago I wrote a little piece of music. This piece of music has been played by our Red Cross orchestra at venues around London and amazingly it has always been received by rapturous applause. I thank God that Sam enlightened me of its merits as a piece for violin and that Evie encouraged me to orchestrate the original score. And I am proud to tell you that not only has it been published, but next month we play it at the Royal Albert Hall with the Symphonic." Frank grinned broadly and thrust the manuscript at his mother. Eliza gasped with delight her left hand flying to her mouth while she accepted the pamphlet with her right.

"Open it," Lily urged excitedly. Eliza hurriedly did so, her practiced eye scanning the score with growing pride, hearing the music written within.

"Are you pleased?" Frank asked.

"Oh Frank it's wonderful. So moving. When did you write it?" Eliza declared her eyes brimming with tears, her heart swollen with pride.

"In the winter. I orchestrated it over the summer. You will come and hear it?"

Eliza beamed. "Frank, darling, I wouldn't miss it for the world. My clever son. Oh I always knew, always said you were special." With unabashed effusiveness she stood and kissed her youngest child.

"Oh Thomas, isn't it wonderful? Isn't our son the cleverest? We should stay at the Savoy and..."

"I'm afraid you will be going alone my dear," Thomas gruffly interrupted his wife's happy babbling.

"Alone?" Eliza queried, confused by her husband's less than conciliatory tone. His frigidity had not gone unnoticed though she had put his mood down to another argument with Samuel.

"Yes alone dear. I am far too busy to take time out to visit London for the sole purpose of watching a concert," his words were cuttingly harsh.

"But..., I thought. It's Frank's...," Eliza stammered not understanding.

"It's alright Mother. Father is a busy man. We all know that. You come anyway," Frank hurried to her rescue. Hurt by his father's cold rebuffal that he did not comprehend, he was well aware of the rapidly developing atmosphere of discomfort and he refused to let the day be spoiled. He sat next to his mother and engaged her and Evie in rapturous discussion for the proposed visit.

Thomas helped himself to more champagne and ignored the contemptuous gaze of his middle son and the puzzled expression of his daughter. Instead he gathered himself with all the self control he could muster and entered a long and exclusive conversation with Robert over the medical advances being made as a consequence of the war.

"Would you care to take a walk?" Robert asked as he noted Lily finish her coffee.

She hesitated thinking she was not ready to be alone with him, not fully prepared to let him down, but as her mother smiled encouragement she found her mind devoid of suitable excuses and consented. He offered his arm as she rose and reluctantly she accepted it.

They did not speak as they passed out into the garden. The air outside was heavy, sultry and hot. A warm breeze carried the powerfully sweet scent of roses into her nostrils but offered no respite from the stifling temperature. It must be the hottest day of the summer by far and there was sure to be another storm before the day was out. She thought the prospect fitting. At the far end of the garden, where it sank away into the river Waveney, she noticed Sam pacing, cigarette in hand. He had not seen them and she thought he looked lost, a restless soul. She sighed.

Hearing her exhalation and following her stare Robert chuckled and offered his thoughts, "He looks out of place here doesn't he?"

"What do you mean," Lily rounded on him with more aggression than she would have liked. It shocked him and he raised his eyebrows in surprise.

"I mean, he is so much the soldier, so out of step with the gentle society of your family."

"I don't know what you mean. He's as much a part of this family as I am and no more out of step as you put it." Lily tried not to sound so defensive. She agreed with Robert, but felt honour bound to side with her twin.

"You think so? I don't think he understands just how much Eliza worries about him. To express his expectation of death was rather tactless," Robert opined referring to Sam's somewhat insensitive answer to Evie's query over his next leave. It had caused a momentary, awkward silence, a painful reminder of an increasingly uncertain future and had cast a temporary shadow over the celebrations.

Lily removed her arm from his and turned to follow a circuitous path away from Sam. "Realistic though," she argued and her words sent a shiver of fear down her spine. She looked over her shoulder towards her brother. He had seen them now, but was making no move toward them. Instead he leant against a willow trunk, watching through a veil of smoke.

"He and your father seem a little cold with each other," Robert blundered.

"They always are," a terse reply.

"But more so than usual. Have they fallen out again?" he chuckled.

"I don't think that a laughing matter even if it were true," she rounded on him causing him to regret his choice of conversation. She was in an odd mood today.

Robert did not press the point. He recognised the obstinate posture. He frowned to himself, took a deep breath and then changed the subject. "So what do you think to Frank's suggestion?"

"What suggestion? I didn't realise he had made one," she answered a little impatiently.

God she was being difficult. Why did she spoil her character like this? Just like her damned brother. "Intimation then. Come on Lily, you know what I mean."

"No I don't. Enlighten me." *Of course you do. Why not admit it and get this over with?* She glanced up at him.

Robert stopped walking and took up her hand, his expression became serious. "What's the matter Lily? Don't you want to talk about marriage? I thought we could decide on a date. It would be something to look forward to, not only for us, but for your parents too."

Lily stared down at her hand in his. She felt her eyes fill and her throat tighten. How could she do this? How could she break his heart? She sniffed.

"What is it? What's wrong? Darling?" he asked his voice full of concern.

"Oh God!" she exclaimed and turned away from him.

He stared at her trying to deny the truth that slowly dawned upon him, to ignore his pounding, fearful heart. *Oh God indeed.* "Lily?"

"What Robert? What do you want me to say?" she spoke without facing him. She could not bear it. The soft pleading in his voice was too much, too painful. Tears spilled down her cheeks.

"I thought I could make you happy. I was wrong wasn't I?" he offered her a way out. So selfless. So noble. She stifled a sob and half turned toward him.

"I'm so sorry," she lamented.

"This damned war!" he forced a laugh, there was no humour in it, it did not touch his eyes and his face bore the pain he strove to hide. She smiled through a stream of tears.

"Is there...? Have you met someone else?" he asked. He needed to know. *Why? Why torment myself further? God she is beautiful.*

Have I? "No. It's just..., me," Lily held his gaze her heart almost breaking as his own eyes brimmed. She almost caved in, almost pledged herself to be by his side for life.

He nodded and looked up into the shimmering sky. "I'd like to be alone for a while," he said very quietly. She thought she detected a quiver in his voice.

"Of course," she uttered and placing a hand gently on his arm she hoped to impart some understanding, some sympathy. He looked at the hand coldly, patted it once and moved away. Lily watched him continue the walk for a few seconds and then headed back to the hotel. She saw Sam, looking her way, but she could not face him yet. She vanished indoors, repairing to her room in order to gain some composure before rejoining the wedding party.

Sam waited until Robert had almost reached the river before he headed to meet him. So lost in his own thoughts was the surgeon that he actually started when spoken to.

"Sorry Rob. Didn't mean to make you jump. You alright?" *Stupid bloody question Sam. Does he look alright?*

"What? No. I mean yes. I don't... Look Sam, do you think everyone would be really offended if I made off? No, of course they would. How selfish of me. I'm sorry. Just had a bit of a shock," Robert gabbled and smiled apologetically.

Poor sod! "Lily broken off the engagement?" Sam asked.

Robert's head swung around from the river he was absently gazing at. "You knew she would?" his words were accusatory, hostile.

"No, although I knew she was having second thoughts. Shitty isn't it?"

Robert studied his companion for a few seconds and then with a sneering laugh agreed. "You can say that again. God Sam, I'm a wreck. I feel like my world just caved in. I thought she loved me."

"I think she does, but...," Sam did not finish. He took out his cigarettes and placed one in his mouth offering the packet to his companion.

Robert helped himself and accepted a light. He inhaled slowly and exhaled at length. "But not enough," he finished the sentence.

"I don't think it's even that. Lily just isn't the marrying type. She's too independent, too selfish, too much like me," Sam explained with a chuckle.

Robert smirked. "I thought all women wanted to marry, have children. I could have made her happy you know. She would have wanted for nothing. She could have lived like a duchess."

"Well that's just it. She wouldn't be happy with that. She needs to fight her own battles, needs to strive to be someone. She couldn't simply be a cosseted wife. It would stifle her. Let her go Rob. Find yourself someone more deserving of your generous nature."

Robert paused working out if there was any hint of mockery, but there was not. Sam was being genuine. He meant what he said. The surgeon nodded. "I think I need to leave. Will..., will they mind dreadfully?" he asked.

"What's it matter if they do? No, I'll cover for you Rob."

"What will you say?"

"Dunno, but I'll think of something. Telegram from your maiden aunt informing you of a family crisis. Something like that," Sam grinned.

"Thanks Sam," Robert offered his hand.

"Don't mention it. You're still a pal. Will you be alright?"

Will I? No, I'll probably never be alright again. My world has just ended. "Yes, of course." Robert smiled faintly and with a short nod drifted away. Sam watched him go and thought once more what a shitty mess this war made.

CHAPTER 42.
September 3rd, Northern France

The Battalion medical officer had returned to Blighty on leave. Joe, for reasons he was now unsure of, had volunteered to fill his shoes for the ten days. It was simply bad luck that *this* should fall within those ten days. It was not a duty Joe had ever imagined undertaking and Lord knows he had tried to argue his way out of it. The uncomfortable fact was a doctor had to make the pronouncement and currently he was the Battalion medic. Simple, undeniable and bloody awful!

The CO had been quite forthright with his expectations. There would be no further argument. The rule book demanded a qualified practitioner must be present. Besides the whole damned Battalion would be present, no exceptions. None at all. Was that clear? *Perfectly.* An example had to be made. The men needed to understand that there would be no leniency in such matters. God knows if they did not deal with this swiftly and decisively the men would start to think they had a bloody choice. This is the British Army, not some tin pot militia!

Joe had seen the prisoner. A great giant of a man; tattooed, strong, a proper Regular. At first glance anything but a coward. How could he be? He stood over six foot tall, his features were hard, his military record clean if not outstanding. The fact that he had thrown down his arms and run away in the face of the enemy distinctly at odds with his record. But there could be no leniency lieutenant. Oh no.

It was not the first time, the CO had patiently explained in a tone resembling a father speaking to a small boy when Joe had expressed his professional view that the big Scot was suffering from shell-shock. Not the first time he had deserted. Just because a man was big did not follow that he was also brave. A condescending and final reply.

Joe had gaped in disbelief. *But the man is suffering from nervous collapse!* He had explained the symptoms, the nervous twitching, the constant, though slight, tremor of the hands. Surely it was obvious that the prisoner had suffered a sort of mental breakdown?

But the CO remained unsympathetic. The man was a serial deserter. A coward and that was that. What made it more abhorrent? He was also a Regular soldier of four years standing. No one had thought he carried such a despicable flaw in his character.

Flaw! The man is ill! Joe's exasperated words echoed around his head as he stared with frustration and impotent anger at the farm yard being swept and cleared of rubbish by a group of kilted Tommies. He sighed remembering the colonel's face turning puce and contorting with sudden rage, the soft Scottish accent becoming distinctly more pronounced as he banged his fist heavily onto the table of his farm house HQ.

"May I remind you Lieutenant, that you are a visitor to this Battalion and that you have a duty to perform while you are here? It is a duty I expect you to carry out without question. May I also remind you that Private Baldwin was found guilty and sentenced by a Court Martial. That he had a fair trial and that a doctor, far senior and far more experienced in these matters than you are, gave evidence that there was nothing wrong with the man!"

"Far more experienced! If you will forgive me Sir, there are few men experienced enough in these matters. No army has been subjected to constant artillery fire and such atrocious conditions before. Thrown into one bloody action after another it's bound to make men..."

"That is *enough* Hepworth! I will hear no more. Tomorrow morning the Battalion will be paraded and Baldwin will be shot. And you *will* be there. In the mean time I suggest you brush up on your history. If you think this war is bloody then you know little of our military heritage young man. Now get out of my bloody sight!"

The colonel had returned to his papers ignoring the MO hovering with barely concealed anger, aggrieved at the injustice, the lack of understanding or pity. He had been fair. He had listened to Joe's petition. Most COs would not.

Staring at the makeshift parade ground taking shape with due military exactness Joe thought the bright morning sun distinctly out of place. It should be raining, should be cold, miserable and damp to reflect the pernicious act about to take place. It should not be warm with a light summer breeze wafting the gloriously sweet scent of early morning into his nostrils. He paced the perimeter of the farm yard; the working men saluted him respectfully and then paid him little heed. He hardly saw them. His mind too full of morbid thoughts he could not shake.

He had taken no breakfast. The thought of food made him feel physically sick. Over and over again he had tried to think of a way to make the Army see sense. But the Army did not see sense; it saw rules and harsh discipline. That was the whole damned point. It did not favour leniency or compassion. It did not recognise mental instability. Could not conceive that a Regular soldier, a man who it had invested time and money turning into a killing machine, could suffer from a debilitating neurosis. Even the Army doctor who had examined Baldwin had prescribed to the same point of view. The poor man's fate had been sealed before he even set foot before the Court Martial.

Joe sighed and squinted into the sunlight as he passed a tall poplar growing at the yard's entrance. The mellow light cast long gold fingers through the aging leaves. Like the summer they were past their best, but on this shimmering morning they rippled with life in the mild breath of air. With eyes closed they almost sounded like a gentle surf breaking on a pebbled shore. Peaceful. Even the guns were quietly distant, a faraway thump and rumble reminiscent of thunder.

A sudden movement startled the doctor and he jumped edgily in surprise as a figure leapt with panic to its feet from beside the tumbledown wall.

"Jesus Christ!" Joe exclaimed his right hand flying automatically to his heart.

The figure saluted and apologised. "Sorry Sir. Did nae mean to make ye jump. Did nae see ye 'til just now Sir." The figure stood awkwardly, staring with clear, striking blue eyes, straight ahead.

"Good God man! You nearly gave me apoplexy. What the hell are you doing out here? Why the devil aren't you at breakfast?" Joe demanded trying to sound authoritative and feeling, as usual, that he had failed.

The young private glanced at the officer and then back into the distance, his fair complexion flushed and his mouth contorted with unexpected emotion. "Did nae feel like breakfast Sir. Does nae feel right," the private replied dropping his eyes to the earth.

"Because of Baldwin?" Joe asked his tone softening.

The private's gaze flicked up to his and then dropped to the ground. "Aye Sir," was all he replied and exhaled heavily.

"It's a terrible business. A sad business. Do you know him well?"

"Not well Sir." Another short answer. He was not giving much away this lad.

"I see. But this bothers you? His execution?" *What a stupid question Joseph. Of course it bothers him. Look at the man, he's only a kid. That moustache he's cultivating is more bum fluff than whiskers.*

"Yes Sir. I'm on the firing party Sir," the slow reply.

Oh God! What in hell's name do I say to that?

The private's eyes drifted back to Joe's. They were full of fear. "I've never killed a man before Sir. Not close up. Not one of our own. It..., it does nae seem..." his words trailed into heavy silence.

"No it doesn't seem right does it?" Joe agreed. The private nodded, his face still doing battle with his emotions.

"I d'nae think I can do it Sir. Not kill one of us. I could nae sleep at night knowing I'd done it," the lad burst out with a long quivering sigh.

"What's your name son?" Joe asked softly trying to keep his rising anger in check. Anger not at the young man before him but at the archaic and unfeeling system that expected so much of someone so young. Did the Army not have any idea what this kind of thing could do to a man? Evidently not. After all they were soldiers were they not? They were not supposed to have feelings. They were supposed to follow orders and be prepared to be punished if they did not. Inexplicably his thoughts drifted briefly to Sam.

"Private Keeling Sir. Sorry Sir. I should'na said that. I know it's my duty Sir," the private hurriedly added thinking he was for it.

"Duty my arse! It's bloody barbaric that's what it is. This whole damned charade. What are you doing here Keeling? You, I and poor bloody Baldwin? Have we taken leave of our senses?"

Keeling stared at the doctor with puzzled confusion. Not what he had expected. Not like their usual MO. Probably a civilian. He looked soft, compassionate. Something about him invited confidence. "I d'nae know Sir. I joined up for King and Country Sir. I did nae expect to be doing this," he answered.

"No, me neither. Try not to dwell on it Keeling. You probably won't shoot him any way. Half the bullets are blanks you know. The Army thinks it better if you think that you might not be responsible," Joe informed bitterly. It was hardly reassuring.

"I know Sir. Trouble is, I'll never ken will I? That's what's bothering me Sir. Not knowing. It'll go round and round in my head. Already is doing. My hands are shaking."

Joe studied the private thinking it a lamentable situation. The lad looked so young. Vulnerable despite his uniform. He smiled and gave some advice that if repeated would land him before a Court Martial as fast as he could blink, but at this moment he did not care. At this moment he wanted to cast aside his stupid temporary commission, his bloody so called duty; he wanted to leave this deplorable war and return to his beloved Dora and his infant son. He wanted to return to something he could call normality. "Well you'd better make sure you miss then hadn't you?" he said.

Keeling stared at him astounded. Neither of them spoke and after a long ten seconds Joe nodded a cheerio and sauntered away. The private watched the doctor carry on with his perimeter and could not quite believe what he had heard. He looked around furtively to see if anyone else was about, if anyone else could have been listening. There was no one. He blew out a huge sigh of relief and vowed this conversation was one he would definitely keep to himself.

Warm sunshine smiled benignly upon rows of sweating men, uncomfortably hot in their rough serge tunics and heavy woollen kilt. The respective warrant officers and officers standing beside and in front of their allotted troops fared no better other than their eyes were shaded by the peak of their caps. The collective discomfort showed on flushed, perspiring faces. A parade in full kit was no fun on a hot day. Even less so with the prospect of an execution to look forward to.

Joe studied the attitude of the Battalion trying to gauge its mood. He thought it subdued; the men looked nervous. He caught the occasional glance towards a neighbour, an unspoken question or shared expression of dread or something akin to it. None of them wanted to be here. It showed on their red, damp faces, in their slightly slumped stance. Standing easy most had lost that classic, proud highlander's upright pose. The troops waited, round-shouldered, oppressed, and it was not simply because of the heat of the late summer day.

Squinting into the endless blue sky and watching a family of swallows flashing effortlessly through the air in pursuit of insect prey Joe thought once more that it should be raining, that the birds should have flown south early. In less than ten minutes a man would meet his death at the hands of his reluctant comrades. The sun was out of place as were the swallows. It seemed indecent. Did they not know? Did the weather not understand what was happening? It should be raining.

A shouted order brought eight hundred and fifty three pairs of feet together, backs straightened; the Battalion stood to attention. A group of twelve men marched into the yard. They passed close by the MO in his position in front of A Company, adjacent to the allotted wall with its poignant wooden post. They carried rifles held at arms and followed the commands of a sergeant accompanying them. Joe recognised Keeling, pale faced, hollow eyed, but the private did not look around. Like the rest of the firing party, the young soldier kept his gaze fixed on the man in front of him, disconnected from the rest of the world. Keeling dare not look around; for one he should not, for another he did not wish to catch some sympathetic glance, some relieved expression that said *poor sod, rather you than me*.

The firing party took up position in the middle of the yard. On three sides the Battalion surrounded them. On the fourth the brick wall with its lonely, ominous post. Keeling and his unfortunate colleagues placed their weapons upon the spotless, swept ground, turned their backs and took several paces away facing, but not seeing, C Company. It was obvious that each stared somewhere high above into the faultless azure heaven and not toward the sea of faces before them and who could blame them? The carefully discarded rifles were loaded with one round, all live, none blank, by a pair of military policemen. Only they and the RSM knew the truth. The firing party would never know.

Joe felt suddenly sick. Sick to his stomach at the unfolding scene. Even bloody executions had to be carried out to some ritualistic script, follow some ridiculous military etiquette. It could not be done in private. Oh no, as the colonel had said, an example had to be made. And in order to set that example the men had to watch their comrade, in many cases, their friend, die. The prisoner not only lost his life but also any dignity and pride he might still possess.

Perhaps some of them agreed with the sentence, thought Baldwin deserved to die. There would be some in this gathered crowd who thought the punishment fair, held the prisoner in contempt. Some who even perversely enjoyed the spectacle of execution. Looking around Joe did not think there were many who did. These men had seen a lot of war, too much not to understand and though many quietly might agree that desertion could not be tolerated, their expressions showed sympathy too. There but for the grace of God go I, those faces said. It was easy to lose one's nerve stuck in a trench, being shelled constantly, being thrown into one bloody useless offensive after another. It wore one down. Ate at the mind.

Joe swore under his breath and caught movement to his right. Turning his head a fraction he found a young subaltern watching him with eyebrows raised in surprise. The boy looked ill. Probably never seen anyone killed before, his uniform was spotlessly clean and flawless, one of the latest draft from home. What an introduction to war! Joe offered a reassuring smile that translated only into a grimace and he resumed his silent observation of the men. He noted that a fair number had dropped their eyes to the floor.

Keeling and the rest of the firing party had retrieved their rifles. They stood in a line, at ease. More than one nervously glanced around, another stared fixedly at the wooden post ahead his face contorted and dark; the others looked pale and nervous. How would they deal with this afterwards? Would they forget? Put it to the back of their minds along with the countless other abominations they had seen or committed. Would they drown their remorse in a binge of heavy drinking and refuse to think, let alone speak, of what they had done? Or would the knowledge they had shot a friend, or at least one of their own, in cold blood, eat away at their souls?

Joe turned his attention to the CO who stood almost directly opposite with the adjutant. Only yesterday he had thought the man a callous unfeeling man; an old school martinet. That might be the case. Even so, the man was here and at his order so was every other officer. This was not a spectacle enforced solely on the other ranks. The colonel was at least a believer in that if an example was to be made it was pertinent to the whole Battalion and not merely the rank and file. He understood the men would never respect his officers if they did not partake of the lesson as well and he was humble enough to include himself in their number. Joe wondered how many executions the colonel had witnessed. Surely it would not have been many. They were not exactly a commonplace pre-war punishment.

The waiting seemed interminably long. Too long. The men sweltered at attention; the firing party seemed to waiver, swaying on the verge of panic, struggling to maintain composure. Years of discipline, years of training, fear of retributions kept them in place, kept them standing, ready.

At last! The condemned man with his escort shuffled into the yard, his feet fettered and hands bound in front of him. A padre led the procession, an armed guard, the prisoner and another guard at the rear. The chaplain walked slowly reading quietly from his bible. The sad figure of Baldwin lurched behind him his leaden legs reluctantly propelling him to his fate.

Baldwin wore no hat. His sandy hair ruffled in the light, balmy breeze and he held his head bowed, gaze rooted to the ground. He seemed a forlorn, miserable figure, devoid of hope for there was none, lacking dignity, pathetic, when suddenly he looked up. He stared around at the assembled Battalion, locked eyes upon C Company and something akin to a smile or a cynical sneer curled his lips. He held this expression for some seconds before glancing with fear at the firing party who fidgeted despite their orders.

The escort reached the post and halted. A corporal unfastened the prisoner's hands and tied him to the wooden stake facing the firing party. Baldwin looked up into the sky, seemed to watch the wheeling swallows. Joe thought he saw those eyes fill and overflow, yet the face bore a serene and wistful smile. A regret for his lost life? A treasured memory brought to the fore? Whatever it was it brought light and pride to the condemned man's face before a coarse blindfold, securely fastened caused an involuntary convulsion and the smile was gone.

Joe shivered despite the heat of the sun. All around him men were avoiding watching the spectacle, trying to avert their eyes, trying not to show emotion while others were drawn to the scene with morbid curiosity.

The padre moved away from his charge and took up a position next to the doctor just as the order was given for the firing party to make ready. On the command six men knelt on one knee, the remainder standing above.

"Such a waste," the padre muttered through gritted teeth, his long pale fingers clenched tight around his bible.

Joe grunted in agreement but said nothing returning his attention to the twelve executioners. The sergeant shouted the order to take aim. Twelve rifles were shouldered. None of them held very still; every one trembled slightly. One man stood muttering to himself, presumably a prayer. Another blinked furiously as if dazzled, though the sun was behind him, beating upon his neck and the raised face of the condemned man. Keeling, knelt in the front row, shuddering from head to toe, barely able to hold his weapon stationary.

A deathly hush descended upon what had already been a scene of apparent silence. For a fraction of a second the world seemed to stop still, seemed that the sparrows squabbling in the poplar tree drew a suspense filled breath and the restless breeze lulled to a sudden dead calm. Even the distant thump of guns faded into oblivion. And in that suspended calm Baldwin straightened his spine, raised his blindfolded head even higher as if with pride towards the smiling sun. It was an act that struck Joe with a deep and profound respect. This man was no coward. Whatever his reasons for casting aside his arms and running away, it was not because he was afraid to die.

"FIRE!"

The shout rang out like a clarion call in the still, warm air. A momentary hesitation and the sharp crack of rifle fire, not quite as one, but stuttered and unsure, rippled from the twelve executioners.

Joe felt his heart leap into his throat and seemingly stick there. The hairs on his skin rose in horror and he knew he had jumped at the sharp rapport. He was not alone. And watching the body jerk and twist as the bullets ripped through it filled him with angry disgust and left a bitter, metallic taste in his dry mouth. Brick dust spat from the wall. Not all the bullets found their mark even at close range. Not every man in the firing party had the nerve to kill their own.

A low moan, audible and blood curdling sent bone tingling shivers down every man's spine. The padre glanced, white faced, at Joe, who blanched with horror as Baldwin's head lolled heavily onto his chest, blood frothing from his mouth and oozing thickly through his tunic. But he was still alive! It was he making the awful groaning wheezing as his ripped lungs battled to breathe, fought the rising tide of suffocating blood.

"Christ!" Joe muttered and hurried forward. A firm hand grabbed his arm and pulled him to one side as he reached the dying man.

"Steady on Doc," a quiet voice in his ear and a restraining grip on his arm. An officer pushed by him, pulled a pistol and placing it against Baldwin's temple squeezed the trigger before Joe could even find voice to protest. The distinctive, piercing crack and the executed... murdered man's head lurched as if struck by a hammer blow. Pale, pinkish-grey tissue spattered onto the floor, the body slumped and an eerie silence ensued.

"Don't think you're needed now Doc. He's gone," the soft voice again, a vague trace of a well educated Scottish accent. Joe wrested his eyes from the dead man, his expression appalled, his heart still beating a pace in response to the grotesque scene. He stared, wide eyed at the subaltern by his side, the same boyishly clean face he had exchanged a half smile with earlier. The young officer offered a sympathetic shrug. It was all he could muster. He too was reeling, his hand trembling slightly though he endeavoured to maintain a brave face.

The escort unfastened Baldwin's bonds and lowered his corpse with extraordinary gentleness onto a stretcher. A shouted command signalled the Battalion file away from the makeshift parade ground and a flag was draped over the body. Joe pulled his arm free from the subaltern's grasp and knelt by the dead man. He was not needed. He knew that. But his professional duty forced him to perform that final examination, to declare death no matter how obvious. He pressed a shaking hand onto Baldwin's carotid artery feeling for a pulse. Nothing. He pulled away the blind fold cringing with uncharacteristic squeamishness at the gelatinous gore that seeped down the left side of the head. The eyes were tight closed. Even with the cloth covering them the condemned man had squeezed them shut in terrified anticipation of his demise or possibly, but hopefully not, in response to pain.

Joe lifted an eyelid, noted the pupils dilated and fixed; no response to the sudden bright light. He sighed and stood, motioning the escort to cover the corpse once more, noting with morbid fascination the neat round hole at the temple and the black powder smudge around it before the pale face vanished beneath the Union Jack.

The doctor turned away and searched the parade ground. The officer who had ended Baldwin's life stood talking, apparently unaffected, to a comrade. The men were filing away sullenly subdued, their heads downcast. A few threw a furtive glance at the mound of human remains as they passed by, but most kept their eyes lowered somewhere ahead. The firing party had shouldered rifles and waited their turn to join the ranks and return back to billets. Shaken and red faced they carried a depressed air but betrayed little emotion. Already they were closing minds to the terrible duty they had undertaken, putting it into the dark recesses of their subconscious. Keeling even managed a smile at a passing jibe from a comrade. Unbelievable resilience!

"Are you alright Sir?" the subaltern asked. He had not moved.

"Yes I suppose so. Are you?" the eventual reply.

The young man shrugged. "Never thought I'd see an execution. The men said he was a safe pair of hands, a steady head. Just goes to show one never can tell can one? I mean, the men never thought he was a coward." His face flushed as if embarrassed and a nerve twitched under one hazel eye. He looked directly at the MO. "Did you think he was a coward Sir? You didn't agree with the execution did you?"

"No, I didn't in answer to both your questions. I think it a sinful waste of a man's life," Joe replied with obvious venom. His companion watched him for a moment with curiosity.

"But he deserted, twice. The second time he threw down his rifle and ran," the subaltern said believing this confirmed the charge.

"But that action did not fit with his previous record did it? There was no evidence before a few weeks ago that he was a cowardly sort. You said the men thought him a steady head."

"Well, obviously they were mistaken."

"You think so? Does it not occur to you that the man may have been ill? Shell shocked even? God, this place is enough to drive anyone insane. We all have our breaking points. Do you know what yours is? How long have you been out here? Three, four weeks? Baldwin had been out for nearly a year," Joe stressed.

"So have half the Battalion and they haven't deserted," the young officer countered half-heartedly.

Joe shrugged. "Like I said, we all have our breaking points, but it's likely that if Baldwin had been given proper rest, a spell of leave, then he would have continued to be a good soldier.

"I don't think he was cowardly. I think we have partaken in a travesty of justice today. Let us pray that God can forgive us for it. Instead of helping a brother in need, we condemned him to the indignity and shame of a firing squad. We did not ask why he deserted. We branded him a coward despite all evidence to the contrary. Well, he may be at peace now. One thing is certain; he will be tormented no more." Joe smiled sadly, and with a last look around the emptying parade ground, walked away.

CHAPTER 43.
Loos, 1915

25th September

    No one spoke much. The occasional murmur, the odd oath. No one felt like conversing. The banter that had been evident before the first battle at Ypres, nearly a year ago, and again at Neuve Chapelle no longer seemed appropriate. In part because many of the men who had enjoyed that confident camaraderie, the pride and feeling of indestructibility, were no longer here. They were pushing up daisies in some corner of a foreign field or nursing their shattered bodies somewhere in Blighty. Those that had been there, had fought through Ypres, Festubert and Givenchy, they no longer suffered that blind faith, the unwavering assurance that victory was a short and bloody fight away. Bloody yes. More bloody than anyone could imagine. But by no means short. For the Old Sweats the eve of battle held no heady excitement, no mysterious glamour, only a weary understanding that not all of them would return.

    The new men, Special Reserve and a happy bunch of eager volunteers, perhaps brimmed with the spirit of adventure, tinged maybe with a little apprehension, but they hardly showed it. The quiet, sombre demeanour of the Old Sweats demanded respectful dignity, not boisterous, childish chatter. Not now. Time for jesting and teasing was past. That time ended with the order to form up and move out.

    Even if the new men had secretly thrilled at the prospect of battle, had shared a furtive grin with a neighbour, their light-hearted jollity soon transformed to awe as they trekked out into a lurid night. Even for those with previous service, nothing in their past, in summer camp, in training, had prepared them for the unremitting crash and rumble of guns, for the constant quaking of the earth, for a night sky alight with a hellish ruddy glow from a hundred or more fires. Nothing had prepared them for the pyrotechnic spectacular that tore the heavy clouds asunder, lighting the dark with beautiful, yet terrible multicoloured light.

    No need to worry about being able to see the way. The mining town of Vermelles, the country and the villages around were all bathed in a gentle, spectral flickering from multiple conflagrations and dazzling star shells. The flares sent everything into stark relief and heralded a fresh onslaught from artillery shells, bursting with their own crimson and gold brilliance, rocking the ground and scattering a deadly rain amongst the mud, the long spikes of uncut grass and the men.

    No one felt like laughing or joking, not now.

    They marched in fighting order into support lines at Noyelles by companies, dropping in one after the other, weighed down by entrenching equipment, wire cutters, water, extra rations, greatcoat, gas mask, rifle and ammunition. They carried enough to see them through a couple of days, in theory. And though the weight was evenly distributed it made a heavy, cumbersome burden. The NCOs had checked each man before setting out. Everyone was properly equipped. Everyone understood exactly what it felt like to be a beast of burden.

    An order passed along the troops to move up and spread out. Got to get nearly nine hundred men in this damned trench! The bottom of the ditch was muddy. They trudged through it cursing and sliding. Number One Platoon, A Company, in the lead, shuffled forward as more and more men piled in behind them. Finally a command to halt, fall out or rather, sit it out. This was as far as they were going for now. They were in support. The rest of the Brigade were somewhere ahead of them. No one was going to see any action for a while. The men peered through the gloom at their sergeant as he squeezed by telling them to rest. *No they could not smoke. Stop bloody grousing*!

"What's 'appening Sarn't?"

"We wait here, that's all I know," the impatient, but unflustered reply. A composed man. A steady influence. One of the original Old Contemptibles, an Old Sweat. A brave, decorated man whose youthful features sat at odds with his experience.

One Platoon slumped against the trench wall just as their comrades were doing all down the support line. They stood, hard pressed against the cold mud, to let Mr Wise, their terribly young commander, pass by before crouching on haunches and staring at the vivid sky above. No one spoke. Without shouting, they could not hear each other so why waste breath?

The sergeant trudged back along their ranks, stepping over and around legs, kicking some out of the way with a grumbled expletive and reprimand. He studied the men carefully. They were alright. They were steady enough, he thought as he leant against the opposite trench wall. There were a few anxious young faces amongst the expressionless resignation of the veterans, but they would be alright. They were all soldiers, most with some experience. He sighed and wondered if the Territorials and the handful of New Army battalions would be as steady. With a Regular soldier's innate prejudice he doubted it. He pressed his head back against the mud and closed his eyes.

This was it. The Big Push everyone had been calling it. Hardly a secret. The British Press had been regaling the country about it for weeks now. Not that it really mattered. Fritz would have to be blind, deaf and stupid not to attach some significance to the build up of troops opposite and the sudden, massive bombardment of their front line trenches. It was obvious that just about every damn gun the BEF possessed had been concentrated on a sector under twenty miles wide.

With their usual unfathomable optimism, it seemed the Staff were confident that surprise was irrelevant. The enemy would be so pulverised, so demoralised by the execrable battering they were receiving, that the BEF would easily walk through their lines. The sergeant, for all his ignorance of the plans of his military betters, did not agree. Had they not been told this assured claptrap before? Was it at Neuve Chapelle or Festubert? Either way, had not the artillery been too short of ammunition to enable the infantry to maintain their forward momentum? There had been an outcry over it in the British papers.

This battle was supposed to be different and he did suppose that the bombardment was particularly heavy, plenty of stuff sailing overhead now. Even so, judging by the amount of iron flying back this way, it did not seem that Fritz had been so totally pulverised or even demoralised. At least his gunners were not. And besides, the sergeant thought, if the Staff were so confident in their artillery why had the Battalion spent three nights furnishing working parties to carry large, ominous cylinders to the front lines?

The cylinders were shrouded in secrecy. No one would discuss them. Questions were discouraged with a blunt reprimand. All the working parties had been told was that they were imperative to the Big Push and they needed delivering to the forward Royal Engineers' officers at the Front. These officers mysteriously referred to the cylinders as the 'Accessory' and became extremely nervous if the men handled them roughly or dropped one, scurrying over to inspect the valve on top or to listen with ears pressed close. Despite the secrecy it had not been hard to guess what the Accessory was. The Company officers had been very keen to ensure that every man carried a gas hood, more so than usual, asking their NCOs several times to make certain of it. Everyone knew that Fritz used gas, but this was a British offensive and the commanders had fretted about hoods with a suspicious paranoia.

A star shell fizzed into life scattering garish magnesium light upon the men in the trench and casting them into monochrome relief, their sinister, giant shadows looming behind them like some portentous spectre of death. The sergeant shuddered and tearing his eyes from the troops turned his gaze to the brilliant white flare as it lazily descended and then snuffed into oblivion. He fought back a wave of nauseous apprehension. Inhaled and exhaled deeply and wished more than anything that he could smoke a cigarette. He glanced across at his platoon catching a few faces watching him and he flashed a reassuring grin.

Another flare and he checked his watch. A little after three thirty. The leading brigades would be over in an hour and a half and then the Battalion would move up into immediate support ready to leap frog through other units. If all went to plan. He knew this much, but little more, and an hour and a half seemed an awful long time to crouch in the cold, waiting.

A great shuffling and clattering of equipment as men were disturbed and stood to make way for Mr Wise as he stumbled his way back to the head of his men. The sergeant pushed himself away from the solid comfort of his wall and assumed an attitude of attentive respect.

The second lieutenant was alright. Came for a long lineage of Army men but did not conform to the usual bombastic mould. He was ridiculously young at just twenty, untried in battle, but he seemed steady and at least, practical. If he had any faults it was a tendency to be overly enthusiastic, a legacy of youth. He had been with the Regiment a little over a year now, but only out in France with the Battalion for two months. He still struggled to grow a decent moustache and the men nicknamed him Baby Wise accordingly, but he was nobody's fool. Intelligent and self assured he set the right example, earning respect for his level headedness as well as his fairness. He treated his platoon sergeant with due haughty reverence and was not above asking his opinion or advice, but it would always be he who made the decision, gave the order. He was one of the new breed. In this war of attrition the old ways were fading, blurring around the edges. As men and officers lived together in appalling conditions relations between them improved and new respect founded regardless of rank.

Wise caught his sergeant's eye and pulled a face halfway between a grimace and an expression of disappointment. "Attack's been postponed by an hour Eppy. The wind is not sufficiently strong to use the Accessory. Zero hour's moved to six. *Damn* this infernal weather! Probably going to rain too. *God!*" he explained with chagrin.

Sam smiled recognising the youthful impatience tinged as it was with mild anxiety. "Never could stand hanging around Sir. Wish we could get moving," he shouted back offering his own thoughts, knowing they complemented the subaltern's.

"Do you get nervous Eppy?" Wise asked loudly. He took out his pipe, stuck it in his mouth unlit and sucked upon it earning himself a few grins and nudges from his platoon.

"Bit. Before we go over. Once I'm moving, not really. I just make sure I move fast," Sam answered with a smirk. He was not going to admit to being scared stiff, to having his heart hammering fit to burst in his chest. He would never tell anyone that the sweat ran coldly down his back and left his hands clammy and slick, so much so that he was afraid of dropping his rifle and constantly wiped them on his tunic or inside a pocket. He hid the fear well, behind a mask of cool nonchalance, but inside his body seethed in a turmoil of barely restrained terror. The officer returned the smile, inspired and settled by the sergeant's sang-froid.

As the first strains of an autumn dawn crept with dubious discernability into the sky the remorseless shelling grew in intensity. For forty minutes the earth trembled and heaved, the din became a pounding torture, maddening, terrifying. Any chatter that had sporadically broken out died away. The men crouched, white faced and contemplative, their eyes wide and staring, their bodies tense and restlessly jittery.

As individuals' features became imperceptibly recognisable in the grey and chilly half-light of a dull daybreak it seemed to Sam that the weather felt as he did. That it too understood and bemoaned the bloodshed occurring below and could not bear to show a smiling sun onto such a shameful place of slaughter. He shivered in his greatcoat, glanced for the hundredth time at his watch and nodded once at Wise whose eyebrows were raised in question. The officer returned the acknowledgment that it was time and Sam shouted the order to remove coats and stow them in packs.

The men stirred, stiff with cold, their breath condensing as a thick mist in the still trench air around them. The bombardment continued to hammer on relentlessly and effectively drowned the combined clanking of equipment and stamping of hundreds of feet as platoon after platoon, company after company, heaved itself into readiness once more. It drowned out the racket of nine hundred stretching, clattering men, but it did not and could not compete with the sudden paroxysm that shook them to the ground again two seconds later. With an inconceivably gargantuan roar, and a quaking of the earth hitherto unknown, the artillery was momentarily silenced by a stupendous force. An explosion, somewhere to the Northwest, sent men reeling and crumbled walls of the shuddering trench about them. Almost immediately afterwards another shock wave reverberated on the heels of the first. Faces reflected the instant of terror, the pulse of fear that coursed through veins.

"Christ they're early!" Wise shouted in his sergeant's deaf ear as the seismic eruption faded into a vague vibration. Sam turned to face him, the usual cool exterior visibly shaken, his eyes demanding answers. Wise smiled. "Mines. They've set the mines off, but they're bloody early," he shouted again.

Sam felt the relief flood through him. He had not known; dared not think what those two tremendous detonations had meant. But now knowing they had been intended, were part of the bigger picture, they made sense. What else had the miners of the tunnelling companies being doing here for the last few months? They were not solely concerned with foiling Fritz's attempts to tunnel beneath the British lines. The imperturbable mask returned and he shouted at the men to form up.

The company commander squeezed to join his youngest subaltern at the head of the column. Everyone was ready. On the given order they climbed as one out of the support trench, across a stretch of grassy field and dropped into the long and tortuous communication trench known as Gordon's Alley. In near silence the Battalion began to move forward, A Company in the lead, Headquarters at the rear. It was six am.

Two hours of struggling against unforeseen or at least unplanned for obstacles followed. Gordon's Alley had been reduced in places to a mire. Flood waters from a thunderstorm two days earlier had been insufficiently reduced and the murky, six inches of glutinous, chalky swamp that comprised the trench's floor showed no respect for the men who struggled through it. Already trampled, churned and deepened by thousands of feet, it mercilessly sucked at legs and boots, sapping warmth from toes and energy from already sleep deprived bodies. It reduced the soldiers splashing and wading through it to a cursing body of miserable humanity. Where the mud finally disappeared the narrow, zigzagging maze of semi-subterranean pathways became congested with countless walking wounded trying to get back to dressing stations, impeded by their injuries, the equipment they still clung to and the men trying to get forward. Behind them the stretcher bearers staggered and laboured with their pitiful burdens.

The trench became impassable. Time and time again the Battalion stopped, unable to move further. Frustrated orders shouted by irate officers to get casualties out of the way. A few more yards progress and then another hold up. Meanwhile a steady bombardment had commenced from the German lines and shells fell all around adding to the confusion, general chaos and trepidation. Evidently Fritz had not been pulverised as the Staff had predicted they would be.

Exasperated by the interminable delays and lack of movement Lieutenant Colonel Yarwood sent the order down through the companies to *leave the damned trench* and head for their objective overland. A moment's hesitation only and the command was repeated all down the line. Without question, whether they felt it a foolish order or not, the Battalion obeyed and nearly nine hundred men clambered out and into the fields of harvested stubble and uncut grass. Shells exploded above and around, confining them to a relatively narrow strip, but the pace quickened. Running and leaping over shell holes. Dodging and weaving around bodies of farm animals, long dead, passing dishevelled casualties dragging themselves to the rear, they ploughed onwards. By nine they reached the collection point in close support trenches and relative safety. There had been casualties, but so far, not too many.

No. 2 ADS

The Advanced Dressing Station was sited inside a ruined house, west of the railway and just south of Hulluch Alley according to the current trench maps. It sat over a mile behind the lines, more if the advance continued as predicted. The first casualties began to arrive shortly after eight thirty in the morning. Walking wounded at first, dribbling in with filthy, bloody clothes and field dressings hastily applied. Then the stretcher cases, carried by sweating, silent bearers, the third relay, fatigued by the weight of their burdens and their struggle up against a tide of advancing troops and guns. The ADS swung smoothly into action, experienced now at filtering the flotsam and jetsam that drifted in and out. Of course they would be overwhelmed. It was inevitable. But at the moment the flow was manageable and the medics and orderlies set to their gruesome tasks.

"What's the story on this one Corporal?" Joe asked as he moved to his next patient. The soldier sat struggling for breath, his pallor greenish with what appeared to be burns around his mouth, nose and red, streaming eyes. At first the doctor thought the man suffered from a punctured lung, but that did not sit quite right with the other symptoms.

"Gassed," Fallon read from the label and sucked in a deep breath.

"What! Are the German's using gas on us again?" Joe questioned with weary incredulity. He had heard of the effects of gas from colleagues who dealt with troops during the April battle at Ypres but had not yet encountered a victim first hand. He bent to examine the man, frowning and grimacing with disbelief that such a weapon could even be contemplated let alone used.

"'S not Fritz. It's our own bloody stuff!" a voice from beside the gassed soldier grumbled angrily.

Joe stopped his work and stared at a private with a heavily bandaged right arm. "What do you mean?"

"What I said. We been carryin' the stuff up for days and they let it go this mornin' just after the barrage lifted. Gas and smoke bombs. Trouble wa', some o' the bloody stuff came right back at our lads. No wind see. Not enough anyway. It just sank back into the trenches where our lads were waitin' to go over and choked 'em," the private enlightened contemptuously, his face contorted with a strange pained expression.

"Good God! Are there many?" Joe glanced at Fallon and back to the injured soldier again.

"Dunno. It were further south. Stuff at our end seemed to be movin' alright. You could see it, like greenish fog rolling across the ground. Suppose most of the poor buggers will have been taken to one of the other aid posts nearer to 'em."

The gassed man started to wretch and cough. He vomited an oddly greenish, bloodstained mess, groaned and heaved in a long tremulous breath.

"*Jesus*! I need water Donal, lots of it," Joe demanded and the corporal scurried away. There was little they could do but clean the man up, wash him down to remove any trace of the irritant gas and rinse his mouth and nose with copious fluids. They could dress his burns and his eyes, but other than that, nothing. He would just have to be sent down the line and hope for the best. Fallon returned and they set to work washing and dressing, encouraging the poor man to rinse his mouth over and over. Whenever he swallowed he vomited, but maybe it helped. Maybe it cleansed his stomach. Perhaps.

Front Line

They had leap-frogged the Twentieth Brigade and entered into the old German front line with barely any resistance. Here they filed up a substantial trench, checking for enemy hiding in dug-outs, heading towards the Quarries, their next objective. Easy so far. The barrage and the Accessory seemed to have done their work. Sam had been doubtful and had even sneered cynically at the RE officer who had bragged to Mister Wise that the Accessory....*Gas, why didn't they call it gas?* That the Accessory had in all likelihood wiped out any remaining Germans left after the devastation of the artillery bombardment.

Well, the deadly vapour had drifted over these trenches. You could still taste its bitter odour, but there were no choking Germans or asphyxiated bodies. What Boche remained in this trench had died from the effects of shell fire, not gas. Perhaps the survivors, and there must have been plenty, had run away at the sight of the drifting smog. Either way, it did not really matter as the first line had been abandoned with barely a fight and was now firmly in British hands. Anxiety had been replaced by enthusiastic optimism and morale was running high. So much so that when the order came holding A Company in reserve within the captured trench whilst C and D moved north to clear the Quarries the disappointment unusually manifested itself in groans and ill-disciplined dissention.

Frustration! Sam kicked at the trench wall. A German trench. Well made and relatively dry. Typical that Snowy had grinned and passed a mocking, derisory comment as D Company pushed through and into the Quarries. Now heavy rifle and machine-gun fire spoke of a fierce fight, but A Company, languishing in the trench, were not part of it. Instead they could only guess at what unfolded a few hundred yards away.

Second Lieutenant Wise paced back and forth occasionally glancing at his watch as if time might improve the situation. He sighed heavily. "Might as well let the men have a smoke Eppy," he muttered to his platoon sergeant through gritted teeth.

Sam grimaced feeling the same sense of impotence and resignedly stood the platoon down. The soldiers slumped against the sticky mud of the trench wall suddenly overcome with weariness as the adrenalin seeped from their veins. They broke out iron rations and munched in silence or puffed away on foul cigarettes.

Wise ventured a cautious peep over what had once been the parados and saw nothing but a stretch of long grass punctuated here and there with muddy craters and the puffs of white and black smoke from the shells that now burst somewhere over the enemy's new position.

The bombardment and machine-gun fire went on. Endless noise. A garbled message from C and D Companies filtered through. They were being held in the Quarries. Something about heavy resistance. Probably the reason for the renewed shelling. Only an educated guess. Neither Sam, nor his young commander were privy to anything more than rumours and supposition.

Just after noon the Germans decided the time was ripe for retaliation. Heavy Howitzer shells thundered into the British lines sending men diving for cover. The Quarries seemed to be bearing the brunt of it, but, as A Company strove to consolidate and reverse their trench, flying shrapnel and other debris caused many a nervous curse and a hurried crouch against the walls with arms covering unprotected heads. There had been a promise of helmets designed to afford some protection from this lethal rain. None had been forthcoming. Another empty promise, just like the shell crisis at Neuve Chapelle six months earlier. The British Army fought against a hail of steel with only their service dress caps for protection. Ridiculous this far into the war. Unforgiveable. It began to rain.

No. 13 General Hospital, Boulogne

The doors banged open and the sombre face of Davies and his fellow orderly heralded the first of the casualties. No longer the singing, laughing boy, his expression held a mixture of shock and pity, his eyes bright with a different emotion.

"Bed one Davies. We'll fill up alternate sides. Hepworth, we'll start together. As soon as the next...," Sister stopped as the doors burst open once again. She frowned and then smiled grimly. "Alright, plan B. You and Parkinson take this one. I'll start on the other.

"Over there please," she indicated to the nearest bed on the opposite side of the ward. "Davies, when we have the next one up I'll need both you and Jarvis here."

"Yes Sister," the Welsh man acknowledged as he and Jarvis carefully lifted their filthy, bloody burden onto the clean coversheet of bed one.

The beds soon began to fill and the routine of combating the deadliest enemy began. Shock. Most of the men had lost a lot of blood, were freezing cold, or both. Later some would arrive that had received better care, who had a better chance of survival. At the moment, with the dressing stations and Casualty Clearing Stations overwhelmed with the human detritus of battle, men were moved who should not be and many who might live given prompt treatment would die through unintentional neglect. The nurses knew from experience that they might save some through basic nursing care. Shock was a killer. The biggest killer at this stage.

With quiet efficiency the nurses and orderlies of Surgical Ward Five swung into action. Pale, ghosts of men were wrapped in warm blankets, stuffed with hot water bottles. Those who could manage were given hot drinks. Dressings could wait a few minutes more. If core body temperature could not be stabilised then changing a bandage would do little good.

In under an hour the ward was full. One man had died, quietly fading into oblivion after holding on for so long. Death had silently stolen him when on the brink of safety. The cruel reality of war. No one mourned him. There was no time. His body was simply covered and screened and attention turned to the living. The task of examining dressings and injuries had already begun. The MO had raced around the ward and hurried away to the next leaving his opinions on priority. He would return forthwith, but not before he had rushed around Ward Six.

Used to a level of responsibility she had never dreamed of in civilian nursing Lily moved to her fourth patient's side and exchanged a sorrow filled glance with Parkinson as the latter wheeled a steaming bowl of water, ready for use. The Staff Nurse drew a deep breath and peeled back a stained blanket exposing the half dressed man beneath. The stench of an unwashed body, stale sweat and blood filled her nostrils and she steeled herself against the instinct to recoil. Coolly she assessed the pathetic bundle before her.

A man of indeterminate age. Not a boy. Somewhere between thirty and forty perhaps. Impossible to tell through the muck. His head and hair were matted with blood and mud. A filthy, sodden bandage stuck grimly to this. Another soaked dressing wrapped around his upper left arm and then a swathe of soiled bandages around his torso which, it appeared, someone had attempted to clean. His stained tunic covered what was left. Obviously either the CCS or the dressing station had made a start on him, but had probably become overwhelmed and he had been moved out. In a hurry. The man looked feverish but Lily could smell no gangrene. Not yet. Warm, lucid brown eyes met hers and crinkled at the edges as he smiled.

"Hello. Still wide awake then?" she said softly. They usually fell asleep once warmed and settled. Not this one.

He nodded slowly and with obvious discomfort.

She studied the barely legible label fastened to a tunic button, looking for a name and any other information. The MOs or orderlies at the dressing stations and CCS usually managed to scrawl something useful, even when beleaguered.

"Private Stanley Pickford. Is that your name?" Lily asked frowning as she tried to decipher the blood smeared, spidery handwriting.

The wounded man nodded again. "Stan," he croaked with a half smile.

"Well then Stan. Nurse Parkinson and I are going to clean you up a bit and make you more comfortable. The MO will be around later to see you. First of all let's get rid of that filthy jacket and give you a good wash. Are you able to sit if we help you?"

The private grimaced and as the two women bent to lift him he set his bottom jaw with determination and clamped his teeth together. Gently the nurses peeled away the tunic, Parkinson quickly bagging it with a frown of distaste at the crawling lice. They made one itch. Even the sight of them and, despite wearing a full length gown with tied collar and cuffs, she knew she would spend half the night scratching at imaginary vermin. They lowered Stan back onto his pillows. He lay there, his pallor white under the grime, exhausted by the pain. *Poor soul.*

With the utmost care they began to wash his exposed skin, covering his body with a modesty blanket while they cut away his trousers and underpants. He wore no socks or boots. His feet were encrusted with the muck of France, red raw and spongy from splashing around for days in water.

Quietly and efficiently the women worked; Lily with an eye on the other men assigned to her as well as on Sister. They had to be fast, but not slapdash. They could leave clothing and general washing to the orderlies once they knew who and what to be careful of. Sister was already moving purposefully amongst the wounded men, giving Davies and Jarvis instructions. She caught her Staff Nurse's eye and nodded approvingly. They had time to finish with Stan. The others were not desperate and the orderlies capable men.

Lily turned her attention to the chest wound. She could not decipher the label and decided the only course of action was to see for herself. She cut through the soiled bandages, prising them away with the aid of a little clean water, washing the skin as it became exposed. The final bloody rags came away with a lump of wadding. She stopped, sucking in a sharp, involuntary breath. Her eyes darted to Parkinson who, having exposed the head wound, hesitated in cleaning it. Beneath the layers of dressings a gaping hole had been packed with what was now soaked gauze. Lily could actually see Stan's pulsing heart beneath her hand. With the utmost care she replaced the wadding and fastened it in place with a fresh strip of linen. This was one for the surgeons. There was little more they could do now. *Where is the MO?*

The doors banged open again admitting two more patients, both in a bad way. One groaning with obvious pain, the other as silent as the grave and deathly pale. Lily rushed to assess the first as Sister took the other. Parkinson could finish cleaning Stan's head. The chest must wait until the doctor returned.

Reserve Trenches

The bombardment continued all day. Slow, methodical, nerve shattering. Not frenzied, but a constant drip, drip of shrapnel and heavies. A tortuous flirtation with the spectre on an unheroic death. Rifle fire echoed around the Quarries where most of the Battalion still engaged the enemy in a bitter fight. Frustration and fear, a soldier's worst enemies, conspired to undermine the resolve of A Company still kicking their heels in reserve. Much better to be in the fray, to use some of that pent up, destructively overwrought energy. But hanging around in a sodden trench, soaked to the skin and surrounded by a conflagration they could not engage sapped their strength.

Darkness came rapidly with evermore rain. The night sky a lurid display of orange, red and white flashes. Mind numbing boredom. They had rebuilt the trench, reversed the parapet. Errands had been run. Ammunition and rations brought forward. Now they had little to do but watch and wait. Try and catch some sleep. *How, with this racket?*

News from the forward companies remained sparse. Details did not filter down to the rank and file. Perpetually, A Company expected to be sent up and pitched into the fight. Disappointingly, the order never came. Occasional wounded staggered through them from the aid post in the Quarries. From these lucky men they gleaned snippets of information. Fritz was holding his own. No progress had been made. A counterattack was expected. Nothing concrete. All conjecture and the rambling interpretation of confused and injured men.

At eleven orders came to withdraw. A Company were going back to the old British Line. The rest of the Battalion would be relieved shortly.

Sam exchanged a sour look with Wise and spat into the mud. He heaved his kit onto his back and shouted at his platoon to form up. They were heading out.

Morosely they began to trudge along the communication trench, now ankle deep in thick, cloying mud. Flares and shell bursts lit their way but the conditions and fatigue made the going slow. They stood aside once to allow stretcher bearers through with another pathetic burden before plodding back the few hundred yards, miles it seemed, to their starting positions of that morning.

A sudden and ferocious outburst of rifle fire broke out from the direction of the Quarries. The men and officers alike looked to their commander. The counterattack must have begun. Surely they would be sent back now. Surely reinforcements were required. A weary excitement lit tired faces. No, there were no orders to advance. The major firmly pointed out this would be where they stayed for the present.

With disbelief and resignation A Company squatted down upon the chalky clay, heads against the trench wall or on rifles firmly planted in the ground. They listened with frustrated impotence at the battle that raged ahead, where their comrades were fighting and dying.

28th
No. 2 ADS

His hands shook. Exhaustion. Completely and utterly spent. Stepping, almost staggering, over the somnolent bodies of orderlies and doctors alike, Joe felt his way into a shadowy recess. He barely had the strength to climb onto his makeshift bed, a trestle table at the back of the dressing station. Flopping, almost falling, onto the wooden surface the sounds of battle, shell bursts, gunfire, the distant crack of rifles, urgent discussion and orders from his colleagues and the soft moans of wounded men, all drifted into a faint, barely audible buzz. The sweet, dark oblivion of sleep embraced him even as his head hit the table. Rest. His body succumbed to it without a fight. Three days without proper respite. Three nights of being dragged from a hastily caught cat nap and thrown back into the fray of battle with death. They had simply poured in, the wounded. Almost nonstop. Or so it seemed. At last a chance to draw breath.

Reinforcements from behind the lines had finally allowed the flagging medical team to collapse into bunks, curl up in corners, and sleep. A brief respite in the numbers of injured reaching them had helped. Thank God there were no more gas cases. No more wretched souls vomiting blood and fighting for air through burned out lungs, blinded and terrified. It had sickened him. More than the torn bodies and shattered limbs. Helpless to do much for them, they had cleaned the men up, rinsed their mouths and noses and eyes with as much water as they could spare, and sent them down the line. An inadequate treatment for an unforgivable weapon and all from their own lines. From the British trenches. Anger had fortified him when his body had cried to rest. He had worked like a demon. They all had. Now they could sleep. For a short while at least.

He did not dream. He did not even stir when Donal Fallon lifted a trailing arm and placed it across his chest before gently wrapping a greatcoat around him with a fatherly smile.

"You sleep Sir. You deserve it," the Irishman whispered and curled up beneath the table in his own coat and dreamt of the dark haired, blue eyed girl who had been his wife.

Neither man woke when the ground shook from the explosion of a nearby shell. Deaf were they to the carnage that raged outside. For seven hours solid they slept. Like the dead. And when Joe and his corporal orderly were woken by a rough shake and a tin mug of tea smelling strongly of petrol they felt like they had never slept at all.

30th
Front Line

Sam shouted at his men to extend along the line as they filtered into Gun trench on the right of the Royal Scots Fusiliers. The rest of the Battalion were somewhere else. Not far away, but it might as well have been Timbuktu for all A Company knew. From now on they were with the Scots. Heavy shells screamed overhead and flashes of explosions, garish white brilliance from star shells punctuated the dark, rain filled night sky. Miserable weather and miserable men.

They had lost the Quarries. The German counterattack had proved too strong and the Brigade to the North inexperienced. A New Army lot, untried and unseasoned. So the Quarries had fallen back into enemy hands and with them the Yorkshires had lost their First Aid Post along with a number of wounded men and the MO. Rumour had reached Sam that Snowy was amongst the wounded. It was only rumour. He would not find out until they were all out of this. *If* he got out of this. Too weary to really care he barked at the equally tired men and cursed the mud and rain.

"This is a bloody awful night Eppy," Second Lieutenant Wise shouted above the din of shell fire.

Talk about stating the bloody obvious. Sam merely grunted in agreement while casting a practised eye along his platoon and to their left where the Scots took up the line.

The OC pushed by, muttered something into Wise's ear and trudged onwards into the ranks of Fusiliers. An odd rushing whine and a thrill of spine tingling fear brought Sam's heart to a pumping frenzy.

"SHELL!" he roared and pushed the lieutenant into the mud. The platoon instinctively threw themselves flat covering vulnerable heads with arms. A deafening detonation and terrible juddering followed by a screaming man and shouts for stretcher bearers. A distant cheering.

"ON YOUR FEET! STAND TO THE PARAPET!" Sam yelled releasing his grip on his commander.

Everyman jumped to the firing step. Covered from head to foot in slime and dripping wet they waited with weapons ready, peering into the dark. A Very light fizzed into the air and the world seemed to shrink into a silent void for the briefest of seconds before an order further along the line and a following ripple of rifle fire brought reality rushing back.

"RAPID FIRE!" Wise shouted and the platoon obeyed, twitchy fingers eager to pull the trigger. They fired into the advancing Germans, oblivious of the stretcher bearers removing dead and injured men from the shell burst, their aim deadly and automatic.

A frenzied ten minutes. Reminiscent of Ypres all that time ago. The strong smell of cordite, the comforting kick of the powerful Lee Enfield and the satisfaction of macabre dancing bodies to their front. When the enemy started to retreat Sam felt almost saddened that it was over.

"CEASE FIRE!" a Scottish accent ordered and the crackling onslaught petered into reluctant quiet only to be replaced by the soft moans of the wounded and the occasional crump of shells. Not for long. The retaliation came swiftly as a barrage of deadly missiles sailed into No-Man's-Land and along the British front line. The big British howitzers behind answered back and the Poor Bloody Infantry cowered in their trenches whilst the heavies fought it out.

By day break the rain had eased and the shelling become sporadic. They stood-to shivering in the pale light of a frigid, damp dawn and the word spread down that the OC had been killed by that fateful shell. The morning blurred into a wet afternoon where nerves remained frayed and the watch vigilant. A steady bombardment continued and the night would see plenty of work repairing the damage if nothing worse should happen.

Sam stood down from the firing step. His place taken by Corporal James. Time to walk around the men. He trudged heavily through the thick mud, hunger gnawing at his stomach, fatigue tugging remorselessly at his body, yet adrenalin and fear kept his brain clear. Yes fear. He was afraid. He would admit to that now. Now, in the relative quiet of a routine barrage. He wiped the sweat from his forehead with a grimy sleeve, wished for the hundredth time that he could smoke a cigarette and did his rounds with his usual efficient diligence.

Early Morning 1st October,
No. 2 ADS

"Put them down there," Foster ordered with a pointing finger as another batch of wounded were stretchered into the ADS. "Hepworth your turn to sort the poor sods!"

Joe looked up from the dressing he was working on and with a grimace handed it over to Fallon to finish. He wiped his bloody hands on a stained towel and stepped over a row of occupied stretchers to four now blocking the entrance.

"And for God's sake get them moved from there will you!" Foster grumpily added as he struggled to extricate a bullet from between his patient's lower ribs.

Some cocked up attack had brought a dozen men from the Yorkshire Regiment into their hands. Some garbled story of Germans taking part of a trench and some fool commander trying to trickle his men through a gap in the wire to retake it. By all accounts the poor buggers had been lit up by German lights and raked by machine-gun fire. These were the result. Foster swore as the bullet slipped from his grasp and he muttered lowly to himself.

Joe took in a deep breath as he neared the new arrivals. He knew these were men from his brother's Regiment and he half dreaded seeing Sam's face staring up at him as unlikely as it might be. But was it unlikely? It could just as easily be Sam as anyone else.

Bending down to each stretcher in turn he suffered a wave of guilty relief that no face was familiar. Two were lightly wounded. He ordered the orderlies to get them out and to the CCS. They could manage the journey. One he had lined up ready for treatment. The fourth, a corporal with light blue eyes and skin like alabaster, was dying. He should be moved to the moribund tent.

"Can I 'ave a drink Sir?" the corporal asked, his voice weak and laden with pain.

Joe nodded. "I'll give you something for the pain too." He caught Private Stubbs' eye and indicated morphine and a drink. Peeling back the man's tunic he winced at the peppering of bullet holes along his upper abdomen. He had almost been ripped in half by machine-gun fire yet the man still clung to life. It never ceased to strike Joe how tenaciously some men held on. It would not be long now though. The corporal was bleeding to death. His body already showed signs of advanced shock.

Stubbs arrived with water and a syringe.

"Here you go old chap," Joe helped the man to drink.

"So thirsty," a feeble reply.

"I know. This will help you sleep." The MO rolled up a grubby sleeve and with the help of Stubbs searched for a decent vein. Already they had sunk and shrivelled as the body vainly struggled to keep its vital organs alive. It was a battle too far. The morphine would help end that battle. Joe depressed the plunger watching the narcotic drug vanish into a pale blue vessel. He sighed and looked at the label hurriedly scribbled on and tied around a tunic button. "Cpl William Pratt. Multiple gunshot wounds to upper abdomen". *No kidding*!

"Well Corporal Pratt, you can rest now. Moribund tent Stubbs please."

A couple of stretcher bearers gently removed the dying man from the floor and laid him inside a cold, dismal tent along with twenty or so similar. An attendant orderly moved amongst the hopeless cases, taking details and occasionally covering a blue face. He nodded at the bearers as they left Bill Pratt and walked over to his new charge. He looked down at a sleeping man, quite serene in the dim lamp light. No pain now. He felt for a pulse in the big carotid artery. Nothing. He wetted the back of his hand and lay it against the corporal's mouth. No breath there. With a sigh, the orderly removed the man's dog tags, made a note of name and rank and fastened one tag with a form that stated quite blandly, Corporal William Pratt, 8408, 2nd Battalion The Yorkshire Regiment. Died of Wounds, first October 1915.

2nd October
Front Line

The promise of relief at last. The rest of the Battalion had already left, but A Company stayed behind with the Scots. Any time now though and they would be marching away from Hell towards a proper meal, not dog biscuits and cold tea, and a proper bed in warm billets.

Working parties had returned, everyone was ready to move, packs on backs, rifles slung. They just waited on the Ox and Bucks Light Infantry. *Where were they?* Never before had Sam longed for the relief with such impatient anxiety. He had survived. Survived another blood bath. Death had walked right by him once again. *Lucky bastard Hepworth!* He was not alone in this thought. The men treated him with superstitious reverence now. Vying to stand close to him in the trench. Touching his shoulder or rifle as they passed as if his luck would rub off on them. He had been wounded. Twice now, but still he was one of the few originals remaining. In truth there were quite a few, but some had been moved to other battalions, some, like Snowy perhaps, were prisoners of war. And they had been lucky this time. Not so many killed. Or so the officers were muttering.

Come on! Where are they? He glanced at his watch, the luminous dial glowing dimly in the dark. *Oh for a cigarette. Soon. Very soon.* He caught Wise's eye.

"Seems to take forever doesn't it Sir," he offered recognising an echoed nervous frustration on the young face.

Wise nodded solemnly. Gone was his youthful exuberance. It had been replaced by the realisation of what this war really meant, of death, destruction and above all weariness. Exhaustion beyond belief. Like his men, Wise wished for food and sleep. Nothing more.

A crackle of rifle fire, distant and brief raised a few incurious heads. It was not the sound they listened for. Sam leant heavily against the trench wall. He glanced up at the sentry. All was quiet the returned nod said.

At last it came. A steady tramp in squelching mud and dull clatter of the odd, unsecured tin. The relief. Making as much noise as a bull in a china shop, or so it seemed.

"Tell Fritz we're moving why don't you?" a private beside Sam muttered under his breath. "Fuckin' useless lot. They'll throw all the iron they can at us now."

But they did not. The relief exchanged places with men who to them appeared as ghosts; pale, filthy, stinking and dead on their feet. The order to form up came. They were going. They were leaving Hell. Without a word they shuffled away, their eyes only on the man in front, their ears straining for the telltale whine of death. Death was elsewhere that night. Trawling some other trench for souls to reap. They filtered down Hay Alley and into the labyrinth of support trenches beyond. As the distance from the Front widened a smile crept to one or two besmirched faces. Someone started to whistle a tune. They were out. They were safe.

CHAPTER 44.
October 2nd, Number 13 General Hospital, Boulogne

The ward had finally fallen into steady routine. They had lost a few. Some had been moved on to Blighty. Lucky devils. Others would be here for a while yet. Against all odds Stan Pickford had survived. He had been operated on, his wounds cleaned daily and somehow he had remained free from infection and his heart, so very nearly torn from his body, beat with the strength of an ox. He sat up in bed now, reading a newspaper as if he had never been anywhere near a battlefield. Only his skin, still pale from blood loss and the swathe of bandages across his chest gave lie to the illusion. Lily looked up from her table in the middle of the ward and caught his eye. A miracle if ever she saw one. He grinned and she tried not to return the expression, but failed and so sticking her tongue into her cheek returned with apparent enthusiasm to her notes.

"Hepworth." It was Sister's voice.

Lily stood. "Yes Sister."

"You are to report to Matron."

A sudden heart stopping fear drained the colour from Lily's face. It must have been overtly obvious for Sister suddenly flushed and apologised.

"No, no it's nothing terrible. I'm sorry, I should have thought. I think you will be pleasantly surprised," she patted her subordinate's arm with a rare show of affection. "I'll take over here. Run along now."

Quite puzzled, Lily obeyed. It was rare to be summoned to see Matron unless one had done something dreadful or unless bad news waited. An intimation of a pleasant surprise was, to say the least, perplexing. She hurried to the nearest bathroom and checked her appearance in the mirror. Clean, tidy..., well apart from that defiant strand of hair again. She impatiently tucked it under her veil with a clicking of her tongue.

Standing outside the oak panelled door on the first floor she took a deep breath and then knocked.

"Enter." A strong voice from the other side.

Lily smoothed her starched, pristine apron and obeyed.

"Ah Staff Nurse Hepworth. Please come in and sit down," Matron said, a broad smile warming her normally serious features. She waited for the young nurse to settle and then decided not to waste time on small talk.

"Hepworth I have been more than pleased with you conduct here. You are a good nurse and though you have a tendency towards what I might call wilfulness, I am more than happy to give credit where credit is due. As a result you are to be rewarded with a promotion."

"A promotion," Lily echoed vaguely.

"Yes. You are promoted to acting sister forthwith. I hope that within the next few months this will be ratified and the position made permanent. However, I do this with a tinge of regret," Matron paused.

"Regret?" Lily's smile faltered.

"Yes Hepworth. Unfortunately I am to lose you to Number 23 Hospital at Étaples. They are desperately short of good, experienced nurses. I don't mind telling you I will be sad to see you go."

"Oh. I mean, er thank you Matron, but Étaples. When do I go," Lily struggled to take in the news.

"Tomorrow I'm afraid. They've asked for you straight away."

"So soon."

"Onwards and upwards Hepworth. I'm sure you'll do splendidly. Now, return to your work. I'll arrange everything."

"Yes Matron. Thank you." Lily stood, bobbed a curtsey and left. Outside she leant back against the door, closed her eyes and let the information trickle into her brain. A promotion. She would have her own ward. The surprised expression gave way to a broad smile and she giggled behind her hand. It would mean leaving friends, dear friends. But acting sister. She started to head back to the ward and throwing her head back she laughed out loud.

CHAPTER 45.
October 17th, Paris

    The brandy tasted rough. Some cheap stuff that suited the seedy Parisian bar he sat in, but it would do its job. Robert finished off the glass and unsteadily poured himself another. His hands shook and he smiled cynically. *Not a surgeon's hands now old chap.* He downed half the drink in one gulp screwing up his face at the sharp, metallic bitterness left in his mouth and spluttering as the liquor hit the back of his throat.
    She filled his thoughts constantly, obsessively. Day and night. He did not sleep. She, or rather the memory of her and the bitter knowledge that she was gone, prevented him from resting. The anguish of his loss consumed him.
    At first he had determined stoically to carry on. He had his work. It was worthwhile, rewarding, and good surgeons were needed more than ever. But deep down he could not believe it was over and the malignant worm ate away at his resolve. He did not understand why her feelings had changed. She had written to him trying to explain. Had professed that she did love him, yet only as she loved her brothers. With a curse, he had angrily cast the letter into the stove that tried to warm his shared tent causing his companion to raise his eyebrows in surprise. Still, he had not believed it. Had not wanted to admit it. The pain grew, gnawing into his psyche, eating at his brain until he could take no more.
    He had packed a bag and boarded a train to Étaples determined to find her and declare his love. To beg her to take him back. He had, in effect, deserted. But he would do anything; give her anything, if only she would love him. It had taken him three days, but he had finally found her. He had walked onto her ward and requested, no, demanded they talk. Oh, the astounded, embarrassed expression on her face. *What a fool!* The ward had fallen silent. Curious eyes had watched with sensationalistic expectation. The promise of delicious scandal. But the eager Tommies had been disappointed. She had remained calm, had quietly led him out of the ward and agreed to meet him when her shift had ended. *He could wait? There was no urgency?*
    No, no urgency, only the frantic beating of his heart, the burning desire to pull her into a passionate embrace, to.... No, there was no urgency, he could wait.
    He *had* waited for her in a secluded café impatiently drinking cognac. When she had arrived, looking pale faced and wary, he was already drunk. It had not gone well. His alcohol fuelled words had sounded childishly desperate. He had cruelly made her cry. It had not gone to plan. She had remained unnervingly quiet while he poured out only half of his pre-planned speech. It had hardly been eloquent. His brain struggled to muddle through the haze of inebriation.
    At last, when he had finished his pathetic monologue, she had picked up his hand and kissed it before softly saying she was sorry and goodbye. He had screamed at her as she left. She had hurried out the door, her head bowed, tears flowing. Part of him had been glad he had hurt her. Glad that she shared at least some of his pain.
    Remorse. It was almost as bad as the other cancer. His world had dissolved into a routine of endless drinking and morbidly obsessive self pity. He had not returned to Rouen. He remained absent without leave and ended up here, in Paris. He wandered the streets for a while watching the seemingly endless stream of lovers; soldiers on leave with some girl, possibly a prostitute, possibly a nice girl from a good background. Finally he craved a drink and solitude. He found himself in a run-down

area of the city, sought a bar and began to indulge himself in the oblivion of alcohol.

He fell asleep, exhausted and drunk only to be roughly awakened by the proprietor demanding in florid French that the lieutenant leave. *He* wanted to go to bed. So, blearily Robert staggered to his feet, his head swimming dizzyingly, his mouth dry. Somehow he walked out into the rain drenched street and pulled his cap onto his head. It was cold, but the alcohol burned a fire within and he did not notice the chill. Fresh air caused his brain to protest more and in a lurching swirl he half fell into a dark alleyway and vomited in the gutter his hands supporting his weight against a grimy brick wall. God he felt rough! With a great effort he turned himself around and leant backwards, his face upwards allowing the rain to splash onto it.

Unseen and unheard a figure slid into the alley and dissolved into the shadows. It watched the handsome British officer for some minutes and occasionally glanced towards the main thoroughfare, taking note of any passers-by. At this late hour there were none. It was safe and the officer would be carrying money. They usually did.

Robert coughed, groaned and rubbed his face vigorously. Only slowly did he become aware of a voice, a whispered threat and demand for his wallet. He squinted through the rain and the dark trying to focus upon the wiry owner of the voice, but everything remained a blur, even sounds seemed distant and surreal. He did not respond to the demand.

Suddenly he was slammed hard against the wall and nimble hands began plucking at his uniform, searching the pockets. Dimly Robert realised that he was being assaulted, robbed and somewhere in his intoxicated mind he registered outrage and reacted. It would have been better to have let the thief alone, submit to the mugging and awake the next morning, wet cold, with a hangover and little memory of what had happened. But his body reacted almost instinctively only much too slowly. Robert struggled and lunged at the man with an uncoordinated fist. The thief was far too quick and side stepped the drunken attacker with a sneer on his thin lips. However, the sneer hid his frustration. He had hoped the officer too far gone to give him any trouble. It seemed this was not so. He pulled a knife from his belt and as Robert half spun to shake free of the arm that now arrested his escape the thief plunged the steel deep into his abdomen.

Piercing pain brought sobriety to Robert's brain. Acutely aware of his surroundings, of his body slumping against someone who backed away rapidly, allowing him to fall. A deep, aching agony in his guts and with horror he looked down to where, even in the dark he could see his hands clutching wetly at his own stomach. Somehow he registered that he had been stabbed. A metallic taste in his mouth making him feel sick. Fevered hands searching his body, tearing at his clothes and being helpless to stop them. Footsteps running and splashing away. Robert closed his eyes; sweat beaded his brow despite the cold. Everything felt oddly distant, different from the drunkenness of a few minutes ago.

Oh God! Oh God!

Desperately he tried to drag himself from the alley, back into the street. Surely there, someone would find him. Paris is the city that never sleeps. There would be, *must* be somebody. With laboured effort he half crawled towards the dim glow of a gas lamp out there in the real world. Too dim. The light was fading. Robert felt terribly cold, his body shivered uncontrollably. Without warning the light went out. An odd, distant rushing sound filled his ears. A moment of panic assailed him as his body fought to survive and fear of the darkness folded around him. He thought he heard a woman. A beloved, soft voice and through his tears he managed to smile. *It's alright Lily's here.*

The young prostitute was on her way home, her work for the night over and she thanked God for it. She saw a sly looking man appear from the alley and then run for all his life was worth down the street. She had slid into the shadows instinctively. This was not a safe neighbourhood and that man had the look of desperation upon him. Too many times, she had run foul of such fellows. She waited only until the dark swallowed him up and then cautiously she continued her journey. She was tired and wet through. It had been a slow night and once again she found herself thinking she needed a career change. Maybe she could volunteer at one of the hospitals. Become a nurse.

By the lamp post opposite the alley she stopped, her thoughts distracted by a strange dragging and gasping noise. The hairs on the back of her neck rose and her heart began to increase its pace. She glanced around and caught her breath, her hand flying to her mouth in horror. There, at the entrance to the alley, a uniformed and bloody man tried vainly to pull himself to his knees. He fell and immediately she ran towards him. She bent near to his ears and in French offered some words of comfort, but even her untrained eye knew it was useless.

Robert did not recognise the words as French. He knew only that Lily had found him and all would be alright once more. The thief had done him a favour. It had all been a silly mistake. She was with him. He whispered her name and held out a hand.

The prostitute hesitated only briefly before taking the dying man's hand in hers. She looked down into a handsome face, the dark unseeing eyes sparkled brightly for a second and then the light within them faded, the body slumped.

"Aide, secours. Un homme de meurt. Venez vite!" the girl shouted over and over, but it was too late, Robert was already dead.

CHAPTER 46.
October 30th, Number 23 General Hospital, Étaples

Lily smiled along the long row of beds of Number 12 Surgical Ward. Her ward. Her patients.

The last few weeks had been hell. The wounded still pouring in from Loos, battered remnants of humanity, but they had broken the back of it now and the offensive had, seemingly, once more slipped into routine trench warfare. The rush of casualties returned to a steady flow and there was time to look after the boys that reached her surgical ward with the care they deserved. Up until now, she had little time to appreciate and reflect upon her achievement. The fact she had been given a position of acting sister, her own ward. It was an honour and a privilege and though it had meant a move away from her friends she thought it worth the sacrifice. Besides it removed her from temptation, from Alex Thewlis, and it gave her a new direction. The nursing authorities had showed her approbation and she would do her utmost to ensure they did not regret their decision.

It was a difficult ward to manage. The men were badly wounded, some of them hideously so. The pervading aroma of gangrene hung heavily in the air despite the liberal use of carbolic and the open windows. Death stalked this hospital hut with a greedy eye and day and night another soul lost the battle to stay amongst the living. It was hard and one had to detach oneself from the relentless horror. Yet not all was doom and gloom. For every death there were several miraculous recoveries. Men who had lain on the brink of eternity would suddenly return to the mortal world and surprise even the most optimistic of doctors. For all its trials and its harrowing drudgery Lily would not have given up her ward for anything in the world right now.

The ward's orderly, Corporal Briggs, had tried to make life difficult, not approving of so young a ward sister. It had taken the onslaught of the casualties to bring him around and then only reluctantly did he offer the olive branch of comradeship. It did not worry Lily. She knew she would gain his respect some day. Either that or he would request a transfer. So far, after the best part of a month, he had not and so she assumed that he, rather grudgingly, regarded her as more capable than he had first thought. His taciturn moods and awkward challenges had diminished and more often than not he now obeyed her without question even if he did occasionally roll his eyes heavenwards or shuffle away muttering to himself. Grey haired and too old to fight, Briggs was a miserable curmudgeon, yet his heart was in the right place and he cared for the injured men with the tenderness of a mother, even if his demeanour said otherwise. Lily understood his sort. He was hard work, but he worked hard and she strove to gain his regard one way or another.

She wheeled the dressing trolley to the corrugated hut's store room. That duty done for the morning it was time to catch up with her paperwork before they served lunch. Briggs scurried around cleaning up and giving churlish orders to the convalescent soldier sent to assist him. Placing the unused bandages and ointments back on their shelves Lily smiled at the impatient commands from the gruff corporal and emptied the bloody contents of the washbowl into a slop bucket for later removal. No doubt poor Melling would get that unsavoury task after mopping the floors.

"Hello Lily," a soft, familiar voice interrupted her thoughts and she jumped around having not heard the visitor approach.

"Joe! You scared me half to death. I wasn't expecting.... What on earth are you doing here?" she demanded a laugh in her voice that suddenly trailed away as dark foreboding replaced the immediate pleasure of seeing a beloved face. "Oh no..., It's not..., it's not Sam is it?" she begged the colour draining from her face and her hand searching for support.

Joe smiled sadly and shook his head. "No. Last I heard Sam was fine. In fact, I will know for certain soon. They're sending me into the front line. I'll be joining his Battalion as their medic. They lost their last one at Loos," he added with determined jollity.

Lily did not know whether to be relieved or worried. The news that Sam was well was welcome, but to know another brother would be at the Front was not. "Oh Joe. I'm sorry."

"Sorry?" He laughed. "No, I'm rather looking forward to it. Must be mad, but I think I'll feel more useful up there and like I said I'll be with Sam." He looked to the floor searching for an opening, a way to break the news.

"Well, I suppose that's good. I'll have two of you to fret about now though and I should think Dora will be horrified," Lily replied. *There's something else isn't there?* He had come here with something more ominous to tell her.

"Dora doesn't know Lil. Please don't tell her," he blurted fearfully.

"I wouldn't dream of it if you think that best."

He glanced at her catching the disapproval. Lily always thought honesty the only approach. So had he until this war came along. He changed the subject. "Matron said I could take you to lunch."

"Lunch! Oh Joe, I don't have time for lunch. I have my notes to write up and then there's the men's lunch and the MO's rounds, and dressings again... Joe, what is it?" she stopped, knowing this was no social call.

"They gave me a couple of days leave before I join the unit so I thought I'd better come and see you in person." God he was making a mess of this. It was not how he had planned it.

"In person? What do you mean? Is everyone...? It's not Mother or Daddy is it?" He was scaring her now.

"No everyone at home is well. You would have heard otherwise before me anyway, I'm sure. Look Lil...," he stepped forward and took her hands in his. She cocked her head on one side and gazed almost tearfully into his eyes. Something dreadful *had* happened.

"Uh, Sorry Sir, Sister. Didn't mean to barge in on yer," Briggs announced loudly with a hint of glee as he perceived an altogether different encounter.

Flushing Lily snapped back at him, "Briggs please get rid of this slop bucket and send Melling for some more towels I've made a list here," she handed him a chit. "This is my brother, Lieutenant Hepworth, we'll be in my office, but I only want disturbing if it's urgent."

"Yes Sister," Briggs took the chit with an expression of disappointment that he had not stumbled upon something more gossip worthy. He shuffled away and Lily led Joe into the small partitioned room known as Sister's office. Bracing herself for bad news she insisted he sit before she took up her own place behind a battered table piled neatly with paperwork.

Joe removed his hat and played with it nervously while he waited for her to take a seat and compose herself. He watched as she stiffened her posture with determined resolve and hoped that she could remain brave and self-possessed when he told her, for he was sure if she broke down, then he would struggle to remain detached also.

"Are you staying in Étaples?" she asked just as he opened his mouth to speak. Ridiculous small talk. Her way of staying calm. She fought the rising tide of panic within and prayed for strength.

"Er no. In Boulogne, but I'm leaving for the Front tomorrow. Lily...."*God, get it over with man*!

"Yes Joe."

"It's about Robert."

Silence. She simply stared at him. He swallowed back his own rising grief. She saw the emotion playing behind his eyes and her heart did a somersault in her stomach.

"Robert is dead Lil. He was killed in Paris." There he had said it. He wiped his eyes briskly and waited for her response.

"Killed? How?" Quite calm. No emotion. Yet.

"He was stabbed. The authorities say it was a robbery. Apparently it's becoming a bit of a problem. I'm so sorry."

"No. Don't be sorry for me. What about you? He was your best friend. Are you alright?" *Don't cry. Don't give in. There is no time for grief here.*

"Yes, I suppose so. It was a shock. One would think one was safe in Paris, but I suppose nowhere is truly safe is it?" *She took that well. In shock no doubt.*

"No."

"Matron is happy to relieve you if you wish to be alone. Or we could go for a walk. Get some air. Do you need some air?"

"There's no need. I think I need to stay busy. You understand. Thank you for coming to tell me in person. I'm glad you did. Would you think it awfully rude of me though if I asked you to go now?" she replied quietly.

"No, no not at all. I understand. If you change your mind though and want to talk I'll be in the Cafe Anglais this evening. Matron is sympathetic and will place no obstacles in your way," Joe said with a sad smile. *God she's courageous. She must be torn apart inside.*

Lily nodded and stood. She took her brother's hands in hers and squeezed them tightly. "Thank you Joe."

"I'll leave you in peace then." He placed his hat back on his head and leaning across the table kissed her cheek before leaving her alone. Outside the hut he almost bumped into Briggs who saluted him smartly.

"Leaving already Sir? Very busy is Sister," the corporal offered almost apologetically.

Joe looked at the middle-aged soldier and smiled half-heartedly. "Do me a favour Corporal and keep an eye on her will you? I've just given her some bad news and I don't think it's sunk in yet."

"Will do Sir," Briggs answered and watched the serious young officer walk away. He returned to the ward and following a knock against the partition popped his head around the curtain. Lily stared at him, her face ashen.

"Everything alright Sister?"

"Bad news Corporal Briggs."

"Oh. Sorry to hear it ma'am. Is there anything I can do?"

"I don't think so Briggs. We just have to soldier on."

"I know. A nice cup of tea will help. I'll go make you one and don't you move out of 'ere until you've drunk the last drop," the corporal smiled with uncharacteristic friendliness and sympathy.

Tea, the panacea for all ills. Lily smiled back despite the overwhelming grief that surged inside her. "Thank you Briggs."

"Don't mention it Sister. You can call me Jack if y'like." He touched his forehead in a kind of salute and ambled away to the kitchen. Tears flooded into Lily's eyes and still she laughed to herself. Through this despicable tragedy she had just made a new friend. Human nature was certainly an unpredictable beast.

CHAPTER 47.
November 8th, Front Line near Givenchy

Another non-stop moaned overhead disappearing wearily into the distance. Joe glanced up at the ceiling of the first aid post and then back to his pile of papers. *Bloody forms!* Forever piling up on his desk. He barely noticed the subsequent explosion somewhere way behind the lines and did not acknowledge the accompanying tremor of the earth. Instead he scribbled notes onto yet another piece of besmirched paper and shot an occasional peep at the three men remaining from this morning's sick parade. Two were running mild fevers, but would be alright after a rest. The third needed hospital treatment for a nasty gash across his knee. Might even get a trip to Blighty with it if he was lucky. Joe looked at his wristwatch and wondered what was keeping the stretcher bearers. He sighed, sat back and rubbed his sore eyes just as the elusive orderlies hurried into the dug-out. Without getting up he pointed to the knee.

"Took you're bloody time," he muttered.

"Got caught up wi'...," one of the men began.

The MO cut him off. "I don't want to hear your excuses Jessop. Just get that man up to the ADS and don't dawdle. Which means no stopping for a brew or a smoke. Clear?"

"Yes Sir," *Christ, he's in a mood today.* The stretcher bearers hurriedly gathered their charge and gladly staggered from the dug-out with their heavy burden.

Joe stared after them and exhaled loudly once more. He had been a little terse perhaps. Still it would not do them any harm. Keep them on their toes. God, he was in danger of turning into a proper soldier. He smiled sardonically and returned to his notes without enthusiasm.

The distinctive shouts of an NCO and steady tramp of marching feet brought to an abrupt stop signalled the arrival of another customer. It was slow today. The weather fine and cold and the Germans busy shelling behind the lines. A day to catch up. Joe eyed the gas curtain covering the post's entrance, listening with grim amusement at the bellowed commands from the trench outside. The voice was more than familiar yet he still struggled to picture its owner bawling at some unfortunate individual. The curtain lifted.

"In! Left right, left right. Mark time. Halt! Salute the officer!" the sergeant growled at a tall, fresh faced and dull eyed private as the latter marched into the dugout.

Joe stood and assumed an expression of suitable sobriety. He looked to his brother for explanation "Sergeant Hepworth?"

"Private Ibbotson reporting for short arm inspection Sir," Sam replied barely able to keep the smile from his face, his amusement more than obvious in both his tone of voice and the mischievous gleam in his eyes. The brothers strove to avoid eye contact. To do so now would end, for Sam at least, in inappropriate laughter.

Joe raised his eyebrows and covered his mouth with a thoughtful hand. "Is that so? And why Ibbotson did you not come forward this morning at sick parade?" he demanded with serious authority.

The unfortunate soldier flushed scarlet and nervously glanced at the sergeant.

"Answer the lieutenant, Private," Sam snapped. The young man jumped visibly and mumbled his reply.

"Too embarrassed Sir."

"Embarrassed? Ah yes. I see. Well, you should have thought of that before shouldn't you? Did you ever listen to any of your health lectures Ibbotson?" Joe managed to maintain a stern countenance and appear unimpressed.

"Sir?" the private queried his expression now puzzled as well as anxious.

Not too bright. "The lectures on sexually transmitted diseases. Did you listen to them?" the MO reiterated with impatience. Sam sniggered in the background earning a quick reproving stare from his brother. *Juvenile!*

"Yes Sir, but I..." Ibbotson faltered turning puce again.

"But what?"

"But I didn't really understand 'em Sir," the forlorn reply which brought a fit of coughing from the sergeant and a deep sigh from the doctor.

"Well let's have a look then. Drop your trousers and pants. You do realise if this is confirmed that you go on report don't you?"

"Yes Sir." The lad fumbled with the buttons on his trousers, flustered to almost feeble ineptness. He trembled with a mixture of shame and dread. His mates had put the fear of God into him. Told him *it* would turn green and drop off. For three days he had suffered the infernal itching and the gnawing terror before, overcome with extreme anxiety, he had sought his platoon sergeant and confessed his fears.

Sam watched with wicked humour from the corner of the dug-out as a pale backside was revealed and his brother stooped, with lantern in hand, to examine the affected organ. He could not help but chuckle under his breath at the comical scene unfolding. It took all his self control not to laugh out loud. Of course he would have been far more serious if he thought that Ibbotson really did have the clap, but he knew otherwise. This was simply a rotten joke played upon an all too innocent and simple lad by his comrades. Mean, underhand? Most definitely. But good sport all the same and it might teach the idiotic kid a lesson. God, he needed one or two. Too stupid by far. Looked like Joe was taking it seriously enough. Good old Joe. Always the professional, but he had almost laughed hadn't he? When they first came in.

"When did you last have intercourse?" the MO asked.

"Beg y' pardon Sir?" the private responded his eyes riveted on the back wall and his ears burning.

"Sex man! When did you last have sex?" Joe demanded with growing exasperation. The young soldier was hard work and everything looked normal. A bit of irritation caused by lice, but nothing suspicious.

"Er, I dunno. I'm not right sure whether I 'ave Sir. If y' know what I mean," Ibbotson replied with an expression of confusion.

An odd choking sound from the corner told Joe that his brother may collapse into hysterical laughter at any minute. Highly inappropriate he thought and cast a hard scowling stare in his direction. "There is a flask of water on the bench over there Sergeant if you need a drink."

Sam muttered something that might have been a thank you and scurried to the back of the dugout unable to control his humour any longer.

Joe looked heavenwards and sighed again. "Pull your pants up son. There's nothing wrong with you," he said wearily.

Ibbotson looked shocked, then relieved and then puzzled. He hurriedly redressed himself and stood frowning not sure what to do, wanting to ask the doctor questions and too afraid to do so. And where had Sergeant Hepworth gone?

"Ibbotson, you do know that you can't catch venereal disease without having sexual intercourse don't you?" Joe began not unkindly. He kept his voice considerately low not wanting to encourage his brother's puerile amusement any further. It annoyed him that someone in Sam's position had quite obviously found pleasure in the unfortunate private's innocence. Everything annoyed him these days.

"Vener...?" Ibbotson struggled with the terminology.

"The clap, Ibbotson!" Joe enlightened irritably and tried to ignore the guffaw from the far end of his aid post.

"Oh! But what about the itching Sir? The lads said it wa'..." the private slowly worked his way towards understanding.

"Lice. The itching is caused by lice. You do understand what I am telling you don't you son?"

"I think so Sir. Just not used to them big words. So I 'avn't got t' clap then?"

"No."

"An' I won't lose me pay an' stuff?"

"No Private, you won't. I think you can return to your..., whatever it was you were doing before you came here."

"Thank you very much Sir," Ibbotson iterated with genuine happy relief.

"Sergeant Hepworth!" Joe called and in a moment his brother was by his side with sparkling eyes and a not too pleasant smirk on his face.

"Private Ibbotson can go. He is free from infection," the intimation said as well you know.

"Yes Sir," Sam grinned in reply.

"And Sergeant," Joe interrupted before the fiasco of marching the young man out began.

"Sir?"

"Will you stay a moment? I'm sure Ibbotson knows the way back."

Sam hesitated, scrutinised his sibling's face and then with a jerk of his head said, "Clear off lad and no loitering on the way. I'm right on your tail remember."

A moment of silence while the private completed his drill and vanished back into the support trench outside. Once alone the sergeant grinned once more and his brother vented his disapproval.

"That was a low and rotten trick Sam."

"Don't know what you mean," the snappish reply. No respectful Sir. No trace of remorse.

"Oh yes you bloody well do. You knew he didn't have VD, that he couldn't have and still you put him through that. What pleasure do you get from degrading someone?"

"I didn't know. How could I? I don't know what they get up to in their spare time. I resent your implication Joe. Anyway, the kid might have learnt something from it." *Bloody typical you moralising!*

Joe exhaled deeply recognising the obstinate stance and set of his brother's jaw. A lecture would get him nowhere and only cause resentment. "How old is he anyway?"

"Twenty one."

"Seriously?" the MO looked sceptical.

"Yeah. He's old enough to be here. Trouble is he's bloody simple. Thick as pig shit. The Army must be getting desperate if he's the best sort of recruit we can get," Sam grumbled.

"He's just innocent that's all," Joe protested quietly. He thought his sibling insensitive in his assessment.

The sergeant laughed cynically. "He's a bloody halfwit. Can't march in time, can't clean his equipment properly. He's a fucking liability. Still, he won't last long. Just hope he doesn't take anyone half decent with him," he spat venomously.

Joe stared astounded. This was an unexpected revelation. "That's a bit harsh isn't it?"

"You think so? I'm sick to death of the kid. He's a liability and the sooner he goes the better for everyone. Now if that's through sickness or a bullet through the head I don't really care."

"You callous bastard! I never thought.... *Jesus* Sam! This is a man's life you're talking about," the doctor retorted angrily. He could not believe his ears. Had never thought his brother to be so hard. Tough yes, but not downright unfeeling.

Sam simply sneered, the insult half expected. "I have thirty-six lives to look after and if sacrificing one for the sake of the rest is all that is likely to happen then I'm not going to lose sleep over it. Yes it's callous, but I can live with that. It's not like it's much of a wasted life is it? I'll tell you something else as well. That lad will run. He hasn't got it up here to cope with things when it gets tough." He tapped his head with a forefinger. "I'll not let any of my men risk their lives for the likes of him. So, the sooner he goes the better.

"Anyway what's up with you? Bloody miserable these days. You'd have had a laugh too a few weeks ago. Thought you were becoming a proper soldier," Sam's tone softened. There had been a change in Joe. He was much more morose than he used to be. The trenches could do that to any man, but Sam thought there was a different reason. He offered his brother an opening to talk about it.

The MO ran a weary hand through his hair and sighed. He did not want to talk about Robert. He had not told anyone of the circumstances behind his friend's death. He did not think they would understand, yet the burden of that knowledge weighed heavy in his mind. He both grieved for Robert and felt ashamed of his desertion. He did not understand what had possessed his closest friend to act this way. He had been the first to hear of the tragic death, his name and unit on a scrap of paper not stolen by the thief. He was the one the authorities contacted and informed of the details. It had taken some persuasion to stop them from telling all to the surgeon's parents.

"Nothing is wrong. I'm just tired that's all, as we all are," Joe replied at length. Sam studied him shrewdly.

"Is it Rob?" he asked intuitively.

Joe hesitated and shrugged. "I..., find it hard to accept, yes."

"He won't be the last you lose. Best put him out of your mind. No point moping about him," the matter-of-fact response.

"Moping? Christ Sam, Rob was my best friend. What about poor Lily, he was her fiancé? How is she coping?"

"Lily broke off the engagement this summer, didn't you know? She'll manage. She's tough."

Joe gawped in shocked surprise. Suddenly everything became clearer. Robert's unlikely desertion, the drinking. "*She called it off.* Oh God! Poor Rob." With a groping hand he sat down heavily on his chair.

"You alright Joe?" No answer. "Joe?"

"Yes. Yes, I'm just fine," a snappy reply, the anger welling within. "And what about you? Don't you feel anything for Rob either? He was supposed to be your friend too."

"Hey, that's uncalled for. Of course I was upset, but I've lost more friends than you can even imagine. There's no point getting cut up about another," Sam bit back. It wasn't his bloody fault that Robert was dead.

"God, you really are a hard bastard aren't you?" Joe accused without thinking. It was unfair and unwarranted, but his own pain blinded him to the hurt he caused.

Sam's jaw set ridged and his lips pulled into an angry thin line. He'd had enough of this. "Are we finished, Sir?"

Joe nodded. "Yes I rather think we are Sergeant," he replied not knowing what else to say, his anger subsiding into miserable resignation. He did not understand. Could not reconcile the Robert he had known with one so desperately depressed that his only escape was a bottle of brandy in a seedy bar in Paris leading to a brutal, pointless death. Who would have thought something like this could have happened to the brightest and best of men? And now Joe had fallen out with his brother, who in his own, clumsy way had only been trying to help. With an increasing sense of despondency he watched Sam leave and returned to his never ending pile of forms.

CHAPTER 48.
November 28th – 30th, Front Line, Givenchy

Evening 28th

Hard, penetrating frosts had rendered the trenches quite tolerable though bitterly raw. Still, dry and cold was preferable to the wet and mud which, somehow made one feel even colder and decidedly less comfortable. Dry and cold would not have been bad at all if the winter clothing had reached the Battalion before they relieved the Second Bedfords in the line. Unfortunately it had not and as One Platoon, A Company settled down to a warming stew dinner no one, for once, complained about their rations. Anything that could increase body heat was entirely welcome.

Sam Hepworth mopped up the remnants of this heartening repast with a hunk of stale bread and stuffed it into his mouth in a manner that would have caused his mother great consternation. As if the thought drifted into his mind he smiled wryly, ran an almost clean rag over his mess tin and packed it away. No point sitting about here. Too damned cold! He needed to be moving about. Besides, he wanted a quick word with young Mister Wise before the men were told off into working parties for the bloody miners.

No one was happy with this posting. When they were not being shelled they were helping the Royal Engineers of the 176th Tunnelling Company, acting as labourers, carrying sandbags filled with earth back from tunnels or bringing equipment up. For most of the men working underground was an alien experience and not one they relished. It did not help when someone reported Fritz doing the same damn thing. Everyone was nervous and resentful that the task of manning this active part of the line had fallen to them. As if they had not been through enough this year! About time some of these New Army battalions faced a busy front. About time the few remaining Regulars were given a decent bloody rest!

Such were the grouses the men muttered in low, grumbling voices through the long dark hours on sentry duty or struggling in the frost or mud to repair shell blasted trenches. It was what they complained of as yet another comrade was stretchered away, another pitiful bundle of shattered humanity, maimed and mutilated or dead. It was what they grumbled about as the miners of the Tunnelling Company changed shift after just six hours underground leaving their infantry colleagues still sweating and cursing with loads of muck or explosives in the dank, dark of their subterranean galleries. Tombs the men called them. Sources of claustrophobic anxiety, of fear of being buried alive, trapped under piles of French earth, slowly suffocating to death.

Morale had definitely taken a dip of late. Hardly surprising given what the Battalion had been through. They had escaped lightly at Loos. A thought that Sam recollected with bitter irony as he remembered the last of his closest comrades. One dead and the other – well, God only knew. Missing, presumed taken prisoner, but Snowy might be gone too; he *had* been wounded. Did the Germans care for injured prisoners? He did not know, but he hoped so.

He cast the memories aside and turned his mind to the present, setting off to find the platoon commander. His concern remained Ibbotson and the impact of the private's childlike fears on the troops. It still amazed Sam how the man had ended up with a Regular battalion, let alone a front line infantry unit. Ibbotson should never have even made it to France. Far better suited to the labour corps, helping farm land back in Blighty. It would be better for everyone if he could be got rid of, transferred to base, anything but remain here.

Sam was not vindictive. This was not some personal vendetta against a man he did not like. In fact, he thought Ibbotson an amiable bloke, but he was no soldier. Not tough enough, aggressive enough or bright enough and God knows, that was saying something as half the Battalion possessed only a rudimentary education at best. Yet there is a difference between unschooled and stupid.

Unfortunately the private's lack of aptitude conflicted with the military requirements. He struggled to understand the necessity of rules and discipline. He became alarmed far too easily, growing agitated and unable to hide or control his fear under any kind of bombardment; even when the shells flying over were from British batteries aimed at Fritz. He had to be bullied and coaxed by his comrades and NCOs when working underground because he could not contain his claustrophobia. Ibbotson was a liability and his constant jumpy terror drove everyone mad, made them all nervous and added to the increasingly depressive atmosphere.

And then there was the scratching. Everyone was lousy. Everyone suffered the constant torturous torment from unwanted insect visitors. But whereas everyone else managed to control their urge to scratch furiously at irritated skin, Ibbotson did not. He rubbed himself continuously, often frenziedly like a mangy dog, breaking his raw skin. He even scratched himself on parade. It was an embarrassment to his platoon commander, his sergeant and his section corporal. It was inexcusable yet he did not learn from punishment. It was another example of his inability to maintain self discipline, another childish trait. And when he began his aggravated scratching it reminded everyone of their own discomfort and that niggling, interminable itch became maddeningly unbearable for all.

Already there were signs of resentment against the simpleton, exclusion at best, outright bullying at worst. It did not add up to a close knit unit of fraternal comradeship and ultimately that could be dangerous either for Ibbotson, or worse, for more useful members of the platoon. He *had* to be got rid of.

Sam hurried along the trench, squeezing by men finishing their meal, and found Second Lieutenant Wise emerging from a smoky dug-out in a close support trench, an officers' funk hole.

"Eppy! I was just on my way down to join you. Smoke?" the cheery subaltern offered forth a silver case of cigarettes.

"Er.., thank you Mister Wise," the sergeant accepted momentarily thrown off his purpose. Officers were certainly metamorphosing into a different kind of animal these days. One hardly knew where one stood with them anymore. Not that he thought it a bad change. Far from it. He selected a cigarette and allowed Wise to light it for him. He inhaled and enjoyed the rush of nicotine and the far superior taste of a more distinguished brand.

"Is something amiss Eppy?"

Sam exhaled and shook his head. "No, not exactly. I was wondering if I could have a word about Private Ibbotson, Sir."

A frown clouded the young officer's face. He looked behind to the dug-out with some concern and then moved a few steps away. "Why, has something happened?" he asked in a deliberately low voice. He knew only too well the problems with Ibbotson, the fact he was a thorn in Hepworth's side and a potential embarrassment to himself.

"No..., not yet. But...,"

A sudden and urgent tramping of feet caused both men to look around and Sam was rudely pushed aside by a mud caked, red faced lieutenant wearing the badge of a Royal Engineer. Out of breath and sweating profusely despite the cold the newcomer wiped a grimy hand smearing more mud across his already besmirched face and demanded, "I need to see your OC now!"

For a second Wise hesitated, irritated by the interruption, annoyed at the bad manners, but the filthy engineer was exasperatedly impatient and any apology or attempt at civility from him seemed, at this time, unlikely. It was imperative he see the officer commanding and now!

"Come on man, don't dawdle. The bloody Germans are beneath the Warren!" he burst out at the same time flapping his arms like a stricken chicken. It would have been comical if it were not so serious. He shot a furtive glance towards the sergeant he had just roughly pushed out of the way, briefly regretted his outburst and then ignored the man. *Too late now*. What was said was said. Too bloody bad if the sergeant blabbed to his mates. They'd all find out soon enough anyway.

Wise blanched and dropped his cigarette onto the frozen mud, stamping it out. He acknowledged the engineer, and turned to Sam, "Later Eppy. Discretion if you please."

Sam nodded his head once, a cold apprehension trickling along his spine as he assimilated the information and understood its potential implication. The entire Battalion were distributed around the Warren; some in the firing trench, others resting in support lines just behind. If the Germans were tunnelling underneath them it could only mean one thing; that they were planning to blow them to kingdom come.

"Of course Sir," he said and watched the two officers rapidly vanish along the support trench and into the dark. His preoccupation with Ibbotson forgotten, he trudged back to his platoon forcing the unwanted images of a premature burial to the back of his mind. He began the usual routine; setting the men to work, some to assist the miners, some to make good any damage to trenches, the sentries changed. Regardless of his promise to Wise there was no point telling them anything yet anyhow. Knowing Fritz was burrowing beneath them, probably piling his tunnel high with explosives, would do no good at all. They would only become windy. At this moment in time ignorance was bliss. Sam only wished he too had no inkling of what lie beneath his feet. *Damn the bloody miners!* Before they came one only had to worry about death from the air, now it lurked underground as well.

29th

Dawn, or thereabouts and the men knew of the threat. The added tension was palpable as they stood-to knowing their lives may depend upon the success or failure of the hastily prepared countermine the 176th Tunnelling Company were due to detonate any minute now.

A reluctant platoon from B Company waited behind the rows of their comrades who, despite standing to arms, cast wary and surreptitious glances at the pale faced group as if to say, rather you than me pal. The platoon had the unenviable task of running forward once the mine was blown to occupy and secure the crater before Fritz could react. They were divided into bombers with bayonet man and working party armed with shovels and picks. The latter would repair any damage done, connect the resulting crater to the trench and if necessary, position loop holes. The chances of enemy retaliation with mortars and machine gun fire once the explosion subsided were high; the job of securing the crater not one any would wish for. As the order to take up position filtered along the platoon, and they began to squeeze their way through the narrow confines of the trench, many a man they passed muttered a word of good luck or administered a bolstering pat on the back.

Sam squinted at his watch in the thin, grey half-light struggling to read the dial clearly. He looked up and down the section of trench where his men stood-to, rifles propped through loopholes, their collective breath steaming in the frigid air. Not all had their eyes ahead, towards the dismal wasteland of No-Man's-Land. Some were still watching the retreating backs of the work party. He hurried along the line gruffly shouting instructions to keep eyes forward.

"Eyes front Braithwaite. Fritz isn't going to come from behind you is he lad?" he chastised.

"No Sarn't," the mumbled reply as Braithwaite obeyed and his sergeant passed by lambasting, in his peculiar measured way, others whose morbid curiosity had got the better of discipline.

Sam reached the last traverse in his section, the men detailed to work on the crater were gone, his own fidgeted with anxious anticipation of the explosion and its possible aftermath. Second Lieutenant Wise smiled grimly his expression betraying his nervousness.

"Let's hope it works Sir," Hepworth offered with a half hearted grin. God, how he hated this place with its constant mining and countermining, where the earth reverberated too often and swallowed up troops piecemeal and buried miners in the bowels of their own tunnels. This was no longer a soldier's war. This was an unimagined Hell!

"If it doesn't Eppy we'll be shaking hands with the Devil," Wise answered with uncharacteristic melancholy. He glanced at his watch.

Suddenly the ground shook, small avalanches fell from the trench walls and a deep rumbling roar followed as the precautionary camouflet detonated. Not a big explosion, but enough to throw muck high into the air and scatter it widely over the startled infantry standing ready for any ensuing action. Instinctively they covered their heads until the rain of debris ceased. Orders echoed all around to make ready to repel the enemy.

Waiting with bated breath they stared across No-Man's-Land trying not to contemplate what might happen if the charge had not worked, if the German mine was still intact. Rather a full on frontal attack than that. Prayers were muttered by men whose only commune with God took place when fear threatened to overturn their usual vaunting atheism.

Silence! For a long, painfully long time, nothing other than distant artillery some miles away. The sounds of men working carried eerily on the still morning air, the clinks of spades on rock, of muttered oaths and clipped, concise orders. On and on the quiet yawned until at last a number of mortars sent louder shouts to take cover as they soared into the air with their characteristic thunk. A number of small detonations from the vicinity of the crater reciprocated by a short, but rapid, volley of rifle fire before the stillness descended once more.

For another hour the Infantry stood-to arms, sweating in the chilly air. With each infinite minute their confidence grew and their apprehension subsided. It had worked. They had not been blown to pieces. The German mine was dead and buried. Relief! At half past eight the order went around to stand down for breakfast. The threat had passed. It began to rain.

"For God's sake hold him still! Lowden, keep his damned arms out of the way," Joe shouted at an orderly as the soldier on his treatment bench thrashed about in a paroxysm of semi-conscious fear and pain. A large mortar splinter stuck out from his right thigh, it pierced the muscle and had lodged in the bone. The man was heavily dosed with morphine, but it did not prevent him from fighting three orderlies holding him as the doctor attempted to remove the offending shrapnel. Instead it made him insensible to instruction and incapable of recognising the agony that burned into his leg was a result of someone trying to help him.

"*Jesus Christ!* Shit, this is a bloody mess. Donal, get me some ether. I can't do a bloody thing with him struggling like this," Joe demanded agitatedly. "Damn thing's wedged well in."

The Irishman scuttled away while two others held the unfortunate private fast. He returned in less than a minute equipped with a small dark bottle and a gauze pad which he placed lightly over the patient's mouth and nose and looked to the medical officer, poised.

"Just a few drops Donal, I don't want him too far under. Hold him fast lads; he's likely to fight it."

Fallon administered a small quantity of colourless, aromatic liquid to the gauze. The private's eyes widened in alarm; the breath snatching quality of the anaesthetic bringing a new terror to his half sensible brain. Lowden and his colleague strained to prevent the man from tearing the gauze from his face with clawing hands and leaping from the bench despite his injury. Slowly the ether took effect and the heaving body fell still, the tussle over. With a sigh of relief Joe straightened and smiled at his sweating assistants.

"That's better Sir," Fallon grinned back and Lowden laughed, wiping his brow.

"Let's work fast," the doctor suggested. "Better keep hold of his shoulders Yardley, just in case he wakes up when I yank this thing free." Yardley nodded, glanced at Lowden and pressed his weight against the unconscious patient's upper torso, his face grim with concentration while the MO wrestled with the splinter. In less than a minute the foreign object was removed, the wound cleaned with water and doused in iodine powder in an attempt to prevent infection. There had been no arterial bleed only a slow venous ooze. A good sign.

The private groaned dully, slowly ascending back to the light as Fallon expertly finished the dressing and Joe wiped bloody hands on an equally gory rag. It made all the difference having the efficient Irish corporal back with him. Joe found the other orderlies wanting both in skill and compassion. It did not help, of course, that most of them were Battalion men, bandsmen schooled in battlefield first aid and little else. They were good workers, well disciplined and cared for their charges in their own rough and ready way, but they were not a patch on Fallon. It had taken Joe some time to persuade his superiors to release the corporal from the ADS, but in the end his persistence had paid off.

"Alright lads, let's get him out of here," the doctor said while tying a label to the casualty's tunic. He watched Lowden and Yardley carry their burden away for despatch to the ADS and beyond and then sat heavily behind his makeshift desk and began filling in paper work. It had been a busy day. The morning had seen a spate of minor injuries resulting from enemy retaliation to the mine explosion as well as the usual number of sick men, trench fever mainly, and a few who were obviously swinging the lead.

To be fair they were all exhausted and Joe felt a certain pity for the weary soldiers who pathetically tried their luck by feigning illness. Unluckily for them, he had learned a lot since those days on the Sussex Downs. Yet Joe had not hardened totally and in his first aid post four somnolent boys lingered, oblivious to the world, the constant noise of men and warfare. He glanced across at their still forms, huddled haphazardly against the wall at the far side of the dug-out. It never ceased to amaze him that men could sleep anywhere and in any position, even standing up, if they were tired enough. He smiled grimly to himself and decided to leave the boys for a while yet. They would be more use to their superiors if they were rested and there was not much happening. No one had come looking for them.

Maybe he was being soft, but from what he had seen and learned this Battalion was nearly done in. They needed more than a few hours sleep; they needed to be pulled out of the line and sent back to rest for a few weeks at least. They were carrying more than a handful of wounded men and a number who had returned in a less than fully fit state from base hospitals and convalescence camps, his brother amongst them. Joe knew Sam still suffered headaches even after all these months.

"Cup of tea Sir," Fallon placed a tin mug on the table bringing the doctor from his brooding thoughts.

"Thank you Donal. What time is it? My watch seems to have stopped," Joe asked squinting at his wristwatch and listening with it close to his ear.

"A little after seven Sir. Bit of activity up front," the corporal replied.

"Is there? I thought is seemed rather quiet."

"No, I mean there's something afoot Sir. Engineers are preparing to blow some mines early. By morning I heard. Something to do with a couple of deserters telling the CO that our sausage eating friends are planning to blow up the Warren," Fallon enlightened.

"Really? I thought they'd countered that threat earlier," the MO sat back, his eyes wide in surprise, his mind rapidly turning to his brother and the other men in the part of the line nicknamed the Warren. "Are they getting the men out?"

The Irishman shrugged. "Don't t'ink so Sir. From what I can gather they've got everyone carrying up explosives. It's proper busy up there. Apparently this morning's blast didn't do much."

Joe would have asked more, had questions piling into his brain faster than he could turn them into words, but he was interrupted by an unknown and very cheery, well spoken voice dragging his attention from worrying thoughts of mines, to the entrance of the dug-out.

"Hello there! Do I have the pleasure of addressing Lieutenant Hepworth?"

"'Ullo, Devil Dodger Sir," Donal muttered with amusement.

The doctor stared passed Fallon at a slim, tall figure standing in front of the gas curtain. "That's correct. How can I help?" he asked curiously.

The figure strode forward and held out a long, slender fingered hand. Joe shook it surprised to be greeting a dog-collared officer, an army chaplain. A man in his late thirties or early forties with bright, intelligent grey-green eyes and oiled or greasy brown hair. The clergyman wore no cap, it was tucked under his left arm and his pink, scrubbed face was devoid of the ubiquitous moustache.

"So pleased to meet you. The name's Graham, Simon if you will. The CO suggested I introduce myself. I rather think he wishes to pass the responsibility of looking after me to you. Sorry about that. It's not inconvenient is it? I'm not intruding? I'm not really familiar with trench life yet, but I'm ready and willing to learn," the chaplain rambled happily, looking around at the same time.

"Er, no, you're not intruding. We've just finished with the day's work. It's likely to be quiet for a while now unless our friends across the wire decide to change their habits. Sorry, I'm a little taken aback. No one said we were getting a new padre. I presume you're here for a visit?" Joe tried not to sound disapproving though he felt certain he had failed as a cloud flickered across the newcomer's face. It was so unusual to see a Church of England clergyman at the Front and the last thing he needed now was a sightseer.

"Goodness, a visit, no. I believe in administering to my flock Doctor, much as you do I suspect. I cannot see what earthly good I could do the men if I'm not prepared to share at least some of their hardships. I hope you don't mind, but the CO suggested that I bunk with you. I think he was rather shocked that I asked to stay."

"Yes, I rather expect he was Mr Grah..., er Simon. Your presence will be a bit of a shock to both the officers and the men. We never saw much of our last padre up here. Always stayed behind the lines. Instructions from the Church he said. The men called him the Holy Ghost," Joe laughed warming to the affable chaplain.

"Holy Ghost?" Simon queried catching the amused glint in the eye of the quietly respectful orderly by Hepworth's side.

"Er, yes. Sorry. Soldier's humour. Like the Divine Spirit they never saw him. It took faith to believe in his existence," Joe explained catching Fallon's expression and fought the urge to burst into inappropriate laughter. However, Graham did so and uproariously, causing both men to stare with shocked amusement.

"Well that is a shame," the amiable cleric said at last. "I hope I will serve them better. Would it be awfully impudent of me if I asked for a quick tour around? Is it too late? I am happy to wait until morning if it is."

"No, it's not too late. Better at night. It's quieter, but the men will be busy. I'll be snowed under in the morning with the fallout from tonight's labours and the sick parade. But first let Corporal Fallon fix you up with a cup of tea and sort you a bunk next to mine. Corporal?"

"Sugar in your tea Sir?" Donal asked.

"Thank you, yes."

"This way Sir. Doctor sleeps back here," the Irishman led the Chaplain to the rear of the first aid post and Joe set to finishing his paperwork with oddly renewed optimism.

Donned in rain coats with collars turned up against the cold Joe led the Reverend Simon Graham through the mud and heavy rain into the firing trench. They had already toured the support lines, looked into fetid dug-outs where up to a dozen or more soldiers huddled to catch a few hours sleep. Already the chaplain had lost some of his jolly humour and his perpetual smile had been replaced by frowning contemplation. He had not expected such dire conditions, such wretched squalor. Still, Joe had to admit he was impressed that his companion managed to brighten whenever they met anyone, that he had a few words to pass with all regardless of rank. Neither did the clergyman appear fazed by the obviously incredulous stares that met his arrival, or the uttered oaths quickly and disconcertedly followed by an apology. That the Battalion was unused to seeing a man of God at the Front was more than evident and their astonishment escaped them, more often than not, in a blasphemous exclamation. Yet Graham took it all in his stride.

They turned a traverse and bumped into a young second lieutenant in close conversation with a sergeant. Both men looked up and failed to hide their astonishment at seeing a chaplain accompanying the medical officer.

"Mister Wise, may I introduce our new padre. This is Mister Graham," Joe announced loudly as a minenwerfer exploded somewhere nearby.

Instinctively the chaplain ducked his head, his eyes wide with shock rapidly followed by a distinct flush of embarrassment that he was glad the dark covered up when he noticed the other men had barely flinched. He shook the subaltern's hand. "Not quite used to this yet," he admitted apologetically.

"It takes a while," Wise replied with a grin.

"And this is Sergeant Hepworth," Joe continued with a half smile at his sibling's unhidden expression of utter amazement.

"Sergeant," Graham thrust his hand forward and Sam hesitated briefly before taking it. It was not only unusual to see a padre at the Front, but one was also expected to treat them as officers and shaking hands was definitely outside of the expected military etiquette.

"Hepworth? You share the same name. What a coincidence," the chaplain commented innocently.

"Brothers Sir," Sam responded smiling broadly.

"Really? Well I never." No other comment. A refreshing change.

"Are you planning to continue along the firing bays Doctor?" Wise asked breaking a momentary silence.

"Er, well yes that was the plan. Is there a problem?" Joe answered.

"No not really, but there are a few places one needs to be careful. You ought to have a guide. Problem is I need to go check on..., er some of my men. Perhaps you should allow Sergeant Hepworth to accompany you. Eppy?" Wise turned to his sergeant.

"Certainly Sir," Sam acknowledged and shouldered his rifle in readiness to act as escort.

"We wouldn't wish to inconvenience anyone Mister Wise. I'm sure we can manage." Joe felt certain they were interrupting something. He perceived a trace of resentment or rather intolerance and frustration in the platoon commander's demeanour. It was politely hidden, but there nevertheless. His brother, on the other hand, merely seemed vaguely amused.

"Not at all. I can spare Hepworth for a half hour. I'm sure your tour will take no longer than that." A barely veiled suggestion that it should not. Wise dipped his head close to Sam's good ear and whispered some instruction to which the reply was a grave nod. "Well then gentlemen I shall leave you in Hepworth's more than capable hands." He bowed his head formally with a gracious smile.

"Thank you. Well, lead the way then Sergeant," Joe requested with his usual discomfort at addressing his brother as a subordinate. It was something that never appeared to bother Sam though, who politely waited while Graham also offered his thanks to Wise, before turning to trudge along the crenulated maze of trench.

They tramped along duckboards slippery with rain and mud, slithering occasionally in the dark, fumbling around traverses and over obstacles the sergeant somehow sensed rather than saw. In each bay, the chaplain stopped to pass a word or two with astonished sentries, to impressively chat to each man as if he had known them for years. He laughed easily with the men and after they had recovered from the shock of his appearance and friendly, unmilitary banter they responded in kind. It was evident already that the Reverend Graham, if he stayed, would be good for morale.

"May I have a look?" the chaplain asked indicating to a loophole in one bay. The addressed sentry looked uncertain for a moment, more because of the polite request than anything else. His eyes automatically drifted to those of his sergeant, who smirked before stepping in.

"Use the periscope Sir, it's safer. I know it's dark but Fritz has a habit of occasionally raking the parapet with machine gun bullets," Sam indicated the trench periscope and the private stood aside to allow access. Graham smiled his thanks and peered with one eye closed through the crude contraption taking in a sombre view of No-Man's-Land.

If the dark had persisted he would have seen nothing only black silhouettes against a slightly less black sky, but as he stared a flare fizzed into life casting the desolate ground in eerie, monochromic light. He stood back gazing up at the flare and then peered once more through the lens. Joe sighed and tried to catch his brother's eye, but Sam was watching the padre intently, studying his response.

For a brief few seconds Simon saw the cratered hell that stretched between this trench and the German line beyond. He saw the thick tangles of barbed wire, the shattered remains of a farm; dead, grotesquely contorted cattle and in the midst, just before the star shell faded, he thought he saw the remains of a number of German infantry. He stood back rapidly as darkness descended once more, clearly shocked. This was his first sight of the real Front; his first realisation of the horrors it held. He had seen the dead and dying back at base, in hospitals, in his own parish even at home. But this was his first sight of such dehumanising brutality. His face blanched, he felt the blood drain away and once more was thankful for the dark.

"Are those men's bodies still out there, on the wire?" he asked quietly and gazed from the sentry, to Joe, to the sergeant.

"Fritz attempted a raid a couple of nights ago, before we moved back up. That's what's left of them Sir," Sam replied matter-of-factly. *Welcome to the war Sir.*

"And they will just stay there? Unburied?" the incredulous question.

Sam shrugged. "Depends whether the enemy wish to risk fetching them in Sir. Not a wise move to walk out into No-Man's-Land. Likely to end up the same as those poor bug..., devils Sir."

"You mean our men would shoot at anyone attempting to collect their dead?" Graham asked disbelievingly, his voice becoming quieter.

"Yes Sir."

The chaplain stared hard at the sergeant his mouth agape in disgust and horror. "But that's inhuman!"

"It's war Sir," Sam corrected laconically his tone soft as if humouring a child.

"Shall we move on?" Joe suggested sensing the need to interrupt. There was no way Graham would comprehend the simple, cold facts of warfare. It was something he had failed to master himself and he remained constantly both amazed and dismayed by his brother's and all the troops' ability to accept this horror with nonchalance and even, on occasion, grim humour. He understood it was a coping strategy, but it took some getting used to. Simon's expression of complete abhorrence and angry disbelief signified that the chaplain did not understand at all. Not yet.

Sam took the hint and commenced along the next traverse. Wordlessly the two officers followed, both lost in different thoughts. They entered the next firing bay and Sam put up a hand to halt their progress. He caught the inquisitive gawp from one of two men positioned by a loophole. The other carefully peered through it and dropped down turning to face the visitors on hearing their approach.

"Willy still there?" Sam questioned.

"Aye, reckon so Sarn't. Quiet though now, the bugger. Uh, sorry Padre, Doctor Sir. Didn't si thi there," the observer offered an apology with a grin that said he knew well enough but did not truly care.

The sergeant sneered at the response before explaining. "There's a sniper got his sights lined on this loophole. He's been there all day. You'd think he would have given up by now. He can't see a thing in the dark, but Willy doesn't work like that. He'll stay all night if he can and take occasional pot shots, especially when a flare goes up. He's hoping that just at that moment someone might pass this loophole. It's a better target than most. A communication trench joins just around this next bend and troops have to pass this way to get to their positions. Very patient man is our friend Willy."

"And are these men simply checking if he's still there?" Graham asked after a second or two in contemplation.

Sam smirked again his expression unseen. "Partly. If a light goes up though they'll be hoping Willy shows himself, or at least gives his position away. Willy isn't the only one who can shoot straight Sir."

"Oh..., I see. Of course," the chaplain mumbled feeling foolish and even more horrified. This life was simply dreadful! For a fleeting moment he wondered whether he had the strength or even desire to administer this wayward flock he had inherited. He had no idea their world would be so devoid of compassion or that his sheep would be so hard-bitten. So much for the glory of war. This was cold, premeditated murder at all levels. He shuddered.

"Perhaps we should return now and let Sergeant Hepworth get on with his work. I know he must have a busy night ahead of him," Joe suggested tactfully reading the situation well.

The pounding of footsteps and splashing of water announced the arrival of someone in great haste and a flustered, out of breath, soldier skidded to an ungainly halt in front of them, "Sarn't, Sarn't..., uh! Excuse me Doctor, Sir, er Padre...," the private stammered clumsily. Suddenly he was not certain whom he should address and his wide eyes roved from one man to another.

"What is it Collins?" Sam demanded.

The soldier snapped his attention back to his sergeant and passed on his message. "Mister Wise needs you at tunnel three Sarn't. It's Ibbotson. 'E's gone bloody bonkers. Won't let anyone near 'im. 'E's flattened Corporal 'Oldsworth and Charlie Benson and t' RE are going nuts. Want to finish chargin' it Sarn't. Mister Wise asked if y'd come quick like."

"I'm sorry Sir, Mister Graham, you'll have to excuse me." Typical that something like this should happen now. Unsurprising that Ibbotson was involved. Sam frowned and wished someone had acted sooner. Then when had the Army ever listened to common sense?

"We'll come with you Sergeant," Joe suggested.

"I don't think that will be necessary Sir," Sam replied. *God, all I want is an entourage!*

"On the contrary. It would seem there might be some injuries. I think I should come at the very least. Mister Graham may also be of assistance," the doctor reasoned.

I doubt that! Sam wavered. He thought the officers more likely to be hindrance rather than a help, yet it would not do to say so or argue. He was wanted now and so consequently he nodded his head in reluctant agreement.

Moving rapidly with Collins in the lead they wound their way out of the firing trench, into a communication line and through a bewildering maze of interconnecting passages to what appeared to be a dug-out entrance. Little wonder they named this place the Warren Graham thought to himself as he plodded behind the others, slipping on wet boards, totally lost. There was no way he would find his way back to the first aid post without assistance. He struggled to keep up and eventually slithered to a halt, out of breath, the rain water trickling uncomfortably down his neck. Peering through the gloom he was surprised to see a large number of muck encrusted men gathered around the dug-out entrance and a lieutenant of the Royal Engineers with a decidedly flustered looking Mister Wise. The corps officer puffed himself up to his full height on the arrival of Sergeant Hepworth and turned his frustration and annoyance upon the unfortunate NCO.

"About bloody time! I assume this damned idiot is your responsibility. Get him out of my bloody tunnel. You infantry are supposed to assist my men not damned well compromise the whole operation. I haven't spent the last...,"

"If you excuse me Sir, I think I should apprise Sergeant Hepworth of the situation in order that he may be of assistance to you," Wise interrupted the lieutenant with firm politeness. The engineer looked affronted but conceded, with a wave of his hand, that the subaltern take over. He folded his arms across his chest and gazed with steely, impatient anger as the story was told.

"Ibbotson seems to have lost his nerve underground Eppy. I know, it's not surprising, you were right. However, the situation is grave. The RE need this mine finished before three this morning. That doesn't give us much time. Ibbotson has barricaded himself in with two other men, whom I think may be injured. He's been making a lot of noise and therefore it is likely that the Germans know of the tunnel's existence by now. I assume you understand what that might mean...," Wise paused and licked his lips. "We need to get the men out quickly. I know Ibbotson looks up to you. I've already tried. It's getting desperate Eppy."

Sam listened, his mind rapidly assimilating the gravity of the situation. The longer this went on the higher the risk the enemy would blow their own mine before the engineers could, with the chance they would kill a good number of British troops by doing so. He looked to the tunnel entrance with reluctance and knew he had little choice.

"It's unlike Ibbotson to be violent Sir. May I ask what happened? It might help in dealing with him," he asked.

"Oh for God's sake man. Just get on with it!" the engineer cried with exasperation. *"Bloody infantry!"*

"I'm not sure Eppy. I think the miners were ragging him pretty hard. Trying to scare him..., you know. He seems to have just snapped. I should never have asked you to place him on this job," Wise muttered lowly out of earshot of anyone else.

Sam smiled grimly. "Don't worry Sir, I'll try and get him out." He hitched his rifle higher on his shoulder and made to enter the tunnel.

"No bloody point taking that in there. Not enough room to swing a cat in the tunnel. *Christ!*" the RE lieutenant remonstrated, pointing at the Lee Enfield.

"Better leave it with me Eppy," Wise suggested.

Sam pursed his lips angrily and handed his weapon to the officer. "Better get Doc Hepworth to prepare for casualties, just in case Sir and sort out some men to help. I'll go in alone first. No point in risking too many of us is there?" he suggested wishing he was anywhere else but here, now. With a sigh he disappeared behind the gas curtain and waited as his eyes were assailed by the relative brightness of candle light. Rapidly the glare dimmed to a flickering yellow stretching away for what seemed an eternity into the long, steep and narrow incline of tunnel number three. At least it was not dark in here, just gloomy, oppressive and stale.

Ridiculously his heart beat fast, an unwelcome response to the knowledge that he was heading deep underground. It was a sensation he fought to control, a fluttering that hinted at panic not too far away, of a childhood phobia he had never quite conquered despite those adventures in the old lead mines above Pateley Bridge with his brothers. Bravado. He had always been scared. Tried to hide it by terrifying Frank instead. But always when Frank ran out screaming, secretly he had wanted to follow and only his desire to maintain his tough, couldn't-care-less attitude in front of Joe had prevented him. Now he shuddered and with his mouth dry and heart pounding in his ears, he stooped to avoid banging his head on the low ceiling and crept into the bowels of the earth.

After about forty yards or so the lights dived downwards, plummeting into an inky abyss up which a steady stream of humid, sour air rose in stifling eddies. Sam stared down the long, wooden ladder descending into the shaft and swallowed back his trepidation thinking the winking candles seemed less comforting at that depth and the air tasted foul and unhealthily devoid of oxygen. "Come on Eppy, pull yourself together," he mumbled to himself and climbed onto the top rung of the ladder.

The sound of footsteps echoing from the tunnel entrance stayed his descent and as he waited, guiltily hopeful of companionship, two men appeared through the gloom. As they drew nearer he could make out that one was a miner and the other an officer, a dog collared officer.

"Thought you might like some company Sergeant," Simon Graham whispered cheerily his face beaming, "And a guide." He jerked his head at the miner.

"Not that y' can get lost like," the besmirched tunneller muttered grumpily. Evidently he was here against his wishes.

Despite his nervousness Sam grinned. "Thank you Sir," he replied, not even attempting to argue. He had dreaded dropping into the depths alone and even grudging company was better than none at all.

The trio climbed the twenty feet to the next level and paused to listen. Way up ahead, sounds of what might have been a child weeping and a soft thudding of indiscernible origin. Hepworth held a staying hand against the chaplain's chest and murmured, "Let me go first Sir. Ibbotson isn't usually violent, but from what's been said he's not exactly acting characteristically. Poor sod's probably scared to death. Pardon my language, Sir."

"There was an intimation of injured men Sergeant," Graham murmured back

"Corporal Holdsworth and Private Benson, yes. Not sure whether they're hurt or he's holding them captive. Likely to be the former I think. Holdsworth's quite handy in a scrap so I reckon he's probably injured.

"Is this the only way to the face?" Sam turned to the miner.

"Aye Sarge. Just keep followin' this gallery. It forks in 'bout twenty five yards, but t' left fork on'y goes another five yards or so. Can't go wrong really Sarge," the miner informed suddenly more cheery than before. Maybe he thought he would be allowed to return up top now. He thought wrong. Rankling at the improper title used, Hepworth managed only to overlook the miner's ignorance of military correctness with ill grace that ensured the reluctant sapper was doomed to remain in the tunnel.

"Right, then you follow Mister Graham. I might have need of a runner," Sam instructed and turned back to the tunnel with a satisfied smirk at the distinctly sour expression given by the guide. A hand on his arm stopped his progress. He looked at the chaplain with an eyebrow raised in question. "Sir?"

"Before we go on. What's the story behind this man?"

Sam sighed. "We haven't really got much time Sir."

"I know, but I might be able to help if I understand."

"Ibbotson's a bit simple. For the life of me I don't know how he managed to pass a medical let alone get posted to a Regular battalion. He's usually soft as sh... Well, he isn't usually aggressive and he responds well to authority as long as it's not too brutal. Problem is he scares easily. Like a kid, you know."

"I see. And you think something has frightened him?"

"Mister Wise told me that some of the sappers were ragging him bad. I reckon they scared him witless and he's flipped," Hepworth theorised with a dark look towards the miner.

"And if he has injured anyone?"

"He's buggered Sir, if you'll excuse the expression. Assault on top of everything else? I wouldn't give much for his chances of staying out of prison. Although to be honest, it'd be a relief to get shut of him. He's more damn trouble than he's worth."

"They won't take his handicap into account?"

"As far as the Army is concerned he has no handicap Sir. He passed A one fit, which puts him at the Front with us and also makes him answerable for his actions. Shall we move on Sir?"

"Yes, yes. Thank you for explaining," Graham uttered thoughtfully.

"Don't mention it, Sir."

They crept forwards stopping at the fork where Sam peered carefully around the corner. Way up ahead, in the dim flicker of candle light, a dark figure rocked to and fro, its back thudding dully against the planked wall while uttering a low mewling cry. It was Ibbotson and at his feet lay the sprawled outline of a body, ominously motionless, while cowering against the opposite wall two infantrymen watched on, huddled together, silent. None of the three showed any sign of having heard the approaching men. Perhaps the plaintive whimpering covered other sounds. Perhaps Ibbotson was beyond noticing. Perhaps the men with him were either too afraid to turn and look or too injured. Sam sucked in his breath at the thought and turning back to the chaplain and placing his mouth close to the officer's ear explained what he had seen.

"Do you think he's killed the man?" Simon whispered back in reference to the stationary, prone figure.

Sam shrugged. "Doesn't look too good Sir."

"What are you going to do?"

"Talk to him I suppose. Best if you stay here Sir, for starters at least. I'll call if I need help." Without a further word or waiting for a response he stepped around the corner and heedless of remaining quiet shuffled forwards. Immediately the two cringing infantrymen looked in his direction one of them half edging himself into a more comfortable position. Ibbotson continued to cry and rock slowly back and forth, oblivious. At a distance of ten yards Sam recognised the soldiers as Benson and Corporal Holdsworth and both alternately eyed him and their captor with nervous apprehension.

"Now then Jimmy, what's going on here?" he asked nonchalantly and dug into his right breast pocket for a cigarette and the silver match box Lily had given him. He did not look at the deranged private or his anxious prisoners while he casually lit up and inhaled the smoke with the needy appreciation of an addict. Exhaling, he finally allowed himself to truly survey the scene before him, rapidly assessing the situation. His heart sank. Benson and Holdsworth were definitely worse for wear. Both had bloody stains on their uniforms. The corporal bore a purpling bruise around his left eye and cheek, while the private's hair was matted and wet looking and his eyes seemed heavy and dull. They were hurt and wary, their eyes flicking from their sergeant to Ibbotson. The latter had stopped rocking and stared at Hepworth with a bleary half vacant expression.

"Careful Sarn't 'e's got a..." Holdsworth began and cringed back against the wall as the simpleton bounced to his feet with amazing cat-like speed and flashed the bloody blade of a bayonet in his direction.

Sam froze, cigarette in mouth, his mind racing and heart pumping wildly. *Jesus.* "Steady on Jimmy. Look, I'm not armed. I've just come to talk to you. We can have a chat can't we Jimmy? You and me, eh?" He half turned his face to where Graham and the miner still hovered in the shadows, way back along the dripping tunnel. Would Ibbotson respond better to a man of God rather than one he was essentially afraid of?

"I'm not goin' anywhere Sarn't. I know what y' want. Y' want to shoot me cos of what I done. It weren't my fault. 'E made me do it. 'E MADE ME!" Ibbotson roared his eyes wild now with both fear and rage. Not so stupid then after all. He understood the severity of his situation.

Sam held up his arms in supplication noting with some satisfaction and a little hope that the private's gaze constantly diverted towards the cigarette. "I just want to talk Jimmy. Here, do you want a fag?" He held out the woodbine and smiled reassuringly though his heart pounded hard and a slight tremor in his outstretched hand belied his nervousness.

Glancing behind the wavering Ibbotson he noted the confined space opened up into a small chamber where a pile of carefully packed explosive loomed ominously. The sight sent shudders of dread down his spine. *Should be safe. It's not primed.* This had been what the men were doing down here. Bringing boxes of TNT and gun cotton for the sappers to carefully place ready for detonation at three thirty that morning. Not much time left then.

The thought that the Germans must know of this mine and were possibly preparing their own deadly welcome did not exactly make him feel more comfortable. It had happened before. Not here, but a little further down the line. There were numbers of miners and infantry buried alive in similar subterranean tombs where they slowly died of suffocation. A cold sweat beaded his brow and trickled down his face. It was a death he feared more than any. Drawn out asphyxiation. Fighting for air, the panic overwhelming him and gradually, slowly sinking into the abyss of darkness. Like drowning. He shivered involuntarily and forced the bitter memory away.

Ibbotson stared at the cigarette longingly, licked his lips and dithered on the brink of accepting. Sam, gathering his wits, ceased the moment and took a step forward. It was a mistake. The bayonet flew upwards and the mad man lunged at Corporal Holdsworth, grabbing him by the neck and pushing the blade of his weapon against the grimacing man's rib cage. Holdsworth squealed out in both pain and fear.

"Fuckin' 'ell Sarn't!" he cried. Sam stopped stock still.

"Alright, alright. I won't come any closer. Look Jimmy, I'm going to stay right here. That's OK isn't it? If I stay here?" he soothed racking his brains for another idea.

"GO AWAY! LEAVE ME ALONE. I DON'T WANT TO TALK TO YOU!" Ibbotson shouted causing all three men to cringe.

A soft footfall caused them all to peer back into the gloomy twilight of the tunnel. Sam bit his lip at the sight of the chaplain purposefully walking towards them, his body stooped to prevent banging his head against the low ceiling. Ibbotson tensed shoving the bayonet blade even closer to Holdsworth's thorax, its sharp point piercing the skin fractionally and drawing a fresh, but unseen, welt of blood onto his tunic. The corporal whimpered at the sudden scratch and closed his terrified eyes tight shut.

"Who's wi' thi? Who've y' brought? Knew y' wa' up to summat. Yer all tryin' to trick me," the captor accused.

"It's not a trick Jimmy. Sergeant Hepworth only wishes to help you. My name is Mister Graham. I'm a chaplain," the clergyman stepped into full view his arms held wide in a gesture of appeasement. "Do you mind if I call you Jimmy?"

The private stared at the officer, took in the dog collar, the placid, well spoken voice, the kind eyes and he frowned with vague puzzlement. At the same time his grip on Holdsworth lessened just a little. "Not seen a padre down 'ere befower," he said suspiciously.

Simon laughed with an easy manner, reassuring and casual. "No, so I gather. Everybody has been staring at me like I dropped from another planet." He grinned and amazingly the private echoed the expression. The infantrymen held their breath and watched on in silent anticipation.

"I believe that I can only carry out God's work if I am actually with the men I am supposed to look after. You believe in God don't you Jimmy? You go to church?"

"Every Sunday. Never missed 'til I came 'ere. Can't go to church 'ere. No churches left. Go to services though, when we 'ave 'em," Ibbotson replied slackening his grip further.

"I knew as much. I knew you were a God fearing man. Mind if I sit down?" Graham continued, pointing to a box next to the body of the miner.

"Suppose not," the private mumbled, his eyes still darting between the officer and the sergeant. The chaplain edged forwards, squeezing by Hepworth. He hesitated briefly when he saw the letters TNT upon the box lid, shrugged and sat anyway. *Must be safe.* He reached down and touched the prone miner's skin, felt around the neck for a carotid pulse. There was none and an awful lot of blood had oozed from the body and mingled with the dirt of the floor creating a dark, muddy puddle. He caught the sergeant's eye and shook his head once.

"You know Jimmy that you can't stay down here don't you? It's not a very pleasant place to be anyway, is it?" he continued in a soft empathetic tone.

Ibbotson's eyes filled with tears and a large gulping sob escaped his lips. "I'm frightened Padre. They'll shoot me cos of what I've done. 'E wants to shoot me!" he pointed the bloody bayonet at Sam with a shaking hand.

"Sergeant Hepworth doesn't want to shoot you Jimmy, but he does want to help you and these other men. He wants to make sure you're all safe. You do believe that don't you? That he only wants to help. He's always helped you before hasn't he?"

Hesitation and confusion. Ibbotson teetered on the edge of wanting to believe, but his fear would not quite release its grip enough to let reason win. "Don't want to go up top," he muttered at last with the sulky petulance of a naughty child.

"You can't stay here Jimmy for God's sake. They're going to blow the place up. Come on man," Sam jumped in with growing frustration. They did not have time for this. The private mewled fearfully and Graham threw a warning glance at Hepworth. *Not helpful Sergeant.*

"It's alright Jimmy. Look, why don't you let Sergeant Hepworth take the other two out of here. They need to see a doctor don't they? It's not very Christian of you to keep them here is it? Let them go and I'll stay with you."

Ibbotson drew in a deep quivering breath. "Alright," he agreed, "But no funny business. I'm not coming out of 'ere."

"You have my word Jimmy," the chaplain promised.

"'S not yours I'm worried 'bout. It's 'is," the bayonet was stabbed in Sam's direction.

"You have mine too Jimmy. I promise I won't touch you. I just want to get the lads out. Is that okay?" Sam appeased.

The captor nodded and released his grip on Holdsworth who crawled hurriedly to where his sergeant stood. Sam dropped to his knees to check the corporal's injuries.

"I'm alright Sarn't but Charlie'll need some 'elp. Took a bit of a clout to 'is 'ead," Holdsworth muttered breathing heavily with the relief of escape.

"May I?" Hepworth asked pointing to Private Benson. Ibbotson tossed his head in agreement and stepped backwards, his weapon still held ready for use. Sam scurried to the injured soldier.

"How do you feel Charlie?" he asked taking a cursory look at the purpling bruise on the man's head.

"Like shit Sarn't. Me 'ead's killin' me an' t' bastard stabbed me in me bloody thigh," Benson replied in a hoarse, wary whisper. His eyes roved constantly towards Ibbotson and the chaplain and back again, never quite focussing, always appearing a little distant.

"Can you stand?"

"If it means gettin' outta 'ere I bloody well can."

"Here, put your right arm around my neck. Good lad. Ready?" Sam hoisted the private's arm around his shoulder and awaited confirmation. This was going to hurt. Benson nodded biting his lip in concentration and then crying out in pain as he was heaved to his feet. His hand clutched tight around Hepworth's neck causing the sergeant to choke momentarily until the grip was released.

"Sorry Sarn't," the injured man muttered, the sweat glistening on his brow. Sam did not reply, merely grunted and with his burden leaning heavily against him he staggered back to where Holdsworth waited. He turned to speak to Graham.

"I'll be alright Sergeant. I shall sit here and have a long chat with Jimmy. We'll be fine won't we Jimmy?" the chaplain anticipated smiling broadly at Ibbotson.

"Yeah. We'll be okay Sarn't," the private answered innocently with a toothy, childlike grin.

Sam did not wait, trusting the cleric's judgement he and Holdsworth helped the bleeding Benson back along the tunnel to where the miner still hovered in the shadows.

"Get back up top quick. We need the MO and some help to get these men out of here. Benson will never make that ladder. Move it man!" Hepworth ordered the sapper. The wiry tunneller did not wait to be told twice. He shot off back along the gallery as fast as his short legs would carry him leaving the others to painfully and slowly trudge up the incline that none had noticed coming in.

It seemed to take forever. Holdsworth struggled with his breathing, clutching his torso and grimacing alternately. Charlie was becoming increasingly heavy and incapable. From time to time his body sagged completely onto one or other of the two men assisting him as if in a swoon. The tight space of the tunnel did little to help. Every few yards they had to stop to give one or other of the injured men a breather. By the time they reached the ladder Sam's lungs were burning with effort and his back, bent almost double with the weight of Benson and the low ceiling, felt fit to break. It was with relief that he saw his brother, a medical orderly and a number of sappers rigging some kind of sling to lift the casualties from the bottom of the shaft.

Lowering Benson to the floor, Sam leant heavily against the tunnel wall as Joe bent to examine the private, Holdsworth crashed down next to him.

"You alright Sergeant?" the MO asked while studying his patient. He did not lift his eyes from the purple contusion, but his voice betrayed his concern.

"Yes Sir. Just need a breather. Is Mister Wise still out top?"

"Yes and your CC. Where's Mister Graham?" Joe replied moving onto Holdsworth. "Ribs?" he queried noting the awkward hunched position of the corporal and the laboured breathing.

"Aye Sir. Bastard kicked me didn't 'e. Beg y' pardon Sir," Holdsworth responded and yelped as the MO felt at his torso.

Sam frowned. "The padre is with Ibbotson. I need to go up top Sir. You alright down here?" he asked feeling he should stay and help, but knowing the situation was not yet resolved.

Joe looked up. "Of course I am. You do what you have to Sergeant," he said with a touch of exasperation that brought a half smile to his brother's lips. He gestured with an impatient shove of his hands. Without further hesitation Sam bounded up the ladder, pushed his way past the busy sappers and ran in an odd, stooping lurch to the gas curtain at the tunnel's entrance. Bursting out into the frigid cold of the night air he almost ran into Wise and Captain Lockwood, the company commander.

Things had changed. It was clear that Lockwood had taken charge. The RE lieutenant leant sulkily against the trench wall with his hands shoved into his coat pockets, an unlit pipe in his mouth and a dark, brooding expression upon his face. Around him waited a number of miners, dirty and sullenly quiet. It was without doubt that they were dreading being sent back underground. Behind the captain and the flustered looking Wise, a number of A Company men hovered, their faces curious and not a little concerned. Both Lockwood and the young subaltern jumped as Hepworth almost careered into them.

"Sir," Sam blustered, lurching to a stop. The captain did not seem to notice he had nearly been knocked down, or more likely did not care. His look of surprise turned to relief and then business-like gravity.

"Sergeant Hepworth. What the devil is going on down there? Where's the padre?" he demanded stopping himself from asking the other hundred or so questions that burned through his head. Hepworth would report accurately anyway. He was a good man, Hepworth.

"Sir. Mister Graham is still with Private Ibbotson. Corporal Holdsworth and Private Benson are at the bottom of the shaft with the MO Sir. They're a bit knocked about, but otherwise they're alright. Ibbotson is refusing to leave the tunnel. He has a bayonet which he is not afraid to use Sir, but he seems to trust the padre. Mister Graham insisted I should bring the others out while he tried to talk Ibbotson around, but...," Sam divulged and paused.

"But?" Lockwood prompted.

"Sir, I don't think we'll get him out by the time the engineers want to blow this thing up, not without taking more drastic action. Ibbotson has killed one of the sappers and had a good go at two of his mates. He might be a simpleton, but he understands the consequences of his actions. I don't believe he intends to leave of his own free will and I don't think Mister Graham will be able to persuade him in time."

"*Jesus Christ!*" Lockwood spat and turned to Wise. "Why the *hell* did you send the man down there if he was unstable, you fool?" he uttered under his breath. The subaltern turned scarlet and looked around self-consciously to see if anyone had heard his rather public reprimand. He caught Hepworth's eye and thought he saw sympathy, but, in the gloom, he could not be sure. He muttered an apology and began a half-hearted explanation, but the company commander turned from him with impatience.

"Do you think Mister Graham is safe Sergeant?" he demanded in a tone that imparted accusation.

"I don't believe Ibbotson would harm a man of the cloth Sir. He holds a deep seated religious conviction Sir," Sam responded his own cheeks burning now. The implication had been that he should not have left the chaplain behind. What else could he have done?

"How the hell are we going to get them out of there?" Lockwood thought out loud, the question rhetorical. No one spoke for some moments and the air hung heavy with tense expectation. "Do you think he'll retaliate and hurt someone if we try to bring him out by force?" He wheeled back around to face the NCO.

"Yes, I think he would Sir," Sam replied laconically. He did not like the way this was going at all. Ibbotson was a dead man now, but the thought of bringing him out by force was far from appealing. Bloodshed seemed inevitable. He became aware of the captain staring at him, his expression grimly thoughtful. An odd sensation of dread filled Sam's stomach.

"Will he listen to you Sergeant or Mister Wise here? Will he follow orders?"

Sam shrugged. He doubted it. "I'm not sure Sir."

Lockwood sighed and glanced at the engineer who pointedly looked at his wristwatch in response. "Very well. Sergeant Hepworth, I want you to return to the tunnel and bring Mister Graham out. Take this," he unclipped his revolver and held it out to the amazed sergeant. Sam wrapped his hands around the cold butt of the weapon. "Mister Wise will go with you."

"And Ibbotson Sir? Sam asked quietly, licking his lips with distaste.

"Do what you have to do Sergeant. We need that mine primed within the hour, which gives little time for negotiating."

"And noise Sir?"

"If the fool isn't playing cricket then sod the noise. He's a dead man anyway. Do I make myself clear?" the captain stressed carefully.

"Crystal clear Sir," Sam replied as a cold chill ran the length of his spine and catching the second lieutenant's eye saw the horror of that intimation written across his young features.

"Good. You have fifteen minutes and then I'll send more men in. Mister Wise," Lockwood stood aside to allow his subordinate to pass.

Stony faced and in silence the two men entered the tunnel and headed downwards. They passed Joe and his helpers bringing Holdsworth and Benson to the surface and ignored his questioning glance. At the bottom of the ladder, Sam waited for Wise to catch up and took the time to check the chambers of Webley revolver, slipping the weapon into the webbing belt behind his back as the officer landed with a thud by his side. Wise swallowed hard and held the sergeant's gaze.

"I'm sorry Eppy. It's all my fault. I... I should have listened to you to start with," he stammered.

"With respect Sir, don't be so bloody daft. I could have put Ibbotson on some other job. It wouldn't be the first time I've done the opposite to what you asked me."

Wise smiled nervously, the expression dropping almost instantaneously from his features. "He meant us to shoot him didn't he?" Confirmation for what he was reluctant to admit.

"Only if we can't get him to come with us Sir," Sam whispered back. Sound carried a long way down here and he was aware that he could hear a conversation droning somewhere ahead and that the young subaltern spoke louder than he should.

Wise took the hint. "Do you think he will?" he breathed.

"In all honesty I don't know. Let's get going, we haven't long."

A restraining hand clamped onto Sam's arm. "Eppy, I don't think I can shoot one of my own men." Wide, frightened eyes, appealing for help.

Hepworth nodded. "Understood Sir," he said and felt his heart rate pick up a pace.

They hurriedly crept forward, aware of the time, pausing briefly at the fork to peer around the corner and gauge the situation. Ibbotson and Graham were as Sam had left them a few minutes previous. The chaplain sat, apparently relaxed, on the box of explosives and Ibbotson crouched next to him, his back against the wall and a wide, stupid grin on his face. He did not appear dangerous though the body of the dead miner gave lie to that assumption. Wise took in a deep breath and exhaled very slowly. He could not hide the tremor in his breath and as he caught his companion's eye he felt a sense of relief that Hepworth also seemed nervous. "What now?" he asked.

"Might as well just get it over with Sir. I'll go first shall I?" Sam replied his mouth dry. He tried to ignore the flutter of apprehension that played in his stomach. He tried to tell himself it would be alright, that Graham would have talked Ibbotson around, that they would all walk out of here calmly and unhurt. He also tried to forget that the enemy might be priming their own charge somewhere on the other side of those walls or in a chamber above. Sweat beaded his brow and trickled down his left temple. He wiped it away with his sleeve aware of the coarse serge on his face, aware of his heart pounding hard against his ribcage.

Wise nodded in agreement and, inhaling sharply, Sam stepped around the corner the subaltern close behind him. Immediately Ibbotson jumped to his feet and brandished the bayonet. Graham sat upright and frowned before smiling broadly and offering a nonchalant greeting.

"Sergeant Hepworth, Mister Wise, how nice to see you both. Jimmy and I were just talking about our favourite hymns. Jimmy likes Onward Christian Soldiers. A good rousing tune don't you agree?"

Sam smirked at the ludicrous conversation yet at the same time understood it as a means of maintaining the allusion of friendliness, of keeping Ibbotson calm. "Prefer Fight the Good Fight myself Sir," he offered and moved closer to the two men. Behind him the second lieutenant was so close he could feel his breath on the back of his neck. He needed more space, more room to move. Deliberately he pressed a hand against Wise's chest. The young officer stopped still and the sergeant took another step forward.

"Another stirring hymn. What do you say Jimmy? Do you like that one too?" Graham continued with absurd enthusiasm, but it seemed to work. Ibbotson nodded in agreement a slow grin replacing the wariness of a second ago.

"How about carols? I always liked carols myself. *O little town of Be-thle-hem how still we see thee....*" Wise began to sing in a quavering, tuneless tenor.

"No Sir! It's unlucky. Shouldn't sing carols when it's not Christmas," Ibbotson interrupted a trace of superstitious fear in his voice. Immediately the officer fell silent. The tension had returned. The private was agitated once more.

"It's alright Jimmy. God won't mind," Graham appeased and patted the simpleton's arm. Ibbotson shrugged the hand away, his relaxed mood vanished, the chaplain's hard and patient work undone.

"What you come back fo'?" Ibbotson challenged angrily, pointing the bayonet at Sam. Why could they not leave him alone? He was happy here with the padre. Felt safe.

Hepworth's right hand slid behind his back and carefully grasped the revolver lifting it from the webbing. Behind him Wise stared with nervous and horrified fascination, a terrible sinking feeling in the pit of his stomach. He licked his lips and tried to swallow, but no spit came, his mouth horribly dry.

"Time to go now Jimmy. You can't stay here any longer," Sam answered the question directly. There was no time for anything else. Besides, it might just work.

"Don't want to go," Ibbotson muttered sulkily.

"I know, but you have no choice now lad. The engineers need to blow this place up. You don't want to be down here then do you? Come on, let's go eh?" Add a little fear. Could help persuade the stupid lump to move. *Come on man. I can see the cogs ticking in that stupid head of yours. Just think straight for once.*

Ibbotson waivered, his soft, pink features deliberating over the sergeant's words. He seemed to sway forwards, even moved one foot half a step, hovered uncertainly and then the face went blank and the shutters came up. He shook his head vehemently. "No! I'm not going."

Wise shivered as a cold chill seeped through his body. With growing dread he watched the Webley move to Hepworth's side, still out of view, but nearer to being used. With his heart in his mouth he cried, "Good heavens man, you can't stay here. You're coming out with us now. That's an order Private." He had to try something.

Ibbotson jumped as if struck. He seemed to have forgotten the subaltern was there and for a moment it appeared that the command might work. The seconds ticked by with laborious slowness. Sam held his breath. Graham stood, sensing the time was right, that a decisive step was needed. He grasped the private's left elbow in his hand with a firm, yet gentle grip. "Come on Jimmy. It's time to go," he uttered quietly.

Ibbotson glanced at the hand; Sam took a step forward never daring to drop his eyes from the private. It was going to work. The lad was going to give in. With growing confidence both the sergeant and the chaplain allowed themselves to believe they had succeeded, but at the last moment they were proved wrong.

"NO! Don't come any closer!" Ibbotson shouted and grabbed Graham by the collar hoisting him backwards with surprising ease and pushing the point of the bayonet against his neck. The chaplain's eyes widened with fear as a trickle of warm blood lazily rolled onto his dog collar. He had really thought he had talked the lad around, calmed him down, but the private was seriously disturbed and only now did he realise the danger of his situation. He felt the tremble of his captor's hands and body, smelt his terror and understood this was a desperate man.

"Jimmy...," he began in as subdued a voice as he could muster though his heart fluttered frantically within his chest and his eyes sought reassurance from the sergeant standing only yards away with one hand outstretched pointing a revolver in their direction.

"SHUT UP!" Ibbotson roared.

"Jimmy put the bayonet down and let Mister Graham go," Sam said steadily but with authority.

"NO. You're gonna shoot me. Y' BASTARD! Yer all bastards!"

"Jimmy, if you don't let the Padre go I *will* shoot you. Don't think I won't. Don't think I'll miss. Come on. There's a good lad, put the bayonet down." A subtle change from threat to cajoling.

"Ibbotson, do as Sergeant Hepworth damn well says you fool!" Wise added unhelpfully. The private held him in a wild, demented gaze, his lips pulled back into a ghoulish sneer. In the flickering candlelight, his face looked demonic, unearthly. He laughed manically.

"You won't shoot me now cos you'll 'it the padre if y' try. See, I'm not that daft Sarn't."

For a fraction of a second doubt flickered through Sam's brain. He saw the terrified expression upon Graham's face, the insane leer of his tormentor. He pushed away the annoyance at Wise's unhelpful attempt at intervention. This had gone far enough. Time was running out. Ibbotson was a dead man now anyway. Had been the moment he killed the miner. He steadied his aim.

"Jimmy, please. This won't...," BANG. Simon jumped violently at the sudden explosive report, his last attempt to talk the private around cut short. He felt something tug heavily at his neck and suddenly he fell backwards. His arms flayed in wild windmills connecting with something soft and then he hit the ground, or rather Ibbotson. He landed squarely upon the private, the air whooshing from his lungs with the unexpected impact. For an instant he lay still then someone pulled him upright. It was Hepworth.

"You alright Sir? Sorry if I startled you," Sam apologised hoisting the chaplain to his feet. As the wide eyed Graham looked about him, he bent down to take a closer look at the private. A small, neat hole darkened the middle of Ibbotson's forehead and his eyes gazed glassily at the ceiling of the tunnel. His mouth was rounded into an O as if surprised by something and beneath his head the ground glistened wetly dark. The bayonet lay harmlessly by his side.

"Sorry Jimmy, you gave me no choice lad," Hepworth muttered shaking off the feeling of remorse. *That was right wasn't it? He had had no choice?* He shivered.

"Is he dead?" Wise called from his original position. He had not moved and his voice sounded shocked.

"Aye he's dead Sir." Sam acknowledged standing once more.

Gathering his wits Graham bent down and signed a cross over the body, whispering a hopeless blessing. He felt wretched. A man had died and he could have prevented it. He looked up at the sergeant. What was *he* feeling or thinking? How did it affect a man to kill someone he knew, one of his own men? It was impossible to say. Hepworth appeared completely in control, almost relieved. Maybe he was.

"Shall we go Sir? We can leave the bodies to someone else," Sam suggested not wanting to stay a moment longer with the ghost that sprawled before him. There would be some explaining to do, an inquest, but it would only find he had acted appropriately under the circumstances. The CC had practically given the order anyway. Only his conscience would mete out punishment.

Simon nodded dejectedly wondering why he had volunteered for front line service. He joined Wise and watched as Hepworth removed Ibbotson's identity disc, then all three men made their way back to the surface in silence.

The killing of Jimmy Ibbotson gave the engineers just enough time to prime and tamp their mine. At three thirty that morning the mines were detonated, men rushed forward to secure the craters created by them. There was no retaliation from the Germans.

30th

"Come on you lot, get a bloody move on! Morris, shift your fat arse!" Sam yelled at the stragglers as they fought through the clagging mud of the narrow trench leading to the consolidated crater that had, until the early hours, been a part of No-Man's-Land. This was the relief, a good portion of One Platoon and they miserably groused at their misfortune at taking charge of a soggy, bloody hole and probably, a missed breakfast. They grumbled and trudged reluctantly by their sergeant who could not refrain from flinging a cruel jibe with an affected NCO snarl at the sullen men.

"Hurry up you miserable buggers, Mister Wise and I will miss our breakfast at this rate! Shift or you'll get my boot up your sorry backside!" The penultimate man eyed Hepworth with scorn, his lips betraying some muttered expletive.

The subaltern chuckled under his breath, "That really is unfair Eppy, you rotten sod."

Sam turned to face him with a sly grin. "Aye, but it makes me feel better Sir."

The last man passed and they fell in behind him, sliding unceremoniously in the heavy muck.

As they neared their destination the men instinctively fell silent and only the clanking of equipment or the odd cough betrayed their presence. Fritz knew there were men in the crater and no one wanted to advertise how many or that a relief was taking place. That would be inviting trouble. Still it was a tense time. The enemy could probably guess what was happening across the wire and lonely stretch of mud between. One could only hope they were similarly busy with sentry changes and readying for stand-to.

Sam slithered unsteadily on hastily laid duck boards awash with watery slime and banged his arm heavily against a stout post cursing under his breath. He felt lousy and miserably cold. His legs ached, he had a low fever and a dull pain throbbed in his head. Even muffled up with as many layers as he could comfortably fit beneath his tunic and jerkin the chill still bit through to his bones. He coughed, bringing thick, yellowish phlegm from his lungs and spat into the mire at his feet. *Christ, what a time to get flu!* And he'd been alright a few hours ago. A bit chesty maybe, but nothing much.

"You alright Sergeant?" Wise uttered placing a hand on Sam's left shoulder. A nodded reply signalled all was well. They struggled onwards into the crater spilling in behind the men and glad to be out of the claustrophobic confines of the hastily dug communication trench.

Looking around to take in the size of the task, where best to place whom, what still needed doing, Sam rapidly summed up the situation.

"Can you see Lieutenant Lister?" Wise asked breathing heavily into his sergeant's good ear.

Sam looked around. Where was the damned lieutenant? In the dim half light it was hard to discern individual's features and uniforms. "Over there Sir," he recognised the distinctive stoop of the tall commander of Three Platoon and pointed just as the latter spotted his relief and with a cheery wave commenced slithering towards them.

"Ah, jolly good. Start sorting the chaps out Eppy. With luck we'll get this shambles over with in time for brekkers after all. Bloody mud!" the subaltern grumbled with his usual good spirits. "And then Sergeant Hepworth, *you* will report to the MO," he added with a knowing expression. Sam opened his mouth to protest but the young officer cut him short. "That's an order Hepworth. You're ill and you're no bloody good to me half dead. Understood?"

"Yes Sir," Sam mumbled, a dark frown clouding his flushed features. Last thing he wanted was to report sick to his own brother. Everyone knew their relationship. The men would think he was shirking; given preferential treatment if Joe sent him down the line. And knowing Joe, he would. The fact that Wise was correct did not figure in his own summation. Irritatedly he shuffled off signalling the men to follow him, exchanging places with the exhausted working party from the previous night.

"And you're fuckin' welcome to it mate," one man muttered with a grim smile as he relinquished his post to a disgruntled comrade who swore back through gritted teeth.

"Keep your bloody voices down!" Sam whispered harshly bringing his face close to the offending privates. Sullenly they swapped places, one waving provocatively at the other as he slid away from the loop hole and formed up with his relieved colleagues at the crater entrance.

Sam shook his head and moved on wondering whether it was simply the thickness of the clay that made his legs feel like lead or whether he really was sick enough to deserve a rest. A rest. The thought whirled tantalizingly through his aching brain. *That is a strange sensation though?* His mind clearly registered an odd vibration through his feet, not unlike that felt on a platform when an express train hurtles through... *Oh God!* He spun around, opened his mouth to scream at everyone to....

The world heaved. Before he uttered a sound his body bucked upwards tumbling amidst muck and other debris. Falling. Something hard hit his back. Was it the ground? A dreadful rumbling, ear-splitting thunder. The air being knocked from his lungs. Blackness!

Joe looked up, startled, as the explosion shook the earth and rent the air with a stupendously reverberating boom. He steadied himself by holding onto the table where he had assembled his equipment in readiness for the morning sick parade. His heart beating fast, his first instinct was that a heavy shell had burst nearby, but there had been no tell-tale whine only a sudden, powerful detonation. Too powerful. It was a mine.

"What the dickens...?" Graham gasped clutching the doctor's arm in an involuntary reaction. The MO faced his companion listening intently. The rumbling finally died away leaving a moment's silence before all hell broke loose. The rapid, staccato fire of a Lewis gun and rifle shots. Worse. The urgent shouts for men and stretcher bearers.

"*Oh my God!*" Joe exclaimed. "Fallon, get this place ready, fast. Parkes, I need as many orderlies as you can muster. No, on second thoughts get all of them. I don't care if they've been up all night. We need everyone now and get a message up to the ADS. They might be busy. Go on, MOVE IT!"

"What is it? Joe, what's happening?" the chaplain asked catching the doctor's arm once more and demanding unwanted attention.

Joe fought the surge of exasperation. The padre did not know. How could he? He had only just arrived. "You'll probably be needed too Simon. The Germans have just exploded a mine. This is where we earn our crust," he smiled cynically and grabbed his pack, half pulling the clergyman with him to the aid post entrance. Graham hesitated and his fellow officer responded uncharitably.

"Thought you wanted to bring God to the trenches Simon. Or was that just talk?" Joe snapped harshly. An unworthy and cutting remark that stung with its unfair insinuation. The chaplain's expression hardened yet the jibe had its desired effect. Shock and uncertainty were replaced by a flash of indignation. It focussed his mind. He grabbed his prayer book and stuffing it into his pocket followed the MO through the gas curtain and into the trench.

Fighting their way through a confused throng of men moving as what appeared to be a panicked mob, they headed in the direction of shouts and small arms fire. A furious, unremitting hail of bullets, accompanied by the occasional trench mortar, harassed the German lines. The two officers were jostled and pushed, carried forwards now by a tide of stretcher bearers, men carrying shovels and buckets. A long moaning whine and the delayed thump of a gun heralded the onslaught of British retaliation as the artillery answered the SOS from the Front and joined in the mayhem. Graham jumped nervously as a number of explosions somewhere across No-Man's-Land indicated the gunners were on target. *This surely is Hell!* He stumbled after his comrade, horrified and at the same time shockingly exhilarated. Shouted orders somewhere close to his ear and the rifle and machine gun fire died away. Let the artillery do their bit now. No point wasting bullets! Men waited, poised by loopholes and peering anxiously into the murky grey wasteland across the wire.

Suddenly the way was blocked by a jumbled pile of debris at which a good number of men dug furiously, with grim determination. With numbing shock, both officers realised that this mountain of muck, timber and wire was all that remained of the crater in which a good part of two platoons were buried. Already a number of filthy, dazed men occupied stretchers, waiting to be taken away. Their stunned, besmirched faces testimony to the ordeal they had undergone. At first glance all appeared chaotic devastation and desperation, but a closer inspection showed the CSM and a number of officers had the situation in hand. What appeared to be confused pandemonium proved to be an efficient operation to dig men out from the mountain of rubble.

Joe did not hesitate. He immediately set to work, quickly ascertaining that most of the men were unharmed. Shocked maybe and understandably, but not maimed. A few cuts and bruises. A nasty bang to a head. With cool detachment he told stretcher bearers to move the rescued away. Fallon and the other orderlies could see to this lot well enough. Nothing a nice cup of tea and an odd bandage could not cure. The worst were yet to come. Moving by his side the chaplain handed out cigarettes and offered quiet words of comfort in his own indomitable way. Both were welcome, especially the smokes.

The flood of rescued men became a slowing stream. Working swiftly with a few competent first aiders, Joe marvelled that it was nothing short of miraculous how quickly they were pulled from their suffocating tomb as their comrades sweated and toiled like Trojans to set them free. Even more astounding that so few were seriously hurt. A relief, but they had not reached everyone yet.

"How many were in there?" Graham asked a mud caked subaltern as the latter shakily staggered with the assistance of a tunnelling company sapper to where the MO had set up his forward aid post. The young man sat heavily onto the muddy ground and dropped his head into his hands. He appeared to be weeping and Simon bent down touching his shoulder. "It's alright son. You're safe now," he uttered kindly.

An exploding shell somewhere out in No-Man's-Land brought the subaltern's head upright in sudden, fearful panic. He clutched childlike at to chaplain's hand. His eyes were dry.

"It's alright old chap, that was one of ours. Here, have a cigarette, the Doc'll see you in a jiffy. It's Wise isn't it?" Graham soothed helping the terrified second lieutenant light his smoke.

Joe's head snapped around from the man whose broken arm he was hurriedly fastening into a sling. "Wise?" he repeated and bent down clasping the young officer by the shoulders, pushing his face close. "Wise, was Sam with you?" he demanded.

Large, sunken and puzzled eyes met his.

"Sam?" a shaky voice mumbled, struggling to make a connection.

"Yes, my brother. Eppy for God's sake! Was Eppy with you?"

Wise frowned, his reeling brain finding it hard to concentrate. His ears were ringing and he wanted to sleep. The MO shook him roughly.

"I say Joe, steady on," Simon interjected.

"Come *on* man, think!" Joe insisted ignoring the chaplain.

"Yes.., I think s..so. Not with me but,... He was over there somewhere. Sorting the men. Sorry.., can't quite remember," Wise struggled in reply, his haunted gaze drifting across the melee before them. Joe stood upright and followed the direction of his stare. His face blanched and he ran a dirty, bloody hand through his hair.

"*Oh Jesus Christ!*" He moaned as a sinking dread filled his soul.

Sapper Lowry nearly jumped a mile when a hand fell from the pile of earth he dug through mechanically. He swore under his breath clutching his chest as if the fright might cause a heart attack and then he looked about him surreptitiously. He thought they were wasting their time now. Surely no one else would be alive. Surely it had been too long and the enemy mortar and sniper fire too hot by far despite British artillery attempts to silence it. They had done enough. Out of twenty five or so men buried, eighteen had been miraculously saved. Surely seven was a reasonable price to pay and better them than he. So Lowry had grumbled to himself as he dug half-heartedly now into the rubble. And then the hand had dropped in front of his eyes. A hand still attached to an arm and presumably a body buried in its suffocating tomb. A hand that fell limp and lifeless. A hand whose wrist bore a rather desirable watch.

Lowry looked around again and licked his lips. The officers were not looking in this direction; the CSM was chivvying marksmen to hurriedly prepared loopholes. No one would notice and the poor bugger under this heap of muck was not going to complain. Slowly the sapper bent down. He did not want to attract attention just yet. Not until he had his prize. Carefully he reached for the hand and took it in his. It still felt warm and he shuddered involuntarily. Casting another quick glance behind, he satisfied himself no one had seen before he turned the hand to get to the buckle on the leather strap.

Suddenly and violently the hand moved, grabbing his with superhuman strength.

"*Fucking 'ell!*" Lowry cried his heart in his mouth and leapt backwards pulling away from the now groping limb. "Sir, Sir! Another live one," he shouted and began to dig.

Icy black water swirled around his body, sucking away the heat, sapping his failing strength. His hands had slipped away from Lizzie's and he felt himself sinking. Panic stricken he fought to gain the surface to gasp at the crisp, sweet air. His lungs burned. A crash and a scream and he became aware of someone else in the water beside him. Something strong pulled him upwards. Someone. He broke the surface fighting for breath only this time there was no pure, winter air. This time as he breathed in his mouth filled with soil and he retched, half choking on the foul stuff. He tried to inhale again, but an oppressive weight crushed his chest and his lungs could barely expand. Confused, his oxygen starved brain sought to understand. Where had the water gone? He tried to move but could not. Something pinned him tight and fast. Trapped! He was trapped in the dark. Underground? Slowly his mind recalled an explosion and remembered that Lizzie had died a long time ago. Realisation of his fate slammed like a fist into his consciousness. Panic swelled and overwhelmed him but he could not lash out. He could not scream. He was going to die buried alive. Justice at last for killing Lizzie. Paralysing fear gripped him and he began to choke once more. It did not register that he was still alive; that he must be buried in an air pocket or he would already be dead by now. Neither did it immediately register that someone picked up his hand and began fumbling with his watch strap until...

Someone was with him. With desperate terror he grabbed the hand. It was snatched away. He groped around vainly for it. Even if he was going to die it would be some comfort to touch another human being. To not die alone.

Slowly he became aware of muffled voices, shouts, a strange scraping sound. The load on his body lightened. They were digging him out! He tired to move and this time managed to shift his right leg a little. The panic turned into frantic hope. He could distinctly hear shovels now. Men's voices became clearer. He could tell what they were shouting. A call for stretcher bearers and the MO. His legs were free! He could moved them. Someone grabbed his webbing. Strong hands. They pulled hard and with a last slump of falling earth Sam Hepworth was dragged from the clutches of death.

"Give 'im air, give 'im air for God's sake. 'Ere Sarge," a rough voice cried and cold water hit his face causing another flash of panic as it ran into his nose, dislodging the muck that stuck there but also stinging and running back into his throat causing him to gag once more. He coughed violently and fought to sit up but someone pinned him fast.

"Steady on lad. Let the MO look at yer first. Might be 'urt an don't want to make it worse do yer," a familiar, steady voice. Different from the first. "No more bloody water. D' yer want to drown 'im yer daft bugger?"

"Sorry Sir. On'y tryin' to 'elp like," a cowed reply.

"Well, it's t'sort of 'elp 'e can do wi'out." The CSM. It was the CSM.

"Mister Mason," Sam croaked and half choked on the dirt that speaking disturbed from his mouth and down his gullet. He coughed hackingly once more.

"Aye that's right lad. Take it easy. We've got yer now. An' 'ere comes yer brother. Won't be long son an' we'll 'ave yer away," Mason soothed.

"I can't see! *Christ...*," another retching cough. "Sir, I can't see..." Panic rising once more. He was blind! But it felt odd. He tried to open his eyes, but just as in the eternal dream they remained shut. "What's..."

"Sshh. Steady on Eppy," Mason held the struggling sergeant tight. "'S alright. Yer eyes are caked in muck that's all. They'll be alright. Just need cleaning up," he added hoping he was correct in his assumption. He gazed for confirmation at the MO who hurriedly dropped to his knees and grabbed hold of Sam's hand. "Ain't that right Doc?"

"Certainly," Joe said and felt his squeeze reciprocated by his sibling. "Hiya Sam, just need to take a quick look at you and then we'll get you moved and cleaned up," he added ignoring military protocol. *Who gave a fuck*! This was his brother. Gently he prized his hand from the sergeant's iron grip.

"Joe," Sam sighed and his body finally relaxed. He was safe now. Joe would make sure of that.

CHAPTER 49.
Early December, No 12 General Hospital, Rouen

Sam opened his eyes to a dim blur of lamplight and a strong smell of camphor. Another hospital. Part of him succumbed to a feeling of relief, the other part battled to remember how he had got here. He remembered feeling ill, an order from Mister Wise to report to the MO. Wandering in a cold grey dawn around a crater and then blackness, suffocating blackness. He could not remember and frowned with annoyance at his amnesia.

"Ooh that's a serious face. Good evening Sergeant. It's nice to see you with us at last," a soft, female voice brought him from his concentrating reverie and his eyes flicked up to a smiling, pale face fringed by a nurse's white veil. He returned the smile without thinking and stared a little too long into the wide, hazel eyes that studied him.

"Now anyone would think you had never seen a nurse before Sergeant Hepworth," she laughed. The expression reminded him a little of Lily, but this girl had dark hair and though she was not fat, she had a more ample figure than his sister. He thought her pretty and only reluctantly dropped his gaze from hers.

"Sorry. Didn't mean to stare. Where am I?" he apologised and realised with odd familiarity the dryness in his throat and mouth. He began to cough.

"Oops. Here you go." Surprisingly strong hands lifted him to a sitting position and rubbed his back vigorously. "Have a sip of water." A glass pressed to his lips.

Sam drank thankfully and when the spasm passed he allowed the gentle, firm hands to prop him against his pillows in a semi-sitting position.

"That better?" the nurse asked.

"Yes, thank you," he replied feeling exhausted.

"You're at Number Twelve General Hospital in Rouen and you've been here for several days now."

"Rouen! That far away?" he stated surprised.

"You've been quite poorly you know. Pneumonia the MO said. A terrible fever and in and out of consciousness for days," the nurse continued without being asked and tucked in the sheets around him.

He watched her working and smiled to himself at her forwardness. Just like Lily. But she was not an army nurse was she? The dress was different. Must be one of these VAD girls. She smelled of a peculiar aroma, of rosemary and camphor, an oddly pleasant mixture.

She looked up, her face very close to his, and caught him staring once more. This time she flushed slightly, their proximity making her self-conscious. He realised her discomfort and smiled.

"Sorry. I don't mean to keep staring. You remind me of my sister," he offered an explanation that was only partly truthful.

Standing upright she returned his expression, "Well, at least that's better than reminding you of your mother."

He laughed and his white, gaunt face transformed into the boy that dwelt within. The nurse dropped her eyes to her hands briefly before facing him again. "Do you feel up to something to eat? Some soup perhaps?"

"Yes, a little. Have you been with me often?"

The question was unexpected and again she blushed. "You were assigned to me yes. I'll fetch you some soup then," she replied awkwardly and made to move away. With surprising rapidity his hand caught hers.

"Thank you for taking care of me Sister," Sam said earnestly and squeezed the cool hand in his. Tactfully she withdrew it and smiled shyly.

"I was only doing my job Sergeant and it's Nurse, not Sister. I'm only a lowly VAD."

"You're an angel," the wickedly teasing response.

Oh he was a quick one this and just round from a fever too. She would have to watch him. Yet deep down his words warmed her heart.

The ward felt frigidly cold despite the two cast iron stoves burning away at either end. One was only yards from his bed, yet its heat seemed not to penetrate the chill air. Canvas and wood did not give much protection against the bitter north wind, did not provide adequate insulation. And the doors, being opened every few minutes, brought an arctic blast with monotonous regularity. Maybe it was better for those further away from the entrance. Maybe the raw bite of winter struggled to invade that far. Sam eyed the furthest end of the glorified marquee with envy. For some reason the MO had instructed he should have a bed near to the doors in order to be availed of fresher air. It would be good for his lungs! But hell, there was fresh and fresh and Sam disagreed with the good doctor's definition. He also thought the cold was more likely to bring back his pneumonia rather than actually rid his chest of the remnants of infection.

Early morning. Still dark outside and there had been snow. The day staff had brought enough of it inside when they arrived for their shift at six. Only ten minutes ago the night sister, her VAD and orderly had left. Sam had watched the comings and goings wearily whilst shivering with each icy blast as the damned doors opened and shut, opened and shut.

He had been awake for an age; since some time in the wee small hours when the choking, claustrophobic nightmare wrenched him from another fitful sleep in a cold sweat. The same dream as always. The fever gone and his memory returned to haunt him in terrifying dreams. Always oppressive darkness, a crushing weight on his body, starved of oxygen and gasping helplessly for air, knowing he was going to die and the panic that thought brought. Yet he never did die. Instead strong hands clutching his and a transformation from earth to water. Being pulled from a frozen lake and the sense that Lizzie had been with him before she floated downwards into eternal darkness.

Sam shuddered and bringing his coarse, hairy blanket high under his chin he settled to observing the day staff set about their business. The two orderlies would go and fetch breakfast and tea from the cookhouse soon. Sister and her young VAD helper would walk the ward, checking on their charges, ensuring everything was as it should be and as ordered as when they had left yesterday evening; that no one had taken a sudden turn for the worst and about to pop off their mortal coils. Death could come suddenly on a medical ward like this and when one least expected it. Men seemingly on the road to recovery sometimes succumbed and died for no apparent reason.

Five minutes passed and this morning he was lucky. Sister drifted to the far end of her ward and Nurse Farnsworth headed his way closely followed by Chigwell and Sandford, the two orderlies. The doors flew open allowing another gust of chill wind and a few swirling flakes of snow to enter as the two men left. Sam cursed under his breath and then caught the disapproving expression of the nurse in the soft glow of her oil lamp. She placed the lantern on the cupboard beside his bed and looked down at him with folded arms.

"Sergeant Hepworth, your language is simply appalling," she chastised softly though there was a barely hidden laugh behind the rebuke.

He grinned but did not speak. He did not want to speak. He wanted to watch her and listen to her voice; a gentle yet authoritative voice and deeper than one would expect. It held a richness that gave it a mildly seductive air, and a mellowness that soothed and calmed.

"Not very talkative this morning?" she quizzed with humour as she scanned the notes pinned to the foot of his bed, though he thought she did not read them. After a moment she sighed and walking around to his left side, she had learned he was somewhat deaf on his right, she picked up his wrist and began measuring his pulse. Was it a little faster now? He thought perhaps it might be. He studied her concentrating. A little frown played upon her brow and her lips were set into a thin line. He noticed a wisp of hair escaping from her headscarf just behind her ear and wanted to push it back into place for her. Did his pulse just quicken again? She put his wrist down.

"You didn't have a very restful night Sergeant?" It was not really a question. She already knew this as fact. Night Sister had briefed them on those men who had given cause for concern.

"Not really," the laconic reply.

"Headache again or bad dreams?" she asked. A lot of them had nightmares. A lot of them were haunted by ghosts.

"Both."

She held his eye for some seconds before speaking again, "You had some painkillers though."

"Yes."

"And has the pain gone?"

"More or less. It's just there if you know what I mean."

She nodded. "Well, we'll ask the MO if you might have some more painkillers when he comes."

"Don't need them. The pain's always there to some extent. It lets me know that I'm alive," he smiled sardonically.

"And the bad dreams. Do you want to talk about them?"

"I don't think so."

"It might help."

"Doubt it. Besides, I wouldn't want to burden you with the rubbish inside my head."

She cocked her head prettily on one side and looked thoughtful. After a pause she said, "I might not see the horrors of the front line Sergeant, but I do see the result of them. I think I would understand. It might do you good to talk."

"Excise my demons?" Sam returned cynically.

"Something like that."

"Nurse Farnsworth, there are far too many demons inside my head to ever excise them all. Don't waste your time on them."

She opened her mouth to say more, glanced along the ward and realised she had spent too long with one patient. She smiled. "Think about it Sergeant. I'll spend some time with you later if you change your mind," she said and moved on to the next bed taking her lamp with her. He watched her go and then cursed again as Sandford and Chigwell crashed into the ward with a huge dixie of tea straggled between them.

"Tea up lads!" Chigwell, the craggy faced corporal shouted cheerily and with his announcement a string of electric lights sparked into life along the tented ceiling and those who were able, sat up in bed.

"Sergeant Hepworth, Sergeant," Nurse Farnsworth's mellow voice seeped into his subconscious and brought him unresisting from slumber. His eyes flicked open and slowly fixed upon her pale, perfect face. With some regret she had woken him. He needed his sleep, looked so tired and drawn. "I'm sorry Sergeant, but you have a visitor...," she paused and appeared to want to say more. Maybe some words of disapproval to the mentioned visitor, but instead she stepped to one side and knew immediately she had made the right decision.

Sam's eyes drifted sleepily from the nurse to the tall, thin officer behind her and his face lit with pleasantly surprised recognition.

"Not too long Sir, he still needs rest," the VAD whispered to the lieutenant as she moved away.

"Mr Fielding, Sir," Sam greeted as he struggled to sit upright bringing on a coughing fit.

Fielding glanced guiltily at the retreating nurse, saw her hesitate and decided to act before she could throw him out. It had been an unexpected delight to find Hepworth. He was not going to miss the opportunity. He dashed forward and pulled Sam upright rubbing his back at the same time, as one might a baby, to try and suppress the cough. Somewhere between each spasm Sam began to laugh and indicated with humour in his eyes to the jug on his bedside cupboard. While the lieutenant hurriedly poured a glass of water his friend coughed a glutinous lump of phlegm into a handkerchief and with a grimace screwed it into a ball and slid it beneath his pillow. Out of sight. He accepted the water and drank deeply.

"Sorry old man," Fielding apologised sheepishly as the sergeant sank back into his pillows with a sigh and a strained expression.

"Don't be daft Sir. Not your fault. What I need is a bloody good smoke, but they won't let me. Said I have to give my lungs time to clear," Sam grumbled.

"Sorry to hear you've been so ill though."

A shrug. "Can't be helped Sir," Sam replied and studied the lieutenant briefly. A little thinner perhaps and maybe a peppering of grey around his temples, but otherwise he looked very well.

"Do you mind?" Fielding indicated to a chair.

"Be my guest Sir. I have to say this is rather a surprise. Not an unpleasant one, but I thought we had got rid of you for good Sir."

The lieutenant laughed. "No such luck. Thanks to you Eppy I made a full recovery. Managed to have a few glorious months in Blighty, but now here I am, back in France." The remark was made lightly, an attempt at couldn't-care-less bravado, yet he knew he fooled no one least of all this stalwart sergeant before him.

Sam did not comment. He understood. "You rejoining the Battalion then Sir?" he asked instead.

Fielding shook his head sadly. "No. I've been on a course down here and tomorrow I'm moving to join a new unit. One of Kitchener's New Army lot. Same Regiment, which is something I suppose, but it won't be the same. God knows how battle ready they are. They've been out since July I think and seen no real action. A spell or too in the quieter sectors of the line, that's all."

"Well if it's any consolation Sir our lot aren't much better. Not many of the originals left. Young Dobbo's out, lost a leg and an eye poor little sod. Ted Little and Jacko bought it at Festubert. Bill Pratt went at Loos. There's loads of 'em gone. Probably wouldn't recognise two thirds of 'em and officers too. Load of eager reservists and new lads now. Good bunch, but green as grass."

The two men fell silent, lost for a moment in their own quiet reflection of comrades lost.

"Hell Eppy, this is no damned good! I found out you were here and thought to come and cheer you up before I left. Least I could do after everything. I didn't want to engage you in bloody miserable conversation," Fielding stated with false cheeriness. The truth was he felt miserable, bloody miserable.

"How did you find out Sir?"

"Excuse me?"

"How did you find out I was here?"

"Stroke of luck really. Bumped into Major Wilson on the course. He told me what had happened with the mine and that he thought you were here somewhere. After that it was a matter of minor detective work. I rather fancy myself as a latter-day Sherlock Holmes you know," the lieutenant explained with almost boyish pride.

"Well I'm glad to see you Sir and I'm glad you're well, although it's a shame you aren't out of it for good. Like me eh Sir. We'll be back amongst it soon enough," Sam laughed without humour.

"Pity you won't be with me though. It would be good to have a friend there," Fielding uttered lowly. This was not going how he planned. He had thought to bring Hepworth some joy and hoped to make him feel better instead it was he who was needing the strength and support of a friend.

"You'll be alright with your new lot Sir. You don't really want a cynical Old Sweat like me spoiling the fervent enthusiasm of all those willing volunteers," Sam joked, but he too felt a pang of disappointment. The lieutenant smiled faintly and looked as if he had more he wished to say yet he refrained and dropped his eyes to his hands before awkwardly meeting the sergeant's gaze once more.

"I'm not sure how one does this Eppy, but I came here primarily to thank you. I wanted to do it in person before..., well you know, I might never get the chance again. It's not the same in a letter and I know they gave you a medal and you hate me for that, but well old man, you did save my life and that makes me forever in you debt. I owe you a great deal Eppy."

A pause. "You don't owe me anything Sir. You would have done the same in my shoes," Sam returned quietly, slightly abashed by the lieutenant's gratitude.

"You think so? I'm not sure I posses sufficient courage."

A clip clip of shoes broke the moment as Fielding turned to see the VAD returning. He brought his eyes back to Sam's, recognised the unspoken sympathy and also respect. They did not need to say more. "It looks like your pretty little nurse is coming to throw me out," he said laughingly.

"Looks like," Sam agreed.

Fielding stood rapidly nearly capsizing the chair in his haste. *Still as awkward as ever.* He nodded at the nurse and held out his hand. "Goodbye Eppy. Make sure you get well."

Without hesitation Sam grasped the hand tightly. "I will Sir. Good luck Sir."

The lieutenant acknowledged the wishes with a shy smile, thanked the nurse and left. His former sergeant, the man who had saved his life, watched him go with an odd sense of loss.

"Seems a nice chap," Nurse Farnsworth interrupted his thoughts.

"One of the best," Sam pronounced facing her.

"You are close? I mean, he's an officer I know but...."

He studied her momentarily. She would not understand. How could she? No one could unless they had been there, unless they had lived through that hell together. "He's a brother," he said simply.

She smiled and held his eyes for an instant longer. "Yes, I know," she replied and wandered away.

At first getting out of bed had left him light headed and feeling strangely weak. Even walking the length of the ward had been exhausting. But it did not last long. He was young and strong and once rested the ravages of pneumonia soon faded leaving only the familiar headaches and the dreams. It was only a matter of time now before they moved him to the convalescent camp across the road. A prospect not to be dwelt upon.

Sam clamped his pipe in his mouth. A compromise. They would not let him smoke cigarettes but a pipe was different and he had to admit that he rather enjoyed it. The pipe tobacco had a far more pleasing aroma than his usual, awful woodbines; fragrant almost. And if one inhaled rather deeper than one ought, the nicotine still hit the spot. He had never thought to use the gift his father had sent, yet now it was a God send. In fact, he might give up the fags altogether and take to this more refined habit out of preference. He smiled at the thought and sat down at the old piano.

The instrument had been gifted to the ward by some well meaning visitor who really had no idea of what was practical in a field hospital, even a more-or-less permanent one such as this. Still, the piano languished mainly untouched, at the far end of the ward. Untouched and out of tune. That was until a certain Sergeant Hepworth discovered it on his first sortie out of bed. The temptation to touch the ivory keys had been too much and he had stroked them tentatively at first, cringing at the discordant notes.

"That is why it remains unplayed," Sister had remarked with a frown as she passed by him. He had agreed the tone was dreadful, but it could be tuned given the right equipment.

To his surprise the necessary equipment had been found with very little trouble by the corporal orderly Sid Chigwell, no questions asked of course, and Sam spent a couple of hours working upon the forlorn instrument. At the end it was by no means perfect, the old piano had long since seen its best, but now it could belt out a half decent tune to sing along to and Sister was more than happy to let him play for an hour each afternoon after tea. It cheered the men up. Took their minds off their ailments and their nightmares.

He sat at the stool and took a moment to light his pipe before turning to the small crowd of men, those who could get out of bed, around him. Others sat up in their cots their faces bright with anticipation. It never ceased to amaze Sam how something as simple as a good sing-song could lift a man from the depths of despair. There was something about music that touched the soul. Equally, he was aware of its darker power. Where it could give happiness, it could also bring deep, aching pain and for that reason he played very few melancholy tunes.

"What'll it be lads?" he asked through a veil of blue pipe smoke.

"Let's have some carols Sarge," a pale, scrawny kid asked.

"Carols?"

"Aye, why not. It's nearly Christmas," another man added.

"Alright, carols it is," Sam acquiesced surprised at their choice. He began with Hark the Herald Angels Sing and the inhabitants of ward six joined in with gusto. A festive medley followed.

"I think Sergeant it is almost a travesty to have to move you out of here," a thin haired officer of medium height and sombre expression said as Nurse Farnsworth ushered the reluctant audience back to their beds ready for the MO's last rounds of the day.

Sam removed his pipe from his mouth, it had gone out anyway, and tried to ignore the instant dread that filled his stomach. He grinned, but something in his eyes must have given away his true emotions.

"Sorry old man, but you're fit enough to leave us now. I've arranged for you to move over to the convalescent camp in the morning," the MO added apologetically.

"Can't be helped Sir, been here long enough. Bored to death and itching to get back out there Sir." Not true at all, but it was what they expected to hear.

The MO nodded sadly and moved to his next patient. Sam closed his eyes and took a deep breath. He remained seated and staring at the walnut veneer for a whole minute while he fought the fear that threatened to engulf him. *Must not give in to it.* He had always known he would go back. *Still, had some weeks convalescing anyhow. Not all lost yet.* He stuffed tobacco into his pipe and lit it once more drawing hard and letting the nicotine rush calm his racing heart. *Christ!* He swore under his breath and began to play the piano, a hauntingly beautiful melody penned by his brother. The piece reflected his mood perfectly.

"That's lovely," Nurse Farnsworth said from just behind his shoulder.

He turned and looked up at her. Such sorrow in those dark eyes, such torment. The sight shocked her and she instinctively touched his face. He grasped her hand and held it tightly. She did not withdraw. Then he squeezed the hand and dropped it, a wide smile forcing away the desolation.

"My brother wrote it. Good isn't it? I don't really do it justice though. It belongs to the violin in truth not this clunky old thing," he patted the piano with affection.

"Well, I'm not a musician, but I would say that you played it very nicely Sergeant Hepworth."

"Thank you," he acknowledged with a nod and a cheeky grin that made her blush.

"The MO's releasing you tomorrow?" she asked already knowing the answer.

"Aye. You'll soon be rid of me Nurse Farnsworth." *What a pity I can't take you out. I'd like to get to know you better.*

"Well, we'll miss you. Do you think they'll let you come and play for us?" A naïve question.

He sucked on his pipe and shook his head. "Doubt it very much. They'll be intent on getting me fit to move back up the line."

"Oh." She hovered uncertain of what to say. She should move away. Sister would be watching and she should be attending Captain Maitland and Sister.

As if he read her mind he gave her the opportunity to leave, "I think you're wanted. Sister has that disapproving look in her eye."

"Oh, yes. I..., hmmm," she dithered and flushed prettily once again. She turned to go.

"Nurse Farnsworth?"

"Yes?"

"Thank you for taking care of me."

"Don't be silly Sergeant it's my job."

"Still, you've made the difference. May I ask you something?"

Oh goodness! What is he going to say? She did not answer, but waited anxiously.

"What's your name? Your Christian name?" he asked.

Relief! She smiled. "Alice," she confided with a slight air of recklessness. *It couldn't harm, him knowing that, could it?* She hurried away before he could ask more. He smiled at her retreating back and returned to the piano keys.

CHAPTER 50.
December 24th – 26th

London 24th

In buoyant mood Frank almost bounded up the stairs to his flat. Under one arm he carried his violin, under the other a neatly wrapped parcel, a present for his heavily pregnant wife.

The concert at the hospital had gone well. A selection of carols, music hall songs, jokes and classical pieces. As usual the men had brought the house down singing raucously and shouting for numerous encores. If anything they had been louder and more appreciative than ever. Perhaps because it was Christmas.

Frank had left the hospital uplifted as always following one of the Davidson Orchestra's performances. He caught the late tram and then the tube, hardly noticing the bitter cold. The present for Evie he had collected earlier from one of his fellow musicians; a middle-aged woman who worked as a milliner. The hat was exquisite to match his exquisite wife.

At the top of the stairs he paused for breath, his labouring heart reminding him harshly of his forgotten frailty. He frowned and inwardly cursed his affliction giving himself a few moments to recover. He did not want to enter the flat half dead. He mopped the sweat from his brow with an initialled handkerchief and hoping she was still awake, for the hour was late, he strode to his door. Tucking his violin case under his left arm he tried the knob, it turned, she was still up. Entering his eyes fell upon the small tree they had decorated together yesterday bringing a wide smile to his bluish lips. He called her name and was about to demand a kiss, but instead stopped in his tracks, his mouth open in a surprised O. She was not alone.

In front of the gas fire, one arm behind his back and the other clutching a large brandy, stood a young man in uniform, immaculately smart, his fair hair cropped close and oiled, moustache neatly trimmed. The soldier grinned at Frank's obvious shock.

"Hello old man. Good to see you," he said.

"Frank darling," Evie heaved herself from the sofa, one hand covering her swollen belly. She beamed at her husband radiantly. "Isn't this a wonderful surprise?"

For a second Frank did not know what to say. He glanced at his wife and back to the dashing officer, then he too grinned and kicking the door shut with his left foot he placed his things on the floor and hurried forward, right hand outstretched.

"James, my dear chap. I'm so sorry. Just a shock to see you. Not an unpleasant one you understand," he laughed.

The two friends shook hands warmly.

"I should have let you known I was back in London, but I have to admit I have always enjoyed surprises and couldn't resist calling on you. Of course I didn't know you would be out. Shame on you Frank leaving your gorgeous wife alone on Christmas Eve. Sorry I couldn't make the wedding," James flitted from one subject to the next his mind seemingly not concentrating on any. He smiled awkwardly.

"Oh don't be silly James," Evie declared and slid an arm around her husband's waist. In response he wrapped his around her shoulders. "Frank does important work you know," she said proudly, sensing the odd discomfort and feeling the need to keep the conversation light.

"Yes, of course. Good for you old man," James raised his glass in recognition and a toast yet his expression did not quite carry the feeling he had hoped to convey. "God, it's good to see you both," he blurted and quite uncharacteristically his eyes filled. He looked at the floor suddenly and struggled to compose himself.

Frank detached himself from Evie and touched his friend's arm. "Here, sit down. Don't stand. Has it been dreadful? My brothers say it's hell, but not much more than that," he indicated to the sofa.

James sat heavily and continued to stare at the floor. Frank took a seat opposite in the threadbare armchair taking hold of Evie's hand as she perched herself upon his knee. They waited in respectful silence their eyes flitting from each other to their troubled friend with sympathy.

"It, it wasn't what I expected," the laconic and unsatisfactory reply after some seconds. James lifted his head quickly and forced a smile that failed to reach his dead eyes. "God it's good to see you both," he repeated.

"It's good to see you too. How long are you in London for? I presume you're home on leave?" Frank asked uncomfortable with the awkward silences and stilted conversation. The man before him seemed a shadow of his former self. It was unnerving. He felt Evie squeeze his hand and realised she felt the same.

"Leave? No. I'm not on leave. I've been transferred to the War Office. Father pulled some strings. Still in uniform, which is a God send. Wouldn't want to be branded a coward."

"A coward? Don't be ridiculous! You've been out there. You've done your bit. How could anyone call you a coward?" Frank remonstrated, the memory of white feathers all too raw.

"Done my bit. Hmm, yes... I suppose so," James mumbled hesitantly as if he did not quite believe those words, as if he tried to convince himself. He knocked back the remainder of his brandy and bounced to his feet taking his hosts by surprise. "Well, better go. It's late. Good to see you old chap." He stuck his hand out.

Rising to his feet, Frank took the hand and shook it warmly as Evie stood to one side a quizzical expression upon her face. "So soon? Do you have to go? You could stay the night couldn't he Evie?" He turned to his wife.

"Of course. It would be lovely to have you stay," she responded dutifully although her tone suggested a reluctance.

"No. I only popped in to say hello. I'm staying with my parents." James drew his hand away quickly, looking troubled. He opened his mouth as if to say more then promptly closed it, the thought unspoken.

"You'll come and visit again?" Evie asked as he stooped to kiss her upturned cheek.

"If you wish." He smiled warmly for the first time and then pulled his cap upon his head. "Must dash. Don't see me out. I know the way. Used to live here you know," he joked. He rocked back and forward on the toes of his feet, looked once again like he wanted to say something else, but then turned with a "Cheerio" and hurriedly left the flat.

The couple stared after him, astounded and disturbed by his odd behaviour.

"How odd. He seems so different, so..., sad," Evie spoke first still gazing at the closed door.

"Yes he does. It's the war I suppose," Frank agreed feeling uneasy.

"Oh Frank, I'm so glad you couldn't go. I couldn't bear to see you in pain like that," Evie pronounced vehemently and wrapped her arms around his torso laying her head against his shoulder.

He kissed her hair and gathered her close to him. For the first time he had to agree. This unexpected meeting had shaken him more than seeing any number of wounded soldiers at the hospitals. Those brave men were the nameless masses. He professionally maintained a protective wall between them and himself, even with Bert Dobson. But James was his best friend. *Had* been his best friend. Had been the life and soul of every party. The gay bachelor. Happy-go-lucky and carefree. The man that had visited tonight seemed only a pale shadow of the James he knew and loved. The spark had gone. Nothing remained of the bright, generous James of a year ago.

Frank shuddered and felt Evie clasp her arms tighter. Yes, he was glad to be out of this bloody war! Suddenly he smiled, bounded to his belongings left by the door and picking up the parcel hurried back to his wife.

"Merry Christmas darling," he said affectionately and kissed her lips tenderly.

Surely next year would see an end to war. Surely it couldn't last much longer. He forced the thought that it might away as Evie threw her arms around him with grateful joy.

No. 12 General Hospital Rouen 25th

Sam hovered outside the great marquee not really sure whether he should enter, feeling ridiculously self-conscious. It was bitterly cold and he shivered beneath his greatcoat and various layers of clothing. The tent door opened disgorging a pair of orderlies intent upon their business. Nearly lunch time. They would be hurrying down to the kitchen tent to bring up the men's dinner. Christmas dinner. One of them stopped short and nodded.

"'Ullo Sergeant. Come back to see us then?" the man asked with a bright smile. He grabbed hold of his cap as a sudden blast of icy wind threatened to rip it from his head.

"Going up the line tomorrow. Wanted to say goodbye and thanks," Sam replied flushing. The orderly knew his purpose and the generalisation of his explanation did not fool him.

"I see. Bit of a bugger eh Sarge? 'Aving to go back at Christmas," the corporal sympathised.

Sam shrugged. "Got to go back sometime. At least I get a turkey dinner. Poor buggers in the trenches won't," he laughed hollowly not even bothering to correct the improper address. There was no point. This bloke was no Regular and things had changed. He straightened his shoulders and sighed. "Will..., is Nurse Farnsworth on duty Sid?" he asked feeling his face grow hot again. *Christ Eppy, what's up with you man?*

Sid grinned. He'd known all along why the sergeant was here. "Yeah she's inside," he replied and opened his mouth to say more.

"Oy Corp, you comin' or am I bringing this grub back single 'anded," the impatient shout from his colleague stopped the witty remark from being voiced.

"Better go Sarge," Sid said jerking his thumb towards his mate. He stuck his hand out. "Best o' luck son," he said. Unhesitatingly Sam shook the proffered hand. He did not mind the unorthodox familiarity. Sid was nearly twice his age. The fact that the orderly was merely a corporal did not rankle. Somehow it seemed different with these RAMC chaps. Well at least with an old boy like Sid. It was the unhidden expression of sympathy that irritated. That look which said so many things. A look that wished him God's protection; that said rather you than I; that carried all the regret and sorrow of a priest attending a condemned man.

"Thanks Sid. Don't take this the wrong way, but I hope I never see you again," Sam joked pushing away the chill of fear the orderly's wishes had triggered.

Sid smirked. "I understand completely Sarge," he said with a chuckle and hurried off after his impatient comrade.

For a moment Sam watched the two men disappearing into the distance, along the long line of vast tents and huts that made up the medical wards of Number 12 General hospital. At length he took in a deep breath, - *don't know why you're so bloody nervous-*, and entered the marquee. It took a moment for his eyes to adjust to the relative gloom. After the brightness of even a bleak winter's day the great tent seemed oppressively dark, it's thick canvas allowing little natural light through. Number Six Medical Ward was lit, as all the marquees were, by a row of electric lights suspended from the roof. Their massed glow, though sufficient to read by, was no substitute for daylight and the effect, he had always found, depressing. However, today there was a festive cheeriness about the place normally lacking. A number of lights had coloured paper shades around them giving the impression of Chinese lanterns. Paper chains in patriotic red, white and blue adorned the canvas walls and in the centre, at the end of the long dining table, a tree stood decked with home-made ornaments. The ward had been decorated for Christmas.

Looking around he took in the lines of beds, all occupied by some sick solider in varying degrees of malaise. At the far end he noticed Sister busily attending to one of her charges whom it appeared was having some awful coughing fit. Probably a gas victim or maybe pneumonia like he had suffered from. Sickness was as rife at present, if not more so, as injury.

He let his eyes wander from bed to bed, but could not see her. Maybe she had been sent on an errand. He suddenly felt disappointed. He did not have long before he had to get back for dinner. But Sid had said she was inside. Then he saw her, or rather she spotted him as she emerged with a tray full of mugs and plates from a curtained recess known to all as the ward kitchen. She smiled brightly when he caught her eye and with a quick, surreptitious look towards Sister, she placed the heavy tray upon a trestle table and walked briskly to where he stood.

"Sergeant Hepworth," she said formally, her warm hazel eyes searching his.

"Nurse Farnsworth," he replied feeling oddly embarrassed. God knows why. She always made him feel this way. Like a kid. Not in a patronising way, but with the awkwardness of a teenager with a crush. It was an alien feeling to him. Normally he was quite the charmer with women, knew what they liked to hear, how to get what he wanted. With Alice Farnsworth it was different. He took his cap off hurriedly and fumbled it into his greatcoat pocket. Her smile widened.

"Have you come to see me Sergeant?" she asked mockingly, not cruelly so, just a little provocative, and cocked her head to one side.

God she is pretty.

He gathered himself together despite the tingling thrill running through his body and the thoughts of what it would be like to kiss her that often, no, always rushed into his mind whenever he saw her. There were other thoughts too, but none he would admit to her.

"Yes. Sorry, I know you're busy and I shouldn't bother you...," he hesitated taking a glance towards Sister. The senior nurse had seen him and was watching from a distance with arms folded. "Look, Sister's watching. I just wanted to see you before I go."

Nurse Farnsworth's smile dropped from her face and she became serious. "You're leaving?"

He nodded solemnly. "Can't swing the lead forever," he laughed. "I'm moving up tomorrow. Rejoining my unit. Well, I think I am. We're going to Étaples first."

"Oh." It should not be a surprise. They all went back eventually, or went home to Blighty - or died. Suddenly Alice found all the Christmas joy deserted her. She felt terribly sad. She should not have these feelings. Not for a patient and especially not for a sergeant, but Sam Hepworth was different.

A momentary awkward silence.

"Look, I'm going to get thrown out in a minute. Sister's looking daggers at us. I wanted to ask you. Two things." He waited.

"Yes?"

"May I write to you?"

"Of course," she smiled and her face brightened. The thrill returned and he echoed her expression.

"Thanks. And tomorrow. We'll pass through the gate at seven thirty in the morning. Will you..., will you come down and see me off?"

She frowned not sure whether she wanted to watch him march away.

"Sorry, you're on duty. It's alright. It was just a thought," he hurriedly added reading the frown incorrectly.

"No.., I mean yes I am but... Look, I'll ask Sister. I'm sure she'll not mind. She's not the tartar everyone thinks she is. I'll be there." The grateful, relieved look on his face transforming into a wide, boyish grin made the decision worthwhile.

"Grand. Well, I'll be off then. See you in the morning," Sam held out his hand. She glanced at it hesitatingly before taking it in hers. He squeezed her fingers tenderly, holding on a little too long for mere politeness, not wanting to let go. She responded to the squeeze in turn and gently pulled her grip from his.

"See you in the morning Sam," she said in almost a whisper. It was the first time she had used his Christian name since she had nursed him through his fever.

He nodded his head, removed his cap from his pocket and with a lusty wave at Sister turned on his heels and hastily vanished through the door. Alice returned to her tray, noted Sister shaking her head with a wry smile upon her lips and blushed in return.

Pateley Bridge 25th

Joe wondered around the frosted garden like a lost soul, a pipe, a new habit, clamped firmly between his teeth. The mellow stench of tobacco hung in heavy aromatic wreaths around his head unnoticed as he stared unseeingly at the valley below. Bathed in golden winter sunlight it was a scene of almost breathtaking beauty with only the chimneys of the brewery giving lie to the tranquil picture. Yet all this passed Joe by. For once the dale held no allure. He breathed deeply through the corner of his mouth, careful not to inhale too much tobacco smoke. It was not a habit he was particularly enamoured with but it served its purpose in calming his nerves.

He glanced at his watch. They would be home soon. The service would be over. They were at church. All of them. Including the servants. Only he and the nurse looking after his son remained. He had no appetite for God. Not after France. Not after Robert. Where he had always wrestled with uncertainty of the existence of a divine being he now knew, unquestioningly, that there was none. It was something he had argued at length with Simon Graham. Amicably of course; intellectually even, yet his new found atheism was unshakeable. Of course it horrified his mother. Poor Eliza, with her blind, pathetic faith. This war was having an untold affect upon her. Her family no longer safe and changed, irrevocably, forever.

Voices carrying clearly on the still air from the drive disturbed Joe's thoughts and with a sigh he reluctantly tapped out the contents of his pipe and sauntered indoors ready to greet them with as much festive joy as he could muster. Had to put on a show. Would be poor form to behave as he felt, the brooding, miserable eldest son, at Christmas. Even if it felt a hypocrisy to wish good will to all men. War had changed him. Much more than he had ever thought possible. The happiness of a family Christmas seemed obscene when men were dying in atrocious conditions at the Front. Any decent civilisation would cancel Christmas when so much death abounded surely?

Joe smiled cynically at his own thoughts. What a curmudgeon he had become. People needed their traditions at times of hardship. Keeping Christmas and to their faith girded morale and helped to dispel despair. He had no doubt the Battalion would be enjoying their meagre festivities despite the cold, mud and the ever present flirtations with death.

"Ooo it's so cold," Eliza's voice from the hall. Agreement from Dora and a chuckle from his father.

Joe deliberately placed his pipe on the mantelpiece and, turning his back to the heartening fire, forced his face into a welcoming smile as his family burst into the drawing room. They beamed with the righteousness only those who know they have made their peace with God can, their demeanour full of festive cheer. Inwardly Joe cringed. Dinner, his last supper before the special train south, would be another ordeal of forced jollity and denial of the truth. How he wished he was alone. How he wished Sam or Lily were here. Someone who would understand. How he missed Robert.

No 23 General Hospital, Étaples 25th

It was a great shame, nevertheless predictable, that the desperately ill Irishman should die on Christmas Day. For an hour or two his passing brought a cloud of sadness to an otherwise happy shift. If only he could have lasted another twenty four hours, then the others would not have had to watch the curtains carefully placed around his bed, listen to the squeaking wheels of the low, wooden mortuary trolley traversing the planked floor, or the mutterings of the Catholic priest incanting the Last Rites. And the poor boy might have gained some final happiness from the carols sung to the inexpertly wielded accordion. But it was not to be and at three minutes past two in the afternoon, Private O'Halloran breathed his last laboured and shuddering breath and was no more.

Lily saw it from her place by the tree where she, Corporal Briggs and the VAD nurse retrieved a sack of presents in preparation for doling them out to the patients. All the men on this ward remained bed ridden and unable to enjoy their Christmas dinner in the mess marquee. All the more reason to give them something to smile about. The day shift had been gathering, hording and wrapping small, simple gifts for the past month for this occasion. Chocolate, tobacco, a mouth organ, a pack of playing cards. Nothing expensive, but the thought was there. Now one parcel would remain unopened.

Lily sighed and placed a hand on Briggs' shoulder.

"Jack, please could you go and fetch Father Riley," she said softly.

Briggs let go of the sack and stood upright. He glanced at the far corner and back at the sister again nodding solemnly. Without a word he hurried from the ward.

"Nurse, the curtains," Lily indicated and she and her VAD help quietly arranged the mobile screen around the dead man's bed.

The ritual was one carried out so often, that the fitter men, those able to sit up in bed, knew what it meant. The cheerful chatter amongst them as they ate their Christmas dinner died away and the clatter of knives and forks became a subdued, barely audible scraping. The assisting orderlies, there to help with feeding the less able men, paused from their task and glanced briefly at one another before encouraging their charges to take another mouthful.

"Is it the Irish lad?" a heavily bandaged Liverpudlian asked his attendant orderly.

"Aye looks like it. Poor sod! On Christmas Day too."

"Makes no odds to 'im upstairs," the patient returned.

Behind the screen Lily sighed. "Thank you Walker, I'll do this alone. Go and make sure the others get some beer with their dinner. We'll delay presents until five. Ailin should have left us by then."

And so the ritual of death began. The priest came, followed by the mortuary trolley. Briggs helped Lily lay the body out, gather the deceased's belongings into a muslin bag and take them to Sister's office ready for sending to the bereaved parents. Later, Lily would write a letter to them and post it with the broken fob watch, photograph of a pretty girl, pocket bible and the almost empty wallet. The mortuary attendant and Briggs lifted O'Halloran onto the trolley and covered it with a sheet.

"I suppose it is a relief," Lily uttered lowly thinking how she had hoped the Irishman would soon be free of his terrible pain. His body had been ripped apart by a shell. The injuries were the worst she had seen, yet the poor boy had lived for five days before the inevitable gangrene claimed him. For four days he had been lucid, but by Christmas Eve the fever took hold and he descended into coma. In many ways that was better, for it was likely he knew little suffering from then on. Still, his death was as much a blow as it was a welcome release.

"Pity he 'ad to go today though," Briggs muttered back. Lily shot a disapproving glance at him, but said nothing. She pulled back the screens and the trolley was wheeled away.

"Right Jack, let's clear up and then we can give out the gifts and have a sing song. Have you brought that accordion?"

"Aye it's in your office," the corporal returned with a grin.

"Is it indeed? And are you sure you can play it?" she countered with a half smile.

"What you inferring Sister? Course I can play the thing," he grumbled with mock hurt pride and ambled away to begin clearing dinner plates.

An hour later and the sad death had been forgotten, or at least pushed aside. Music, of a kind, filled the ward and Lily's sweet, clear voice led the singing. Only occasionally did she grimace at the dud notes squeezed from Jack's wheezing accordion. No one cared that it played out of tune. The boys were enjoying themselves, propped on pillows or turned gently to watch. The ward lights spread a warm red and green glow through their makeshift shades and a few candles leant atmosphere to the rather splendid tree that Jack had somehow purloined. Lily had not asked questions. The men sang happily and the carols changed into music hall tunes, cheery and comforting. They brought forth thoughts of home. A home, most of them would be seeing soon, if death did not come knocking first.

The clamour for more was deafening when Lily declared the final song. Amazing how much noise badly injured men could make. They banged their mugs and shouted and whistled. Fearing they would disturb the neighbouring ward Lily held her hands aloft and acquiesced to one more tune. They begged a solo. Without accompaniment, for she was sure Briggs would not know it, she began 'Pack up your Troubles' and the ward fell quiet to listen.

Unseen a uniformed figure crept inside and stood leaning quietly against the partition to the store room. The officer smiled broadly to himself and enjoyed the angelic clarity of the voice he loved. He watched the injured Tommies gazing at their sister with more than profound respect and suspected that at that moment a number of them had fallen hopelessly in love with her. Their eyes never left her form; their expressions were bright, yet at the same time wistful. At last she encouraged them to join in the final chorus which they did with a surprisingly gentle air. The intruder felt himself lost in the same spell as they; he hummed along tapping his fingers against the partition. For some reason he felt curiously nostalgic and more than a little disappointed when the song ended. He was not alone. The men begged for more, but Sister was adamant.

That was enough. They needed to rest now. Too much excitement was not good for them and the MO would not be pleased if they were agitated when he made his final rounds. To good hearted groans, Lily stepped down from her orange box stage. Only now did she notice the figure standing by the store room. Her heart turned a little flip and she bit her lip in an attempt to stem the sudden and unexpected rise of emotion.

"Nurse Walker, please prepare for the MO's rounds," she said to a surprised VAD. Never before had she been entrusted to prepare for such an important event.

Lily did not hear the reply, she was already on her way to the waiting figure. She stopped about a yard in front of him. He stood upright and grinned.

"I'd forgotten how lovely you were and how beautifully you sang," he said in a soft Canadian drawl.

"Alex...I mean Captain Thewlis, whatever are you doing here?" she managed stammeringly, shocked to see him.. She had not expected this. Ever again. Though there was no reason why their paths should not cross. Her eyes held his and she experienced that old familiar thrill of pleasure as his smile broadened.

"I thought you'd be pleased to see me," he teased.

"I... I hadn't expected..., this is a surprise. I thought you were staying in Boulogne."

He shrugged. "I asked for a transfer."

"You're here now? At Number 23?" her eyes widened incredulously.

He laughed drawing a few curious stares in their direction. She stepped into her office ensuring he followed.

"Sure am. I couldn't let you disappear from my life you see. So, here I am and this evening I am going to take you to dinner."

"I'm sorry? I'm afraid that's impossible. I don't get off duty until seven and then I will be far too fatigued for a late dinner. Besides it's against the rules remember." Somehow she managed to remain aloof, to give the impression of propriety. She hoped he could not hear how loudly her heart thumped in her chest.

"To hell with the rules Sister. It's Christmas and I'll be damned if rules are going to stop me having dinner with my favourite girl," Alex returned.

She flushed. "Your girl? Captain Thewlis, I don't think it entirely appropriate..." she began suddenly guilt stricken. Her mind drifted back to Robert and absurdly she felt unfaithful to his memory.

"Aw come on Lil. It's Christmas.?"

"I'm sorry, but it just wouldn't be proper," she replied firmly, her momentary weakness mastered.

"I'm not suggesting impropriety, only dinner with a friend," he tried. She turned away from the hurt in his voice.

"Look, think about it. I'll be at the main gate at eight," he said hopefully and with a smile left her alone. Outside her office he almost bumped into Briggs. Had the man been listening? Impossible to know for sure. The corporal saluted him and knocked on the partition wall. Lily's voice bade him enter and as Thewlis hovered uncertainly he disappeared inside with a wink of one eye. Alex grinned broadly and swung from the ward whistling.

"Jack, what is it?" Lily demanded a touch waspishly as she heard the cheerful whistle fade with Thewlis' departure. She pretended to be busy with a pile of paperwork, feeling her face flushed and knowing exactly how the shrewd orderly would read it.

"Was wondering if you wanted a brew before MO's rounds Sister," the corporal answered.

"There isn't time is there?" She questioned with uncharacteristic uncertainty.

"'Alf and 'our yet."

"Oh, is there? Well, in that case yes. Thank you."

Jack hovered.

"Is there something else?" Lily queried.

"You really should go you know?"

"I beg your pardon?" she stiffened and her face coloured even more.

"To dinner with that captain. It would do you good," Jack ventured.

Lily opened her mouth to tell the man it was none of his business and reprimand him for eavesdropping, but he cut in before she could speak.

"I don't think your young man would mind. He's been gone a while now."

The sister stared at her orderly. She could hardly believe he had spoken so forthrightly. She should be angry. She should severely reprimand him for his familiarity. Speaking to her as an equal and offering unsolicited and unwanted opinions. Instead she experienced something like relief.

"It's against the rules," she stated simply at last. An inadequate reply, but all she could muster.

"Well, I won't be telling anyone Sister. You go out and enjoy yourself. You deserve it," Jack returned with a big grin and left to make tea. Lily gazed after him her head in turmoil.

Lily sat awkwardly sipping what was really a very good Bordeaux in a rather shabby restaurant in Étaples. Her eyes flicked nervously to the door as she dreaded anyone entering who might be in uniform, who might catch her having dinner with an RAMC captain. On the other hand, he was charming and entertaining company and for the first time in weeks she felt a burden of guilt lift just a little from her aching shoulders. She blamed herself for Robert's death, whether rightfully or not.

"You don't have to worry. No one will come in. Monsieur has opened only for us this night," Thewlis laughed his eyes alight with his usual half mocking humour.

"Oh? And how did you manage that?" Lily asked her tone obviously disbelieving.

"Because I've paid him for the privilege of being his only clientele. He drove a hard bargain I can tell you."

Lily stared at her companion. *Is he serious?* Uncomfortably she realised that he was. "Alex, I don't want you to think that because I..."

"Don't worry. It's only dinner. I wouldn't dream of anything so outrageously caddish. I'm an officer and a gentleman you know," he interrupted.

She eyed him suspiciously, but a slow smile crept to her lips. His boyish charm was infectious. "You shouldn't have gone to so much trouble. I dread to think what you've paid," she said at last as she twisted her glass with mild embarrassment.

"Worth every penny," he replied softly.

She caught his eye and flushed. The mocking facade had gone. In his gaze a different light burned. She took a gulp of wine and fought to remain impassive, but inside her breast her heart beat a furious pace.

"I've embarrassed you," he suggested, not unkindly.

Lily smiled shyly. "A little, yes."

"I'm sorry," he reached across the snowy table cloth and picked up her hand. She did not pull it away, but she dare not look into those eyes again. "God you're lovely. You know that don't you? You know that I'd walk to Hell and back for you?"

"Alex..."

"Ahem. Le dejeuner Monsieur," a polite cough and firm announcement from the proprietor brought a sudden return to reality. Their hands flew apart and their posture straightened like naughty children caught up to mischief by a school master.

The plates were placed before them and with an amused twitch of his ample moustache the proprietor bid them "Bon appetite".

Lily glanced at Thewlis and they both laughed out loud, any awkwardness between them dissipating.

"Well this looks wonderful," she said gazing at the plate of chicken, potato and cabbage.

Thewlis pulled a face. "Not exactly the Savoy, but it's the best he could come up with. Merry Christmas Lily," he held his glass up in toast.

Smiling broadly, Lily chinked her glass against his. "And the same to you Alex. Thank you. Thank you so much," she stressed.

"Thank you, for coming. Now tuck in, before it gets cold," he returned and watched for a few moments as she self-consciously cut a piece of meat. Yes it was worth it. *Every goddamned penny*. She felt the same he was sure. This was the beginning of something truly wonderful. He smiled to himself and began to eat his meal with more relish than the simple repast deserved.

No. 12 Convalescent Camp, 26th

"Right lads, form up!" the sergeant major shouted and with a well trained scrabble of feet and clink of equipment the mixed ranks of men straightened their mien, and smartly, rapidly organised themselves into a long column of fours. One would never guess they were mishmash of different units, all moving up to rejoin their various battalions at the Front. There was no banter, no chatter. This was a solemn occasion. No one enjoyed the prospect of returning. All had hoped for a return to Blighty. Not to be. The war needed them. They had recovered from whatever wound they had suffered or illness that ailed them. It was back to the fight and the constant promise of death and bugger the fact that it was Christmas. War did not care for holy festivals. Not this year.

A pompous captain of about thirty joined the sergeant major on a quick inspection along the ranks. A pair of base wallahs. Never seen the Front either of them. Not in this war at least.

"Right-ho Sergeant Major. Let's march these lucky lads down to the train," the captain announced loudly with inappropriate jocularity. The warrant officer winced at the insensitive joke and, with uncharacteristic sympathy for one of his kind, gave the order to quick march out of the camp. The long column seemed to utter a collective sigh but obeyed and were soon swinging out of the gate and into the eternal lane that ran between the convalescent camp and the hospital, straight as a die, towards the rail head and their journey north.

Sam set his face into an expression of grim determination. He was not going to show his fear. The fact that three times now he had spent a considerable length of time in hospital because of this war weighed heavy on his mind. All in the space of, or a little over, a year. His luck could not hold forever. If one could call it luck. He had been blown up twice and buried alive once. It only left getting shot. Would he survive that one too? He thought the odds were against it. And as the Staff continued to insist on sending their best troops, the few remaining Regulars, to the slaughter, then it was only a matter of time before a bullet with his number on it ended his life. He shuddered, but not from the cold. *God Eppy, pull yourself together!* He forced his mind onto other thoughts and wondered if she would be there. It brought a faint smile to his lips.

"NOOoo!" the anguished scream brought the column to a shuddering halt and the sergeant major hurrying back along the line. Sam glanced at the corporal to his right, a man from his Regiment, but a different battalion, with raised eyebrows.

"That kid from the DLI. Poor bugger," the corporal muttered in response with a shake of his head. Sam nodded remembering a boy standing alone sobbing quietly to himself while they waited for the officer to arrive to take roll call. He looked behind and saw the same officer berating the young man now as the latter cowered, prostate on the ground, shaking his head repeatedly and crying.

"*Christ!*" Sam mumbled to himself. Everyone stood watching, their faces blank and unsmiling. Most could sympathise.

The charade carried on. The captain ranted, calling the boy a coward and a disgrace to the Army. *Bastard! What did he know with his cushy desk job a hundred miles from the Front?* He never had to face fear on a daily basis. The sergeant major stepped in as the officer threw his arms up in despair and bent over the soldier. He spoke encouragingly, not unkindly, but with the usual stern authority of his creed. They could hear his deep, resonant voice along the whole column.

"Now then lad. This ain't no good. Let's be 'aving you now. Time to go." He bent down to pick the private up and the boy wailed loudly, lashing out with his arms.

"Stand aside Mister Crawley," the captain addressed the warrant officer and drawing his pistol pointed it at the cringing soldier. Crawley looked horrified but obeyed. The low murmuring that had broken out amongst the troops instantly hushed.

"On your feet now Private or I'll bloody well shoot you!"

"*Fucking shoot me then you bastard!* I ain't going back. *You can't make me go back,*" the young soldier yelled.

Appalled, Sam broke ranks before his corporal companion could stop him. He ran along the line, his rifle banging heavily against his back and thigh, his pack clanking. Everyone stared. Both the captain and the sergeant major looked up in surprise.

"Get back in line Sergeant," Crawley growled in warning.

"No Sir. Sorry Sir, but let me try," Sam blurted. To hell with unquestioning obedience.

"Don't be ridiculous Sergeant. Do as you're bloody well told," the officer snapped angrily.

"Please, Sir. Let me try. It's better than shooting the poor bugger."

"He's not even your Regiment lad," Crawley added but his voice signalled he had relented. He did not want the death of a young soldier on his conscience.

Sam did not wait for a reply. He hunched down next to the quivering, sobbing boy and began to talk very gently and so quietly that no one else could be sure of his words.

"Stuck up skrimshanker'll do it son. Don't give him the satisfaction. Think of what the bugger'll say over his fuckin' brandy and cigar with his CO. He has to justify been out here somehow. Don't let him use you as an excuse. If anyone's the fuckin' coward it's him. Never been within a mile of the Front."

The private lifted his head slightly, his tear stained face taking in the owner of the subversive words. He glanced at the puce officer and almost smiled. But not quite. "I can't go back. I can't stand it anymore. Don't let 'em make me. I'm scared shitless Sarn't," he pleaded in a whispering breath.

"I know pal. So am I. We all are. It's a shitty deal but there's nothing for it. If you don't go this prick'll do for you and tell all his base wallah pals what a good egg he was. How he did his duty and all that tripe. You're better than him. You're one of us."

The boy glanced at the medal ribbon upon the sergeant's chest and shook his head violently. "No, I'm a coward like 'e said. I'm not like you. Any of you. None of you want to march with me," he cried.

"You think? Can you see anyone objecting? We've been there, all of us. We know. Come on son, stand with me." Sam stood up and held out his hand. The private hesitated and glanced from the friendly sergeant to the glowering captain and the contemplative sergeant major. With a shuddering breath he accepted the help and got to his feet.

"That's better. What's your name son?" Sam asked with one hand still supporting the youngster. He looked like he might fall down at any moment.

"Michaels Sarn't, Eric Michaels," the private mumbled with head bowed.

"Right Eric. Head up. You're DLI aren't you son? Show 'em you're proud to be," Sam returned encouragingly. Almost there. Memories of Jimmy Ibbotson crowded into his head. *I'm not losing this one.* He pushed them away and turned to the captain. "Private Michaels will march with me Sir," he stated.

The captain flushed angrily. He could not believe how this sergeant was talking to him. No respect, no deference to rank.

"Like hell he will Sergeant. He can get back in line here and you can join the rest of your Regiment back up there," he pointed his revolver in the direction from which Sam had come.

"If I may Sir," the sergeant major intervened and muttered lowly into the officer's ear. The captain turned even redder, looked as if he might explode for a moment and then with a resigned wave of his arms, holstered his pistol and stomped off to the head of the column. The old warrant officer smirked to himself as he watched him go.

"Right then. In line both of you. You lad...," the sergeant major pointed at the man in position next to where Michaels had stood. Leg it up there. I'll not 'ave bloody untidy lines. *Imshi!*"

The startled private hurried away and Michaels regained his position Sam flanking him on the outside. "Thanks Sir," he said quietly.

"No Sergeant, thank you. Between you and me, the captain's an arse'ole, but I never said that," the sergeant major replied with a tap of a finger against his nose, before bellowing at the top of his voice with the order to quick march once more. The column clanked forward. Michaels threw the odd curious glance at his new companion. Noted the confident air and the proud carriage. It was infectious; his own posture straightened and head lifted.

"Thanks Sarn't. I lost me sen there," he said quietly.

"Did you? I thought you found yourself," Sam smiled back and pulled out a battered tin whistle from his top pocket. "Time for a tune don't you think?"

Eric Michaels nodded and as the first notes of Tipperary floated out into the darkness of the frosty morning his was the first voice to pick up the song.

Victoria Station, London, 26th

The station filled with acrid soot and a fog of steam as the troop train chuffed and hissed to a final standstill at platform four. Before its laden cars had even finished bumping together to a clunking stop the doors were flying open and hundreds of steaming, smelly soldiers flowed onto the welcoming London concrete, tired, dishevelled but gloriously happy. The leave train shuddered and halted. Shouts and laughter, a thousand sparking footsteps. Girls rushing forward to offer a kiss or something more. A few sweethearts or wives, those who lived in the Capital and knew their man would be returning, if not on this train, then maybe the next. For many there was no one only the secure knowledge of being safe for nine days and another onward journey to some village or town in the North or the Midlands.

Joe watched with the unguarded jealousy of one whose leave was over, whose thoughts and destiny now lie in that uncertain horror of the trenches. He sighed and put down the newspaper he had been pretending to read in order to torture himself.

The boisterous Tommies quickly dispersed and just when the train appeared to be completely empty a small gaggle of nurses tripped from the First Class carriage. They too were a little careworn, yet clean and pink and smiling brightly. Their girlish voices betrayed their happiness at a spell in Blighty with loved ones. Despite his melancholy Joe smiled at their vivacious laughter, understanding that feeling of euphoria as one stepped onto British soil after so many months of toil, death and destruction.

It had been a good leave he supposed, even if a little strained at times. At least it had been restful. And now he was going back. He could feel the weariness upon him already. As if he had never been away. He thought of his wife and his son. How the little chap had grown! How brave she had been when he had to leave. Dear, gentle Dora. How could he have deserted her again to return to God knows what unthinkable horror?

He looked around the men upon his own platform. Hardly any spoke. Their gaze too was distant or slowly, mechanically following the retreating backs of the nurses across the line. None of them looked to the long, black snake of carriages waiting to take them back to Hell. Those carriages, whose open yawning doors beckoned darkly, waiting to swallow them whole and spit them out into a world of blind terror and barbarism. None would enter until the whistle blew. Every man tenaciously held onto what precious few minutes he had left in the light. But it was a light that was fading fast. Already the locomotive was building steam, the guard had left the engine driver and all too quickly marched to his position near the rear of the train, checking his watch while he did so.

Let it leave late. Let us remain here for another hour. Another minute, another second.

A shrill whistle and a shouted "All aboard!". Three hundred weary, laden souls climbed heavily to their feet, NCOs and military police shouting and chivvying them along. Joe shivered and carefully folded his paper. With great reluctance he rose from the bench along with his companions. He did not know them. They had not spoken other than a morose hello. They were simply fellow officers returning to France, feeling the same foreboding and dread as their men.

The soldiers shuffled stiffly onto the train, squeezing their burgeoning kit bags into rapidly vanishing corners, sitting in corridors when compartments filled, staring blankly out at the vast emptiness of the station platform. Not many to see them off. Most goodbyes had already been said amongst tears at other stations all over the country. Though there were enough friends, lovers and family to give an air of grieving, a stifled sob, a crying child.

Joe forced his legs to carry him to the First Class carriages. No squeezing in here. An orderly, spacious, comparative luxury. The first three compartments were full. VAD ambulance drivers and nurses in one; young, white faced subalterns in another. He found a seat amongst a quiet group of officers from some Cavalry Regiment. He did not know which and neither did he care. They moved feet aside to allow him passage and to his surprise he found himself sitting by the window. Perhaps no one wanted to look out at their country any more, now they were leaving it. He stowed his valise in the rack above the seat and took his place just as another shrill whistle sounded and the train jolted forward with a long hiss.

The carriages clanked and groaned, the powerful locomotive forcefully pulling them into a gently swinging motion. The strong smell of soot once more as the exhaust rebounded from the station's vaulted ceiling, swirled thickly around the receding platform and re-entered the train through open windows. No one seemed to notice, or at least no one cared. Already the compartment had filled with a mixture of pipe and cigarette tobacco.

Joe grimaced and stifled an involuntary cough and pulling his own pipe from his greatcoat pocket clamped it, unlit, between his teeth. He stared out of the window at the vanishing drabness of the station. Squinted as a relatively bright winter dawn dazzled the carriage occupants as the labouring train broke free into the real world. The real world that very rapidly became a stream of familiar images, of coal yards and sidings, houses and streets. The very ordinary and mundane. The last views of London disappearing into a blur of fields and trees. The real world being left behind and they hurtled towards the beckoning nightmare.

Joe closed his eyes and slept.

No. 12 Convalescent Camp, 26th

Alice stood with a small group of snowy headed nurses by the main gate. They could hear voices singing, the clatter of equipment and the steady rhythmic stamp of marching feet long before they could see them. She hoped she would catch a glimpse of him. That he would see her and be fortified by her presence. *Was that presumptuous?* Probably. She hoped she would not cry for she suddenly felt quite emotional. It was the cheerful singing. It sat at odds with the reality of the situation; the fact that all these men were returning to untold horrors. That many of them may never see home again. A treacherous lump swelled in her throat and she swallowed angrily to force it away.

Soon the leading men came into view. At their head a pompous looking officer, then rows upon rows of young men all singing as they marched. As they passed the little group of nurses they waved. Some blew kisses, winked an eye or even called out. "Wish me luck girls." "Be seein' you next time." "Keep a bed warm for me sweetheart." Cheeky, but harmless banter. Some of the nurses feigned shock or giggled behind their hands. Alice ignored it all, intent only on catching the eye of one man. He was a long way down the column. Not with the other men from his Regiment. *Strange?* She grew worried she had missed him and a frown grooved her pale forehead.

Eventually she saw him and waved. He was playing a whistle and when he caught sight of her he stopped and smiled widely. She was there. They kept their eyes locked for the few precious seconds as he passed through the gate. Eyes that conveyed a hundred unspoken feelings; a deeper understanding than words could have expressed. Then he was gone marching smartly with the rest. He raised his hand above his head in farewell. She returned the gesture though she knew he could not see. The tears began to flow and this time she could not stem them, but she had been strong while he went by. She had not shown fear for him.

The tin whistle started again. Some lusty voice amidst the mass of singing men shouted out, "Are we downhearted?"

The echoing roar "NO," answered the question and the men tramped away into the gloom, their step and singing fading with their ghostly forms.

****

This book is dedicated to the memory of

8408 Corporal William Pratt

2nd Battalion

Alexandra Princess of Wales Own Yorkshire Regiment

(The Green Howards)

Who died of wounds on 1st October 1915

Printed in Great Britain
by Amazon